ASCENDERS
X-CATCHER
BOOK FIVE

ASCENDERS
X-CATCHER
BOOK FIVE

C.L. GABER

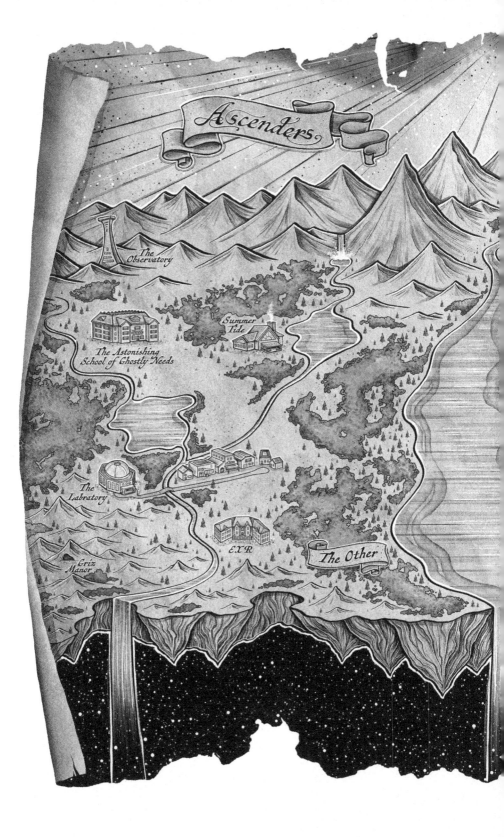

BOOKS BY
C. L. GABER

Jex Malone

Ascenders Series
Ascenders
Ascenders: Skypunch (Book Two)
Ascenders: Omorrow (Book Three)
Ascenders: 11:11 (Book Four)
The Claires (An Ascenders Novella)
Ascenders: X-Catcher (Book Five)

This book is dedicated to J. With love.

Think you're escaping
and run into yourself
Longest way round
Is the shortest way home

– James Joyce

I was never insane except upon occasions when
my heart was touched

– Edgar Allan Poe

Never tell me the odds

– Han Solo

PART I

ONE

1.

The Other Side of the Other Side isn't a place for wandering. It's a realm for wondering.

All the people are dead, but human curiosity never really leaves the building.

You could listen to the speculations of, say, a music teacher named Kurt who wore faded flannel and used to have this band.

One day, he stood in front of my classroom at the Academy, a high school for the recently departed. The man who brought stringy hair into the great beyond told us about the hereafter of his hopes and wildest dreams: "When I was alive, I believed that when you died, you were completely happy. That there was this positive energy. It would be peaceful and beautiful."

Kurt with the angel blue eyes.

I, Walker Callaghan from third period Music 101, row four, beg your pardon.

Quite obviously, when alive, you didn't know shit.

3

2.

The bullet broke the sound barrier, a tiny rocket traveling at supersonic zoom and spitting fire. Tor's fingers were on the trigger of a 9 mm pistol I guessed—of course, I've seen one in about ten thousand movies, but as the song goes . . . *ain't nothing like the real thing, baby.*

Warning: Your afterlife is not a weekend blockbuster complete with a large soda and the mega popcorn.

It's a gun that you spot in just a glint of bright moonlight.

It's a heart, your own, that longs to sprint from the devil.

And it's a seventeen-year-old on the cusp of annihilation, standing on a second-story terrace of a grand cabin. She sways in a place between heaven and hell in the crosshairs of a serial killer.

Turns out the sound of a gunshot is a lot louder than what you expect. It's a mind-blowing *BANG* that leaves your ears shrieking followed by a deeper *BOOM* that causes every human nerve to waver.

The first slug was a whirling torpedo detonating into a virgin night sky. The bullet spun and swirled until it drilled a deep canyon into the fleshy part of my upper chest. Blasting through muscle and tissue, the invader sent shock waves through my reverberating rib cage. Sinking deeply, the trespasser stopped when it met bone.

You can hear your demise, and it's the most awful sound of all. It's a cracking from deep inside, much like a rock shattering a car's windshield with just one bounce off the glass. You kid yourself that it won't splinter. But one crack leads to two . . . three . . . ten and then a million fissures and fractures.

Remember, getting shot is not cinematic.

Your knees buckle. You break. And then you fall.

3.

Midnight in the afterlife. We were barely gone twenty-four hours from our beautiful limbo home called the Midst. Our post-life education had been temporarily put on hold for good reason. Our little band of renegade teenagers was forced to go on the run because we were being hunted by our savage Principal Dick and his corrupt administration of fools, devils and con artists.

It forced us to open and then perilously venture across a barrier wall into a lawless place for the dead known as The Other. Think of it as the Wild West of your next existence.

Strange the things you remember when your time is slipping, but despite my newfound murkiness, I was a student reporter, so I forced myself to stick to just the facts, Jack:

My name is Walker Callaghan.

I am seventeen.

I am already dead.

I am almost naked. Well, wrapped up in a bedspread.

Or was it a comforter . . . or a blanket?

"Details," my journalism teacher Mr. Mongan insisted, "make the story."

Focus, Walker, as you lay naked bleeding on the patio deck. The comforter, I had decided, had tiny, pretty red roses on it. But what the hell was the difference? And who the hell cared?

Before I was shot, I was reading. A letter. From my living mother.

She sent an actual letter . . . to the afterlife . . . to me.

Who knew that mail could cross over, but it does. To recap, when it comes to the afterlife: we don't know what we don't know – and we don't know most of it.

Sadly, I couldn't read anymore. Maybe never would read anything ever again.

I was spiraling into nothing.

Dead girl down.

4.

Random facts on being shot: it doesn't hurt at first. Damn it, you think you beat this thing because we deep down believe that we come with endless get-out-of-jail-free guarantees.

But you're not Bruce Willis—and neither am I.

All that bravado is, medically speaking, known as shock, and once your adrenalin stops pumping hard, the hole in your body burns like a bitch, which is why I'm curled into a tight ball crying for my mother.

The pain is so excruciating that I'm white-knuckling it. The reset I've enjoyed in the Midst—sparing one from suffering physical angst—is spotty on this side. Right now, it's gone and I'm wishing I was never born. I curse my body, which has served me so well thus far. But this isn't just flashes of agonizing hurt. It's something worse because it's slow-release torture. This agony? You marinate in it.

A head-to-toe numbness follows, which is the most frightening thing of all.

Pain, my friends, is your friend, your beacon, your lifeline. It's a personal highway sign: You are here. You go on. You are on the right side of that proverbial, all-important line.

I felt nothing all of a sudden, so I placed my shaking, bloodied hand to my mouth to be sure I still had air.

All I heard was breath on flesh. Turns out, it wasn't mine.

It was his.

5.

"YOU WAKE THE FUCK UP! Do you hear me!" he demanded.

Why was he so loud?

"You hear me, Callaghan? I know that you do. I will never let you rest in peace. I will haunt you until the end of time, God damn it."

Then he slowed it down. "God. Damn. It!"

Daniel Reid was wired tight during the best of times, which this clearly wasn't. His adrenaline was usually pumping at a ten. This was a one billion plus. He leaned down to blow words into my ear. "You don't go . . . *places*," he demanded. With that he bit my earlobe until my eyes went wide, which meant they popped open again.

"That's a start," he growled. "You stay with me."

Daniel was primal. Large and protective, he was . . . *and then he wasn't . . . there anymore.*

The world began to tilt. Here, on this side of the afterlife, if you were lacking that tricky, above-mentioned reset and you died of "natural or any other causes," which was entirely possible and certainly probably, you ceased to exist in any form, anywhere, ever again. Your remains turned into particles that defined the idea of dust in the wind.

My eyes fluttered down because it was so gentle, peaceful and tranquil. . . .

Serene . . . did I say peaceful? Tranquil?

Soaring through mist and cloud, I sailed through time and space. Oh, the colors, the pretty lights, and why was his mouth on the center of my chest? Why was he sucking so hard? *Just let me glide, baby.* I was sliding away like the groove of a sharpened skate on fresh winter ice. I was one with the slide. Going fast . . . faster.

I even heard the strains of one of my favorite songs in the far distance:
"Give me the beat boys, and free my soul.
I wanna get lost in your rock 'n' roll.
And drift away."

6.

Someone was calling my name. He was leaning over me, jabbing two icy, long fingers directly into the bullet wound. He began to root through flesh and muscle. I knew Daniel was a natural healer, but this was pure agony. "Son of a bitch, we're losing her," I heard him call out.

Better to take off again. A lightness filled my head and my eyes were a blanket of star-born sparkles.

I felt the moon on my face and the stars in my hair.

One thing about losing everything: you have all the dreaming room you could ever want.

7.

Human eyelids are life's great ending. They're like theater curtains. They can drop from the top, but often there is a tiny line where those heavy drapes do not meet and you can still see a sliver of light. That is life, too. Keep your peepers open just a bit and there is hope.

Let's be honest. In the theater and in existence, in most cases, no one really wants the show to be over.

If you're lucky, you have enough human will to see through the crease and open your eyes wide. One last time.

In my crease, I see a rugged face. I look at him. *Really look at him.* And then I think, "I really love you. Not just making out love you, not having wild sex love you, not having tender sex love you or laughing until we cry love you. Not even love you when we're making peanut-butter sandwiches together at four in the morning, getting half of it on the counter and licking it off each other love you.

There's something about him in this moment—his determination, his mad skills, and his fire at inferno level.

I even loved the way he uses words so economically.

"Got it," he thunders.

I feel his tears fall on my face like salty rain. What breaks your heart, opens your eyes.

My lids lift.

8.

A single bullet drenched in dark red dangled between Daniel Reid's teeth. The rest of his face was covered in my blood. Rotating, he spit the bullet to the ground and then his hands went to work.

Palm on my wound, he pressed. He caressed. He used the fleshy meat on the back of his hands in long strokes to seal my skin like he was suturing it.

I felt the tingles as my skin began to knit. Sweet relief. The pain dipped quickly from white-hot to none at all.

A hard press and my heart surged.

Euphoria mixed with relief is a heady combo. An energetic fuel raced through my blood. I wanted to walk. Screw that. Run! We were gonna race for pink slips later tonight.

Daniel is the fixer of broken things—gifted in the art of healing in ways no rational person could ever explain or attain without it in their DNA. There was no doctor who could do what he did. It's a God-given talent he doesn't discuss.

Not that I'll ever let him get a big head about it.

"Shitty bedside service," I gasped as he used his body weight to keep me down on the deck because that asshole down there was *still down there*. "But otherwise, five big Yelp stars," I whispered while he secured my body in the blanket again, covering all my parts.

He isn't having it. No jokes to smooth it.

His lips, my blood, my lips, our kiss.

Our story met hard in the middle—so what else was new?

9.

Peter Reid was outside, too. Funny, I hadn't noticed it before, but he was probably here the whole time (and later I would find out that he was actually present for the whole gunfire extravaganza).

On his face was the sweetest toothy grin. He had the whitest teeth for any bookish hunk in training—small white squares like that gum, Chicklets. I saw his arm go up like he was waving to the shooter down below. *How oddly friendly of him.*

There that arm went again. Up. Up. And up.

He looked like a big dork who was raising his hand in class. Only, he was wearing a rather large, oddly shaped glove that looked like an oversized catcher's mitt that covered his entire hand, wrist, and most of his arm. He lifted that arm with each loud crack of another bullet breaking the sound barrier.

All I heard was the dull thump of contact with the contraption at the end of his wrist.

"*Yee-haw!*" Pete exclaimed. The young man who could catch *anything* without even looking. He dropped five long gold bullets down by his brother's feet.

"Asswipe needs time to reload and revamp. Gun's jammed now and my reset works just fine, *yee-haw!*" Pete yelled with glee.

"You're catching the bullets?" I said.

"All five, except the one that got you. Sorry, sis," Pete said.

"Sorry is the best you can do!" yelled Cass, bursting through the mesh of the patio door. Hovering over me, he put his hands on the top of my shoulders. "Are you hurt? I heard gunshots. I was sleeping. Can you talk? Damn it, you can't keep her safe for—"

"Stop," I begged.

Daniel and Cass locked eyes. My face swiveled in slow motion to look at both.

"Don't," I growled at each of them.

"Mine," Daniel roared. I misunderstood until I saw his gaze wasn't directed at Cass. It was set way down below.

"God damn it. You don't go . . . places," I snarled back at him.

Daniel Reid was over the banister in a single bound.

10.

My killer smacked the bottom of the magazine of his assault rifle to make sure it was in place. Viciously, Tor yanked the charging handle and listened as the rifle snapped back forward making a *clack-clack* sound.

Daniel, unarmed, rolled on the ground. Raw and dangerous never won a gun fight, and I had no choice but to press my face to the slats of the terrace to watch in horror.

"Go help him, Cass," I begged.

"No," he said, using his entire body to shield my every move.

Someone inside had flipped the outside flood lights on and in an amber haze I saw the smug, satisfied smile on Tor's angular, almost albino face.

Tor would finish the job because killing was his birthright. Just like in every high school, there was always an overachiever.

Tor wasn't even exactly his entire name. His full name, only one word, was Distortion. In our regular afterlife realm, he was one of Freak U's finest student specimens. In fact, his freak flag flew higher than Mount Everest.

If you got lost in his stare, he would literally change your view of things until the entire situation altered course. Not so long ago, I got trapped in his stare and almost found myself raped followed by murdered in a past time loop, which meant I would never have been born in the future.

Silently, I began to pray.

Daniel emitted a low, deep throat growl that served as a battle call. With one hand, he ripped the iron out of Tor's slim hand. I heard the splash as the weapon landed in the dark lake. A lone bird wailed and the water sloshed.

Tor enjoyed a little conversation during his psychotic episodes. Why not? Teachers, the ones who lived, always praised his mad verbal skills.

"I came here to kill her. Brilliant, isn't it?" he enunciated slowly in his hybrid British accent. "Kill her as in gone. But I wanted to hear her scream first. I like that sound. You should have heard her wailing. When I had her in my bed. In New York."

Sadistic, son of a . . .

"Wish this could take longer," Daniel said in an equally composed voice made up of grit, stone, and determination. He was so dispassionate that it sent chills up and down my arms.

"Unfortunately, you'll go fast," Daniel continued. "What did you say? Oh yeah. Kill you as in gone. Dead as in never setting eyes on a son of a bitch like you again. Just a good guess, but no one is gonna miss you."

In the silence that followed, punctuated by a rustling in the trees, the man who kicked soccer balls eighty miles an hour exploded and landed his foot directly into the middle of Tor's jugular.

11.

As his throat imploded, Tor croaked the most horrifying sound, as if he was gurgling spoiled milk. As he struggled for breath and voice, he leaned back. Then tumbled.

My heart began to pound when Daniel fell directly on top of Tor. To finish it.

Daniel's hands were around Tor's throat. My tormentor's mouth was open in a silent O now as blood gushed from his lips while his fingers tried to pry Daniel's iron grip away.

"Don't look him in the eyes, baby," I cried. "He wants it. He wants you to fall into his trap."

My sweet love didn't answer, but continued to press, as Tor's arms slapped at the cool night air.

He continued to press. Tor's jabs landed softly now like caresses.

He continued to press. Tor's arms fell to his sides as he resigned himself to his fate. Blood and white foam sputtered from his mouth, dribbling into the earth.

He continued to press.

Tor's eyes were bulbous now, bulging out of their sockets.

He continued to press.

Life fights for life. One last time, Tor found a little thrash and buck.

Daniel continued to press.

Tor's head fell to the left.

He continued to press.

Then after he was sure, Daniel finally rolled off him.

Tor laid still, eyes skyward, like he was just another young man gazing up at the stars on a pleasant evening.

Leaning over, Daniel checked Tor's pulse and then stood up.

"Happy trails, muther . . . ," Daniel muttered.

12.

I felt my head loll back. Lifting my arms to the sky, I asked why without saying a word.

When there wasn't an answer, I couldn't stop crying and crying and crying.

Back home in suburban Chicago, Madeleine Callaghan was standing on the deck of her new home in suburban Wheeling, Illinois. It was unseasonably warm for late December, but she just chalked it up to good luck combined with the global warming that everyone in charge denied, but she knew was true.

She had just placed her newly adopted quadruplets in their cribs for the night and she could hear her baby daughters snoring, just a bit. She had to get some new batteries in the monitor because it sounded more like hissing.

Her attention was diverted when she looked straight up on impulse and saw the strangest cloud. It looked like a large white bird with its wings stretched out across the wintry night sky. The first drop hit her forehead and then another plopped on her right cheek. It was odd because the weather forecaster didn't predict any rain. When several drops landed on her lips, she was compelled to taste them.

She could have sworn that they were salted.

TWO

1.

My name is Walker Callaghan and if we're meeting now, it certainly won't be face-to-face. There will be no mulling over my promising future, SAT scores, or obscenely expensive pale pink prom dresses with the little strappy straps. That ship, honey, has sailed.

Embrace the suck, as we say at the Academy.

Of course, dead at age seventeen is a relative term. The young dead in the Midst, the realm that holds my feet on the ground now, exist in a way that is quite close to the daily doings in the living realm. We look the same, feel the same, and even have cheerleaders.

We've just moved —way, way out of town.

In death, we shed what doesn't work. And we move on.

The rules of our afterlife are simple: there are none. It's teenage existence on your own terms with one caveat. You are never allowed to visit your former life as it's dangerous to your soul's future. Slithering, flying, ragged-tooth demons lurk there to extinguish your very essence. There are the fragments of your soul that you left behind. They're ballistic now. Pissed off to infinity. And they're waiting to devour what has abandoned them.

In the Midst, we are not lost souls, but the ones who are processing into a new existence.

Truth is: you don't die.

You level up.

2.

I'm not in the Midst at the present moment. This is thanks to another kind of devil, the corrupt new leader of the Academy, a high school for the recently departed. Principal Dick fully lives up to his moniker as well as the street use of the word. A former disgraced US president with a penchant for taping every conversation, Dick and his henchmen (and woman) on the "school board"—called the Higher Authority here— issued a warrant for my arrest. And Daniel's arrest. We had no choice but to live the immortal words of the very much alive Bruce Springsteen who sang about tramps like us. We didn't run out of town; we sprinted.

We slipped through to The Other, the lawless, unexplored other side of our afterlife realm. It was where our former principal, the stalwart, honest and decent Dr. Marvin King was hiding. Presumed extinguished, Dr. King followed Daniel and I when we broke the sacred rule and returned to the living realm so long ago to find Daniel's little brother Bobby. Dr. King was trapped on that side, presumed eaten by demons and thus the nefarious Dick was appointed principal.

It remained unsafe for Dr. King to reveal his true whereabouts, especially after Daniel and I were tasked to explore time loops of the past to find the last, lost works of Albert Einstein. It turns out the great brain uncovered something in his youth that he hid from all humanity *for his entire lifetime*. Einstein knew that humans couldn't handle what he found. That they would abuse it. What he unearthed was something that would change everything for the living and the dead.

It's why Principal Dick came to the Academy. Desperately he wanted Einstein's early work known as the Omorrow Project. Those pages revealed the exact coordinates to a place where the living and the dead could visit each other and truly communicate. Dick had a laundry list of those he wanted to have a little chitchat with to help him mastermind a future so bleak and dark that it was unimaginable. Their names: Hitler, Bin Laden, Manson, among other evil forces.

There was no choice but to hide those papers and then bolt to The Other.

To reach this anarchistic place, first you had to find the force field wall and then open it with special coordinates that sealed the two sides of the afterlife. Upon our arrival and a "swim" through churning ocean waters, the wall locked again, leaving us trapped until someone could figure out another code to open it.

Until then we would be forced to live here.

Some called this outlaw land the "wild, wild west of post-existence."

Yippee ki-yay.

You know the rest.

3.

I'm lucky not to travel solo.

Daniel Reid was my ride or die, my "shotgun," and he brought with him a bad-boy exterior plus a strong body, protective nature, and badass attitude, which is why tats covered most of his canvas. Underneath a forbidding stare at first sight, I found a heart of gold that he showed to very few.

He was a game shaker, magic maker, and my push comes to shove. He refused to allow me to play small with my new future. He was my meteor ride.

One look into those steel-gray eyes and I was in my right zip code, but at a home I had never known before. This one had vistas that stretched beyond edges and spaces that were as wide open as a true deep breath.

"All in for all time," he whispered now, cupping my shaking hands in his calloused ones.

It was our battle cry, but right now I needed a status report on our last battle.

He answered the question in my eyes.

"Tor's dead, baby," he said. "Dead-dead. Pulse not pulsating. But, forget that. How are you, really?"

He was highly suspicious when I said, "Never better."

"But I need . . ."

"To see the body. Of course you do, Callaghan," he said planting a hard kiss on my lips.

He knew I was planning on becoming a *New York Times* reporter *if only* I would have lived. The foundation of that plan lingered. I still possessed a desperately yearning, never satisfied, not easily quenched need to know just the facts, and all of them. But I would be forced to put my rabid curiosity on check. At least for the next few minutes.

"Who wants waffles covered in real maple syrup?" asked Auggie, my XL, ponytail-sporting, band-geek friend from the Academy. The six-foot-four lug snuck over to The Other to help, which was just about the sweetest thing in this world or any other. Poor Auggie was only eighteen, with very few street smarts, when friends bullied him into trying heroin at his cousin's beach party. Almost immediately, he went into cardiac arrest. It was a one-way ticket to the Academy where his permanent record and our wonderful admissions director Miss Maude Travis was waiting.

Auggie was one of my best friends—a walking, talking ray of sunlight who was wearing a big red onesie that he packed for the trip. It made him look like Santa's dorkiest elf.

"Really?" I teased him. "I'm thinking about bodies and you're thinking about breakfast? Nice onesie, by the way."

"They're theme pajamas and they're yummy," he replied with a grin.

"You look like a blood clot, Aug, and I could eat. Just saying . . . but I could . . . even in my emotional state," said Eddie Wargo, who just magically appeared on the patrol. During my shooting, he had been hiding in the living room . . . behind the couch. Behind Bobby . . . who was six.

Alabama born and raised, tough-guy Eddie really wasn't that tough, but I always liked him. He had crazy hair that went every which way, and a southern slang for any situation. He was a former bully who now had a metal fruit bowl over his head for protection. We met him when he was incarcerated at ITT—the Institute for Troubled Teens—which is also located on our side, the Midst. Eddie had become an unexpected ally, although dealing with him could work your last nerve.

"I could eat grilled dough. And bacon," Eddie offered. "Or I could eat anything that goes with trying not to shit in the only pair of pants you have with you while some wacko is shooting outside in the middle of the night. Do they have Walmart here? I might need more pants."

"You need a hug and then waffles and maybe a little Rocky and Bullwinkle. The video collection is in the den," Auggie offered, placing an arm around a still-shocked Eddie.

Aug wasn't in such good shape either.

"On vacation, still existing and living my best afterlife," Augs said, trying to convince himself.

4.

Before the flour hit the waffle maker, Daniel wordlessly scooped my body up like he was lifting air. He was broad shouldered in a black shirt and tight-fitting jeans. When I first met him, I knew he didn't belong in any high school. He was much too rugged and looked a little battered, too, thanks to a childhood spent at the mercy of his abusive father, mob lawyer Edward Reid of posh Lake Forest, Illinois.

Daniel had reckless hair, jet black, and shorter on the sides than on the top. It looked almost blueish in certain lights and was wildly hand-combed off a masculine, square face that was marked by about a day's growth of facial stubble. You could barely see it, but his shadows were always there and made him look older and dangerous.

Those laser eyes were laser focused now as he lowered me down and I found the garish, bloodied spot on Tor's blackened throat. His skin was so pale that each mark was amplified. When I put my hand in front of Tor's blue lips, I felt the finality of his nothingness.

"We beat the Dutch," I said. "Squad goals."

Daniel was confused. My crazy and quite alive, Listerine-loving, lint-phobic Aunt Ginny didn't translate easily.

"It means to beat the devil," I whispered.

As I said the words, it happened so fast that I could barely blink. Black and glistening, it began a slow glide out from under Tor's body. It was a long, wriggling streak of forward flow that sparkled in the glimmer of midnight. It stopped fast, rose when it sensed our heat, and then inched up a third of its thick body that looked as if it was made of tire rubber. The snake opened a wide jaw, hissed, and then inched its facial skin upward to reveal two deadly fangs that seemed to glow a ghostly iridescent white.

"Son of a bitch." Dr. King rarely swore, but he did now while holding a pointed steel garden shovel in his hand. Three hard jabs into the ground and the snake was cut into parts.

"Now that I have the makings of a new belt, do you want to tell me what the hell is going on here?" our principal demanded.

5.

We had faced many storms together, Daniel and I, but none as upsetting as the shit storm we walked into now.

"Can someone please tell me why I heard six shots ring out . . . and why is there a dead body in a trench coat on my back lawn?" demanded the nineteen-year-old version of my fifty-something principal.

Quick note: Teachers at the Academy were there because they chose to pass on knowledge to the next generation of souls. They weren't paid in money, but in pride and various "perks." One such mind-blowing extra was they could age themselves backward and forward depending on their moods or the needs of the times. Funny, but most settled at an age where they were happiest, which wasn't always when they were young and in the best shape or prettiest. For Dr. King, his sweet spot when it came to aging was somewhere in his early fifties during his glory days as an assistant high school principal in Detroit.

19

We were used to seeing a slightly gray-haired, physically fit, but older Dr. King—a vast improvement over when he was a one-legged educator in Detroit who suffered from the ravages of diabetes. But times being dire in the afterlife now, he de-aged himself recently (but not permanently) to enjoy the physical prowess of youth during what was soon to be fighting times.

The rub was he still spoke in a rich baritone of someone much older . . . and wiser. But, he looked like . . . us. He also made it clear he was not one of us, and wouldn't take our crap. He was now, and always would be, our principal.

Daniel was not one for long-winded stories, which is why on the not-so-long walk back into the house I observed my right to remain silent while my beloved thought up some sort of half-baked explanation. I was still drawing a blank when I made a mad dash upstairs to ditch the blanket and dress in a warm sweatshirt and black leggings, no socks, of course. Naturally, I looked for wounds in the bright bathroom mirror and couldn't even find a scratch from the bullet.

It wasn't fair to waste more time, so I slowly walked back downstairs to fill in some blanks.

It turns out that Dr. King wasn't familiar with Tor at all, so we educated *him* for once.

"Tor stands for Distortion, which is why he attended Fredrick Reardon," I said.

The school for those with oddities in the Midst was known as the Frederick Reardon Establishment of Academics and Kinetics, lovingly called Freak U by its students who celebrated their rarities and reveled joyfully in the heady gift of true weirdness.

"He's from Russia. He has been alive for over a hundred years with this power to stare at you, make eye contact—which is key—and then distort your reality just enough to change outcomes," I explained. "He has amassed quite a body count as many kill themselves in his presence, if he doesn't torture and kill them first."

"I don't want to hear it, but go on," Dr. King bit out.

"In a past time loop, he lured Callaghan to his house and almost raped her," Daniel said, fists clenched and jaw set.

We were in the living room now, sitting on those soft leather couches when Dr. King rose like he was ripped to his feet. "Is this true?" he boomed.

"Yes," I said. "I, um, had to go to his house. *His house in the year 1945.* I guess he has homes all over the globe over vast time periods. He lured me there to rape me. I was caught in his gaze. He distorted things to . . . uh . . . make me think he was Daniel."

"And then!" Dr. King yelled. "No comment on your regularly scheduled social life."

"And then, I sneezed," I said. "It was enough to force me to close my eyes because sneezes are an involuntary bodily response where the air speeds up to a hundred miles per hour in your lungs then throat and nose. In ninety-nine percent of the cases, you will close your eyes. It was enough to break the trance he had me in."

"Fascinating. So, you raced out of his home," Dr. King demanded.

"Not exactly, sir," I said. "First, I slashed his throat. And then I hog-tied him with his computer cord, which is actually tougher than rope. Another mindless fact. And then I watched him bleed out a bit before my friends arrived and we left his house."

Dr. King just stared at me.

"I was . . . in the moment," I said in a soft voice while looking at my feet. When I glanced up, I could see Daniel was smiling, which wasn't good in this situation.

"He's gone now. I choked him out and don't give a shit," Daniel finally said. "I wish I could do it again." He looked at our baby-faced principal who looked like a young Denzel Washington and added, "What I meant to say is I don't give a shit, sir."

"You want to run this bullshit by me one more time?" Dr. King demanded. "Mr. Reid, the floor is yours so make the most of it."

Yep, that sounded a lot like the old Dr. King. I looked at Daniel as in, *Here we go again.* Daniel Reid had never exactly been Dr. Marvin King's favorite dead teenager, despite the fact that on some level he respected him. For a rich kid, he knew that Daniel had street smarts to spare and was brave as f—.

"Tor will now be classified as Existence Compromised," Dr. King quickly affirmed as he paced around that lovely living room in the cabin. He pivoted toward Daniel. "Mr. Reid, if you're not too busy, as in currently, get back out there and remove his decaying bones from my lawn. These might be wild lands, but most existing here do frown upon tripping over human remains."

"Yes, sir," Daniel said.

"One more thing," Dr. King said. "Stay frosty. That snake was a venomous king cobra. It might have friends who also share enough neurotoxins to kill an elephant. That was a baby. Most are eighteen feet long. Another fun fact."

I felt queasy.

In the next moment, the former assistant principal from Detroit turned into Tony Soprano before our eyes.

"There are flashlights in the garage. Strip that young dead man naked. Dig a deep hole by the vegetable garden. By the tomatoes. Say a prayer. Sing a song. Plant him deep. There are bricks in the garage. Put bricks on top of him to prevent any animals from digging him up and having a midnight feast. Then burn the clothes and any ID, so he can't be identified. And don't get bitten by any living creature because I don't have any antivenom on me. I don't want to be digging two plots tonight."

"Eddie, let's go," Daniel barked.

"I don't know any funeral songs," Eddie moaned as he followed Daniel outside into the blackness.

6.

Casually, I slipped away, but I was afraid enough of snakes to stay in the house. Instead, I went upstairs because the bedroom I shared with Daniel had a much better vantage point of the entire situation. Who did I find sitting in the middle of our bed, lotus style? It was Tosh, clad only in a long ripped pink tee.

After grabbing and hugging me, she punched me in the arm as hard

22

as a former ballerina turned anorexic turned dead girl could. "You scared the crap out of me, Walker," she said.

"Ow," I said, rubbing my flesh. *What was the deal with the reset?*

"Pete was pretty spectacular out there," I said, knowing she had a major crush on Daniel's younger brother.

Tosh jumped into bed, dragging me with her.

"I know," she replied, smiling. "Dr. King gave him some souped-up catcher's mitt he said was made of tungsten, which he said was the strongest natural metal. He said it was very dense and someday would be used for the military in the living realm, but not until they worked out the kinks here in The Other. I guess they do a lot of research here to help the living. Anyway, I guess when Howard Hughes stayed here at his cabin, he was developing those tungsten mitts to avoid germs."

Howard H, the now-dead former billionaire, was the principal and headmaster of Freak U. Just thinking about him made me smile, although Tosh had other subject matters on her mind.

"Did Pete mention me when things got dicey?" Tosh demanded, collapsing onto her stomach to lay prone with her face propped up by her hands.

For the first time tonight, I had to laugh.

"Yeah, honey, while he was catching bullets shot by a psycho killer with his Captain America souped-up glove, he said, 'Tosh, Tosh, I love you, Tosh! Tosh is the only woman for me . . . in this universe or any other.'"

Toes pointed, she kicked me in the side. It didn't hurt. The reset was back.

"I hate you," Tosh said with glee and a quick giggle. Then she reminded me, "Everyone deserves a great love. By the way, what's the deal with Daniel playing doctor? Don't spare any details."

Before I could open my mouth, the door burst open.

"How are you doing, sugar? I saw Daniel go outside and since boy wonder was gone, I wanted to make sure with my own eyes that you're not hurt. I'm saying this in a totally nonsexual way, but can you lift up your shirt? I want to feel your skin for wounds," Cass said.

23

"That is the lamest pick-up line ever," Tosh whooped. "But, you can feel my wounds. I'm not committed to anyone here. I have an opening for a hunky boyfriend who is good with salve and bandages."

"Tosh!" I said.

"Then again, I don't think we know each other well enough, Cass," Tosh said with a sparkle in her eyes as she gave him a quick once-over. Yes, she liked Pete. But the truth was that Tosh pretty much liked anything male, especially when he came with long, flowing, dirty-blond hair trapped in a leather tie; a big square face; and an almost six-foot-three frame built with muscles.

"I smell burning waffles," I said.

We were interrupted by loud voices below, which made me casually detangle the situation by slipping past both of them until I could reach the top of the stairs for a better listen.

That's when I heard Daniel—who was back in the house—say what seemed impossible.

"The body is gone."

7.

"What do you mean gone?" Cass confronted him. He had followed me downstairs and now he was smack in the middle of the fray.

"Gone as in gone. Not there. You should know how that goes . . . gone as in people are being shot and you're basically doing jack shit about it because you're basically gone," Daniel stated, glaring at Cass. "It's not everyone who could basically do nothing while the rest of us are the bullseye in some psycho's target practice."

"Hey, asshole, I was there protecting Walker. But if you want to step outside . . . ," Cass began.

"I've already been outside," Daniel stated. "To save Callaghan. As you would say, Maverick, mission accomplished."

It was going to get ugly if Daniel brought Cass's days as a marine into it by quoting lines from the wrong branch of the military.

They would never get to finish it that night. Little Bobby was also out of his bed. He had secured a yellow bath towel to his pj's and put on his best Spider-Man onesie. His weapon was an actual small sword—a priceless and quite deadly antique he must have found in the house.

My feet raced to grab it out of his plump, sticky hands.

"I can fllllllyyyy, Walkie," he screamed. "For reals. Gimme my sword back and I show you."

"Hey, little man, weapons down," I said, keeping the blade just out of his reach.

"But I need my saber. 'Cause it's growing," he informed us. "Gotta kill it again."

"What's growing?" Daniel said, dislodging the sword from my fingers to put it on a high shelf.

"The monster on the grass," Bobby repeated, jumping from foot to foot in his excitement.

"Not growing," Pete amended after gazing out the nearest window. "Holy shit! It's . . . *glowing*."

THREE

1.

"I'm not saying it's aliens, but do you think it's aliens of the big-eyed and green variety?" Auggie interjected. His spatula had fallen to the floor.

"I mean, if something out there is glowing, and/or growing, it could be something that descended from a UFO and I don't want to be the subject of medical tests. I mean, I watch *The Twilight Zone*. I fear probes."

"Will Smith," I said to him. "Take it down a notch."

There is a reasonable explanation for everything under the stars and su--" thus began Dr. King, but the rest was cut off when he gazed out the window. Even he was rendered speechless.

If only our most frightening moments came in carefully marked boxes with the label: Horrifying memories, the lasting kind, await. Do not open.

2.

Under a dappled night sky, we made the trek outside only to find the impossible.

The body had disappeared—as in not there. But something freakish was left in its *exact* place.

It was human skin.

The top layer, no thicker than two pieces of notebook paper, lay on the ground now as if someone peeled it off Tor's entire naked being. What remained was almost translucent and it took on an odd, golden glow. Despite objections, I dropped to my knees to look closer.

The skin was intact, making what looked like a fragile form of a tall man. It was cloudy, like a thin layer of milk spilled on plastic wrap, but it formed a layout of his long legs, muscular body, narrow feet, and elongated arms. I stared at his arms, which were complete with ten perfect piano-player fingers.

Daniel tried to pull me up, but I eluded his grasp. My eyes scanned bumps where his ribcage belonged and then darted to a slender, almost aristocratic, neck. I focused on the mask of his face with cutouts for those dangerous eyes, two nostrils, and a small mouth. The ears were there, too, wisps of skin fluttering in a smooth kick of wind.

"How could a dead man skin himself?" Pete asked in an almost whisper.

"Look," I said, pointing to tall, evergreen bushes in the near distance.

Hanging from the branches was Tor's trademark trench coat, black pants, white shirt, and black running shoes.

"Callaghan, move!" Daniel shouted.

This time I had time to jump to the side as another large, black snake with slits for eyes slithered out of nowhere. It was moving slowly, inching forward in twitchy little spasms, as if it were injured.

It was Cass who took a hunting knife out of his pocket, flung it, and sliced the snake's head clean off. Just like Dr. King, he knew to cut it once again. Just to be sure. Feeling bold, I kicked over the middle piece and then looked at it carefully.

"We should check the woods. Maybe something bigger did this to him," Daniel said, looking down at the glowing skin that remained.

"There are thousands of miles of woods," Cass interjected. "You could be checking until the end of time—and you don't exactly have survivalist written on your forehead."

"Bury it—not each other," Dr. King interrupted, glancing back at the shimmering epidermis. "Put what's left of that boy in the ground before some animal wanders along and decides to snack on the outer shell. There's nothing else we can do tonight, which means we wonder, but do not wander. Don't make me tell you twice."

Our principal began to clomp away, and as much as I didn't want to leave Daniel and Cass to fight it out, I needed to talk to Dr. King.

"How can this be?" I began, my feet sinking into the marshy grass with each step back to the cabin.

"Miss Callaghan, I just don't know," said Dr. King, who moved at a fast clip when he was especially perturbed.

"Something about his right arm," I said, keeping up. "Or what was left of it."

He stopped on a dime to whip around and stare at me.

So I told him about how I saw two small holes in the skin by Tor's pulse that looked like bite marks. It had to be bites because he wasn't suicidal and I didn't peg Tor as a cutter.

"Did you see the middle of the snake that Cass killed?" I said. "Its midsection had a distinct wound."

"The knife wound," said Dr. King.

"No," I replied. "It looked like something made from human teeth."

3.

In the end, we did what most people do after a long, troubling day. We went to bed.

No one really wanted waffles anymore, which was fine with Auggie who told Bobby stories until the little guy drifted off. Pete went upstairs to his room to read while Tosh slipped away to pout. I never saw Cass come back into the house. Eddie said he was going to drown his nerves in a big bubble bath.

Daniel, however, refused to allow me to stay up all night and pace.

"You're going to bed . . . and no funny stuff," he said.

"If I had a dollar for every time I stood over a dead body in the moonlight and someone wanted to take me to bed *just to sleep*," I began with a tilted lip.

"Do me a favor," he whispered. "Let's try to exist. Until dawn."

"You're so damn demanding," I said.

When our breath mingled, this world, that world, and all the others fell away.

In that soft bed covered by a warm cloud of blankets, I felt his heart beating against my palm. It was soothing in ways I could never explain, but I was beginning to understand.

Those tiny little throbs meant one thing: With each tiny strike . . .

We.

Go.

On.

4.

It turns out that monsters don't sleep under your bed. They live inside your head. It's why I slept hard for about an hour until the nightmares of Tor began.

When my eyelids flew open with a start, I saw his beautiful face. I felt him in my bones—real, pure goodness. Daniel's middle-of-the-night kiss was that dip in the road that sends your belly to your throat.

A gritty voice was crooning into my ear, "Baby, baby you know it's true . . . there ain't no one in this world for me, but you."

I had to giggle because this tall hunk was actually the world's worst singer.

"How are you, really?" I asked when the song was over.

"Juiced, but feeling the dread," he said. I followed his gaze out into the darkness of the window. "It's a big, unexplored world out there, isn't it," he said. "And you?"

"Scared shitless, but there's a thunder inside of me. I want to run out there and see it all," I said in a rush. And then for the sake of sanity, I added, "When it's morning. I can wait that long."

"Good thinking, Callaghan."

He pulled me closer—and closer—and closer, legs tangled, arms twined. We used our lips, but not just for what seemed obvious. Words tumbled out as we shared our deepest fears and most impossible dreams for this part of the ride. That's the weird thing. People think intimacy is just about sex. Real intimacy is about truth.

When you tell your truth that's when you are the most naked.

5.

4:00 a.m.

We couldn't possibly sleep, so he built a fire and wrapped both of us in the thick white comforter, though it really wasn't that cold. I watched with an easy heartbeat as the flames danced and flickered. In the amber light, he checked for where the wounds should have been, but they were not because of his handiwork.

"Show me where it hurts."

"All over," I teased.

"You need your rest," he said, worried that I was still somehow damaged.

"Kiss me now," I retorted. "Or live with regret for the rest of forever."

His eyes caressed mine and then he used that same power to examine the soft hollow in my neck. When he reached forward to play with the tangled ends of my hair, I began to softly trace the lines of a large tree tattoo that started on his hard forearm.

One small kiss. A head tilt. Exposed skin. His lips on the side of my neck. A tiny bite. Inevitability set in when he moved forward until we began to devour each other.

He tried to pull back, again and again, once stopping cold to just stare at my lips. Daniel ran a calloused thumb over my bottom one.

"Why look at the menu if you're not going to order anything," I teased.

"Callaghan . . . ," he began.

I removed my hand from under the covers and raised it.

"Present," I said.

"Yes, you are," he replied, slowly sliding both of us down into the fluff.

Later, I knew that if someone asked me what the word *beautiful* looked like—if I had to draw it—then I would sketch a picture of my head on his shoulder, his strong arm loped over my stomach.

This was beautiful.

6.

5:30 a.m.

An uncertain sunrise was still a dream away and Daniel was snoring away when I slipped out of bed. Three low knocks on a door across the hallway. No one answered.

A wide-awake and shirtless Cass didn't seem surprised when I opened the heavy wooden door and slipped inside. His long hair was out of the holder and fell into his face in a messy tangle. "Sugar, please tell me this is not a dream—or maybe it feels like a dream I had about two hours ago," he mumbled, face planted into a fluffy pillow. I noticed he was shirtless and probably everything else "less."

He moved the covers back with a sweeping arm movement.

"Come on in," he murmured.

I got it, but sat down in one of his straight-back chairs because I didn't want to muddy the waters. We were something else, as in check the "just friends" box. At least one of us felt exactly that way.

Because he was smart, helpful, and personally invested in this situation due to his sisters, the Claires, I needed his help. He knew this was business when he spied a piece of paper in my hand. "You're killing me, sugar," he said, sitting up. "You just wander into my room in the sweet spot of dawn when lovers should be greeting the day. Next time, do it naked."

"Cass," I said, clearing my throat. "I have to show you something." I handed him the letter I was given here in The Other. It was why I was standing on the outside porch when Tor decided to use me as target practice.

That letter, and several others, came from across the realms that separated life from death. Turns out that all those balloons and bottles the living sent into the air or tossed into the sea ended up somewhere. If you were very lucky and dead (not the lucky part) then one of those messages would float on a current, slip through a fissure between worlds, and follow you into the afterlife. There were post offices for the dead to pick up their mail.

I couldn't wait to read mine

"My mother adopted your sisters," I blurted to a shocked Cass who apparently when half-asleep was a slow reader, of all things. Now, he was swinging his legs around to face me. Draping his large frame over the side of the bed, he didn't seem to mind when the covers slipped to the floor. Yep, he was naked. And oblivious. And quite the something. Leaning forward, he caught his face in his hands, which he always did when he was thinking deeply.

Every breath I took sounded garishly loud. It wasn't just that I was in this room alone with him. I didn't like keeping any secrets from Daniel. But he already had enough on his plate with both of his brothers here and me to protect, in addition to finding his sisters who went missing months ago. The girls were hidden away in some past time loop, probably by their insane father, Edward Reid.

Daniel didn't need to worry about how my mother had adopted Cass's quadruplet clairvoyant sisters—who died in unison only to be "reborn" as babies and adopted by a new family or a single mother. That was bad enough. Making it worse was the fact that just prior to their demises, they kill the current mother, which meant my favorite person on earth was now facing a certain death sentence.

Even dead, I would not let that happen.

"So, what are we going to do about your sisters and my mother?" I blurted in a half- crazed whisper.

"Nothing for now," Cass said, smiling over at me. "But we're going to think about it. And we're going to figure it out before they do one thing to your mother."

"I can't ask you to—" I began.

"Kill them?" he posed. "Yes, you can. I know you remember Claire C stabbing me in the back when I was alive. You know, they say payback's a bitch and there's not bigger bitches that deserve some payback than my sisters."

"But, you're not the type to—"

"Sugar, there's a lot you don't know about me," Cass said. "A lot of falsehoods you've been told about me by my darling former sisters, I'm sure. I came here to help you, but also to help myself. That's a tale for another time."

"I'm here right now," I whispered.

"I want to tell you," he said in a soft voice. "But after you make love to me. Not after you make love to him."

An uncomfortable silence, the kind that made you want to burrow into the center of the earth, followed. I gazed at his bedroom door and then stood. What else could I say? I gave him a tiny wave and tried to retreat.

My hand was on the door lever when he said, "As for my sisters and your mother, it's horrendous, but here's one given that should put you at ease for a little while at least. We have seventeen years until they're grown. They don't get dangerous until they've come of age."

"And," I said, facing him again. "I can go into the past well before that happens and somehow—"

"Take them out?" Cass offered. I thought he might judge me, but his smile was wicked and complicit. "Your only choice will be to take them out—and I can help you do it. It would be my pleasure. We'll call it a date night."

I nodded.

"I honestly do not believe that my reincarnating sisters should *ever* come of age in Chicago, Illinois," said Cass, who knew the city well—as did I. It's where I met Cass. I grew up in the burbs and he was a college student there who could "see" and talk to the dead.

"They'll be little girls when we find them . . . and kill them. Can you stomach it?" he asked. "And your mother will be devastated."

"My mother will be alive," I said. "Did they—"

"Kill my mother, yeah . . . and me . . . and someone else who meant a lot to me," Cass said. "I don't want to talk about that part. Not now."

I almost made it through the door before Cass softly snuck up. He put a gentle hand on my shoulder, spun me around and gently kissed my forehead. Then he placed his fingers into my wild mane of auburn hair.

"I have to go," I said in a low voice, removing his hands.

"Then I already miss you," he said, allowing his fingers to linger until I walked out of his grasp.

FOUR

1.

The plaque outside our current residence read: Summertide, but it was an injustice to simply call it a log cabin. A wooden shack was something rustic that had bugs in it and a heater that kicked in if you were very lucky.

This "home base" in The Other was a striking, three-story rustic retreat belonging to industrialist Howard H. in his saner days before the long nails and germophobia set in. A young and impossibly rich Howard wasn't shy about demanding the best, which was why this was more like a log mansion, with floor-to-ceiling windows in back revealing the bluest lake and a horizon hugged by tall green trees. Those pines were dusted white because it was . . . wasn't it? Yes, it was the day after Christmas.

We didn't have a tree or presents here, but someone thought to sneak downstairs early and light a small blaze in the enormous stone fireplace in the great room and it *snap-crackle-popped* merrily, shooting off bright orange-and-white sparks of light. Dr. King, a man who "lived" (but not literally) to make it better, somehow managed to wrap a few boxes for

Bobby. He had strung some greenery across the fireplace mantel. It was just enough to make my heart do that little holiday flip.

In the warmth of our borrowed bedroom, I couldn't find Daniel. In fact, he was long gone when I opened my eyes and rolled over in an empty bed. So, I put on my shorts and sweatshirt and made a plan to follow the distinct smell of sizzling bacon combined with the joyful aroma of freshly brewing coffee.

Still in blue flannel jammies, Pete was the master chef this morning and he bid me hello with the wave of his spatula. A glance to the right and I found a barefoot Daniel in his black shorts and black tee pouring some dark brew.

The best feeling in the world was when I looked at him . . . and he was already staring.

Drifting just close enough, I waited for his long, muscled arms to extend, drawing me into his vortex.

"Merry post-Christmas, Callaghan," he whispered, mindlessly yanking me all the way in. Bone on bone. Skin on skin. Curves and slices fitting like puzzle pieces.

A potent flicker of joy ignited his face and it made my heart surge. He used the offer of my parted lips to dive right in. Hard. His kiss tasted warm and rich; his heart pounded against my ribs. The only thing I needed was to stay in this spot for the rest of eternity.

How could death feel so alive?

"I love you," I whispered into his shirt, trying to create privacy when there was none.

"If I know what love is, and I do, it's because of you," he whispered with warm lips on my ear. Shivers ran riot down my back.

"I love you, baby," he said.

I could wander in the world, on wings of gold or on the back of his Harley, and it would be all right if I could always come home. It wasn't a house of bricks and wood, but of bone and flesh.

"And what about me?" said Auggie, who suddenly hovered over my left shoulder and looked so forlorn. I had to laugh, then reluctantly untangled. In the absence of anything worldly, there was only one thing to give this holiday season and it felt like more than enough. I drew Auggie closer with my free arm.

"Don't hurt me," Auggie begged Daniel. "I've always been this needy."

"He is a big ball of need," Eddie sniffed. Someone had given him yellow flannel pants and a matching shirt, so he looked like a frowning, lonely, desperate Big Bird standing outside our little circle.

"Get in here," I grumbled, grabbing one of his crayon-colored sleeves.

Eventually, we had to unwind—which couldn't come quickly enough for Daniel. Food was a good diversion and Pete flipped too many sunny-side up eggs without breaking one yolk.

"And he cooks, too," I stated the obvious, as I helped Tosh fill glasses with fresh OJ.

"Yes, he cooks," said my friend in a leotard and shorts, her standard operating gear. "I don't settle for half-assed men."

That dangled in the air while I pressed another orange into the juicer.

"Hey, good morning," Cass said, finally joining us. It should have been awkward for him, but he wouldn't allow it because the former marine was used to life in the corps. Without being asked, he started to set the table, which was fortunate. Tosh wasn't one for manual labor. She had already retired to the cushy leather sofa, a woven Indian rug on her feet for warmth.

Cass looked toasty in a big white sweater and jeans. He was always ready for action, and to that end, I handed him a few stray paper napkins.

"How are you?" I asked when he purposely allowed his fingers to brush over mine during the handoff.

"I'm vertical, sugar," he said.

"How's it going?"

"It's going—for a guy who had very little sleep."

Daniel didn't miss much and the fact that he was now outside bringing in firewood was a lucky break. Cass might have pushed it another few miles, if it wasn't for a diversion that came in the form of a small missile plowing directly into his knees.

"Holy shit, why are you still here?" Bobby inquired.

Cass was faster and had animalistic instincts when it came to an impending attack. He grabbed young Bobby Reid by his yellow towel superhero cape and hoisted the boy in Iron Man jammies off his feet.

"He's taken a prisoner! Death to the last survivor!" Bobby yelled, swinging his arms and legs wildly until a laughing Cass was forced to put him down.

Bobby just glared up at him.

"She's not yours . . . you know," the kid said, sticking out his defiant Reid chin. "Get your own girlfriend. She belongs to us."

"Are you six or twenty-six?" Cass responded.

"Didja know my brother calls you a douche?" Bobby said. Then he turned to me. "Walkie, what does that mean?"

"It means it's time for breakfast," I said. "Everybody, let's sit down and someone put on some Christmas music. Crank it to ten."

I was mortified when I saw Bobby flash double middle fingers at Cass. The kid wasn't playing.

2.

It felt so normal. It felt like home. So, why was I so keenly aware that this day was fleeting? The clock ticks.

You can't hold on to the seconds.

Relentless. That's what time is.

The breakfast bubble burst when Daniel returned and I could see Cass glaring at him.

"Hey, man," Daniel said.

Cass was the one who didn't mince words.

"Hey, man, glad we all made it to today, especially Walker after you got her shot last night. You should be proud."

"Let's just try to get along . . . and I'm fine," I interrupted.

"My bad," Cass said.

"Just not bad enough," Daniel said. "Story of your life . . . and now your death."

He had a full-blast grin on his face with a hint of merriment behind it. Cass just shook his head in disgust. Both stared at me in the kind of way where I wanted to jump out the window to cut the tension.

"Weird how you run into people when you're out of town," I said, summing up the situation. So much for deflecting the tension with a joke. It didn't work, so I put my hand on both of their chests because they were already too close to each other.

"No reason to elevate my cortisol levels," I said.

"Or mine," Dr. King grumbled before adding, "Mr. Reid. Mr. . . . . I'm sorry, Cass, I don't know your last name."

"Danko," Cass muttered.

"Mr. Reid, Mr. Danko, it's going to be a long afterlife, not to mention an endless mission, if the two of you almost come to blows every other minute. In other words, knock it off and act like men."

Speaking of which . . .

"Mine," Eddie said, matter-of-factly, after grabbing the last five pancakes off the stack. He poured a sea of syrup on them until the plate was swimming and lifted his fork. Eddie didn't have too much to eat growing up with his two brothers, no mother, and barely a father in a rural town that America forgot. The afterlife for him was horrific. At his prison school, he was starved, which is why he never failed to stack his plate high.

It shocked me when he glanced at a pouting Bobby whose pancakes were gone. "Nah, it's for you," Eddie told the kid, sliding over his own plate. Since he was only six, Bobby didn't need to be told twice, but paused before he dug in.

"Sure?" he asked in a hopeful voice – the kind that broke your heart.

Eddie patted his stomach. "I'm as full as a tick on a hound dog," he told the kid.

"Very nice, Edward. You're a giver," Tosh said, sizing him up and smiling.

Obviously inspired, she offered Pete the last piece of bacon, which he ate from her fingers.

Yeah, he liked her, too. And there would be seconds.

When the last dish was cleared, Dr. King didn't say a word, but pointed to the living room where we fell into various nooks and comfortable places: Daniel and I reclined on one of the worn brown leather couches sitting close. Cass sat alert in the chair across from us forming an interesting triangle. Pete and Tosh made their way to the fireplace ledge to warm up their backsides, supposedly, and heat up already overheated hormones (now that Pete was around, she didn't give Cass a second glance). The "boys"—Eddie, Bobby, and Auggie—hit the floor to play with some little metal trucks Dr. King found in the garage and had wrapped for Bobby as a delivery from Santa.

I watched as Eddie shivered—meaning his reset wasn't working so good either because we never got cold.

"It's colder than a penguin's balls," he said. When Bobby "got it," he burst into gales of laughter. Even Auggie laughed before standing up to get a plate of freshly baked Christmas cookies. As he walked into the kitchen, Eddie shouted out, "Don't let the door hit you where the good Lord split you!"

It took Bobby a minute. "You mean ass?" he cackled.

"Now, that we've had that lovely holiday exchange," said Dr. King, "perhaps I could interest you in other subject matters, like survival."

He had my attention.

Our principal didn't sit, but stood in front of us because that's what leaders did before sending their troops into battle.

The party was definitely over.

3.

Dr. King didn't usually stand on ceremony. He was direct and blunt.

"Students, I need to know your intentions," he said. "I know you've only been here one hell of a day and night, but there are choices that need to be made and positions declared . . . and the sooner the better."

"What are the choices, sir?" I asked. He smiled briefly because it felt like all those days at the Academy when I'd run into our principal in the hallways. I asked; he answered. It was always a lovely exchange like playing verbal ping-pong. No filler. Keep your eyes on the ball.

"We could all stay here. Form our own small society," Dr. King said. "We have some of the building blocks of existence. We have shelter. This cabin is well beyond a luxurious choice of a dwelling. There are animals. We could hunt for food, grow vegetables, and just stay in place."

"What about Principal Dick?" Daniel took a shot.

"The force field between the two sides is locked closed. The only one who knows the code to open it is the X-catcher who is on this side. The X-catcher is a person—just one—entrusted with the new code. Every time the wall opens, the old X-catcher retires and a new one steps up. Who appoints this person? I don't know. But he or she is already in place with that code," Dr. King said. "If you find the X-catcher and plead your case, he or she might give you the code to go back home. Or not. It's entirely up to this person.

"And here's the rub," he added. "The longer we're here, the X-catcher could change. If the current X-catcher feels that he or she is in danger, they will give the code to someone else thus making them X," he said.

I took a moment to digest. Basically, we were looking for a phantom.

"Don't let this news steal your sunshine," Dr. King said with an ironic smile. "All of what I just blathered provides a nice buffer between Principal Dick and Walker and Daniel. He can't get here to find the X-catcher. Again, he or she is on this side. My intelligence agents are seldom wrong about these kinds of things. Opening the force field is entirely our decision from this side."

"Sir, what are the dangers of just staying here?" I asked. "What if we chose just to *be* for five minutes?"

"There are other factions out there who might want this house. There are few as luxurious on this side or that hold so many," Dr. King said. "We could come under attack. These people won't just hurt us. If they came in greater numbers, they would kill us. All of us." He looked around the room. "But we have enough strong fighters here, myself included now at my new young age, that I think we could save the ranch, so to speak. Plus, this place is on few maps. You'd literally have to stumble upon it or know it was here in order to find it.

"And there is one more thing when it comes to this topic," Dr. King said. "Follow me into the war room."

"War room?" I saw Tosh mouth to Pete. We shadowed Dr. King into a room I thought was an extended pantry past the kitchen, but it was filled with small computer screens and home monitoring equipment. Dr. King was a one-man FBI.

"Look at monitor one," he instructed. I could clearly see the front of the house then the back and the sides on the screen.

"It's snowing outside," I said.

"The machine has a one-second delay," said our principal.

"Miss Callaghan, press button one," he commanded. They were clearly marked, but my hand still trembled a bit when I pressed the number and a warm green light came on.

"Look at the monitors again," said Dr. King.

I did exactly as he instructed, although this time my eyes popped and my breath hitched.

The house was gone. No front. No back. No sides.

"If we have advanced warning that we have 'visitors,' then we can activate this invisible mode. If the visitor is several feet away, it will appear as if there are only huge pine trees—although if they had a reason to advance and reach out, they would actually find the house by bumping right into it," he said.

"Does this mean—" Eddie began.

"Keen observation, Edward," said Dr. King. "Yes, everything and everyone in the house is invisible to outsiders when this mechanism is rendered."

"Nice toy," said Cass.

"Necessary tool," said Dr. King.

Once again, we gathered in the living room to hear the rest. I glanced at Daniel. It sounded a lot like retirement at age seventeen if we stayed and relied upon the gizmos in this amazing house. It also brought up several unsettling questions such as: *What would we do here for eternity? What would we aspire to be? How would we ever level up?*

"We wouldn't level up," Dr. King said, almost reading my mind. "We would remain in our current states for as long as we stayed."

"Pass," Cass said. "I'm bored already."

"There is, of course, a Plan B," Dr. King said with a nod of his head. "Of course, it's a lot more dangerous than Plan A, but hear me out.

"The Academy is imploding," Dr. King continued. "Dick's plan is to strip the students of every single freedom similar to Nazi Germany or any totalitarian regime. He knows that teenagers by their very nature are rebellious and will resist. His phony war of rules versus the students is a ruse.

"Soon, he will send the most progressive thinking teachers away to other realms. There will be no one to fight for the students. Every infraction will carry a severe penalty. Drop a napkin. Shout a swear word. It will be the perfect reason to ship the rebels off to ITT and cage them. Even the most obedient will slip up. Off to ITT. That will leave him with only one thing."

"The building. The actual structure," I said, "with all of its magical and one-of-a-kind elements like the Hall of Yearning and other supernatural peculiarities."

"Prime afterlife real estate," said Dr. King. "And isn't that what mankind always fights for in life and now death? Real estate."

There was more to Dick's plan.

"Once he figures out where you hid the Omorrow project, he will find that realm Einstein discovered where the living and the dead can meet and talk. He will bring back the worst of the worst. He will house them at the Academy. Imagine Charles Manson in control of the Hall of Yearning. What would his dark soul yearn for now?"

I shivered just thinking about it.

"Plan B, if you have the balls," Dr. King stated. "We find the X-catcher, open the force field wall, slip back in under the cover of night, find certain hiding spots that only I know of, and make a plan. We enlist only the most courageous students under my leadership and we fight for the Academy. We avoid the Higher Authority, which is corrupt, build a student army, continue to hide the Omorrow papers across time and realms, and eventually wipe that son of a bitch Dick and all of his followers off the map."

"And Plan C?" Auggie asked.

"There is no plan C, son," Dr. King said. "Be grateful in life if there is a Plan B. Not everyone is lucky enough to have a second option, let alone a third."

"I guess I'm greedy," said a dejected Auggie.

Our principal was having none of it.

"I guess you're human," he corrected.

In the end, we decided to take a silent vote. Bobby passed out little pieces of paper and one crayon each. Funny how the fate of something so precious would be decided by holding a child's writing instrument with the word *magenta* on it. Dr. King insisted that we write one of two words: Fight or Stay.

The end tally was thus:

Auggie: Stay
Eddie: X for Stay. He didn't read or write.
Tosh: Stay
Pete: Fight
Cass: Fight
Daniel: Fight
Me: Fight
Bobby: Fite

"It has been decided," Dr. King said, a slow smile spreading across his face. "We fight."

"We go home," I said.

"You know that's impossible, Miss Callaghan. You can't go back to Chicago."

"Home is the Midst now," I said. Then I confessed the rest. "I haven't had many homes to call my own. If we're talking about eternity, I want my own front porch, my bed, and that kitchen table that isn't level with the floor.

"You have no idea," I said, looking out the window into a vast new land, "what I wouldn't do to get home."

Daniel put a period on it. "You have no idea what I would do," he said.

4.

"Home it is—we'll all go back to the Midst after we find the new X-catcher," said Dr. King. "I do have a few ideas of who might have been appointed—and how to find this person. I have a lead telling me he or she is in north country. It's quite far away."

Dr. KingHe shook his head.

"Ah, the beautiful rub of it all," he said. "An X-catcher can figure out the code to the force field because this person is extremely proficient in math. The universal joke here is that even in death, you still have to do the math."

"Who chooses the X-catcher?" I queried, the questions flying off my tongue now.

Dr. King nodded and launched.

"No clue, except they do have a murky governing board on this side called the Council of Curiosities. As for the rest, let's start with a quick geography lesson," said Dr. King, who began to pace like a jungle cat. "We're not really in The Other. We're on the outskirts of the places. They allow strangers from our side to stay on the fringes, no questions asked. None answered either. If occasionally one of them drifts to our side, we allow them a few spare rooms on Freak Island. That is our outskirts. Sometimes someone just needs a brief change of location."

"What do we need to get into the actual Other?" I challenged. "A passport?"

"Worse," said Dr. King. "You will have to take a physical and mental exam. There are special doctors here. They will probe every inch of you. I'm telling you this now because if you don't want to go through the exam, it's fine. No one will think less of you. You can stay here at the house where the only exams will be the history, math, and English tests I will give you."

"Did you say probe? Because I'm at a place in my new life where I don't really like to be probed," Eddie interjected.

"It's a complete mental and physical exam, Edward," Dr. King said. "They want to make sure that you're capable of survival once they do let you in."

"Who or *what* are we, um, surviving?" I asked.

Again, Dr. King ignored me and stuck with his agenda. "Think of it like going through immigration at Ellis Island. Again, if you find this distasteful, that's fine. There are seven of you here. I only plan on sending five of the strongest. Two of you will stay with me."

I opened my mouth to protest.

"Not up for discussion," Dr. King warned.

"Those who trek into the wilderness of The Other will be gone months or longer. A few of you must remain to protect the cabin."

His words rang in my ears.

He would only send five.

"I need five who will be able to survive this journey. To do so, the five will have to keep wheedling their way in," said Dr. King. "They will turn every corner, dig every hole, and go through each dark tunnel. Against all odds, they will keep moving forward, following their angels and their feet."

Every cell in my body began to tingle like it had been revved. This was exactly my kind of road trip—one where there might be no recognizable road.

5.

My excitement was not contagious.

"Do I have to get naked during the exam?" Eddie whined, because he was obsessed. *I kept doing the math in my head. Eddie shouldn't go. One down.* "Because, generally, I have no problem with nudity," he said.

"Neither do I," said Tosh, flashing a smile at Pete, who looked down but was still smiling. What fifteen-year-old male wouldn't be?

"I'm assuming you will be naked," said Dr. King. "They will look for any kind of weakness. Your strength, both mental and physical, is key, because The Other is a big undertaking. The land is vast and dangerous. The cost will be paid in bone and blood."

"Sir," I said, keeping my voice level in order to not show any trepidation, "What exactly is out there?"

"What's not out there?" he answered. At least he was funneling some information this time. "This is a place for misfits and rebels who want to tap into different states of consciousness. They live in various domains or settlements. Some have powerful energies or mind-blowing forms of intelligence. They've crossed the great divide between life and death to find this place where they can celebrate their Otherness."

"Robert, look up the word *other* in the dictionary on the table," Dr. King said.

Apparently, the six-year-old had received advanced tutoring—and quite a lot of it—during his time here. He cleared his throat after finding the word in a nanosecond. "Other," he recited, "used to refer to a person or thing that is different or distinct. Dis . . . disturbingly or thr-threat-threateningly different."

Daniel and I glanced at each other. The kid even powered through the hard words. Score one for Dr. King.

"As in other places with rigid points of view, most of these settlements do not get along with each other, so there is fighting and even small wars," Dr. King pushed on. "You will not get involved. Keep your head down and push on. You'll have a great distance to cover and stopping to get involved with the locals could mean two worst-case scenarios:

the X-catcher will slip through your fingers or you will be killed. Killed means you're dust particles. Gone."

"What do you mean by states of consciousness?" Cass asked. "When I was in the military, there was either conscious or unconscious, which is how I preferred to keep the enemies."

"Cass," said Dr. King, "think of states of consciousness as being in a tall building with many floors. Most of us live on only one or two of those floors. But there are others who dedicate themselves to exploring each floor. It makes them powerful."

"Drugs?" Cass asked.

"No, there are no drugs here," said Dr. King. "In The Other, your senses are tuned up naturally in a place that's simply open to possibilities. What that means is if you were ever to experience any type of bonus skill—one that even seemed unimaginable—well, this is the place you'd want to be, because expanded consciousness means stronger, longer, leaner, meaner, and more active—or greater—in every way.

"It doesn't happen overnight. The longer you're here, the more your natural abilities are honed," he said. "What's fascinating is personal choice plays into it. The dynamics of who you want to be as a person is recognized and allowed."

"Walker is already the Questioner," Tosh teased. "That's her superpower."

"Very true," said Dr. King. "But there's actually more to it. Your genes modify for this atmosphere. For example, what if Walker already knew the answers to most of her questions? What if Daniel could throw a punch with his mind? "Robert, come over here," said Dr. King to Bobby. "Let's show them what we've been working on. You've been a very good boy in keeping it a secret."

Three heads—mine, plus Daniel's and Pete's—were on a swivel as we locked onto our small hellion. *In the weeks that Bobby had been hidden here, they had been working on something that was . . . clandestine?*

"Robert has been here for some time now," our fearless leader. said, picking him up, straight up, by the back of his little checked shirt. "That is why he can do a few nifty things. Neat things. Things boys his age only dream of doing, but few actually do.

"*Alate!*" Dr. King said.

At first, Bobby just dangled, bare feet pointed toward the ground. Dr. King waited a beat or two, and I expected him to put Bobby down. But, he didn't place the little one's tootsies on the cold wood floor. Dr. King removed his hand.

He let go.

Arms jetting out over his messy hair, Bobby didn't just hover a foot in the air, but he actually *flew forward* about an arm's length before Dr. King reached out to grab him *midair* and then he placed him gently on terra firma.

"*Alate* means lifted in flight," said Bobby.

"We sorta got that part," I replied in a stunned voice.

"I fly now, but I dunno how to land. Yet," Bobby said in a calm voice. "My friend Stan here on this side help'ted. Dr. King teach'd me. You know, Stan. He comes over somedays and helps me draw comic books."

Bobby whispered extra loud in Daniel's ear—as kids do. "He knows Spider-Man. For reals," he said. "He nin-vented him."

With that news flash, Bobby took off like a terror and returned with an artist's portfolio filled with pictures he drew with his friend Stan to pass a boring afternoon: Spider-Man, the Hunk, Iron Man, Black Widow, Captain America. They weren't just childish drawings, but perfectly professional and amazing.

"He draw'd it and I colored it," said Bobby proudly. I could see that these were little works of art from a master with a six-year-old trying to stay in the lines.

"Stanny know'd a lot superheroes, but he says I'm the super-est," Bobby said. Then his tiny hand flew to his mouth.

"Shitballs," the kid exclaimed. "That's 'nuther secret."

6.

"He is only in the preliminary stages of learning to do what his heart desires, which is flying," Dr. King said. "I don't think we have to worry about him taking off for a long, long time. And not to worry. He can only do this in The Other, we're almost sure."

"Wanna fly up and over trees," Bobby yelled before going back to his trucks. Like what just happened was no big deal.

I heard Daniel swear under his breath.

"We can discuss this more later," Dr. King said. "But back to what I was saying before. You will hopefully pass this physical and then you'll be sent into the actual Other realm. And if I were a guessing man, which I'm not, I think I know who the next X-catcher is and where he is located.

"We need to find this person and ask for the punch code," Dr. King continued. "Again, it's encrypted and trusted to only one. There might be others who will try to steal that code from you as you make your way back here. There are rumors that some settlements here would like to carve out some choice real estate for themselves in the Midst. They want to infiltrate the Midst. One person who comes to mind is a self-declared sheriff of sorts here. She has hired herself to keep the peace since there is no formal law here. Stay away from her. We don't know her true intentions. And she hates newcomers."

"Name?" I asked, producing a thin, tall reporter's notebook from the waistband of my pants. It was my way of accessorizing.

"Sheriff Pristine. No first name," said Dr. King.

"Some matters in The Other are dealt with by the Council of Curiosities. I mentioned them earlier. They're sort of like the United Nations between the Midst and The Other," he continued. "They're more into investigating and tracking the abnormal . . . and it's all abnormal here.

"The only thing is, it takes forever to get them a message . . . and even longer to get an answer. The good news is they haven't been corrupted like the Higher Authority back in the Midst."

It was a lot to take in, so I took a deep breath.

"How far do we have to go?" Daniel asked.

"To put it in layman's terms, it will be like walking from Florida to California," said Dr. King. "But I do have a car for you, and hopefully it won't be stolen. It's vintage. Howard likes his cars to be returned the way they were lent out—or else."

"Wait just a second," Eddie said, dropping his truck. "The only kind of walking I like is *The Walking Dead*."

"We *are* the walking dead," I retorted, standing up to walk the floorboards.

Dr. King stopped me when he put a gentle hand on my shoulder. "Walker, you don't need to go. Stay here with me and Bobby, plus one more."

"She'll stay here," Daniel interrupted.

"And that's nonnegotiable," Cass concluded.

7.

For a minute, the world pivoted off its axis. I couldn't draw one more breath. Staying at the cabin was insane starting with the fact that *the two of them had finally found common ground*, which was protecting me, damn it.

"It can't be nonnegotiable because we're not negotiating," I informed Cass. Then my eyes swayed left and locked. "And my staying here is, in your case, not on the table," I said to Daniel. Our eyes locked—all six of them—and I saw *his* granite and *his* conviction mix with the fortitude of a daughter of a steel worker. Epic love equals epic wars, and Daniel and I had already had a few. I felt a fresh one brewing.

As for Cass, his opinion didn't count here. Because I wasn't giving him an opinion.

Our fearless leader *just ignored me. He couldn't possibly consider this settled?*

"After your physical, you will begin in the Tunnel Lands where it's light at night and dark during the day," Dr. King said. "There are those who will want to take you as a slave there. You'll have to elude them."

Cass shook his head—and this was before it got worse.

"It's important to know that the people here are either hunters or gatherers. This is key," Dr. King said in a determined voice. "Some gather other humans; others hunt them. I know Miss Callaghan wants to ask: Who would take a teenager slave? Answer: Anyone who needs workers for their settlement. There are mines here where special entities are sourced. Hard labor doesn't mean workers. It means slaves—teenage ones make a strong and hearty workforce."

"That wasn't my number-one question," I blurted.

Everyone ignored me.

"Is this like the Midst? Are there mostly teenagers here?" Cass asked. He was an expert subject changer.

"What else? Dragons?" I said in my most sarcastic tone.

"I hear that was last century, son, but you never know," said Dr. King. "Don't interact with them either."

"Portals?" Daniel asked, and I could read his mind without having that power. He was thinking about taking a little detour and going into the past to find his sisters who had been hidden there by Dick and his horrendous father, Edward Reid. There was no way in hell I would let him do that without being by his side.

"There are no portals to the past," said Dr. King. But then his right eyebrow twitched in a way that was almost unperceivable unless you had taken many journalism courses in body language. I was a pro.

He was lying.

"How do we know who is good or bad?" Pete asked.

"Anyone trying to annihilate you . . . they're bad," said Dr. King.

"Easy enough, team," said Cass who obviously just assumed that he was going—and would be the leader because of his military training. I could see by the dark clouds on his face that there was no way in hell Daniel would report to anyone, especially the blond wonder who had feelings for his girlfriend.

"What kind of weapons do I need to give the other four?" Daniel inquired. Already, there was a war brewing for top gun positions. "Guns? Knives? Swords? Ourselves? I've been trained to use all of the above."

"You will be provided with some interesting choices," said Dr. King.

"My aura is tingling, although I'm thrilled not to go," Tosh said looking at all three of our alphas, which apparently also included Pete.

"I'll take all of those weapons you listed above," Pete said as I remembered his time out alone on the fringes of The Other before we found him. "Do you have a grenade launcher? Tank? Bomb?"

Everyone has questions. "What if someone does steal the car?" Daniel asked.

"Well, son," Dr. King said. "Then you fall back on something my granddaddy James, a sharecropper, used to say to me: an individual can go as far as his yearning can reach."

8.

There was only one monumental decision that would be made in the next minute. To that end, Dr. King passed around a pad of paper to sign up for the mission, but I couldn't wait.

My arm shot straight up. I could see the resolved looks on both Daniel and Cass's faces.

"I didn't come this far to only come this far," I said in a defiant tone.

Dr. King looked right at me—and then right past me. The five realm travelers to The Other in no particular order:

Daniel, Cass, Pete, Eddie, and Auggie.

Auggie, WTF. There was no fight in him. Just love.

Tosh and I would stay at the cabin with Bobby and Dr. King.

Decided. In stone.

FIVE

1.

"No," I said under my breath. "No!"

"Callaghan," Daniel interjected. I was stalking around the room now and he was my roadblock. His quiet resolution stunned me. I could deal with his rage, but this new serenity was odd to say the least. "When I say I'm going to take care of my partner, you, I don't just mean sexually or romantically," he grumbled. "I also mean physically. I'm going to take care of you in all ways, which means you're not going, baby. Not today. Not ever."

"Walker," Cass said, unlocking Daniel from his lethal stare. "It's really for the best, sugar. Just stay here. We will be back before you know it."

I glared ice at both. WTHF now translated into what the holy f—.

Knowing their collusion, for lack of a better word, made me started ranting.

"Forget about the blatant sexism of it all. Forget about the fact that the two of you know nothing about the art of preparation or fact finding. Forget that I've saved both of your sorry asses—and numerous times I might add, if I was a bragging person. Forget it all, suckers." Now, I was seething. "Someone might take a moment to remember that I'm trained for this kind of mission. Better trained than Eddie or Auggie. So put an apron on one of them and have them stay at home and bake cookies or clean the toilets."

I found out the reset had kicked back in when I kicked the coffee table hard with my shoeless foot. *Nothing.*

"I'm going upstairs to pack," I declared.

The hell with both of them.

2.

I bolted upstairs. About five second later, the bedroom door quietly closed.

Daniel smelled like fury, but his walk was deliberately slow across the wood floor, stopping only when I could feel his breath on my hair. I stared squarely at his chest, watching him breathe, which was when he put a finger under my chin. My head was tilted up.

"You're delusional, Callaghan, if you think I'm going to take you on a trek through some unknown dangerous abyss," he said.

"Exactly my kind of vacation," I responded.

"Walker . . ."

"I'll see you out there. If you don't let me in the car, I'll wait until you leave and I'll walk—or I'll leave right now," I said, tossing my socks, extra pants, and my lucky rabbit's foot inside my pack. I was done with being reasonable.

Reasonable was why I died at age seventeen.

We didn't have much, and I was already accustomed to packing at record speeds. Nothing like having to gather your gear when flying demons are attacking.

"You're working overtime here, baby," Daniel said in that low, slow voice. He made every word sound like its own sentence. "You're. Not. Going."

Dr. King was the one who stepped in the middle. He didn't even knock, but simply flung the door open.

"Save your wrath for that pile of wood outside, Miss Callaghan," he said. "It's going to be a cold night and we'll need more wood for the fireplace. You, alone, will chop the wood and bring it in. Maybe you can work out some of your feelings with an ax." His rich baritone voice of authority forced me to stop in my tracks and turn around.

"You shouldn't give me an ax," I warned.

"Sorry, sugar," Cass said from the hallway. He wandered into the room, taking up too much space. "You're going to have to trust us. You've been through enough. It's okay to coast."

"Hey, she can have my spot," Eddie offered in a hopeful voice. He stood in the door.

"Shut up, Wargo," Cass yelled.

"What is this . . . a conspiracy here?" I blurted. "All of you suck. Auggie, please come in here." He was there in a nanosecond.

"Auggie, honey, you're not going," I said.

"Thank God," he blurted, tears rolling. "I'm not good outdoors."

"Go fucking pack," Daniel and Cass said in unison.

"You don't have to be rude about it," said Auggie who took his tears to his own room.

I pushed past all of them, ran down the stairs, and blasted out of the back door.

3.

The slap of a crisp north wind felt good as it turned my face a winter red. Ax in my hands, I swung for the fences; and each time the blade connected with a piece of firewood, I felt vindicated. *I will not stay*, I thought, pulverizing the poor wood as the velvety snow mixed with fresh tears.

Some kind of warrior you are. You're a worrier, my head screamed, in the body of a rejected wuss.

All day long, I heard it. It was that little voice inside of me that said, "Go. You must take this journey." Ironic, wasn't it? All I truly wanted to do is find a space in this vast universe to call home. I longed for that place and yearned to plant myself.

But this wasn't that place and I already felt itchy to roam.

I spent the better part of the day speaking to no one except Bobby, who was making numerous plans for us. When he came downstairs carrying a red towel, I was curious. My eyes welled when he glued a ribbon to it and then draped it across my back.

"You're my Wonder Woman, Walkie," he said.

"I'm glad someone has faith in me," I retorted, ignoring Daniel who blasted out of the back door and headed toward the woods.

Eventually, Daniel returned home and took my lead. He didn't say a word about the trip, but kept mostly to himself, watching and observing. I returned the favor by staying inward and never making eye contact with him. While putting away the dinner plates in the kitchen, he came close to me and whispered into my hair, "Baby, don't make me beg."

I turned around to face him. "Then don't make me beg," I replied.

After the last of the roast beef and mashed potatoes was put in the fridge for a midnight raid, I was sequestered in the living room pretending to read while those going on the trip had a special meeting in a back office.

If they wanted to kill me again . . . this was the way to do it.

I left Tosh and Bobby playing a mean game of Monopoly to sneak down the hallway and listen at the door, which was cracked just enough for spy purposes. Dr. King was talking about the particulars of the mission and I took out that little notepad again to jot a few things down.

"I lied earlier today because the fewer who know the particulars the better," Dr. King said.

"Let's start with portals to the past, which will be present along your journey. Time travel is actually allowed more freely here on this side.

You'll find these portals in interesting places, I'm told. You might even stumble into a few of them by mistake, so be careful.

"It's always tempting to go visiting, but don't get stuck in the past. If need be, you can run there," he warned. "But remember, we need to get the code. Time is of the essence if we want to save the Academy and beyond.

"And remember how dangerous it is to stay in a past loop. If you die in the past, you will never be born, and thus cease to exist in the future," said Dr. King. "It's also difficult to extract you from the past."

Daniel spoke next. "My father sent my sisters into the past. They're his hostages somewhere in another time because he wants my little brother back. He will bargain away the girls if we give him Bobby, which will happen when hell freezes over."

"Son," said Dr. King, "my first act when I'm restored as principal of the Academy will be to take you with me through the Principal's Portal and find your sisters. You have my word."

Daniel nodded, but through the sliver of door, I saw it on his face. If given a portal and a few clues, he would find Andy and Jenna. The knowing glance of future daring he gave Pete, which was returned, just sealed the deal.

The Reid boys meant business.

"Here, in The Other, they call portals to the past a Rewind," he explained. "There's also something you've never encountered before called the Now, which is truly tempting because you can go into a room to catch a quick glimpse of how life is going on without you in the living realm. It's an afterlife spy mission that can be found at one of the special schools here. Don't get stuck in watching life going on without you there instead of living your current existence here—although, believe me, it's tempting."

Dr. King decided to move on. "Remember what I said about how your senses are turned up here on this side. The way you will find the X-catcher is to get in the vicinity of this person. He or she will sense that you need help and that your motives are just and sound.

"He or she will come to you—or not," Dr. King added. "It's a choice based on free will and a sense if the wall will be opening for reasons that make sense."

Chance. Danger. Extinguishment.

So, I guess, it's just the same old, same old, I thought.

4.

He found me sitting outside with no coat on, slicing back and forth through freezing cold night air on one of the old wooden rockers that Howard kept outside on the best of the wraparound porches. I could feel his intensity, even from a minor distance. Silently, Daniel sat down at my side in the other rocker, but he didn't move. He simply watched me for a few minutes. When he had enough, he stood and swept me out of my chair, sat down in it and placed me on his lap.

I waited to tell him that this wouldn't work. That it was far too dangerous for him to do this without me. It wasn't ego, but based on our past together in these situations. This was our rewind. I was often the brains, he was the cunning and brawn. It wouldn't work in parts.

But I didn't say anything about those absolutes. Nor did I list the reasons why I needed to be traveling with him. He couldn't romance me out of it, talk me out of it, or scare me out of walking out that front door.

"I'm going with you . . . or by myself," I said in a matter-of-fact voice.

"I know."

"Who is going to tell Dr. King?"

"You can't beat the devil every single time," he said and his voice caught. "There comes a time when he beats you."

"How do you know the devil is male?" I retorted.

"Callaghan . . ."

"Hold me closer," I said, staring up at a clear winter's sky and catching the powered snow that fell from it onto my lips. It melted when his warm breath bathed my face.

"The one thing they can't take away from us is time . . . this time," I said, cupping his face with my hands.

We rocked until dawn.

5.

At six in the morning, we wandered inside to find a few early risers. "Candy," said Dr. King, who was sitting at the table with two others. "Sound it out," he instructed them.

"I'll go first," said Bobby, who did what I had taught him at home in the Midst. "*Ca-ca-ca* is the first part," he said. The kid was a fast learner and always got it at all levels. I watched as he slid a piece of wrapped chocolate over to the other person at the table. "Here ya go, Eddie," Bobby said. "You get a piece of candy just for trying. And so do I. Let's go get it."

"*Ca-ca-n-n-d*," Eddie began. Even though age eighteen, he couldn't read because he was mostly out of his local school system in Booneville, Alabama. Eddie's father preferred that his three sons take local jobs on farms where they picked veggies from sun up to sundown in order to help with the bills. Bobby slid him another piece of chocolate.

"That was very close," said the little boy. "Now, try again, but put a girl named Dee in it."

"*Ca-ca-n-n-dee*," Eddie said, slowly.

"Masterful work, Ed," Dr. King boomed. "And quite a magnificent incentive, Robert."

"Now, what has four legs and takes a shit on the rugs?" Bobby posed.

"*D-o-g*," Eddie said.

Eddie Wargo was *reading*. And for some reason that made me want to cry.

We didn't want to embarrass him, so we casually walked into the kitchen to pour some orange juice and crack some eggs. Daniel took care of the rest. "Dr. King," he said. "Can we have a word?"

Our principal was up in a single bound and stood by the stove in the kitchen with us.

"I know, she's going," Dr. King said. "It was a futile endeavor to bench Miss Callaghan, but I had to try."

He nodded. I nodded. *Thank God.*

My blood stopped boiling.

"Not going would be like opening the door, but not stepping outside,"

I said.

"Now you'll have one too many," Dr. King said. "The car seats five."

"Take Pete off the list," Daniel said. "That way, if anything happens, well, he can be with Bobby and find Jenna and Andy. I'll talk to him about stepping up for the family."

"As you wish," Dr. King said. "Now, put on your outdoor gear. I have a refresher course for you to take today and additional meetings to cover some of the pit stops along the way. You'll be leaving tomorrow morning."

"I have a list of questions," I said with a grin.

6.

After breakfast, Dr. King had arranged for one of his "training" buddies to come over to size us up. Pat used to play pro football, but then joined the US Army after the September 11 attacks, but sadly was killed in Afghanistan when he was shot three times in the head. They ruled it as friendly fire.

He was twenty-seven.

Here on this side to help with training for special missions, he was big and brawny with a square face and searing blue eyes. Cass almost lost his mind and shook his hand reverently. I found the courage to walk up to him and ask him why he was hanging out in The Other. "Just passing through," he said, "but I feel a passion for this place. And passion is what makes life interesting, what ignites our soul, fuels our love, and carries our friendships. It pushes our limits.

"Now, I want to push your limits, Walker."

For the first hour, he had us running around the property and through the woods where he hid and nailed us with big, red paintball splotches to prove Dr. King's point.

"People here are hunters or gathers, which makes you either the hunted or the slave," Pat said. "In other words, kids, remain observant. Exactitude will save your asses as will meticulous alertness." And then came time for the real fun. "Your femur is as hard as concrete," he said, pointing to the area that ran from the hip to the knee. "Remember that when you run . . . and when you kick."

He looked at Cass before the two engaged in a particularly brutal punching session. Pat and Cass circled each other several times like lions fighting for the same den. Neither was winded and Pat didn't have any trouble talking through the inevitable blows. I had no idea that calm Cass could turn into savage Cass in a nanosecond.

"Think of it this way. You have a steel core. If someone throws a punch at you, imagine that they're going to break their hand," Pat shouted. When he actually did break Cass's hand, I heard the crunch and then said a silent prayer of thanks when the reset kicked in and mended the bones. I wasn't so sure that Daniel would heal him.

My own personal meticulous alertness was diverted, which is why I didn't see Pat looking at me. He actually jumped me from behind, dragging me down until my legs buckled and I was eating dirt. When Cass and Daniel took steps toward him, Pat put out a mud-caked pointer finger and growled, "Stand the hell down."

"You were just taken prisoner! Now, what do you do Walker Callaghan?" he demanded.

The reset was back and I felt like I could run/fight/flee forever. It's why I nailed the side of his head with a head butt that caused his neck to snap back. When he righted it, I had one of my throwing stars, previously tucked in my sock, at his throat.

"Walker, nice to meet you," Pat said with a laugh while I continued to hold his hair in a tight grip in my other hand.

"If these two idiots," he said pointing to Daniel and Cass, "get out of line . . . that's exactly what you should do." Pat was delighted when both he and I broke into mad laughter. The guys just stood there staring us down while Pat roughed my hair with his hand.

"Get in line, Pat," Cass said.

"There's no line for you, Cass," Daniel said. "Just the cheap seats."

"Ignore them," Pat said. "Five more miles, boys!"

The rest of the day was spent with Pat *motivating*.

"COMMIT to the fight," he shouted, "Every punch deserves a breath. It will make you faster and stronger. Exhale sharply with every punch.

Drive your elbow and not your fist into every punch. Go for the head first and then the body. Every single time."

"If you think you're going to get destroyed, out crazy them," he continued. "Fact: most people won't mess with crazy."

Daniel took that last bit of advice to heart during a bloody session of roundhouse kicks with Pat. In the heat of battle, he ripped off his black tee and emitted what could only be called a jungle monkey screech. It stopped Pat long enough for Daniel to nearly rip his head off. Cass tore his own shirt off, Hulk style, as he sparred with Daniel. He smacked his chest and then grunted, "Bring it, rich boy." This was followed by a hand gesture. Daniel took a shot to the face while Cass went for the right ear with his fist.

"That's all you got? Of course it is," Cass grunted. "Typical Daniel, bringing piss to a shit fight."

"Okay," Daniel said. A man of few words, he took time to crack his own neck and then responded with a spinning elbow to Cass's gut that made him toss part of his breakfast and then fold like a portable table.

At one point, both were screaming and roaring. Pat seemed to delight in that one, noting, "I see you both have a yen for the young lady. Which means, pussies, I want to see real throw down."

Both went for bone marrow and it was a sweaty brawl of two matched opponents. Daniel didn't mind if there was a reset or not, but I was curious if his was working. He landed a fist to Cass's jaw. Cass returned a particularly nasty front kick to Daniel's chin.

Poor, poor Auggie. When Pat threatened to kick his ass, he looked like he might cry. Auggie stopped, forced a smile, and actually ran for the main house. I thought he'd never come back, but he did return a few minutes later.

"What was that?" Pat demanded.

"You said you were going to kick my ass, so I went inside and padded my pants with paper towels."

Pat looked at him like "next."

"What will follow is my super-mega-howling-wolf-claw-punch," Auggie announced, his shaking, tuba-playing, peace-loving hands at his side.

"Kid, you don't provide a menu of what you're gonna do," Pat said with a laugh.

"Okay," said Auggie who crouched down. I thought he was going to fake a faint, but he actually grabbed Dr. King's metal clipboard and hit Pat in the side of the head with such a force that I felt the impact down to my toes. *Boom!* Knocked him out instantly because his reset was also spotty.

"I'm sorry. I'm sorry!" Auggie rushed while Tosh clapped.

"No," Pat said, coming back.

"That was good, kid." Then he joked (I think), "What year is it? Where am I?"

In the end, there was no moaning, no blood, no breakage—despite the intentions in the moment.

"Reset kicked in," Daniel griped, glaring at Cass who also looked no worse for wear.

The two had gone back to neutral corners, which meant one stood by a mighty pine and the other leaned against a naked oak.

"I don't care what you think you can do . . . show me what you were *made* to do," Dr. King yelled. He was going through all the training, too, in order to protect the home front.

I watched in awe as our principal, dressed in all black, stood toe to toe with the former NFL player. Turns out, when he was an assistant principal in Detroit, Dr. King trained in his spare time (for fun) at a place called Savage Martial Arts. This was in his twenties and thirties, the years before diabetes rendered one of his legs almost worthless.

Turns out, the place lived up to its name.

In the afterlife, with all parts healed, he mixed Krav Maga and jujitsu to deliver explosive kicks to the body.

A savage, indeed.

Pat had me do a quick sparring session with him in an area of shoveled snow. It was slick and slippery, but I was agile and fast, which should have impressed him. "Is that the best you can do, Walker?" he asked. "Hit me with your best shot."

My spare throwing stars were in a neat little pile on a nearby picnic table.

"My reset is working just fine," Pat said. "I've been waiting for you to kick my ass all day. Use your anger. Turn it into strength."

It was Bobby who carefully handed me three stars.

"Ass whipping, toots," he said with glee.

I gripped the stars.

"It's a war for our souls, suck it up, buttercup," Bobby insisted.

"Kid has a mouth on him," said Pat, laughing under his breath, although we all tried to pretend it wasn't funny.

I nailed Pat twice in his chest and another time on his neck. He just smiled, pulled out the blades, and the reset immediately handled any wounds. "Finally, a girl who isn't trying to fight like the guys. Let them try to fight like *you*."Forged in fire and darkness," Pat added.

I thought he was talking about the steel throwing instruments.

"Not those things," Pat said. "You, Walker Callaghan, are an imploding star."

I tossed the last throwing star into the thin skin on top of Pat's hand. This time he winced, pulled it out, and heaved it back in my direction. I flew right.

Ass whipping? Not today.

When dusk arrived, Pat had a few last lessons. "Train hard every single day. Keep your body strong. Eat when you can. Drink water. Sleep in case the reset isn't working," he said. "Above all, don't throw away your shot at getting the code. Sometimes people only get one shot—and when it's done, all that's left is that it's over.

"Duck and move. Remove anything in your way," Pat told Daniel. Then he asked him, "Can you do that while you're worrying about her?"

Pat swung back to me.

"I can multitask," Daniel said.

He even handed Tosh some ballet shoes that Dr. King had rigged.

A dancer in her former life, Tosh could leap through the air like a deer. Now that Dr. King had reinforced her point shoes with sharp ends, she was literally a dancing weapon, which was what might be needed because who knew what visitors might show up at the cabin while we were gone.

Pat had spent time earlier showing her some moves.

"So, this is what you people do when you're missing school," she said. "Awesome!"

"Slice to kill," Pat said, looking at me. "Of course, if all else fails, he can save you." He pointed first to Daniel and then to Cass. I knew Pat was just trying to piss me off.

"I don't need a knight," I retorted. "I need a sword."

7.

Before he left, Pat asked us to make a circle and put one hand in the middle. I never wanted to let go. I grasped Daniel's hand on one side and felt Tosh and Pete's hands over ours, topped by Cass, Eddie, Auggie, Bobby, and Dr. King. Pat capped it.

A soft early evening fog dotted the sky rendering in almost blank. The winter felt deliciously cold against my sweat-ravaged skin.

"Remember, life, even now, is a race. Life in this form is also a fight. It will always be a race against time and a fight against the odds."

"*In omnia paratus,*" Pat concluded and we repeated.

Translation: Ready for anything.

SIX

1.

The only thing left to do was tell Pete he wasn't going on the journey. It didn't take a genius to know that he would go ballistic. "Of course I'm going!" he shouted. "You treat me like I'm a kid and I'm sick of it."

To which, Daniel slammed two doors and yelled louder. "If something happens out there to both of us—which is probably a given—and we don't make it back, then Edward gets Bobby. The girls are never found. The Reid family. Done."

"Son, I could use a fighting man to help protect the cabin," Dr. King mentioned.

Against his seething will, it was decided. Pete would hang back and those going now would include Daniel, Cass, Eddie, Auggie and me. Why Auggie? He wasn't a fighter, but he was big enough at six foot four and over 250 pounds to look tough and hold the line.

"Hot dog," he said with terror in his voice. "I better go to the bathroom again."

"Nice," Tosh said. "Why don't you just leave him with us. He's like a

67

friendly Saint Bernard."

"I'm seconding that motion," Cass jumped in. "He's a liability to the team."

"Listen to me," said Dr. King. "We need five in case someday it becomes four, three, two, or . . . ," Dr. King began.

It was a dismal conclusion, but someone had to say it.

"One," I finished.

Last man standing was a game we played in the Arlington Heights, Illinois, community pool when I was growing up. You walked deeper and deeper into the pool until the water was touching your chin. The last little man or woman with their feet on the ground holding their breath was the winner.

Why did it feel like it might be the same conclusion here?

2.

Daniel and I took on the chore of packing silently because we spent a good part of our relationship throwing our worldly possession into a bag that could be strapped to our backs for purposes of running or evading. We were the afterlife's homeless or hunted depending on how you looked at it now.

Sadly, this wasn't one of those processes where you had half of your wardrobe laid out on the bed and did a quick game of pick or ditch. We only had two changes of clothing each, plus a slew of small sword-and-blade-like weapons, including my standard throwing stars, chakrams from our Midst trainer Johnny, and a few "newfangled turbo gadgets" he had concocted and given to Daniel to save our asses when they were in a proverbial sling. "I'm old school," Johnny said. "Until I'm not." Endless batteries were invented in the afterlife.

Truth is I could have stayed in this cabin forever with my favorite educator and most of my friends. My heart ached for the ones we left behind at the Academy, including Bertha and Izayah, plus I yearned for Daniel's missing sisters Jenna and Andy. It was such a big, big universe that it made me want to hold tight to what I could grasp.

The idea of opening that front door tomorrow morning and leaving was like punching a one-way ticket to Narnia.

When you go off into an unexplored world, the odds were slim that you would return this way again or in the same manner. That's why constants were necessary. At one point, I held up Daniel's vintage Springsteen "The River Tour" T-shirt, which I had sort of stolen and slept in about a hundred times. I jammed it into the bottom of my bag along with my lucky rabbit's foot, a small ruby ring Daniel had given me for my birthday, and a few photos of us with the kids.

The idea was to lighten our loads because Dr. King explained that our trek would be partly on foot through ragged mountain ranges in all kinds of temperatures with these hunter or gatherer types, plus a wide range of animals that weren't part of our world in the Midst.

What could possibly go wrong?

Dinner that night was all wrong. The food was unmemorable and tasteless. What I could eat went down in chunks. I hugged Tosh and Bobby, held hands with Daniel, and gave a little soothing smile to Cass.

The clock was ticking.

Desperate times meant one thing: Love everyone you can. Love them hard.

There was Auggie bringing in the mashed potatoes, and I squeezed his hand after he put them down. Bobby, half crying, half eating, was fussy and slid off his seat under the table to sulk. He reemerged when Dr. King threw up a little whammy that made for some interesting dessert conversation.

"The seasons move backward here in The Other," he said. "It's December now with the New Year looming. When the clock strikes January one, we go backward."

He had our collective attention, which wasn't an easy thing to wrangle.

"The progression is dead of winter followed by the last gasp of autumn, but then sparks of life . . . trees that turn golden followed by their browning turning into ripe summer green with warm temperatures and then life shrinking down for the renewal of spring. What cannot live through the harshness of a rebirth will die again in winter . . . never to be seen again."

"The circle of life, yet backward," said a fascinated Pete.

"Excuse me, I don't get it, but can you pass . . . oh my God, what is it? If this is my last meal, I'm going out in style!" exclaimed Eddie who lived in the extreme now. He was always all about the circle of life that went from plate to stomach.

My own head and stomach were full after Dr. King's last-minute instructions and three-layer chocolate cake, a recipe handed down from his grandmother, Jennie.

He went through it one more time for the cheap seats. "The people are settlers. Hunters who will hunt you; gatherers who will want to collect you and keep you."

I couldn't even begin to process it, so later that night I held up that vintage Bruce shirt and came clean about my thievery. Putting the shirt on and nothing else was just a way to . . . display the goods?

"Should we take with? Do you like?" I asked Daniel, who as a guy was already packed. He sat on the end of the bed contemplating, but his head popped up when I cornered him with fashion.

"Do I like?" he repeated, eyes vibrant and alive, "No, baby, I love."

3.

Music. It was the only answer. There was an old-fashioned vinyl record player in one corner of the room and enough classic platters to play us to the moon and back. I put on Sinatra and found a song that was low and slow, which fit my mood of trying to make the next eight hours last forever.

Daniel cut the lights.

A blazing fireplace on the far side of the room crackled like tiny bolts of thunder as yellow sparks danced.

He was attractively grizzled with a day's worth of stubble that made him look pleasantly dangerous and ready for anything. "Are you a hunter or a gatherer?" I asked as he slowly approached, wearing nothing more than his tats and bronzed skin.

"I think when it comes to you, Callaghan, tonight, I'm a hunter," he said.

Like water, I slipped from his grasp until he checked my sideways right move and yanked me into his arms. "First you hunt, then you gather," he explained, ravishing my mouth with a passionate kiss that must have lifted the roof off the place because all I saw was tiny white stars.

Strong arms bandied around my waist and then lifted me straight up until I was at least a head taller. If only he wouldn't have stumbled, but he did. Gravity did the rest. It always did.

It's why we landed in a heap on the rock-hard floor. It gave him just a moment of pause, enough to roll us onto a fluffy white rug placed in front of the fire by someone who believed in miracles. The soft fibers on my back felt like thousands of tiny caresses; the man hovering above was millions of wishes fulfilled. I yanked at his shoulders until our lips met again and our fears lay in a heap. The fire made his skin feel hot while his rough hands touched all of the shadowy spots that only a good lover knows exist.

"All we have," he said in a throaty voice.

"Is all we need," I whispered.

As the world slid, he said words I would need to remember: "Baby, we don't end. We go on."

After, he smiled for the pure joy of it and I started to grin. And then he accidentally sucked down air through his nose and it made a loud chortling sound, which made me giggle in that way where it's not just funny, but you laugh so hard that it hurts. He began to choke, which made me suck air and then enter the hiccup zone. His deep, warm chest laughter was so consuming that his entire body began to shake.

This was joy.

That was the thing about being frozen at this age. You could still laugh in a way you never could if you grew up and lived. All the way.

4.

At 3:00 a.m., we were in that sinfully comfortable bed naked, twined, and under a comforter so thick it was like wrapping yourself in a cloud. The gaps left too much time to ponder what our rootless future had in store.

"I'm like freaking Dorothy, always leaving home," I said. It was meant to be a joke, but he took it entirely the wrong way.

"I read a poem once about home—and what it means," he said in a reverent tone.

"You read poetry?" I choked. He worked on motorcycles, played soccer, and slayed the occasional demon, but I didn't think *poetry* was his thing. Apparently, I didn't know everything about Daniel Reid, thank God for major favors. Who wants to know it all about your lover? The surprises were the fresh cement.

He cleared his throat.

"If we're separated, meet me at night in the woods of our dreams. We'll sit on the ground, make a fire, look up at the glittering eyes of the stars and pretend we can fly above the oldest trees. Go there. I'll find you," he recited. And he meant it.

"We'll find joy," I finished it, quoting C. S. Lewis. "Joy is the serious business of heaven."

"But, this isn't supposed to be heaven," Daniel whispered. "All evidence to the contrary."

"Yes," I said staring back at him. "It is."

He kissed the small of my throat . . . just because. Because we were young and impulsive and both wondering if we would ever be like this again. Anything could happen to any of us. Five-four-three-two-one. I guess that wasn't much different from daily life back in the living realm. Numbers thinned daily.

Maybe it was too heavy, too heady, and that was why this was his cue to roll us, comforter and all, off the bed in one move and onto the floor. Legs tangled, I fell on top of him. "Just checking the reset," he said, grinning.

Yeah, that was just part of it because his hands were moving lower in order to save me from the cold, hard wood that was our perch. Again. "I'm absolutely fine, thank you, Dr. Reid," I said.

"No, you're not."

"What are you doing? But do it again."

"What am I doing?" he repeated. "Losing my mind, but finding my rhythm."

Daniel had wild brilliance. Forget butterflies. He made me feel like I had a kaleidoscope in my eyes.

5.

In the wee hours with a dry throat and an itch to get started, I tucked a snoring Daniel in and snuck downstairs to find Dr. King sitting at the kitchen table sipping hot tea and grasping quantum physics from a thick textbook. *Just a little light reading before dawn.* Seeing him there in the dark contemplating big issues with a fat candle flickering was the best/worst feeling ever.

Why couldn't we stay? Why couldn't I do exactly this every middle of every night? Let the Academy take care of itself. I imagined wandering downstairs and having endless philosophical discussions with our moral compass until the sunlight broke along with the eggs that made their way to the pan.

Why couldn't I ever take the easy way out?

Screw finding this X-catcher and getting a code that would lead to us going back. *And going back to what?* It could also mean our demise at the hands of Principal Dick.

And then I heard my father's words so clearly that I swore he was actually here. When I struggled with taking the training wheels off my bike and fell two, three, ten times, he wrapped my bloody knee and said, "Babe, it's going to mean a whole lot more if you get there hard than if you get there easy."

I would make tea. Sit. Contemplate here. Maybe for the last time.

Getting there hard was the route fate had decided for me when I was born. *Good five-star plan for Walker*, I thought as my shaking hands dropped the tea bag twice on the floor before pouring burning hot water from the kettle onto my fingers by mistake. *Let's make it as rough as possible on her*, my mind echoed. *What else is new?*

And when I had logged enough time at my personal pity party, I sat down beside Dr. King, my chair scraping in a way that sounded loud and garish. I was hopeless in the stealth department, but he remained quiet and undisturbed. Dr. King knew that sometimes all I needed was another body in the room.

An old wooden grandfather clock ticked mercilessly in the hallway and I counted the clicks until finally he spoke. "One thing, Miss Callaghan," Dr. King said. He didn't look like the voice of authority in his Detroit High School T-shirt and black sweats, but his warm, rich voice held most of the answers. Of this I was sure.

I waited for some practical Dr. King lesson about frostbite or navigating the wilds, but he surprised me.

"In the end, everything will be okay. If it's not okay, it's not the end," he said.

He wouldn't take credit.

"That was courtesy of John from Liverpool. Lad had a wicked way with words," Dr. King said with a chuckle. "In fact, I heard that he applied to be a philosophy teacher at the Academy recently, but I guess the place isn't big enough for peace-loving John and Principal Dick, who rejected his application."

"How can we possibly end the reign of a madman intent on destroying everything we know?" I asked. The hint of hysteria in my voice didn't rock Dr. King.

He put down his book, took a slow sip of his cooled tea and said, "It's the possibility that keeps me going, not the guarantee."

6.

Later, I snuck back into bed, expecting to hear Daniel snoring away. His eyes were wide open and he was silent. By now, the sky was a bruise signaling the beginning of our leaving day.

Sometimes, it's not the words that break you. It's a look that attaches to the face of the one who knows you the very best. A jaw muscle twitches, eyelid descends. In that moment, if you're very lucky, you don't have to speak at all. Your own personal "to be continued" is in good hands. It's covered. Three of the best words in the English language: *I got this.*

Daniel Reid was good at the get.

My hand slipped into his and we waited. At 6:00 a.m., we received our first wake-up call when Bobby slipped into our bed and into our arms.

"I got this, little man," his big brother told him and the little boy believed it enough to bow his head and cry just a little bit longer.

7.

Alarms blared around eight and suddenly the house came to life.

One way to avoid my own emotions was to focus on the rest of them. Tosh had so much nervous energy that the former ballerina did continuous spins in order to relieve her anxiety. Pete was all business as he packed up Auggie . . . and I never saw Cass.

Traveling with Eddie was like transferring a serial killer between prisons. He was slippery and threatened not to go at all. Then you'd catch him and want to cuff him to a chair just to contain him.

A fully awake Bobby cursed a blue streak while pushing around his pancakes and swore that soon he would "fly" and meet us. Silently, I said a prayer that this wouldn't be possible, but I wasn't exactly sure what was probable here.

Tosh took every chance available to touch Pete's shoulder, his hand, and even his chest when she took care of a syrup stain with her bare fingers. I swore I saw tears in her eyes because she was staying and he was sticking, too. It filled her with a kind of relief that was palpable. I saw Pete actually grab her hand under the table and squeeze it.

Auggie hovered over all of us like some kind of mother hen. "Do you have socks, Walker? Do *I* have socks?" he asked. "Do you want my socks? What about tissues? No matter what. You/I always need tissues."

I watched as Eddie fit what I estimated to be ten packs of Twizzlers into his pack. "Got any weapons in there?" I asked. "Or are you just going to take out any undesirables with a stray hard Twinkie."

"Twinkies don't expire, Walker," Eddie said. "Neither do Ding Dongs and I have a few packed. You'll be begging for a handful of my Captain Crunch powder when we face near-starvation."

"What is Captain Crunch powder?" I asked.

"An entire box of Captain Crunch crunched down into powder form," he said. "Genius, I know."

"Glad you've spent so much time dealing with the major issues," I said. "I feel so much better now knowing that we have pulverized breakfast cereal with us."

"You're welcome," Eddie said with a grand smile.

8.

In the cold, blue light of the winter's morning, I wandered outside to a driveway overlooking a green-blue lake. I knew I might never see this place again. Daniel was inside making sure all the weapons were packed and saying his last good-bye to Bobby, which left me with Cass, who had been mostly MIA. Standing alone in a black parka and camo-colored pants, Cass looked like Aquaman crossed with The Hulk. His wild, longish blond hair had been pulled back and tied with a leather string. Strapped to his side was a long, high-powered rifle.

He looked like he was ready for anything—and I cursed myself for feeling safe and cared for in his presence. His gaze said it all. It said, "*I'll wait.*" Not so long ago, he told me, "Your future isn't with him. It's with me." I couldn't/wouldn't even think about it.

When I approached him, he gave me that stoic smile and then put his warm hand on my upper arm. He left it there for one beat, then two, then three . . . then ten. Then came the full-blast Cass smile, which felt superheated like the California sun on a cloudless beach day. It was entirely harmless, if you believed in fairy tales or people who tried to convince themselves of what was harmless. If you had to ask . . . it wasn't harmless, as a general rule.

"I was just thinking about you, sugar," Cass said. "I don't know why. But I always think about you."

"Where have you been? You missed breakfast," I said with a warm smile. There was nothing wrong with us being just friends who cared deeply about each other. At the moment, Cass wasn't so concerned with the status of our relationship. I had never seen him this ready, willing and available for damage.

"As a marine, before we go on a mission, it's all about the planning. We prepare and then we prepare again. By the time we get there, it's like we've already been there," he said, waving a piece of paper that was a last-minute checklist of supplies. "The only problem with this mission is we don't have many particulars other than people are psychos . . . and some like to enslave teenagers."

I shivered, and Cass took that as an opportunity to run his hand down my back *for moral support.*

"Yeah, they don't have this trip on Travelocity," Auggie noted as he approached with his pack. "Maybe Dr. King forgot to tell us about the good parts of this road trip like when we work on our tan and read a few books."

Pete was a wonderful bookworm type and packed the only literary thing we needed for this road trip. It was H. G. Wells's *The Time Machine,* a tome that had served us well in the past as the chapters had a unique way to navigate various decades when we were time traveling.

For instance, if you wanted to go to 1925, you had to tab page 19 and then page 25. The book never failed, which was why we needed it.

"A little light reading for the road," Pete said with a wink.

"Yep," I said. "Best to keep the particulars under wraps."

Daniel arrived carrying coffee for both of us. He flashed at Cass and addressed the small group.

"All we have to do is camp out, get the code, go home, and save our school from a madman," said Daniel, who flanked my left with an extra pack filled with reinforcements. He dumped the packs at our feet and thrust his hands into the pockets of his jeans.

"Easy enough—if there is an actual plan and we're not just winging it," Cass challenged. Then he stared hard into Daniel's face. "I hope you don't find my honesty offensive."

"No, I just find your fake friendship and sugar-coated bullshit offensive," Daniel snapped.

"Anytime you want to have a go at me . . . I'm available," Cass taunted.

"I have no prior commitments right now," Daniel challenged.

"Okay, okay, okay," I said. "Let's go through the checklist one more time."

"Gladly, sugar," said Cass, who scowled as he blazed through each item one more time. Finally, he stopped at what someone wrote in for Eddie.

"What the hell is Captain Crunch powder?" he asked.

Eventually, I moved Daniel a few feet away under the pretense of having to tell him something, which was better than the two of them going at it on the back lawn.

"This could get dark—a wandering journey with friends and enemies," Daniel said, staring at Cass who returned the alpha-male challenge. "I could get dark."

"I'm not afraid of your dark," I said.

We were interrupted by Dr. King, looking so lean and limber in a black Academy polo shirt, with the gold "A" crest, and dark jeans. I watched as Dr. King walked back to one of the garages, flipped the big door by hand, and then emerged again.

"Damn, I forgot the keys," he said and ran back into the house.

About three minutes later, he was walking down the driveway again in the same black shirt and dark jeans, but his black hair was suddenly gray and there were lines on his face and small bags under his eyes. In a matter of seconds, he had aged himself back into his midfifties again.

"Pick your jaw up off the driveway, Miss Callaghan. People age-morph easily here," he said. "In seconds."

"I wanted to show you how quickly it can occur, so you're not fooled by it," he said, insisting, "Take one look at this middle-aged man before you—me—who needs a good shave."

Once again, he walked to the garage, but this time I heard what sounded like some kind of big engine roaring and rumbling like thunder. A colossal boat of a car came backing up until it was right in front of our faces.

I couldn't focus entirely on the car. The man driving it was muscular, lean, and fit enough to take on the world. Dr. King had aged-morphed back into a seventeen-year-old.

"This is Howard's car," he informed us. "It's a one-of-a-kind 1953 sky-blue Buick Roadmaster. He has one message for all of you: Don't mess up his baby. Or you will be deader than dead."

9.

It wasn't just a car. It was an experience, a piece of history, and one damn-fine motor machine. Long and sleek, the steel, two-door tank was painted ice blue except for the roof, which was angel white. An arc of polished chrome raced from the passenger's side door all the way to the front; both the rear and back bumpers were made of that same shiny silver. The whitewall tires looked so clean that I wondered if the vehicle had ever been driven.

"There are so many custom touches, including the fact that the car's twelve-volt electrical system has been supplemented with a separate twenty-four-volt system," said Dr. King.

"So, it drives like hell," Daniel said with a slow smile.

"Howard also installed a power auxiliary system—the kind that jump-starts aircraft. Plus, the ventilation system was removed and replaced with a custom air-conditioning and heating system that functions independently of the engine. Even if you run out of gas, you can always heat or cool yourself in the car."

"What else?" I asked.

"Perceptive, Miss Callaghan," said Dr. King. "Actually, there is a special dust trap and antibacterial filter in the car for our germ-hating

Howard. He was so intent in operating a germ-free atmosphere within his car that only the driver's window opens. The rest of the windows are forever sealed as are the firewall vents. Hughes Aircraft did all the work."

"I'll drive," Cass and Daniel said in unison.

"No," they both repeated at the same time. "*I'll* drive."

10.

"Are you ready?" Dr. King asked us.

"I am not prepared, but I'm so f—ing ready," Daniel said.

"Are you ready, Eddie?" Dr. King asked.

Eddie Wargo stood in the same black parka that had been given to all of us, heating pads inside activated, and gloves covering his meaty hands. He had never had such nice gear, and was embracing the joy of such luxury.

"Ready, willing, and unstable," Eddie said.

"Eddie, turn down your psycho before I have to turn mine up," I said.

"Crankin' it down to nine, kid," Eddie said.

"Cass?" Dr. King asked.

"Yes, sir, ready to surf the ups and hate the downs," he said.

"Auggie?"

He froze in place and clutched his pack tightly. I swore I heard his knees knock.

"I'm ready!" cried Bobby, who raced around his brothers now in his favorite Batman pajamas and a blue towel from the bathroom as his cape. Daniel and Pete both kneeled down to hug the crying little madman.

"If you go with us, who will protect Pete, Tosh, and Dr. King?" Daniel reasoned. "We need our wingman on the home front."

When I hugged him fiercely, he pulled back in tears.

"I know, baby," I said. "I know."

Dr. King took the lead again and this time he called my name.

"Miss Callaghan?"

I nodded.

"Team, when nothing is certain, everything is possible," Dr. King said, putting his hand on my semi-shaking shoulder, "That's on loan. It's exactly what I used to tell my daughters and sons."

He had children? A wife, maybe? Funny, but all this time and I didn't even know that much about his former life.

Suddenly, I was wicked pissed for having to leave the party early. Again.

We huddled in a small circle and Dr. King said in a reverent voice, "We pray to be guided by those who have gone before us and leave something for those who go after."

"I know Pat gave you his favorite Latin line, but here is my own," he said, and then looked at everyone but me when he recited, *Per aspera ad astra.* Through hardship to the stars."

And to me, he added, "As always, Miss Callaghan: Grit."

He reached into the car and pulled out a large box. "Put them on," he said to me.

I opened the box to find shiny new boots. "But, my boots are fine," I said.

Years of being dirt poor with my mother had taught me to use an object until it collapsed.

"For me," Dr. King said. "Put them on. Use them well."

Inside the car, I rode shotgun next to Daniel with Cass, Eddie, and Auggie in the roomy back seat. No one could see it, but before he slid the car into drive, Daniel and I linked pinky fingers. He wasn't just my touchstone. He was my true certainty.

He rolled the only window that worked down and the blast of winter-cold air felt good on my tender skin. He pumped up the music for me and luckily the sound system had been rigged in later days to play a variety of CDs. Jay-Z was in the house; I buckled up because even off to your own demise, you had to be careful.

"Let's go for a ride," Daniel said.

SEVEN

1.

For the start of an epic journey, it was strangely . . . normal. Pedestrian, as they say. Day didn't turn to night; seasons didn't click backward—at least not yet. We raced on a regular two-lane road with tall evergreens blotting the upper ceilings of the sky. Were we on the way to our demise? Or picking up milk at the local grocery store?

The nerves in the car, however, were like a thousand drumbeats.

It's going to be fine, just fine, fine as wine. But I didn't drink wine. *Get a grip,* I reminded myself as I stared at the blur of snow-covered greenery that looked exactly the same as when we arrived here a few days ago on foot.

It was a winter wonderland with some kind of dark vibe behind the wonder part.

It's not frightening. It's not even odd. And there has to be good people here, I pep-talked myself, which I had never been very good at doing. Nope. I didn't believe a word of it.

A quick mental channel change.

"There are always good people," my mother used to tell me. "Just stick on the side of the angels, Walker."

"Yeah, Mom," I answered in my knee-jerk seventeen-year-old way at the time. We were standing in Aunt Ginny's kitchen and I was about to take the train by myself into the big, bad city for the first time. I taunted her with the "danger" of it all. "Look around, Madeleine. There's a shortage of wings," I snapped. I was a junior in high school for crying out loud. If there were helicopter parents, my mother was a Gulf Stream jet.

That was me then: The social commentator—life expert with zero experience. I was the one who knew everything and knew nothing. How could I ace geometry and flunk life? By that I mean *what I wouldn't give for her to go anywhere or nowhere with me now.*

Oh, Mom.

Focus, Walker. Break it down to the facts like any good reporter would on the beginning of a long assignment.

What we had right here, right now, was enough wide-open space to pretend you were on an unexplored planet. There was blacktop and it was bleached white in spots from the harsh conditions of winter's ravage blasts.

No road signs. No speeding signs. No arrows pointing toward Poughkeepsie. I loved words and the idea of a place called Poughkeepsie made me laugh. Daniel caught the sides of my lips curling for a second and leaned sideways. He knew me well enough not to ask. He knew me well enough to whisper, "Way to make the best out of the bullshit, baby."

I squeezed the side of his leg. We didn't need to say it in words. Glances and touches were our secret language, important in ways that could not be described.

In the rearview mirror, Cass's face. Impatient. Waiting.

In the infamous words of Eminem, snap back to reality. Maybe here in The Other, no one wanted any markers. Perhaps no one wanted to interrupt such a scenic view. And there was something to be said of a place with absolutely no coming attractions.

Famous.

Last.

Very last.

Words.

There was nothing on either side of that nameless road—no stores, no houses, not even a shack or a promise of a pit stop with both gas, a *turr-lot*, as Eddie would say, and a burger—although not necessarily in that order. No town name or city limits. It was as if we fell off the face of the earth into a new one that looked familiar, but operated on its own mojo.

Given no limits, Daniel pushed it to prove he was in charge.

He was flying about a hundred miles an hour in that big tank of a car, but to where? Before we left, Dr. King just point forward and nodded as in "that away." There was no "back" at this point or we could have returned to the cabin and the lake. I might have failed to mention that the road we were on went only one way. And when I glanced back, it looked as if the trees were swallowing the blacktop we had just driven over.

"A map?" I asked Cass—and when I turned around he greeted the question with one of his full-face enveloping smiles that felt like a warm blanket just out of the dryer. Yeah, he was loving this type of adventure. The fact that he was sitting directly behind me felt just a bit too close given the way he felt, but I couldn't go there now.

It was a no as far as a map was concerned. Before we left, Dr. King informed us that there was almost no cell service here or Internet. A few rough patches of service existed in these parts making The Other either a throwback or an advanced society. There was no better living through a screen here.

"Life—well, you know what I mean—is your movie now," Dr. King had said.

Oddest of all was the fact that we were the only freaking car on the road. I half-expected to see some drifter on a motorcycle or an explorer in an RV or a wayward hiker with a pack half his or her size, but they were also figments of fantasy. This car was it, take it or shake it. And we had no choice but to take it.

"It's like we're driving off into a void," I told Daniel. "Who knows what kind of wake we're leaving or who or what is in those trees watching?"

"Callaghan, really?" he said. "Did you have to go there?"

"Sorry. Keep your eyes on the road."

"I'd rather keep them on you."

His gray eyes temporarily left the road and caressed my face in that way he had of pushing you forward toward the next thrill.

"Just sit back, enjoy the ride," Daniel said with a sexy wink.

Why was it so warm in this car? I had to look away for fear of blushing.

Trees always centered me. They were bigger, older, and bolder. They knew how to grow, to last *no matter what* and give up what was required, so the core would rejuvenate.

We blew by a patch of massive, stalwart aspens, solid to the naked eye, but vulnerable with their paper-white trunks secured for thousands of years in the ground and with tips that touched the sky. I remembered a strange fact from bio class. Their bark was photosynthetic, meaning that growth was still happening after all the leaves had been dropped and died off. It reminded me in a weird way . . . *of us.*

Way in the distance were the snowcapped tops of ragged mountain ranges that made the Rockies look like bunny hills. They pierced low sooty-gray clouds thick enough to make you really believe that the sun had permanently checked out.

A quick glance backward. In the rearview mirror I saw the beautiful wide face of a terrified Auggie playing air guitar (*Really? Well, why not?*) while Cass stared out his unopenable window at the road, eyes narrowed and ready for anything. Eddie was Eddie. I heard wrappers crinkling. And nervous chewing of Twizzlers taking their last stand.

After 17.5 minutes into the journey, clocked on the new, multifunctional watch that Dr. King strapped on all of our wrists at breakfast—"a belated Christmas present—and compass. Don't take it off"—I began to settle in.

Maybe I wasn't officially born to run, but I was certainly born to roam. I decided to list my "likes" so far, which is a game I used to play when I was younger and afraid. I liked the fresh, dank smell of mossy dirt as it wafted in through the wide-open driver's side window. I liked the safety of a blanket of a few inches of fresh snow and the big, red, ripe raspberries I saw growing on some of the low bushes that suddenly brushed the road, but just in one direction. I liked this watch, which had interesting buttons with just letters on them. Finally, I liked the fact that we had choices.

Because now there were two roads up ahead in the near yonder.

Or, more specifically, the road forked and Daniel slammed on the brakes.

Why not?

We were the only car. The chances of getting rear-ended were zero.

We idled.

We all knew there were duel options now, although they looked identical. Naturally, they would present entirely different choices. Like I said, neither was marked, which made it worse. We couldn't play the name game, deciding our fates on which one sounded better. We could simply hang a right or pull a left. There wasn't a third choice.

"Which one scares you more?" Daniel asked the group.

I could see that despite all of the bravado, he was honestly *unsettled* and his absence of rebel conviction rocked me to my own core.

"When did you become such a pussy?" Eddie demanded. At his current sugar levels, the eldest of the Wargo brothers heard the glitch in Daniel's vocals, too.

"Ya go right. Ya always go right. Right is right. Most of us are right-handed," Eddie reasoned. "You use your right hand to . . . well, you know. But you can also use your left."

"We get it," I said.

"Go right if you want to avoid being wrong," Cass said.

"Callaghan, call it," Daniel said.

"Yeah, sugar," Cass piped up, putting his hand on my shoulder from the back seat. "I trust you and the lucky penny in my sock. Just go with your gut and—"

"Eddie?" I said, knowing that despite appearances he had something that many would call souped-up gut instinct. I was beginning to think of it as Wargo Wisdom.

"Cowboy up," Eddie said. "Give it all ya got and go right."

Daniel gunned it, careening right for about one-two-three seconds and then I heard the dull, hard *THWACK* bouncing off Howard's unbreakable glass. Our scenic view was obliterated.

It's what happens when a river of fresh blood pours down your front windshield.

2.

"What the hell? I said go left!" Eddie yelled. "Go left!"

"Did we just hit something? Did we hit *someone*? Don't stop," Auggie rambled. "Whatever you do . . . just drive faster. Go, man, *go!*"

But he *couldn't*. Blinded by the red flow covering the entire front windshield, Daniel had no choice but to slow the car by pumping the breaks one, two, ten times. Slamming one hand in front of me for the inevitable fast pitch into the dashboard, my chest crashed against his formidable forearm.

"Brace!" he roared, gripping the wheel tightly, while the car finally came to a whiplash-inducing final stop.

My neck flew forward and then back, and forward again. The reset was once again my friend and to prove it I touched my neck, temples, and even my forehead which had been flung sideways as I smashed into the passenger's side window.

Cass was no worse for wear. He was learning forward, head poking into my space to assess the situation. My face fit into his gentle hands as he inspected for damage, his finger reluctantly pulling away when he realized I was fine.

"Sound off," Cass demanded. "Is anyone hurt?"

The reset was in high gear.

"This is messed up," Cass said, and for some reason it did appear to be *unreasonably dark for seven in the morning*. It wasn't the clouds. It was night again.

"The minute we hung the right, the world went black," Cass said, adding, "Stay frosty, my friends."

Daniel nodded as they locked eyes in the driver's rearview mirror.

"No bullshit," Cass said.

"No bullshit," Daniel echoed. "Eddie, are the packs in the back seat with you?"

"I put them in the trunk," he said in a frantic voice. "I didn't think we'd need them from inside the car!"

"In the trunk . . . *shit*," said Cass.

"Except for two of the packs filled with the extra clothes. Everything is in the trunk. Dr. King said to keep them in the locked trunk until we cleared our examination," I said, knowing that I had two handy throwing stars in my pocket. Just in case.

"Son of a—" Cass began.

"Hey man, it is what it is," Daniel finished it. I watched as he tapped on some small button by the steering wheel.

I could hear a stream of windshield wiper juice blast several strong streams of cleaning fluid onto the big glass. Through the car vents, I could smell something sweet mixed with the pungent smell of iron. Since this was Howard's wheels, the cleaning fluid was a wide stream that seemed to power wash a thick swatch in a matter of seconds.

It was clear in that moment that the car had been drenched in only one substance. It was fresh and red . . . and there was quite a lot of this thick, apparently sticky juice.

"Maybe we hit a deer. We'll find a safe spot, pull over, and weaponize. We should have done that from the jump," Daniel said, flipping the windshield wiper button. "Just another second or two and we'll see the open road and look for some trees to pull into in order to regroup."

Impatiently, Daniel pressed down on the fluid button several more times and that's when I saw it.

No moose. No squirrel. It was a blood-drenched man.

3.

He was standing smack in the middle of the road about three inches in front of the car.

Armed with a large gun, he didn't hesitate to pull a trigger that launched a fresh pouch that burst upon impact. Syrupy red fluid with the iron smell of blood washed over our window again rendering us sightless. A voice inside me calmly preached the law of physics. *He shot us from the front . . . turn toward the sides. The sides. The sides.* When I whipped around to glance in my side mirror, it was perfectly clean and clear.

Five men in big orange parkas walked out of the woods.

My breath was ragged now. "The people here are hunters or gatherers," I reminded myself, digging deeply into my pocket for my throwing stars with shaking hands. For some reason, I was rusty and my winter-numbed fingers were partially paralyzed from fear and cold.

"Run those mothers over," Cass bellowed to Daniel. "Gun it! Just go!"

It was one thing to fight demons, but we had never killed a man.

Not in cold blood.

Daniel revved the car, but those side men never walked in front of us. They flanked us, three on the left, two on the right.

They had wide hands. A few easily reached for the door handles. Almost on reflex, Daniel went to punch it, but it was too late. Had we thought to lock all the doors, we might have regrouped and hit them at ramming speed, but our driver was otherwise occupied. Two of the men opened his door and began to rip him out of the vehicle.

Viciously, my door was yanked open in a way that made me think the steel slab would fly away. A six-foot-four man in camo with black binoculars around his thick neck and rusted knives on his belt yanked me out of the car like I was feather-light.

Slamming me face down to the road, I didn't wince. The reset, thank God. A minute ticked. Then another. I could only see a thin shaft of light and the actual black asphalt an inch from my nose. He was good at wrestling what moved, and pressed into the center of my back with an enormous, muddy hunting boot that smelled of fresh kill.

When he crouched down, I smelled foul breath, rancid with the remains of old chewing tobacco. It spread across my face and filled my nose, abolishing everything but the animalistic scent of him.

"Bite the ground, bitch," he hissed.

The boot moved up until it smashed into the back of my head making me actually kiss the oil-slicked road. He was so big that I couldn't move and I imagined myself suffocating as tiny bits of gravel embedded in my face and flew into my mouth until all I tasted was warm chemicals and grit.

One thing was clear. If he was the hunter, I was prey.

To prove my future, he dropped a long rope by the side of my face. "Lots of fun we can have . . . just you, me, and this rope, girlie. Haven't seen a girlie as pretty as you around these parts for some time. Makes a man want to—"

I blocked his last words by closing my lips and screaming into my own mouth.

Meanwhile, two of his "friends" were taking care of Daniel, who kicked and punched valiantly, but it was hopeless. Every move was checked and the hoots and cheers from the men confirmed it. Craning my neck, I could see Daniel was down on his knees, hands behind his neck, and already tied with a thick black cord. My eyes filled when a rag was stuffed into his mouth by two gargantuan men, all in orange vests, camo pants, and with cowboy hats on their heads. Long rifles were attached to their trigger fingers.

The man with the fancy grenade launcher shot another round of blood. He hit Cass squarely in the face, blinding him until they could tie his arms behind his back and his legs together. Stifling a cry, I watched as his body was dumped in a heap by the side of the car.

Auggie was the least physical of all of us and he only had one day of hard training. I heard him cry out like a wounded child and then even worse. Silence. But he wasn't gone. Couldn't be. *Please God, no. He didn't belong on this trip. He couldn't perish after just one hour.* One of the men talked loudly about Auggie being his "type."

A fast look up the road make me sick to my stomach. On the ground, in a neat row, were the carcasses of at least ten gutted "fresh kill" deer. It's where the blood came from for the rocket launcher. This is how they did it: they filled paintball pods with it after they slaughtered those poor animals who were simply trying to find their evening meal.

Those spent deer were now frozen, although it looked as though they were casually sleeping in the middle of the highway.

"Now, whadda we have here, Billy Ray," the man holding Daniel addressed his friend. He took a long swig from a flask. "It looks to me that the woods have a species that we love to hunt even more than we like to blow the brains out of John and Jolene Doe. In more respectable parts, they call these highly overbred species teenagers. Over here in The Other, we just call 'em vermin. Too many of 'em, if you ask me."

His friend, who had Cass in a chokehold, picked it up from there. "We call teenagers vermin because they're wily, they steal what you need to survive, and they're so damn moody that you'd swear they were all rabid. And you know what we do with rabid things?"

His words hung in the air like a cloud.

When no one answered, the man above me kicked me hard in the middle of my back.

"When it comes to vermin, it's *always* huntin' season," he said.

He poked me in the side with the gun. When I twitched, he did it again, but this time he laughed.

"Your type tastes good . . . grilled." He bent down. "After we have our fun."

4.

One word kept pounding my brain.

"Water," I heard our trainer Johnny tell us. "When trapped by the enemy, you must imagine that you are shapeless, formless, like water. When you pour water in a cup, it becomes the cup. When you pour water in a bottle, it becomes the bottle. When you pour water in a teapot, it becomes the teapot. Water can drip and it can crash. Become like water, my friend," he suggested.

I pictured myself flowing away from here, but first I would rush over the predators in front of me. It was enough for me to lift my head to the point where it felt like I was severing every ligament in my neck, but no matter.

I had to see where my flow would go.

From my vantage point, I could see a man in a bright orange parka, up ahead, draining the blood of the deer and placing it into plastic bags that he fed into that rocket launcher. "We stun 'em and then we gun 'em," he said to his friends. "That's what we do with the Abandons. Aimless foundlings like you kids who happened to wander into these parts."

"We're meat hunters," a voice to my hard left announced. He was Daniel's captor and I made a mental note of his position. I cringed at the sound of a gun cocking from that direction.

Daniel was in the driver's seat, so it made sense they nabbed him and dragged him into a ditch about ten large steps in front of me and slightly to the left. "I didn't plan to beef a man today. Good thing this one has a little meat on it, which you certainly do, muscle boy. Or should I call you Big Nuts to Crack? Oh, how we're going to have some fun carving you into bite-sized patties," he said.

"I think he will taste best," said the one on top of Cass. "He's stockier. Done some time in the gym, boy, haven't you? Muscles are chewy, but your innards will make a nice meat stew."

His voice was about thirty degrees behind me, which meant that Cass was back near the pine trees. I knew he would have done something if it wasn't for the fact that these guys were well-armed and trigger happy.

It was too soon to do. Best just to let it play out for a few seconds.

"I do like the girlies the best," said my hunter. He brushed my hair with the back of his hand like he was petting a dog, smashed my head back down, and then ran his hand down to cup my ass.

"I think I keep this one like a pet 'cause she's a-feared of me. Take her to pound town. At least for a little while," he opined. Then he informed me, "Don't worry. Some of the others will leave you alone. They'll want your friend. The marshmallow. They'll toast him and then roast him real good."

He had to be talking about Auggie.

"I'll smoke the two big ones and Russell, you take the girl and the fatty into the woods and have us a hog-killin' good time. Take them into Mother's Cave," he commanded.

"Sex, drugs, and rock 'n' roll!" he whooped, shooting his gun into the air three times.

"All beer and Skittles," he shouted.

I heard Auggie cry out and then the crunch of thick boots crushing tiny pieces of something fragile . . . his bones or his glasses. I knew that we would be their playthings. Until they tired of us . . . and then they would shoot us.

Auggie knew it, too. "Get your filthy hand off me!" he yelled as the men just laughed at my tuba-loving best friend. They had nefarious plans for him. "By-and-by, pudge-boy is a live wire," the one who was referred to as Billy Ray said. "I say we give him to Little Bob first 'cause he's the biggest toad in the puddle tonight."

If they moved either of us into the actual woods, I knew one thing. We would never come back the same.

You never went to a second location riding shotgun next to a psycho. That's where they do their real damage. The permanent kind.

That fact is why I did it.

And I did it loudly.

Because as bad at math as I am . . . I could still count.

"His name is Eddie. We call him Eddie Wargo. He's from Alabama. And he likes to drive cars—and fast," I shouted. *Of course, I was talking about Auggie, but they didn't know that.*

"Who gives a shit what fat-ass calls himself. We're not gonna be pen pals!" Billy Ray said.

My adrenalin surged as I frantically watched two of the hunters march Daniel and Cass down the lane toward the dead animals. Soon, they would be nothing more than carcasses facedown on a lonely road. It was their smartest move yet. Take out the big ones before they had their fun.

"Eddie is a bit of a reckless driver," I continued to yell. My water was at a boiling point now.

"He keeps his eyes on obstacles in the road!" I yelled into the night.

My water overflowed. *He just had to burn the breeze. Ride at full speed.*

"Go!" I screamed so loudly that the syllables reverberated in my own ears.

Like a snarling lion, the car roared to life.

At ramming speed, Eddie barreled toward Daniel and Cass's captors. They were like the deer, frozen in those amber lights. Daniel had time to head butt his captor and fling his body into the ditch. Cass bit his tormenter in the right cheek and then dashed forward, jumped high, and purposely slid off the hood of the car like he was body surfing the metal machine. His body rolled into the wet, wintry mulch.

Eddie ran down those captors and then drove his front wheels off the back of the third hunter attending to the deer. In the headlights, I saw the wicked gleam in his eye as he used that steel tank to obliterate them. "Dang!" he cried out of the window. "Like lickin' butter off a hot knife." I watched in awe as he twisted his head, nodded, and then shoved the car into reverse. The two hunters behind him? Roadkill.

"All balls!" Eddie screamed out the open window.

It was Auggie who stood first and slashed at the beefy killer hovering above us with the star I put into his hands. Auggie went for his wrist, which didn't dislodge the knife, but instead made his captor grip it harder and slash recklessly into the darkness. I took three steps back and flung hard, nailing him in the jugular.

I hadn't thrown in a long time, but turns out, it was like riding a bike.

5.

Here's how it happened: Eddie Wargo had managed to go incognito. It was a historical first.

The Buick was big enough that when we stopped, he slid to the floor and flattened himself in one of the darker recesses of that boat of a back seat. A black blanket back there helped as did the two packs with the extra clothing that fell on top of him. The hunters never really looked inside the car after ripping the four of us out of it. No one assumed there could be five. Eddie's silence saved his own ass . . . and later ours.

"Callaghan," Daniel yelled, racing up to me as Eddie blasted the passenger door open. I flew into the vehicle as did Cass, Auggie, and

Daniel who shoved their way into the back seat.

"Eddie," I said with tears in my eyes.

"I'm an excellent driver," he said, mimicking a certain movie starring Dustin Hoffman and Tom Cruise.

He proved it by driving backward at seventy miles an hour in a perfect line until we reached that fork in the road again. Slamming the car into drive, he hung a hard left.

The road not taken was our only choice.

6.

This time around it was a young girl—tall, lean with white hair in braids—standing in the middle of the road with a stop sign.

"Swerve?" Eddie said. "Hell yes or hell no?"

"We can't hit a kid!" I screamed.

Cautiously, we pulled up next to the girl and Eddie rolled down the window just an inch or two. The only reason he didn't gun it is that the girl seemed lost. A closer look revealed that she had piercing blue eyes that were covered in the milky sheen of someone who was probably blind.

She was wearing what used to be called dungarees with a black-and-red checkered shirt tucked in, and snow-white athletic shoes. She had an open wool coat over the entire ensemble, but refused to secure it as if she was dismissing the wintery air. Eddie rolled the only working window down and said words that made me cringe.

"What's up super freak?"

"Eddie," I hissed.

"State your business," she said. "Or don't. I can't allow myself to care anymore."

"We're seeking entry," I said.

"Aren't we all?" she replied.

Her voice had a homespun twang, but remained emotionless when she rattled off words she probably said a million times—and would say a million times in the future.

"Good evening, my name is Sara. Would you have the kindness to help a girl sitting here by the side of the road doing her penance?" she asked.

"Can I ask what is required? And what are you doing penance for . . . if you don't mind." She answered the first, ignored the second.

"What is required is your silence in this moment," she said and I went optimistically mute.

"I'm supposed to say to you, 'Welcome to The Other,'" she said. "Now that I said it, I'm supposed to tell you that you're only on the periphery. It's a safe zone, which some find ironic because it's really not that safe. But we digress. For true entry to The Other, you just go through the border, which is ahead. You will face an immigration board that will conduct certain tests.

"You will only be allowed to enter if it is decided if you are mentally and physically fit and possessing an aura that jives with this part of the beyond," she said. "No use asking me any questions or making a hullabaloo about what will account for the rest of your night. I don't have the *partics*."

She slapped a parking permit on our windshield and I read it backward. When you unscrambled the letters, it read: Examination.

"You can proceed ahead to that white building off in the distance," she said as I continued to stare at her. How the journalist in me longed for the time to ask her about her own story and how she became the gate guard of the afterlife's Ellis Island.

"I lost my sight when I was fourteen years old," she said, almost reading my mind. "I didn't wear my science goggles in chemistry class. Who knew that teachers were serious about that one?"

"The chemicals killed you," I said in an astonished tone.

"Went right to my brain," she said. "Boy, did that teacher get into trouble, but that's neither here nor there. Let's just say that they never experimented with battery acid. Ever again. And every senior after me was forced to take boring botany instead of chemistry. The lesson was that science is dangerous, but ultimately worth it."

"But every physical limitation is restored in the afterlife," I said.

"If you truly yearn for it to be healed," she said.

She reached into her pocket and put on two eye patches. "I don't want to see what happens here. You won't either."

A chill ran through my system. I barely had a follow-up.

"How will we survive it?" I whispered.

"Protect your parts," she repeated, leaning into the car. "Hunt those who hunt you. Finish it! Sometimes, it's the only way."

"And wash your face," she added. "You're a mess."

"So, you can see?" I marveled.

"Not with my eyes, but yes," she said. "Over on this side, we all see."

EIGHT

1.

A wooden sign got to the particulars: Before you enter The Other, you must be examined and granted an access pass. Proceed to the main building.

For fun, someone had placed a less official marker next to the main instructions. It read: Little Ellis Island. I got it. We were immigrants and "they" were the law, whomever they might be in this situation.

The only thing was . . . there was no island. No water. There was just one building that looked like some high-tech office complex set in the middle of a grove of ancient Redwood trees. They stood majestically, tips reaching the sky. Maybe the building was fifty or sixty stories in a singular column tower made out of cobalt-blue glass that gleaned like moonlit forest.

Other aspects were familiar.

The parking lot out front was dimly lit like a mall parking lot in the living realm, but it was obvious by the perimeters that we had reached the proverbial end of the road. There was one huge lot and then the trees.

I hated to leave Howard's car, but at least it was in good company. The lot was rather packed with choice rides: red Camaros, black Mustangs, and even a steel-gray Buick, circa 1940s.

"Obviously, there are a lot of others knocking on The Other's door tonight," I said to Daniel who swiftly found a spot and then gazed at me first . . . and then the others.

"Stay frosty, baby," he said before addressing the rest. "We probably only have a minute or two before these assholes descend. Stuff things into your pockets. Grab your packs. Keep them tight."

"Or don't do any of the above," Cass barked, sending out completely opposite orders. "There is no way that we won't be searched here. The packs will be taken. Why have it all confiscated now?"

He took it upon himself to rip the keys out of Eddie's hands. "Hey," said the hurt Wargo. "You could have asked."

"I don't have time for manners," Cass said, in full commando mode now. "I have the only keys. This trunk triple locks, thanks to Howard. They'd have to burn the car to get into the trunk or totally destroy it. Dr. King put a tracker on the car. He told me there is an app on our watches that will help us find it, no matter what."

"So we walk in there unarmed. Great plan, genius," Daniel bit out.

"Yeah," Cass drawled. "Some of us know how to fight with our hands."

"You know where you can shove those keys," Daniel snapped.

2.

There was only time to grab three more stars and shove them deeply in my pockets.

By then the dogs had arrived—just as Cass locked the trunk—and they had a canine festival sniffing and then barking at us. A tall guard in a dark blue immigration uniform held leashes that were loosely draped across his arm.

He announced loudly, "Loitering the parking lot is not encouraged. If you have anything to declare, as in possessions, you can put them on the table in front of the building. They may or may not be returned."

If our things were to stay our things, the best chance was actually inside the trunk of that tank of a car.

"Where *are* you putting the key?" I asked Cass in a low voice.

"Sugar, you don't want to know," he replied.

"I could make a really bad joke about now," I whispered.

"Please do," Cass said with a wink.

Just like at the real Ellis Island in New York City, we were swiftly guided inside a place that operated as its own universe. There was only in; out was dangled as a future event.

The massive electronic doors that didn't just shut, but locked hard behind us. The air was heavy; the walls were thick. Guards were milling around and there were enough of them to make the hair on my arms stand tall.

What happened next reminded me of my glass jail cell at ITT. Once you stepped inside, the idea of your former life was just a dream.

Of course, my entire body went off in the metal detector.

"Miss," said a female guard who outweighed me by about two people. "Do you have anything metal on you?" She waved the want by my feet. "Fancy boots with jingles and jangles on them," she said as her censor beeped when she waved it over the hardware of those new shit kickers. "Anything else?"

I shook my head as she swept her wand over my pockets. Thankfully, I wasn't hiding any stars in there.

Her wand went off by my mouth in a way that I thought I set off an entire alarm system. "A lot of metal cavities?" she suggested and I looked down and nodded slightly again.

It wasn't until we sat back down that I oh-so-carefully removed the two throwing stars I had put in my mouth in order to keep them. No one ever wanted to look inside your cheeks (above or below), so it was the safest place, if your tongue didn't get ripped to shreds. Mine felt just fine despite the slight iron taste of a few nicks.

Score one for my new TV series that I would propose someday called *Self-Defense When You're Scared Shitless.*

3.

Another guard silently guided us inside a waiting room where we were greeted by a blast of forced heat and the smell of lemony industrial cleaner. I hated when places were overheated—it actually made me feel dizzy—but this was okay because along with the tropical temps, the room was created to look oddly comfortable.

"What is . . . the opposite of the Midst? Welcome to The Other," said a certain young man known in his life as a beloved game show host. He wasn't here-here, but on a flat-screen TV where his greeting announcement seemed to run on a loop. "We pride ourselves on being total individuals on this side," he said in his usual scholarly way. "Nonconformity is our vibe. Only those with wide-open minds will be allowed to enter."

"I'll have 'We're Screwed' for five hundred," Cass whispered.

Once the PSA flipped off, our regularly scheduled program returned to their latest rerun of a fan favorite at my house, *Everybody Loves Raymond,* and someone thought to leave large plates of chocolate chip cookies and containers of milk on the tables. Eddie was already treating this like he was in some afterlife VIP lounge.

"Do you have chocolate milk?" he asked a smiling attendant who looked to be all of sixteen or seventeen. He was in white, which meant janitorial here. The place was so clean that the clean-up crew wasn't even dirty.

"No, sir."

"Chocolate shakes?" Eddie posed.

"No, sir."

"Twix?"

Interestingly enough, there were other teenagers in the waiting room, but unlike immigration in old New York, the object here wasn't an endless wait. A nurse type in green scrubs named Sally Jones was soon upon us with clipboards, which was unnerving. I remembered how Dr. King said that this was also a naked medical test.

"Don't get all jittery. Just fill out the paperwork," she instructed. To Cass, who was walking around touching things and trying to look over her computer on the desk, she purred, "Don't be touching things, handsome. You sure got yourself some brass tacks."

For a moment, I thought it was a compliment.

It wasn't.

"We don't like that here," Sally said.

Then she reconsidered. "Well, some of us like it," she told him with a wink before purring, "Welcome to The Other where no one is your brother."

She handed each of us a clipboard and said, "Fill it out, hun. It's just the basics starting with an emergency contact."

I took Eddie's clipboard away from him quietly knowing he couldn't read or write.

"Emergency contact," Eddie said. "Just put Jesus."

4.

"Line up according to gender," said one of the technicians who was flanked by two interns. All of them wore long, white lab coats and black pants. I knew that like the real Ellis Island, we would be separated, but I just didn't expect it this quickly. I wasn't ready for it. My mind kept screaming, *Divide and conquer.*

"I'll take the woman," the guard announced.

I was trained to follow since age five. Weren't we all? Some sort of instinctual code made it impossible to move. My feet rocked in my boots while refusing to advance. *What did my feet know that hadn't yet traveled to my unformed frontal lobe? I remembered in that moment that your brain doesn't fully form until you're twenty-five years old.*

My feet were street smart. They knew we were at the point now where one step felt like it could lead to oblivion.

I was someone who already had walked enough lost miles leaving a trail of blood.

Daniel Reid, my rebel heart, rushed wildly into an upright stance. He was standing with me. Then he was kissing me so hungrily and for so long that I forgot to be petrified.

When he pulled back, he looked at me, *Really looked at me.*

In a soft voice that was like liquid honey mixed with a chocked rasp, Daniel whispered into my hair, "Each time I see you, I remember what it's like to be alive again. When I touch you, I exist." When I opened my mouth to speak, he kissed me again, hard and with a finality that made me want to scream.

There were first kisses—and last kisses.

This was the end credits for now.

"Walker . . . Walker Callaghan, I won't call you again," said another type named Matthew Jarvis. His name badge also included his position, which was head examiner. The only thing was he was young, about seventeen, in an ill-fitting black suit—that pooled at the hips and knees— white shirt, and tie. The fact that he had what looked like a high-tech Taser gun attached to his hip made my hands shake.

Given no choice, I backed up to take that first step into my uncertain future. As I passed a sitting Cass, he reached out to touch my hand, but oddly missed and settled for my upper hip. Then I felt it. He wasn't just saying good luck with an odd pat, but he inched his hand up my leg to drop the car key into the pocket of my jacket. I jiggled it down a little further.

I wanted to remind him that I didn't really drive. I was a city girl.

Cass stood, big and aggressive, and there was a danger in his attraction. I thought he might embrace me, which might have led to an altercation with Daniel. But the way he looked at me with so much longing and trust—with nary another touch of a fingertip—was so much worse and it left me shaken. It was as if the idea of seeing me across the room was enough. And not just for now. It would keep him going for the rest of the day—or forever if fate wasn't kind.

He reached low and rubbed his thumb over mine. Then he squeezed my hand in a way that the bones began to protest. Quickly, he pulled back as he leaned down. "Do you still feel my hand? I know you do. It's for later, sugar. For always," he whispered into my hair. "I press hard, so you can still feel it. If this doesn't turn out so well . . . "

"How do you . . ."

"Know it won't turn out well?" he whispered. "You know it, too. Just survive. No matter what. You get through. You exist."

My feet walked, but my heart began to slide into oblivion. I took one last look at these faces wanting to memorize them, but my shaking arm was grasped and another door closed with a slam.

Story of my life.

Story of my death.

At the internal exit door, a stern-faced, young administer whose nametag read Jacob Andrews was lurking. He was cooled out with a buzz cut top flanked by longer sides and wearing one of those standard black suits. Absentmindedly, he wrangled me into a herd of about twenty other girls, all frightened out of their freakin' minds, and complete strangers.

"*Grant* Callaghan, make yourself plainly known," he announced.

At first, I was confused, but then I got it. Slowly, I raised my hand.

"You didn't fill in one of blanks," Jacob said. "What sign were you born under, Grant?" I would learn that they wanted to take the sting out of the former word, so they shortened it to Grants. As in, we were the ones who needed to be granted permission to enter these parts; they were the ones to grant our wishes . . . or not.

Several males were brought into the room including Daniel and Eddie. I wasn't sure what they did with Auggie and Cass.

"What sign was she born under? A warning one," Daniel shot out. From across the room. It caused over a hundred other Grants to break into uproarious laughter that can only reach these decibels when a group of this age is mocking authority.

Mental note: not a good move as far as moves went here.

Jacob glared at Daniel.

"Do not make me render you as one of the hopeless," he said.

Another uproarious shout from the crowd. It was always amazing to me how the masses always went for the easy laugh and often gave it to the wrong side.

Score one for The Other.

5.

Everyone here was in some kind of rabid hurry.

"Move quickly, Grants," Jacob demanded. "We don't have all night."

Actually, we did have all night. And all the nights after this one. What else did we have to do, except walk in a single file line like we were back in elementary school. But this wasn't an institution of learning. It combined minimalism with your basic hospital blankness.

The scrubbed-clean whiteness of the place creeped me out, including the pictureless bright-white walls; shiny white-tile floors in long, thin rectangles; and heavy white doors marred by serious silver locks. It made the place look like we had just traveled through Marie Kondo's version of a perfect world.

Even the elevator doors were polar-bear white and Jacob practically shoved all of us, totaling about twenty-five females Grants, through them.

"Ow," a twelve- or thirteen-year-old cried.

"Unless we've hit an artery, I don't really want to know about it," Jacob blurted. I watched as he typed the word "coddled" into his phone over her photo.

My ears cracked and popped—not a good sign for the reset—as we took that ascending box thirty-two stories up into the sky. Looking around in that confined spot, I noticed there was one other male species in the elevator with us. He was a young man, about eighteen or nineteen, who was alone. I'd learn in the next moment that flying solo in this building was not an acceptable thing.

"What floor do you work on? And where is your badge?" Jacob asked.

No answer.

"Grant, you have one minute to comply," he said.

"I don't work here," said the young man.

In a whip-fast move, the Taser was out and Jacob pressed it to the young man's heart. All of us watched in horror as his knees buckled and he dropped to the floor thrashing like a fish out of water. I couldn't stand it anymore when I smelled burning flesh.

"I got the Kadota," Jacob said into his sleeve. When the doors opened, two orderly types in blue scrubs picked the guy up off the floor and carried him away.

"What's a *Kadota*?"

I knew it wasn't the right time to ask. It just slipped out.

"Someone who has disappeared. Slipped through the hands of inspection. It's a capital offense. Do it once and you will be labeled one of the Faded," said my handler. "Don't choose to fade because in this building we can make you disappear. There is a portal to a prison realm—and not your candy-ass ITT—for those who choose not to cooperate."

If nothing else, it was a warning. Play their game.

Or there would be no game.

We reached floor forty-seven and the routine was like being at the doctor's office. All of us were assigned to a room on the right side of the hallway. Exam Room #18 was like a glorified white (what else?) closet that was so small, I could reach out and touch the four walls. A nurse, the nonfriendly type, came in, took my vitals, which weren't so vital in my present condition, and encouraged me to lay down on a small white table.

I sat straight up like an arrow.

Outside of #18, I heard what sounded like Auggie being taken down the hall, which made sense. The guys would enter rooms on the left side. It sounded like he was crying. *Oh, please, Augs, don't resist,* I thought. *You don't know how to handle these situations. Just go with the flow, so you don't fade. Don't be on one of the . . . what the hell did he call it? The Kadota . . . WTF did it even mean?*

I jumped when a door in the wall opened.

"My name is Dr. Peter Shaw," interrupted the bald young man who was maybe a few years older than me—and I got it. Unlike the Midst, where there were more adults, it seemed like most of the workers here were young. Except these were teens with titles.

"When did you have time to go to medical school?" I spat.

"Walker?" he responded. "I'm not that kind of doctor. This isn't a hospital like the one you encountered in a past loop. This isn't about healing at all." He was talking about where I took Pete when we were on our mission in New York. It was called an Actaeon and was a hospital for wounded spirits floating through certain time periods.

"You're Grant 1,670,582,896," he declared. "This session is being recorded for training purposes. Here we go. We only allow fifteen percent of those who come into this building to enter The Other. Your passport in or denial revolves around your intentions."

I nodded.

"Why do you choose to enter?"

Dr. King had prepared us for this part. "We're students of the afterlife arts seeking knowledge, foresight, and training at a certain school here called the Astonishing . . ."

He wouldn't let me finish, but seemed to approve of my answer. I could read backward and he was scoring my chart with your standard A, B, C, D, F. So far, I was an A minus GPA here.

"The Astonishing School, of course. It's the Harvard of the afterlife," he said.

The school was actually one of our stops directed by Dr. King.

"I need to photograph you," Shaw abruptly said. "Stand and follow. It's your only choice."

Another long, white hallway and we reached what looked like one of those old-fashioned photo booths that was just plopped in the middle of all that pristine tile. It was black, almost touched the ceiling, and looked like the kind of throwback machine where you made funny faces with your best friend on a Friday night at the mall.

Shaw motioned for me to enter what could have been a portal to anywhere.

But it wasn't. It was a photo booth. Of sorts.

Inside, it was pitch black and nothing happened. A few minutes later, I was told to step out without even one light flickering.

"Is it on the fritz?" I asked.

"No," Dr. Shaw said in a matter-of-fact voice.

"Then what did you just do?"

"I took the picture I needed."

"Of my face?"

"Of your soul," he said.

6.

After the impromptu photo shoot, we wandered down another hallway inside this maze and finally settled into Room 2117. It was the size of a gymnasium, but there was nothing athletic going on in here. Inside, there were about a thousand cubicles filled with packets of paper and pencils. Two folding chairs flanked each desk. This part would involve a written Q&A, but we would do no writing.

You were assigned a student intern.

"Describe to me a hell of your own making?" asked mine, a kid named Jeremy Pride (from his name tag) who wore a white lab coat, black pants, and had frizzy dark hair and black-rimmed glasses. He reminded me of my science-loving friend Arnie at the Academy.

What a neat parlor trick. They would ask you for your version of hell . . . and then probably make it happen.

"Puppy commercials," I declared.

He paused for a long minute.

"Do explain," said Mr. Pride.

"Did you ever stay home sick from school in the living realm" Inevitably, there would be the abandoned dog commercial. Cute dogs. Unloved. Unwanted. Then a country music star with big hair would sing some weepy song as they cuddled some sad dachshund who lived her tragic life behind bars. I wanted to adopt every single one of them, but I couldn't because my mom and I lived at Aunt Ginny's apartment. "Watching those commercials—a hell of its own making," I summed up.

"I don't watch television," he said in a clipped tone.

There were hundreds of other questions that seemed to take hours and some pertained to my past, my "associates," and my deepest desires, wants, and wishes. He also made inquiries about my deepest and darkest fears.

"I guess you're afraid of car crashes and deer," he said.

I had gone along with their nonsense, but this felt like a slap. My death was private.

I just shrugged.

"Directory of the Dead—documentation of your past," he said. "Eighty some years ago when I started working here, we had to actually get out this big book, which was so heavy, not to mention dusty. But now it's all digital, which I guess you could call progress."

That's when it dawned on me. Most of these people looked like teenagers . . . some were . . . and some were not. They were just age shifters. Older adults who moved their ages backward just like Dr. King.

He pushed the forward key and jumped ahead as he read my story.

"So, what the hell happens to me in the future? Do they have flash forwards?"

"Oh, it's an epic story," he said with eyes that were too wide. "But, we don't provide coming attractions."

Jeremy chose not to elaborate. Instead, he finished his paperwork and sent me back out of the double doors.

As Springsteen would have sang . . . the hallway was jammed with almost broken heroes. My heart raced when I saw the familiar and oh-so-welcome faces of Daniel, Cass, Eddie, and Auggie together in a line about to merge left. There would be no breaking ranks because even a step out of line would be considered a mutiny.

I nodded at Eddie who looked like he was about to cry.

Auggie stood half an inch from him, looking worse. If Auggie got any closer to Eddie, they would be dating.

Cass and Daniel were in front. Side by side. Feet planed. Stances wide. Cass nodded in my direction while Daniel's eyes burned.

It reminded me of the day we were taken to ITT to serve eternal sentences. Daniel reminded me that my steelworker father Sam was with me in spirit.

"Steel, Callaghan," he said, raising a fist before they took him away.

Right now, he clenched his right fist, lifted it, and then seared the paint off the wall when he looked at me again.

I clenched my fist and touched it to my heart.

7.

What followed was the worst of it, thus far. Another white little room and I was naked on a steel table, hands over my bits, when she approached with a little square machine that flashed numbers and letters. Her name was Kimberly Guscia, MD, a girl genus who looked like the Doogie Howser of the afterlife.

"Where exactly is that thing going?" I demanded, sitting up.

"It's called a bio read," said Dr. Kimberly, who weighed about ninety pounds and actually looked to be about sixteen. She had a diamond chip in her nose and ink-black hair that was so un-doctorish. She even had a few acne spots, plus a sweet, round face prone to the occasional zit riot.

"A bio read is the latest in physical examination," she explained like she had said it a thousand times a day and probably did. "Sorry about the naked part. Someday, they'll be able to do this with clothes on. The living will do it on their kids. They'll do it for fun and read the guy next to them on the subway. But for now, we just wave this machine over you and it checks for cancer, growths, a slow metabolism, heart disease, bone spurs, pregnancy . . ."

She stopped at my stomach and pressed a button for a further reading. Her eyebrows shot up.

My eyes went wide.

"Just kidding," she said with a giggle. "Gets the girls every single time. But you did do a little horizontal mambo this morning. It can tell that, too, from your presenting temperature and hormonal levels."

"Are you waiting for a confession?"

"None required."

She wanted to know what age I died.

"Seventeen."

"Shame. You probably would have lived to a hundred," she said. "But don't lament. The world is equally wide over here. And it's a beautiful thing to fight for even a moment of breath."

"Still is," she added.

We were silent for a few moments while she checked off some boxes. When she was done, her doe eyes looked so sad that I asked what ended it for her. "Oh, it was silly, really," she lamented. "My parents owned a farm in Iowa, and kids at my high school used to tell me that I smelled, but I couldn't help it. I had to feed the pigs and cows every morning before the bus.

"So, I became obsessed," she said. "Smelling good was my quest. I began to buy ten cans of deodorant at the same time. I liked the spray kind. Every morning before I went into the barn, I'd spray my whole body again and again with the stuff until I couldn't even smell a thing anymore."

"And then?" I prompted her, hating the fact that I was such a sucker for a good story.

"It was winter. All the windows in my room were closed and I died thanks to butane gas inhalation," she said. "Medically speaking, I sprayed my body with so much deodorant that I couldn't get enough oxygen."

Shit.

"Funny thing about your own personal world ending," she said with a wry smile. "What few know is that it begins again on this side with the next conscious thoughts."

"Proving nothing really changes."

"Exactly—well, mostly," she replied.

8.

I would ponder her words even after I was ushered into a much larger auditorium-like room bathed in a deep blue light. *Were we getting a break to see a movie? Maybe I could suggest one of the Avengers films. . . .*

There were over a hundred Grants in here and the longer I stood, I could pick out the ones who actually meant something to me.

Daniel was way up front, oddly next to Cass and Eddie, who was now crossing his arms overhead like he was landing a plane. Turns out, he spied me early on and I pointed at him so he knew that I saw him.

Auggie was two rows behind me looking for a seat. He waved furiously.

"Hiya, Walker . . .Walker . . . over here, Walk—" Auggie said frantically as he was told repeatedly to keep quiet and sit down. "For me, I am being quiet," he insisted as his rear end brushed several other people on the way to his landing spot. "Excuse me, excuse me, sorry, excuse me, apologies," said my frantic friend, as he climbed over throngs of seated people, stomping on feet and almost falling into laps, while navigating the narrow space. It wasn't long before he was hovering over me.

"Wouldja mind? Couldja move? I really need a hug, but not from you . . . ," he rambled to the girl sitting next to me.

She was up like a shot and relocated her seat.

Then he plopped. And turned. Auggie enveloped me like we hadn't seen each other in years—and I hugged him back like I would never let go of my afterlife bestie. It wasn't long before we were told to quiet down and warned not move again. But it was worth it. I pointed straight ahead and gave a little wave to Cass. He flashed a tender smile. Daniel was next to him looking brain-surgery serious.

As I began to wave, I couldn't see my hand anymore.

The lights were cut.

That American actress. Her face filled a big white screen.

Wait . . . *wasn't she still alive?*

Maybe she was allowed to come here from time to time if she did these little public service announcements.

Her milky-white face and searing red hair loomed in the flickering light.

"Welcome to the Aura-torium. Are there any light workers in here? Magic makers? World shifters? Game shakers?" she asked in one of those wondrous voices.

I couldn't be sure, but I didn't see a single hand rise. There seemed to be a whole lot of average in these seats.

I celebrated the ordinary.

"Young people, your aura is the physical manifestation of your energy. It's the first step in knowing your true destiny," she insisted.

Hello? Who gave a shit about a destiny? I just wanted to pass these tests, join everyone else, and find a nice Ramada to settle in for the night.

"Your aura is a terrible thing to waste," Shirl droned on. "This is why, children, you're at this gathering post to figure out what type of aura you possess."

"Or, as I once heard on the streets—several lifetimes ago—thou shall not let low-vibin', sketchy energy penetrate a pure aura," she said.

God forbid.

Perhaps my aura could be described in two words: smart and ass.

This is what I learned:

*We all have an aura, which is a rainbow-colored energy field that is invisible to the naked eye.

*Aura energy comes from our seven main invisible energy centers called chakras, along with other energy sources within the body.

*Existence—noise, pollution, television, cell phones, and all electrical things or toxins along with negativity, criticism, meanness, and bullying—depletes our aura. Which means one thing: existing is hazardous to your aura's health.

*Kids pick up on auras easily because they're pure energy.

It's why a kid draws a girl with a blue light around her. He or she is just drawing the aura that they see plain as day.

"In the special lighting of this room," she said, "your aura will be easily seen. Your seats contain a number on the armrest. When your number is called, you will stand to have your aura recorded in your Record of Permanence."

And so it went with body after body rising and sitting. Number 32 was Daniel who stood defiantly. Even I could see the red surrounding him. I looked down at a small booklet that was left on our seats like a program. It read: Red is for those charged with action, survival, courage, and determination. Red = Daniel.

His plusses included that he was a passionate lover. (*Um, obvious. Embrace the vole.*) Minuses: Short-tempered and a nature to erupt. (100 P).

Cass was a Green for love, fidelity, trust, harmony, and spiritual growth. His positives included a loving heart that was beyond generous and deeply committed to love and romance. His negatives included conflicting emotions and emotional dependency. "Loves unwisely and too much," I read from the booklet.

When I stood in this special light, I couldn't miss the pale, almost snowy glow around my being. It was like someone had traced me in light.

I had a white aura. A quick glance down at the book and I was fascinated. White meant limitless potential, boundless energy, and a free-flowing life force with a soaring spirit. I was what they called a "quester" or innovator. The plus was that white meant a highly evolved person with a unique soul path. Someone who would make a difference in the world.

"Walker," Auggie whispered in a reverent voice. "It says you draw pure, undiffused light from the cosmos to reach higher levels of consciousness on your quest for the truth."

"A queen," he said.

I rolled my eyes. "Not even a princess," I said. "More of a peon."

9.

Our assembly ended swiftly after the last name was called and we returned to our original exam rooms. Thankfully, I didn't have to do the naked dance again.

This time the nurse's name was Jupiter and she was seventeen, and extremely inquisitive. "Call me J," she said while adjusting thick, black, cat-eyed glasses. She motioned me to sit on yet another cold steel exam table.

"I love your dress," I said of a long black sheath covered with a white hand-knit sweater. She smiled, but was having none of my icebreakers.

"A few final questions," Jupiter said. "What period is your soul derived from in the large sense?"

Most of the time, I was extremely fast on my feet, but she had me at the world derived. "I have . . . no idea."

The cat-eyed glasses slid down a long, thin nose. "If your travels take you to the Astonishing School, you might get a beat on that."

Most of the other questions were odd . . . but answerable to some degree.

"What mythical creature would you like to be?"

"Uh . . . Samantha from 'Bewitched.' You know, twitch your nose and make it happen. It's good, too, if your nose itches."

"Your spirit animal . . . wolf, bear, owl, or snake."

"Owl," I blurted.

"Wolf," she wrote down. "Same as your delightful boyfriend, Mr. Reid."

"What time period would you like to live in . . . Dark Ages, the Industrial Era, the Renaissance?"

"The eighties," I said. "Good music and I like the idea of leg warmers."

Smiling, she shoved a piece of paper at me. "Look at the list, Walker," she said, struggling over my name as if she had to glance down to remember it. "Circle any special extras that you brought into the universe."

It was a lengthy list that required a few second glances. Did I have:

astral projection or the ability to project an astral body anywhere; breath or the gift to breathe underwater; clairvoyance or the ability to see the future; energy vampire tendencies or a person who steals the voltage of others; indestructibility or someone who is impervious to damage or remote viewing, which I learned is the power to track people or objects from afar.

Mind Control? Precognition? Regeneration? Levitation? Biokinesis? (That last one was the ability to control organic tissue and the ability to heal others, which is exactly what Daniel possessed—not that he would tell them. I was sure of it).

Daniel could literally heal by flushing out illness or pain and replacing it with healing energy. This sheet offered several notes about it, including one that left me unsettled. If one who possesses biokinesis heals another with biokinesis, it can affect their energy and cause them to lose their power. In that case, they would never be able to heal again.

"I got nothing," I finally told my inquisitor. "Too bad there wasn't a line that read: Scrappy with inflated dreams to save the world."

"There is a line. You can fill that in," Jupiter instructed. "Write your name and status at the top of the page."

"Status?" I replied, looking at a laundry list of choices I didn't understand.

"You're an Angelica," Jupiter told me. "A young, unmarried woman who isn't tethered. You'll be coveted. Some even hunt for that type here. At the very least, you need to be aware to fend off advances or to cooperate and tether – which is akin to marry."

My face read one word: Horrified.

There was one last topic.

"In the Midst, you were told that the knowledge you gained at the Academy would be judged by only one—you," she said. "That's true . . . over there. Here, that knowledge will be tested."

Before we could explore it, she handed me a little blue booklet that looked like a passport.

"Here's your passport. Good luck out there."

"I passed!"

"You're saying it," she whispered, "like it's a good thing."

10.

When I was young, I was given a reward each time I went to the doctor.

My mother would stop at the Sugar Bowl, a timeless ice-cream shop that opened in 1921 and used to be a soda fountain and candy store. Pennies being pinched hard, I was allowed to get a one-scoop sugar cone filled with anything my heart desired, like their homemade cinnamon vanilla.

Milly Jackson, the extremely old lady who owned it, felt bad for me in my winter coat with the matted fake fur and sleeves that stopped about six inches from my wrists. *Way to squeeze out another season, Mom.* Milly's scoops were XL for certain customers wearing jeans that could be classified as flood pants (i.e., if there was a flood, the bottoms wouldn't get wet).

For those who had less, she gave more.

It was a bit different in The Other, although they still believed in the concept of quid pro quo. In Latin, it meant "something for something."

It went this way: You consented to be examined, poked, prodded, and questioned -- and passed. Now a little love would be sent your way. This was in the form of a long, silver folding table on the way out offering what smelled like freshly baked oatmeal raisin cookies and some kind of trippy-looking purple punch with red berries floating at the top.

There was a line.

Warning: Never get in line until you know what's at the top. Don't be a lemming.

A quick glance around and no Daniel, no Cass, no Eddie, and no Auggie. Just like any other starving teenager, I grabbed for my first cookie and then stole a second. No one said to just take one. We were all loading up because anyone who had reached this point had passed. I was happy to grab a water to wash it down, but a sweet-looking teenage girl named Olivia, with her brown, slightly curly hair pulled back in a loose bun, smiled at me warmly as she filled red plastic cups full of that punch.

"What is it?" I asked.

"Camu-elderberry something," she said and smiled. "Tastes like grape juice, but we don't have grapes here."

I took my first sip tentatively like it was poison, but soon began to gulp. It was grapelike and so pleasantly sweet that once my tongue emerged from a sugar coma, I asked for a second glass.

"I had no idea I was this hungry or thirsty," I apologized as my face went red.

My mother always said that you should rarely grab for seconds in a world where most don't get firsts. If only my body wasn't on some kind of autopilot, craving any kind of liquid or chewable substance. I would have eaten my own hand at that point. I stuffed half a cookie in my face when I wasn't drinking and then held my cup out hopefully, pitifully, for another refill of that grape swill.

"I got you," Olivia said, filling it to the brim. Then she asked me an odd question.

"Will you be a hunter or gatherer here?" she inquired.

It was one of those awkward moments when someone asks you an important question while you're chewing. You speed it up, teeth mashing fast, and choke it down while trying to think.

"Neither," I sputtered, brushing the crumbs off my sweater. "I'm just a student."

"No one," she said, the sweetness draining from her face, "Is *just* an anything here."

11.

An official-looking guard in blue cut her off.

"Passport," she demanded.

"What?"

"You are Walker Callaghan?"

"Yes."

"Blue door to your left," she said. "When you step outside, you will wait."

"For what?"

"Blue door," she repeated.

I found myself in a remote parking lot where there was only a sea of asphalt and no cars parked. I was the only one out here. *Where were they? Where were the vehicles?* Then a little voice reminded me that I didn't need to jump to the worst-case scenario. I wasn't alone. I was just *the first*. It was lonely, but not a tragedy.

When life gives your curveballs, swing like Stevie Wonder with a light saber. I heard that somewhere.

A light snow began to fall and it just added to the soundless night. I remembered from science class that fresh snow absorbs sound, lowering the ambient noise over a landscape. That's why the world went quiet when it snowed.

Tonight, the quiet was earsplitting.

I couldn't worry about it in the moment because I really, really, really had to pee. This presented two choices. For once, I chose the safer option, but when I tried to walk back into the building I found that reentry wasn't exactly an option. From the outside, there was no lever or knob on the door.

Once you were cast out . . . you were out.

There was a hard concrete bench at the top of the asphalt, so legs crossed, I sat on it and stared up at the foggy winter sky. That took up about thirty seconds of time. It was cold enough to see your breath, so I made several large Os in the air, which occupied about three more seconds.

Suddenly, I couldn't wait any longer. *If you know what I mean.*

Guys had it so easy.

Luckily, there was a cluster of tall trees in the near distance. I was born minus the camping gene, but this technically was an emergency, which is why I found myself in territory unknown.

Yes, the woods were lovely, dark, and deep, but there was something else here that felt sinister. Maybe it was the encounter with those hunters. My eyes were peeled open in case they made a quick return.

"Trees are not sinister, ding-dong. And no one is out here in the middle of the night," I scolded myself. A deep breath. It smelled pungent and fresh while the snow felt crisp and cold, awakening my senses. It smelled like a fresh start, which should have calmed me.

I always considered the forest my sanctuary, but in this particular matter, I was anxious.

"You're losing it," I told myself.

I could hear the rock-concert loudness of my own breath . . . and with each anxious moment, the volume was cranking up. *In, out. In, out. Intake. Release.*

Deeply surrounded by the trees by now, I did a fast, half spin like some kind of freaked-out ballerina. The dead winter leaves didn't rustle, but thundered on a stray breeze.

A muffled whispering wind played as if someone was screaming my name.

"Walker, keep it together," I warned myself, sliding my leggings around my ankles before I burst.

Yogini that I wasn't, I crouched down, rocking in my boots to keep my balance on the mulchy ground. Suddenly, I felt a bit light headed from the pose, the nerves, and what had happened that night. Maybe I was having a panic attack. But I had never had one in the past. Not that it mattered.

Sweet relief.

Until I saw her.

Watching me.

12.

Those damn leggings remained around my ankles like elongated rubber bands, tipping me forward. A hand out to the next tree stopped my fall as I yanked at what felt like a straight-jacket around my legs.

She advanced.

I couldn't have been more vulnerable.

"You looking for something, friend?" I asked, yanking at my clothing.

"I'm not your friend."

13.

She had silky, straight, black hair that could only be described as wind-whipped in a brisk winter breeze. Her blanched skin, the color of fresh white paint, refused to redden in the frigid conditions. She was Asian, maybe seventeen or eighteen, and extremely tall at close to five feet eight or nine, I guessed.

She sparked a Camel cigarette and flicked the ashes wildly while sparks ran down from her fingers to her exquisitely black leather booted toes.

She walked like death itself, dense and heavy with a finality about it. I don't know why because I wasn't a violent person, but I wished I had one of my throwing stars at the ready.

"Out for an evening stroll?" I said, noting that she had what looked like a Glock attached to some kind of leather holster she kept at her hip. It was like she read my mind as she traced my gaze. "Sig Sauer P226," she said. "I left the Remington 870 shotgun in my cruiser."

"Cruiser? Sounds official," I said.

"Do you often shit in the woods?"

"I'm not shitting."

"Several hunters were run over tonight by what must have been a large truck or tanklike vehicle. Not too far away from here. Did you hear anything? See anything?" she snapped in a voice that was just a little too much on the side of the hunters.

"Did I . . . what?"

If all else failed, I would fall back on generic teenage confusion.

"You heard me."

Okay. She wanted a story.

Please. All teenagers are novelists.

"I was too busy being prodded by the welcoming committee in that big building. Over there," I stated.

"You arrived for inspection just after the offending incident," she said.

"Thanks for keeping tabs."

"Funny how your hearing is fine now," she taunted.

"At the risk of repeating myself, although I will . . . did you hear anything? Such as their screams as their bones were breaking? Or perchance you saw something like them trying to stand as their lungs filled with their own blood. Maybe you heard them gurgling when they began to drown in their own bodily fluids?" she suggested.

In that moment, I knew there was only one answer.

No answer. Followed by a shrug.

In the moonlight, you couldn't miss one of those old-fashioned sheriff badges with a name engraved in the middle. A glance down. Her belt contained handcuffs, an-old fashioned walkie-talkie radio, baton, pepper spray, another round of ammo, a Taser, flashlight, pens, pencils, and keys.

Her ill-fitting puke-brown cargo pants were matched with a colorless, long-sleeved shirt that looked like some last-chance discount rack giveaway.

It was clear that she put this ensemble together.

Then she confirmed it.

"I created this uniform," she said.

"Does that costume come in black?"

"No, Walker," she said.

"Not fair that you know my name," I replied slowly, because it helped to slow it down during these kinds of *oh shit* moments. "And I can't exactly read yours on that badge because you're standing in the shadows now."

"My name is Pristine. That's it. Or you could call me Law Enforcement Officer Number One."

14.

"Some call me Sheriff Pristine. No first name," she continued. "I was born and my keeper said, 'She's Pristine.'"

Keeper? Perhaps that went with the gathering part of this place. I'd file that one for later, if there was a later.

"Dr. King told me about you. He also said this was a lawless place."

"My, oh, my, oh . . . you're a wordy one," she said.

Suddenly, I didn't feel so wordy. It was an icy, almost glacial fear that raced around my insides while she looked calm and collected. At that moment, my mother's voice filled my ears. "Walker," she would say, "never compare your insides with someone else's outsides."

"I am the law," she said, breaking and entering my mental playback. "I am the law in a lawless place. Someone has to keep house. There is always a first."

"Authorized by whom?" I put it out there.

"Why are you here?"

"School project," I shot back.

No one could *ever* argue with it. Life. Death. It was all a school project.

"Tethered?" she asked.

There was that word again.

"I don't give a shit about your fake school project from your candy-ass half of this realm," she announced. She spit out the next words. "The Midst. That's where you're from . . . isn't it?" The way she laughed about it made me burn.

"Bitch, I'm from Chicago," I stated.

I felt a wave of something coming on that had nothing to do with my rage. My head began to swim in some kind of light fog.

"Too much juice," Pristine said with a smile. "Greedy, greedy, greedy. All you teenagers—especially in the Midst—ever do is care about your own needs. You're overgrown children with self-inflated visions of . . ." She kept ranting, "A false belief in one's own superiority, greatness, and intelligence. With overwhelming evidence to the contrary."

Maybe, she was about to say grandeur . . . wait, is that how you spelled it?

I felt a hit that went to the nectar of my being. As my knees began to buckle, she shook her head, the cascade of slick black hair flying from side to side.

"Remember one thing, honey. The first step off your high horse is always a bitch," Pristine said. "Tuck and roll. Just tuck and roll."

I tucked my arm around my middle. And then the entire world began to roll.

NINE

1.

Chuff-chuff-chuff-chuff.

In my haze, I heard the sound of blades punching through the atmosphere. Pristine lifted me up in the air, a veil of her black hair draping over my face, suffocating me. She carried me to what felt like the solid ground of the asphalt parking lot. Something even louder began ripping through the air and piercing my ears. I heard someone on a walkie-talkie.

"Do a bio read. He said to make sure it's her. All of our asses are on the line."

I tried to raise my hand, but it felt so damn heavy. Like it was dipped in concrete. "What . . . why," I began to mutter, but Pristine leaned closer as she rubbed her cold hand across my forehead. "Just sleep, little rebel. You'll be home soon enough."

She placed me gingerly onto a leather seat in what felt like a cold box. Someone put what felt like hard earmuffs over my head and then I felt myself being belted in place. "Daniel," I tried to say, but it wasn't him. The man had reddish hair like me—a ginger, which you often didn't see in the opposite sex—and his words along with my own just reverberated in my own head as a rotor noise became increasingly louder.

There was something about relaxing. Something about not *fighting it*. Whatever it might be, which was unclear.

We were lifting, accelerating forward, pushing through air. Something was slapping the wind and I felt a juddering as I began to bounce up and down, my lower and top teeth hitting each other in some kind of rhythmic pattern. The ginger's voice in front of me said, "Hang on. They don't call it a chopper for nothing."

I was lost in the sudden molasses of my own mind combined by the ever-present pulsating. *A chopper was a what? Chuff-chuff-chuff. Of course, silly, silly Walker. It was slang for* . . . a helicopter, and I had never ridden in one. It's like I had a chopper waiting in Arlington Heights, Illinois, in my school's parking lot waiting to wing me home. *Wait, did I?* No. I couldn't focus.

"I don't want to go," I insisted, but it came out sounding underwater. No one answered me. Which, of course, was an answer. Now I was beginning to scare myself. "I can't go anywhere," I mumbled. "I'm waiting . . . for people. People who need me . . . to be waiting for them." *Who was I waiting for now?* Their names. I forced myself to say them, although no sound came out: *Daniel, Cass, Auggie, Ed—*

As I began to whirl above this world, I heard those blades transporting me.

Taking me.

Elsewhere.

2.

Training taught us what to do in a hostage situation. You tap your wrist. Every tap is a second away from where you started. *Tap, tap, tap.* Second thing: you listen to the sounds outside to identify your current locations. I heard what sounded like silence punctuated by rushing water and marked by the scream of a hawk followed by the smell of fresh snow over freshly tarred roads.

My nostrils filled with burning, but it wasn't a crackling log of wood on a winter's night. This smell curled your nose hairs. It was strong . . . and took your breath.

Something was being cooked. Or someone.

That was the last thought I remembered as we plummeted.

Sometime later, there was a large bed and I was in it.

It was thick and surprisingly cushy, like sinking into a cloud of fancy fluff. It must have been a queen size because I could roll. Somehow, I widened my arms and they remained on the mattress. It wasn't so easy to do with my right hand, which was attached to something bigger via a plastic cable. I was bound, but to what? When I moved to pull on it, my strength left the building and I forgot what I wanted to do in the first place.

Hours later, I was semi-awake again.

My training taught me to memorize the particulars, and I began to count them down while I was still able: silky, cold sheets; expensive down pillow; thick comforter . . . *whose bed was this . . . and I was totally buck naked in it . . .*

When I woke, my heart began to pound.

3.

Facts, Walker, facts: There is a man standing over you. Thick black hair slicked back over a square forehead, dark brows, light eyes, bloodless lips pursed together, small ears with one of those CIA communication devices in the right one, decent chin.

Maybe he was twenty-five or thirty, tops. His forehead was smooth accompanied by slightly tanned skin and a perfectly sculpted nose. He looked movie-star handsome and distinguished in a way that was achingly familiar. Then it dawned on me. He looked like a model. No, that wasn't it. My brain scrambled and searched. . . .

Six o'clock. On the dot. Aunt Ginny and my mother gathering around the old TV practically salivating. "He's so beautiful. I'd let him explore what was under my pantyhose . . . even if he wrote the ad for them," said Aunt Ginny. To which I would make a disgusted face and say, "Aunt Ginny!" Sometimes, there weren't enough exclamation points in the world. Mom would just blush. Yep, they watched it in a way that reminded me of crack addicts needing their fix.

And now the man staring at me had an uncanny resemblance to that actor my mother refused to admit she had a crush on because she only "had eyes for my father." I knew she drooled over the guy who sat in his office in the 1950s and smoked a lot of cigarettes when he wasn't sipping something amber in a highball glass.

He looked like the main guy from *Mad Men*. Like his much younger just-got-out-of-grad-school self.

The man filling my vision was formal in a white, silky dress shirt and I'm assuming dark pants of some sort, although I couldn't see that low because he was hunched over me looking concerned. I wanted to scream, "Hey pal, just get me on my feet and give me a glass of water to clear my head and I'll be leaving." But for some reason, words would not form. My brain felt muddled like there was a short circuit or a disconnect, but I could still log in a nurse type in an all-white standard hospital uniform— not much older than me—who stood next to him.

Why was she pushing a long, hurting kind of needle into my otherwise dead right arm? Didn't she know that I hated shots? *WTF?*

He leaned down to smooth the hair out of my eyes.

"Don't worry," he said. "You're home now."

Historically—or was it hysterically—speaking, the moment a total stranger, who just kidnapped you, promises that you are "home" is the exact time to run like hell.

My lips were moving. I was trying to form words, unsuccessfully.

"I am . . . not . . . home," I said in a raspy voice. "Where am I?"

"You are experiencing day one of your new existence," he said. "You're welcome."

I felt cold and shivered.

"You are naked," he said in a low voice. "Shivering. Exhausted. Bleeding. Pigheaded. And probably won't listen to a single rational thing. Let's start again. My name is Xavier and you can trust me. I'll keep you safe—and you need my protection.

"I provide homes for many wanderers here," he said. "I'm sure you've heard the line, 'Not all who wander are lost?' I collect lost things."

His face dipped and he put his lips on my forehead as if he was checking for a fever. I tried to twist my head away, but it felt so heavy. When he placed a light, welcoming kiss on my right cheek, a tear slipped, damn it. I couldn't appear weak or emotional, but I didn't have the strength to turn, so he also kissed my left cheek. *How very European of him.*

"You're a very lovely girl," he said. "I should know. I got you ready for bed."

My hands were under the covers, but they began to tremble.

"Lovely verging on beautiful," he said, caressing my hair, which was splayed out on the pillow going every which way. "As they say around these parts, it's proper nice to have you here."

4.

Sometimes later—hours or days—when it was dark, I woke up again and heard voices in the hall. He was talking to the one who brought me here. "Pristine, you've done exactly what I wanted. Now, you can go back to the original plan," he said. "You will be handsomely rewarded."

"We went back and dropped the rest off where you wanted them," she said. "Proper nice not to have to worry about any of them ever again." Pause. "I assume my bonus is waiting for me in the basement."

"Not yet," he said. "First, you will go hunting. You will hunt until I say stop. Only the finest of specimens will do."

5.

When I came to again, it was blindingly sunny—maybe midmorning or late afternoon. I sat straight up and called out for him. "Daniel!" No one came to my rescue or my joy. I was clothed now in a thin, gauzy, white cotton nightgown, the expensive kind with fancy lace on top that itched like hell.

To my horror, one of those IV stands stood next to the bed, making this look enough like an upscale hospital room. I was attached by a line and tape. When I went to yank it out—and it didn't hurt—I knew the reset was back, my sweet friend. I kicked my foot into the side of the bed. No bitch of a stubbed toe. *Victory.*

I'd take a header out of one of those lovely windows. Whatever was required.

Freedom was outside of these walls.

I counted four windows to the right of me, the old-fashioned kind with dark wood embedded into the glass that made large diamond formations. The glass must have been thick because the blast of sunlight made triangle prisms on a creamy white wall. The windows were the large, floor-to-ceiling type.

I just needed a few tools. . . .

There was a dark brown dresser, new, but trying to look old and expensive, plus a matching tall wooden cabinet with an intricate design of small swirls on the front and another filmy white dress, much like the one I was wearing—no, make that three of them—on wooden hangers.

I could smell the lemon Pledge furniture polish on most of that lovely bedroom furniture, including on the big sleigh bed that had room for two. The walls were an oatmeal color, painted in slightly raised swirls. There was no TV. No radio. No magazines. No books. No computer.

It wasn't a bedroom. It was a cell.

I was being monitored. Just to prove my point, I looked up at the four corners of the wall and smiled broadly before flipping a small black camera-like device on the ceiling the double bird. A quick trip to the bathroom revealed a wealth of towels. I stood on a chair and tied one of them over the camera. A small red circle on the wall began to swirl and make an ultra-annoying beeping sound.

There wasn't much time.

There was enough however to make it to the windows (locked) and the door (solidly locked). *Shit!* The knob was turning from the outside.

I didn't have time to make it back to bed. So I stood in the middle of the room looking like someone who was guilty of everything, although no one had exactly explained the rules. I was a rules girl. Tell me the rules and I'll figure out how to break them.

"You pulled out your line," the handsome man said. What the f— was his name? Xavier. He was stepping back into the room and this time flanked by another youngish nurse in the typical white uniform and dark hair in a bun. She looked to be about twenty, which made her nursing skills dubious. I mean, where did she go to nursing school? Walmart U?

Unlike before, he looked shorter and more compact this time . . . maybe five feet seven or eight . . . athletic build . . . muscular arms . . . black sweater tied around the back of his neck over the nice white shirt . . . weirdest part of the whole thing: he was also wearing black driving gloves.

"I have to go," I said to them both. "If you could give me back my real clothes and my boots then I'll be leaving, as in right now."

"Travel is unwise at this juncture, Walker," Xavier said. "In fact, I must insist that you get back into the bed. Later, I'll have my chef bring you a nice bone broth and some crackers."

Crackers. Who the hell wanted crackers?

I saw her pull something plastic out of her pocket. She removed the cap and the silver of another long needle caught a glimmer of light by my highly polished nightstand.

"Don't," I warned, sticking a finger into her face.

In the end, I pulled the shooter out of the dime-store nurse's hands. She launched and I stabbed her hard in her upper arm.

The nurse fell to the floor, knees buckling. The man took that as his cue to pick up a silver tray on my nightstand, chuck the drinking glasses to the floor, and then smack me on the side of the head hard with the silver metal. No reset. My head was suddenly made of filmy pieces of nothing.

"I think we're going to need another nurse," he said.

6.

I had fever dreams of Daniel. We were standing on the edge of a cliff. The gentle pastels of the muted evening sky pulling an exit bathed us in soft light.

It felt otherworldly and perfectly regular at the same time.

Daniel pointed at snowcapped peaks while I focused on clouds backlit by the kind of light saved for this type of awe.

He wrapped strong arms around my middle and allowed me to sink effortlessly into him, every groove fitting so perfectly. Puzzle pieces clicking into place. I felt so relentlessly needy that I leaned harder, inched deeper, greedy in how I grabbed extra millimeters of his skin. The shame of wanting so much swept over my face in a hot wave.

He held my fingers like they were lifelines. Then he said words into my hair that would linger forever because they were trapped in time, longing, and loss.

"Once upon a time, a boy loved a girl," he said in a scratchy voice, "and when she would cry, it made him want to move mountains."

7.

Consciousness returned when I smelled freshly brewed coffee and heard the hushed voices of several others in the hallway outside of my prison cell. I logged it in my mind. Laughter slipped under the door as did cigarette smoke and what might have been something else burning like bacon left for too long in a greasy pan. In a total betrayal, my stomach began to rumble. I put my hand to the center of that cotton nightgown and heard the door click open again.

I rushed the open portal.

On wobbly legs, from a lack of food and water, I didn't get far. In fact, he was back and gently walked me backward until I was near the bed. He put one finger on my chest and pushed. I had no choice but to sit on it.

"Walker, right? Charmed, I'm sure," he said. "I don't want you to get hurt. I know you have a million questions, but for now, let's just be. Over time, you'll see that this was for the best. Some might call it fated, but it's impossible to predict fate, so we'll just have to embrace all that is current. Acceptance is the first step."

Acceptance, my ass.

"This doesn't have to get violent," he warned. "Your choice."

"I must warn you. I'm pretty good at violence . . . something you might have to accept," I said.

He smiled. Like he was enjoying this little verbal sparring session.

"So, you're a witch," he said with a smile.

"I'm not a witch. Nothing supernatural. No *woo-woo.* I'm just a pissed-off teenage girl who doesn't like to be grounded." "Did I say witch? I meant to say bitch—and that will conclude this portion of our conversation," he said.

In the Midst, our master trainer Bruce told us once not so long ago to draw a mental picture of our opponent.

He must have come from a workout because there were sweat beads on his forehead. Otherwise, he looked like a walking advertisement for that swish company in dark sweats and a matching nylon jacket. Were those dark-blue eyes real or some sort of stab at vanity via contact lenses? I could smell the hair gel combined with a strong pour of some kind of manly man cologne.

Focusing better now, I began to explore the rest: he was in his physical prime. And so was I, which is why I sprung up suddenly, hooked a leg behind his knee, and dropped him on his toned ass.

"Spirit. Spunk," he announced, bouncing up to stand eye to eye. "I won't underestimate you next time."

As I raced for the locked door, he put out his hand and clasped it in his other palm.

I jiggled the knob. It didn't move, and I had no choice but to turn back around.

He held out a small, weight-lifter's gloved left hand for what was going to be a formal introduction.

"I don't know if you remember much from last week when you arrived here, but you can call me Xavier," he said. I ignored the hand. *It had been a week.*

"Where is Daniel? Cass? Eddie?"

"Who?"

"My team."

"They were probably taken by hunters," he said, matter-of-factly. "It happens here a lot. It's not a good thing. What I do is help people. So they're not taken into slavery here. You were actually saved because I sent Sheriff Pristine to help those who appeared in need. You can thank me later."

"I need to get out of here."

"I need you to stay still," he said. "Thus, we have conflict, although you shouldn't resist. This place is a fortress. No need darting around like a jack rabbit. We kill little stray rabbits here and turn them into stew."

"I'm more partial to the cheetah," I retorted. "They move faster. . . . Where are my boots? You cannot keep my things. It's called robbery."

The grin widened. "How much fun is this? Sparring together. A partner with a razor- sharp brain. A coveted asset."

"I'm not your partner. Is Daniel here? Locked in one of your little rooms?"

"No, you're something different. You're my captive," he said in a suddenly serious voice. "Enjoy your day here in paradise."

8.

Legend says when you can't sleep at night it's because you're awake in someone else's dream. I had my memories of that rough face with a hint of a smile. The attitude combined with a creative mind and stubborn personality. Ah, that loving soul.

He was an artist when it came to his love, a deep-thinking creative with an open heart and the most loyal blood.

When I woke, I looked at the spaces between my fingers. "Remember, that's where my fingers fit," he once said.

My hand fell off the side of the big bed.

There was nothing. Just space.

9.

Hours or days later, I felt two cold fingers taking a slow trek down my right cheek. It was the gentle caress of an ice cube on naked skin to wake me. "There is food and I suggest you eat it to maintain your strength," Xavier said, helping to prop me up on the pillows.

The tray contained scrambled eggs, thickly cut toast, strawberry jam, and there was a big mug of almost boiling coffee with a silver pitcher of cream on the side. Damn it, but it was my hand that plunked three sugar cubes into that steaming cup of heaven. Then I grabbed for the fork and ate so ravenously that I looked like a teenage barbarian. My mother would have been *mortified* that I was shoving chunks of hot bread into my trap, but starvation made you forget your manners. It made him laugh for some reason.

"My last partner ate like a bird, which was for the birds," he said with a warm smile.

"I eat *Game of Thrones* style," I said, swallowing in gulps. "And I'm not your partner."

"I've always appreciated a woman with a healthy appetite," he said. "Take what you need because we have plenty here. There's nothing to be ashamed of because you haven't eaten in a long time."

"How long?"

My pathetic attempt to keep a time table was met with zero resistance.

"Fourteen days. You were drugged, but fed and hydrated by IV," he said, which made my eyes pop. A lot could have happened to the others in two weeks. Saving me wasn't on the agenda.

But why didn't he even try?

Dread filled my veins. *Maybe he needed me to save him.*

"And we're all animals needing substance," I finally said on my third piece of toast.

"Some," he said, "more than others."

The food was making me feel much stronger.

"Why am I here?" I demanded. "And where am I?"

"You're here to tether to someone. It's the equivalent of getting married in the living realm," he said, slowly. His cobalt-blue eyes were pensive and never left mine.

"Let me explain the deal because existence is just that—a series of deals," he said. "You will tether to someone who is a thinker and developer in these parts—me—but you won't be a slave. You'll be a wife, which is a much better thing. You will be expected to do the normal wife things like sex and support, but you won't have to dig in the mines or work in any fields. You'll have all the food you need. Shelter. Material goods. This home, which is a substantial one. Also, I have children who will need a mother. Their last one is gone."

"Gone?" I said.

He raised a hand, joined his fingers, and made a birdlike fluttering motion.

"Gone," he repeated.

"And this is happening because . . . ," I began. "You can't figure out another way to get a girl?"

"Good behavior will be rewarded. Quid pro quo. You stroke me; I stroke you."

"There is a shortage of suitable women, or women at all, for men of my stature in The Other," he said. "So, yes, you could say that I had my associate Pristine on the lookout for a suitable, beautiful, young female to claim as my own."

I sat up tall. "I don't tether. Plus, I'm already in a relationship. In fact, if my boyfriend knew what was going on here, he would kick your ass from one side of The Other to the other side."

"I look forward to it," he said.

He decided to explain things to me in the way that you might to a child. "In case you're not familiar, tethering is the action of linking or binding one thing to another. You tether farm animals with a rope and chain. You link people for eternity here with a short tethering ceremony. It's short and sweet. They only ask the man if he'd like to tether. Women have no rights here."

"How eighteen hundreds of you."

"If you try to leave this place," he said, standing from the straight-back chair. "I'll have you extinguished on the spot. If you prove too much trouble, I'll have you extinguished in your sleep."

He came close enough for me to breathe him in.

"You do know that demons come in many forms."

10.

I didn't see him again for days or maybe even a week, which put my captivity past one month. Over time I wasn't drugged anymore and slowly came back to my regular senses. Once I had my wits about me again, I was on one hundred percent escape mode, one hundred percent of the time.

It was nearly impossible. There were no sharp-edged tools to pry open a door and the windows only opened a bit, but did it matter? It was at least seven or eight stories up. I couldn't jump, but I would sit here thinking about doing it. If only I could only be absolutely sure the reset would kick in.

The thing was, I couldn't.

Be sure, that is.

Another issue is I didn't have my traveling clothes. Even if I made it outside, I wouldn't last long in a place where blizzards occurred daily and after the flakes fell, the air was below zero as the winds kicked the ground into the sky.

Each time the fog rolled in, I imagine Daniel walking out of it. I saw his tall frame and broad shoulders, mist-kissed. He would instinctively know which window was mine and put up his hand. As in, just a second.

Baby, I'm coming. I'm here. I will never leave you, Callaghan.

But he didn't arrive.

It was just fog.

11.

Wait for the ironic twist.

I was now in the company of my very own servant. Naturally this luxury was high on my teenage wish list—when I was alive and kicking—probably part of every adolescent's dream life.

Now, in captivity, I had one—and she was my only link to the outside world.

Three times a day—breakfast, lunch, and dinner—she would enter the room to take care of my needs, which were in no particular order: food, liquid, TP, and fresh towels.

She was one of "them." At first, I ignored her.

Which was hard.

For starters, my maid could carry a tune and she sang disco songs under her breath including "I Will Survive." She was also a song stylist who wrote her own material, hence the bathroom boogie: "I'm folding your towels. Yes, I am. Yes, I am," she crooned, dipping and dabbing as she went along. "Folding is molding and holding. Yes, it is! Yes, it is."

I sat in a chair. By the window. Glaring.

My inner Taylor Swift suppressed.

There was a joy about her, damn it all to hell. I had no room anymore for joy in this afterlife. There was only resentment during the day and longing at night. But, I could study this creature from a perfectly professional journalistic perspective.

She was maybe seventeen or eighteen with soft folds of skin on her neck like a neat stack of freshly folded towels. She was five foot eight. Or nine. And round. She always wore a long, white, flowing shirt over black tights.

"Commiserations to you," she said each visit as a greeting.

"Commiserations back," I tossed out one day just to make sure my voice was actually still working.

"Isn't it Walker—if I may be so bold to call you by that name," she said, lifting a silver covering to reveal two tuna fish sandwiches and a mountain of potato chips. I hated my stomach for rumbling. Her face looked so wide with warm brown eyes sparkling. She was so . . . hopeful.

She stopped dusting and a smile burst across her face like instant sunshine.

"I'm Bitty Gibbons—and you may actually be so bold to call me by my given name," she said. "He said not to talk to you, but I don't excel in obedience."

I burst into sobbing tears and Bitty Gibbons did the only thing she could think of under the circumstances. She went into the bathroom and brought out the huge bath towel.

Then she sat in the chair next to mine. For the next five minutes, we had a good body-shaking, mascara-running weep together.

Two teenage girls. One million tears.

12.

As for her first name, all evidence was to the contrary. Her spirit was large and she owned it from the red silk head wrap tied in a bow on the top of her head to the large framed glasses on her kind face. She was *extraordinarily* light on her feet and moved swiftly like she was made of part wind. She zoomed in sure, graceful steps—never breaking eye contact—like a dancer on speed.

I was the klutz who just walked quickly into the bed. The reset—AWOL. Wincing, I shook my head before checking my shin and spewing some choice words.

"Idiot," I said to myself. Under my breath.

"Bad self-esteem isn't going to get you out of here, although I used to be plagued by terrible self-esteem, too," she said as my head lifted. Maybe it was too much for a personal maid to divulge because her subject change was as fast as her moves.

I stared up at the camera overhead. "The house is full of cameras," she said. "They can only see; not hear. The kid they have in there spends half of his time playing Fortress. But he does look at the screens from time to time, so be careful."

We didn't discuss it, but I had escapee written all over my face.

She was back the next day. "I made you some iced tea and a corned beef sandwich. I'll leave it on the table. Fresh towels and lovely gardenia soap by the tub. Will you be needing anything else?"

"Yes, a key to the door, a weapon, and my pants," I said. Then I looked at my bare feet. "And my boots."

"Okay," she said. "I'll go look for them."

13.

One rainy afternoon, she had rolled up her sleeves so they didn't get into the cleaning fluids. It's why I noticed that she had about a million little dots on her lower arm like someone had put them there with a magic marker. They looked permanent like tats.

Shit. She saw me. Examining her.

"Will I help you escape? I can't because they will hurt me," she said. "Will I tell you about the dots? Please don't. I won't. Don't ever ask me about them."

My head swirled as Bitty went back to business.

"Do you want one sugar in your tea or two?" she demanded, lowering those glasses. "And they're not dots. They're . . . something else. It's not contagious, which is all you should care about. Okay?"

"So many," I said, pushing.

"So many more in the future," she replied. *Was someone hurting her? They couldn't . . . or could they be . . . wounds?*

I sat at the little table that served as my dining spot in captivity. It was round with a black onyx surface and flanked by two plush chairs with embroidered roses. With my hands, I split the lobster roll in two and put half on a napkin for myself. I had lost my appetite, but needed to eat to keep up my strength, but I didn't need to eat alone. I pushed the plate with the other half next to the empty chair and put out my hand.

"I can't eat this," she replied.

"Vegan?"

"No, I can't eat it unless you give me your pickle."

Wordlessly, and without taking my eyes from hers, I pushed it on her plate.

She sat with such speed that for a minute I thought something was wrong with my brain or my eyes. I took a big bite. She took a bigger one. The way this was going, we were going to need another sandwich.

"Why can't you find my original clothes and leave the door to my room unlocked?" I finally asked her.

She continued to chew.

"Xavier has your clothes and things in his bedroom now. I also clean his room," she replied. "He would notice if they were missing. He likes to . . . it's too gross."

"Tell me . . . please."

"Smell them," she replied. "And if I tried to take them, it wouldn't matter. There is an armed guard sitting in a chair outside your room. I'm even afraid of him," she said.

"Don't even try it, Walker," she begged.

It was time for a quick subject change.

"How did you—" I began.

"Originally die?" she said. "Are we sharing? Is sharing caring? Are we already at that point?"

"In the Midst, at the Academy, we're so used to talking about our life exit that it's like discussing what you had for breakfast," I said.

"They don't feed me breakfast here," she said, gobbling down her half of the chips. "Reducing a subject's fat layers leads to a purer draw."

I looked at her quizzically. "Draw?"

"We'll move on," Bitty said.

"My ascension plan was a car crash," I blurted, which caught her attention. "A deer. A car. A trucker. A snowy night. I went flying out a windshield into the great yonder. It's how I died. I guess it was big news the next day at my high school. They did the grand announcement. A few of the popular girls even said that they would reevaluate me. Boys I didn't even know said they dated me."

In journalism classes, I learned one thing: you give; you get.

Your turn, Bitty. Your turn.

"Gonna eat those cookies?" she said, staring across the room at a platter of fresh chocolate chip wonders she had placed on a small table by the window.

"I'll go get them," I said, standing.

She put up a finger.

"No," she said. "Let me."

"If you insist."

Bitty Gibbons moved like a rocket, thrusting across the carpet so quickly that her entire body blurred and dust stirred at her feet. Her return was even faster—and the proof was that the ponytail holder on my head snapped and my hair blew back as if I was in a Corvette convertible on the autobahn where cars went over a hundred miles an hour.

"You're not just a maid," I stammered.

"I'm not *just* an anything," she replied. "None of us are."

14.

Death Story: Bitty Gibbons
Age of Demise: 18

She was the kind of storyteller who jumped in . . . at the middle.

At first, it was my size. Five foot seven in the sixth grade. Then it was my weight. Too many LBS in a land of XXS. The bad self-esteem came from the fact that I was bullied in school because I looked so . . . creatively different.

My obvious mastery of the color wheel was another issue. I went to class with a bunch of neutrals when I was a bold blue eyeshadow with purple hair tips. Suffice it to say, I just didn't fit in.

I hated to interrupt her with the details, but I needed her "vitals."

"Where?"

I'm a Southie from Boston, MA. Land of dropping the final "r" to make "car" sound like "cah." Or to put it in a sentence, "I would pahk the cah in Hahvahd Yahd." I wanted to go there someday. To study physics. But, I digress . . .

It was your standard bullying menu. No one respected a walking art project—red lips, sixties beehive hair wrapped in a scarf and big glasses despite that my sight was 20-20. I loved to mask my face with the frames. They were like my mask. And I felt like a superhero.

Sixth grade. I was afraid. Seventh grade. Petrified. Same thing with grade number eight. Then one day, the summer before I entered high school, I just said, "Screw it. I knew all those years of feeling less than were just wasted moments. But I learned from it. I didn't stay in it.

When they would bully me, I'd simply say the word "override," first in my head and then out loud. I'd slash into those negative thoughts and find that kind of empowerment with just one word. Sometimes I would smile when they would taunt me because I had already put an "override" on it. Those bullies thought I was stark raving bonkers and became a little afraid of me.

If they only knew the real truth.

She didn't talk for a long time. And just as I thought she would never tell the rest of it, Bitty Gibbons put an override on her fears and let it rip.

I was born with astral projection, which is the ability to have an out-of-body experience and separate the astral body from the physical body at will. It means I can focus and travel—body, mind, and soul—to another location.

I looked at her in awe.

I was able to do it a few times as a kid, although many times it happened in dreams. I'd go to sleep, dream of a new place, and wake up there. When I'd close my eyes, and think of home again, I'd be back in my bed—under my covers and generally shaking with a mean need to pee because the whole thing was just so weird. I decided that I would grow out of this oddness, but no go.

High school was so emotionally exhausting, between the teachers who looked at me oddly and those bullies, that my yen to travel became even stronger. Over time, I tried to project during the waking hours and staged little experiments. Such as, I'd project myself out of school to places like the woods or a local pub for a "tawnic"—or as you would say, tonic—or soder—soda. Or, I'd project into a big open field to stare up at the stahs.

Once, when Mom grounded me for not doing my chores, I projected myself all the way to California and went to the beach for the day. I was back in Boston for that chowda by dark with my hard-to-explain tan in the middle of January. In history class, we talked and talked about the beauty of Paris, so I snuck into one of the stalls in the girl's bathroom and projected there for the rest of the day. While my classmates at John F. Kennedy High ate slop for lunch, I was strolling the Champs-Élysées with a chocolate croissant in one hand and the world in the other.

As my powers expanded, I felt empowered in a way no one could touch.

My trips became daily ones. I was in Machu Picchu one day; the Great Barrier Reef the next. I walked the Great Wall of China while telling my parents I was on a week-long school field trip; Stonehenge was during spring break. Man, they have the best hot chocolate there.

One day, I sat in my bedroom and then projected myself to Maui where I hiked the Haleakala volcano and drank out of a fresh pineapple. The pearl earrings dangling from my ears now are from another trip to Grace Bay in Turks and Caicos. It was there, standing on pristine white sand, that I banished the fact that my locker had been destroyed by some of the mean girls who painted Bitch inside of it.

I looked up at the purple sunset, which took my breath, and said, "Now, I live for me. I'm imperfect, which is perfect. I'm atypical, which is typical. I own it, meaning I own me. I own MYSELF."

What I didn't know at the time is that I'd only have one more day to be me in the living realm.

It was our annual school field trip to one of the tallest office buildings in Boston at One America Tower. The top floor is all windows, so you can see the whole city. In groups of ten, my AP history class rode up an elevator that went so high and so fast that your ears popped and popped. I stood by myself while I heard some of the guys on the football team—Jimmy Jackson and Ryder Holland—laughing and crunching something up. They kept staring back at me for some reason and I didn't want to think the worst. I would override any negativity and remember, "I own myself." I approached them and Jimmy smiled.

"Hey, Bits," he said. "Press your face to the glass. It's a trip, man. It feels like you're flying."

I shook my head. I already knew what it was like to fly from one spot to the next in a matter of nanoseconds.

"What are you," Ryder taunted, "chicken shit?"

I was never much one for dares, but soon a small group gathered and one of the girls, faux friendly Megan McCallister, said, "Bitsy, you go first and then I want to do it."

So, I did it.

I went up to the glass and leaned against it. It didn't break, but there was this sound.

Of something unsealing.

Pop! Whoosh! The entire panel burst out of its frame and I plunged to my death . . . thirty floors to street level, face first.

I guess natural weathering made the window frame unstable and it had been reinforced earlier that day. The guard supposed to be watching the spot was on a smoke break.

That unbreakable window fell with me, landing on my face, as if I was just a photo now.

A still life.

In just a few seconds, I arrived in the Midst. Some beautiful old lady named Miss Travis had my papers waiting. She was lovely, but my first night in the dorm, someone came to collect me. He said I was graduating. I said, "Hey, bub, how can I graduate when I haven't even been to school?"

I guess no one cared what I thought about it. I was fitted for a gown and went to my graduation ceremony the next day. I ended up here. Wandered the deep woods when some guys came and asked my name. It was like they already knew me. They knocked me out and brought me to this house of horrors.

"I know what you're thinking," Bitty said. "Why not just escape? I did two or three times when I first got here—and this was before they did . . . what they did to me. I projected myself back into the woods, but they hunted me and found me. My powers don't work the same here because I don't know the landscape and it seems there is nowhere to go. And then they started to work on me."

"Work on you?"

"They drain me daily before bedtime. There's a laboratory inside the house where they draw countless vials of my blood, which leaves me weak. They work me all day and night as a maid, which makes me tired. But he believes in hard work. Then at night, the real work begins. They withdraw bone marrow and inject it into their test subjects to see if our powers can be transferred. That hurts like a bitch for both parties, by the way," Bitty said.

I wasn't sure what to say.

"I wondered when you came here if you had extras," Bitty said. "But when they never dragged you to the hospital, I knew it was something else. Maybe something worse."

I glanced at her, horrified. *What could be worse than having your insides drained?*

"Good-bye, Walker," she rushed. "I know I've said too much. And you know what happens to most science experiments when they're no longer needed."

The frogs we dissected. The baby pigs we examined. When it was over, we kept the knowledge and discarded the carcass.

15.

In the darkness, I made my future plans. I didn't have clothes or weapons, but I had just one tool in the form of a little plastic knife that Bitty forgot. Well, she didn't really miss it when she left. I slid it down my shirt when she wasn't looking.

I used it to try to unseal one of the windows.

I worked overtime on Shawshanking it, but I remained outraged and caged.

At precisely 6:00 a.m. when the sun rose and the window was as cemented as ever, I heard noises from downstairs and then a small rumble in the hallway. *Click!* My eggs arrived perfectly runny with three gorgeously toasted golden bagels, cream cheese, and homemade jam. I wondered if Gordon Ramsay had kicked the bucket and ended up in the kitchen here.

This time, I watched Bitty in fascination. It wasn't her outfit of a big purple shirt with black dots and leggings. It was her actions. She was standing next to the bed and a blink later, she was by the bathroom door. Fast didn't describe the way she moved; she was supersonic.

She smiled.

"Despite all of it . . . I still got it," she said.

I reached out to touch her arm, but she pulled away with a ragged gasp.

"It was a rough night," she said. She winced when I touched the arm this time and since it felt hot, I gently rolled up the sleeves.

The dots were higher now. They passed the crease of her elbow and were moving well up to her shoulder. This close, I could examine her and these weren't ink dots.

They were fresh bruises.

"Oh, Bitty," I began.

"Walker," she interrupted me. "I own it. Remember."

"But, you can always share it," I said in a soft voice.

TEN

1.

She shared a lot of other things over the next few weeks including her love for music, dogs, and art. She was going to be a singer or music teacher and that she wanted to somehow communicate with her mother just one more time. We certainly had that in common. I told probably too much about Daniel.

"And he's *your* boyfriend?" she said. The shock in her voice made me laugh.

"Ouch," I said, pretending to be wounded.

"No, sorry. Me and my big mouth. I didn't mean it that way," she said, laughing.

One day, she came limping in with a big white bandage attached to her right hip. I could see it through her leggings.

"Bitty," I gasped. "What the hell?"

"I fell down the stairs," she lied, her eyes the widest. Then, she fled. When she entered the room later with steak and potatoes, a fresh green salad, and lemon pie, I motioned for her to sit for a minute.

That's when I noticed that she was pale and her hand was bandaged. Obviously, she had been on an IV between breakfast and dinner.

"A lot of draining last night and a surprise session this afternoon. More tonight," she said. "We started after lunch and . . . well, I might need the day off tomorrow."

"Bitty, what are they doing to you here?" I demanded. "Are they mining people?"

"They're making me normal—at least that's what they tell us," she said. "My worst fear."

"How many others?" I asked.

No answer.

I didn't see her for the rest of the day.

2.

Late at night in the silence of the room with escape an impossibility, I found my exit through my dreams.

From a time beyond memory, I see him. I can feel him strong and sure. I can smell him . . . sweaty tee mixed with a maple and pine smoldering fire pit stirred with worn leather and a liberal dose of sexy musk. He always said I smelled like vanilla-laced jasmine.

He lights a candle and shows me a way. He is a good man. There is no bullshit. "Baby, we're stuck somewhere between nothing and what if," he says. "I prefer what if. Are you with me?"

Where else would I be?

We stand on my window ledge in this prison room and prepare to jump. Can we count on the reset? We won't know until we know. Our odds are literally fifty-fifty, which makes me sad for some reason. *What if . . . No, f— it.*

"Baby, level up," he says as the faint light of morning rises to meet us. I loved the early morning because it was the most honest part of the day. He stares into the light of chance and then brings that spark in his eyes to ignite mine.

Hard love. Was there any other kind?

Big chances. Was there any other way?

"Callaghan," he shouts into the world. "The sunrise has never failed us yet."

A hard yank. We are falling several stories to earth. I hold his hand in a true death grip and think, *Daniel Reid. You are so loved.* We are falling and he must have read my mind. I watch his eyes crinkle at the corner as he entire being dissipates into the ground.

3.

I wake up screaming and sweating, but she is there with a cold towel.

"You have to pull yourself together," Bitty says. "He's back."

After a brief hiatus to conduct business, the Big Man was back in the manse.

"A dinner date," I said, my jaw on the ground. "I'm not going on anything vaguely resembling a . . ." She wouldn't let me finish, but she couldn't know the particulars. This date was just one big step closer to becoming his wife.

"You're going. And you're going fancy. Those are my orders. And you're going to scope out the house for the future, for your escape. That is my dream, so get out of this bed," Bitty said, motioning me to follow her to the armoire. Inside of it was some strappy, low-backed navy dress that would provide too much skin for his wandering hands.

If he touched me and I could get my hands on a butter knife, I would gut him.

Just what every man dreams of as his dinner date—a woman who knows how to slice and dice.

I sank into one of the chairs, head in my hands. Bitty pulled open the nightstand drawer to reveal three big Hershey bars.

"You have eight hours to get dressed and get high on this chocolate. You're welcome. By the way, I put a bag of makeup in the bathroom. With some extras."I repeat," Bitty said. "You can thank me later. You need to get out of this room or your brain will turn to mush." She looked at me hard. "Look at everything in the bag. Merry Christmas."

"But it's not Christm . . ." She was already gone.

Turns out, nothing went with a simple evening frock like a key out of your cage and a small, jagged knife hidden in the lining of a small silk purse.

4.

In the confines of my bathroom, I tucked the key deeply into the silk dress pocket. The knife rested in the other just in case my dinner date had any crazy ideas about what followed dessert.

I dressed with newfound hope. Maybe I wouldn't be able to leave tonight, but a fresh breeze of freedom was making me feel giddy and antsy at the same exact time.

I would listen to his stories, feed his ego, and then insist that I wasn't feeling well. I'd go to bed early and sneak out later. It would be an early evening, I vowed, as I stared into the mirror to complete the womanly art of getting ready to be a display object. A thing.

I wasn't good at this stuff. I never went to prom and my mom couldn't afford much makeup. If I put a little mascara on before high school in the living realm, it was a big day. The few times that I amped it up for Daniel created no bigger effect than me barefaced at the end of the day or at first morning's light.

The navy dress fit perfectly, as if it was custom made, which it probably was given that he had my other clothing and knew my sizes.

Of course, it had those thin spaghetti straps that easily slipped down. I stared into the mirror and pictured him. A finger would linger on a strap that wouldn't hold. Even in such bleak times, those strong arms would wrap around my waist as he moved closer.

Daniel, I will move the molecules. In every bad situation that's what you had to do. Move the molecules.

A smear of lipstick. Another coating of mascara. I put my hair up in a high bun.

Another glance in the mirror and I saw myself frowning, which just would not do.

Play the game, Walker. Make him think you're grateful for his thrilling conversation, roast beast, and soggy veggies. Act defiant because that will seem normal. Throw a few snide comments in there. He won't believe you if you're too nice. Maybe a dinner roll with real butter will be involved. I would laugh at his jokes. If I could without vomiting. I would look for windows with shoddy locks and doors that were not manned by goons with guns.

I wrote all of my fears concerning this night into the palm of my hand with the black pen Bitty left in my nightstand because I had asked her for paper and writing utensils:

I wrote: captivity, imprisonment, confinement, incarceration, detention, physical pain, mental torture, loss of loved ones. The last was the worst. Then, as my mother taught me to do when we did this together because it was free and it worked, I crossed them off one by one, deciding not to allow them to have any power over me anymore.

Each *X* felt like I was in control now and not the enslavement swirling around me.

Was this crazy? Yes.

I wouldn't wash that hand.

I would wear my crazy.

Proudly.

5.

I heard the door unlock from the outside, but no one stepped inside. Instead, there was a shaft of light because for once the slab of thick wood was actually open.

For a split second, I thought about wildly running. Out of there. Into the yonder. A small voice inside screamed: *That's what they were expecting.*

This was obviously a test. If I passed, I might be granted additional freedoms like a walk in the yard or some time downstairs, which I could bank for the real escape. It was crucial that I played by their rules, which is why I casually and slowly walked down the winding wooden staircase, praying I wouldn't trip in those, sorry to say it, hateful Sarah Jessica Parker Manolo whatever stilettos. It was a wonder that I didn't klutz it up and tumble down what were actually five flights of carpeted stairs. Carpeted stairs were silent stairs. Score one for the prisoner.

I was in the front foyer now. Ten steps to the front door.

Just maybe . . .

A few hard leaps . . . and then I would run.

I took a hard step toward my release and then I saw them through the front window.

The guards were outside standing by what looked like a school bus. Odd. But they were right there making escape futile.

I turned the opposite way remembering the words of my trainer, Bruce.

I am free, I told myself. *As you think it, so you shall become.*

There were several opulent rooms, including a lavish living room to the left and I purposely made a wrong turn into it. It would do me well to admire what he had put there to admire: a deep-blue velvet couch, hand-carved wooden tables, and an elaborate shelving unit filled with priceless glass and porcelain antiques.

If one of the guards stopped me, I was just a girl without a map.

There were two oversized French doors that ran the back of the couch. *Were they locked? Was there a yard before wilderness? Was it fenced?*

I took a wobbling step toward the doors. *Walker, no. He wants to see if you will check the exits. Do not take the first offer because there is no out tonight. It's just biding your time.*

Casually, like any other girl on a dinner date at a mansion in the wild, I wandered out of the living room and into a kitchen where three young male cooks—Bitty called them the Confident Morons because they were about sixteen and told really stupid jokes. It was actually more than jokes. Bitty said that the Confident Morons said things that were wildly incorrect, but with enough confidence that they wanted you to believe they were speaking the truth.

At the moment, they were actually making something that made my mouth water. "You're a vegan, right? We made you steak," said the tallest one who wore a Kiss the Cook apron over white pants and a white shirt. He blew me a kiss.

"Your salad is burning," I retorted and he laughed. *They would be easy to corrupt. Perhaps, they were my way out.*

It was an executive kitchen with the professional stove, red knobs and all—and a stainless-steel sub-zero fridge that looked like you could move into it like a small, albeit always cold, apartment. There was a large patio door in the kitchen that wasn't covered by blinds or curtains. It led to a patio where one of the Confident Morons was actually grilling the steaks on an outdoor barbecue grill. Willing my feet to stay in place, I looked out there, thrilled by the first fresh natural breeze I had felt in a long time.

I memorized it. *Patio. Grill. Grass.* Not much of it, maybe half an acre, and then the side of a mountain. How freaking rustic. I heard some kind of creature howl in the distance. Two words came to mind: mountain and lion.

There was deep snow next to the rock wall. Green grass in the yard covered by a thin coat of ice. I smelled fresh roses blooming.

"What month is it?" I asked one of the Morons. It was just small talk. *Blah. Blah.*

"September," he said. If that was true, I had been incarcerated . . . no, it couldn't be true because the others would have saved me by now. But it was true. There was a date on the fridge in greenish digital lights. It was September 25, year unknown.

I had been here over three months. Ninety days. Twelve weeks. I had to force myself to remember that the months went backward here. Dr. King said that was a fact.

I wandered out quietly, casually admiring the garish wallpaper of birds and trees and then looking up purposely to memorize where the cameras were located. They were in the north and west corner of every room. I would have to evade them one day . . . make that soon.

Along the way, I spotted a lavish office with a dim light still on from a computer sitting on a glossy mahogany desk. A few steps later, there was another room where a man usually sat in front of about thirty computer screens. This was the tech center or the heart of the house, so anyone coming or going would be filmed and thus there would be no surprises. I noted a large steel water bottle on a side table. Maybe soon that computer system would be getting its first "bath" when water was spilled all over it.

I slept on the fifth floor. Xavier's master bedroom was on the sixth. Oddly enough, there was something under the kitchen/living room level. A basement? That screen was filled with little white dots like it was currently blurred out.

The bottom left monitor was of my empty bedroom. I wasn't a techie, but it was easily marked, plus I left a towel hanging off the side of the desk chair. There it was.

There was a button under my room monitor. Three choices.

I hit the pause button. All one could see now was that chair and the towel.

Hopefully, no one would notice.

Deed done, I wandered back to the front of the house.

There was a double front door with an armed security guard in a black suit sitting in front of it on a folding chair.

He didn't say a word, but his message was clear. I wasn't walking out the front door.

Not tonight.

He tilted his head to the left. I nodded.

I stepped over an invisible threshold and entered the dining room.

6.

The thick maple table could have easily sat twenty heads of state, plus a stray queen. The entire room gleamed in the low light of a crystal chandelier that threw golden prisms of light into the shadows. Each dark wooden chair offered snowy white cushion with bold maroon stripes running up and down the most expensive of silk fabric.

A large matching wooden hutch was filled with glistening china and sparkling crystal. Perhaps someone had borrowed the large diamond-cut cobalt-blue Baccarat vase from there, the one that was now on the main table and filled with at least thirty long-stemmed red roses.

A waiter type who was maybe eighteen in a black suit with an earpiece in his left ear handed me a champagne flute. My calloused and scarred hands almost bobbled the delicate glass. *Was I supposed to sip? Or wait? Could I sit? Or should I stand? Was the liquid drugged?* The fanciest restaurant I had ever visited was an all-you-can-eat Italian place in Chicago where splurging on diet soda was encouraged while ordering cheesy garlic bread.

His voice distracted me from such a pleasant memory.

"I expect you to be on time to these dinners. You're six minutes late. Being late insults your dinner companion, a fact that your mother should have taught you as a child unless you grew up in a barn. It also angers the other person who is waiting," he lectured.

"Nice to see you, too, Xavier," I said, blandly.

He was in his dress propers: a perfectly tailored black suit, crispy white shirt, no tie . . . and shirt unbuttoned by two to reveal skin. The black hair was cut shorter and now barely graced the top and sides of his head making him look like some kind of action movie star. He had a little stubble along his jawline and upper and around his lower lips that made him look dangerous. Many women would dare say sexy.

We were about the same height, but he still felt taller as he approached. I noticed that he was wearing black gloves on both hands. A glint caught my eye. He was wearing gold cufflinks to close the sleeves of that fancy dress shirt. How old-fashioned of him. *What was next? A ride in his horse-drawn carriage?*

"Do you want to explain to me why you were tardy?" he said.

Dude, get over it. I was scoping out the house.

"I'm sorry. Next time I'm kidnapped, I'll try not to underestimate the time it takes to travel from one room to the next."

I took a step closer to him. I would not shrink.

All things considered, this was not a good idea.

I shuddered when he tried to kiss me on my right cheek and then my left. My deep lean backward almost threw me off those big-girl shoes. An impending collapse was checked when he put an arm around my back and then shockingly landed a sneak-attack third kiss. Somehow, he missed my lips and landed on my neck, which made me shudder from revulsion.

"All in good time," he said, harshly pushing me upright.

I took a sip of my drink. This is why I needed the drink for after all. So I didn't upchuck my internal organs.

Xavier laughed.

He seemed to find me . . . amusing.

"Walker, let's just . . . start over. Have a nice dinner. Talk," Xavier offered. "I'm not the big, bad wolf that you seem to think I am. I am a reasonable man. Single. In the company of a beautiful woman for dinner, which isn't my usual lot in these parts. Let's just resolve to be friendly. It will be easier on both of us to tether if we can get along in all ways."

"I'm in a relationship," I stammered.

He lifted his glass.

"Cheers then to the people who loved us, the losers who lost us, and the lucky bastards who are with us now," he said with a top spin to his words.

"Why me?" I asked, calmly. I really did need to know.

"You're quite intelligent. I've seen your permanent record. That's why I had Pristine bring you to me, among other things." His voice softened. "You will see that it was best. You will find some peace. It's not wise to be unwavering in your heart. Things change. People come. And go. New people arrive. Be resolute in adapting to change. At least, think about it."

There was no time to reply.

"The first of seven courses—the aperitifs," said a servant, "have been served."

There was nothing else to do but sit down next to him at that enormous table. It was far enough away for him to end an awkward silence that had set in by him lobbing a hard dinner roll at my head. I almost ducked as it grazed the side of my face. I tossed my roll right back at him and it landed on his nose. This seemed to delight him.

"See, Callaghan, it's not so bad," he said with a smile.

It was like being shot again.

"Don't you dare," I bit out, "ever call me that again."

He looked at me oddly. "Lighten up," he advised, "and try the shrimp. It's quite delicious tonight."

7.

He set the "date" back on track.

"I thought we'd enjoy an authentic seven course dinner tonight. Have you ever been to Paris, Walker?" he asked. *I had never been to Milwaukee or Sheboygan, let alone Paris.*

"I know it sounds fancy, but the aperitif course is really just crackers and nuts with a sweet, fruity drink and a few olives," he chuckled, popping a bottle of champagne that was waiting in a silver ice bucket encrusted in what I assumed were real rubies.

He caught me staring at them. "If you like jewels, I can get you quite a few," he offered. "They would look beautiful with your red hair."

"That's . . . okay. But thank you. It's lovely," I said. It didn't serve me well to spar with him constantly. I needed to ask him questions, get the lay of the land, and reinforce my body by eating his food.

He stared at me.

"Lovely," he repeated, locking eyes. "In this context, yes, it is."

It was a fairly tasty culinary journey from someone who had decided to "pull out all the stops." Olives and crackers were just the start of what was a virtual food marathon. That course was followed by one of the Confident Morons bringing in the appetizer course, which was a tray of fruits and vegetables along with smoked meats, followed by cantaloupe slices "to cleanse the palate for the next course."

One of the Morons tried to serve dessert next, but a frown from Xavier had him scurrying back into the kitchen only to emerge with a lush raw-vegetable salad of greens, beets, tomatoes, and mozzarella chunks. I was already stuffed, but my host only shook his head.

"We haven't even touched the main course," he laughed, just as long pieces of freshly baked baguettes were placed on the table next to exotic oils and vinegars. It was to sop up all the fresh juices from the perfectly grilled chicken breasts covered in herbs de Provence.

It was during this course that I learned that Xavier considered himself a man of business focusing on the science of new inventions, although he also dabbled in other things such as hunting, fishing, and his true passion, aviation.

Once the entrée plates were cleared, the cheese portion of our meal arrived, since the French often bridge the meal and dessert with flavorful French cheeses such as Gruyère or goat milk's cheese or a strong blue cheese made with sheep's milk.

"You have sheep on this property?" I queried.

"We have several breeds of wild animals here from the sheep to cougars to mountain lions. I wouldn't advise even trying to take a walk in the woods alone," he said. "Wouldn't want to run into a mama grizzly who hadn't had her lunch. I'd rather hunt that mama and make her my lunch."

I wanted to recoil because violence against animals was so vile. But I smiled.

"Did your father hunt?"

"For bargains at Target," I replied and he laughed.

"I'm sorry about his untimely demise," he said.

"I don't go there," I replied. "Too painful. And, in case you're wondering, I don't have Daddy issues."

He changed the subject. And I went through all the motions of listening to him while seldom speaking, which was fine because he was a man of many words, theories, and life lessons. He stopped every now and then to ask me a question, and I was quick on the draw. I would babble on about a subject while he feigned interest.

He was the kind of man who didn't really listen to you, but waited politely until he could speak again. There was a remoteness in the way he nodded, like he was mostly checked out. Women in his life probably served two or three purposes. Conversing wasn't one of them.

He caught me staring at his hands while he talked and he let them drop to his side.

"Why the gloves?" I asked as dessert arrived. It was a dense chocolate cake with sprigs of lavender baked in, along with steaming coffee with pieces of melted chocolate stirred inside. I had to force myself to take a bite because I was that full.

"I had a condition in life called Raynaud's disease. Gloves were needed to keep my blood vessels under control. Otherwise, my hands would render themselves so cold that they were inoperative," he said. "The gloves keep my hands a reasonable temperature and prevent tissue damage."

"I'm so sorry," I said. "But aren't all medical things corrected in the afterlife?"

"I'd prefer not to talk about it," he said. "And you should realize that when one is sent to The Other, the rules are different. Physical ailments in life are not necessarily corrected."

There was an awkward pause.

"But, why focus on one's shortcomings on such a beautiful evening," Xavier said.

I was checked out, mindlessly nodding, when he finally caught my attention.

"Would you like to take a walk outdoors?" he posed. "I'll protect you from those grizzlies."

I stood.

8.

The idea of fresh air was so tempting that I wanted to run out of there and do a freedom dance. Instead, I wobbled on the shoes, walking slowly out of the dining room and through the kitchen to those French double doors. He punched a code into the side of one of them and both sprang open. I tried to memorize it: 7, 19, 8 . . . damn it, or was it 18, 7?

"It's freezing outside. I do have winter coats in varying sizes," he informed me. "But, perhaps your reset has kicked in and then we can avoid a jacket. I'd hate to cover that beautiful dress. It was on the cover of *Vogue* two years ago. In the living realm. We get the second runs here, apparently."

A Callaghan wearing a dress from *Vogue* from a designer named Givenchy. My mother would have fainted since our usual dressmaker was known internationally as Salvation Army.

I shook my head when it came to the coat offer. I wanted to feel.

As the first icy breath of space and freedom washed over my being, I took the deepest breath known to human lungs. The fresh air was intoxicating and I wanted to dance in it or run wild on a wind current. Kicking off my shoes, I left them on the patio and raced ahead to try my naked toes out on the frosted lawn.

The moon was sitting low in that winter sky, but bright like a shiny pearl gleaming in the distance.

He put a hand up to stop two security guards who were lurking. They followed us outside, but waited for his command, standing like tin soldiers until he made his wishes known. One was directly ahead of me across the lawn. There was little chance I would make a break for the mountains in a backless cocktail dress with naked feet.

"My wife used to dance in the grass," he said with a smile.

His words brought me all the way back.

"Is she in a different realm? Is she . . . ," I asked, trying to politely inquire if she was still alive.

"Something like that and no. I was the last surviving member of my family," he said as he slowly made his way out onto the lawn.

He put out a hand and I took it, allowing him to twirl me in a slow circle.

It was only right for me to pull away, but I'd give him just a tiny taste as a way to barter for any freedoms before my escape.

Speaking of which, I saw the helicopter that brought me here parked on the far edges of the property. He traced my gaze and tossed me the keys from his pocket.

"I don't fly," I said, sadly.

"I'll teach you," he promised. "I can teach you wonderous things, Walker."

A beat passed. Then two. Then five. He hadn't asked for the key back yet, but a razor-sharp man like Xavier would never let me keep it. Sweetly, my stomach churning, I handed it back, which pleased him.

"Why did you want to become a reporter for the *New York Times*?" he asked.

Mindlessly, I talked about my love of journalism, freedom, and the truth. "But in my current situation, I will never become a reporter," I said with a shrug.

"It's never too late to be what you might have been," he said.

I bit my lip.

"What if I started a newspaper for you," he said. "Your own."

Bribery?

"I do believe in the attainment of our wildest dreams," he said. "Usually, you find that next big thing when you feel as if all hope is lost. Like you do now. For instance, I wasn't always this wealthy. I know about a hungry stomach and an empty wallet. Life's greatest lessons come from moments that are the bleakest."

So, kidnapping was a "teachable" moment. Not exactly Oprah-approved.

He took my hand. I took note of the periphery of the property.

He smiled at me. I smiled back, looking just slightly over his head to estimate how tall the mountains in the distance were and how high in case I had to hide out in them.

"We should go in. You're getting cold," he murmured.

"Thank you for a lovely evening," I said, wondering if this was how Meryl Streep did it.

9.

When I went back to my room, I knew that tonight wasn't the night to go rogue.

Xavier certainly had the guards on high alert. He knew that a young woman who had tasted freedom would want a larger bite. I wanted the whole pie.

No, tonight was for contemplating.

Preparing.

I heard the words of our trainer Liam from the IRA: "Do not assume you will be rescued. Always keep your mind on the other option . . . escape, but only at the right time. Complacency is to be expected, which gives the captive the leg up on their captors. As time passed, you become part of the routine. The eyeballs on you wander. That's when you escape."

I fell to my knees and pulled out nails from the furniture with a small cuticle knife in my bathroom that Bitty had given me. Then I worked on yanking stray paint chips off the wall. The house was old. The metal from the air vent wasn't easily pulled off, but I would work on it.

It was time to put my plan on paper. I had asked for paper and a pencil, but wrote in my own code, keeping careful notice of when the guard shifted his metal chair on the hardwood of the hallway. It made a high-pitched squeaking sound. These men ate three times a day, leaving the chair empty for at least the ten minutes it took to wander to the kitchen for some grub, followed by a slow pee.

The times matched up: 7:20 a.m., noon while Bitty was in here, 9:53 p.m., precisely.

In the darkness of my bedroom cell, I worked out by doing sit-ups under the bed. I pumped weights holding onto the steel lamp from the desk. And then I did an hour of sprints in the bathroom by running in place.

The world is your gym.

10.

The next day: same hell, different devils. Bitty was in and out with the breakfast and lunch, looking more battered and bruised than a car crash victim. When I went to touch her arm, she cried out and then patted my hand. "Last night was a rough one, but I remember what my mama used to say," Bitty said in a strangely distant voice. It was as if she was half here, half gone.

"What was that?" I asked her. When she didn't immediately answer, I quietly said, "What did your mama say?"

"Look for the best in people, but expect the worst . . . and don't be surprised by either," she muttered.

I sat in that room all day wondering when I would start looking outside of these walls. For surprises.

Xavier played right into my hands. Around 5:00 p.m., I noticed that a black Cadillac suddenly sat idling on the long driveway, clearly visible from my window. I watched as a driver in a black suit climbed out of the front seat, went outside, lit a cigarette and perfected the art of the lean against the vehicle.

Tilting his body back against the fancy paint, he took a long drag and waited. It wasn't long before the great man himself, Xavier, trekked outside hauling his own small overnight suitcase. *What's in there? Plutonium?* Obviously, he had plans outside the compound. Maybe some fancy dinner or meeting. He walked at a fast clip, barking into a cell phone as he dumped the bag at the driver's feet. I wished that my window would open so I could overhear him, but that wasn't on the menu.

A maid who wasn't Bitty, but a young girl named Sonja, brought my food the entire next day. Boring oatmeal, a tuna sandwich, and then . . . pay dirt. I wasn't so excited about the steak and baked potato or the fine china plate, but what was covering it. It was one of those silver, domed food covers you might find in fancy restaurants put on top of plates to keep the food warm.

After she left, I shoved down the food for strength and then shut out all the lights. Darkness was my best bet and I put that food dome in my bed and placed the covers over it. With any luck, the guards watching my room on their TV screens would get bored watching a dark room. If I really spun the wheel of good fortune, they would believe that it was my big melon head, the silver thing, which I covered with a towel. I placed it in the exact position in the bed to show a young woman who was sleeping away her depression from being here.

It was my insurance policy. I couldn't be sure if the screen to my room was still on pause.

Next, I went into the bathroom where I quietly dressed in the clothes Bitty hid in my fresh sheets. She knew that I would be going soon. To that end, she tried to be helpful, but first asked for a favor.

"I put an envelope in the back pocket of the jeans. I want you to keep it under your nightstand. I'll check it from time to time. Do not open it until you're far from here," she instructed.

"Bitty, just tell me," I begged her.

"If you want me to help you . . . promise me," she said.

I nodded, which was why there was a pair of jeans that might fit and a warm XL black sweater, and even an old pair of Nikes that she found somewhere. The key to the room that Bitty left me days ago was still here. I had hidden it the night after the big date by carefully removing and then fixing a bathroom tile. Grabbing it now, I made my way to my bedroom door, crawling low in the black recesses.

The door didn't meet the floor and in that gap, I could see the legs of the guard outside my room. I had to wait about ninety minutes until his bladder or hunger pains gave way. Eventually, the legs stood and moved in the general direction of a bathroom down the hall.

My hand rose slowly as I prayed hard that this key actually worked. It didn't.

Again. I jiggled it hard.

It didn't fit.

The third time, when my hand stopped shaking, the universe cooperated.

Click-click-click . . . and out.

Freedom. I closed my eyes tightly.

It smelled good.

I took a deep breath. It tasted even better.

11.

Silently and slowly, I crept down the stairs.

I bit my tongue from screaming when I saw two armed guards stationed at the front door. I snuck a quick left and retreated to the back of the house. The shadow of an even larger watchman paced in front of the patio door. If there was a side exit or another way out, I didn't know it.

Regroup, my mind shouted.

There was one obvious place to do so: The king's liar.

12.

Xavier's downstairs office was marked by the mingling smells of old cigarettes and strong, male cologne. Slowly, I shut the big wooden door, which left me in a dark room except for the stray strands of moonlight filtering in the ornate windows. It was locked from the inside. Damn. I tried it seven times. Just to be sure. And then I muttered every swear word known to almost silently voice my displeasure. As a native Chicagoan, I possessed a large swear vocab.

The good news: the guards and household staff probably made few visits in here unless they wanted to be part of a place where Paco Rabanne came to die. That is a gross guy's scent. I reassured myself of this assumption, knowing that with his controlling nature, most likely there was an invisible warning to stay the hell out of his office.

My feet walked across the thickest beige carpeting past tall bookcases made of dark mahogany. I ran a finger along the side of a massive desk. There it was. Plain as day. His daily schedule for today/tonight. In the dim computer light, I saw he was in phone meetings most of the day followed by a dinner tonight at a place called LB267. I half hoped it was on Pluto.

Someone had used a yellow highlighter to emphasize that he wouldn't be home tonight for "The Draining." The box next to the ten o'clock hour was marked: Delivery. Five Specimens.

The smart thing to do was hide under the desk until the house went to sleep and I could slip out.

Turns out I wouldn't have to kiss the floor. His desk chair was one of those big leather types with a large back that hid my entire body when I turned the tallest part of it to the door.

If I didn't move, I could sit here, maybe all night.

13.

He had one of those top-of-the-line Apple desktop models with the XXL screen, the best that money in life could buy. In the afterlife, they just gave you these things, if you asked nicely.

My fingers didn't hesitate to linger on the smooth hardness of those beautiful white keys. To a writer like myself, it felt like a drug when I ran my fingers lightly over them.

That blank Google line glared back at me.

Really? We had that here, too? Then again, it didn't really say Google.

It didn't say anything at all. There was just that box to type in your key words. When I typed the words DANIEL REID, the machine whirled for a moment and then actual words appeared. *Please, please,* I thought, but it wasn't what I wanted.

It was clear: Access Denied.

I looked up Madeleine Walker and the computer went to work. I closed my eyes, knowing that my access to anything was probably a moot point. But, it wasn't. *Oh, dear God, would this serve as an update?* A story popped up in the *Daily Herald* newspaper, the official source of knowing in Wheeling, Illinois. The date was a year after my death.

My heart raced when I read the headline: Oh, Baby! Local Woman Adopts Quadruplets.

My eyes scanned the first paragraph. It was obvious that the writer, someone named Sydney Pearlman, took great care with the intro paragraph.

It read: "Madeleine Walker thought she would never love again. She lost her precious daughter, Walker, seventeen, in a horrific car accident not so long ago. The pain never leaves, but on days like today, it is tempered by a new daughter she refers to by only an initial: V. 'Ouch, honey, that hurts,' Madeline says with a little laugh as the bald baby with big curious eyes sinks her nails into her new mother's upper chest."

Did that "thing" draw . . . blood? Murderous rage raced through my veins.

I didn't want to read another word, but I couldn't stop.

"'My new daughter has a strong will,' said the former teacher who was working at the local orphanage when she fell in love with motherless quadruplets. V just gurgles and throws her tiny fist up, hitting her mother squarely in the eye. 'Honey,' the new mother hushes the child, 'you're killing Mommy.' The other three babies in a nearby playpen somehow stood and clapped at those words, proving they, have advanced senses of humor at six months. Their cackle pleases all but the family cat, who strangely hisses, teeth dripping, claws at the ready. 'Walter the cat is jealous,'" said my mother.

Walter is a genius. That cat has a backbone like a ramrod.

Last paragraph: "Mrs. Callaghan lives in Wheeling, Illinois, where she is raising her new brood including daughters C, S, and A. The mother of four realizes one of her wishes for her new babies will never come true. 'I only wish they could have met my first child, Walker,' she said.

Oh, Mom.

I had sixteen years to save her. The Claires always died at age seventeen. But first, they always killed the mothers.

Reluctantly, I stopped typing.

It was ten minutes to ten. I knew that it was time to call it a night and began to panic when the long beam of a golden headlight swept through the front window. But it wasn't the Cadillac. A small van had pulled up. I knew it wasn't carrying the big man. He would never travel in something that looked like a plumber might ride in.

In a pool of darkness, I watched as a large, square driver, the tall kind that resembled a bodyguard, got out, tossed a lit cigarette onto the driveway, and then proceeded to the double back doors. He waved his keys in the air and then unlocked one side. Four small people didn't step out. They practically fell out.

Who were these people?

They were kids. And teens. Four or five human bodies. Some tall, some small, some whimpering, some begging for an ounce of freedom. All were wearing shackles on their feet, chains on their hands, and thick silver tape covering their mouths. I could see their eyes— impossibly huge and scared to death—when burly men placed thick, black burlap bags over their heads.

Efficiently, as if this was a common drill, they were led across the driveway, like animals during a roundup. Additional guards materialized—tall, muscular men holding small stubbed-nosed guns. In the bright moonlight, I caught the glint of a semiautomatic in the hand of the driver. He stood at the ready position with the gun pointed at his "guests."

It was the perfect time to sneak out of the office, hunkering low in the back hallway until I could make it to the main staircase. Turns out this wasn't a good spot because the inside guards were too close, so I took a chance and made a break for the kitchen.

It was just my luck that there was a person standing by the island counter.

Bitty put a silencing finger to her lips as the package of oats she had been holding spilled everywhere. She pointed to a back staircase and my feet didn't fail me.

For a second, I stopped because I could see she had been crying. But there was no time for even a small hug. She shooed me away when I moved in closer.

"Go, Walker," she whispered. "Go now. If they find you, they'll take you down there."

"What's down there?" I rushed.

"Endings," she whispered. "It's where the guards are taking those kids."

A loud noise had us scampering. I hid by the side of the island where I willed myself to stop breathing.

The others were already in this room. A guard led the pack with chained prisoners in the middle and Mr. Machine Gun keeping up the rear. Bitty seemed to know this drill because she scurried to the back door and opened it wide for them to have easy access. She bowed her head, refusing to make eye contact.

Silently, I watched as the group was led like cows taken to slaughter. Only, this time, it was a short walk through a back door and then down a close-by concrete staircase to whatever lurked in the recesses below the house.

Bitty pointed harshly at the stairs.

I made my dash upward, thanking my lucky stars that my guard was on another bathroom break.

I wouldn't sleep that night.

I wouldn't escape, either.

14.

Luck shined my way a few nights later. I found out from Bitty that the big man had left the building again. I spied him from my window for confirmation. He was in a dark suit and some minion was jogging alongside of him carting his luggage, which indicated an overnight stay somewhere else.

I bided my time and did the downstairs slither. The guards made it easy. They were having a heated game of poker in the living room. The youngest guard, around nineteen with headphones on, watching some movie on his watch, was still in place by the front door . . . and the kitchen and back doors were being eyeballed by guards going back and forth to fill their plates although they seemed more interested in beer than deserters.

Once again, I was prepped to leave, but this time it felt even better. I was in leggings and sweater—my own—that Bitty delivered to my room after Xavier left.

As usual, escape wasn't easy. But it was still on the agenda.

I was at the ready, but I had to wait for the house to go to "bed."

Once again, his office had the smell of him. Stuffy. Oppressive. Lingering.

Bored out of my mind, I allowed my typing fingers to graze his computer. I had already explored my mother's current plight, which meant tonight I would pass the time trying out new names. Again, I typed in Daniel Reid and Cass Danko. Nothing. Then for some reason, I typed the name of Daniel's eldest sister into the computer. I will never know why.

Access Granted.

Jenna Reid.

There was an odd picture that looked *vintage*. Pretty Jenna had her glossy dark hair in an old-fashioned bun and her gray eyes were red from crying.

Current Location: San Francisco, the past.

Occupation: child bride.

There was a stamp over her face. Four little letters that read: Sold.

ELEVEN

1.

It must have been a joke. She was only thirteen years old and slept with a retainer. She had crushes on movie stars with names like Timothée and Justin. Who in the world would marry a little girl? What father in this world or any other would offer his daughter up in this way . . . as if she were property?

My stomach twisted.

A note dated three weeks ago appeared on the screen. It was in Jenna's loopy handwriting.

"I, Jenna Reid, do not accept my tethering," she wrote. "I am of sound mind. Of sound body. Of sound will. I will not be led to this abnormal union. Not to that man. Not in this time period. Not in any lifetime."

She signed it . . . in Latin.

Flectere si nequeo superos, Acheronta movebo.

It took me a second to pull up a new screen and translate.

Jenna—who just got her adult teeth, loved vampire books, and was afraid of thunderstorms—wrote: If I cannot bend the will of Heaven, I shall move Hell.

2.

"Jenna, my Jenna, where are you?" I whispered to myself. "Your father . . . he sent you off to be married in the past, so he could get rid of you. You're just a little girl."

Frantically, I searched for more information, but there was none.

My heart sank as I typed in the name of Daniel's youngest sister, Andy Reid. *Nothing.* With shaking fingers, I replaced it with Andrea Reid. Her full name and picture popped up. Beautiful Andy, eleven, with her black glossy hair and trademark slate-gray Reid eyes. She was smiling in what looked like a high school yearbook photo from years ago. Under her name were the words "Current Location."

It was listed as Colorado, the past.

Colorado, when? Pioneer days? Last week? Why this place? These past visits were usually tied to some kind of historical event. What? Why San Fran and Rocky Mountain high?

Daniel Reid. I punched it in. Access Denied. Again and again.

Then, I punched in Bobby Reid.

A video of the impish six-year-old came up. He was eating dinner at the same impossibly long dining room table I had been forced to sit at a few days ago. The blue vase was in the middle filled with deep-orange fall chrysanthemums. The video was dated several months ago . . . when Bobby was here in The Other, but before Dr. King found him.

It couldn't be. My heart battered against my rib cage. Implosion was next.

"Eat your dinner," snapped a curt voice. The camera was on the little boy the entire time. I couldn't make out the man.

"Don't you like it?" cajoled the man. "It's expensive. We only like things of great worth."

"It tastes like deer shit and shark shit and every kind of shit ever shitted," Bobby replied. "You're a shitty shit, too."

"Eat it, young man—or you'll be sorry," demanded the man in a clipped tone.

"Screw you," said the kid. "And I am sorry."

"That's better," the man barked.

"Sorry that you're my daddy," Bobby cried.

3.

The camera swung around. It wasn't his father, but my captor, Xavier, who was doing the talking. He was younger than Edward Reid, far more handsome, and his hands were gloved but in working order. Edward Reid only had one hand. His killer made sure of it.

"You're a shit Dad," Bobby railed on him. "Shit Dad when you looked old . . . and still shit now that you had your 'peration and they made you look more normaler."

What in the world was Bobby talking about now? I was a pro at translating and figured that the man had an operation.

I watched in horror as this man whipped around the table to strike Bobby. He was furious by now and fast. Something did, however, annoy him. He swatted at the child with one hand, but couldn't strike him beyond a quick glance.

My eyes widened when I watched him rip off the gloves. One hand was perfect, but it wasn't his right or primary one. That one stopped at the wrist. There was nothing more to it.

Coincidence?

It had to be.

I wanted to throw something, and that's when I saw what looked like an ashtray on a dark corner of the desk. It would do . . . just fine. In that moment, I didn't give a shitty shit, as Bobby would say, if the guards heard and I was dragged back to my room by my hair.

I picked up that crystal piece of crap, cocking my arm back. The pointy thing inside tumbled into my hand, nicking the skin because the ends were sharp.

"Ow," I whispered under my breath, dumping the hard, little piece onto the desk. It had a twin that went with it and both tumbled out of the ashtray and fell onto the wood like dice.

I picked both little gold pieces back up and then stared at them in my hand.

Cuff links. Obviously, they belonged to Xavier and he must have taken them off when he was typing something before he went out tonight.

I saw a glint of diamonds on the flat face. The initials sparkled in the low desk lamp light: EXR.

I couldn't breathe.

The top drawer of the desk was locked, but with a few moves I learned from our trainers and a paper clip, it opened easily. The first thing I found was boxes of colored contact lenses in dark shades of blue.

There was a photo album tucked into his bookshelf. If it was Edward Reid, I knew that he was too much of a narcissist to feature photos of anyone but himself. With shaking hands, I picked it up.

Inside were various pictures: before and after shots. First, he de-aged himself much like Dr. King did. Perhaps it was easy to do in The Other. Then he had his face "fixed." The photos were various stages of plastic surgery. He signed off on each "improvement" using his legal designation.

Edward Xavier Reid.

I wrapped my arms around my body and began to silently sob.

The devil was in the details, and I had missed all of them.

4.

The intense rush of terror was cut by a blinding light flooding the windows.

A small yellow school bus pulled up and two guards emerged, large guns slung over their shoulders. Next came their nightly prey . . . children as young as thirteen or fourteen. Their legs were chained ankle to ankle because this age group wasn't dangerous. They were just simply slippery and whip smart. And there was no fence around this property to block any attempts to haul ass out of there.

I wanted to run through the glass of this window and go with them, but the window was reinforced with thick wooden inlays, which made it shatterproof. It did have one of those little silver arms. You could open it just a sliver, which was enough to hear the sound of barking humans.

"Form one line. I'm sure all of you 'tards can count to one. No talking. No screwing around," snarled the guard. "If you leave the line, you leave this afterlife. We'll feed you to the mountain lions who are always extra hungry for young, tender meat."

"I gotta take a piss," said one of the more defiant boys.

The guard ripped the boy's pants off him. "Do it right here," he demanded.

There was nothing I could do but watch the snow turn yellow. Boys that age were defiant, which was a superpower in its own right.

A pair of eyes spied me doing it. Bitty came into the office through a back door and whispered, "He's on his way home. He didn't go out of town. Go back upstairs. If you want to continue to breathe."

If she wouldn't have looked so exhausted, I might have actually complied to save my own ass. But she was beyond wobbly on her feet. Her right arm sported a fresh bloody bandage that covered the fleshy white inner skin of her elbow to her wrist.

"What the hell is going on here with the kids?" I bit out.

She shocked me with her answer.

"You're part of the reason they're here. You opened the force field when you came to this side with your friends and it stayed open all night. The hunters crossed to your side and came back with their spoils. Many are still stuck at immigration, but that Pristine woman alerts Xavier when they're free.

"The hunters have been poaching a place on your side called Freak Island," she said.

"What do they want?"

"To drain the freak right out of us," she whispered. "And figure out a way to inject it or implant it in themselves. Who knew that your own personal freak was your most coveted asset. The irony is in the living realm, we spent our entire lifespans trying to push our freak away. Hide it. Deny it exists."

"What can we do now?" I whispered.

"Pray," she said before slipping out of the room.

5.

The front door opened wide and guards with Taser pulse weapons and semiautomatic shotguns walked through it.

"This is Dave 289. Stay frosty," one of the guards said into a device in his sleeve. "Last night, we had a runner. He had to be contained—and we won't bag another one like him again. Body is DOB." I knew from Cass when he talked in military terms. DOB was dead and buried.

Six kids in chains filed in. Someone quickly removed their hardware. To the naked eye, it looked like the field trip from hell with scared faces and looming adult captors.

"Copy," said another guard into his wrist. "No excuses tonight. Bag and tag the resistance."

I saw a slightly older boy, maybe sixteen or seventeen, still in chains with a pole attached to his neck, arms cuffed behind his back. There were two girls flanking him, maybe fifteen and sixteen, with their hands zip-tied in front of them. A younger girl sounded strangely familiar, although I couldn't place her because her head was hung so low it almost hit her stomach.

"You can't keep me," she cried. "My sister said you just can't."

One of the big picture windows in the foyer acted like a mirror and showed the sister standing beside her. Both wore the same strappy yellow sundress covered in cheerful white daisies. It was the worst possible ensemble for this freezing-cold place.

I looked closer, trying to memorize their faces. That's when it hit me. I knew these girls from Freak Island. It was the partially invisible twin sister duo that called themselves Deuce. Molly and Matilda Malone were twins, fourteen years old and always beside each other. You could easily see Molly, who once, long ago on Freak Island, told me, "We're happy to meet you."

"*We?*" I had asked her, gazing at one smart-mouthed kid.

"Aren't you happy to meet *her*, too? She never did anything to you—at least not yet," she had said. "And it's rude to play favorites. We hope you're not one of *those* rude girls. We hate rude girls."

She instructed me to look into the reflection of the water on that windswept beach.

And, there she was. The other girl wasn't visible to the naked eye. In the water's reflection, in that sliver of moonlight, plain as day was her invisible sister. They held hands and both spoke.

"Duh. We're twins," blurted Molly, who'd informed me that one died in utero and was stillborn while Molly lived until her death in a car crash as young girl. The truth was Matlida was born in her own way: invisible and only seen in reflections of glass or chrome or water. Always there. Anyone with a fast eye could see her. Lingering. Eating. Talking.

Being. In life. And in death.

They dubbed themselves Deuce. Two for one.

"Why are you here?" I mouthed. A normal human would have never heard it. The only thing was: these girls weren't normal, thank God.

Molly glanced past the guards and our eyes locked. Her voice was little-girl shrilly when she answered, "They know about us," she said in a frantic rush. "They saw Matilda on infrared and took us away."

I could see better when they were forced to move closer to me. Someone had put duct tape over the invisible Matlida's eyes and mouth, so they could easily track her. It floated, attached to what appeared to be nothing. Molly's hands were tied in front with thick rope.

"Help us!"

Matilda used sign language, which I knew from my mother who volunteered to work with the deaf. "Someone. Anyone. It's so dark here and my beautiful eyelashes will be a wreck," she signed.

When she began to race toward the front door, I shook my head hard as in "no."

The guards laughed when she ran into a wall, bounced off, and then the tape was seen close to the ground where she fell. Molly chose to ignore me and took off for the front door, her sister upright again, trusting her and racing by her side.

Molly with her hands tied made it all the way to the front step again.

Go! Run away. Head for the woods! Fast! My mind was screaming. *Take me with you.*

"I have a ten-eighteen. Escapee," said the unnervingly calm guard into his sleeve.

"Take the shot. Put it out of its misery," a voice commanded. I heard it come out from the man's suit jacket. "We only need one of them."

In dire times, Molly was a howler. She was born that way as the more visible one. As long as I heard her, she was still here.

Click!

A shot rang out and silence. I heard the thump of the little girl crashing. Flesh and bone on a bed of concrete. Fresh blood ate the yellow away from her dress.

No! God no!

"Containment," said one of the guards into his sleeve.

6.

An excruciating wail came from the three slices of duct tape. It splintered my bones, searing my tissue as it lacerated my heart. No matter how hard I tried, I would never be able to erase the sound of that invisible sister watching her beloved twin hit the ground. A guard carried her tiny 14-year-old body into the foyer and allowed her to melt to the ground.

"It's you we wanted, freak. The other one is just baggage," the guard said to the floating tape, which he tried to grab with both hands, but Matilda kept slipping through his fingers. Angered, she stuck to his eyes and then his hair, laughing loudly now when he tried to swat her away. Still invisible, she raced left, then right, through his legs and then around the small table in the foyer. He was no match in speed as she continued to elude him.

"Your sister is dead meat now. You're the package," he taunted. "Now, get over here!"

His burly friend came back into the house.

"Drug the invisible one. She gives me the effing willies."

"You drug her," he snapped. "You gotta catch her first. I can't even f-ing see her!"

He didn't know the half of it. As twins, Molly and Matilda *always* experienced the exact same emotions and pain.

I watched wide-eyed as the tape stopped moving and something rather curious happened. The gray pieces of duct tape began to bleed midair . . . large splotches of red floating, attached to nothing. After a minute, the blood droplets separated, flying high and then regrouped, pouring down a creamy white wall, trickling slowly until it pooled in a large puddle on the fancy floor.

"Shit, this isn't sanitary. You could catch Ebola or something," cried one of the guards.

Another stared and then took a step back.

"I ain't taking the blame for this. Big Man wanted the invisible one."

As for the more visible Molly, blood poured from her ears, nose and mouth, escaping trails of liquid life form that raced away from her physical body. The destination was to mingle with her sister's blood, which now was forming a tight circle around the corpse. When the ring was complete, the liquid moved together into a tight pulsating ball.

"This is beyond my pay grade," a guard yelled as he backed way up.

And then another with more seniority barked: "Clean all this shit up and toss it outside. The wolves will eat good tonight."

I just stood and watched as the blood ball flattened. In the middle of all that red, I saw two little hands, fingers twined.

It dawned on me in that moment that they weren't dying. They were fusing.

"Move your little asses!"

That was directed at the rest of the "kids."

Horrified and silent, the rest of the child prisoners silently followed another guard through the house in a single-file line.

"Load 'em and code 'em. Use cells zero to six down below. I gotta take a piss," said a female voice that made my arm hair rise at attention.

It was self-proclaimed Sheriff Pristine, the woman I met in the woods, the one who drugged me and brought me here.

My hands were shaking and tears dropped to the ground as I stood paralyzed.

If I made a sound, I wouldn't be able to help them.

I would be one of them.

7.

I couldn't breathe.

I couldn't think.

All I could do was slink back into the bowels of his office and sit in that big swivel chair and cry silently. A few minutes later, when the office door fully opened, all I had left was the element of surprise. But he was smart and saw it coming from the moment he had me kidnapped.

Even now with the high back of the desk chair turned toward him, he knew that I was in it. He reached out a hand and spun my chair around. Hard.

His smile was predatory as he went in for the kill strike.

"Walker," he said, feasting on my fear. "It's like I'm seeing a ghost."

8.

He looked like Xavier, but that man didn't exist. That model was just a souped-up Edward Reid who had the entire makeover package in The Other. He was de-aged, nipped, tucked, worked out, and worked on. He even sounded younger, which was no excuse for not making him earlier. Tonight, he chose not to wear the glove and I wondered why. He lost his life after the son of one of his victims made the great Edward Reid back up and up into the rotating propeller of his prop plane. I wished they had stuffed his head in there.

In the afterlife, all physical ailments in life were fixed, but not for him. The hand and arm were back, but not right. It looked as if a wild animal had chewed on both and the remains were sewn back on.

"No Hollywood kiss?" Edward said.

When I didn't respond, he went down a different road. "What are the chances you'd be here? In The Other?" Edward posed. "It's really odd and absolutely synchronistic."

The tight lipped, pensive smile. The sweaty skin. The fine lines that would someday become crater-like grooves. The full head of inky dark hair, farmed from fake materials. I should have seen how easily it could thin in the future into some sort of sad comb-over. But not now. He had been refreshed. Refurbished. Reorganized.

Regenerated in The Other.

"What are you wearing?" I asked. "Someone else's face?"

"What I enjoyed most about turning back the clock was picking the age," he said. "Of course, I didn't want to age too far back into the teenage years. The frontal lobe of your brain responsible for judgment just isn't there," he said.

Dr. King went back to his teenage self in body, but kept the mind and spirit of his fifty-something self. Obviously, he knew how to level up the process.

"It was tempting to go all the way back with the mind—the ultimate do-over," Edward said. "As you teenagers enter puberty, your brain spouts more dopamine than it ever will again in your life. This is the stuff that signals enjoyment. It's why laughing with your friends, having sex, eating a cheeseburger, listening to your favorite band or driving around with the top down on a hot summer night will never feel as good as it did when you were a teenager," he stated.

Was that a compliment to the young?

"This fact is why so many are you are so stupid," he added. "You can't assess danger. All you feel is the reward lurking. And science tells us that you take even more risks when your friends are around."

"Is there a point here?" I interrupted.

"When I was offered a chance to de-age, I took it," he said. "It certainly fooled you. Who would expect to find me looking just a few years older than my vile oldest son?"

My mind was on overdrive. My mouth still silent.

"Nosy little trailer park bitch that you are, I knew it wouldn't take long for you to follow the clues in this house and seek out my true identity," he said. "Edward Xavier Reid . . . I always enjoyed my middle name. It's so commanding. Almost king-like. I'm so glad you could enjoy it, too—and will come to say it fondly in the future."

Revulsion. I swallowed hard to keep the contents of my stomach from launching.

"Oh, you kids made it so easy. I waited for all of you to come through the force field. I knew that things were getting too hot with Principal Dick for you to stay in the Midst. After you arrived here, it was a done deal. All I needed to do was put Pristine on the hunt and gather you for us to arrive at this point."

"And what point are we at, Edward?"

"Containment," he said.

"Where is Daniel?" I demanded. There would be no whimpering. No pleading. If I were to be contained, I would leave this world with answers.

"Little bastard is gone. Leveled up. With my help. Should we take a minute and cry about it?" he said with a top spin to his voice. He was enjoying. Feasting.

"You're a sick bastard," I began.

"He was screaming your name as he left town," Edward offered.

"He said, 'Say good-bye to that cheap little whore whose name I can't quite remember now. Tell her it was nothing more than practice. Remind her, I'll won't go trolling in the swamps next time for a bed warmer. But I'll always remember that a Reid takes what he wants and then he throws her away."

In the silence that followed, he walked to the cabinet and poured us each a drink in a crystal high-ball glass.

Then he slid my drink across the desk hard enough that part of it spilled on that fancy wood. I had never shot whisky before, but I had seen it done in countless movies. Maybe it was the loss of Daniel and now Deuce. I tossed my head back and drank fire that burned all the way down.

"I am positive you will align yourself with the right side—once and for all. Your mother didn't raise a fool. A psychotic, cold-hearted, inbred, social-climbing piece of white trash with a vile mouth and average body. But not a fool," Edward said.

"Leave my mother out of it," I warned.

9.

It didn't take more than another minute for Edward to outline the plan he had in mind. In the end, I was to be "married." To him. Immediately.

"We will tether together tomorrow at sunset, which is like a wedding ceremony here. And then you will be mine. All of you will be mine. I will own you."

"We will enjoy all the pleasures of our tethering. Every single night," he promised in a husky voice that told me he was looking forward to that part of it.

"Why would you tether with me—the foul-mouthed, inbred, white trash? I'm sure The Other is full of bimbos who will do. Maybe they even glow in the dark."

"You're right. You are not my type, but I can mold you. Plus, you have the Omorrow papers or know where they are, Walker," Edward said. "After we tether tomorrow night, I will own them because on this side, all that one partner owns after tethering is also the property of the other. You will also tell me where that bastard Dr. King is hiding my youngest son. I will bring him back here and cut off one of his little fingers for each day you don't tell me where those papers are located."

"And if I refuse any of the above?" I challenged.

He had it covered, too.

185

"Then, I will make sure that the already heinous fates facing Jenna and Andy will quadruple. I'll bury them somewhere interesting after making sure they suffer horrifically. Maybe they can burn in the great Chicago fire of the past or how about sink into the icy ocean after the Titanic hits that ice cube. You know how much I enjoy a good water death."

He looked down at an expensive gold Rolex watch like he was concluding any other business deal. "I'll work out the particulars—or not—based on your cooperation," he said.

I ran for the door, but he easily blocked me.

"It's late, dear, and you need your beauty rest. Unless you'd like to start joining me in my bed tonight, I'll send you back up to your room for your last solo slumber. Please do something with that *ethnic* hair and wear a decent dress. When I send out announcements of our tethering, I don't want it took like you just stepped out of a double-wide at the RV park."

Edward moved closer. I began to taste my dinner again.

"You certainly served yourself up to my son on a tin platter. Naked, night after night in that little hovel of a house screwing like rabbits, I'm sure. And now, I will make you forget about my son. In every single way."

"I'm sure you will enjoy it," he boasted, adding, "we only have eternity to find out."

Edward put a hard finger under my chin and tilted my face upward. "Good night, darling," he said, pressing his lips to mine.

When I twisted away, he did it again, but harder.

I wiped my mouth with the back of my hand. He grabbed for me again, embracing air, but finally snaring me in arms that were much stronger than what I expected. He was muscular, and panic filled my system because I was being suffocated. He used pressure, tongue, and a hold that almost snapped my neck. I felt waves of sickness. I could feel below that he was aroused by it.

"*Fung chu*, Walker," he said while I choked for air.

TWELVE

1.

We were taught an exercise to deal with our darkest, middle-of-the night fears. You had to identify your surroundings. Simple as that. "Picture, paint, wall, dresser," I began to list, "doorknob, rug, sink." The exercise took you out of your panic and restored you back into the present moment.

I felt my stomach calm and said the magic words: "You are bigger than your fear. You are better than your captor. You have come back to the present moment grounded in reality."

I would be forced to tether to Edward Reid.

It would not kill me. Almost. But not quite.

2.

I heard the click of the door being unlocked and tensed. There was nothing else I could do but grab the towel rack pole I had dislodged earlier that day and hid between the mattress and the bed. But it wasn't

Edward. It was an exhausted and depleted Bitty who caught wind of the chair, moved it, and then proceeded to bring in bags and bags of goods along with a clothing rack sporting several "options."

"I'm so sorry, Walker," she said.

I watched as she brought the bags into the bathroom and then rolled my eyes when a virtual makeup counter-worth of ivory and pink shadows, golden blushes, thick mascaras, and the like were set up for my transformation. He wanted me to smell like gardenias hence the bottle of bubble bath. When Bitty was done, she placed the clothing rack in the far corner of the room and removed three plastic garment bags.

The wedding dress should have been hideous, but it wasn't. It was a pearl-white, biased-cut slip dress that just grazed the floor. The accessories were elegant including a long tulle veil and sheer gloves.

There were written instructions in the bag: wear your hair in a low bun and make sure the makeup looks natural. As regal as he planned the wedding, he had other plans for the wedding night. There were nightgowns in the other bag: one short, black, and lacy, another was red and sheer in all the wrong places, and the other virginal white made out of silk with a low dip in front and fitted to the ground.

"I don't know what to say," Bitty said, shaking her head.

I shrugged.

"What if I could do one positive thing for you?" Bitty offered. "They're in the bathroom. Behind the toilet."

I hoped it was a gun or knife, but it wasn't. But for some reason, my heart did the kind of leap that might have been unwarranted.

My shit-kicking new boots. There they were.

Shined pretty.

3.

Funny thing about having nothing to lose. It makes you risk the little bit you have left.

At three in the morning, I stood outside in the cold. I made it out of my room with my key, past the sleeping guard, down the stairs, and out the back door. It was bitch cold outside, maybe ten below with driving winds. I didn't have a coat, but wore an XL black man's sweater and dark leggings that Bitty left me, plus the boots.

What I hadn't counted on was the three guards who stood at the perimeter of the lawn smoking and making sure the property was middle-of-the-night secure.

They were looking for wild animals. A girl on two legs wasn't on their radar.

My good fortune was short-lived. When their guard "friend," probably just steps behind me, walked out the back door, I had no choice but to hustle for the only hiding spot, the basement stairwell, where I hid in a dark space.

There were maybe twenty stairs, possibly thirty. At first, it seemed like a proper hiding spot, but as I sat chattering from cold (thanks, reset), I found myself inching lower—a stair or two at a time. As I descended, I kept reminding myself, "There is nothing you can do for the children they brought down there. You don't even know why they're there. You have no weapons. No backup."

All I got today was the boots.

When my feet hit the cold concrete of the bottom stair, I straightened myself like an arrow and hid in a sliver of blackness by the single metal door. It had some kind of numbered lock on it and a small window in the middle.

It was a heavy door.

An unlocked one.

I went right in.

A fine blast of manufactured warmth blanketed my being. Someone had cranked the heat up to old-lady—eighty-five solid degrees—but, despite the blast of soul-affirming warmth, I still felt a cold chill in the pit of my stomach.

It wasn't the temp, but the smell of what was going on inside here that raised hackles on my skin. It was something *sterile*.

The walls were white. The floor was made up of marbled ivory tiles placed closely together so it looked like a river of milk. Every piece of furniture was colorless. It looked like a hospital wing and confirmation wasn't far away. There was a sign across a white check-in desk that read: Reid Laboratories.

In small letters below was the mission: Dedicated to the advancement of the ingenious human functions.

I wish I could report that no one was behind the desk, but damn the luck. There was a woman, maybe in her forties, who was about five foot seven and big in shoulders and hips. She stood like a redwood tree, impressive and powerful, as if she could devour whatever walked in that door.

"Bus early tonight with offerings?"

She thought I worked here.

I don't know what possessed me. Or maybe I did. It was called self-preservation.

"Yes, ma'am," I said.

She swung around the desk and put long, tapered fingers on my shoulders. She had paperwork attached to a clipboard and a pen.

"Don't worry, Betina," she said, pressing pen and board into my hands. Her hard stare and plastered blonde bob made anything but worry an impossibility. She handed me a paper cup and for a minute, I thought we were doing a pee test. "I suggest you drink water now. Once the testing begins, there will be no food or water."

She held out something that looked like a large Q-tip.

"Open, Betina," she demanded, towering over me. "We haven't had one like you before."

"Open what?" I asked. Then, it dawned on me. This was a case of mistaken identity at its finest. She didn't believe I worked here. *She thought I was one of the "specimens."*

"DNA swab," she said in an exasperated voice. She grabbed me by my chin, which caused my lips to part. Shoving the stick into my mouth, I choked as she rubbed it on the inside of my facial cheek.

There would be no running out of there. An orderly type in a long white coat grabbed me from behind and muscled me into a smaller room down the hall that was made out of concrete bricks. I had to stop him before he went too far. "I think you've made a mistake," I said.

"That's what y'all say."

He wrapped a fat rubber band around the skin at the bottom of my hand and when I went to take it off, he called for two additional orderlies to hold me down. The needle that he stuck into the paper-thin skin on the top of my hand was long, and the entire area began to burn.

"I wouldn't move or you'll tear your vein," he said.

When I flinched, he looked at my chart and smiled. "If you can't handle a little blood draw, I'd hate to be you during a bone marrow aspiration."

He drew three vials of blood and handed them to a nurse who popped her head in holding a tray for samples.

"Rest," she said. "The next procedure will be conducted in the operating room."

Leaving me alone in there, untied, was a fool's mistake. The minute they were gone, I took several steps toward the little door, which wasn't even locked.

It must have been around 3:30 in the morning by now and a long hallway was vacant. I couldn't possibly walk out the front door, but figured there must have been a back way out. I wouldn't walk too quickly or slowly. My body on autopilot, I made my way down the long concourse where at the end someone had made a sign on a white piece of paper. The arrow pointed right and read: Fifth Avenue.

Of course, that was a fancy street in New York City where only the best shops were located. Turns out Fifth Avenue at Edward's house of horrors was a white room with fifty padded leather recliners where he kept his finest "experiments." There was wide gap between the rows, hence the avenue. But this wasn't some R&R area. Each chair was hooked up to several medical machines including IVs and other whirling gadgets that pumped something from point A to point B. There was a simple silver coat rack in one corner and rather quickly I donned one of the lab jackets.

The nameplate told me the jacket belonged to a woman named Dr. Cassandra Hopkins. Each chair had the word Specimen on it and a number. Several were occupied by what I assumed to be patients. I guessed the age range went from about twelve- or thirteen-year-old preteens to those just a bit past twenty years of age.

As I walked down the avenue with a borrowed clipboard to make it look legit, I saw that most of the machines were withdrawing blood from arms although a few of the patients had medical equipment hooked up to hips, mouths, and their lower abdominal regions.

Most were lightly sedated. Some were totally gooned. Some had headphones on. Others just started into space. A few were twitching or withering in pain. Most of their eyes were closed.

Strong fingers reached out to violently grab mine. He had long, sinewy arms and was large, athletic, and toned. As hard as I tried to recoil, he held on tighter in a death grip.

"Run," he said in a low voice filled with the gravel of one who wasn't well.

4.

"Flick? Chris Flicker?" I whispered as my Freak Island friend.

Trapped in a medical chair, looking pale, and barely "there," he gave me a look of pure hatred. There were IV lines snaking from his lower arm into a bag that was deep red and constantly mixing with a clear substance. His other hand kept mine in a death grip.

"What . . . why?" I stammered.

Then I stared at the bag again. I wasn't a medical pro, but it stood to reason that when they gave you medicine, it flowed into the tube. This was the opposite. Blood from Flicker's arm was being pumped into the bag.

"Why . . . are . . . you . . . here?" I whispered.

"You are the reason I'm here, so listen to me, damn it. You opened the force field between the two sides," he muttered through blueish lips.

"There was a raid at Freak Island. This is your fault."

It was the answer I least expected—and it hurt to the core.

"That night in the Midst." He paused to catch a labored breath. "I had dinner that night in the cafeteria at Freak Island and then came to the mainland. I wanted to take a walk in the woods. Clear my head. So many of us from Freak Island walk in your woods late at night. It's against the law, which makes it even more enticing."

I rubbed his free arm and it was ice cold.

"They trapped me with nets. For a split second, I didn't fight. Thought it was some senior year prank, but this was no joke. They collected many of us. Put us on a boat that traveled such a tumultuous sea. I lost my dinner and lunch and breakfast," Flick said. "Don't remember the rest of it because I was eventually drugged. I woke up naked in a little white room. They examined me for days. And then my 'counselor' explained what happened. Apparently, they have people watching constantly for the force field to open—even for a few minutes. Then, they go poaching."

Man hunted for various reasons. For sport. For food. For collecting. The reason why this hunting took place made me feel physically ill.

"They're draining our insides. Stealing our birthright, our DNA," he said. "Here, we're not considered humans. He calls us the Specimens and we've had numbers tattooed on our wrists, as if we're nothing more than inventory."

I was never a science genius and my confusion registered.

He took a deep breath and found some kind of inner reserve to explain it to me. "Even in death, our DNA remains, Walker," he said. "DNA is contained in blood, semen, skin cells, tissue, organs, muscles, brain cells . . . you really should have paid attention in science class."

He paused to wince in pain and my mind raced to listen while thinking of ways to unhook him.

"Hair, saliva, mucus, perspiration, fingernails—all DNA hot spots . . . ," he rambled.

"They're harvesting all of it from us . . . blood first and later our organs," he said in a rush. "They're extracting our DNA. It can be stored for a long period of time. Up to five years at room temperature. They're only doing this with the 'gifted' or 'special ones' who have extraordinary powers. "He wants what we have," Flick snarled. "Edward and Dick, and some of their associates, believe that their own ultimate power will come when they can mix 'extraordinary' DNA with their own normal strands."

"Does it even work that way?" I asked.

"Who knows—but they find it too tantalizing not to try it," Flick said.

My heart was racing. But before I could figure out how to release him, he did something odd.

He put up the hand with the IV attached.

"That's it. Now you know," Flick said. "You can leave now."

It hit me like a shot.

"Flick, don't be crazy," I cried, looking for the exit. "Why are you acting like you don't know me?"

"Because you are a liar!" he stormed. "I saw you from the window, over there, in a pretty dress. A few nights ago. On your date. During my free hours when I'm caged in one of those little white rooms, I ran your future without you knowing it. Congratulations, sugarplum."

"Congratulations for what?"

Marrying the big man. An upgrade from Daniel, I suppose."

"That is not going to happen," I said in horror. "How dare you—"

"I don't need any favors from you, *Mrs. Edward Reid.*"

He squeezed my hand tighter. Violently.

"Don't call me that," I hissed.

"Explain it to me then, Walker. Why are you spending time with the Big Man? Having dinners with him. You're about to make the ultimate mistake. I call it a disaster," he said.

What happened next zapped him of so much energy that he moaned in agony. Flick still managed to nod at a blank wall.

"Showtime, dear," he mouthed.

He showed me three quick movies. Of my future.

My hands began to quake.

5.

Chris Flicker, Freak Island's finest, had the God-given gift of projecting three versions of your future life on the wall. Only one was true. But you never knew which one until you "lived" it. This time the "coda," as they say in film circles, was clear because the endings were all the same.

In each of his projections, I was Mrs. Edward Reid.

Mrs.

Edward.

Reid.

"No!" I moaned into my hand.

Flick's arm became stiff like a wooden board. He was shaking now, his entire body in some herky-jerky dance that made him slouch forward and then backward in that leather seat. Immediately, instantaneously, I unbuckled the belt that kept him sitting and watched in horror as he slid spinelessly to the floor.

He was unconsciously quaking, his fit body contorting into odd and grotesque positions. Along the way, he had pulled out his IV and blood sprayed from a nurse-inflicted wound onto my legs, racing until it hit ground again and slid into the grooves of the tile grout.

There was no 911 in hell.

There was only my voice, screaming.

"Help!" I cried, kneeling next to him. "He needs help!"

Two medics came running with blankets that provided some kind of cushion. A minute later, they strong-armed him into some kind to submission and gave him a long needle filled with what was calming. In my peripheral vision, I saw Flick wind down to a puddle of flesh, neck folded, head hung low.

"Walker . . . Get. Out," he croaked, "Of. Here. Now."

But, it was too late. My stealth break-in was now public knowledge.

"Get her to her feet," said one of the medics who ripped me upright and then tied my hands behind me with a plastic zip tie.

"Zap her."

6.

It was Bitty who stopped them from running an electrical current down my spine.

"Big Man sent me," she warned the guards. It was no lie. He did send her because she was the fastest thanks to her astral projection.

"You have no authority," the guard began, but he was stopped short. The Big Man had arrived in a dark blue business suit, eyes narrowed, a cigarette burning his right hand. His mouth set in a hard line.

"Can't I enjoy a simple coq au vin and chocolate soufflé without interruptions," he stated while glancing at me with a mixture of wonderment and disgust. "Ah, Walker, you always make it interesting," he said to me. "What disgusts me is you're sweating like a pig and your hair looks like rats are nesting there. You're . . . so . . . dirty, darling—and not in a good way. Is that blood on your legs?"

"On legs that belong to me now."

To Bitty, he commanded, "Bathe and sedate her. And if you do anything more or less, I will extinguish you."

7.

Bitty grabbed my hand and we flew—literally—out of there, back into the house and up the winding staircase.

We beat Edward, but not for long. He was suddenly there in the room, flanked by a guard, a nurse, and someone else who held something that smelled like fire.

Edward demanded that I change into a fresh nightgown and I complied. When I took a gown out of the big armoire, I pivoted toward the bathroom, but the guard stopped me by standing in front of the white door. "You can change right here. In front of us," said the nurse.

I locked eyes with Edward, refusing to allow my torment and humiliation to bubble into torrents of fresh tears. In that moment, I did not cover myself. I let the long coat drop. My leggings came next and then the sweater. Then, I crouched to the ground and slipped on the new gown.

They would not break me.

"I hope it hurts," Edward said. "Let's take her to the bed," he added.

My fight factor was amped I struggled with the guard, kicking and flailing until I looked like a rabid forest creature. It was to no avail. Bitty stood in the corner crying while the guard held my shoulders and Edward grabbed my legs, forcing them apart.

I smelled something familiar, which was the rubbing alcohol.

"Hold still," the nurse demanded, pressing something red hot to the fleshy side of my right hip. Immobilized now with my eyes wild, I took one last look at Edward. He smiled as the nurse pressed forward. She brought the silver wand closer while I screamed "no" at the top of my lungs.

Her words were ones one woman should never say to another while doing the deed of some man: "Butch up, little missy."

I floated. Mentally, I went back to a place and time when this seemed improbable.

I imagined Daniel coming through that upper window to save me. He would take out my tormenters, one by one, emerging from a path of destruction to grab my hand. "Callaghan, you want the last one," he would say . . . just in the nick of time, placing one of my throwing stars in my right hand.

There were no stars. No sky. I would not come from a long line of great love stories, but instead just a dot.

The window was sealed shut. There was no last-minute reckoning.

Just burning skin.

He had me branded on the side of my hip with his initials EXR.

Right on cue, the train wrecks.

THIRTEEN

1.

On my wedding day to Edward, the sky should have been angry and brooding, but a fat winter sun illuminated a fresh, thick blanket of snow below the window. The world was made of tiny sparkles surrounding a house of dull and doom.

"This is hard," Bitty said, biting her bottom lip as she began to place the gown on a long silver clothing rack that had been brought into the room so she could steam the garment.

I stood at the window for the longest time, picking at the grout until my fingernails began to bleed.

"What are you going to do, Walker? Take a header out the window?" Bitty demanded.

I gazed in that direction and wished that I grew wings. Even if the reset was working, it was a long way down. And then what? The house was surrounded by endless woods and framed by tall, peaked mountains. Even if somehow—emphasis on the bleakness of the situation—I got out . . . then what? The nights still tipped into below-zero temps. If the reset failed me, I wouldn't last until dawn.

"I'm going to take a shower," I said in a dead voice.

"Your Daniel would want you to go on," Bitty said in a low voice. It was a warning of sorts.

"I'm not drowning myself under the nozzle, Bits," I reminded her. "I'm just going to stand there, let the hot water burn me because existence is good at burning me. And then I will remind myself of my Daniel, as you call him, knowing that the universe is full of beautiful things that don't last."

"I'll sit on the toilet while you shower," she said, "and I will remind you that today will be bad, but soon he will tire of you and move on. He tired of me."

"Oh, Bits," I mouthed.

"Most of the household staff. He has 'dated' the majority," she said. "Guys. Girls."

I make it a point to never forget all the times when I was pushed beyond what seemed survivable. Or even when I felt like I couldn't breathe another second," she said. "Remind yourself of all the times you almost gave up, but you did what you just did a minute ago. You got out of bed. To try. Just one more time.

"We're all the same, Walker. We're women. We proceed."

No answer.

"I'll go get your shower ready."

"Bitty, I want to smell like hell," I said. "You go enjoy that nice hot shower."

"Don't mind if I do," she said.

2.

He was waiting, sitting on the edge of my bed when I returned to the main room. I was in a towel, excess water dripping on his expensive stained oak floors. He was in a black business suit, white shirt, and a fancy, formal silver tie. The cuff links were in place. His hair was gelled back.

He gazed at me as if I were late to a business meeting and it annoyed him because this reeked of incompetence.

"Well, there you are," Edward said. "I dressed for you."

Did my future rapist expect me to tell him that he looked nice? Handsome? Somewhat attractive? None of it was true, but the narcissist within him wanted the validation.

"I've assumed we're going to dress for this ridiculous event," I stated.

It earned me a quick, stinging, humiliating crack across the cheek.

As suspected, the rest was a business meeting—no fluff.

"Six o'clock tonight will mark our tethering," he informed me. "There will be a short ceremony followed by a dinner and then we will retire to our quarters for private activities." He glanced at Bitty. "Where, I know we will not be disturbed by anyone until I call down the next morning for breakfast."

Bitty stared at her feet.

"Do not expect some last-minute save. My eldest son has been contained," Edward said. When he walked closer, it took everything in me not to step away. I couldn't appear afraid. I wouldn't give him that much.

"My son is just a pale imitation," Edward said, seizing my arm to draw me in closer with a hard yank. He rancid breath—cigarettes mixed with stale coffee and bourbon—made me sick to my stomach. "You'll see," he promised with his usual bravado. "The original is braver, stronger, and smarter. Better in all ways, as originals tend to be. It will be the best sex of your life. The best time of your life. You'll see."

"Six o'clock," he repeated, releasing me with a hard push. My feet swayed on the cold floor, but I remained upright.

The letter *F* began to form on my lips.

"Don't make this harder on yourself than necessary," Edward warned.

I wanted to scream, but I had perfected the bland stare of a coma victim.

"Try to look presentable, darling," he said before slamming the door behind him. "I'd like our tethering announcement to reflect the joy of this extraordinary union."

I could pretend all I wanted it wasn't happening, but the facts were clear.

In a few hours, he would own me—body and soul.

3.

It was a chilled day, a time when even the smallest of animals find holes to hover in small places. I wish I could have found my hole. Even the light had escaped to places unknown leaving just a meager offering of bright. It was easy enough to imagine yourself diminishing until you were nothing more than those paper-thin leaves that drift away on autumn breezes.

Bitty brought out the wedding gown, which was a column dress in off-white—strapless with a back zipper concealed in hook-and-eye closures. *And really, Edward? A side slit? How 1980s, Dynasty, Melrose Place, slutty.* I imagined my freshly shaved leg rearing up through that split with an unchecked, wicked roundhouse kick right into his smug face. *In sickness and hell, darling.*

Yes, here comes the bride. All dressed in white. Ready to kill.

I wondered if this tethering was even legal, although it seemed to be the norm around The Other. Bitty tried to console me by insisting that it was more of a promise than an eternal vow to love, respect, and blah, blah, blah. For some reason, my mother's words kept floating through my mind: *Your word is your promise. You can never break your word.*

There was no veil to hide my disgust, but there actually were ankle-strap black leather stilettos to complete tonight's farce. When Bitty began to pack other clothes into the garment bag, I gave her a questioning look.

"For the wedding night," she mumbled as I grabbed the bag.

I pulled out some slutty looking white spandex and satin slip-like thingy that probably wouldn't clear my thighs. The front was some faux virginal lace bra made of the thinnest possible material making up the barely-there rest of it. There was a carbon copy of it in black and red in case he wanted some variety. Even in the Other, he managed to find clear stilettos with pink feathers, the hooker kind.

I pointed to the closet. They were muddy, hot damn.

"No, I can't," Bitty said. "He wouldn't like it."

"Do this one thing for me, Bitty," I said. "Please."

I gave her a pleading look and she shook her head.

She was right. He would have probably hit the roof, but at least it would be me. The real me.

Representing.

4.

There was no wedding march.

There was only a slow death march down that tragic winding staircase where I was flanked by a unformed guard in front of me and Bitty behind me. "I put your things in the master bathroom myself. Unpacked certain things. They're under the sink. I'm so sorry, Walker," she said.

I stared straight ahead until we reached one of the downstairs sitting rooms, which wasn't decorated in any "wedding day" finery. It was just another cigar-reeking, dank room in his mansion of horrors—all dark-wood framing, a large fireplace ablaze with flames, and deep-brown velvet couches.

The groom was pasty white because his skin rarely saw sunlight. He was obviously antsy. There he stood in front of a large picture window with light snow falling outside in the darkness. He was a cruel and dangerous man in his black tux now with a white bow tie. His hair was still slicked back to perfection. He had small hands like lobster claws and I imagined his fingers as jagged pinchers.

On his right hand was a thick gold band with an obnoxiously large diamond in it.

He took one look at me in my satin glory and a pointed tongue licked his lower lip.

"You are very skinny," he remarked.

The rest of the conversation was mentally muted because he never said there would be guests, but the overdone room was filled with strange faces. There were three men in business suits, two looked to be in their late sixties and the other was younger with a full head of reddish hair captured in a ponytail. And then there was Sheriff Pristine, who stood next to the bar sipping something from a small, crystal glass, the glints of which caught in the amber light.

Her long black hair fell in slabs around her muscular frame. She wore her official khaki-colored uniform with the gun in one pocket and what looked like some kind of stun device in the other.

"I kept the guest list down to my closest friends here," Edward boasted. Adding, "If it was not for Pristine, then this situation wouldn't have resolved itself so blessedly."

"A pleasure," said Pristine who twirled a gold band around her left ring finger. Obviously, she was tethered, too. Her glare toward me was not obvious. I wasn't sure why she had this instant dislike for me when it should have been the other way around. She was the reason why I was here today.

"Let's get this done," Edward said in a brisk voice.

My head began to throb. With one hand, I flicked some of my hair back. I had left my mane loose and unruly knowing he'd hate it that way.

A man stepped into the room in a dark suit, holding what looked like the Bible. He had one of those kindly faces that betrayed what exactly was about to happen.

"Good evening, I'm Minister Malone," he said, introducing himself with a lifted hand. I gazed at it. That was all because I certainly wasn't going to shake. I had no party manners.

"Edward was right," he remarked. "Lovely—and headstrong. She reminds me of your uncompromising late wife, Mr. Reid, although I'm sure with time, the inflexible will become flexible."

"Please take hands."

Edward grabbed my palm, holding it hard in his calloused, lumpy hand. I felt his fingers crushing mine. Still, I made sure that my skin felt formless, which made him press even harder. It was a test. Was I malleable? The answer was no. I wasn't clay. I was human. And boneless.

My quiet rebellion. Did it even matter anymore in this hopeless time?

My eyes were downcast when the ceremony began. I wore my heartbreak on my ashen face, remembering another time when I said actual vows to Daniel in that Central Park chapel with white benches. It was snowing outside, but inside it was warm and vibrant. On each bench sat several of the ghosts that haunted the park each night. At the altar, we fell to our knees with the centuries as our witnesses.

"I can't say in sickness and in health or for richer or poorer. Those things don't mean anything to us anymore," Daniel had said. *"I will promise to hold your hand when it needs holding."*

"I will smile at you first thing in the morning, every morning," I said.

"I will sit next to you forever," he said.

"I will love you at three in the morning when you can't sleep," I said.

"I will love you first, best, and last," he said.

"Now and forever."

5.

The tethering ceremony was akin to the traditional marriage vows, but with a few twists. Edward offered the ring first, a blackish-gray opaque stone with metallic luster. It was almost silver.

"It's a hematite stone, which is one of the main soul-transforming stones they mine for in The Other. It's very important," Minister Malone related. "This one helps transform negative energies into more positive vibrations."

Some gaudy rock was supposed to turn me into the good little wife.

In his dreams.

"It's time to bleed the bride," said Minister Malone.

This was new to me, and I stepped back, out of the circle of no trust. Pristine was right there, and gave the center of my back a slight shove forward.

They came at me from all sides.

The minister grabbed my hand and cut a diagonal line into the pad supporting my thumb. In most cases, I would have jumped at the sight of a knife, but he surprised me with a cut that was deep enough to draw dripping blood.

It didn't hurt.

In fact, my wide smile made the men uneasy. It wasn't blood lust on my mind, and certainly my sudden idiotic grin had nothing to do with this farce.

The reset was back.

6.

My stomach churned when he cut an opposite diagonal on Edward's hand. The big man winced, but that was short-lived due to appearances. He smiled when the minister put our hands together. "You form the perfect X in blood," Minister Todd said. "Two distinct pillars of support. Perhaps the couple would like to say their own vows?" he suggested. "We will start with the bride."

I wasn't much of an on-the-fly speech maker, but I did have something to say about current events. Before my words, I would do things that proved unnerving. I started by staring so hard into Edward's eyes that he rocked back in his shoes.

And then I spoke.

"Why do you even want me? You don't even like me. In fact, it was hate at first sight."

"Your spirit excites my demons," Edward replied.

"That was lovely," said Minister Malone who quickly added, "Do you, Edward Reid, tether to Walker Callaghan?"

"I do," Edward snapped.

"Do you Walker Callaghan . . . in good times and perilous ones...in death and all the levels that come after—"

"Get on with it," Edward interrupted. "This isn't *Romeo and Juliet*."

"It's not even *Outlander*," I said in my most wiseass tone.

"Do you Walker Callaghan—"

I opened my mouth to say no.

"You are officially tethered," said Minister Malone.

Edward's upper lip curled in a way that morally superior creatures perfect over the years. He was a paper champion gloating over his faux victory.

7.

What followed was Edward yanking me toward the fireplace for a quick and highly confidential marital confab.

"So, you will cooperate," he posed. "At least, lie to me and say that you will."

"It's no hassle in the castle, Eddie," I replied.

We both knew I was full of the deepest kind of shit. He refused to shovel it tonight.

"You'll get to a place of peace and acceptance—or you won't," Edward hissed under his breath while maintaining his movie-star smile for the guests who came floating in the front doors.

"If you say no to me ever—about anything—I'll extinguish you and everyone you ever loved," he vowed. "I'll wipe you out. For good. Don't think I'll spare my own. I'll kill the girls and Pete. I'll do it for sport. I'll save Daniel for last. Killing is too good for him. And then I will have my friends down below deal with your mother."

I nodded. With just a hint of a bottom-lip tremble.

The latter wasn't acting.

There is one more thing," Edward said, shoving me hard toward the middle of the room. Wealthy, older people were happily swilling champagne and shoving their faces with hors d'oeuvres from the kitchen. Waiters in tuxes passed around the shrimp puff and steak bites while others kept the crystal glasses filled to the brim.

"It's time for the toast," Edward said. The corners of his mouth curled into a winner's smile.

I lifted a glass full of bubbly gold fluid that he jammed into my hand. And then I interrupted him.

I learned long ago to never trust Edward Reid with anything you valued, especially your dignity. In this particular matter, it meant a few sparring words as the teenage bride gave the toast.

"Cheers to the people who love us," I said, proudly. "To a special man."

I lifted my glass. "The one who taught me how to love, but not how to stop. I will never stop loving him."

The guests happily lifted their glasses because they thought I was talking about Edward, who knew that my toast was to Daniel.

"Please follow the lit path for dinner in the dining room," Edward said, clasping my hand in a bloodless grip. "Walker and I will be retiring to our quarters, but first we bid you good night."

They went left in the direction of the massive feast and why not? I was on the newlywed deprivation diet, meaning he could dress me up, take me in public, but he couldn't exactly trust me. It's why Edward dragged me to the right with my now-bruised arm. We made our way, the unhappy couple, through the slick marble entryway of the house. One of us took powerful steps while the other was ice-skating across polished floors, dragged her heels in tipped stilettos.

His head guard led the way, oblivious to my . . . well, I couldn't say pain because once again, the reset was working fine and I felt nothing out of the ordinary except humiliation, dread, and the fear of being raped repeatedly, night after night, by Daniel's father.

Unsatisfied by gripping my arm and yanking, Edward snaked his right hand into my mass of hair. Bitty had advised wearing it in a bun— and finally I figured out why.

"If you want to be treated like a pack mule," he fumed under his breath, "then I will grab you by your reigns."

And it's exactly what he did, yanking and dragging me up the bottom stairs, a handful of hair coming out in his hand causing me to almost fall forward. He made up for it by digging deeper until his fingernails were embedded in my scalp. With each stair, he physically lifted me— sometimes by the hair, other times by my left ear, which I swear would rip off.

"It's like leading a horse who thinks she can't be broken. How does one do that? You grab her by the mane. You beat her. You break her. You train her to be ridden . . . no matter how long it takes. You do it until it takes and she just gives in.

"I've been married before," he fumed.

"And she probably preferred death than to be married to you," I shouted.

The air trembled for a moment. And then with his left hand, he cracked me across the face, which made me tumble backward, cascading down all of the stairs until I was back on that hard marble foyer floor.

"Get her," Edward shouted to the guard, who did just that. In my momentary confusion of hitting my head on the hard marble floor, I was dazed enough for him to lift me like a sack of potatoes, toss me over his massive shoulder, and then make the way back upstairs to the honeymoon suite. It was the top floor, which I had yet to explore. From my vantage point now, I could see that there were no guards up here. There was nothing except brown double doors at the end of the hallway.

It was his room.

"As you can see, the bride is a bit anxious about the wedding night. To make her feel more comfortable, no matter what you hear . . . no matter how loud the screaming, do not disturb us under any circumstances until ten tomorrow morning.

"Do you understand me?" Edward demanded. "No matter what you hear – or how loudly you hear it – you will not approach this floor."

"At ten a.m. promptly, we'll have our eggs delivered. Poached with toast—or do you prefer scrambled?" asked his flunkie.

Was he asking me for my breakfast order?

The guard put me down with a thud on thick black carpeting.

"Eggs all around," he said to the guard who nodded and quickly turned on his heel to go back downstairs.

No one wanted any part of this part. They would, as usual, ignore the screams.

"Move," Edward thundered, hooking his hands under my armpits and dragging me to my feet.

8.

His bedroom was the size of a small gymnasium, but divided into sections: A desk area for working. A large closet area for dressing. A bathroom for those needs, plus showering. And there was the bed in the middle of the room. It was surrounded by low burning floor lights as if his place of slumber was some exquisite art exhibit.

Oddly, there was a vase of black roses by the California king, which was covered with a thick white comforter. Garish piles of rose petals were strewn over the bed like this was some romantic fantasy instead of a horror show. On the other nightstand was a big ice bucket and a large bottle of champagne. Other amber-colored fluids were waiting on a nearby table, which also had a tasteful fruit platter.

Rape and snacks. Edward had thought of everything.

My legs felt like they would buckle as we stood in the entranceway. My stomach lurched as Edward not only closed the door, but bolted it on top, locking it with a small key he placed back in his tux pants pocket. He pointed toward what I assumed was some sort of changing or bathroom area.

There would be no chitchat. He was ready.

"You have ten minutes to make yourself presentable," he said. "There is a closet just beyond the bathroom where your new things—beautiful things—are now located. You can thank me later for my generosity."

"Go to hell," I hissed.

He just stared at me like a boss who was giving out orders to some uncooperative underling.

"You will wear the white negligee, so we can all pretend that you're some kind of virgin, which I know you're not because you've been slutting all over the afterlife and the past with my son. And I left a bottle of Creed White Flowers perfume. It was my late wife's favorite. Don't douse yourself with it. Just a bit behind your ears. And thighs. Oh, and I prefer red lipstick."

"Behind my ears. Or thighs?"

"On your lying lips," Edward said, calmly. I prided myself on being able to keep eye contact with him, which is why I didn't see his fist, which he barreled directly into my stomach. Air rushed out of my lungs as I folded in the middle, breathless, but as the reset kicked back in, I forced myself to fall lightly on my knees. I made myself cough wildly.

I didn't feel one damn thing.

"The bathroom is to the right," he said. "Don't make me wait."

I made a slow show out of standing up ever so slowly, unfurling myself inch by inch as I feigned great pain at the center. I took those first painstakingly tiny steps and soon I was standing on the opulent white marble floor of that fancy bathroom. First things first: the lock had been removed from the door.

I spun around. All I needed was a window now, but to my horror there was none in this room of two sinks, an enormous shower, and a toilet.

At least there was a radio. It was time to test his theory about the guards ignoring any sounds coming from the upstairs bedroom on the top floor. I found a great Pearl Jam song and cranked it up to ten.

Life is always better when you turn up the music.

I waited a minute. Edward finally entered the bathroom, yanked the radio from the wall and slammed the door behind him.

"If you want to start on the cold tile floor, you can stay in there and I can join you," he bellowed from outside the door.

Inside the closet, the short red, white, and black nighties hung from a wooden rod. They were the cheap, slutty kind that had more lace and straps than actual material. I had no choice but to twist and turn as I navigated the zipper of the wedding gown until it finally gave and then I viciously ripped the rest of it off my body, delighted as material shredded in my hands. I tossed the remains in to the tub, smiling as the water rendered it useless.

I stood naked in Edward Reid's bedroom. It was freezing in here and I longed for a robe or anything that would cover everything. There were only the nighties.

Forget my bravado.

This was inevitable.

At the sink, I brushed my hair as fat tears fell into the porcelain bowl. My hand shook as I tried to slather my lips in fire red. I couldn't find the damn perfume, which for some reason made me cry harder.

At the mirror, I looked into my own eyes and they were dead.

How would I ever survive this . . . how would Daniel? I don't know when I picked up the brush again, but I did and I worked it convulsively through my hair. Tears fell with every stroke.

Daniel.

Dad.

Dr. King.

Cass.

There would be no last-minute save.

"Don't forget the shoes," he bellowed from the other room. They were on the floor of the closet and in my current state of panic, I would have missed them if he hadn't reminded me. White kitten-heel slippers with fur and feathers on them. This is what it took to twist his knob. He had Bitty leave them for me, and when I looked down again, I saw it wasn't all that she left.

Next to them was the bag. Nestle inside were my last pair of shit kicking boots.

I would wear them now. Because he would hate it.

I'd wear them with his disgusting little hooker outfit.

If he was to have me, he would have all of me . . . down to my favorite shit-stompers.

Dr. King had given me these boots before we left on our mission and the black leather was still perfect and formfitting. It was my only familiar thing in this room, which is why I ran my fingers lovingly over every inch of them. *My babies.* They felt glorious. Familiar. My fingers slid along the side of the right boot in order to feel something that was normal. That was strong.

God help me. That same something was cutting into my skin.

Was that my blood dripping ever so slowly and brightly onto the fine marble floor?

I still didn't feel pain, but my hand returned wet, a pool of darkening fluid collecting in my palm and racing to my wrist.

"What the hell? How could I cut myself on smooth leather? It must have been one of the embellishments."

I yanked off the one boot and examined it closely. In the rush of leaving the cabin and after what happened with the hunters and immigration, I hadn't really taken the time to look at the new boots. *Really look.*

There was one quarter-sized stud on the outer sides of each one—a strange nod to cowboy culture style from Dr. King, a man who wore serious black pants and nondescript sweaters almost every single day.

Sadly, the embellishment on the right boot was ready to fall off. Instead of losing it, or a finger, I tugged gently until I was holding it in my hand. It sparkled in the bathroom—glints of hope bouncing off jagged duel-spiked blades that ran a 360-degree course around the entire stud. I had never seen something so beautiful in my entire afterlife. And there were two of them because thankfully I had two feet.

Turns out, guns are not your friend because they can run out of bullets and jam. However, a circle of cold steel in the form of a lethal training star never lets you down.

"Walker!" Edward fumed from outside the door.

FOURTEEN

1.

Hand on the bathroom doorknob, I twisted until the white wood opened. And then I stepped back into the outer room.

I wasn't the first woman to pray for wings to just fly away. I mouthed a silent oath.

"Are you talking to yourself?" he boomed, downing his drink. "Come closer, so I can see you."

I wasn't the first woman to want to evaporate in place.

There I stood in a short white nightgown with lace over the breasts, slut-red lipstick smeared on my ashen-white Irish face. I did accessorize. There were two hidden, small throwing stars carefully tucked into a fisted palm.

I had two additional things to offer my "groom": a dirty boot on each foot, both sporting a tiny hole on the side.

He was waiting by another fireplace that some minion set up with crackling white logs spewing tiny blue sparks. The Vegas of it all made me throw up in my mouth. He wore red silk poured over his being from neck to knees. He looked like a dictator of some small country donning ceremonial robes.

He was certainly excited to see me. I knew because he purposely didn't tie the robe, which caused revulsion on my end.

He had an amber glass of fluid in one hand over a small brick of ice. He downed the liquid in one gulp and allowed the glass to slip out of his hand because things were expendable to him and everything was a thing in his world. It bounced but didn't break when it made contact with an inlaid-wood end table. My nerves in overdrive, it sounded like a small bomb exploding.

He was not pleased with my . . . anything.

"Take off those boots immediately. You look like trailer park trash."

My feet firmly in place, I rejected his offer.

Disobedience was never high on his list, which was evident because he moved closer to look me hard in the eyes.

He took a finger to slip one of the tiny straps off my shoulders. When Edward Reid pressed his cold lips to my own and invaded my mouth with his tongue, I froze in place, not moving, not feeling, not reacting . . . it just would not do.

He tasted like old cigarettes and revenge.

Finally, twisting his lips away, he shoved me backward toward the bed.

"Your will is so strong, it's like you're staring at me in Caps Lock," he said.

Another shove.

The bed was about three feet away. I continued to stare hard, but this time my eyes were downcast monitoring his growing lust.

"I waited for this moment for a long time," he boasted. "Just because I deplore you doesn't mean I don't want you. And as for my son, think of this as an upgrade."

No answer was an answer.

I would not react. Not now.

Not ever.

2.

"Take those hideous boots off. I will not tell you again," he said when finally stopped. We were here. The side of the bed was a stopping point and the hard mattress grazed my satin-covered backside. It was one of those super tall beds where you practically had to jump into it. He attempted to shove me back into it, but I just bounced off.

He went to Plan B.

"But first, this . . . ," he said, sliding both straps off until the lace almost evaporated and the bodice of my dress fell, fully exposing my breasts.

He shook his head because he was instantly disappointed.

"Small," he said. "But you'll do."

He leaned forward until his wet mouth was on my shoulder. Sinking his teeth into my flesh, he bit me. Some might call it a love nip, but it was enough to almost draw blood." I felt it, but the reset kicked in and the teeth mark and fluid were instantly gone.

He watched the entire process. Edward knew about the reset. He was fascinated by it. And he wanted to test me.

He bit me again. In the same spot.

It disappeared.

His fist was small, but lethal, and when it connected with my jaw, I staggered backward. He hit me so hard that it should have been broken, but the bones mended.

He allowed me to slip out of his hands and stagger back a foot or two. Somewhere in his deranged mind, he voted himself the early winner. And I couldn't deny the logic of it. My body didn't ache, but my mind was yowling.

He was stronger and faster and motivated. People took over countries with far less in their war chests. All he wanted to take was a seventeen-year-old girl who was standing almost naked in his bedroom.

It caught him off-guard when I did a slow twirl. He must have thought he had corralled me into doing to do a little striptease show, an activity he obviously enjoyed, and on the menu with his girlfriends.

It was humiliating, but I allowed the entire gown to slip to the floor, but spin in fast circles again and again so he had to strain to beyond my long hair that acted like a shield.

I spun halfway across the room, which excited and unnerved him. When I got closer to the bed again, I stopped. He was excited when I bent all the way over to remove one of the boots.

"Move that mop of hair. In fact, I'm going to get scissors and cut most of it off, if you don't," he warned.

When I sat down in a low leather chair, he smiled. It sickened me to remove half of my hair so my right breast was exposed, but it was the only way.

I put up my index finger. Waiting was sexy—and he was slipping into a hazy state.

Carefully, I grabbed the other boot from the side and slowly slid it off my left foot.

My eyes never left his.

Quickly, he shoved his own robe away until it pooled at his feet. Edward was completely naked. His excitement punctuated the air.

One of my hands remained fisted.

In his sudden lust haze, he didn't notice. Until he did. "Don't ever think of punching me. And if you ever strike me, it will be the last thing you *ever* do," he warned.

He couldn't be sure I wouldn't do it.

So, he would strike first.

Edward was a small tornado. He jettisoned across the room, grabbed me by my bottom lip and ripped me to my feet, letting go of my flesh just long enough to slam me hard into the wall.

"Where's the piss and vinegar now?" he taunted as I bounced, but was still standing. "You're not so full of yourself when you're naked and alone."

Only one thing raced through my mind when my back hit the hard oak of that door. Hell, yes, I was naked. I was alone. I was scared shitless. But I had me. It was always enough.

I uncurled my hand.

"Just go stand by the bed. I'll join you," I begged.

He enjoyed gut-wrenching pleading.

"Let's not make this worse than it has to be. Please," I cajoled.

"No more games or you'll be dissected in my laboratory by morning," Edward warned. "I'll send you back to my son in pieces."

"No games. Just the truth," I promised. "You will have the real me—all of Walker Callaghan—in just a second."

3.

Edward stood proudly by the side of the bed, facing me. King of the world. Ready for his conquest.

I rotated my wrist. Something fell to the floor with the tiny but explosive ting of metal hitting wood.

No, God, no! I dropped one and there were only two stars.

"What do you have in your . . . ," he began. The word "hand" melted into the air.

One shot. One chance. I aimed, flicking my wrist so hard I thought it would shatter.

Random thoughts: we learned in sex ed once that the average penis head has four thousand nerve endings in the tip and that's exactly where the star cut through tender skin and embedded.

The blood didn't pour. It erupted in a volcano of carnage and rage.

In the silence of his rape room, he was the one whose screams shook his entire body and perhaps the entire realm.

4.

Edward fell to his quaking knees, body contorting right and left, fists clenched, like he was having a seizure. Between animalistic, high-pitched sobs emitted from a face as white as chalk, he began to choke, bubbling foam pouring out of his mouth as the great one convulsed on the floor.

"I . . . will . . . kill . . . you," he agonized as if each word required his last breath

Just in case there were any guards, I screamed out, "Edward! Edward, stop! Stop!"

I knew if they heard a female voice during the commotion, it would swing the story. They had probably been through many of those nights with Edward and his younger conquests. I heard loud laughter from down below followed by music. He hired a band.

As predicated, no one came to the door.

He told them that under no circumstances should we be disturbed.

But just to be sure, I looked for a cloth to stuff into his mouth. I couldn't allow him to yell that loudly again and as my brain scrambled to find ways to mute him, I grabbed the red silk tie to his robe. For once, he did me a favor.

Edward Reid—a man without a reset—passed out cold.

With shaking hands and my own blood frosted in rage and adrenaline, I grabbed the white nightie and somehow lifted it over my neck, never noticing that it was inside out. I couldn't run in it; I'd freeze. Inside his closet, I found a sweatshirt and a pair of matching pants, but they were huge and would fall off. It was the sweatshirt over the nightgown. There was no other choice.

Those beautiful weaponized boots managed to find the right feet and my numb toes slid into them like my legs were made of water.

My eyes drifted toward French doors that led to the third story terrace.

I had one choice: do it now or stand here and cry every tear that had been inside of me since the day I was born.

Sometimes, there is no third option.

5.

The French doors weren't locked. Why would they be? He was a chain smoker. In fact, Bitty had opened it just a bit to allow air to flow into the staleness of his old cigarettes and cigars.

Swinging the wooden, slatted barriers fully open, I said a silent prayer of relief. It was a large opening and I stood in it with the wind ripping through my being. Was I in my right mind? Hopefully not for this sort of swan dive. A certain amount of crazy was necessary when you're about to jump six stories onto a concrete driveway.

Almost every other phobia on the planet is based on the fear of death. Instinctively, we go for self-preservation. We want to live. That's why, given no other choice, we roll away from that moving car, we race from the fire and . . . we jump.

I landed hard on the roof of one of his Chevy Escalades, which was now deeply dented as were my bones and other organs. That reset kicked in a blink later and I found my feet as the fresh snow crunched underneath them. Fully operational, although not dressed for the elements, I ran at one speed.

Blazing.

I ran for my life because movement is life.

I ran for my existence.

6.

The expansive backyard was covered in a fresh seven or eight inches of the kind of wet snow that felt like quicksand as I tried to trudge through it.

All you need to do, my mind screamed, *is make it across a football-field-sized lawn and get lost in the woods. You know the woods. The woods know you. The trees are your compadres. Your true friends. The deep forest is your home.*

Ahead was true wilderness in the form of snowcapped gray-black skyscraper mountains. A question remained: Once I reached the edge of the House of Edward, then what?

I felt the icy wind blowing against my naked skin. I was wearing nothing from the hem of the nightgown, which was just below my business to the top of the boots.

My past living in Chicago made me a bit of a weather expert as all cold weather mammals have their interior thermostat. It was Antarctica cold with temperatures around ten degrees with wind chills that would soon feel like thirty below. If the reset became spotty again then hypothermia would set in.

I wouldn't have hours. I would have minutes.

In a wild panic, my feet pounded hard, disbelief carrying me, gusts of Mother Nature's wrath lifting my feet at points until I felt as if I might just fly away.

Winter is not why I stopped in my tracks. I swore I heard their names in that unrelenting wind.

Bitty.

Chris Flicker.

The newly fused Matilda and Molly.

Earlier today, as a subject changer, Bitty told me that the basement had mostly been cleared. The only current Specimens (along with herself) were Flick and Molly/Matilda. That's what he called them; that's the name he buried them under when he was done. Specimen #1, Specimen #2, Specimen #3 . . . as if they were just worthless pieces of nothing.

She had also informed me that Edward gave all but a few necessary cooks, maids, and servers the night off for the wedding festivities and that big dinner that we had skipped. The Specimens were locked in cages like rejects at a dog shelter. The guards were most certainly drunk and in their rooms by now.

But what about tomorrow for the Specimens? Edward's scientists would be back at it. Draining them, operating on their parts, stealing their DNA, and collecting their blood. When it became too much they were dumped into the cold ground, empty shells with unmarked graves.

I could leave now and take my chances of survival in the mountains. Of course, there was an alternative. Shit. Wasn't there always?

I could go.

Back.

7.

I took three steps in the direction of the woods. It was beginning to snow hard again. No one would blame me. No one would ever question it.

He would hurt me bad this time, as badly as I hurt him—and probably worse. He would make me feel every single pain. He would cut things off of me. And then he would do it all over again. And then I would be in the ground. Prized Specimen #5. Someday, he would lead his oldest son to my grave and laugh.

His voice filled my ears.

"Embrace the vole," Daniel had once said. It meant to risk everything in hopes of great rewards. But not this . . . certainly not this. He would never expect me to take a chance with my very existence.

My feet pivoted on a slick piece of ice. Was it fate that turned me around or words embedded in the wind? I would never know.

Free a few from a lab of human specimens in the middle of an arctic storm?

What the hell? The cold never bothered me anyway.

8.

There was a nurse behind the counter about ten steps from the door. She was my first line of resistance. She was a large woman who stood suddenly from the chair where she was dozing off in front of a *Sex and the City* episode. It was the one where Mr. Big gets engaged to someone who is not Carrie. My hair was wild enough that for a split second I swore she thought I was Carrie come to life.

"Is this the local Hilton?" I asked.

"What?" she replied in a confused voice.

She snapped to it quickly, possibly recognized me, and gave me a murderous look. Poor Anna – per her nametag -- not only missed her wedding invite, adding to her woes was a teenage girl advancing toward the desk as if I broke the force field between peon and authority figure.

Who was in charge here? I didn't get the memo. Instead, I locked

Anna's arms behind her and waited for her to kick with one of her legs. And when she did, I used her lack of balance to haul her into what looked like a messy back-breaking bend.

The last part was the most brutal.

I imagined each of my fingers to be knives, and dug each digit into her throat. She hit the ground from a lack of oxygen in record time. She wouldn't wake for a long time unless she had a reset. I waited one minute, two. No such luck, bitch.

A big keychain was in her pocket. I smiled when I saw the numbers taped to each key. She was organized and had a sheet right in front of her identifying who was who among the specimens tonight.

Cell #1 opened with a hard click.

"What took you so long, buttercup," Flick said with a big smile. "I had already projected three versions of your future tonight on this wall and I knew that bastard wouldn't 'have' you . . . and I knew you would be saving my sorry freak ass. "I'm sorry about the other day."

"Forgiven. And Flick," I interrupted him with a hug, "less talking. More moving."

"Right, chief," he said, his eyes scrambling while putting a thin blue blanket over my shoulders.

Cell #2 was empty. Bitty was in a chair in the main area being drained and I leaned down and said into her ear, "Wanna go on a field trip?"

She ripped out her IV and I handed her a wad of gauze to stop the bleeding.

"Spectacular," she replied with a big smile.

"Are you strong enough to walk?" I asked her.

"I could crawl. Anything to blow this place," she said.

Cell #3 was also empty, but not really. "Matilda, I can't see you, honey" I said. "But I feel you. You have to come with us, angel."

I felt small invisible fingers slip into my own.

Flick punched out the guard who was doing his rounds. He fell with a thud, but his partner was more agile. I grabbed a loaded syringe off a tray and stabbed him in the heart with it.

"Sweet," Flick said. "But how are you, really, Walker?"

"Pissed," I said. His eyes caressed my tear-streaked face.

"Oh, dragonfly," he said with great remorse.

"Not now," I said. "If you pity me, I swear, I will rip your head off."

"Let's go," Flick said. "The house is stirring. Edward has regained consciousness and is crawling toward his desk phone. We must leave this place."

The three visible ones of us, plus one, blasted out of the basement door. I was lucky to run like crazy by their sides until I could take the lead. I followed my past prints and we made it across that expansive lawn with invisible Matilda making small snow prints in her wake, so we knew she was there.

As the house got smaller, it was every person for herself. The kid was much faster than any of us as she raced for the mature fir trees and giant sentinels that were at least two hundred and fifty feet high.

"Split up," I said. "Regroup later. Run hard. Survive."

9.

Somewhere along the way, I noticed that my skin was bright red. I still had the sweatshirt, but little else in terms of clothing. With nothing to weigh me down, I flew through the trees like any other forest creature.

Under that big, black sky, I pounded. A mantra floated through my mind: *Go forward. Do not stop.*

Yes, you might get caught. But not easily.

Do not go gentle.

10.

Where were the others? Did it even matter? I swore I saw Mr. Jack Mongan, teacher extraordinaire of sophomore English, explaining strange vocabulary words I would never need . . . until now. "Are you a solivagant, Miss Callaghan?" he asked me.

The fact that he stumped me was written on the blank slate otherwise known as my face. "A solitary wanderer," he explained.

Yes. Yes, I was. And that fact made me sad.

He asked me if I had words to share with him.

Shit. What was it with teachers putting you on the spot at the worst possible moments?

"The universe always falls in love with a stubborn heart," I blurted, because I once wrote that when covering a story about a girl in our class who had stage four cancer for seven years and refused to leave the planet.

Translation: No one is going to save you. You not only have to save yourself. You have to actually believe that it is possible because then it is probable. The universe just works that way.

PART II

FIFTEEN

1.

My bleary eyes saw only a primitive world with no shelter, no food, no light. I had virtually no clothes. No underwear. No socks. My head was hatless. My ears. My feet. My hands. I couldn't feel them anymore and my fingers had turned a color that was cobalt black. They were so cold, I felt like I could snap them off, digit by digit.

Maybe this is what it really felt like to be dead. You lost pieces of you until the you of the past was annihilated.

No one was following me, so I could stop. Catch my breath. Hide behind a tree. No, they would find me. And by "they," I was sure that Edward had been found and sent out his guards. They had snowmobiles, which is why I tried to walk through dense brush where they couldn't drive them. Was that the sound of a motorized engine?

I found what looked like a small crater in the ground and used the last remnants of my strength to bury myself alive in forgotten leaves and discarded sticks. Even Ma Nature threw out the trash.

Inside my little cocoon, I felt heady from the cold and a lack of oxygen.

But I could . . .

Dream of a puffer-coat parka. A thick red woolen scarf. Gloves so thick they were like little homes. No, mittens. Cocoa hot enough to burn your lips. Daniel close enough to blow the steam from the top of my mug.

My eyes began to droop.

Reset, gone again.

Hypothermia. So be it.

The shivering had long since stopped. My nose felt like it was made out of wood. My cheeks were solid. Like someone poured cement inside the skin and let it dry. My knees refused to quake. My legs felt like they were made out of stone. I was winding down.

I would freeze solid.

In the woods.

At least I'd be going-going-gone on my own terms.

If there was a better way to go, I wasn't sure what it . . .

Was.

What was I talking about? And where was I going? Up the coast? Down the shore? To the road? What was it that people said when they were leaving, maybe forever . . . I'll meet you up the road. Did roads go up or down—and why the hell did anyone debate this kind of thing when there were so many more lively discussions to be had?

The winds sliced at the top of my head like small swords loping off their chunks. I would not close my eyes even though snow in my lashes had made the lids a heavy burden.

Would I ever see another sunrise? Probably not, but I had witnessed my fair share. Once more for all time, I stared way up into a black night sky with no moon or stars. Here was the world. Beautiful and terrible things happened in it.

The horrid was looming. I wasn't resting.

I was expiring.

Next lifetime, I vowed:
Less talking, more listening.
Less planning, more doing.
Less chocolate, more kale.
Less bitching, more gratitude.
Less wondering, more Belief with the big *B*.
Less lists, more living.

2.

Was it five minutes later? Or five eons? Infinity being relative and all that stuff that was fun to debate with science types and Star Trek geeks, and I say the g-word with great respect.

I heard my booted feet runching over freshly fallen snow. Somehow, I had crawled out of my hole. Yes, they were my tired limbs, suddenly moving again in this soundless world. The old trees refused to even make a whisper.

I walked even though I still couldn't feel many parts. For hours. Until there were mystic lights above that made the sky look a deep purple with pink streaks running through it.

It was almost dawn.

I stopped for a moment to make sure that I wasn't running in circles. My clue was the timber and greenery. Even in the lightening darkness, I could see the side of the trees with the sparse amount of leaves. Trees are naturally lopsided and the side with more branches and leaves always pointed south. Sparse leaves meant the western side.

Thrust forward. Push on.

As I limped along, I thought about Daniel.

"Why the long face, baby?" he would ask, running hands up my bare arms. "It's not good for the world, you know."

"The world doesn't care about me," I'd say.

"You are the reason I smile. I breathe. I love. I can be," he once said.

My lover wrapped his arms around me and I buried my face in his strong chest.

"Really?" I spoke into his flannel shirt.

"Really," he spoke into my soul.

3.

Dawn.

I drove forward into a sky that was the most dazzling coral peach. It was an arctic winter light and it looked otherworldly. As the sun rose, I found the gentle pastels of soft pink and yellow blazing across the ice and snow.

Just one more step. Then, I would take a break.

Random weird thoughts when you're at complete exhaustion:

"Everything the light touches is our kingdom."

Now, I was really losing my marbles. I was either quoting Shakespeare or *The Lion King* with smart money on the second one. Wherefore art thou, Simba?

I felt the first splash. Son of a . . . not again! I was walking on a frozen river until I hit the exact spot where the ice was thin. The splash was loud and obnoxious and I didn't even bother holding my breath. What was the point?

I fell face first into a deep freeze, cartwheeling several times until up was down and down was up and limbs much bigger than me were plundering overhead.

"Getchu," he said.

4.

I was cocooned.

Tucked tightly in blankets and then covered by a thick external shell that looked like a partially shredded purple sleeping bag. A woven winter skullcap was pulled low over my eyebrows. My eyes were blurred and I was on fire, sweat pouring from my temples.

One blink. Two. I lifted my head ever so slightly.

Maybe blurred was better.

It was ceremonial in a way that was almost beautiful. There were candles, hundreds of them, misshapen, and each lit by a single flame dancing in some kind of imaginary breeze. Above me, rock. Below me, rock. Sideways, the walls were made out of some kind of stone shooting thirty feet straight up. It was a shelter of some sort carved into sediment.

When I looked way up in this cave, I found that it made my neck hurt. What I'd soon learn was that the corridors were two hundred feet long, often thirty feet wide, filled with deep, winding gorges and recesses or other shelter rooms.

In this particular rock room, there was a circle of gray stones in the corner with thick slabs of hickory-smelling wood, a delicious smell, creating a crackling fire. A spit hovered above it and a big black pot suspended from it. Whatever was bubbling on the inside was making my stomach do gymnastics from hunger.

I always had a slight case of claustrophobia, so the idea of my body encased in bedrock left me feeling a bit lightheaded. I couldn't even think the c-word or I'd have some sort of panic attack, but the truth was undeniable. Somehow and some way, I had either transported myself or I had been taken into the recesses of this cavern.

Maybe I had spiked a fever and was delusional, but when I listened hard, I swore I heard something that was definitely alive and making a growling sound.

Maybe it wasn't growling. Maybe it was purring.

Yes, that was it.

Fingers that weren't my own touched my forehead. Something moved me a few inches to the right and then it curled around me like we were spooning. I heard it make other sounds that I couldn't easily identify.

A wild panic came from deep within the center of my terrified soul and curdled in my throat. My entire body shook in horror as my own monster sound—desperate, ear splitting, and full-throttle hysterical screaming—reverbed along the rock walls.

It screamed back.

5.

He had a shriek that caused the kind of vibration that made my teeth chatter. It was like he swallowed an ambulance siren and the sound coming out of him was that type of shrill mixed with an animalistic yowl. He had already dislodged and since he was standing now beyond the top of my head, I couldn't see a thing. All of a sudden, I was pushed upright into a sitting position, my cap plunked off my head.

He was unwrapping me.

First, the sleeping bag fell to the floor and then the blankets were unraveled until all but the last one rested in a pile on the jagged floor.

I did a quick inventory. Five fingers on one hand, check. Five on the other and none were black blue. The reset must have fixed the frostbite. Toes, fine. Ten in total. My hair was long, wild, tangled with dirt and a few branches within it. I found that my nightgown was gone and replaced by a checkered fleece shirt, down vest, and some kind of blue jeans that felt way too big. *Something had undressed me . . . and then dressed me again.*

I tried standing and my legs worked, but my pants went south, pooling at my ankles.

There was no time to be self-conscious as I stood in my new wool socks that went from my toes up to my knee caps.

Whatever was in here with me was still here. I darted around in a circle and didn't see it, but I still heard whatever was probably about to eat me. It was breathing hard.

"Hiya," it said in a deep voice.

6.

He looked like a cross between a bear and a man. A few blinks later and I clutched my fist tight knowing there was no way I could physically fight him. He was a Gigantor at approximately seven foot five, a mountainous being who was the size of a grain elevator. But, he wasn't a creature. He was . . . human with an abnormal amount of hair growth all over his face and body. I studied this in biology class. It was a rare condition known as congenital hypertrichosis. *Why did I remember the damndest things at the damndest times?*

All I could do was go stealth because the quieter you become the more you can figure out. Unfortunately, my body had another plan.

I took a frantic step backward. He took a fearful step backward.

My eyes went wide. His eyes went wider.

I hid my face in my hands. He covered his face with hairy fingers. When I scratched the back of my head with one hand, he used two.

His eyes were a dull black brown, but inside had their own sparkle. There was some kind of exuberance about him . . . her . . . him, I think.

Him. For sure.

When I flipped my long hair forward, he approached.

And he spoke in a guttural way of hard syllables.

"Wat doin? Wat doin?" he kept repeating and I finally translated.

"What am I doing?" I said. "Well, I'm trying not to piss my pants."

"Pis pans," he tried to repeat.

"Very good start," I said. "Next, we'll do my top ten swear words starting with holy shit burgers."

"Holey shit," he repeated, grinning. Then he reached out one of those long arms that weren't only hairy by DNA. He was wearing some kind of elaborately sewn long coat made out of animal skins.

"Frens?" he asked nervously, patting the top of my head. His hand shook in fear.

I just hoped my head would still be attached to my neck when this moment of bonding was over.

"I mean, not the kind of friends who have known each other forever and send texts and pictures, but the kind of friends who meet under dire circumstances and are forced together out of survival needs. When this sort of thing happens," I said. "So, yes, friends."

I had lost my mind. Rambling probably meant I was going to be the other-other white meat.

Or maybe not.

He took one step. Then another. Closer.

Into the light.

"Frens," he repeated.

"Frens," I said as I reached out this time to touch the top of his hand.

7.

He was in possession of a baby face, albeit one that never shaved, so it was covered in patches of dark, overgrown hair. No grays. I aged him at about eighteen or nineteen with pale skin and onyx black long hair that was wildly pushed back by long, wide fingers.

He stepped closer and there was one reason—and a singular why—I didn't take off running.

When his full lips curved, I couldn't stop staring. It was the kind of sincere smile that stopped you in your tracks. I wanted to memorize it. Maybe it was the most hopeful smile I had ever seen.

There was such a sweet gentleness in those walnut-brown eyes that tears sprung to my own.

I finally realized that I had seen him the first night we arrived in The Other, right before we reached Dr. King's cabin hideaway. I found him hiding behind a tree. He had no shoes on that night or tonight, and maybe size fifteen feet that were covered in black fuzz on bluish skin. He looked like an actual bear with a human face, walking upright. It didn't help that he wore a big black coat covered in fur skins from past hunting expeditions. The feathers and fluff went from his neck all the way down to his ankles.

Daniel had seen him, too . . . once upon a time go.

I remembered his exact words and even now it made me smile: "Callaghan! What the f— . . ."

Before Daniel could go into testosterone, ultra-protective mode, I yelled out, "No, no, no . . . don't hurt him. He's . . . fine. I think. Maybe, I know."

But, I didn't. Still couldn't be sure.

That night upon our arrival, the Gigantor was frightened and made a dash into the trees, but didn't go far. I saw him standing on a rock with his face partially shadowed by a large pine. He held up a peace offering—all that he had. It was his own giant palm. He had crinkled his extremely long fingers, flexing each one at different times.

He was . . . waving? Maybe. I lifted a hand back then and waved wildly like a little kid. That time he nodded his head furiously up and down. He curled those enormous fingers until they were clenched and he was fist-pumping the sky.

"Walker," I yelled.

"Grrr," he growled. When I recoiled, his eagerness turned to show. Then it dawned on me. He wasn't snarling at me, but trying to actually say something.

"Grrrr . . . i . . . z," he enunciated. Then he darted away.

8.

I watched as he took a small pile of dead leaves and dried sticks from a corner and threw them into the fire, topping his creation with dried acorns that crackled and popped, shooting amber and yellow sparks into the air. Agile and fast on his feet, he was gone again, but returned in lightning speed. He was carrying something heavy, another black pot, and it had two large slabs of cracked ice sticking out of the top.

I was never much of a camper, so I was fascinated to watch as he took the ice pot and put it over the fire to melt it. Drinks. Why not? It's not like I could ask for a Dr. Pepper.

So what if his home wasn't a tasteful two-bedroom condo. I was done with luxury real estate. Caves were one of the oldest known places of human habitation. I remembered learning about them in science class when Mr. Woodberry told us that caves were actually the way to go out in the wild because you're avoiding the weather, plus oddly they have stable temperatures and naturally become warm in the winter and cool in the summer averaging about forty to sixty degrees. The only bad things: critters, lack of air, and collapse to name a few deathtraps.

Griz motioned with a large hand, encouraging me to come to him. I stood on shaking legs and took a few trusting steps toward the fire. He had taken the icy pot away from the flames, long chunks of freeze still sticking out, but the rest half melted.

"Yu wanna?" he asked.

He grabbed what looked like a coconut shell tied with a leather strip to a long stick. Gently, he lifted his makeshift cup to my dried lips. I cupped my hands around the sides of the shell and began to gulp the coldest, purest water I had ever tasted in my life. It was cold and delicious and I could have downed gallons of it. Some of it even spilled out of my lips onto his large feet.

Griz laughed.

"Gud," he said, pausing to dip again and then chug-a-lug with great abandon.

"Good . . . no, make that great," I said. "Thank you, Griz."

He was shocked that I remembered, but it pleased him. Maybe I was nuts, but I swore I saw his eyes mist like he might cry.

9.

I needed to thank him. I tried to make my face radiate the gratitude I felt for him bringing me here and saving my ass. I stuck out my hand to shake and he flew backward three large steps and cowered in the corner beyond the fire. I shrank inside.

Did he think I meant to hit him?

"No, Griz," I said in a soft voice. I forced a smile.

"Griz, good," I reminded him. "Walker, good."

He stood up, his head down, and took one step closer.

"Walker," I said, standing in place, but pointing to myself. I didn't want to frighten him again. I placed a hand on my chest. "My name is Walker.

"Me," I put the other hand over my heart. "Walker."

"Wa-WA-WAAAA!" he cried.

"Yes!" I said, clapping my hands. "That works!"

Almost in slow motion, I took off the down vest because I was warm again. Then, I rubbed my stomach area, my fingers slowly moving over that soft fleece.

He pointed toward the cook pot, which was indeed some kind of meat stew plus extras including carrots, celery, and root vegetables bubbling away.

"Yu wanna?" he asked me.

"Yes, Griz," I heard myself say. "I wanna. Yum. Yum."

He didn't know that word, but at least it didn't bother him. Slowly, I pulled a blanket off my makeshift bed and placed it on a smooth part of the floor.

"Sup," said Griz.

It was such a Midwestern term and I hadn't heard it in a long time. In the Midst, we called it dinner. In Illinois, where I was raised, we convened for supper at the end of the day. Dinner was steak or sushi. Supper was Thousand Island dressing and tuna noodle casserole.

God, how I wanted sup.

10.

He had several mismatched bowls, clean and waiting by a nearby stalagmite. They were wooden and probably hand carved by the chef himself. There was rudimentary silverware including small tree branches to stab your food. The oddest thing of all was the monogrammed coffee mugs with EXR on them.

Griz obviously went poaching for things. In the dark. I wondered how far away we were from the house of horrors, but figured it this way: Griz would be in that lab if Edward knew he existed. Therefore, we must have been far enough for him to remain safe.

He laughed when we both heard my empty stomach rumble.

"Ta-ka," he said, handing me some of that stew, which he scooped with a curved rock into another cleaned-out coconut shell.

"Thank you," I replied. And I'll never know why, but I accompanied my next grin with a double thumbs-up.

He was like a kid and put down his scooper to lift his large thumbs. I smiled and clapped, which made him happy. Clapping was good, real good.

He didn't eat with me on the blanket, but preferred a semi-dark corner, sliding his back down a rock wall until he occupied a big portion of the floor.

I did the same on the blanket and looked like an ant while his shadow from the candles made him look like the Incredible Hulk. I took the first bite and then . . . the hell with manners . . . shoveled in three more, vowing I would slow down.

"Gud?" he asked. Odd as it was, he ate gingerly without an ounce dripping from his lips. *Who had taught him inside manners?* He was almost refined.

"You just knocked it way out of the park and down the street," I said, laughing now. It was so good that I wanted to jump into that stew pot and eat my way out.

He looked confused, but my friendly-happy-crazy tone told him everything he needed to know.

"Gud, gud, gud, GUD!" I repeated, putting my bowl down to stand up and do a little happy dance. I had to keep one hand on the too-big jeans before they took a run for my ankles again.

He waited until the meal was over to offer "dessert," which came right out of his pocket. It was delightful the way he counted out ten fresh and sometimes smashed huckleberries for each one of us, the red juice staining both of our hands.

He licked his and then mine until they were clean. Well, maybe he wasn't *that* refined.

I devoured them.

I was nothing if not a gud guest.

11.

After dinner, he motioned for me to stand. I followed him around a jet-black corner and through a narrow passage where I didn't dare look up, but I heard them. It was a freaking cave, which meant the flapping wings just over our heads were bats. For some reason, they didn't swarm us as we finally made our way to a small opening in the rock. I smelled an evergreen-laced evening wind. A few steps later and we emerged into the deep woods where the sky was smoked with fog.

Griz pointed to one of about ten thousand trees.

Of course. It was time to do our business, which out here meant a little privacy in the form of the wide bark of a redwood. When I was done, I found him waiting by the hole in the cave. There was nothing else to do but go inside, pray the bats were sleeping, and eventually slip back into the cocoon of my makeshift bed.

Griz curled up in the corner, but left the candles burning as our nightlight. I forced a smile while trying not to think about enclosed spaces closing in on me. My head began to swim and before I went into panic-attack mode, I tried to fix it by remembering what my mother said about meeting new people: "Be safe. Be smart. Be humble."

I leaned forward and tried to talk to him, but it had to be basic.

"How did you find me?" I asked. Then I berated myself because it was too many words.

Quite impossibly, he understood every word.

He pointed to his nose and sniffed hard like he was sucking the air out of the room.

"Wow, thanks a lot. You *smelled* me."

I sat up and pretended to smell under my pits. It had been a long run through the woods and—wow—he actually had a point here. A sniff to the other pit made him burst into what could only be described as the giggles. He had a loud kind of laughter that was contagious.

"Smella . . . myyy . . . els," he said.

It took me a minute, but I took it phonetically.

"You can smell someone who is miles away?" I posed and he nodded hard. "How many miles?"

His communication skills were lacking, but his brain was sharp and someone had obviously schooled him in the basics.

He put up all ten fingers.

"Ten miles? He could smell from ten miles away. He shared that trait with my mother who could smell my messy room from just about the same distance.

He shook his head no.

Then he flashed all ten fingers and quickly eight more.

"Eighteen miles away?"

He nodded.

"What do I exactly smell like?" I had to ask.

He pointed to his big ol' feet.

"I stink, I get it," I said, laughing. "I smell like naked feet."

I had read somewhere that there were beings who could smell what the soles of your shoes were made of and if you smoked and what you smelled like naked. I would learn later that Griz had a sense of smell that was seven times stronger than a bloodhound.

It meant that if you entered his realm, he could smell you over distances measured in the double digits or miles. Why not? He lived in a place where smelling meant either a free meal or that you *were* the meal.

I reminded myself that this was the land of hunters and gatherers. I pegged him as a hunter and a bit of a scavenger, although I wouldn't know the half of that until the next day.

For now, he was a gatherer.

"Myn," he said, looking at me.

12.

Griz snored loudly, which wasn't unexpected. I kept replaying my situation starting with the EXR branding on my hip, the tethering, the freeing of Flicker and Bitty . . . and then being saved from freezing to death in the woods. I was safe for the moment, but the question remained: What now? And where were the others? And where was Daniel, Cass, Auggie, and Eddie?

The answers never come at 3:00 a.m. unless you're in a movie starring in your own video montage.

My own movie had no opening credits. It was Daniel on the beach in black jeans and a black tee wearing mirrored sunglasses. He hadn't shaved in days and it made him look darker and dangerous. I couldn't see his eyes, but he was holding out his hand. The surf roared in the background and why not? Our love had always been crazy, wild, and borderless. I ran to him, but when I got closer, he backed away until his back was level with high tide. He fell backward as the sea swallowed him whole.

There was nothing left but the foam.

It was cinematic in a way. If you liked hard endings.

I didn't like them. But, I lived them.

SIXTEEN

1.

The human bear woke before dawn. And he went to work like a whirling top, spinning, spinning, spinning.

The proof was a bright fire where filleted fresh salmon steaks were grilling in a large cast-iron fry pan. I wasn't sure what he used for spices, but the smell was so delicious that my mouth actually watered onto my hand.

What was next? Licking my chops?

He smashed oranges with his big palm, catching the juice in little glass jelly jars that were taken from places a bit more civilized. As a kid, I never liked the pulp. Now, I'd be happy to drill a hole in those oranges and suck out the juice myself.

Starvation has a way of making even the pickiest eater into a glutton.

There were fresh clothes left next to my bedroll. Where he acquired the glasses and the female clothing, let alone his own XXXL sweats and oversized Wham! T-shirt from the 1980s confounded me. Today, my "stylist" had chosen much smaller jeans, an actual black belt, plus a roomy black-ribbed turtleneck sweater and a partially ripped green parka. Tears filled my eyes. A pair of mismatched mittens—one red, the other black—were next to shoes in three sizes. I didn't need new shoes. My books were by my bed.

"Ta-ka," Griz said, pointing a finger at the new duds.

"Thank you," I said in a rush.

Griz beamed. I returned the sunshine.

"Tank you," he replied. "Picka the preta thins, Wa."

"Love the sweats, my man," I said. "Wide legs. George Michael. Very eighties chic."

I had no idea if he had any idea what I was saying. For once, I didn't care. He had a warm, safe vibe; I had a warm, safe vibe. Sometimes, it was all that was necessary.

2.

Griz crooked a finger indicating that I should follow him. It only took a minute or two before that first blast of sun-warmed cold air entered my being.

Outside under a baby-blue sky, I surveyed the world, eyeballing the situation straight up past the tree line. All we had here was cave, dirt, trees, and maybe a lake and it was enough, especially when capped by that "vault of heaven," as Aunt Ginny called it, up above.

A little eye frolicking way north toward the wild blue yonder reminded me of a quote I heard a long time ago. "Keep looking up. That's the secret of life." I wish I could say it was some great philosopher—and maybe it was . . . the author was Snoopy.

I focused on a wee orange, green, and red hummingbird dashing through air currents. She dipped down to do a little dance in front of my nose. For the first time in a long time, I felt my spirit rising.

I had a funny feeling that most of Griz's days in The Other were spent like any other forest creature. He was hunting for things that would ensure he would view that next sunrise.

I didn't want to freak him out, but I was examining Griz as he walked the labyrinth of trails. It wasn't in a getting-to-know-you kind of way, but through a reporter's eyes where no detail was too small. For instance, he walked quickly and gracefully, navigating rock and old logs without missing a beat. There was also a childlike sense of wonder when he got down on his knees to examine a baby fawn who, in her speckled glory, walked right up to him for a pet. He was gentle and kind with all living creatures, using just one finger to reach out and touch.

It felt good, almost empowering, to get back to work. I put handfuls of fresh blueberries and raspberries in a bucket Griz handed me. And then I held a large burlap sack while he found bits of kindling for a future fire. In a way, we were at the market, but now the woods were our grocery store. I stared hard at him, wondering where he got that deep cut on his right forearm that had garishly scarred over. What would his face look like, I mused, if he could find a razor and let me give him a good shave?

If Griz knew more words, I swear he would have said, "Are you stalking me?"

"No, kid," I'd reply. "Just binge researching."

He wore the pelts of some dead forest creatures, which I reminded myself were just for warmth. He just had few hygiene habits, which should have caused him to smell foul, but he didn't . . . for a reason I soon figured out. I watched as he picked fresh eucalyptus leaves and rubbed them on his skin. Nature's perfume.

I rubbed a few on myself, knowing I didn't smell like roses either.

Was he was raised in the woods, perhaps by parents who died, which explained why he was on his own? Or was he actually just waiting for his family to join him? Were they so-called "normal" size or extended? And what about the other parts? He had strong hands thanks to all the rock climbing he did in the name of existing and I noted that the flexor muscle that traveled down and across his forearm from the elbow to the wrist seemed enlarged and almost pulsated when he moved like he had extra in there.

Yeah, that did sound kind of medical. Let me explain.

I took AP senior anatomy when I was alive, figuring it would come in handy someday when I covered crime cases. A random thought floated into my brain: "Man always adapts to his surroundings to maximize survival. The world doesn't evolve. We do," said my teacher, Ms. Bianca Singer. So, it made sense that a boy/man who lived in the trees would grow strong of the hand, mutating in ways that made sure that he became one with the terrain. "The goal is to make it through each day," said Ms. S. I wished I could tell her that she was right.

But there was no time for flashbacking.

"Les du is," Griz said.

This time, it took me a moment.

"Let's . . ." I sounded it out for myself. "Do. This."

Ah-ha! Someone must have said this to him. I wonder how many people he encountered; how many encountered him. Were they afraid— or did they give him a chance? How did he know whether the next breathing being was safe—or not?

Griz motioned for me to keep up, and it took everything in me not to trip on the deep roots on the ground or small, snow-covered bushes. He didn't talk much as we walked about ten million miles, but seemed to understand more words than he could form himself.

"Twee," he said to me, pointing to an apple tree in the distance. He looked hopeful.

"Tree," I confirmed.

"Appy," he said.

"Apple," I corrected.

Was I really starting to understand him?

"Yo say," he grunted.

"You want to talk. Me say things?" I said, clomping along hard to catch up again.

Oh, I could talk until his rather large ears fell off.

"Griz, it's lovely in the woods," I told him, putting my hand next to his on the tall oak he was touching. "I love trees, too. They're there for all the seasons. In the heat. In the sun. In the pouring rain, the freezing ice, and snow."

"Sno," he said, picking up a handful of it on the ground and eating it.

He was getting it. To celebrate, I picked up a fistful of snow and ate half of it.

"I love trees because they endure. They go on. It's not like us. This same tree will be here next summer and in the fall. It lingers. A tree has stories to tell. Think of all the human backs that leaned against that bark."

I wish he would have answered. Instead, he picked up another handful of snow and threw it in my face.

"Watcha doin?" I gasped, trying to speak in his language.

Laughing, he began to climb up a redwood next to the oak and he was as fast as a monkey in the jungle. When I looked up . . .way, way up . . . I could see what looked like a nest up there. Something inside told me it didn't belong to some man-eating bird, but that Griz built this thing. It was actually a small platform made of wood covered in branches and topped with a giant fur pelt. A penthouse with a view.

All of a sudden, he climbed down again. He was crazy fast.

"Up," he said, stabbing me lightly with a sturdy pointer finger. He was strong as a bear, but had a surprisingly tender touch. His melon was another story.

Was he nuts?

"No, I can't even do the rope in gym class," I said. "I totally suck."

"Suck," he repeated, placing a padded palm under my armpit. When I didn't get it, he pet my head and then grabbed my hands, putting them on his shoulders.

No, no, no. I wasn't a fan of the heights thing.

Yet, I clutched him. Why? I was rabidly curious despite my wildest fears, so I grabbed onto him and closed my eyes while he climbed straight up with me hanging on for dear life. My head was swimming when he plopped me on my behind, about fifty feet up in the sky, on all those fur pelts he kept in his perch.

I cracked an eye.

It was magnificent.

"Tolja so," Griz said with delight.

Told you so. *Really?* Those were fighting words.

I felt giddy, and he got it. My joy made him smile, which was enough. What I would remember the most about him forever is his laugh that started in his toes and simmered until it reached the top of his head. His lips would part with the last explosion of joy.

"See," he said, with another deep belly roar. "See, Wa!"

Oh, I could see for miles. And I forced myself to keep smiling because otherwise he would have reacted to the fact that my heart was now in my feet. I spotted Edward's house of horrors in the distance, but consoled myself with the idea that objects were indeed farther than they appeared. There was at least thirty miles of hard terrain along with trees and tall, craggy mountains that pierced the clouds separating us. I willed myself to look away and due north. I found another object of curiosity.

There was a big hole in the ground. It was like The Other's version of the Grand Canyon.

"What is it?" I asked, pointing.

"Pitta, bad," Griz said. "BAD!" He began to hiss.

Bad. I was used to translating Bobby. But what was a "pitta?"

"Bad, bad, bad pitta!" Griz began to rant. He shook his head violently. When his eyes filled, I touched his hand and rubbed his cold fingers.

"Relax, Griz," I said in an even voice. "You're okay. I'm okay. No pitta. We're in our nest. We're birds."

"Birdies," he said, thrilled when I flapped imaginary wings.

When he looked away, my eyes wandered back to that big hole. I wasn't sure what it was, or who made it. Perhaps it was nothing but a geographical anomaly. But, probably not. It was coal black and had a strange effect on the clouds above it. They seemed to surrender as they tried to pass.

As if they were extinguished.

We sat up there until we were illuminated by a pale-green moon. It wasn't long before a night-cooled mist set in, which made me think that Griz and I were floating on a cloud. As the white wisps passed in front of my face, I reached out to touch it. Even as a girl, I pretended that fog contained our lost loved ones. The wisps came by for a quick hello as part of a swirling, eternal dance between sky and earth.

I delighted when the mist took shapes like long spikes, which I pretended were their arms reaching down. Quite often, I'd raise my own limbs to catch them, willing myself to pull them back to me, but somehow, I could never reach far enough. We were prisoners of our own fate and the rest was just gaps.

3.

The days here were simple, but profound in their own right. Griz found wild purple daisies and put them in a chipped coffee cup. In my mind, it was the world's most gorgeous bouquet and more beautiful than anything sequestered in crystal.

His generosity was a thing to behold. His surroundings were meager, but he was eager to share all that he had. When I woke from a deep sleep later that night, I found a rough amethyst crystal, the size of my palm, shimmering by my side.

"Found-a," he whispered. "For Wa."

One of the purple flowers found its way into my hand and I brought it to him.

"For you," I said, pressing it to his palm, which he rested on his chest before closing his eyes.

He trusted. Maybe it was the instincts he learned from the creatures out here; maybe it was just full-tilt Griz, an original, who called his own shots.

The temps one night were freezing cold and I wondered if I'd wake up a block of ice. He solved that by putting a thick animal pelt over me in the middle of the night. I said a silent prayer to PETA and dissolved in all that soft fluff and slept so deeply that I woke up with one hundred percent clarity.

As we forged for just enough food for that day, it dawned on me.

Out of all the animals hunting today, I feared the human ones the most.

4.

The skies were gray the next day, but the lake water shimmered with an opalescent sheen.

We just went to the water's edge to watch whales, puffins, eagles, sea otters, and salmon jumping up and down as they played in what looked like a turbulent green sea. Thunderous winter surf pounded whitewashed rocks. Breathlessly, I realized that we were only a small part of a much bigger story. I heard my mother's voice in that wind. "Take a moment to enjoy the moment," she would say.

I went down to the part where the ground gave out to sand and listened to the pounding of water, which when I closed my eyes became almost hypnotic.

When they opened, I took a look.

A good look around.

There were high ridges and the apex of a trail that looked too steep to conquer. High mountain walls were above us, and the sea roared below. Mount Something loomed in the distance, beckoning. I bent down to pick up the oddest rock with a large hole in the center. It was a hag stone known for protection, good luck, and making wishes come true. It came from the water and I closed one eye to peer through it. A hag stone was rare and extremely magical stone tumbled by tides and winds through time, which wore a natural hole in the rock. It was known to ward off any evil.

Daniel was gone, but I could hear his answers in my head. "Stay here. It's safe, baby. Stay forever."

Griz's natural joy soothed the loneliness. He tried so hard, my little dumpster diver, and before dinner presented me with a big black yummy sweatshirt hoodie that felt as if it had been washed about a thousand times. So what if there were a few rips on the bottom. It was perfect.

Griz stood, head hung down. He wasn't sure if I would like it—and that broke my heart.

"Love," I said, making the heart sign with my hands. He had no clue, but he had a feeling. His soft brown eyes misted.

That night, I tried to teach Griz how to sing. He had no rhythm, but he enjoyed me crooning every now and then and he tried to grunt along. "Let's try again," I suggested, adopting my best rap voice. "Been spending most our lives. Living in a gangsta's . . ."

"Dice," Griz grunted.

"Paradise," I corrected. "But. very, very good."

I continued. "Tramps like us."

"Baby, burn to ron," he said.

"Gud!"

I gave him two extra berries that night.

It was perfect in the most basic way. I had downsized not only my existence, but my expectation of what happens in a day. How I got there was easy to explain. A hungry stomach, an empty wallet, and a healing heart can teach you the lessons of a lifetime.

5.

Beyond the flapping noise of a stray bat or two, nights in our rock house were long and solitary. There was literally nothing to do, but think (dangerous), workout (Griz liked when I taught him sit-ups) or eat or sleep.

Griz suggested something else. He pointed in a way that told me he wanted me to follow him deeper into the cave to places I had yet to explore.

"Ya wanna go. You do, Wa!"

He moved fast, grabbing my hand to pull me along.

We walked for a good fifteen minutes until I began to sway-move. We were deep-deep in the cave now and I could barely see a thing. It smelled like some kind of metallic ore, which wasn't that pleasant, and when I pinched my nose; Griz did exactly the same and made a mock throwing up sound.

He was one step ahead, literally. It was so dark that I thought we'd bump into walls, but he knew the layout instinctively. At one point, he dropped my hand, reached down, and rubbed two sticks together until they produced a flame that he used to ignite a much bigger piece of wood with some kind of device on top. He knew where to find it. It was a primitive lantern that he built—and left there.

The city girl in me couldn't stop her jaw from dropping at the sticks into fire thing. Who knew that this actually worked?

That stream of golden light revealed something shocking. It wasn't that we had entered a large and entirely brand new "room" of the cave. We had also walked into . . . the Target of the afterlife.

There were shirts and pants, piles deep, along with socks and shoes and boots and even soap and shampoos, plus extra pots, pans, and a stray ceiling fan and half-broken rocking chair. A guitar and a lawn mower rested against a rusted claw-foot bathtub.

Turns out that Griz was . . . yes, I watched the show way back then . . . an afterlife hoarder!

He wasn't messy about it like some hoarders, but displayed his "findings" on smooth rounded rocks while hanging other pieces from the jagged rock points on the cave wall. He lit several other torches, positioned strategically, so one could see all of the goods. It was all quite professional and peculiar at the same time. My favorite thing so far was a hat that was embroidered with "Wake Up. Kick Ass. Repeat."

"Ta-ka," he kept saying. "Ta-ka, Wa."

I put the hat on and heard a low, guttural chuckle.

Inside Griz's personal resale shop, after a deep dig into some men's clothing, I hit the jackpot. It was the perfect large, long-to-almost-my-knees black sweater that felt super soft because it was made out of exquisitely warm cashmere. With my prize in hand, I lowered my head. As far as cave guests went, I didn't want him to think I was some gold digger. This beautiful sweater was enough and I planned to never take it off.

I waited a beat.

"Pick-a, mor" he said again and again. "Yu wanna, yu wanna, yu wanna!"

This time, I waded deeper into what must have been hundreds of items collected—a virtual junkyard of afterlife artifacts in all shapes and sizes—and curated from I don't know where. Well, I knew where a couple of times—especially when I found an old Gucci top-end briefcase with little Gs imprinted into buttery leather. I'd take this back with me to my bedroll and study it later. Jeans and a few long sleeve shirts were added to my pile.

My own super shopper grin was firmly in place until I felt it and my stomach sink to my knees.

6.

There were, of course, millions of backpacks in the world. But only a few had a small, distinct *A* for the Academy embroidered on the front zippered pocket in the far-right corner.

My finger traced the small name in the left. When I got past the *C* and the *A*, I blinked hard. *Cass.*

It was the first concrete thing I had seen or felt of "them" in a long time and it made me feel lightheaded.

I lifted the backpack and forced myself to continue to smile so I wouldn't upset Griz, who was hovering over me. He was clapping his hands because suddenly I was so interested in his big find.

Slowly, I unzipped the pack, which miraculously was still heavy enough to contain several weapons including Cass's former marine corps knife, one of those multitool gizmos that folded into a metal center. A few times in the past, I went to touch it and he always pulled it away.

"Sugar, you don't want to lose a limb," Cass would joke.

I held the knife up to Griz.

"Please," I begged him. "Me ta-ka?"

"Doit, Wa," he said and patted me on the head.

Inside the backpack was a caltrop weapon and jagged blade knife. I didn't want to scare Griz, so I didn't take them out. I fingered the shiny US Navy Medal of Honor and held it for a moment in my palm. It begged the question: If the bag was here then where was Cass? One more reach into the pack and I felt a thick piece of paper. In the tiny light, I could see that it was an aged photo, browning in spots with the side curling. I had never seen this before.

"Cute kid," I whispered under my breath. She was maybe three or four with long red hair and a glittery crown on top of her head. Maybe it was his cousin. Or a friend when she was little. I knew it wasn't his little sisters. He would never carry around a photo of his devil-siblings, the Claires.

"More?" I asked hopefully.

"Haf fun," Griz said, moving to the other side of the room to pick out some pretty candles for later.

I put the bag off to the side and dove back to the pile.

It was worse than I expected. Horrifyingly so.

The next bag was filled with wrappers of candy that had long-since been eaten and two pairs of nunchucks fell to the bottom underneath a change of already dirty and smelly clothes. I was careful not to get stabbed by his madu made from two sharp, small points of a small antelope's shredded horns with a crossbar connecting them.

Were they attacked? Captured? I wouldn't go there . . . but I had no choice. Extinguished? I drew my lower lip between my teeth.

Eddie's bag was followed by Auggie's. I knew it before I read the name. Auggie kept a small stuffed elephant with him with the tusks up for good luck.

There were two more. When I reached inside the first, a small leather pouch practically fell into my hands. When I unzipped it, I was staring into my own eyes. It was a picture that Pete took a long time ago of Daniel and I dancing on our front porch. My eyes filled, which seemed to upset Griz.

"No gud! No gud!" he began to chant and I did the impossible. I took his big hand in mine and faked a laugh.

"Ta-ka?" I said, hugging the bag to my chest.

"Where go wit dis?"

"Nowhere," I said.

He didn't look so convinced. When I grabbed the last bag, which was my own, I touched his other hand. I pointed at me and then I pointed at him.

"Mine," I said. He brightened as if he knew that word.

"Myn," he repeated, pointing at me.

7.

In the end, I couldn't take them all. I took my pack, along with the ones belonging to Cass and Daniel, with me and allowed Griz to lead me back to the main room with the midnight snack of fresh vegan stew and the makeshift beds waiting. In a dark corner, I put on my own leggings and that new warm sweater.

I put the packs on my bed, collected myself, and then said, "Where find? These belong to my friends."

Griz didn't understand—or maybe he did. I could see he was tired and maybe this was enough for one day. But I couldn't stop myself from asking.

I never could.

"Where ta-ka?" I asked him.

Griz looked like he might cry now.

"Griz gud," I said. "Wa likes Griz. Griz gud," I said.

Now that his reputation was settled, he smiled before curling into a ball on the floor. He took a dirty old comforter and wrapped himself in it with his furry feet hanging out one end. I stood and walked over to a second blanket he had in the corner. Gingerly, I lowered down and placed the second piece of cloth over his toes.

"Tank you, Wa" he said.

"No," I replied. "Thank you."

And then in the dark:

"Not ta-ka," Griz whispered. "Find-a."

"Where go?" I asked. Then I said a silent prayer that he would understand—and he did.

"Pitta," he said. "Griz go by pitta. Bad, bad Griz boy."

8.

I knew I wouldn't sleep tonight. Griz had found the bags by the pit or the big hole in the ground meaning Daniel and the rest weren't that close to here, but they were not that far.

I also knew that I need to tread lightly with Griz or I'd push him over the edge. Something bad happened to him by what he called the "pitta." Maybe I would have to find out exactly what transpired to make him so afraid . . . I couldn't push. He moved through the world quickly, but he was emotionally just a little boy.

"How old are you, Griz?"

In the dim amber glow, I counted the fast flash of fingers. Just like me, he was seventeen . . . no, make that eighteen. He held up one additional finger.

"You are eighteen," I said. "Wow!"

"Wow," he repeated.

I looked at him again and grinned.

"I'm this much," I said, flashing seventeen fingers.

Griz could count. I saw it on his face. "Wow," he said. "Fren is sam."

Same. Or close to it.

9.

We went shopping again the next night, but this time it was different. Griz took me a little deeper into the cave into a corner that he filled with candles. It took a few minutes to light enough of them to see what was there, but when the room finally burned bright I marveled at how he had made himself a little study or den. There were the remains a cushioned chair, although now some of the stuffing was striving to escape the extremely worn leather.

He motioned for me to sit, and I did. Much to my delight, he reached to the side to pull a lever that had me reclining way back.

"Layzee Buy," he said.

I got it. It was once, and partially still remained, a La-Z-Boy recliner even if it was one that looked like someone had put at the end of the driveway for trash day. Aunt Ginny had a better version in her living room and I believe that La-Z-Boy was surgically attached to her body because she never left that chair.

"Griz, where to do you come from?" I asked him. It was futile, obviously too many words, and he looked at me blankly. There had to be a better way of saying it. I would think of one while he lit the candles.

"Griz boy," he said.

"Yes," I cried. "Griz as a boy. Ta-ka there?"

He shook his head and went off to another part of the cave for what seemed like the longest time. When he returned, he tossed a dusty book onto my lap. I looked at him and then it, slowly opening the cover. It was a worn version of *Lord of the Flies*, but I didn't think he wanted me to read to him. He wanted me to read about him. I knew that much when several yellowed newspaper clippings fell out of the book, which was nothing more than just a holder.

Gingerly, he touched the paper. Then his heart. Next, he poked me in the head as I stared at the picture of an extremely tall whipper.

I got it.

"*This is you*," I said, looking at the faded picture dated ten years ago.

In it, a seven-year-old boy with a smooth, very large face was frowning at the photographer. He was flanked by what must have been his seven-foot mother, who looked like a female version of the current Griz and an eight-foot father. The adults were almost naked except for little cotton skirts that covered their privates.

The oddest thing amongst the other peculiarities was the kid. The young Griz was maybe five foot nine or six feet at the time.

I did the math. He was in the first grade.

10.

Death Story: Griz
Age of Demise: 17

NEW MEXICO. The locals call it Wheeler Peak, but such a bland name didn't give the place it's due. The land was always far more majestic that mere words. At 13,141 feet straight up, the area is the highest natural point in the state. It's also where "they" live if you believe local lore or have been wandering in the dark woods very late at night.

Perhaps you've come upon what looks like a family of giants—eight-foot humans with seven-foot children hunting quietly at night. They wield bows, arrows, and small knives and never take more than is needed for survival.

Juan Rodriguez, a local resident of the nearby town, reported to TIME, "He looked like a bear. And maybe they were. It was the strangest thing I've ever seen in my natural life. They wore pelts. Or was it their own hair and fur coming from weathered skin? One thing I know for sure," Rodriguez said. "They had human faces."

His encounter happened last month, around two in the morning by Williams Lake near the Pueblo Viejo Mines.

"I was camping and went behind a tree to do my business, if you know what I mean. There I was squatting and looked up. Way up! All of a sudden, I saw four giants fishing for their dinner by the nearby lake!" he said.

What did he do? "Well, I cramped up, but then yanked up my pants and ran even faster," he said.

Archeologists and local historians will probably attest to the fact that these "beings" didn't follow. It's not in their nature to interact with many, tribal leaders in the area told us. Scientists will agree that Mr. Rodriguez's situation was not a one-time sighting.

They call the tribe of extremely tall beings the Darklings because, among other things, they are hairy all over and mostly come out at night to forge for food, water, and other survival supplies. "They are weathered old souls who have been around these parts for at least 150 years. In the olden days, miners would try to capture them as children and raised them to do the heavy load lifting," said Dr. Brendan Hughes, who has studied such tribes around the globe for his Society of Unexplained Beings. "We've tracked them to Wheeler Mountain in New Mexico where they live in the woods by that ski resort that closed during the recession. They like to be where so-called 'normal people' are not," said Dr. Hughes.

He explained that the Darklings, born with genetic abnormalities including thick hair patches all over their bodies hence the bear comparison, were forced to live in the deep woods after early settlers in the 1870s forced them from towns and cities. They cleverly keep out of sight during the day and live in cave dwellings in family units. "They bond to each other," said Dr. Hughes, adding, "We can't be sure, but we do think they had a rudimentary language picked up by silently observing campers and other villagers.

Tribes would migrate after being discovered, as Darklings weren't always trustful of their smaller human counterparts, especially the slavers who worked for the mine boss in nearby excavation areas. Capturing one of them was a prize because they were hearty workers who lived long lives. It was up to the Darklings to evade, and they were good at it.

"You see them once, and that's about as good

as the view's going to get for a long, long time," said Dr. Hughes. "They're masters at the art of disappearance."

A camper once reported what he called "a deranged Bigfoot type foaming at the mouth," stealing his Bic lighter, extra tent, and hiking boots. "He made off with the fuzzy dice from my truck, too," he told police. When asked if the being was evil, the camper added, "No, it wasn't evil. It wasn't even that furry if you didn't count some extra werewolf-like facial hair. It looked to be a teenager."

"The thing surprised me when I was going down to the river for some water," said his wife. "I grabbed my shotgun, but I missed. My son came running and I had to shield him. At least, I thought we were in danger."

"It hid behind a tree and stared at me," said their son, Calvin, ten, an elementary school student. "It wasn't bad. In its eyes, I saw kindness. Curiosity."

It was Calvin who during a hike later that day slipped off a ledge into Pueblo Viejo. His mother fell to her knees praying while his father raced to the edge to save his son from falling. As the rocks began to recede and the boy's hands were slipping, Mr. Rodriguez reports that "a creature raced from behind the trees, lifted a paw, and ripped into the dangling child's shirt, pulling him to safety."

"I had no choice. He growled at us. He went, 'Gggg . . . rrrr . . . iii . . . zzzz,'" said Mr. Rodriguez, who had grabbed his gun and shot the Darkling dead. "I'm sure he saved my son's life in order to eat him. I shot the other two bigger ones. Dead-dead. I pulled the trigger when they came running from the woods to kill the rest of us."

Calls to 911 resulted in a US Marine helicopter

attempting to retrieve the carcasses of an adult female Darkling, an adult male, and a teenage male specimen. The episode was called "a tragic hunting incident where a loving father saved his wife and son from a family of rabid bears."

"I would have liked the bear heads for my den. Three of them! Now, that's a major wall of trophies," said Mr. Rodriguez who with a shrug added, "but, by the time those slow asses at 911 arrived, all three carcasses were gone. Just disappeared. Creeps me out every time I think about it."

11.

Dappled candlelight played on the canyon walls sending coppertreaks down to our feet. It calmed me knowing there was something bigger here and he trusted me with it. "Ma, Da, me . . . no morz," he said, sadly. "I comez here. By self."

I wondered what happened to his poor parents, who were certainly "out there" residing somewhere in the afterlife and maybe even looking for their boy.

"Griz, I'm so sorry," I said, putting my hand over his large one. "Your ma and da tried to save you while you tried to save that boy," I said, tears forming. When one slipped, he slid a large finger across my cheek to remove it.

"No sad, Wa," he said. "Griz ok-doe-key."

I smiled through his pain. In that moment, life seemed so temporary and fragile.

But, there were also soft spots. In other clippings, I read that the local government suspected someone in town was helping the Darklings and brought them food and medicine when they needed it. That same person left the newspaper article by their cave in the living realm, knowing they probably couldn't read it, but would recognize the tribe's images in a photo. Or maybe somebody, someday, could read it to them. That in itself was a revelation.

Somehow, the newspaper made it here.

"Griz, someone helped you," I said, touching my heart. "Helper."

He nodded. "Boys," he said. "Smalz."

Small boys helped them. Kids, probably without any parental permission, took them on as a special project. They kept the Darklings' whereabouts a secret and brought things like aspirin, antibiotic gel, and even cough medicine and stolen prescription drugs from their parents' stashes. They brought these things because even the kids knew. These people were rare and beautiful.

Maybe there were kids here in The Other who helped Griz.

"Griz, I need your help," I said, immediately having second thoughts about it.

"Hep?" he repeated. "Griz hep Wa."

"I think my friends are in the pitta," I said. "Or somewhere near there. Need help to find them."

"No pitta!" he screamed so loudly that his voice reverberated in the cave. Petrified, he stood and stamped his feet. That's when it dawned on me. Bad things happened for him when there was a ledge and then nothing but a big old hole in the ground.

We were silent for a long time, which was too much for Griz. When he started making little funny faces at me, I pet his hand and laughed. He was smart enough to know that this joy was a temporary fix.

"Want gunna do?" he asked.

"Whatever it takes," I said, grateful that he didn't understand me. Frankly, I didn't understand me either half of the time. But, for the first time, in a long time, despite the unfairness of my own recent spin, I felt my blood race.

My soul was stirring.

SEVENTEEN

1.

When I woke up, Griz was cleaning and cooking a large catfish. I was so hungry I could have eaten the metal pan, but I watched patiently as he cut at the gills and tail and then down the length of the fish to isolate the fillets. He worked like a surgeon and ate like a savage today. I wasn't much better. We scooped up the fish, licking the back of our hands, and it was the best meal of my life.

When the last morsel was devoured, Griz jumped to his feet.

"Let go, Wa," he said.

If you had wanderlust, the place was a ten.

This was the land of deep glacial lakes, ice-capped peaks, and wave-carved cliffs like the one we stood on right now. There was even a higher plateau above us and the runoff created a crashing waterfall that settled below into twenty plus feet of white foam.

Griz walked us farther today until I was staring into a mirrorlike crystalline lake of iridescent blue water with needle-sharp rocks jutting out here and there.

Nature's palace was to be enjoyed with all of the senses. If freshness had a scent, this was it. As for the sound around me, I heard a few honks, but there wasn't a car or vehicle in sight. The sound came from a large gray seal, a mama, who was sunning herself on a smooth gray rock barely surfacing in the middle of the lake. Mama S was surrounded by three big-eyed white pups. They squeaked each time she placed a squirming fish into an eager pup mouth.

I kept a careful watch because there could be bears out here or maybe a stray moose, goat, or elk going about their morning business. My job was to blend in. I wouldn't say a word; not that anyone would hear me. Griz had disappeared for a while and my only audience was the 250 foot fir trees that pierced an unforgiving slate-gray winter sky.

We weren't on a sightseeing mission.

We were fishing for our dinner and the local salmon heading upstream in the icy river provided nature's buffet. I watched as Griz simply waded into that freezing water and stood on rocks in his bare feet. He had extraordinary balance and knew the shallower spots where the water only met his chest instead of crashing over his head.

With both hands, the size of small plates, he combed through the water to scoop fish right out of that rushing river. He threw eight or nine squirming gifts—tuna, salmon, and catfish—in a bag he had slung over his shoulder.

I admired him for not taking more than we would need in the short term. Why not give those fishes a shot? Scaled survivors took the risk of being spotted. Jumping out of the water into the brisk air, the fish danced merrily in the breeze, and then evaded capture by belly flopping back into the churning drink.

Griz looked like a young man without a care in his world as he bobbed up and down. He was multitasking: collecting food, gathering water, and taking a bath at the same time. At one point, to show off, he bit right into a squirming salmon. He chewed the head up, gulping it down raw without the benefit of ginger or wasabi. After he filled his stomach, he chucked the remains for the other animals to enjoy.

"Sushi sampler," I said with a smile.

2.

The entire time I stood on a smooth rock on the shore, watching and wishing I had a camera phone to keep these memories forever. An hour passed and I watched as the seals and her pups moved on to a spot on the beach where they could rest on the bigger boulders. They took their spots, flapped around, and then picked fights with other seals who had no concept of social distancing. I felt their boredom and was ready for a change of scenery, too, so I stretched my legs and took a few cautious steps toward the woods behind me.

I always felt at home in the woods. It was my church.

Three steps led to six. Six led to twelve. Nature was filled with diverse vegetation and I picked three apples while enjoying the sweet smell of the white blooms of the cherry blossoms that rained down in the light breeze. To my delight, I saw a blanket of wild strawberries racing across the mossy dirt covered by half-melted snow.

My hands were greedy as they picked as many plump berries that could fit into the hood of the jacket I removed when a slice of midday sun came calling with warming rays.

I vowed not to go too far, fearing a close encounter of a human kind.

If I knew one thing it was this: your last mistake is your best teacher.

3.

If there weren't peaches on the tree up ahead I would have never seen the little cabin up ahead.

I was always fanaticizing about other people's houses. Maybe that's why now I naturally gravitated toward the wood structure with the tarred roof in the distance. It was a charmer. Or maybe I had that *Little House* gene in that small wood homes always gave me a tingling feeling.

Three crumbling stone stairs later and I was in front of a small pine door. The place didn't even pretend to have "security." A quick twist on the rusted doorknob proved that there wasn't a lock. Perhaps that was to help others who might be lost in these parts when the weather dipped or the storms blew in. Two clicks; I was in.

The hairs on my arm stood up straight.

Discovery does that to a human being; I hoped it always would.

4.

It wasn't the dilapidated or "rustic" nature of the cabin that caught my attention. Sure, the place was the second one. It was small, maybe a single room or two, and stripped of color after surviving countless winter and summer in isolation. Houses had a way of dying too when unoccupied. The only promise in this one was that its booty backed up into lush fauna and tall trees.

Dirty windows were curtainless. There was no fire coming from a small red brick chimney. Even the air in here had expired. I could see little dust dots floating through it as I moved to the center, clomping with each step. The floors made a hollow sound, as if they weren't that secured to whatever was underneath.

I walked all the way inside, and then got an assist from a northerly blast of wind. It slammed the heavy pine door behind me.

"Great," I muttered, twirling around. But there was no monster. Nothing with teeth. All my actions did was kick up about two decades of dust, which now was making me choke.

On the plus side, this outdoor "charmer" was certainly unoccupied—I really tried to convince myself—if you didn't count the three fresh apple cores on the floor.

Four-letter words formed in my frontal lobe. I wasn't a detective, yet . . .

The apple cores were brownish yellow, which meant that whatever put the teeth marks into them was still in the near vicinity. I always ate my apple first every day at JFK HS. By the end of the lunch period, the bite marks, if I didn't finish it, were yellow-brown. If I kept the apple into the next period, it was tinny brown. Lunch was only thirty minutes, meaning that whomever or whatever crunched that fruit had been here. Not very long ago.

Shafts of bright yellow sunshine pierced the filthy windows on the other side of the cabin. It made it easier to take in the décor including a small, handmade wood table with long benches on both sides, a fireplace filled with the remains of now-black logs, and rows of cabinets that obviously contained nonperishable canned goods. There was a small metal can on the far side of the table. Fact: It had been opened by something with hands. The proof was the cold remains of vegetable soup in a small soup pot that had been placed by the small fireplace.

The human need to know will do you in every single time. I roamed. Touched the pot.

Luke freaking warm.

What forest animal would leave food? Anything worth its weight would eat it all . . . and then maybe the can. *And they wouldn't warm it up, Sherlock.*

One step became two and then three. Someone had taken a full-sized bed mattress and placed it in the corner. It contained no sheets, no blanket. From the dust on the floor, I could see that it had been next to the fireplace not long ago.

The door remained closed, which was little comfort when I heard something with a heeled shoe walking. But it wasn't inside the cabin. It wouldn't materialize no matter how many times I whipped around.

It was underneath me.

5.

The floor consisted of large planks of world-weary oak secured in place long, long ago with large, now-rusted nails.

When I heard the feet move quickly below me, my eyes darted down to my feet. *How low did it go below? Was there a cellar? But where was the staircase?*

My gaze darted toward the back of the cabin where there was a back door, but there was no time to make a clean exit.

The nails from four of the planks were moving. Because someone or something was moving them. It was now pushing with all of its might until they were dislodged. I had only a few seconds for the wood to be shoved violently away, which gave me no time to race to the front or back door.

I still tried, my feet in motion, the dead air at my back.

I heard the wood scrape as one plank was removed.

Then, two and three.

It was in the room.

It rushed me causing me to drop to the ground, but it was powerful and forceful. It plundered, seizing my middle in a grabbing crush and taking me all the way to my back on the wood floor. The shock attack knocked the wind out of my lungs. I gasped for breath that was denied. Wheezing in and out, I prayed that I didn't black out. Or maybe that would be more humane in this case? What you didn't see couldn't— wouldn't—haunt you forever.

Full consciousness returned as my head wrenched left. Was I breathing or hallucinating?

It had my hands, both of them, pinned above my head now. The rest of it covered me, sinking in by inches, because obviously suffocation was the way it killed. I struggled to pivot, to grab that next breath, to twist away, but was denied by gravity and the sheer size of this animal.

My legs, pinned. My arms, not operational. My head, on lock.

My hoodie. Ripped down.

I felt its hot breath puffing on my neck. The jaw tightened, the teeth flash and when the lips parted, I knew it would be a slow killing. Memorable. Closing my eyes tightly, I waited for teeth, for pain, for darkness.

I felt a butterfly soft caress.

And then . . .

It kissed me hard on the lips.

6.

"Walker?"

"Cass?" I whispered.

A mountain of a man, he had moss stuck in that long, blond hair, which tumbled as wild and free as these surroundings. There were dead leaves embedded in a flannel shirt that had once been an actual color, but now it was dirty black, same as pants that were caked in mud and twigs that snarled and embedded into the fibers.

His face was the kind of dirty where the water just left streaks of muddy marks.

As for his warm lips and shaky, shallow breaths, I cursed myself, but I did feel like something that was close to a homecoming.

"Walker!"

Cass gripped me, folding my limbs and enveloping every cell of my being. His hands were strong but gentle when they cupped my face in order to press a torpid open-mouthed kiss onto my lips. It happened so fast, and I erased any guilt by defining it as a kiss of hello after a long and perilous journey. It wasn't passion, but gratitude for the familiar—at least that's what I swore. It was a gesture, like a toast. To life; for life. For lost things, found. Then his lips touched mine again.

Tender and slow.

I pulled back before the kiss could deepen.

"No, Cass . . . ," I began. "Just hold my hand and I will be thankful to the end."

"I know, damn it," he whispered, grabbing my fingers. Before I could think, he rolled us over and now I was on top. He held me tight and then tighter with one hand, looping those strong fingers through my hair. I was glad to see him. And that couldn't be wrong. Not with everything that had just happened. This wasn't that . . . it was about connection.

He was confident in a way that was not conceited. Courageous, yes, and generous, and gentle. His masculine side was proven tough and bold, yet he was brave enough to allow another to take control. I moved a hand over his forehead and the other on his chest.

The door crashed open.

He went from lover to warrior in a flash. Flipping me over hard, my back landed with a thud while his mouth captured my ear.

"Sugar. Do. Not. Move."

7.

Griz could smell him from a hundred miles away. He stood tall now occupying every square inch of the cabin's small door. He dropped a giant basket of fresh berries and I watched them roll across the floor like red and purple marbles. I smelled Griz's fear at first . . . followed by his rage. He roared in a way that sounded like a thunderclap.

Before I could open my mouth, I heard Griz start to yowl now—a child's scream that told a story mixed with terror, pain, confusion, and anger. I felt it to my marrow as that high-pitched wail pierced through skin and bone. I knew how it looked; I blurted words to explain. But, we were past that point. With steadfast speed, Griz charged like any other forest animal in peril while at the same time Cass shoved me upright until I stood on my own wobbling feet.

He was military trained and lived by the motto of "kill or be killed." He had been taught to kill fast, and I gazed in horror at the glint of a knife in his right hand capturing a stream of sun. The dust and the light seemed to swirl as Griz lifted all ten fingers, bending the first crease like claws.

"No!" I screamed. "Fren. Fren! FREN!"

And then: "Cass, don't you dare hurt him. Do you hear me! Back the hell off."

But they were both in alpha-male mode, crouched, circling, and ready to strike. One more breath, another crazed rush, and there would be no going back. There would only be a pool of blood.

A child's game floated through my panic.

"Everybody, FREEZE!" I shouted.

"Freez," Griz repeated, stopping dead in his tracks. He finally got it as I wedged myself between the two. I grabbed Cass's muddy shirt with one hand and took Griz's hand with the other.

"Frens, damn it to hell!" I yelled.

"Frens," Griz whimpered.

Quickly, I knitted Griz's fingers into mine while doing the same with Cass's on the other side. It was clear. If they wanted to hurt each other, they would have to hurt me—and neither would do it.

Eventually, the whole thing seemed rather funny because that's how Griz rolled. He was more of a lover than a fighter.

"Damn it to hell-o," Griz mused, laughing now. "Bad wors. Don't say bad wors, Wa." Then he pointed down. "Picka berries. Wat berries doin' down on flor? Silly berries."

"Don't say *hell*, Griz," I said. "Say, h-e-double-toothpicks."

"H-e-toothpickies," he said.

"Close enough," I said with a nod.

Gently, Griz dropped to his knees to pick up every single berry as three very large salmon fell out of his right pants pocket.

"What the . . . ," Cass began. I saw his knife hand drop to his side.

8.

It was time to sit down and regroup, which is why I dragged both of the to the table with the benches. Cass sat on one side of me, Griz on the other. "So," I concluded, "that's how Griz saved me from freezing to death in the woods.

"Griz is gud," I said. And then added, "Frens forever." I made the heart sign with my fingers and touched it to Griz's chest.

Griz interrupted, smiling shyly. "Forever, dam it to hell-o," he said with glee.

"Bad wors," I said with a smile. "But who gives a shit?"

Cass was fascinated.

"Gonna share your berries, buddy?" he finally asked my new "fren" in an animated voice.

Cautiously, Griz passed two berries over to Cass because he wasn't in a hundred percent trust mode yet. Then, he took one back with stealth speed. This friendship would obviously be a process.

"Berries, myn. Wa, myn," Griz announced, eating the rest quickly as the fish sizzled in a fry pan we found in the cabinet. He put a large hand over mine.

"Myn?" inquired my former protector.

"Mine," I translated, my entire body still on high alert from the last ten minutes.

"Yeah, right," Cass said with a grin as he stood to flip the fish. "Shit, get in line buddy. Get in effing line."

"Bad wor," Griz said clapping his hands. "Bad wor."

"No double toothpicks for that one, buddy," Cass said.

9.

Griz went outside to pick more berries, which left just the two of us in charge of getting the protein part of this lunch ready. The minute my feral friend left the building, I cornered Cass by the small fire he made in the hearth.

"Where is everyone else? Are they . . . just tell me. Say it fast."

"Take a breath, sugar," he said. "It's complicated."

"When isn't it?"

"Real fast: I escaped yesterday from a mineral mine down the road where they operate via slave labor. All guys. Treated like work animals. Fifteen-hour, back-breaking days, barely any food and you sleep on concrete slabs in barracks, which are several hundred feet down. They beat you—or worse—if you try to escape or refuse to work."

"You never passed immigration?"

"They—as in the immigration people, plus some deranged female sheriff—drugged us with some kind of juice and then I woke up in chains on what looked like a prison bus. They need strong workers. I heard it wasn't always that way, but the system has been corrupted by the Higher Authority on our side and one Edward Reid, who has some stake in that mine, on this side," he said.

I was so impatient that I wanted to rip the words out of his throat.

"They took all of us prisoner. Edward arranged it. No way was he letting his oldest son roam free on this side," Cass said. "It has been all hard labor followed by a slice of cheese and old moldy bread. Nights were the worst. No heat. No blankets. This makeshift sheriff is in charge and she's tough and smart. That sheriff I told you about just a second ago. Her name is . . . starts with a *P*."

"Pristine," I blurted.

"You met her?"

"Yeah, in the woods the night I was waiting for all of you to be processed after immigration, and . . . at my wedding."

He almost dropped the pan.

"Your what!"

"To Daniel's father."

"Son of a . . ." Cass bit a nasty stream of foul words under his breath. When he drop-kicked a stray log all the way across the cabin, I shook my head.

"Did he touch you?" he turned to me and asked gently.

"No, there was no honeymoon. He tried to go full-tilt boogie, if you know what I mean, and ended up naked, humiliated . . . wounded," I said. "And I'm not talking about emotionally wounded."

Cass's face burst into a giant smile. "I hope you cut his dick off," he said.

"Perceptive, grasshopper," I replied.

"You did cut his . . . ," Cass said with wide eyes. "But, hey, whatever works. No judgment."

"Not all the way off," I said in my own defense.

"I'm going to tell this story once, but only when all interested parties have gathered," I promised. And as much as I hated to do it to him, it was the perfect time for a subject changer. I had to ask.

"Daniel?" *I had waited long enough to mention him, even though my insides were screaming.*

He flipped the fish again and went mute.

"Please," I said. *Either way, I needed to know.*

"Pristine liked him . . . a little too much," Cass said. "When he didn't return the feelings, she made him work days and nights. No rest.

I saw him collapse and then he tried to escape. They hunted him down," Cass said.

"And?" *I would will him to say that he escaped and was running free. I was manifesting those words although the outcome of my precision wishing remained to be determined.*

"Sugar, I just don't know," Cass said. "I used the commotion of the guards bringing Daniel back one night for my escape. The last thing I saw was someone carrying him down the hallway where the slaves slept. There was a lot of blood. There was no way I could save him because there were just too many guards, so I broke out, snuck into a service elevator they weren't using, and ran into the mountains. They couldn't chase two of us. Whatever was happening to Daniel was my diversion.

"I heard shots," he said, "I'm sorry. I mean it, sugar."

"Sowree, Dan-yell," Griz repeated under his breath. "Sowree. Sowree. Sowree."

EIGHTEEN

1.

Griz provided enough diversion during lunch by butchering songs I taught him, and then trying to teach Cass his unique form of language. In return, Cass carved an apple into a smiling face, which delighted Griz. Two berries for eyeballs and they were becoming fast friends, which meant Griz trusted Cass enough to invite him "hoe-me."

"When I was hiding from the Taliban in Afghanistan, we had a similar setup," Cass said, admiring how Griz created his "kitchen" in the cave. "Very nice work, Griz," he said. "Thank you for having me."

"Come wit?" Griz invited Cass.

One of them looked confused.

"Wat doin? Not movin. Come wit," Griz prodded. He poked Cass in the arm urging the newcomer to go with him into the deeper bowels of the cave.

I nodded, although most of my head was elsewhere. I didn't even eat the lunch, which caused both Griz and Cass grave concern.

"He's going to take you to the T.J. Maxx of cave life," I said. "You don't

274

need cash or a credit card. Everything has been carefully chosen—and Griz has everything."

Cass returned with a fresh outfit in one hand, a winter parka in forest green, and a cowboy hat. I had already given him his pack, which was now dangling off his shoulders. It remained filled to the brim with his favorite weapons, including several badass knives, ropes, and other military mechanisms.

"Best shopping I've ever done," he told me with a wink. "This kid is A plus."

"Griz roks," said the tallest one.

"I taught him to say it," said Cass with pride.

"Well done," I praised them both.

"Free Brat-ney," Griz added.

I gave them both a thumbs up.

I almost smiled when Cass demonstrated how he taught Griz to fly a high five.

"You got it," I said with a small smile.

Cass crouched down in front of me. "Yes, I do," he said. "You know, I could spend the rest of my afterlife out here with the right person, a friend like Griz. And maybe a dog. You always need a dog. Run into any in the mountains?"

My worried face made him switch gears.

"Where does a guy get a shower at this five-star hotel? I must be carrying some serious stink," he stated.

"Cass, we have to . . ." I wanted to explain that we had to leave now and find Daniel and the rest. I refused to believe that Daniel was forever gone because I just didn't feel it. *Certainly, I would feel it.* And I didn't care if Cass smelled like roses or old fish when we blasted into that mine and killed every single one of those bastards before taking our friends out of there.

But how could I ask him to return to this place of torture?

Escaping *just once* was his miracle.

And now I wanted him to throw that all away and probably place himself back in captivity—or worse.

He was a deserter who beat his captor. They would take it out in flesh. I couldn't tell him any of it, so I downshifted.

"Maybe you smell like wet rhino," I said and two of the three of us laughed.

"Griz has about a thousand bars of soap," I said. "I'll go get you the ten bars because that might just do the job."

"I missed you, sugar," Cass said, putting his hand over mine.

"Myn," said Griz who put his own digits over both.

2.

Griz set it up.

He knew that bathing in the lake would lead to frostbite on bits that shouldn't be frozen. In an attempt to avoid hypothermia and amputation, he decided to draw Cass a bath inside. Only thing was, I had never seen his version of a cave spa.

It was in a small grotto – a smaller cave -- that offered some privacy and an actual spa experience. Griz apparently collected towels because there were about two hundred of them in the room: plush ones, beach ones, and even towels with rainbows and unicorns on them.

It took forever for him to heat enough water in his pots and pans and then pour them into a deep circular "tub," but our host loved a challenge.

Everything in this rock room had been filched from someplace else except the tub, which was a bubbling hole in the ground. Griz even provided aromatherapy with vases filled with lavender that he had picked from the local fields.

He ran a fine soak, which was obvious as he brewed the liquid for the bath and then in a separate cookpot seeped evergreen leaves, which he also had me sip as tea in the morning. The smell was intoxicating, and Cass told me that the concoction was nature's very own detox brew.

"All you need, sugar, is right out there," he said, pointing outside the cave. Then he smiled. "I could live in the wild forever. If I wasn't lonely."

"Tub time," I said, interrupting his fantasy.

This bubbling, steaming tub of earthly delight was big enough for three, which was the idea. After the hot water cooled to lukewarm, Griz presented us with a wide variety of robes he had "borrowed" from other settlements in these parts.

I couldn't deny the truth: I smelled like a dead fish, too. It wasn't fair to the others to breathe in my stink. That was why I hid in a dark corner, stripped down to bra and panties, all the while covering myself in that delicious coat of thick, never-worn terrycloth. Cass and Griz weren't as particular with the whole nudity thing involved with bathing. Both stripped down to skin, ignoring the robe, tossing the clothes onto rocks, and then maneuvered their large frames into the bath.

The ground swallowed both of them

Griz lit candles and placed them everywhere, so the entire room shimmered. It smelled like Christmas. It looked like a romantic date. *For three.*

A guy. A bear. And a nerd . . . that would be me.

In this temple of steamy mist and swaying flames, I tried to figure out how to do it . . . as in get in the tub without doing a striptease show. I could stand and just drop the cloak, proudly revealing my everything. *How soft-core porn of me.* Or I could crouch down, quickly drop it, and then with my hands covering everything jump into the tub. *How seventh grade of me.* Either way, it meant maximum skin exposure and both of them were looking. And not at each other.

My face flamed and I looked straight up to avoid their stares.

A glint of something bright way high up caught the corner of my eye because it seemed to spark like a tiny lit firecracker. On second glance, it was nature's chandelier made of jagged blue-white ice crystals that shimmered in the low amber light. I would gaze up and just do it.

Three, two, one . . . mortification.

I stood straight, dropped the robe, and quickly took off the only bra I had, so it wouldn't still be soaking wet in the morning. Same with the undies. Griz could have cared less because he was busy looking sideways now to soap his own pits, and then contorted to do the same with his toes. It made me smile. He was so . . . hygienic about it.

Cass was another story.

He looked.

Really looked.

Shit, shit, shit, shit, shit.

"So, Caspian, what do you make of Chicago Bears season? I think they are woefully lacking in defense." *As was I!*

"You are stunningly, astoundingly gorgeous, and, damn, that's the least interesting thing about you," Cass marveled.

3.

There were no words. Not for him. Not from me.

Cass continued to stare as I sunk in the water so low that only my blushing face and neck was visible.

And then it got worse. Griz was up, out of the tub, draping about five towels over his head. He crouched by the side of the tub, so I could tie one like a turban. I guess having clean pits marked the end of his bath. I caressed that sweet face with one hand. "Thank you, Griz," I said. "You are a wonder."

He smiled. He didn't know what I said. But he knew it was good.

"Night, Wa, night, Gas," he said, happily tripping along until he was out of sight.

And then . . .

There were two.

4.

Cass leaned his head back against the side of the tub like a guy with absolutely no place in the universe to go. He had no issue with the human body—his or mine. Under the fragrant, warm nirvana of water, his arm brushed my leg. Or some body part. I evaded; he waited.

"I like to bathe naked, so don't look," he teased when he purposely jumped out of the tub to fetch a small glass jar. "Remember, our senses are supposed to be heightened here—a scientific tidbit I plan to enjoy. Now, turn around. I won't bite."

"Excuse me?"

He turned me around until he was behind me and his clever fingers were rubbing small squares of salt across my shoulders. Cass mumbled something about how this was a medical treatment (*uh-huh*) to release toxins. I was too exhausted and worried to argue with him or science.

He scrubbed lower, easing every ache of the day, skin and bone surrendering as my tight muscles were soothed. Today was a day when the reset was apparently on the fritz, so I felt the pain of existing in the wilderness. When he reached around to my sides, I felt . . . well, I *felt*. Shivers were running rampart, so I thought of something mundane like cleaning up the kitchen or doing algebra homework. *Way to ruin a mood, Walker.* But, I couldn't deny – as much as I tried -- the little jolts he gave me when the water made his hand slip and slide, accidentally touching the side of my right breast.

I slid away to the other side of the tub.

"You're not going to do my back?" he said, sounding hurt. It was such a simple and dangerous request. Possibilities lingered in the air until I waved them away with my wet hand.

"No," I said, with one-hundred percent sureness.

"At the end of the day, it's not you and him. It's not me and you. It's you and you," he reminded me.

5.

He brushed a hand over my hand and let his thumb rub the inside of my palm. The rest of his fingers felt so good resting in mine.

How do you keep your distance in a not-large-enough tub? Answer: you move to the furthest part and try not to do anything alluring. Questions raced through brain matter. Why didn't I have a ponytail holder? But I didn't, and I knew in all this humidity my hair would be wild and wavy. If only I had my damn glasses.

I sunk down further to just above my nose and posed a perfectly leading question that would make this the least passionate place on earth. Cass was psychic in life and I never asked him if he could still communicate with the living while he was in The Other. I was sure it would provide fascinating answers—interesting, nonpersonal ones.

"It's a dangerous question," Cass said. "Easiest thing to do here is to tell me what you want to find out and I'll focus on it before I go to sleep. Maybe I could invade your mother's dreams. Just do a little check-in if that makes you feel better."

He was one of the most giving people I had ever known and my heart loved him for it, even if I wasn't passionately in love with him.

"Just a quiet check-in," I said, "And by the way, thank you."

"Cass, is there ever anyone you want to check in on?" I asked. It seemed like a fair question because he knew everything about me, and I knew very little about his time in the living realm before he punched his ticket to the afterlife.

He had full lips that usually stretched across that big, lived-in face. Usually, they were smiling, but not now. His eyes were suddenly quite far away. All that blond hair was falling in his face as he tried to hide the unmistakable face of grief. I knew that he had lost his mother when he was in high school. Something about a terrible car crash, but he rarely talked about it.

Cass had an instant solution to his sudden mood change, which was to submerge his entire body and head under the water.

When his head came up, he was inches away and in my face. My breath hitched.

"You know something, Walker, I've loved and lost quite a few people in my life. Someday, I promise, I will tell you," he said in a low voice.

What followed was a silence that was suspended in time and this unusual space.

"It's why I'm so sure with you. And I know you feel something, too," he said as the candles flickered.

When I looked down, he took a wet finger and cupped the bottom of my chin. His other hand rested on my knee. In that moment, I felt protected. Safe.

"You don't have to say it. You can pretend not to see it. But, you can't deny it," Cass said. "The love you choose to never see . . . well, it's still there, swirling all around you."

He put a finger in the water and swirled it around hard until the outer bands of the circles touched parts I kept hidden.

"Cass," I whispered.

There was that smile again.

When Cass laughed, he really laughed. He laughed with his entire frame, shaking as he tilted his body back. These were deep, full-throttle releases that made the air dance. His laughter was contagious and soon I found my belly shaking.

I didn't want to do it, but there were times when I remembered. There was the one time when we almost made love. A ghost of a kiss always lingered. It was from a moment that would never be again. We had an evolving, complicated relationship.

Love him?

Yes. No. Yes.

Daniel was my soulmate. There are many soulmates, but only one understands the howling of your heart.

Once upon a time ago, very late at night, before I would soon be a virgin no longer, Daniel asked me, "Baby, are you sure?"

"With you, I am."

And I still was.

6.

"Cass, you're such a genuine soul. You have integrity. I like the way your mind works. You radiate confidence and love," I began, but he put his fingers to my lips.

"Not now. You're killing me with each word. Someday say those words to me because you'll mean them in another way. You'll also bring up my devastating good looks, sugar—especially when I'm jackass naked like now. But we don't have the time for this now. This moment is for the rest of our team. We have to save as many as possible."

I nodded.

"Before you hit me in the head, I'll help you try to save Daniel. We'll leave in two days. There are less guards on the weekends. It ups our chances. We're not taking the bear child. I don't even want to take you, but I will because you'll insist," he said.

He stared hard in my watery eyes. "But if there isn't any saving possible, I want you to realize something I never thought was possible after I lost *them*.

"A broken heart is an open heart," he said in a quiet voice.

He put a finger to my lips. Again. "I know you have a lot of questions, but let's not do that tonight. We'll make a plan to get into the mine tomorrow. Sometime later, we'll tell our saddest of sad stories," he said, turning away from me.

"Tonight, in this liquid heaven, I'd like to ask you—the girl asking me to go back into hell to save her boyfriend—to do one thing for me."

"Anything," I promised.

"In the interest of good hygiene, soap up my back," Cass said with a grin. "Slowly, sugar. I have a dirty mind when it comes to you—and an even dirtier back.

"Soap my six," he added.

"I'm assuming that's your shoulder blades."

"It's not," he said, "but it will do."

7.

Sleeping fully clothed in my leggings and sweater on a flat rock, covered by blankets past my chin, seemed like a plan. A clean Cass occupied another corner. He had found a down vest, jeans that fit, and a dark-green cable-knit sweater. Hands folded over his wide chest, he mostly closed his eyes, his back "relaxing" against a stone cave wall, marine style. He didn't snore; he barely slept. Cass existed on full alert.

Time was a relative thing, but I figured it was the middle of the night when I woke with a start again. I did a quick roll call in that dim candlelight: Cass was gone.

A wicked thought entered my mind: *Maybe he waited until I fell asleep and then went back to the mine himself to save the others? Wouldn't that be just like him? Evade, so he didn't have to go in with a team, meaning me?*

I raced outside, half relieved, half disappointed at what I found. There he was sitting on a flat rock near the cave opening, eyes wide open and staring at a slivered fall moon. Seasons still moving backward, I could feel the chill of winter giving way to the more tempered coolness of my favorite season, autumn. The dying time.

Cass hated to be pinned down, and maybe the wide-open space of an endless forest felt appealing. Before he could see me, because it was that dark, he must have felt me. I watched him hitch left; a large, calloused hand patted the rock.

He always made room.

I slid in next to him and he took a giant blanket and put it over both of our legs. In front of us were large fir trees that raced upward; way above us was a black slate, except for that one burst of luminous in the foreign sky.

Cass twisted his head to look at me. Really look at me. In a way that made me feel naked and vulnerable.

"Ladies, first," Cass said. He ran a stray fingertip across my cheek, pushing back a runaway hair. I felt treasured and safe. It's why I opened my mouth to speak, but hard, breathless sobs escaped a place so deep that I felt like I had never visited there ever, alive or dead. *How could I ever let the bruises on my insides go?*

"Four little letters," he whispered. Sometimes, I thought he was reading my mind.

"H-o-p-e," he said. "You heal with hope."

"Hope is not . . . a plan," I sobbed.

"It is in my book, sugar," Cass said. "First step onto the hope train . . . then toss the rest of it on the tracks."

For what felt like hours, I poured it out. Every moment with Edward. Every feeling being a prisoner in that room. The tethering. The wedding night. Every second from my time spent in EXR hell.

And when it was over, Cass didn't try to put Band-Aids on critical wounds. He was actually rather matter of fact about it all.

His tone dipped darker. "Well, the dickless bastard will never be able to have sex again. What you did will cause scar tissue. Every single time he even gets excited, he will remember you, Walker, in a haze of excruciating pain, which means he will come after you for payback. Someday—sooner versus later—I'll extinguish that soulless prick for you," he vowed. "I'll rip his insides out."

"I think there's actually a long line for that job," I said.

It just slipped out. And we laughed because really what else was left?

"He can go to hell," Cass bit out. "I'll meet him there."

"Why would you be going to hell?"

"Because of what I did . . . what I didn't do. I'm not this perfect person, Walker, although for you I try to get as close as humanly possible, which is still not close enough."

"Why don't you just try to be yourself," I said, a hand on his chilly cheek. I tilted his head toward me. "The truth is I know very little about you."

"You know the most important thing. You know the deep down," he said in a low voice.

His eyes told me that he loved me. I didn't know what to do with it. With him.

"And I loved her, too," Cass said.

And there it was.

"I know you probably think I only came here for you. I only wish, sugar. But, I came here for both of you."

Cass had been in love?

"Her name is Megan."

NINETEEN

1.

Cass placed a large, warm hand over mine and for several moments, we just sat in that big night, remembering. Existing. It was cold enough to see your own breath, and for some reason that proved endlessly fascinating. It affirmed that we were, indeed, *here*.

He took those strong fingers and touched my face in the most calming way. It wasn't romantic; Cass needed the connection and I stared deeply into his deep blue eyes. He didn't flinch, but looked so hard, I swore I saw pieces of my very soul.

"Walker, ever since I met you, I felt something strongly. It hasn't been that way for a long time. It's called trust," he said, "At the same time, I've wanted to tell you something about me thousands of times, but I didn't want you to carry it. I knew that you would try to carry it with me—and then you would want to help me fix it."

"I have strong hands," I whispered.

I moved my fingertips over a scar on the bottom of his jaw and lowered my eyes, but I couldn't deny what I felt. He was crying now and

285

his tears washed over my fingers.

"Cass," I said in a low voice. I took his hand and pressed it against my heart. "Just tell me. We can figure it out."

"I wanted to tell you . . . only I wanted to keep it close," he said in a choked voice. "Keeping it close is the only way I'm able to go on each day. It's the only way to bear it," he said. I felt his hand slip into mine. "Oh my God, Walker, you have no idea. No idea."

I blew out the tiny candle he had lit, so now it was pitch black. Maybe if we were in total darkness, he would feel safe enough to *finally* say it.

"Cass, let's start small," I said. "Where did you grow up? I met you in Chicago, but you said it wasn't your hometown. You said something about California and then you moved to Chicago with your dad."

"Santa Monica," he said, slowly. "We lived there. Me. My mom and dad. My sisters. The Claires—although I didn't know they were 'the Claires' back then. They were just my extremely strange sisters."

I tried not to visibly react.

"I was eighteen when it happened; my sisters were sixteen, about to have another turn around the sun. Remember, they die when they turn seventeen. They spend the last year of their many lives—and they've had more than you'll ever know—living recklessly for themselves and killing others."

"This is a story about you and your sisters?"

"No . . . yes . . . I don't know what I'm saying anymore," Cass said. He dropped his head into his hands, trying to settle himself. I looked away when I saw his back shake. He sobbed for just a moment. Then he said evenly, "It's a story about me . . . about her. About best friends."

"Who?" I asked, gently. Then, the lightbulb flashed.

"Oh . . . you had a girlfriend," I said, it finally dawning on me that he was so smart, loyal, and handsome that, of course, there was someone special.

"You fell in love—and someone dumped someone. She broke your heart."

"No!" Cass said, suddenly rising to his feet while swearing under his breath. I watched in horror when he kicked a large pile of wood that

Griz has built for fires and then took several individual logs and smashed them as hard as he could onto a nearby rock. The sheer violence of it made my eyes go wide, but I didn't move.

When he returned, he lowered his head and buried it in my lap. His breath shuddered several times while I sat too shocked to move.

Daniel would certainly understand why I put a hand on his shoulder and began to smooth his skin with light, calming strokes. It was the humane thing to do. At least, I convinced myself.

Cass cleared his throat and words that had long since been buried began to tumble.

2.

Death Story: Megan Caspian Danko
Age of Demise: 4

Her name was Annie and she soothed edges, Cass began.

She lived next door and I had known her since the beginning. I was always a big, lumbering kid who felt like the Hulk; she was bony-thin with long, reddish-brown hair spilling halfway down her back, a sprinkling of small freckles, button nose, and heavy lids hiding sparkling hazel eyes. She was the most beautiful thing I had ever seen until I met you, Walker, and my world was a better place when she was happy, which wasn't always.

We were five. Best friends. Forever.

Every single time I saw her, it would go this way: Three birdlike taps on the back door of my house. She would open the door.

"Well, look at you," Annie would say, sidestepping me as she walked in our kitchen. She was always an eclectic dresser to stay the least. In high school, she'd wear this thrift store yellow sundress, black leggings, a Mickey Mouse watch, and cat-eyed sunglasses that made her look like Audrey Hepburn's stunning younger Irish sister.

I couldn't stop memorizing her.

She always said the same thing. And, so did I.

"Well, look at you, sugar," I'd respond. "Now that you're here, I guess

we're out of the woods." I think we heard it once in a movie—or maybe we just made it up. No one knew. All I did know was that her ruby-red lips would curve into a wide smile while her brilliant spirit brightened the room like twinkling light jettisoning across the night sky.

Just being around her made me feel like we were indeed on terra firma, riding shotgun under a blaze of stars.

Annie's mother, Samantha, flew the coop the summer between kindergarten and first grade. I remember the night when the woman with those same hazel eyes stood in the sway between the front lawns in our otherwise boring suburban neighborhood screaming that she didn't want to be a cop's wife anymore—and certainly not the wife of someone who constantly asked her, "Where did you go? Who did you talk to? What did you do? Who do you know? Did you talk to any men?"

Trusting, her husband was not. His name was Gene and he was my father's partner at the LAPD. That night, he hovered in the door, half in his old life and half in his new one as a single father—although he didn't know it at the time. Big, not-so-bad, warmhearted, control-freak Gene, bald and 250 pounds of muscle, had always been my father's trusted pal, but he was in a different kind of trouble that night than what they usually encountered on the streets of LA.

Samantha had been "fooling around" with her boss, although I was just a little boy and didn't know what that meant in those days. The only part I "got" was the fool part, which seemed to describe Gene, who was begging his wife to stay.

My sister, Claire V, slipped through distracted parental eyes to wander outside, despite the fact that it was just shy of midnight. Before my father could stop her, the four-year-old demon who lived in our house looked up at Samantha, smiled sweetly, and said, "You will go off to die—and die you will."

"You're a horrid little girl," Samantha railed on her.

The night her mother fled, my best friend in the entire world—Annie from next door—was outside, clinging for dear life to her mother's long legs and short skirt, although Samantha was quick to shuck her off. She peeled off her daughter's fingers like she was removing alien tentacles that kept reattaching. Annie fell to the ground like wounded animal and began to scream.

"I hear the sound . . . of tears," my other sister, Claire A, began. She was suddenly there. From nowhere. The girls had an uncanny way of feeding off the pain of others and this was a five-star buffet.

Five hours later, they found Samantha's body on the I-15 outside of Vegas, twisted and mangled in a five-car pileup thanks to some college kid in an SUV who took an unplanned snooze while driving. I got a black suit from the local Sears, the sad kind for a little boy, who only needed those kinds of duds for either a wedding or a funeral.

My mom had her hands full with me, my four sisters including Claire C and Claire S, and the semi-orphan girl next door who got all the mothering she needed. I never got along with my sisters who would hit and trick me, so even as a little boy, I stuck to Annie like glue.

Best friends.

Two peas. One pod. Confidants. Never more.

Until a couple of months before high school graduation.

It was a middle-of-the-night, needy, stupid, but beautiful mi—

Wait, I never call it a mistake. That would be a lie.

It was something else.

A marvel.

Cass stopped for a moment and put a hand over my kneecap.

"You okay, sugar? You want to hear more?"

I nodded and smiled at him. As usual, I wanted to hear it all.

Annie and I went to Tommy Malone's party on an unseasonably warm night in Venice Beach. We trusted it was safe to eat the bean dip that we later figured was laced with pot, and a lot of it. I mean, most of us know to question the brownies, but this was chip dip. I had asked if the food was clean because I didn't do that. Tommy lied.

Welcome to your so-called social life when you have to BYOE (bring your own everything) or take a chance.

Life is full of those roulette moments and we got a good-bad spin.

After, we couldn't go home because we were high (neither of us went for seconds, but took liberal firsts). Our fathers were cops and would want answers that led to names, angry accusations, fists, and bail. What followed was a plan to squander a little bit of time until our pops were snoring in front of their respective wide screens.

Annie and I, our second chapter, began with an impromptu semi-clothed midnight swim on a starry beach—my best friend doing a little strip-down hidden by the shadows of night. It wasn't long before she was swinging that tumbling red hair forward before daring me, "Cass, live a little."

My clothes evaporated, and in my haze, I put them too close to the water. A flirty swim had me chasing her, holding her and then . . . why were her arms now wrapped around my neck? Water games were followed by a small, roaring fire—drying my pants and sweater, and her flimsy new green spring dress on weathered sticks—and then wrapping our underwear-clad bodies in a blanket I found in the back of my Jeep.

I convinced her that we were cold, but it was Indian summer warm. It was the kind of summer heat that makes love to your layers.

This was trailed by one of those midnight talks you can only have with someone who knows you down to your DNA. Annie's face looked like she wanted to blink those pretty eyes and transport herself to places unknown.

"My dad doesn't really want me to go to college. He's irrational when it comes to the idea of his daughter having a real future," she said. "He just won't let go. And he wraps it in all these fears about how dangerous it is out there. All this cop shit. I can't take it anymore. The thing is he won't allow another person he loves to walk out that front door."

"Everyone leaves—eventually," I told Annie, not knowing how true those words would echo.

I stayed quiet, but my legs opened and then my arms. She climbed in, I closed any gaps, and we melted together while she continued to pour out her heart and her future.

"I have to do something drastic to get out of here," she said, her eyes welling up. "It's live like this—his idea of life–or create something beautiful on my own."

I felt her entire body shake and when she started weeping. I broke and held her even tighter. When she wiggled around to face me, I dried her cheeks with my fingers, like always, but this time I allowed my skin on her skin to linger.

That's when I knew.

We were crossing a line. We were falling down that slippery slope where loneliness leads to companionship and all vague ideas of friendship become love.

One minute, we were just talking. The next, she pressed her lips to mine and then no one moved. It would have been so easy. Just a lean back. A subtle signal of no.

And then we spit on fate. I kissed her back.

A few weeks later, the Claires made full use of their special gifts of "sight" and future predictions and made an announcement over an otherwise boring chicken dinner. V informed both of our families, and us, that "we" were pregnant.

Walker, are you still with me?

No judgment. *Although, I wasn't sure how I felt about this love story.*

No questions. *Although, I had a few hundred million of those that were strictly none of my business.*

"A baby," I said into the night wind, which didn't erase what was now forever spoken. *He had a baby! Cass was a father.* That fact didn't bother me. What hurt was the idea of how much we really do not know . . . about the people we think we know. Do we really know anyone? The fact that we probably didn't know as much as we wanted made me want to cry. And later, I would hate myself for willing the tears for my own selfish notions.

He saw the question marks and quickly went back in.

We didn't even make it to dessert. Annie ran for the hills, and by that, I mean first the Hollywood Hills and then her rich friend Bec Multack's house in Malibu. It was one of those ten-million-dollar beach houses that only the very rich and very famous could afford. Bec's father ran a movie studio, so no one was worried about cash flow. Annie and I knew Bec from her poor days when she went to school with us and her dad was a junior agent.

You didn't need to be a detective to figure out that Annie would run there. It was a great place to think. I guessed right and the crashing waves of the Pacific drowned out the screaming in my head when I rang Bec's doorbell.

Annie saw me pull into the driveway. She was on top of things now and had one of those home pregnancy kits.

"Well, look at you," she said with a hint of a smile.

"Well, look at you, sugar," I replied.

She told me to sit on her friend's front step while she stayed inside and took the test. "You mean, I'm not invited in?" I asked her because for some reason that made my bones hurt. She grew up in my house, but she would give me the door.

"It's easier," she said in a fake breezy voice, disappearing for a good fifteen minutes.

I sat and listened to the gulls dive for their sushi dinners and I thought of all of the positives here. If she was, then she was. We would work it out and make it beautiful. There were ways.

And then she was back, waving something in the dark. It was the pregnancy test stick.

"All good," she said, handing it to me. Before I could look down, she grabbed a bag that was stashed in the half-closed front door.

"I'm going, Cass," she told me. "Please don't follow."

Words wouldn't form as the knife twisted. "Wait, Ann," I called out. But it was too late. She had made her plans and I wasn't included in them. A car pulled up in the driveway. She had called an Uber from inside the house, and suddenly my future was barreling at me.

I trailed after her, but she was walking fast now. I began to list all the reasons she needed to stay. I told her it didn't matter if there was no baby. We could still be together. We could still be us. We could go away together after graduation and see if what happened on the beach that night was an offer of a new life or just a one-night whim.

"Tell my father that you looked for me," Annie begged.

Her words barreled at me. "Tell him that I might be in Malibu with some friend from school. Buy me a few days to figure it out—and get far. I'll be in touch."

"But where are you—"

My words were cut off as she stopped, turned, and kissed my forehead. I'll never forget what she said next: "I guess we tested fate, Cassy," she whispered into my ear. "I'll never regret it. In fact, I just did it again."

I watched her walk into the distance and with the opening of a car door, out of my life. Her friend Bec came out a few numb moments later and began to offer kind and useless words about it all working out one day or someday and how young love is always tested.

"So, it was true," Bec said. "Sorry, Cass."

What?

She was staring at my hand, which was dead at my side.

A quick glimpse down at the plastic stick in my right hand and I couldn't breathe. There was a pink plus sign. In case, you're a total moron, it also tells you in words.

Pregnant.

"Holy shit, Cass," I said, shuddering deeply.

By not looking down, I missed it. But that was life. Moments swinging one way or the other based on what we did see . . . and what we didn't.

On and off for the next three months, I drove the lonely man's highway, living in my car, stopping at gas stations to refuel, and then checking out states and spots that seemed reasonable. If she ever mentioned it, I drove there to look around. And then when all hope was gone, I would be off, merging with the rest of the seekers, on my way to the next probable location.

I bought doughnuts and stayed in a cheap motel in Idaho where the TV didn't work and the giant black screen gave me entirely too much time with myself. It was my last stop because I was out of money, so I went home to Santa Monica. My plan had always been to join the marines, but I hesitated because what if Annie and the baby came home? I needed to be there.

And I was there, sleeping, on the day of the Claires' seventeen birthday. I didn't tell you yet about how my mother was facing the medium-to-later stages of Alzheimer's disease.

Cass stopped for a second, allowing his words to settle. There was a part of me that believed he would end the story there. The last part was often the worst. Why even say it to the trees? Why give it meaning in a world that often had none?

I could see that he was crying softly again, and I put my hand over his and allowed our breath to sync. In and out. Out and in. I leaned over and kissed him gently on the forehead. He hadn't been touched there in a long time and he squeezed his eyes closed.

Cass needed to know that no matter what I would protect him now. He cleared his throat.

Annie came home on a rainy morning in Santa Monica on Christmas Eve. She wasn't alone. All I can remember from that morning was the baby in her carrier—a beautiful little girl with big hazel eyes and wisps of reddish hair that made her look exactly like her mother and a lot like you, sugar. I guess the dimples came from my genetic pool.

Annie called for me, but I was sleeping with my earphones in and heavy metal music blaring to drown out the ghosts.

What I couldn't know back then is that the Claires always kill their current mothers before they punch out at age seventeen. They do this on their own death day. They handed my mom her purse and car keys, knowing that she wasn't allowed to drive anymore. By the time I finally made my way to the kitchen, I was stunned at the sight of Annie and our newborn daughter.

"I named her Megan," Annie said in a low voice to make the impossible moment private. "Megan Caspian."

"What a stupid name," V vented.

Another beat. "MC . . . what is she . . . a DJ?" sister A taunted.

A quick breath. "No, she's just another mistake in Cass's pitiful world,"

C said.

All of this talking bought them time. We heard a car engine roar to life in the garage. Mom was behind the wheel. My feet pounded through the back door to stop our mother who was backing out of the rain-soaked driveway. Annie was always faster, and raced to the driver's side window.

"Stop the car, Mrs. D!" Annie shouted, opting for Plan B, which was swinging the passenger's side door open and jumping in the vehicle. She opened it in a single move, hurled her body sideways, and bounced right in, slamming the door shut, so she didn't fall out.

Mom floored it. In her fog, she was looking out her side window grinning at our house when half a block down, the Thursday garbage truck meandered down the street. She couldn't possibly see it because Mama was going sixty miles per hour by now.

It was no real contest. The truck would be deemed the winner.

Annie was wedged inside the front seat, her legs and chest crushed, and when I felt for a pulse, I only found a thready one that was slowing by the second. I began to scream one word—"No, no, no, no!"—at the top of my lungs.

"Cass," Annie whispered. "The baby. Forever."

"Forever and always," I said.

Knowing I might kill them all, the Claires locked themselves into my father's relic of a Cadillac that he kept in the garage and tinkered with from time to time. It was V who calmly went back inside the house and picked up the baby carrier. She placed it in the back seat of Dad's big, honking-white machine, a steel tank. Sisters A, C, and S climbed in the car after closing our always malfunctioning, garage door while breaking off the key in the lock.

My sisters were on some kind of autopilot driven by what they described as an ancient curse. Meanwhile, the garage couldn't be opened from either the inside or the outside without a lot of time and tools. A force that was not their own, they claimed, turned on the car's ignition.

I didn't see any of those manipulations. I was in the middle of the street, helplessly watching Annie and Mom die in their crushed car. When

Dad rushed up to the sight, his knees buckled. He had a thunderclap heart attack that almost ended his life.

I stayed with Dad until the ambulance arrived and he was stabilized. When I finally walked into the house, I smelled the car fumes coming from the garage and raced in that direction. That's when I saw V in the other car. With the others.

It was V who, through the haze, pushed the baby carrier onto the passenger side window. She held up a little pink blanket to the car window and I heard her laughing. It was a winner's laugh because she always hated me. "We cut Mom's brake lines. Bye, bye, bitch," she gloated.

I was doubled over choking as I tried to break the windshield out first with a Louisville Slugger Dad kept in the garage. Then, I used my own fists. It didn't take long before my fingers were soaked in blood, which I wiped all over those windows as I punched and struck that glass until the skin was ripped to the bone. By the time I smashed a garden shovel against the car's bulletproof and unbreakable back window, I was barely lucid.

Fade to black.

It was Annie's father, Gene, who revived me.

When I could breathe again, he placed her in my arms.

It turns out the Claires had taken the baby carrier and pink blanket into the car to scare the shit out of me. They left the actual baby between pillows on my bed with a note: "Be seeing you. Both of you. Scratch that. All of you. The Claires."

A shot of murderous rage shot through my system. I would kill them with my own hands before they harmed my mother. But, this wasn't about me now.

I cleared my throat and watched while Cass reclined all the way backward on the smooth, cold rock. I sat, flush with him, arms touching, and asked the inevitable questions: "Do you miss your little girl? Who takes care of her now? How old is she?"

"What you're really asking is: Why the hell have you never mentioned this before?" he said, looking blank for a moment. His tan face went milky white. "Yes, Walker, I miss my little girl with every molecule of my being. I don't know who takes care of her now. She is four.

"I'll finish it now," he said in a low voice.

The baby was only six pounds with big eyes that looked right at you. I would carry her, day and night. Her mama was gone, so I'd take off my shirt, her skin touching my skin.

I'd talk to her all night long. If I really wanted to torture the both of us, I'd sing. She didn't like her formula at first and wasn't gaining weight, so I fed it to her an ounce here and another ounce there. Until it was a full meal. One day, she drank the entire bottle and it remains the biggest victory of my life.

It wasn't long before she laughed each time she saw my face. Her crib was in my room and she would clap when I opened my eyes in the morning. Imagine having someone next to you who is just happy that you've opened your eyes. It was a love I had never known.

She grew and became a curious little girl who loved animals, her grandpas—including Annie's grief-stricken father Gene next door—Winnie the Pooh, and the rain.

I was her big Poppa and she was little girl. I'd read to her, so it all made sense.

"Sometimes," said Pooh, "the smallest things take up the most room in your heart."

My dad—now a widower —and Big Gene, were champions. They babysat, fed her, and sat on the ground with her laughing like fools. They were big cops scrunching under a little girl's pink table having afternoon tea out of fake plastic cups. They loved it. At the same time, they pushed me hard the following year to enlist in the marines. "We have nothing else to do in life but raise and protect that little girl," Dad said. "It would be our honor, son. Now, go. We'll be here waiting. You're her father. Build a life for her."

So, I did.

I went to Texas first and then Afghanistan where I made it into an elite marine combat unit. I shipped home for Christmas that year and found my dad in the laundry room wrapping those solid arms around me in a giant bear hug. He has not only survived his heart attack, but was thriving again.

Dad kissed me on the forehead. None of that macho bullshit was between us anymore. When we pressed flesh now, we put heart and soul into it.

"Is that our famous spaghetti sauce I smell?" I said. "The kind with the whole bottle of wine in it?"

"What's three more drunks on Christmas Eve in the City of Angels, son?" Dad said.

"Who you calling drunk?" I said.

There was Gene behind the stove stirring like a madman. He put down his big wooden spoon long enough to walk over and grab my enormous duffel bag. "Of course, it's pasta and gravy, Cassy. Is it Wednesday? Are we still on the planet earth?" he said.

What followed was the same real hug over and over again. It was just a small family unit now, but it was tight and solid.

He pointed to the living room. "You better get in there," Gene said.

I swung through the living room portal and the little monkey didn't miss a beat.

"Poppa! Poppa! Poppa!"

"Sugar!"

The little redheaded girl with the bright hazel eyes flew into my arms like a small missile. I got a grip on her and then stood, spinning her around and around until we were both laughing, hugging, and kissing. "Did you grow a tree bigger?"

"Just half a tree, Poppa!" she said. "Can I have a puppy for Christmas?"

"Yes, I said. "Anything you want, MC, princess warrior of this fair land and all the lands in the universe."

Six months later, I was back in Kabul on a brutally hot summer day. We lost two men to IED bombs hidden on roads, so I was already raw when my captain handed me the note to call home. My stomach dropped. "Shit, Dad had another heart attack," I thought. "Maybe it was Gene's turn. He eats like crap."

But, as usual, nothing bad ever happened to the men in our family.

"We found a pediatric specialist and he has made amazing strides with childhood leukemia. It's the most common type of cancer in children. But we don't know yet if that's what we're facing," Dad told me.

I flew home the next day.

MC had the flu in January after I left, and then what might have been food poisoning a week later. She had been tired and sluggish for weeks, which made the grandfathers go into hyper drive. A visit to the kiddie doc led to a scary road of hospital tests.

A natural redhead with pale skin, she looked almost albino when I walked into her hospital room.

"Hi, Poppa," MC said, barely sitting up in her bed now. "I don't feel so good. You can't spin me today."

"It's okay, sugar," I said, holding her tightly in my arms. "It has to be okay. It has to be . . ."

"Chemotherapy is the main treatment," said the doctor, who ordered weekly treatments followed by radiation.

I was honorably discharged from the marines and spent the next year in and out of chemo sessions with my daughter. "Read it again, Poppa. I want to be Cinderella," said the wee voice in the hospital bed after another blood transfusion to fight infections that had become wars.

"Sugar, I'll have your pumpkin waiting for you when you get out of here and two beautiful glass slippers," I said.

"And a puppy named Bingo?"

"And a puppy named Bingo."

Another night before the antibiotics kicked in and her fever raged, my baby said, "Poppa, tell me about Mama. I see her sometimes. When I'm sleepy. Like now. There she is. Over there. Behind you. With grandma."

I couldn't turn to look. I would shatter.

"If you want, Megan, you can run to her," I began with a clogged voice. "You don't have to stay here for your poppa. You can go if it hurts too much. You know what to say."

MC cleared her little throat as she shivered under the covers. She knew this by heart. I used to say it to Annie all the time.

"I will say, 'Mama, well, look at you.' That's what she used to say to you.

Then you, Poppa, would say . . ."

"Well, look at you, sugar," I said with the kind of grin that always made my baby smile. It took every ounce of strength inside of me to find it.

We buried her later that week in the town cemetery next to my mother and Annie.

TWENTY

There were no words. Only one question formed: "How do you wake up every morning and breathe?"

"I don't know, sugar. My mom used to say, 'Cass, collect your hurts, but don't dwell on them.' And I geek out . . . a lot. I put songs on. Really loud. I dance to them. She liked to dance," he said.

"Your mom?"

"No, my baby," he said.

I'll never know why, but I stood and I, Walker Callaghan, the world's worst dancer, began to do a slow twist. I couldn't resist moving.

"I go crazy for that stuff," Cass said, joining me.

When he put his hands on my hips, my face tilted to meet his.

"All I ever wanted was to find the right someone. Spoil the shit out of her. Give her my heart," Cass said as he began to twist. "I wanted to take her out. Show her the world. Make love to her everywhere. Get a dog. Eat hot dogs. Smile. Watch movies. Sleep naked in the fall. Say I love you. Hold our baby."

"You don't want much," I said staring into his sweet eyes.

"I want everything," he said.

In those deep, nameless woods, we twisted to the music in our heads.

"I needed someone to turn the lights on," Cass said, a lone tear racing down one cheek. "No one did for the longest time—and then I met you."

In that moment, I knew exactly who Cass Danko was as a man. He was the one who would go the extra mile, keep his word, and give it his all. He would expect absolutely nothing in return.

I wanted someone to love Cass as fiercely as he loved and with as much devotion as he would give. I wanted him to receive love the way I loved Daniel. Yet, at the same time, I knew he wouldn't leave my side because he believed in his wildest dreams that we had a future. . . and he would wait for the someday.

He was a patient forgiver who would ignore each time he saw me with another. He would adapt, adjust, and remain suspended while he waited. He didn't mind flashing his vulnerability, but he wouldn't use it against me. Cass would trust the process. He would stay the course.

It made me feel loved and guilty, worthwhile and ashamed.

2.

As time passed, a hint of early morning sunlight dared to pierce the tall canopy of trees above us. It was easier when it was dark because it was more private. When nature turned the lights on, we just had our truths, the private ones we shared. We had an unbreakable bond as two lives cut short, but not as early as a four-year-old girl who lost a battle to cancer.

Where was she now? Where did the children who died young go? Would she be with her mother who was also in the afterlife? If so, then, why wasn't she reunited with Cass when he arrived here? I was almost sure of one thing: children were not wandering the realms by themselves.

The time for questioning was over.

Now that it was light, Cass placed a finger under my chin and kissed me hard on the lips. It wasn't romantic. If I had to describe it; it was more of a contract with a period on it to seal the deal that we would tell no one about what was said here tonight.

"How do you go on?" I asked him for the second time tonight.

"I love everyone I can," Cass said. "And I think a lot about how she proved to me what C.S. Lewis wrote."

My eyes were blurred again, which obscured his face when he said words I'd never forget.

"You don't have a soul. You *are* a soul. You have a body," he quoted.

"Meaning?" I asked.

"She's out there," he said.

And then Cass told me the real reason he was in The Other.

"Her soul and her tiny body. She's here to be found," he said. "Ever since I was a little boy, the spirit world has reached out to me as a messenger. Finally, I reached back to them to ask just one question: Where do I find my daughter?"

"And the answer?"

"Kids who pass young are revered in the afterlife. They're treated like little princes and princesses—especially the little ones—and live in small clusters in camps with loving caretakers," he said. "And the best news of all? They're waiting to be claimed.

"In MC's case, she hasn't been claimed," Cass said. "Annie, her mother, is AWOL. And the spirits have told me and keep telling me that my daughter has been waiting in a place called The Other. I didn't know where that was until I came to the Midst and overheard you and Daniel making plans to escape Principal Dick.

"When you said that you were going to The Other, I began planning," he said.

He had me on lock as the sun began to rise above the mountain ridge. "If she's here, Walker, I will find her," Cass said. "I will claim her, if it's the last thing I ever do. But I do need a favor—and it's a big one."

"Anything."

He nodded.

"If something happens to me, promise me, you will find my daughter and take her with you, Walker. You look enough like Annie to be MC's mother. You can talk your way through it and pretend that you are here to claim her.

"She shouldn't be alone," Cass went on. "Even my own mother came to me in a dream once and told me MC was here . . . waiting and safe, but she wasn't allowed to claim her when there was a parent who could. "There is no one else I could trust with her except my father and Gene—and they're no help because they're alive. You can give her to them after they pass, or keep her. If you fall in love with her, you could actually be her . . . well, that's a conversation for another time."

If I fell.

How could I not?

The idea of it made my heart fill, proving I had endless empty spaces to fill.

We all do.

3.

There was one more thing—because wasn't there always.

"I don't want to name it, qualify it, or define it," Cass said, "but I do believe you and I keep running into each other for a reason."

"Some might call it fate . . . ," I began, but I couldn't finish. It hit me like a comet landing on your head.

"I saw you once when I was alive," I rushed. "A lot of my life that last month is murky, but I do remember it now. It was right before I died."

"I didn't remember it either for the longest time and then I thought you would think it was odd for me to bring it up," Cass said. "We bumped into each other walking by Lake Michigan in the living realm. You were alive; I was alive. You were wearing a white sweater with the price tag on it."

"I was invited to Northwestern for a student journalism conference," I recalled slowly. "I ran into this guy by Lake Michigan."

"You called me a palooka and informed me that you had pepper spray," Cass recalled, smiling for the first time in a long time.

"I didn't really have pepper spray," I said. "I was wearing a sweater that I planned to return to the store on Monday."

"You had on a name tag . . . one of those: Hello My Name Is things," Cass said. "I remember the odd name for a girl. Walker."

"I told you I was trying for a scholarship, but it was a longshot. You reminded me I had my whole life in front of me," I said, a bit of sadness creeping in.

"I died three weeks later."

"You told me to—and I remember this now—you said to 'Go slay.' And you still can," Cass reminded me in a voice that was like a caress.

4.

Morning was always God's way of saying, "One more time." Cass's swimming-pool-blue eyes were clear and content because what was hidden was now shared. And there was a plan because it was just like him, just like everyone, to constantly want more.

Just like Daniel, he lived by a motto: Just keep moving toward the yes.

Another yes man was in my face.

"Wat doin'?" Griz asked with a grin. He found several packs of bubblegum last night on one of his treks and knew how to blow big bubbles.

"You're Bubblelicious, Griz," I said and laughed.

"Licious," he repeated, giggling as he blew so hard that the gum shot right out of his mouth.

5.

It was an uncommonly warm autumn morning and I decided to go out and pick wild blueberries for our breakfast. I heard the wind in the trees as I filled a small wooden bucket with my spoils. Cass and Griz were much faster and had twice as much as each dared the other to fill their basket the fastest.

Thus began a high-speed chase with berries being crushed on faces and knees being scraped from hairpin turns in the bramble.

"Yee-haw!" When Cass laughed, he really laughed. He laughed with his entire frame shaking as he tilted his body back. These were deep, full-throttle releases that made the air dance. His laughter was contagious and soon I found my belly shaking.

Griz looked so big and tough from the outside, but I knew enough to be careful with the people I met along the way. He was just a little boy inside of a lot of skin and hair. A tender beating heart looking for a family.

I wanted to know him forever. And I knew why when I picked him a wild sunflower.

He cried like a baby.

6.

It was Friday. At dawn, Cass and I decided to leave on Saturday to find the others, and it made my heart race and hurt at the same time. I couldn't stay here forever, but I sure would miss Griz and his gentle ways. I tried to teach him a few words, too, along the way. He put up his big right arm and spread his fingers wide.

"Hi fife," he said with a laugh.

There was no reason to mess with his happy existence, which is why I hung back with Cass before entering the cave for our meal. Griz was making this concoction of dried bison beef, a cup of those berries, and lard that he had on hand from a hunting mission. He mixed it together and cooked it in a pan. When it cooled, he cut it into what looked like big squares.

"It's called pemmican," Cass explained. "Ancient cultures ate it because each square is about three thousand calories of energy. It meant that when food was scarce, you didn't have to eat for a long time."

I took a bite of what tasted like a meat energy bar.

"We have to make a plan for tomorrow. Don't even start with the idea that I'm not going with you," I began.

"Yu wanna go," he mimicked Griz.

For some reason, my gaze went west to the mansion on a hill way beyond here. I couldn't see it, but something inside me felt it, which is why I began to shiver on what was a seventy-degree day. He knew I was thinking about Edward.

He pointed in the general direction of Casa de Hell.

"Yep, no choice. We could spend weeks searching the other settlements in The Other for a car to jack or go to where we know the vehicles are plentiful," Cass said, looking the same way. "Before we go forward to the pit, we have to go back. And one thing," he hissed. "I see that son of a bitch and he's mine."

The plan—minus the testosterone bravado—was simple. To break into the mine, we had real weapons in our backpacks, but we lacked wheels. Cass wanted to go alone to Casa Edward to find a nice sturdy SUV to drive there, one that was big enough to hide and use later to evacuate Daniel, Eddie, and Auggie.

Cass wanted me to stay here with Griz, but knew it wasn't practical. He needed backup. He also needed someone who knew the lay of the land.

When I told him about the cars, the weaponized guards, and the science lab, I could feel his inner marine begin to stir.

"Me go," Griz suggested with a happy smile. "Me stealz there all da time."

"No, Griz. This is dangerous. It's a bad house. Never go there again," I said. I couldn't explain to him that this was way beyond your basic dumpster diving. If Edward ever caught him, he'd end up in that lab being torn apart.

"House, bad. Pitta, bad. Griz stay here," I insisted.

"No pitta for Wa," he cried. "No pitta!"

"No pitta ever, you promise," I demanded.

"It will take us a good day to hike to the house," Cass said. He drew a little map for us that included a steep hike over a mountain passage that separated the house with the cave.

"No walka," Griz said. "Rida."

"But we don't have a car, honey," I said.

"RIDA!" he shouted.

It dawned on me that Griz didn't walk all the way to that house for his occasional looting sessions. He must have had a quicker way to get there.

"Show us," I begged him.

Griz motioned for us to follow him back inside the cave, racing ahead through the rocky twists and turns until we ended up in a previously unknown section that was lower and dramatically colder.

"Looka," Griz said, pointing at a long, metal canoe. It was perfect for a guy who liked to spend his solo evenings on junking missions because there was plenty of room for his finds and treasures.

"Rida," Griz insisted.

Oh, no problem. We would ride there in a ramshackle boat through an underwater cave passage that was not on any map, hoping that our oxygen didn't run out and the walls didn't close in on us or collapse. I failed to recall the Girl Scout's badge for that one.

"We have no idea where this lets out—and it looks damn dangerous," Cass fumed. "I don't like it. Too many things can eff up."

"No eff up. I hep yo," Griz promised.

7.

Later that night, I tucked Griz into his bedroll for the last time, kissed him on his forehead, and said what I told him every night, "Thank you for saving my butt." He responded with a smile and a push of his hand on my shoulder. I exaggerated and did a backward somersault and he laughed like always.

When he was snoring, I went through my pack, which had at least two hundred throwing stars. Cass was in possession of various knives and even a small flamethrower device. All he needed was a fuel and *ka-frickin-boom*. These were dangerous toys, and once you dipped into the treasure chest, they became quite addictive.

What we still needed was wheels to get the hell out of there with three prisoners who might not be healthy enough to walk rough passages.

"Tell me about the mine—the pitta," I said to Cass as both of us tried to sleep. I was on the slab wrapped in blankets and he was just below me in his coat with a big hat over his head and a knit scarf behind his head like a pillow.

After his personal revelations of last night, it was almost a relief for him to sit straight up and give me a science lesson.

"It's about two miles deep. The Grand Canyon is one mile for comparisons," Cass began. "It's about 200 miles long; 18 miles wide.

"The pit plunges straight down, vertically, six hundred feet. That makes the plunge taller than Seattle's Space Needle or twice the height of the Statue of Liberty. It's a straight downward descent of about fifteen hundred feet.

"Oh, that's a relief," I whispered. "I mean, challenge us."

"There are rock walls all the way down and the clever people of The Other have built a complex system into the rock, including elevators, sleeping rooms, a medical and administrative office," Cass said. "They call the top of the pit the Attic and the bottom, the Basement. Everything in between is called the Dark Fantastic because it is really dark in there. As for the rest, all you'll see is miners or slaves suspended by ropes with tiny hard hats on their heads and small lights beaming from the center of their foreheads."

"You'll hear their picks," Cass said. "It's a twenty-four-hour operation," he said.

"What are they mining?" I asked.

"Youth," Cass shot back.

8.

"In a nutshell, the "pitta" here is one of a kind because it's filled with rare earth minerals," he began. "These are elements that are part of a group of seventeen metals and have unique properties that no other elements in the world contain. Some believe they were first created eons ago in a supernova explosion at the dawn of the universe . . . before heaven and earth, and everything in between, existed."

"But you can find these elements in the living world?" I asked.

"Yes, but not so much in the US. China controls the lion's share of rare earth deposits as in ninety percent of the global production," he informed me. "But they don't use what they have because mining and refining these minerals is a bitch. They're sunk deep in the ground."

"I'm still with you . . . go on," I insisted.

"Tectonic activity has jostled and moved the ground over the centuries, making some of these rare earth minerals find their way closer to the surface. It's true in the Midst where there is a small mine just past ITT. And it's true here where there's a mine about an hour away by car.

"In the Midst," Cass continued, "some of the ITT prisoners on B and C Block take turns in the mine. Here, it's harder to get a workforce together, so apparently the bigger guys who go through immigration are taken slave to work in the mines. The sentence: Eternity.

"It's a grueling day of digging because the minerals bond to dirt and rocks and other natural sediment," Cass said. "When the reset disappears, it goes from boring work to backbreaking."

"I'm not exactly a student of science," I reminded him, "but how does this create youth?"

"The mineral is called lanthanide," he said. "It's an energy source for humans," Cass reported. "You mix it with water, drink it, and it creates an age reversal. It's how the teachers here age themselves back and forth. It's better than the fountain of youth because you can regain your strength and looks of the past, but your mind remains your chronological age.

"It not only stops the oxidizing of cells, but reverses all aging, which immediately and literally turns back the clock," Cass said. "A few sips and you won't recognize yourself."

"Look at Dr. King. It's like he entered a time machine," I said.

"Dr. K sipped a little tea and de-aged from a man of questionable strength in his fifties to his prime in his early twenties. There's another mineral tea which immediately reverses it. It's his choice if he wants the strength of youth or the more comfortable, lived-in feeling of being older," Cass said. "Sip a little and you can zero in on an exact age range. You can experiment with it. Want to re-age yourself to what's on your birth certificate? Stop your exposure or quit sipping and your body will age back to normal."

"Can you even begin to imagine how this would be coveted in the living realm?" I said. Then, it dawned on me.

"How young can you go?" I asked.

"Pretty far back, but it's not like those babies on Freak Island," Cass said. "I'm not talking about revisiting age five because your bones and physical frame doesn't shrink that much. But, as you do de-age, you will easily add lean muscle mass while all fine lines and wrinkles disappear. Elasticity returns to your skin. Your youth mojo, at least physically, is on ten. Stamina, it's back. Strength, you're at your peak. You can go back to your late teenage years, or if you drink less, you can land in your twenties or thirties. It's your choice. Just ingest more or less. It's like putting one packet of sugar in your tea or two. Then wait for the results, which are almost immediate."

"These rare minerals must be highly coveted and difficult to find," I said.

"It's buried deep in rock. It's you and a pick. They work you twenty-four hours in the mine. You must be in the mine by three a.m. sunrise and work until ten p.m. There is no food all day long. Just water. One meal a day. A small dinner and sleep break."

"And Daniel?" I implored. He didn't like rules under the best of circumstances. His middle finger was always clearly raised to authority.

"He was classified as a refractory," Cass said. "It comes from the Latin *refractarius* or obstinate. I saw his file when I cased the office during a delivery. Daniel was branded 'refractory to standard work protocol.'"

"What the hell does that mean?" I rushed.

"Not able to be rehabilitated," Cass said. "And by that it meant that none of their torture treatments worked on the only one who refused to go out there and dig. At night, reportedly, he refused other things for a certain officer of the law who visited. A woman named Pristine."

She was everywhere.

"What kind of torture?"

"Denial of food, witnessing the mistreatment of others, knowledge about family members in peril, or news of their extinguishment—and then it gets worse," he said. "Threats of harm to family members, sensory manipulation of sound, temperature, and light. Restriction of space and movement.

"He was chained to a bed, preventing any sleep, and forced to listen as a form of mental torture. And then there was the Ice Box," Cass said. "I didn't want to tell you this, but now you need to know. It was a meat locker where he was sent. The temp was between zero and minus five degrees Celsius. A few hours there and then he was sent to a sweat box or cold night baths. Very few has survived those baths. They hooded him, making him lose any sense of day or night. Then it was back to the ice baths. That goes on long enough and it can send even a healthy young man into a stroke or heart attack."

"What did they want from him?" I said through a thick veil of tears.

"Domination," Cass said. "I played the game, pretended to submit. I was even made a team leader, which is why I was delivering paperwork each night to the main office. He refused to dig. Why the hell couldn't he just go along with it?"

"Maverick," I whispered.

"Then, one day, he tricked the guards and ran," Cass said. "Sirens began to blare and a troop of guards mobilized and fanned out. They hunted him down . . . and the rumor was that he wouldn't stop, so they—"

"They what?"

"Shot him," Cass said. "I'm sorry, Walker. I didn't want to tell you, but now I have no choice. All I know is he lost a lot of blood. And no one took the bullet out because there is no medical treatment there. No hospital. Workers are like animals. When you stopped functioning, they took you out."

"And?"

"When you were done, they flung you off a ledge to land in the bowels of the Basement," he said. "There's a mass grave down there. I'm guessing he's in the company of several other Mavericks."

9.

3:00 a.m. Give or take a few eye blinks.

Waves of missing Daniel hit until my heart began to ache. I remembered the mornings across our kitchen table, eating Cheerios, talking about things un-profound, which were profound. *Would I meet him behind our favorite tree? Did he steal my sunglasses? What bad-for-us food could we fix for dinner? Why were we here? How long would we be here . . . together?*

"Most people just get tired and stop looking for so many useless and useful answers," Daniel once said.

"Never, baby," I vowed. "I'm a professional observer of life. I'll ask the same questions over and over . . . and I'll get answers. The universe respects a stubborn heart."

I imagined those words drifting on some invisible night breeze until they reached the one person that understood them.

Understood me.

"I love you, baby," I signed off and blew the words and a small kiss into an imaginary breeze. I imagined this care package floating to him in some kind of way where it all made sense.

Night messages work that way. You send them; they travel.

10.

The next morning, reality of riding Griz's underground water ride was beginning to sink in—no pun intended.

"It's too risky," Cass ranted. He did this thing where he set that square jaw like it was a roadblock to future endeavors. Then, the lips came together. Barriers were being set in place.

"Walking is much safer," he said.

"We have no time to walk from our survival shelter to the big house because then we have to wait another week for a weekend where there are less guards," I explained. "We lose two days, maybe three on foot to get to the house alone. And then another week of waiting where anyone could perish. I'm riding there—with you or not."

The harsh whip-around head tilt came next. Cass's eyes were steely blue like cold water. Yes, he would give in, but he wouldn't make it easy. He would make his point because deep down he was *that* . . . unnerved. His personal danger meter had mine in the red.

"There is an intricate system of underwater water caverns, which I completely expected," he said. Truth was it made me feel like Indiana Jones for a minute. But, turns out, screw that. I didn't want to be Indiana Jones.

"I'm guessing there will be moments where the walls and ceiling close in around the boat, so keep all parts of your body in the boat," Cass instructed as the three of us descended down a steep, rocky pathway into the bowels of the cave. "And there will be creatures. Don't feed a few fingers to a croc or an iguana."

Why was travel always such a bitch?

"The water recedes during the dry season, which this isn't," Cass said. "I'm just worried that there will be parts where the entire cave passage will fill with water from top to bottom and we'll have to hold our breath as the water slushes us off a cave shelf or through another watery passageway."

"We get stuck and it's over."

"They don't have this ride at Disney," I said. "How long . . ."

"Can we old our breath?" he finished it. "With the reset, probably a long time, although your natural instinct will be to suck in. One word of advice: don't.

Wait for it. Scenario number two.

"In the case of no reset, marines can hold their breath underwater for three minutes or more. My unit had breath-holding drills during high-surf conditions at night, like the SEALs. There is one SEAL who holds the record with a time of eleven minutes and fifty-four seconds, though that is not the norm."

I could barely hold my breath through the airport connector tunnel near O'Hare when I was dared as a kid.

"Sugar, I'm not kidding about the creatures," Cass said. "You know how we're standing in this deep, dark, foreboding cave? The fish, crabs, and other delights that live down here take on a transparent appearance and even live sightlessly in this dark home."

Creepy, see-through, eyeless primate creatures. Why not?

"Eyes are rendered unnecessary down here," Cass said, winking at me.

"Is that in the brochure?" I replied, adjusting my pack as we walked. I was back in travel clothes of black leggings and a black sweater. Cass was in dark pants, a black waterproof shirt, and a thin coat.

My breath formed puffy cold clouds.

In the distance, I heard the hard pounding of rushing water and remembered a lesson learned not long ago from writer Yung Pueblo. He insisted that water teaches man four important lessons: What you see is often your projection; what is soft can also be powerful; persistence can break barriers; change is always happening.

It was freezing cold when we reached the next lowest level and I watched Griz push ahead, almost on all fours as if he was one of the creatures down here. *Weren't we all?* He took those sturdy fingers and pulled a large silver boat off a rock shelf. *So, this was how he did it.* He didn't walk miles at night, but used an intricate cave system of waterways to travel to the outskirts of various settlements where he did his dumpster dives for supplies and brought them home in his boat.

Griz noticed my tears of admiration. *Where there is a will.*

"Donna cry, Wa," he said. "Go on bot rid!"

He had a pliant heart. And it dawned on me in that moment that there was bravery in being soft.

I said a silent prayer for the woman I would be when we got out of this cave. I hoped that she was smiling, aware, in one piece, and unapologetically taking care of business.

Everyday.

In every way.

11.

First things first.

"I com, tu," he said, jumping from foot to foot while carrying the boat down what looked like wide stairs that were rock formations centuries old. "Haf to com."

"No," I said with conviction. Damn, this broke my heart because he wouldn't understand.

"Danger. Bad people. You go home. We'll see you soon."

"No leaf Griz. You said frens!" he cried when I hugged him. "Frens haf to go." He grabbed me to his chest so hard that I could barely breathe. "Ta-ka!" he begged.

"Baby, I love you," I told him. "You need to go back to your house. Eat your breakfast. Start your day."

"Ta-ka! Go with yu, Wa!"

I cupped his face in my hands. "Frens forever," I said. "I will see you again."

"NO SEE," he cried loudly. "NO SEE NO MOR. Yu go and no see."

When he calmed, I held his hand in both of mine.

"Ta-ka," he implored in a small boy's voice. I couldn't stand it anymore. At least he moved, so Cass could check out the boat.

"Fam. Lee," he sat down on a rock and kept saying, "All lone. No frens. No fam. Lee."

I stood on a rock to once again take his large face between my two freezing hands. I couldn't stop crying, guttural sobs that came from deep within. "Family," I told him. "No one gets left behind. No one is ever forgotten."

I handed him my lucky green rabbit's foot.

"Griz, I'm coming back for this. You can borrow it. I will see you soon . . . brother."

I touched his heart with my hand and then my own. I kissed the rabbit's foot and placed it on his face.

Fat tears ran down his innocent face.

He knew—one way or another—we weren't coming back. It's why he ran, sobbing, in the other direction toward his resumed solitary life in his little room. We had no choice, but to push ahead.

TWENTY-ONE

1.

The entrance to the cave's deep-basin underwater transport system was carved by nearby glaciers blasting into solid rock. Icy meltwater that was so cold it promised instant hypothermia to any sort of living flesh churned in the near distance, a blood freezing crypt issuing a warning and a promise.

Nature's frigid drink was also beautiful in its icy splendor and made the room glow a stunning silver blue. It was like walking into a sapphire gemstone.

This was an unforgiving place.

Striking stone formations had created a dazzling and endless underground tunnel system of cavernous chambers and halls. These watery routes were stabbed in spots by stunning stalactites, stalagmites, and helictites that reached down from above and then raced back up well beyond what light a man could hope was there.

The natural crater was framed by narrow, sheer walls that were slate gray and the water cut through the middle of them with loud surges and violent thrusts. It flowed on rocky tracks dug deep into the earth. The shimmering glaze off the top made the room look like a temple.

I had that reverent feeling of standing in a sacred cathedral and bowed my head for a moment.

At first glance, I estimated that the ceiling here was about twenty-five feet high, long beyond where the eye could detect, and maybe thirty feet wide.

Cass was all business now. "Walker, get your head in the game. We'll see Griz again. But now it's time to keep in mind that there will be parts where the cave's ceiling will be so low that we'll have to flatten ourselves onto the bottom of the boat as we try to make it into the next passage."

"Looking forward to that part," I said sarcastically.

"Me, too, sugar," Cass said, deadly serious.

"We'll ride the stream from here into the second chamber and then the third until we descend deeply enough into the belly of the cave to find a natural track that will shoot us up and out," Cass said as he put out a hand. I handed him my pack, which he tossed in the dented silver boat followed by his own.

"Seal motto: The only easy day was yesterday," he said.

"Hoo-yah!" I used a battle cry common in the corps.

"Hoo-yah," laser-focused Cass bellowed, his voice reverberating through the walls and my entire system.

Our boat was a small silver canoe with absolutely no steering capabilities. Paddles meant some realm of control and I had a vision that Griz probably just used those long arms of his to navigate the inevitable twists and turns. Cass took the spot in front. I hunkered in back, my fingers white-knuckling both sides of the canoe.

Cass pulled the tiny rope that anchored the boat.

There was no reverse. The power and vastness of the water moved us rapidly in a jerky fashion as if we were on the most dangerous of amusement park rides. I bounced left, then right and then my stomach felt it when it was all forward thrust.

Just like your standard roller coaster, we moved forward cautiously and then all hell broke loose. "Hang on!" Cass yelled as we ascended about fifteen feet in the air only to run out of water. The boat was airborne and we were flying without a landing pad.

As we fell, I heard Daniel's voice. I knew he could beat anything. You couldn't contain him. Not alive. Not dead.

He needed to live because there were adventures to be had. "Wander often. Wonder always, Callaghan." he would say.

"But wait," I would say. Sometimes, I needed to catch up.

"Later becomes never," he would say, ripping us both forward.

The boat crashed into a churning rush of blackness and I heard something alive hiss.

2.

There wasn't time to meet fellow cave dwellers.

The world blurred as we moved at rocket speed, suspending midair, and then crashing fast again and again as we made our way. My left side slammed against the back of the boat and a spray of blood hit my face from a newfound arm gash.

Cass tried to shield me, but it was like trapping a wet, slippery animal. His hands were on me and they melted away as gravity rammed his body to the front of the boat where he hung on as we dropped several wet shelf floors and then settled onto the next watery track for a full-speed rush into darkness and oblivion.

Limbs flailing and wet hair plastered to my cheeks, I closed my eyes as we slammed forward at speeds I imagined topped a hundred miles per hour. They flew open to the sound of harsh scraping. "Sugar, wrap your arms and legs around me," Cass yelled. I snaked an arm around his midsection and my legs over his center as the walls closed in. His body shot left taking me with him, then hurled right, bashing and banging like we were playing bumper cars with our flesh and a rock wall.

I don't know why, but I looked up. The most concerning thing was the ceiling, which was *lowering* by the second. It wasn't smooth, but made of abrasive earthy chips. It descended in inches until I could stick out my tongue and touch it.

Every claustrophobic cell in my body began to shriek in agonizing pain as I imagined the boat stuck between the top of our new world and the watery bottom. Lunging forward whiplash-style, I knew I couldn't allow my breath to become ragged and forced. If I passed out now, I would suffocate and then what? This would be my final tomb.

Rock ceiling scraped our heads, forcing both of us to tumble to the bottom of the boat where we clutched each other out of sheer desperation.

3.

A blink later and the ceiling seemed to be opening wide for us now as we twisted around a bend that sprayed my face with thousands of pellets of stinging ice.

"Holy shit!" Cass screamed.

Before the "what" could escape my lips, I felt the frosted water splashing into the boat. We pitched left as the water levels began to rise dramatically, offering the deepest "deep" end I had never even imagined existed.

"Cass!" I screamed as thick waves of liquid death began to rush into the boat.

"Keep your pack on your back!" he yelled into my face. "And hold your breath—NOW!"

It was the last I would see of him for some time.

The world turned absolutely black. My numb limbs seemed to float off my body as I desperately willed my fingers to hang onto my pack. But I wasn't sure if they were operational or just simple remains now.

The mother of all waves had us in her sights now and rapidly it rose, crashing over our heads. In the blast of watery confusion, my legs seemed to wrap around my own neck.

Nature had taken her best shot and for a moment, all movement stopped and then it began again in an agonizingly slow manner. We chugged forward, but the trajectory was sympathetically slow now.

Then it dawned on me: I was still holding my breath. When the side of my rib cage scraped cave wall, I didn't feel pain, which meant that there was either hope for the reset or full body hypothermia had set in. I let out three bubbles of air.

The inevitable began to set in. Drowning isn't a violent end. In fact, most victims just slowly drift out of this life and into another realm. It's almost like sleeping underwater, but waking up somewhere else.

4.

As I descended this existence, I brushed against something slick and rough. The world was less black now and I could see that it was translucent and had pale green eyes ridged in scales. It had teeth and when they opened, I knew this was real – and I was just a part of the natural world. It would probably eat me, which would involve seismic pain. Our eyes locked for a moment and then I gazed the other way. No need for the cow to watch the person eating the burger.

In the end, the beautiful unpredictability of water saved my sorry ass.

The liquid world around me violently rushed forward, as worlds do, saving me and denying this thing his midday nibble. I could still see it, serpentine tail ramrod straight and flicking hard, trying to swim closer, desperate for sustenance. Water. The great equalizer had the upper hand.

All we could do was ride the current, one of us white-knuckling it to the maximum, but not close enough for teeth, tail, or human appendages to connect.

We were two travelers. Same road. Different journeys.

Van Morrison lyrics filled my head and they would be fine last thoughts given the situation.

"And ev'ryting looks so complete.
When you're walkin' out on the street.
And the wind catches your feet.
Sends you flyin', cryin.'"

5.

With a thump that was nature's great belch, the water burped me out of the cave and onto hard, rocky land. Wind rammed into my spine, which was in the prone position on a hard rock. I could see from here that the sky was laced with black-shaded clouds. A storm was on the horizon and it lingered past a dense forest of red cedar and hemlock trees.

On shaking legs, I scrambled to stand and find my feet. When those limbs were too numb to hold me, I fell and rolled until I was covered in scrubby compost. At least there was one positive: whatever that thing was that had followed me did not enjoy the sunlight and did a "nice try, but no dice" U-turn back underground.

A giant gulp of air suppressed the shrill scream I trapped in my chest.

"Cass!" I screamed into my closed mouth. I could see the mansion in the not-so-far distance. The guards often did forest patrol to shoot creatures and children visitors who escaped.

"Cass!" I whispered loudly. *Did he make it? What if he was gobbled up by stone and water . . . and creatures that didn't see the light?*

"Hellauva ride, sugar! Whadda you doing Wednesday? Let's do it again," he said in a breathless rush. This was followed by me jumping into his arms to hug him hard. He caught me mid-jump and plastered those thick arms around me like he would never let go. He said the strangest thing, especially under the current circumstances.

"What if love was contagious?" Cass whispered into my ear. "Me to you. You to me. And beyond. Be a better world."

"That's what you were thinking about when you were drowning?" I whispered.

"That's what I think about a lot these days," he said before kissing me on the nose. "Isn't this a great date, sugar? It's not boring. There's time for talking. And wet clothes look real nice on your body," he smiled. "It's a win-win over those guys who would just take you to a movie."

"Cass," I began.

"Now . . . run," he said, grabbing my hand as he supercharged it through the giant oaks.

322

6.

I heard it, too.

A muted scratching sound made me realize a walkie-talkie that was malfunctioning.

Cass put a hand out as we got closer and gingerly we put down our packs. A deep dive behind thick redwoods gave us a shield, but still allowed us to hear two of Edward's personal guards—his muscle—on some kind of piss break talking about their day.

"Doc just left. Big Man is still recovering from his accident," one said. "He says it's stomach issues, but I'm not so sure. How could his little bride give him stomach issues?"

"I hear he can't wear pants—that he's bandaged . . . in the crotch area, if you know what I mean. And that's why he hasn't left his room since the wedding," gossiped the other one.

"Some honeymoon," he joked. "I guess she was real rough with him."

The next words were muffled and Cass raised an eyebrow.

"He still has the roads closed—I guess he thinks someone else will come looking for his bride," Number One said. "No one gets out of here unless we say they're getting out of here—and with the storm approaching no one is going anywhere today or tonight."

I had no idea we were going to get some staff gossip, plus a weather report.

I was the one who reacted and screwed it up. A leg twitch led to a step forward and the breaking of a slim branch.

I might as well have detonated a bomb.

7.

These guards were former Secret Service agents. They heard all. They saw everything.

Number One advanced forward as if it was second nature to him . . . and it was. "Look what we have here. The blushing bride," he said. "Is she allowed out of the honeymoon suite?"

He was too embarrassed to tell them that I had escaped.

Number One fingered a large knife on his belt. "We've been instructed to detain you," he said.

"I've been instructed to nail you," I replied, tossing one of my stars at his forehead. Blood spurted into the mud.

"You are a badass beacon of divine light," said Cass, who had already shocked the other guard with a deeply penetrating knife wound to his leg. I knocked both out with a rock.

"Solid," I said, knowing that they were wounded, but not gone-gone.

"We take no chances," Cass said, pulling a large hypodermic needle out of his pack. I watched as earlier today he melted down a combination of GHB, or gamma hydroxybutyrate, Rohypnol, and ketamine and put it in syringes that he brought from the Midst. I didn't even dare ask him where he found the stuff. He brought a lot of things from home for the trip, Marine things.

Some guys give flowers. Cass kept two hypodermics and gave me the other two. They were one-size-fits-all shitheads we might run into on this journey.

"Honey, you shouldn't have," I said.

"Then I'll give you my heart, my soul, and two needles loaded with enough juice to tranquilize an elephant. Same shit worked on . . . well, never mind," Cass said, sticking it to Edward's elite guards.

"Nighty night, assholes," he said. "The best part of GHB is that it wipes out your memory. So, even if these two wake up, they're going to wonder why they're napping in the dirt."

"Napping and bleeding," I added, doing a quick scan of our surroundings. Cass had already mapped it out on his watch.

"Left to the HVT," he said. Cass was no-nonsense. All business. *He lived, breathed, and ate this marine lifestyle.*

The high-valued target in this case was Edward's swanky and unusually guard-free *gee-rage*, where he kept his most expensive toys that involved wheels. Edward never figured any of the prisoners of his home sweet home would make it to the far outreaches of his property.

That's why the small side door of the drab gray painted building was the one thing we desperately needed: it was unlocked.

8.

By garage, I didn't mean a three-car number attached to the main house.

During one of our insufferable "dates," Edward took me on a stroll around the sprawling property where he revealed an enormous warehouse-looking building he had filled with top luxury cars and other vehicles that cost in the millions in the living realm. How he found them and imported him here was anyone's guess. Maybe there was Carvana in the afterlife.

In good times, my mom and I figured out how to pay two hundred beans a month for a rundown Honda in rusty blue. We weren't exactly what was known as "car people."

To play the game, I asked to take a closer peek at his toys, which like any man of his age appealed to his ego because the cars were like extra body parts to him. He even offered to let me drive his 'Vette, with him in it. "I don't drive," I told him, sweetly—and it was actually true for once. *Play the game. Don't allow him to think you might escape. What I meant is I could barely drive.*

He was barely listening. Edward lingered at every car, caressing them, and giving others longing looks as if these metal machines were his lovers.

"Have you ever sat in a Lamborghini?" he asked.

Yeah, and then I plopped my rear into the Space Shuttle and did a few loops around Saturn.

I did make detailed mental notes about the doors in the warehouse, how they were unlocked, and how the inside was filled with rugged all-terrain vehicles, Mercedes, and the stray Black Hawk helicopter or . . . ten. Edward didn't go small.

"On second thought, I'd love to sit in a Lamborghini," I said.

And then I watched him go to a back right wall where the keys to all those vehicles were kept in a long black box. I was giddy, and Edward thought it was the heady smell of new car leather and his vintage old man cologne, but it wasn't.

It was typical for cars to pull in and out as minions did Edward's business. We would slowly pull out of Dodge and then drive the two hours down to the mine—which is what Cass figured it would be based on his escape route. We were sure that in the moment that we would find a way to get in there. A bonus: he knew the least guarded side, which was to the west.

It was a half-assed Op, but the best we could do.

For now, we just had to find the perfect vehicle and we crouched low against the side of a Cadillac Escalade while trying to determine if we were indeed, alone, in this vehicle heaven.

"Why are you breathing so hard?"

"I'm not," I whispered.

In an instant, I was both revolted and terrified. Just the sight of Edward was horrifying and hideous. I caught a glimpse a flash of the side of his pale face and those expensive leather shoes that shuffled across the gray painted floor.

Every molecule in my body began to scream, "You don't belong here. Not against him. He will win."

Cass put his hand over my mouth. He didn't know what Edward looked like, but he could only assume that the man who appeared to be in his late twenties and on a walker just had a very serious accident. He was still de-aged as the young Xavier/Edward, but his body was too injured to paint a healthy picture.

I watched as Edward moved slowly, hunched a bit in the middle, his resting face a hard grimace. A thin trickle of sweat ran down to his neck. *It was obviously still painful for him to walk. I had deformed him, which was something he would never forgive let alone forget. He would torture me, if he ever had the chance again.*

His one joy: caressing the black paint of a BMW like it was a lover.

My own breath hitched in my throat because the fear was overwhelming. I remembered something young Deuce once told me: *"Just exist,"* she said with a grin. *"And do it with the confidence of a four-year-old in a Superman T-shirt. Now, that's confidence."*

I felt Cass begin to straighten to launch and dug my nails into his leg.

"No," I mouthed. *One call for help from Edward and it was the most over as over could ever be. They would take Cass to the basement and drain him for his psychic abilities. And I would be carved. Into pieces.*

"Let me," Cass mouthed back. "For you."

"Don't," I repeated. "For me."

9.

Breathlessly we waited over an hour while the great man of the Reid dynasty spread his love to everything metal. When he was finished making mental love to his possessions, it took him several minutes to put the walker aside. Next came the painful swing of a leg into a waiting BMW complete with driver.

Nasty animal sounds were emitted from his core. "Son of a bitch," he yelled.

For once, there was no one to help their "boss."

We watched from a spotless window as both made his way to a small road parallel to the great lawn.

"You want to do this . . . let's do it now," Cass said, moving toward the black box of keys. I spent my time surveying the near distance and then I saw it hanging over the side of a vintage cherry-red '68 Mustang.

We were given few breaks in this afterlife, but this one was monumental if it contained what I thought it might. I picked up Edward's jacket and hit pay dirt.

A quick pat down of his pockets produced his wallet, which I threw in the front of my pack. I also found his cell phone for these parts.

There was no time to dwell on our good fortune.

With every deep breath I had to keep collecting, keep moving forward.

10.

At the box, Cass's eyes narrowed. Auto theft also looked good on him and he carefully considered exactly which vehicle we would filch.

"Hey, what the hell—" began the mechanic who snuck in the side door and shocked us by his presence. Cass took the first punch and I grabbed a fiberglass bumper replacement and finished it.

Cass shook his head and put up a wait-a-minute finger to make sure our surprise visitor didn't bring any friends. When he was sure the coast was clear, he snuck back to the offices and returned with two gray jumpsuits. I looked at him quizzically while I put one over my clothes and he did the same. I looked like a dude *who worked there*.

He grabbed my arm and yanked me out the door, stopping at the first runway in front of a rather large helicopter.

"It's Black Ops," Cass said. "Edward has friends in military places."

"I don't care if it's Pink Ops," I said. "You can't be serious."

"Pretty damn serious. Because he has the roads blocked," Cass reminded me. "The guards told us. And anyways, it's a clear shot in. Helicopters arrive day and night with new workers and supplies. It's constant noise. Comings and goings. No one will think twice about it. We'll be there in half an hour.

"Ever been in a copter?" he asked.

"Yes, it was my preferred mode of travel to high school along with the city bus when I didn't have copter money."

He swung his body into our new whirly bird. Silently, I followed.

Inside, the panel lit up like we were on a spaceship.

"You don't really know how to fly this thing?" I said in a breathless rush. "I mean, you actually know what to do with all these little knobs and levers and thing-kabobs?"

"Sugar, the kabobs are my favorite. And I'm going to pretend not to be offended. You ask the guys in the forty-third in Afghanistan if

I know how to fly this thing. I can fly it when surface-to-air missiles are exploding because they've been fired at me, but I hope the skies are friendly today," Cass said with a shit-eating grin.

"Anyway, what's the worst thing that could happen? You're already dead. But, I still need you to buckle up."

11.

Three.

This was insane.

Two.

Cass checked the seven million instruments, knobs, and panels that were brightly lit now like Christmas lights. He put my hand on some lever with his over it. My fingers felt bloodless as the "stick" began to tremble.

One.

Liftoff! My palm was being guided over the controls as he pushed on certain fingertips of mine. I wanted nothing to do with the fact that we had just risen from the earth and joined the sky.

Holy . . . please don't let us crash.

My shaking hand fell away and he punched it and up, up, and up, above the trees and way over the mansion of horrors.

HOLY FUCK.

A copter ride isn't smooth, but bumpy to the max, so when he took a hard right toward the pit, I grabbed my own kneecaps and pretended those weren't dark black storm clouds around us.

The copter shook left, bounced right. A toasted cloud spit us downward while another, glazed dark green, seemed to have tentacles that reached for us like death mist.

"Are we having fun? Or is it the end of the world?" I yelled, because it was deafening loud and my heart was a catastrophic one.

It was almost as if Cass could read my mind. *He did that. A lot.*

"You have an apocalyptic heart, meaning you're always struggling between two major, if not monumental, things," he said over the loud noise of the blades swooshing hard. "Life or death. Kill or be killed. Me or him."

Just what I needed. A philosophizing hunk with a crush who put twenty thousand feet between my boots and the ground.

"Shut up, Dr. Phil, and just fly this thing," I said, one of my shaking knees touching his granite one.

"Yee to the haw!" whooped our flyboy, who was clearly high in every way that counted for him.

"Little less living in the moment. Little more flying," I begged.

"Sugar, we own the moment," Cass said, punching it.

12.

The pit—or *pitta* according to Griz—was cut into three sections that had nicknames: the Attic on top; the Stuff in the middle, which is what was mined; and the Basement for eating, housing, medical, and burial grounds.

We landed on the top part, or the Attic, Cass became serious Cass again. "Go through Edward's wallet, fast," he instructed me. "Find his security card. He's a major investor now when it comes to the mine. He must have an all-access pass. All the honchos do."

It was an easy task because it was the second card in a wallet full of plastic. Why he still kept his black American Express card in death was beyond me because we didn't pay for things in money anymore, but he recognized it as a status symbol, even now. As I got to the end of the deck, I found his library card and social security card from his youth. There was a yellowed picture of a much older man, one of those crumbled, folded relics from when cameras were first invented.

"Look around, sugar," Cass said, descending as carefully as possible because of the sudden, hard rain whipping us from angles. "I need a baseball cap or some kind of head thing and glasses. There has to be sunglasses somewhere. Check the compartments, pretty please."

I could barely make my shaking hand work, but somehow, I popped open a small storage compartment between the pilot and passenger seat. As expected, there were two sick pairs of silver Aviator Ray-Bans, plus several EXR—Edward Xavier Reid—baseball caps in an unlocked box near my seat. I handed a pair of the shades over and Cass put them on, which made him look super cool and dangerous. With a free hand, he scooped his hair into a ponytail and I helped him tie it back with a rubber band I had in my pack.

"Now you, so we're not so easily recognizable on the cameras," he instructed, and I tied my hair back and put on matching mirrored shades and the cap.

The copter swayed left to right, right to left, but Cass still managed to land that lucky hunk of metal on the big *X* painted on concrete near the mine. It surprised me to see three copters parked there at the ready. "Switch," Cass commanded, and before I could ask why, I was suddenly in the pilot's seat.

What happened next was so fast that I couldn't protest. A uniformed guard from the mine tapped three hard times on my window and I gave him the universal pilot's sign of the thumbs-up, everything is A-OK, Houston we got no problem. I had seen it in a thousand movies.

"Now what?" I whispered frantically to Cass.

That's when I heard the click.

"Now, sugar," Cass said, squeezing my stray hand as he took off the cap and the glasses. "You turn me in for escaping."

13.

My head twisted hard just as the guard tapped my window another three times.

"I will not. They'll torture you—or worse," I began. *And then it all became crystal clear. This was Cass's plan all along. He would trade himself for Daniel—and then try someday to heal from however they hurt him and try to escape again. Self-sacrificing, yes. The marine way.*

"No options," Cass said, closing silver handcuffs around his hand hard. He found them in one of the compartments and slid his wrists into position. "We can't just breeze in here and say, 'Excuse me, we're on a field trip. Can you point us in the direction of our slave-worker friends, so we can smuggle them out of here?'"

"Cass, I will not! That option is out. It's terrifying."

He nodded a sure *yes*. "Open the door. The latch is on the side."

With his fingers, he passed me a small key. "Keep this handy. Don't lose it."

The guard continued to tap until I cracked the door open. Around us, the world was one watery blur. If this jerk guard wanted impatience combined with a woman pushed well beyond the edge, he had come to the right place.

"Excuse me for making you wait," I sniped, opening the door wider because I had no idea how to roll down the window in a helicopter. Then, I let it rip as the rich bitch wife of one of the most prominent men in the realm might.

"I'm returning a prisoner to the authorities here on the authority of my husband, Mr. Edward Reid, who is still quite ill. And I'm scheduled to take three back to the mansion for further tests and exploration. Mr. Reid believes they might be harboring special extras and can better serve in our lab. He has scheduled several of your slaves for his personal testing."

The guard was twenty-two, lean, lanky, and armed with what looked like a semiautomatic handgun. We could take him. But then what? We could only attack our way so far into the mine before they outnumbered us.

Cooperation would make this easier.

"You can leave my chopper here, but first fuel it up," I barreled on. "It won't be longer than half an hour given the storm. I need to get back to base immediately." *I wasn't kidding about the sky above, which had turned a putrid pea soup green.*

The guard eyed me suspiciously. Maybe it was too much talking. He heard bullshit stories all day long. But there was one difference here. It was Saturday. He wasn't the A-team crew. He was backup. A weekend worker who was happy to let things slide. In fact, the guy looked ready to take a snooze or watch some college hoops. His voice was monotone, his breath laced with the pungent smell of Doritos.

The power of his gun made him believe he had the upper hand.

"You can leave the prisoner with me. I'll call down to have him transferred to one of the jail cells pending a decision about his afterlife expectancy," he eyeballed me and said in a monotone. "Give me the names of the others. And I'll need to see some ID."

For some idiotic reason, I had my student ID card from the Academy in the front of my pack. I slapped it onto the guard's clipboard. He surveyed it and gawked at the picture.

"What kind of name is Walker?" he said.

"That is Mrs. Edward Reid to you."

"Card doesn't say Reid."

I slapped Edward's ID down on the board. "My husband said there would be pushback. He personally asked me to make this run because I can fly this copter and he's not feeling well. If you . . ." I looked at his nametag. "If you, Martin Brown, have any more questions then we can interrupt Mr. Reid's afternoon nap to discuss your idea of being a team player. I'm sure he'll be thrilled," I stated.

"Yeah, tethering ceremony last week? Heard about it," Martin Brown said. "Congrats. And no need to call the Big Man. No one needs that in their afterlife." Brown began punching the names I wrote down on a pad into his tablet.

"Your friend August or Auggie can be found in the same cell block as Eddie Wargo—Number 12 D. Just take the elevator down to the eighteenth subterranean level. They're on an oxygen break. Too much time in the mine and they need an infusion of clean air. As you know, they will look different from dealing with the mineral."

"Naturally," I said. *What the hell did he mean by "they will look different?"*

"And Mr. Daniel Reid doesn't work the mines. Never has during his time here because of his pedigree. In fact, he's in his chambers. Basement. Level One. It's the room he shares with his wife."

14.

It was like a bomb going off.

His wife.

His wife. Not allowing me time to dwell, Cass was pushing me out of my copter seat because sooner or later, someone who didn't buy into bullshit stories would be in our faces.

I swung out and grabbed Cass by his handcuffs hard. At the same time, the guard handed me a key card. "For the elevators, ma'am."

"Move!" I boomed at Cass, shoving him hard in the back. He stumbled forward like a pro.

TWENTY-TWO

1.

There were three large industrial elevators set against a misty backdrop where rolling fog had replaced sky and the steam of moving parts shot straight into the atmosphere. Each cold steel door was in the closed position meaning we would have to wait. Cass lowered his head in almost a prayer position, which didn't bode well for my rapidly beating pulse rate. A simple map on the wall explained the very few options: Attic, Mines, Basement.

For the tenth time, I punched the square button on the wall to send us an elevator car. When it still didn't respond, I hit it another twenty times *because that always helps.*

"Which one will open first?" I whispered, frantically.

"Two," Cass shot back. "My lucky number."

"I feel so much better now," I retorted under my breath. "We've going for Vegas odds."

Two official-looking types, men in black suits, approached holding several file folders. *This was no time to look guilty.* I locked eyes with the

335

first one and gave an official head nod. *Yes, that's how you do it. When you don't belong, you pretend you do. When you're exposed, you don't hide. You boldface your moves.*

I noticed that both had small clear tubes buried deeply into their nostrils attached to a small box linked to their belts. They were being supplemented with pure oxygen, which didn't seem odd at all in this place. The air here was revolting, noxious boarding on vile. Each breath was laced with something atrocious that smelled sour as if you mixed the sulfur from a hundred matches with the sickening smell of sour eggs.

The more I thought about it I wanted to gag, but I stopped myself. Anyone who was familiar with this mine would know how to deal with it. If not, you put yourself on oxygen and that wasn't an option.

Door number one opened.

Oh, Cass. Wrong already. So much for luck, dumb or otherwise.

"Punch it," Cass whispered. I hit SL or subterranean level ; the suits pushed Level 2, which a quick scan later was administration within the mine area. A few seconds later and they were gone. Alone again, I slipped Cass the key to his handcuffs. We walked out on the eighteenth floor, my fingers on one of the throwing stars in my pocket and Cass's hand on the knife he taped to his side.

It was only a short walk to the bunks.

2.

Bunkhouse #12

The room housed around twenty, but only ten or so were inside of it now. Their front door indicated this was their two-hour sleep break, which would be ending in exactly forty-six minutes. When we opened the door and slipped inside almost everyone was sleeping hard, coma-style. It was the kind of slumber borne out of total exhaustion.

A quick scan and it looked like a preteen ward. No one in here was over age thirteen or fourteen. The boys had sweet faces and bloodied hands and arms.

One of the boys was awake. I found him sitting on a hard, bottom bunk bed crying. He didn't make any kind of eye contact, but looked down like a beaten dog. His nerves, however, were his greeting. He compulsively swung gangly long legs as if that might get him somewhere other than here. If his feet were on the ground, the kid might have walked a few miles already.

The other kid who was barely awake had wild brown hair that stuck out everywhere, making him look a bit like a lion. He covered his face in his hands and moved them around to force consciousness. After, he stood and walked to the corner of the room oblivious, like his friend, to our presence. He was the angry one of the two, harshly kicking a hole in the bottom part of the wall. I don't know if he was trying to escape or simply destroy.

Both boys had smooth baby faces, sweet and hopeful eyes, and lips made for sly smiles and raucous laughter. Each came complete with rosy cheeks and just a sprinkling of freckles, but no red acne bumps. They looked like seventh graders.

"Kiss my aching ass," announced the one who was standing. "And that covers anything you want including pulling an extra shift to going down to medical. You can kiss my sweet Alabama—"

"Eddie?" I said, because the boy in front of me looked as if he could be Eddie Wargo's tween son. He looked up and the instant smile that followed was a ray of full-blast sunshine.

In pants that were baggy and arms yet to grow muscles, he looked at me like I was that ray of light, too.

3.

Eddie didn't look much worse for wear, except he was younger. *Much,*

much younger. He had dropped about twenty additional pounds of Eddie and his muscles look deflated. He was lean, gangly, and looked as if his body didn't exactly fit. He lasered in on me with a broad, grateful smile and his eyes practically sparkled.

I swore I saw tears forming. "No matter where you go, there are always prisons," he said. "Ain't that the shits?"

"Eddie, what the hell?" I whispered.

"We're around the de-aging stuff, night and day," he explained. "It does a number on the workers, too. I look like I'm 12 again – and that wasn't a very good year."

"Eddie, we're getting out of here," I said frantically. There was no time to deep dive into what had happened to him now and hopefully plenty of hours for that when we reached safety. "Cass has a helicopter waiting. Where's Auggie and Daniel?"

A large, completely covered lump on the next bunk rolled over, but didn't pull the covers down. "Hey, Eddie," he said. "I had a dream that Walker came to save us. I think I heard her voice."

"Ready for this to rock your socks, kid?" Eddie said. "She's here. Look, idiot."

The kid grunted.

"Everything the light touches is our kingdom," the de-aged Auggie—complete with baby-smooth skin, tiny shoulders, and a lanky frame—quoted. "Who said it?"

Auggie loved to trade profound quotes with me—and I tried to never disappoint him. This, however, was a cake walk.

"Mufasa," I replied. "We've only watched *The Lion King* together about ten million times."

Auggie whipped the covers off his wide, generous, beautiful face.

"I knew you would save us," Auggie said through his tears. "Because, well, sometimes you just deserve a dream that comes true." He flew into my arms and I held him hard. But only for a few seconds.

"Boys, reasons turn into seasons here. Let's move," I replied, leading the way to the door.

338

4.

First impediment: the guard who had been around the corner when we snuck into this room. She was in our faces now.

"Do not take another step—or you'll force me to use this," she bellowed. I took three quick mental pictures. *Click! Her tool belt featured a large knife, a taser, and a baton. Click! Her body was thick and she stood about five foot eight. Click! She appeared motivated thanks to a little light that burst into her challenged eyes. It said, "You or me, kid."*

"Problem," I stated as I stood in front of her with my hands in my pockets. "I'm really tired of being okay with things I'm obviously not okay with."

"Mute yourself," she snarled. "And slowly take those hands out of your pants and put them over your head."

"On a day-to-day basis, do you often walk right on the line of losing your shit?" I inquired. It was part of my newfound disdain for authority.

"You really want to push this over the edge?" she asked.

"Yes, I really do," I said as she reached for her taser.

I lobbed a star into the side of her neck. Cass pulled my hand back before I could get in another shot. He punched the woman under her chin, causing her head to fly back like a punted football.

"Don't waste ammo," Cass cautioned as a puddle of blood formed and the woman passed out. "Expensive, and we can't run out of it."

Her guard friend surprised us, well, one of us. Cass grabbed a towel from a nearby laundry cart and slung it around the guy's neck. He swung for the fences until the man was off his feet and then gasping on the ground.

"Now, *that's* losing your shit," he grinned.

Preteen Eddie took out the third with a hard kick to his privates—enough to send his backside bouncing off the rock wall. "If you can't run with the big dogs," Eddie taunted him. "Then piss on the porch." *I hadn't realized how much I missed him and his Eddie-isms.*

I nailed the last guy with a star to his right ear. Cass smiled and shook his head.

"Dirty—and costly," Auggie said with a smile.

"Due to the rising cost of existing, dirty deeds can no longer be done dirt cheap," I informed him, pointing to the right.

5.

Getting out of situations fast was our calling card. Our fastball.

The only problem here was the place was lit low with rust streaked, towering stone walls and corridors bleeding into hallways dotted by locked doors. We tried the elevators again and felt ourselves being lowered until a female voice said, "Basement Level." Was it my imagination or did I hear a chorus of moaning in the distance?

This maze was cold enough to see your own breath and smelled like something was decomposing.

Dead ends were everywhere and exits were prized fruit. I hadn't seen one blaze red in a long time. "I almost snuck out once—and I ran into Daniel. He's down here somewhere and he looks normal, as in his real age, because he's not working the mine," Eddie rushed. "Just don't lose me. I know I can find the spot again, I think."

It was an enormous place of caverns, twists, and turns. As we ran, I began to play a game I often initiated during the most difficult times. My mother taught it to me when I was a little girl: "When the negatives come up, sweetheart, allow them to come and then at the end just say to yourself, 'Not true.'"

I will never see Daniel again. Not true.

He will never hold me in his arms. Not true.

I will never leave this underground grave. Not true.

Eddie found a staircase, raced ahead of us, and was swallowed by the darkness.

Next level: Executives only.

Not true.

6.

"Eddie, stop," I whispered.

"No," he cried, flying down an almost black hallway lit only by occasional red emergency boxes with switches that brought immediate guard attention.

"It's this way. No, that way. Come on!" Eddie cried.

"This way" gave way to a series of doors on each side, numbered and, even stranger, named. There was the Lancaster Suite, the Smith Suite, the Lewis Suite, and on and on. Some of the suites has silver trays pushed up against the rock. *It was room service!* Below were the crumbs of half-eaten sandwiches, scraped-clean fine China plates, and empty champagne bottles. *This wasn't for the workers.*

Eddie bent down, grabbed the rest of a ham sandwich, stuffed it in his mouth, and motioned for us to follow him.

At the end of the hallway was a brass fence over a white door. Someone had thought to put fake plastic ivy over it to make it appear more festive. The marker contained two words: Honeymoon Suite. The slim lever on the fence seemed to melt open when I grabbed it. The front door? No resistance, but there was a note taped to it.

"You're late. We're sleeping. Leave our food on the desk and take the dirty dishes."

It was female loopy, cursive writing.

"Wait," Cass mouthed, pushing me behind him to take the lead. I tried to race in front of him, but he kept me back with one strong hand and a body that seemed to check my every try to nav around him. In the other he held a large serrated knife. I had my hand on a throwing star, or three.

Eddie and Auggie were behind us, armed with smaller blades given to them by Cass. They were no less determined even if they still looked like junior high school dorks.

Inside the room, it took a second for my eyes to adjust, but my nose was right on time. Someone had practically jumped into a tank of rose-scented perfume. I assumed it was the one whose black lace bra was dangling off the desk chair.

A blink . . . then two.

The small living room was pitch black, but as my eyes adjusted I could see by the light of a small clock that it was similar to a simple hotel room with a blue couch, a wide-screen television, and a small kitchen area and bar deck. There was a bottle of open champagne, an empty glass, and one that was still full. Full and flat. Those bubbles had left the building some time ago. The ice in the bucket was warm and melted into submission.

Blood red roses that were now drooping tried to keep their petals up, but it was far too late. The heads fell forward in a death pose; the leaves had already crisped. Cass turned back to shrug. I pointed straight ahead to the only other room. The door was cracked open just a hair. Music floated out. It was soft, dreamy, and the words the singer crooned promised endless love. Really? She was into Mariah?

Three fingers. Cass held them up, meaning we go on three.

He held up one . . . then two . . . and then slowly swung the door open.

It was a scene that will always stand the test of time. Man and woman were snuggled in bed together.

Call me sexist, but the movie version would probably feature his arm draped over her, his leg over hers, twined for safekeeping. This was the other way around. She had what gym rats call big guns and logs for legs.

He was her slumber prisoner.

7.

She was overdressed for what was happening in here. In fact, she had on so many layers that she could have stood on a highway, been hit by a car, and never had known it.

I knew her personal dress code because she had kicked off the thick white comforter and the satin top sheet that covered most of him including his face.

She did believe in layering. Her lace camisole was covered by a larger black nightgown and then a plaid red-and-green flannel shirt. The latter was due to the fact that it was cold this far underground. Even the best heater couldn't cut the chill.

Her legs were absolutely bare and she had gone commando, meaning no silk pants and no underwear. Her feet were wrapped in at least three pair of socks, the tall kind that almost reached her knees and seemed to highlight about a month's worth of leggy hair growth.

Eddie tapped me and whispered into my ear, "Those beige pants are so tight I can see her religion."

"She's not wearing any pants. That's . . . *her*," I whispered back.

It was appropriate that Eddie looked like he was fourteen. He snickered under his breath and stared hard.

I didn't care about her; only him. The other side of the bed was occupied by a man who was tall and had shoulders. He was deeply under the covers, but I could see a flash of what looked like black hair. I couldn't be sure.

He was alternating between panting followed by gasping and grunting noises that seemed to come from deep within. *Was he hurt? Maybe Daniel was still in pain.*

She stirred first and we froze as an arm jetted out to the side. Eyes still closed, she reached for the small nightstand and moved what was now an empty wine glass in circular motions, slamming it down again when she realized that it was empty.

Silently, we watched as she swung her legs out of the bed, planting them on the floor like tree trunks. Maybe Plan B was a pee stop.

This part required lifting her lampshades. And when she opened deep-set brown eyes and stood as if it was an effort, she jumped in her own skin at the sight of four strangers in her bedroom.

Quick scan: She was a bigger woman, maybe five foot eight and about two hundred plus pounds. She had dark brown hair cut in a severe, chin-length bob that was sticking out in all directions.

When her arms flailed forward, I braced.

"What the hell? I told you it was our wedding night. Don't you know what do not disturb means? You can clean the damn room tomorrow!" she hissed, squinting hard. "Is that you, Isabella? You better have brought extra towels, you stupid bitch."

It's never right to be rude to the help.

Eddie planted his fist in her face and we felt nothing as she felt the floor. "She's the head guard of the women's wing. We call her Jules Roberts," Auggie whispered. "She's nasty. She beats kids. And someone said she was getting married last week—which seemed like the biggest joke of all. Who would marry her?"

The mister in question sat up with a load moan.

He put both hands up in the air so we wouldn't hurt him.

"Sugarplum?"

"Chris Flicker?" I whispered as he jumped out of the bed. He was stark naked, which was a sight I had never seen. I was so shocked that I looked, by accident, which made him cover himself with his hands. For scientific purposes: he looked his exact age because he wasn't a miner. He wasn't breathing the stuff all day.

"What are you doing here . . . and where is Daniel?"

"I took a wrong turn in the woods," Flick replied. "They brought me here to the mine, but that . . . that woman . . . the guards said she was celebrating twenty years down here. Her present was she was allowed to keep me. Like a pet! I showed her three versions of her future, which all included her getting hit in the face. But she didn't care. They tethered me to her earlier tonight."

"Did you put out?" Eddie asked. "Cause if you did, I think you need some shots or something."

"I didn't put out, Edward. I passed out," Flick said. "I drank so much and fast that I puked, which grossed her out, and then apparently she undressed me and dragged me to bed. Nothing much could happen. I'm not good with alcohol."

"Can you walk?" I asked.

"Walk, yes, I think I can walk," he said. "My sugarplums didn't have that kind of wedding night."

"You didn't take her girls out of their boulder holder, did you?" Eddie taunted. It didn't take long before he was on a roll. "You certainly didn't shake the sheets! Play nug-a-nug? Have a horizontal refreshment?"

Auggie doubled over in laughter.

"No," Flick responded. "I did no sheet shaking. I didn't touch her nug. There were no refreshments of a horizontal nature."

"It doesn't matter now," Auggie added. He looked down. "She's spread out like a cold supper." He paused and said, "Obviously, I've been spending way too much time with Eddie."

Flick grabbed my hand. He projected three images of Daniel on the white wall, but they were dark and hard to make out – except for one. "Follow me, honeybee. It's not far," Flick said. "I just hope we're not too late."

8.

We snuck out of the suite and made it halfway down another dark hallway. Took a hard right.

Maybe I felt him first.

9.

He was my birthday, July Fourth, and Christmas Eve at midnight the minute a light snow bursts from the sky.

He wore black working boots and a nondescript gray prison jumpsuit.

In his hand was a mop and he was bent over it, slowly pushing the wet fibers across a clean floor. He didn't see me at first, so I moved closer and then closer, so nothing else would fill his field of vision.

Finally, his head lifted. I saw his eyes were glazed and his face looked flushed. I lifted my hand like a child waving hello. In the past, it always worked. Someone held a hand out and the other was there to take it.

Something was very wrong.

Before I could reach him, his hand fell to his side.

"Callaghan, you have a cut by your eye. Does it hurt, baby?" he finally said. It came out rough and raspy, as if the words were caught between his heart and his throat. Before I could answer, his face twisted in agony. When he turned slightly and I saw upper back of his uniform was stained black and it was soaking wet. It wasn't the water from the mop bucket or even sweat. It smelled liked rusted iron, which meant that it was blood.

My hand lifted to his forehead, which was burning hot. He was feverish and his body shook. And when he collapsed into my arms, slowly I lowered us to the ground.

"Oh, baby . . . no," I whispered. I didn't even know that I was crying.

His hand barely stroked my face and I caught all of his ice-cold fingertips in my hands. In that moment, I remembered something Daniel once told me after he picked a flower from our garden.

"Never give back something that someone gives you. It could be all they have to give," he said.

All I had was his hand.

10.

"Cass," I whisper-screamed. I heard his hard footsteps. The rest was white noise including the two guards who were on full blast until Eddie and Cass borrowed a few stray mining picks and made sure they were facedown kissing the hard rock floor. My dark little heart skipped a satisfied beat when one of the guard's head became personally acquainted with a wooden handle that was now part of his forehead.

Karma. It was a bitch—and in this case, so was I.

Cass grabbed Daniel, slinging him like a sack of potatoes over his own shoulder. "Elevator," he said, pointing and trying to run, which wasn't easy with dead weight slowing every step.

In the blur of what happened next, we made it into the steel box and punched it for the above-the-earth deck thirty floors over our heads. Eddie, Auggie, and Flick were ready, but the elevator was excruciatingly slow. I held my breath and grasped my stars as the steel doors finally parted. The box was empty. With a tight fist, I didn't request our floor. I pounded that button, demanding it.

Cass stopped to look at his watch.

"Balls-thirty . . . shit," he muttered under his breath. He was in full marine mode now and quickly translated. "It's thirty minutes on the hour, meaning it's time for a security sweep. All the guards will be roaming the top now looking for strays."

Back in the Attic near the copter landing strip and parking lot, Cass had no choice but to put Daniel down on the hood of a Mercedes in order to embed his now-free elbow into the face of the guard who greeted us with a loud "What the hell?"

With his other hand, he grabbed enough of the man's long hair to grip his head and implant his face through a front windshield. Eddie took out two others with a karate neck chop he learned at ITT. With Auggie's help he opened an unlocked trunk of a flatbed truck, found some rope and hog-tied them. The finishing touch? Tossing their flailing bodies into bottom of the bed.

I felt Cass shoving me toward the copter while Eddie and Auggie carried Daniel – one had his feet, the other his shoulders. The copter doors opened and Auggie and Eddie grabbed the passenger side front. Daniel was carefully placed on the floor in back. Flick and I crammed into the two seats in back and Cass took the pilot's seat, which accounted for everyone—and somehow we fit. It was as if we willed it that way.

"Hello, barf bag," Eddie said. "Just kidding. Does someone have a bigger seat belt?"

I squeezed his arm as the top propeller whirled like a mini tornado.

"Cass, skip the safety demo!" I yelled. "Go!"

"Alpha Mike Foxtrot, sugar," he shouted back.

Translation: Adios, muther . . .

11.

Booming thunder rolled overhead. Black clouds had dipped precariously near our takeoff spot, so in no matter of time, we were riding the storm.

The copter shook hard and then fell several hundred feet. Cass was on the stick and pulled hard as he tried to achieve any kind of altitude.

I closed my eyes as we careened sideways in the sky. A crackling boom and a streak of lightening put a garish spotlight on electrified patches of terror all around. Blinding light sizzled across the side windows had me covering Daniel's body with my shaking one.

Forward thrust had us surfing angry storm clouds and for once I welcomed the darkness until I heard the hard drumming of relentless rain. It sounded like a machine gun had our small whirlybird on lock, but not for long. The rain stopped like someone flipped a switch. And the sky cackled and cracked as if it might split right down the middle. Bomb-like claps of thunder were followed by brilliant shocks of white.

Daniel's head was resting in my lap and I refused to focus on the fact that his breath was shallow and his open eyes weren't focusing. I held him tightly because we didn't have seat belts while Eddie and Flick reached around and held me in place with their legs and their hands. It was almost pointless. Cass flew high and then lost five thousand or more feet in a drop that felt like we were plummeting off the world.

As we bounced hard, bones grinding into other bones, I could only imagine how excruciating this was for Daniel. The last time he was cloud surfing in a raging sky, he had nowhere to go but down.

Daniel and his entire family crash-landed in a field and thus the kids began their collective afterlife. Was he thinking about those last moments? I would never be sure. Right now, as his eyes rolled to the back of his head, he was unable to speak.

When I removed my hands from where they were resting on his back, they were beyond bloodied.

I began to pray. It was the kind of prayer of those facing last resorts. Of all the people in the copter, it was Eddie who did the same thing, but out loud. "Heavenly father," he began.

What bound us wasn't age or circumstance. We were all just chasing hope. That's all most of us really do. Every single minute.

I leaned down to whisper into Daniel's ear, "If love can save you, you will exist. I will exist. *De shior.*"

Translation: forever.

TWENTY-THREE

1.

The wind didn't want Cass to touch the bird down, but somehow he manhandled the stick —left and right and right and left—until we swaying sideways and then somehow leveled long enough to actually land.

I knew we were in a field not far from the cabin and insisted that we disembark. Auggie with Eddie's help carried Daniel to the cabin. Before I raced after them, Cass touched my arm.

"Be right back, sugar," he said. I was shocked when moments later, I heard the *chop-chop-chop* of the copter blades. I knew exactly what he was doing. Cass took off again to hide the bird in a field farther away so we weren't sitting ducks for Edward's guards. It was still raining in sideways waves, which would slow their search, but we had to cover all bases.

The wooden cabin door blew open, which announced our arrival to only one.

Griz was waiting for us inside. Eddie entered, took one glance and ran out of the cabin screaming for his mother.

2.

Griz held a freezing-cold Daniel in his arms while a half-petrified Auggie scanned my face. I squeezed Griz's arm tightly to say hello and then raced to the corner of the room.

As torrents of rain pounded the roof, Auggie and I lifted an old, dusty mattress from the corner. It fit neatly on a wooden table in the middle of the room. Griz could smell the blood and gingerly placed Daniel on his new bed.

Griz ran back to the cave and returned quickly and proudly, carrying a large armload of comforters to cover the half-delirious man. He disappeared again only to come back with flashlights, candles, and a large pot of fresh river water. On the third trip, he brought eight pristine white towels, smaller washcloths, and what he considered a medical kit in a rusted box. Inside was a new knife, scissors, and a box of Batman Band-Aids for little kids.

"Oh, Griz," I said. "I love you."

"Boo-boos," he replied, pointing to his knee. I don't know why, but I blew his poor scraped knee a little kiss.

"Wa," he cooed.

Griz had been taking care of himself for years and knew a few primitive techniques. He dipped one of the smaller towels in the water, folded it neatly, and put it on Daniel's forehead.

"Brokin," he said, taking gentle fingers and moving them slowly over my beloved's fever-slicked, ashen face. Daniel's eyelids were too heavy to control, so he kept them shut. His body began to convulse.

Every prayer I had ever known was overlapping in my head and on my lips. They were pleading prayers for the expiring . . . for those souls departing . . . for those who begin to shrink in this life form as they transcended for another . . . in front of our wailing hearts and tearful eyes.

I wrapped my arms around Daniel and rested my head on his cold chest.

Chasing hope . . .

I took off his shirt off, rolling him gently onto his stomach to inspect the damages despite his guttural moans. I wasn't an expert, but it was easy to figure that he had been shot in the upper right shoulder, probably during his escape attempt. *Over a week ago.* There was a hole and it had turned black along with a patch of skin around it that was greenish black. Griz was the one who leaned in closer and twisted his face.

The wound smelled.

As serious as death itself.

3.

It seemed to take forever for Cass to return but only a second for him to take charge. "We, meaning everyone, better deal with it, man," he said. "Or we're going to lose him in the next few minutes." He was especially talking at a freaked-out Eddie who was back. "Griz, take Eddie into the cave and heat this water to boiling. Make bubbles, kid," Cass instructed. When Eddie went white at the thought of helping with anything medial, Cass towered over him. "Suck it up, Wargo!" he demanded. "You're in or you're out."

"Sucked," Eddie confirmed after Griz offered him a half-melted, stolen Twix bar from his pocket. Eddie decided that they could begin to trust each other: Eddie would trust that Griz wasn't some forest creature who would eat him, and Griz would trust that Eddie might be a new fren.

Cass broke up their newfound bromance. "Griz, go into the cave and make the water hot," he commanded. "We can light a fire in here. Auggie, go help him. I'll also need the biggest jar of honey Griz can find. He has a bunch of them in his storage room. Or sugar. Both stave off further infections. Bring lemons and fresh garlic and cooking oil. And I need booze. Any kind of liquor that is in Griz's collection from his dumpster dives although vodka is the purest and would be best."

"Like the guy has Jim Beam," Eddie mocked.

"He has everything, so shut the hell up and just get on it," Cass cut in.

He threw a few of his knives in the bottom of the pot. "Boiling hot water," he instructed.

"Auggie, on the way back dig up some thick mud, put it in one of the clean pots, and bring it back. Enough to fill a large spaghetti pot," he said. "Flick will stay in here with me to restrain the patient."

And to me he said, "It's best if you go wait in the cave until I come to get you."

"Not going anywhere," I said. "Do you . . . know what you're doing?"

"I'm taking the bullet out," he said. "I've been trained to do it. I've done it under less ideal circumstances like when you're being shot at in the desert with no shelter or you're being held hostage by the opposition. It's not easy to watch."

I was frozen in place. "Most things are not easy to watch," I said.

Cass said nothing for a long time.

"Why?" I had to ask him. Cass spent so much time telling me I was destined to be with him, which begged the question: Why save him now?

"Why?" Cass said, locking eyes. "Because I love you. I'm doing this, sugar, for you . . . even if it kills me. But let's take me out of it for a minute. These aren't the best of circumstances. This wound has festered. I don't know how much I can do, but I'll do my best so you don't hate me forever. So I don't hate me forever."

"What we really need is some penicillin," I said. "I'll try to go figure that out."

"You do that," Cass said. "Get out."

4.

The last thing I saw of Daniel and Cass that night was one reaching into his pack and pulling out something really odd. It was a small tape player, the old-fashioned kind, and he hit play. The song "Rock On" suddenly filled the cabin.

"Motivation," Cass said to the lyrics of "*Hey kids, rock and roll. Rock on, ooh my soul.*"

5.

Alone in my thoughts outside, I went there.

Everyone has a *there*.

There is where the deepest fear lives.

When I was done dwelling, I looked to the night sky, which seemed to answer back.

It said: But you loved.

Then fear shouted back: The world is full of beautiful things that don't last.

Then a question was presented: Does the universe fight for lovers to be together?

Then an answer: Unconditionally. The universe whispers to lovers, "Hearts that echo deserve forever or nothing at all."

I would not return to the cave, but to my old friend, the woods. The rain had stopped by now and everything smelled clean and fresh like a virgin world. I sat on a large rock and cried my heart out.

Over the next hour, I heard Daniel scream. Then, there was silence. I didn't know which was worse.

What if he never recovered?

What if the big save was for nothing?

What if I never saw him again?

Tears didn't help. Neither did cursing our fate.

Then, in the dark, wisdom spoke. She said, "One's coming of age is not a given. It must be earned."

6.

"Do you think this might help?" a young girl's voice whispered into my ear. But there was no one there.

I watched with wide-open eyes while she materialized. Matilda and Molly, both 14 morphed into one girl right in front of me. Mentally, both were quite present in one mind that split to occupy both. They called their collective self, Deuce, although either could appear to overtake the one body that was available now. It was their way to maintain some individuality. "Hey, Walker," Deuce said, stepping out into the darkness to greet me with a quick hug.

"We're literally one now," said the invisible Molly. There could only be one visible—and like any kids have done since the beginning of time, they tried to take turns.

"We share one being because of what happened. I'm the dominant and Molly steps out when necessary. Her old body was broken beyond repair, but since we're twins, we use the same vessel."

"Pretty cool, huh?" Molly said with a wicked grin as I hugged her and left my arms open. "Close 'em now," she said, and I knew I was embracing the other girl.

She gently placed three small vials and two syringes on the flat rock.

"We've been here hiding in the cave for a few days," Matilda said with a giggle. "At first, we were afraid of the big guy who looks like a bear, but Griz is an excellent cook. And he's very nice although his language skills are not so hot.

"When you left, we snuck back to Edward's lab in our totally invisible mode—the coolest thing is we can do that now as one. We borrowed some penicillin and a little bit of melatonin in case anyone needs help sleeping tonight. We stole some other medicines. Just in case. But we knew we needed the penicillin because your mission sounded dangerous. Mama gave it to us when we were really sick lots of times. Daniel's really sick now, isn't he? We have penicillin for him."

"Did anyone see you?" I gasped in an incredulous voice. "Did anyone see you?"

"Nope, silly," Molly said. "Works the same way it did on Freak Island. Anything we touch goes invisible, too. And we stayed translucent all the way back to the cabin.

"Suckers," she added. "We're bosses!"

"Girls," I sobbed, embracing air until they moved into the space. I imagined young limbs entwined with my own.

"It's good to be us," Matilda said with a smirk. *I loved that no matter what happened, they moved on and embraced it.*

It wasn't long before the three of us made our way back to the cabin. I handed Cass the penicillin and he nodded. He was ready to operate, so I had no choice but to go back outside. He didn't need me now because my emotional baggage was suffocating the room.

But I couldn't really go. All I had was a tiny, dirty window and I spent hours looking through it. "Loving on you a little harder tonight, Daniel," I whispered into the dense night air. "You. Me. Us."

I felt an invisible hand slip into mine.

7.

Cass treated the room like a triage unit you'd see in the field. He boiled his favorite knife, called the Riptide, in the water until its long silver blade began to gleam. Next, he was ready for the booze that Auggie handed him. He took that bottle of Billionaire Vodka, officially the world's most expensive at three million a bottle in the living realm, stolen from a supplier making a personal delivery to Edward, and liberally poured it over Daniel's oozing wound.

The irony of it was thick.

"Alcohol is the best disinfectant for deep wounds," Cass said as he worked quickly.

He ripped his leather wallet in two pieces, placing one between Daniel's teeth.

"For when the pain gets to be too much and you're wailing, just bite down, man," he said. "If you want to throw up then spit the thing to the floor first and hurl down below, so you don't further infect the situation."

Cass stopped for a moment. Looked his patient up and down. "No reset, sucks to be you," he said.

Then I watched as he leaned in close to Daniel for a private moment. "I don't know why I'm saving your sorry ass," Cass hissed. "Do me a favor and check out for good. Do *her* a favor for once and just slip slide away, you pain in the ass rebel son of a bitch."

In one lucid moment, Daniel lifted is head. "Fuck you, asshole—and thank you," he said.

Cass took a big swig of vodka straight from the bottle. It must have burned on the way down.

"This is gonna hurt, honcho, but pain is the problem of the patient. It's not my immediate priority. I'm here to save your life because I am a candy-ass do-gooder and I made her a promise. Feel free to check out at any time, jackass. The least you could have done is stay gone after you escaped. I didn't," Cass replied, sticking his middle and index finger into the wound and pressing for a short time to stop any recent bleeding.

He knew those words might be enough for Daniel to actual survive with the hope of someday beating the shit out of him.

There was no anesthesia. No drugs. It's why Cass had Eddie and mostly Griz hold Daniel, stomach down. Then he made the first cut into his shoulder to fish out the bullet and Griz started to cry.

I watched Daniel bite down and then I heard him scream.

"Many, many nights, I felt like screaming when I saw you with her," Cass continued as he took a substance out of his backpack called Quick Clot and spread the liquid over Daniel's wound.

His bedside manner was questionable . . . and loud enough for me to hear. "Dumbshit, I could dig you a nice grave tomorrow and we'd all have a good cry. Well, a few of us would shed a tear—not me. I'd drink the rest of that expensive shit from your daddy's house," he said. "Would certainly make my life easier. I'd give her the time to mourn before I had her join me in my bed. But no, here I am. Doing the right thing again, damn it."

"Auggie!" Cass barked in the next second. "Do you know CPR?"

"Yes, I was in Boy Scout Troop—"

Cass cut him off.

"Be ready if he stops breathing with mouth-to-mouth and CPR. If you feel like it."

"I'm a first responder," Auggie marveled. "And that was Troop 786, in case you need references. I do box knots and have a Citizen of the World merit badge. I do CPR and wound care." To Eddie, Auggie commanded, "Go fill a clean jug with three-quarters water and one part vinegar. Griz has some in the cave. It will keep the sutures clean."

It was amazing what secret skills lurked in the past of my friends.

I heard Daniel emit a guttural growl as if he were a wild animal pushed to the limit, one who would bite at any moment.

"Cass," he grunted.

"The patient wants you," Auggie stated.

"What?" Cass snapped.

"You're . . ."

Cass would wait for it.

"You're a dick."

"One more word and I'll filet you," Cass responded.

"I get it," Eddie said. "I really do. His anger is keeping him alive."

8.

Cass had already washed his hands in water as hot as he could stand for the third time. There were no gloves, so he used his naked hand to root around in Daniel's back, pushing with his other hand. At the same time, Auggie had one hand on Daniel's lower back to make sure that his chest was rising and falling.

Cass cut deeper into the skin, which made me wince. "Just one more inch because whoever got you, got you good," Cass grunted while keeping pressure with his lower arm on the wound. Griz practically draped his big body over Daniel to keep him in one position.

"Just a little bit to the right and . . . eureka. A twelve-gauge buckshot. You could bring down an elephant with this thing. Props to Dan over here for walking upright after he was shot," a sweating Cass exclaimed.

He only gave those props because his patient was passed out cold.

The ting of a large piece of metal hit the glass jar where Cass saved the bullet. "These things make wide wounds like this one. If they don't get you with the shot, they get you with the infection that follows if you don't remove the bullet and treat the wound," Cass said, adding, "Someone should blow up that mine."

I watched as Cass cut away additional skin on Daniel's back along with a nasty green swatch of infection. He was a quick worker, springing up to dunk a glass bowl into a now boiling caldron of water. The former marine fished it out and began to . . . cook. He took a cup of cooking oil and mixed it with thick honey out of a jar, lemon juice, and bits of garlic.

Gingerly, he applied the mix to an unconscious Daniel and then slowly wrapped ripped strips of the cleanest white T-shirt he could find over his upper back. Before he applied the mix, he took his palm and placed it just above the injury site to slow the bleeding at one of Daniel's vascular pressure points.

"You won't smell pretty, but you never do," Cass said to an incoherent Daniel, "but this stuff's better than Neosporin when it comes to staving off further infection. It's what they put on me when my leg was . . . well, never mind. These elements fight any natural bacteria and disinfect wounds."

That was the end of the medical lecture. Griz, Eddie, and Auggie had each collapsed against a wall from exhaustion and fright.

"I gave you my best. And here's my best advice. Don't stop when you're tired. Stop when you're done," Cass told his patient.

One last thing.

"Now, if you die again . . . it's on you, muther . . . ," Cass bit out as he stalked out of the cabin. He slammed the door. Hard.

9.

Moments later, when I slipped back in, Daniel was still passed out. His entire shoulder was covered by a bloodied towel over the initial T-shirt dressing. His hands, dangling from his perch on the table, were soft and warm like the world in summer.

"Time is his doctor now," Cass said to me as we passed each other. One was on a path toward eternal love; the other was going for a long walk in the woods.

"Will he be okay?" I said as my eyes shimmered.

"I certainly hope not," Cass said coldly.

Turning his back to me, he put a period on it.

10.

Hours later, Cass returned to glance at his mostly unconscious patient and the girl sitting on the floor holding his hand. The three of us in that cabin felt like there were three million of us. Our emotions seemed to crowd every single corner and sucked up each free molecule of air.

"What did you do with the helicopter?" I asked, because if there was ever time for a subject changer, it was now.

"I set fire to it in the lake. And it exploded, which could have been explained as a hit of lightning. The rain put out the fire," Cass said.

"Thank you, Cass. For everything."

"Some nights, you go full Griswold," he said.

"Big kaboom," Auggie said, joining us. "Oh, and one more thing. I found Deuce and we went back to the big house for more medicine. Through the big windows, I saw Edward and all of his merry men, gutless wonders, stuffing their faces in the kitchen because they are invincible, right? Deuce ran to the lab. Got bandages, disinfectant, creams, pills. Mission accomplished."

"Is that all?" Cass asked.

"Nope," Auggie said. "I went into the house and found this fob. There must have been a million cars in that garage, but I pressed the thing and luckily one of the Caddy Escalades at the bottom of the driveway lit up. I've never seen one in person. Only on *Cribs*."

"I love that show," Eddie said. "Does this cabin have WIFI?"

"It doesn't have a bathroom," Cass stated.

"We have a car now," a visible Molly came out and said with glee. "We parked it in the deepest trees. I'm an excellent driver when you can see me. Otherwise my invisible feet put no pressure on the pedals."

"We ain't going anywhere," I said, glancing at Daniel.

"Not until we know . . . one way or the other," Cass said.

I looked around the room at this ragtag group of misfits, but they were mine.

The secret of a good day every single day?

Find your tribe. Love them hard.

11.

For the rest of the night I sat on that floor by his side. He was still out, but breathing, which I convinced myself was some sort of small victory.

There was a moment when he returned to the world. Our eyes locked, but his were swimming in some sort of clear liquid. I could say the same for mine. Leaning over him, I whispered, "Love. Is. Everything."

His answer was to shut the windows because the cruel twist was that Daniel could heal others—just not himself. When his eyes closed again, lids heavy as if they weighed thousands of pounds, I cursed my fate, wishing I could go back in time to those happy days and nights in our little craftsman house in the Midst.

Alas, unless, you time travel—one of the most dangerous things of all—you can't wind the clock backward. There is only one moment that actually exists. And that is right now. Even if we could rewind, we wouldn't belong there anymore.

But I could remember the past as perfect, as one does on long nights where dawn simply won't arrive. We lay naked not so long ago under a blank midnight sky. Daniel touched his soft lips to that sweet spot on my neck and then wrapped his arms around my middle.

"You are my only certainty," he said.

Love. Is. Everything.

12.

When his whole body began to shake, I screamed for Cass who burst in and gave Daniel another shot of antibiotics and put cold compresses over his legs, feet, and head. The fit stopped as Cass called for Eddie to get freezing lake water and keep it coming to break Daniel's fever.

"How do you know this?" I stammered.

"Everyone knows something you don't, sugar," Cass said with a smile as he shrugged off his parka vest and got to work. "Military training is a crash course in crashing. You're out on a mission with your team and someone has to play doctor."

"It's funny," Cass said around four in the morning while the two of us sat wide awake on the floor, our backs pressed to the wall. "All of us spend our whole lives looking for the right person. Nobody is trying to be the right person," Cass said. "I'm trying. For you. For MC, my other baby, my daughter. Maybe someday . . . I'll stop now."

He was a formidable force combined with the biggest heart.

"Go outside. Go now," Cass said in a low voice. "I'm going to change his bandage. You don't need to see it, plus Griz and Eddie are out there trying to communicate with each other. I'm teaching Griz some dirty jokes."

I walked into the brisk night air.

Through the window, I heard Cass in a stern voice tell Daniel, "We're all tired, asshole. We all want to sit it out. You want to sleep forever . . . remember this: it will take only a second for you to break her heart and leave," Cass said. "But, I'll spend eternity fixing it. You want that to happen . . . just let go. Slipping away is easy. You just drop the threads and drift."

Outside on the small front porch, Eddie was medicating his nerves with food. What was remarkable was the fact that the longer they were far away from the mine, the more they looked like their regular age. Both were almost normal, which meant a quick trip to the cave to get their backpacks and change into clothes that fit.

"Hiya, Walker," Eddie said between bites. He took one look at my worried face and said, "Don't sweat it. Dan-o will be okay. He's too much of a tough bastard to perish from a buckshot to the shoulder. Once I got shot in the ass by my drunk uncle, and I made it all the way back to home, slept on it for a weekend, and then went to the free hospital where it was a three-day wait to be seen and have the bullet removed."

"You've led an illustrious existence, Ed," I said fondly. "You remain a work in progress, too."

I looked down to see Griz curled up on the ground with Molly and the invisible Matilda curled into him like three peas in a pod. Auggie was right next to him, hunkered down in a sea of blankets our forest host had provided.

"Why are you still awake?" I asked Eddie.

"'Cause I got friends. Got lots of 'em," he replied with a smile. "I always had my brothers, Billy and Daryl, but it ain't the same. We were never close—always fightin' for food and a bed. This feels different. Tighter. Gotta protect it."

There were times I couldn't believe he was the same person I met at ITT many months ago. "I never had no real friends back in Alabama," Eddie said. "It doesn't make no sense, but I don't mind being here. Not if you guys are here."

"I'm glad you're here, Eddie," I told him, reaching out to touch his arm fondly.

"I'm into exploring my inner man these days."

"Well, of all the doors in the universe, I'm glad we're in the same room."

"Me, too," she said, sneaking out from behind a clump of trees. She had mud-streaked cheeks and her hair was in messy top bun. But those oversized glasses with the punched-out frames were there in thick, nerdy, black plastic—my favorite of the many she had collected.

"Bitty?" I whispered.

Eddie was speechless for a moment. But then his goofy face was transformed by what could only be described as that look of love. He almost shoved me away to get to her.

"Well, howdy, hottie. Unless I'm dumb as a box of rocks, you're obviously a friend of Walker's," Eddie said with a wide smile. "I might could meet someone new tonight. That's what I said to myself. So, take a seat, and stay a spell." His hand slapped the porch floorboard next to him and in the darkness, I could see the dust fly.

"You must be Eddie," Bitty said with a grin.

13.

We sat for a long time, Eddie and Bitty trading different parts of very different life-and-death stories. When she mentioned the atrocities suffered at the hands of Daniel's father and how she had been hiding in the woods since her breakout, I could see Eddie both fascinated and visibly upset.

"That's as screwed up as a soup sandwich," Eddie summed up.

"Ya reckon?" Bitty said. *Who knew that she spoke Wargo?*

Then she put her hand on mine. "Walker, he will be fine," she said. "And you will be fine. Women can handle it. We can handle it a thousand different ways if you give us a thousand different days."

Auggie poked his head out the door. He formally greeted Bitty with a hand and a head nod. "I'm August, nice to meet you," he said. "But you can call me Auggie or Gus. Or August."

"Or you can take your pea-pickin' heart and go back to sleep, Aug*mented*," Eddie suggested. *Was Eddie jealous?*

I almost smiled and Bitty stifled a real laugh. "I think I just peed my pants a little," she informed all of us.

One thing about Bitty, she never held back.

"That's good, darlin'," Eddie said. "Panty sweat is always good luck."

14.

By 5:00 a.m., dawn still playing hard to get, the fever seemed to break. I dabbed off Daniel's face and he looked almost peaceful. Cass pulled back the bandage and packed it with a new dose of his honey concoction. Maybe I was imagining it, but the deep wound looked less angry.

"I'm going to go shower in the cold lake to wake myself up." Cass grumbled. I walked him to the door. Before he left the room, he leaned down to kiss the top of my head.

"Walker, you are coated steel," Cass whispered into my ear. "No matter what happens, you go on. It's an admirable trait, sugar."

Somehow, I dozed off from my spot on the floor near the table-bed. When my eyes opened, I was greeted by a mellow yellow sun. It was the type of kind morning light that made the world new after a storm.

"Everything the light touches is our tomorrow," I whispered, glancing at the brilliant prisms around the room. I returned to the floor and took Daniel's cold hand in mine.

"Don't blow out the candle," I prayed. "I can't stand the dark any longer."

15.

When I opened my baby greens again, the bed was empty.

My legs hurt from exertion and from sleeping on the floor, but they still worked and I began to run, out the cabin door into a world awash in a fierce and purple sunset. The whole day must have passed, which seemed sad for some reason because I didn't like the past tense.

Breathlessly, I pounded hard on bare feet. The sun was fading. The air was full on intention. I looked to the left and saw true friends.

I looked to the right and saw nothing.

I just felt his breath in my ear.

TWENTY-FOUR

1.

I felt him, which wasn't enough. I had to see him and when I tilted my head, my eyes collided with the warrior stance. The rest of me was frozen in time and space. Feet: stuck. Lips: frozen.

His grin widened. "Don't make me move mountains," he said.

"How many are you going to move?" I asked.

"Every single one in my way."

I was too young to predict happy endings.

I was too old to deny that they existed.

A step forward. And another.

You have to walk toward the things that you love.

We stared at each other's lips. Nervously. He ran his thumb over my bottom one, removing it slowly.

"Please," I said, wishing I didn't sound so needy. It's not enough to want it. You have to go get it. I grabbed the back of his head and drew him in with a force that shocked both of us.

Daniel kissed me hungrily for so long I forgot to be afraid. That was destined. Small kisses and words I'd never remember followed. I slid my hand into his hair; he slid his hand behind my neck.

Then he pulled away and kissed my forehead.

Everyone knows.

Forehead kisses are kisses meant for the soul.

"I have decided to hold your hand forever and walk with you. Just walk with you. But first, I'm going to kiss the hell out of you again," he said.

"There you are," I whispered.

2.

He was a man of his word.

3.

When we pulled back, I realized that beauty is not in the face although his looked luminous in the dying sky. Beauty is in the light of the heart.

I wish I could turn back the clock, find him sooner, in order to love him longer.

When he smiled, it was like being underground and finding a magic eye, an opening above, a skylight, a spyhole that's a straight shot to the heavens.

It's that feeling of every tear dried.

"Damn, Walker," Bitty said, looking Daniel up and down. She was the first to break it up. "He is *exactly* how you described him. *Damn.*"

"Personally, I'm going to vomit," Eddie said. Then he almost slugged Daniel in his injured shoulder. "Sorry, man. Oh, shit! But, good to see you, master of the void. My divine madman."

"How is everyone doing?" Daniel asked in a crackling voice.

"It's been a shitty week," Auggie confirmed. "I went through puberty again in the mine. I mean zits, hormones, aching bones."

"A horror story," Eddie said.

"Now, I'm just trying to keep my vibrations high," Auggie added, enveloping Daniel in a tight hug. I counted down until he was gently pushed away.

"I could hug you forever," Daniel said, dragging me into a tight embrace.

"I'd call that cosmic ambition," I said.

"Where have you been all this time, baby?" Daniel asked, running a warm finger down the side of my face.

I couldn't tell him that I had been tethered to his father who was only miles away. I couldn't say: "I've been kidnapped, nearly froze to a second death in the woods, almost became the bride of Frankenstein, nearly raped, and then a seven-foot guy took care of me in a cave.

"I've been hanging out in the caves," I lied.

He read me in a glance.

"Callaghan, maybe you'll actually tell me the truth later?" Daniel said in a low growl.

He grabbed me tightly, drawing me in. Eventually, he loped a hand around my stomach and let his thumbs linger on the top of my jeans. It felt good resting there.

Griz stood in the shadows.

"New friends to meet," I said in a happier tone. "This is Bitty who has helped me so much, and that is Griz who saved my life."

Griz peeked his head out from behind a wide redwood.

"Hiya," Griz whispered.

"Hiya," Daniel said. "I remember you. We ran into you when we first got here."

Griz grinned. "That me!" he said.

"Thank you for helping Walker," Daniel said. "I owe you."

"Frens," Griz said with a wide smile as Molly and Matilda stood tall on his wide shoulders.

It was the first time I had seen Daniel look up to meet another young man's eyes. Way up.

Overhead, I watched as a crow flew low overhead. I knew from ancient legend that one crow signified bad luck and possible death. Two crows meant good luck or a change for the better. Three crows meant a celebration or even a possible marriage. Quickly, I did the math and counted eleven of those black birds circling above us until they settled in one of the taller branches in a low tree.

"There are ten of them," I said. "That means something overwhelming."

"Eleven," Cass said, returning from a spot farther down on the lake with three large bass in his hands. "That means uncertainty."

Daniel and Cass eyed one another.

"Alive . . . shit," Cass grumbled.

"Sorry, man," Daniel shot back.

"He's better," I said in a hopeful voice.

"Unfortunately . . . I told you so, sugar," Cass said with a wink. "And he's a lot better. The reset finally kicked in, which means he's all better now."

"I hear I have you to thank—I could have expired last night with no reset. I'm grateful and I mean it. Thank you," Daniel began, holding out a hand.

Cass slapped a big dead fish into Daniel's hands. "Now that you're better, you can carry something." Then he said something really odd. "Someday, I will have something to thank you for—and you better deliver," he said, walking past us and slamming the cabin door behind him.

We didn't see him at all for the next two days.

4.

It was time set in slow motion.

Bitty, Eddie, Auggie, and Deuce were enthralled with Griz and the feelings were mutual. They knew enough to leave Daniel and I alone to get reacquainted although at night we pulled up a bedroll next to them in the cave where we slept with one ear trained on the distance.

You could never be sure in these parts.

I went to apply Cass's concoction of natural medicine, but a funny thing happened. Daniel healed completely due to a sudden restoration of the reset. There wasn't even a scar.

369

He tested the reset in all kinds of ways. Several of us jumped in the bathtub and Daniel stayed underwater for just a little bit too long.

Either he had turned into an amphibian or the reset was back. It was odd because I was in the same tub, but suddenly I felt a bit shy around him. I wore a bathing suit and shorts into the tub so he couldn't see where his father branded me. We kissed and cuddled a bit, but the sudden emergence of Eddie in a Hawaiian bathing suit was a mood buster.

"Rub a dub," Eddie said. He was back to his real age in appearance, but still had his boyish personality.

Daniel and I spent the days taking long walks in the woods at the oddest hours.

Wide-eyed because I didn't need sleep anymore (hello, reset, nice to feel you), we greeted one of the brilliant dawns. A hard middle of the night rain brought out what looked like thousands of dandelions waving in a gentle breeze. I kept reminding myself that the months moved backward here, which meant we had left the deep-freeze months for the more tepid temperatures of early autumn.

"Callaghan," Daniel finally said. "We need to talk."

"About your wife," I shot out as we sat outside, dangling our feet off a rock as we stared at the crystal blue lake.

"Some bullshit tethering thing," he said. "Nothing happened. She had a ceremony, put me into some kind of suite downstairs, and then she was called away. Never came back—until I saw her one more time looking down the barrel of a gun. She was the one who shot me."

"Does she have a name?" I asked.

"Pristine," he said.

We walked in silence, deeper into the woods, until we found the perfect spot to really talk.

"You're married to the one who looks like Mulan. Who thinks she's a sheriff?" I said in a shocked voice.

"Baby, yes . . . but no. This is their crazy system. We're not anything to each other—nothing that would matter anywhere else in the universe," Daniel replied.

"She's the one who captured me while I was waiting for everyone in the woods outside the immigration building," I said. "Maybe because she wanted you."

Yes, it was true. I was white-hot jealous. Did she kiss him? Did you try to do more with him?

Again, he read my mind.

"Full disclosure: she kissed me. I kissed her back so I would have a few freedoms in order to escape. She tasted like beer and mint gum. Nothing pleasant about it," Daniel admitted. "She tried to turn it into more, but there was always pressing business calling her away."

"One night when she was gone for a few days, I escaped," Daniel said. "I punched out several guards and made it to the top of the mine. I was in the parking lot when I saw that flick of black hair flying in the breeze.

"Pulled a gun off her shoulder and shot me in the back—no questions asked," Daniel said. "And they don't have a hospital in the mine or even a doctor. If you perish, they just toss you away into the bottom of the pit."

"What did you do after you were shot?"

"I tried to clean the wound myself, but I couldn't remove the bullet. Eventually, it got infected. I guess all that happened about two weeks ago."

My eyes welled and that's not what he wanted. Instead, he went for the joke.

"At least I didn't have to work in the mine. I couldn't let you see me at age fourteen. What a dork," Daniel teased me.

A bit later, we linked our feet as we soaked in that blissfully hot water of a warm spring we found in the woods. He had stripped naked and jumped in. I left on my underwear because of the branding.

"I'm sure you weren't a dork," I said in a sullen tone because I was still jealous. It lessened when he pulled me in for a kiss. A few days' stubble made him look dangerous and ready.

"Maybe you looked like your standard nerd," I gasped as he devoured me.

When he came up for air, he asked the most loaded, innocent question of all. "And how about you, baby? Did anything weird happen to you when we were separated?"

"Everything is weird here," I replied.

At least it was the truth.

5.

That night we wandered the wrong way in the cave until we reached Griz's storage closet of things borrowed. Daniel was a man on a mission, grabbing one of the thick comforters and walking with a crooked finger until I followed him outside. It was a bit of a hike, but he settled upon a wide cliff ledge hovering high above crashing river water.

It was only us, the water, and a beautiful red-black sky that was on fire.

Daniel moved around the ledge swiftly, creating what looked like a nest out of those blankets and my body sunk into the thick cotton and feathers. Redwoods framed us, tall protectors of the ages. For the first time in a long time, I could breathe.

"I love it!" I said. Yet I still felt guilty-sad about not telling him the truth and the whole truth, but Daniel was too explosive. If he found out, there was no telling what he might do.

It was far safer to feign memory loss or live in a delusional state where only good could happen.

"Boots off, young lady," he said, grinning. He helped me pull them off one at a time. The fact that my pants came with them was just a curious byproduct of fashion. There was another cover to put over us, and Daniel slowly pulled it up my legs. "You are so very considerate," I said, holding back a smile.

"Your hair smells good," he said, coming closer. "What do you call that?"

"River water," I said.

"Ah . . . you smell good. What do they call that?" he asked, helping me like the Boy Scout that he was to take off my sweater.

"I call it anticipation," I said with a shy smile.

With one hand, he unburdened himself of both his pants and his shirt in two swooping moves. Carefully, he placed the clothing away from the ledge, back on solid ground. "Just in case any forest creatures need to borrow some jeans," he insisted.

"A special offshoot of PETA," I murmured nervously. We had been together a lot of times, but this felt new. "Clothing the creatures."

"I try," Daniel said, shooting two fingers off his forehead like a Boy Scout salute.

He was nervous, too.

Daniel lowered me down into the fluff to kiss me gently and it wasn't long before he was devouring my mouth with kisses so hot that I actually whimpered. I was the one who took his head in my hands to reclaim his lips when he broke to breathe. He was always liquid and melted forward to consume me, tongues mingling, little nibbles making me dizzy.

This was the great mystery of life. I hoped to never solve it.

"Callaghan," he said, playing with strands of my hair.

"That's me. Erratic. Damaged. Insecure."

"Just three reasons I love you," he said with that sure strength that was so comforting.

"But there is one thing driving me a bit mad," he said. "Do I have to kill Cass? It might be awkward now that he saved my ass, which brings me to the question I won't ask you."

"Cass is a friend," I said. "Nothing more."

"He certainly doesn't think so, baby."

"That can be filed under his problem," I insisted, because it was true.

It wasn't perfect timing, but I spent the next half hour explaining the story of his daughter as both of us reclined on our backs, holding hands, legs tangled. I felt his lips grace my bare stomach while he considered what I had just told him.

"What he wants most of all is to get his daughter back," I said.

"If we help him," Daniel said, "we pay him back. For what he just did."

"All in," I said.

"Mostly in," Daniel replied. "If he gets his kid back, he will be too busy to bother you. A win-win."

The whole time, as the words tumbled, I could hear him breathing. It was faint in my ear, like a wisp of night mist floating over a sleeping city. Butterfly soft, he pressed his lips to mine when I was done. When he began to speak, he allowed his lips to remain in place, each syllable becoming a soft and almost unbearable touch on mine.

The world began to slip away.

"What do you want, baby?" Daniel asked in a low voice. His words were as exciting as his touch.

"I want to spend my days with you waking up with the warm sun on our faces and laying in spiked summer grass. I want to feel the wind on our faces and then slowly kiss you as the sun dips behind the clouds," I said. "By the end of the day, I want to smell you. And have you smell me. And me of you. Otherwise, I want to run around in pajamas and bare feet with you with water pistols soaking each other and laughing so loudly that it hurts."

I took a deep breath. Now, it was my turn.

"Daniel Reid, what do you *know*?"

He propped himself up on one elbow.

"I know that I'm going to hold onto you harder and love you deeper now than before because I almost lost you."

The whimper that came from a secret spot in the back of my throat refused to obey a silencing order. His strength was one thing, but his tenderness reduced me to a quiver.

He became a blind man reading me with his hands as the gentle night breeze fanned our faces and raw spots.

"And I always knew," Daniel whispered, touching the soft part of his bottom lip to the trembling part of mine, "that once I tasted you, I was done.

"I knew I'd fight for you," he continued as his hands moved to my center. "Someone once told me, 'If you don't fight for what you love then don't cry for what you lost.'"

Naked on the cliff, wind at our backs, he kissed me deeply while guiding me backward until my head was cupped in his hand.

"Wait a second," I whispered as the world sparkled. "Who said you were going past first base tonight?"

"Walker, I'm going home," he whispered.

6.

I knew I would breathe this night deeply into my soul. It wouldn't just linger, but imprint.

Sometime in the middle of the darkness, he began to trace his finger over my trembling neck. "According to some old myths, birthmarks show where you got killed in your past life," he said. "You have this little dot under your left ear. What happened?"

"Stabbed by pagan warriors while defending the kingdom because the king was a wuss," I said, playing along. Daniel was a wealth of information, which he used as a weapon. Many dismissed him as some surly tough guy. They would be wrong.

"Um," he said as I returned the favor. He had a small birthmark on the side of his neck and I moved upward to nibble on it. "Explain this one," I teased.

"Well ma'am, there was this hangin' in the Wild Wild West. My gang had just robbed that bank, saved a few fair maidens, and then we were ready to ride but my horse was slow and the rest is history."

He ran four fingers down my side. "You're so beautiful," he murmured, unexpectedly settling on my hip.

"What's this?" he said. His fingers traced the fresh scar.

"Nothing."

He had been there before – when it wasn't marked.

The one thing he forgot was a flashlight or I'm sure he would have done a quick inspection.

"It wasn't there before."

"No."

He would never let this go.

"Pristine found me and took me to this house," I said carefully. "I had to stage a breakout and they didn't like it. I guess around here you are nothing more than property. Like cattle. The boss man was upset and he took out this poker . . ." My voice caught because if I somehow thought I was going to be able to talk about this without crying, well, it wasn't happening.

"They branded you," he said slowly. "Roll over."

"No—and it's too dark," I insisted, hoping he didn't see my bottom lip tremble. I was that close to a cloudburst of tears. "I'll show you tomorrow. But while we're on this topic, that same boss man decided I should do that tethering thing with him. There was some stupid ceremony, but I escaped on our so-called wedding night."

Daniel was on his feet.

I didn't even want to *try* to talk about it. My time with Edward was unlike anything else horrifying in my life. There was even a reminder forever burned into my skin.

"WTF, Walker. Were you going to tell me about this?"

"Yes," I stated calmly. "Somewhere between the helicopter ride and your raging fever and your cabin surgery, I forgot to tell you. It was nothing—"

"It's not nothing. Who did this to you?"

"I escaped on the wedding night before anything happened. Ran into the woods. Met Griz who took care of me. He's a total hero here," I rambled. "And then we found you. End of story."

"It feels like initials," he said.

It didn't take much for him to sit down again and try to feel it, but it was far too dark and I squirmed just enough to almost fall off the cliff ledge. He reached out to grab me hard and I used that moment to push him down gently and roll over him until I was on top.

"Callaghan."

And then in his serious voice.

"You need to tell me."

"And I will," I promised, snuggling closer to him, "But, not now. Not here. Not tonight. It's not what I want—and I'm sick of not getting what I want."

"What do you want tonight?"

"I want to fly. I want to get high on you. I want to feel like I might pass out each time you touch me. And I don't want to think of one damn thing but how good I feel, how alive, how eternal. And the only word I want to say—that will be said—is your name. Your name is a complete sentence, Daniel. It's a paragraph. It's a story. Our story."

He ran his fingers down my spine and pressed his dreams up against my own.

Lying here with him, it was everything. Because *that* is love.

Everything is everything.

7.

Saturday morning. The sky was an electric blue and down below silver-white waters shimmered with tiny sparkles. It paled next to those intense gray eyes that had me on lock.

If you want fullness in your life, you have to stop for it.

As for Daniel, you could never contain him. He stopped for life.

After a morning reuniting, he rolled me under him and said breathless words that would linger, "Baby, let's keep setting the edge."

We hovered precariously close to it, literally, which was fitting. Where else would we be?

In the bright morning sunshine, he flipped me over, but not for fun. I couldn't stop him forever and felt the tears well up. He saw the letters distinctly: EXR. Then he moved his hand over them as if to erase the pain.

"Walker," he agonized. I expected him to scream and swear, but his lamenting was my undoing. The tears began to roll.

And with no other choice, I told him while he held me tightly. "And so," I concluded with shaking hands, "I tossed the star and it landed in an unfortunate place. There was a lot of blood. A lot . . ." I left out certain parts like his father making me strip, but I had to explain the branding. "A lot of blood," I repeated as if it might even the score.

But there was no even score until Edward extinguished us or we extinguished him. There would never be.

Daniel being Daniel finally stood up. His eyes were enraged, but he kept the rest of himself under perfect control. I expected him to punch a fist into a tree or scream every obscenity ever created. Just when I thought I knew him, I didn't. His current madness made me stealth as he internalized his outrage. It was beyond venomous, as violent as death and as serious as the grave.

"Before this is over," he said in a lethal voice, "I will kill my father."

"I'll do it," I promised. "I'll finish it."

For a moment, he didn't say a thing.

"Callaghan, you want to play it that way? Then I'll watch," he flashed fierce, almost savage, as if the words themselves were leaving his throat raw.

"Edward Xavier Reid won't regret the moment I was born," Daniel swore. "He'll regret the moment I was conceived."

"He will regret the day you met me."

We didn't know it at the time, but under those redwood trees in a fierce summer sun, we were actually taking a killing oath.

Any further talk of extinguishing Edward Reid was cancelled when we had a visitor in the form of a red-faced Auggie. He put his hands over his eyes.

"Hi . . . uh . . . food . . . Griz scrambled eggs . . . apparently he has chicken friends . . . and protein does a body, even a dead one, good . . . sorry for the interruption. Have a nice day . . . peace out," he said, blushing a bright crimson red.

"Clothes," I said.

Mortified.

8.

We were leaving later that day although mostly it remained unspoken. Griz had outdone himself and was one omelet chef short of winning wildlife caterer of the year. It was a case of "eat up now because there might not be a later." The only variable was the return of one of our missing and I was happy to see that Cass was back.

"Sugar," he said, hugging me hard despite Daniel's stare. "You should have some protein. You might need your strength."

I shrugged, which was enough for Cass to quote a higher authority.

"Extinction is the rule. Survival is the exception. Carl Sagan. Now, eat some scrambled eggs, pretty please with sugar on top of it, sugar," he said.

"Pass the ketchup," I said, filling my plate.

He nodded to Daniel who grumbled another thank you that bounced off Cass like he was made of some sort of protective coating. Maybe he was.

I heard Daniel and Cass going at it in the corner while I fetched some OJ.

"I heard about how you helped my girl," Daniel said.

Cass smiled. "Let's just say we had a moment."

"Orange juice," I said, breaking it up.

The others had done their job while Daniel and I were camping out. Flick packed the "borrowed" black Cadillac with rows and rows of bottles containing fresh water that Griz had collected. Our packs were restored to their original statues minus a few stars that I used and couldn't get back. We strapped on our watches that Dr. King had given us.

Bitty had created a first aid kit for us filled with sterile gauze dressing, triangular and rolled bandages, safety pins, tweezers, sterile gloves, and the rest of the antibiotics.

"You could get us to the spot at supersonic speed," I teased her.

Her sad smile made my heart sink.

"Edward drained me for so long that I'm lame. I don't work so good anymore," she lamented.

"You just need to build yourself up again," I said, hugging her.

What we couldn't pack is what we needed the most. Hardness is what was required to survive this place: determined, sacrificial, never-shuddering, steely strength.

"If we get caught again, I wish we had something to put up as ransom money, but you don't need money here," I said.

"What do we have to trade? Eddie's virginity?" Flick suggested.

"Whatever," Eddie said as flashed a middle finger and tripped over a rock under his feet.

Bitty looked . . . concerned.

"Is she . . ."

"Going? Yes," I said. "I wish we could take Griz, but he's better off on his own turf."

Deuce decided she would stay with Griz who had all but adopted her. She materialized in the flesh to eat both of her breakfasts and remind us that she was old enough to decide *exactly what she was going to do with her afterlife.* She punctuated that with four eye rolls while sitting atop Griz's massive shoulder.

"Beefs," Griz said to her.

"BFFs," she corrected, but he didn't like it. "Beefs," he cooed.

They promised to mostly stay in the cave except at night when she would fade to invisible to help Griz with supplies.

"We will come back for you, if that's what you choose," I promised both of them. Each has already said that life in the Midst sounded more promising than staying here. I could see Griz living at the Academy or in the nearby woods. Dr. King would figure it out.

"So, it's decided," Cass said. "Daniel can drive. Walker shotgun. Next row in the car is me, Flick, and Auggie. Back row is Bitty and Eddie, if that works."

Somehow, it always did.

9.

Griz was devastated by good-byes. He screwed up his face and cried for a good ten minutes. I touched his beating heart with my hand and he put his palm on top of my head.

What an astonishing thing another heart can be. It's a beating machine made from muscle and tissue, but it's also a doorway.

"Ta-ka," Griz said to me. He reached into his pocket and pulled out a gold necklace with a dangling moon on it. I wasn't sure if he had it for a long time or had just found it, but I was touched.

"All ways, Wa and Gr . . . i . . . zzz," he grunted, sniffing the air. I knew he could smell seven times better than a bloodhound.

"Do not try to find us. We will find you," I told him.

"Griz no list," he said, shaking his head.

"Please listen."

He was my age, but emotionally much younger. If I had to pinpoint why it was because he had that kind of young about him where things were wide open.

The fact that he wore his best handmade pants and newest checked shirt broke my heart. He dressed up for me, which made my eyes well.

Griz hung his head and I reached up to kiss his soft cheek.

Hard endings lead to new beginnings.

"I will think of you with love in my eyes every single day. Every. Single. One," I promised him. Tears fell on my cheeks. Griz tried to collect them and put his wet finger into his shirt pocket. "You and Deuce take care of each other. I love you."

"Luv yu, my Wa."

10.

They waited in the woods for me to say that good-bye. But the minute they saw me, they both grinned.

Standing in the woods by an old oak, Cass's baby blues twinkled; Daniel did the thing where the corners of his silver eyes crinkled. They stood near the main road by the trees, biceps straining against their shirts and muscular backs. Both had strong jaws, the stamp of determination.

I squinted into the sunlight and mouthed the words, "Want to stay?"

381

But I knew that was impossible because Edward's goons could find us. Another thought popped into my mind concerning the rest of this journey. If it was this hard already, how could we possibly think we had a chance. I know it would be nice to echo some Hallmark statement now. A positive mantra. Pretty words you'd put on a Post-It.

Five words: we are all so screwed.

I looked at Daniel to center myself. Cass stared back like I had just ripped his heart out.

So absurdly screwed.

Winsome Cass had hidden the car he "borrowed" from Edward's fleet by the cliffs where the trees were thick and the road nearby. Before we left, he walked us to the exact spot where Daniel and I had spent the previous night. It turns out, he wanted to talk about history, but not the recent kind. "Lore in The Other has it that a group of farm horses leaped over the tallest section of this mountain range, which is exactly where we are standing. It reminds me of us."

An enthralled Bitty nodded. "I know everything about the history of The Other," she said. "And they call this place *Aillna Searrachs.* Translation: Cliff of Colts."

No one planned it and I would never remember if it was a sleepy Auggie or fetching Eddie in a new red sweater who put an arm in the middle joined by Bitty, Cass, Daniel, and finally I put my trembling limb on the very top of the pile.

"And so, we ride," I said. "Colts, all. Colts, forever."

TWENTY-FIVE

1.

The drive north would leave us on full-on coast mode. All we had to do was go straight on Route 167, which was a mostly empty four-lane highway through thick alpine trees providing enough shade to convince you that it was one long perpetual twilight. It was eerie in a way; relaxing in others. Most of the time my eyes were peeled to the sides.

The sides are where small settlements would spring up, for which the journalist in me salivated. People gathered; like attracted like. Why not live together? This was how The Other formed their micro societies. Some of these groups had evolved; some not. Some were "good," some violent psycho killers. Roll the dice and pull the car over at your own risk.

We were told early on that this was a place for those who had powerful energies or mind-blowing forms of intelligence. And there were others in The Other who seemingly sought a different type of life.

There would be no sightseeing. No dealing with the people of The Other, a place of misfits and rebels. We would just drive north as Dr. King had told us until we reached a point where we couldn't go much farther. His theory was the X-catcher was hiding way up there and would reveal himself almost immediately. We had a real need for the code; the X-catcher was certainly tired of the burden of keeping it secret. Dr. King said when fate aligned like this the answers were predestined.

I could try to enjoy a nice car ride where. . . .

Was it my mind playing tricks or was the guy in the Chevy next to me Andy Warhol? The flash of white hair and wide eyes put my money on a yes.

I also remembered Dr. King saying that strange things would happen to our own bodies the longer we were here—and it was necessary to contemplate. "Your senses will be turned up to maximum," he said. "Accept it. This isn't the time to fall into the trap of second guessing what is obvious. Don't ask yourself if *this* is really happening to your body and senses because the answer is always the same: *It is.*"

Even now, for instance, my eyesight seemed extra intense as if I was looking into binoculars. Or maybe, I was just open to the possibilities.

"I feel longer, stronger, leaner, and meaner," Daniel said earlier this morning. It was true that he was full of claw and fight again.

The others brought that fight into the stylish Escalade with the fine sound system cranking the alternative channel.

"Can you move your seat up just a little," Eddie demanded from the way back.

"No," said Cass and Flick in unison.

And then there was Daniel who was driving ever-so-slowly because he didn't want to attract attention. We were moving about fifty miles an hour when I began to see that our stealth act was truly an impossibility.

2.

In a blink, the four-lane highway we were traveling down had morphed into a two-lane road. It was odd how this happened because the trees stayed exactly the same, but the road instantly narrowed as the other lanes disappeared. It wasn't gradual, but happened in a blink.

What I couldn't possibly reconcile, however, was the car desperately trying to pass us. It was a cherry-red DeSoto sedan with perfectly round headlights that looked like eyeballs. Behind us was a Studebaker sedan coupe in baby blue.

If this was rush hour in the afterlife so be it, but why were people driving cars that hadn't been made for over fifty years or since the 1940s?

In that moment, I glanced down at my electronic watch. Oddly, the time, date, and all other applications had been erased from the face while the glass face of the watch gleamed like it been dunked in glitter. When the fog from the middle cleared, the watch face mirrored the trees flying by in the distance. The only thing: I wasn't filming the trees and they were still being shown live and in real time on my watch.

"You better look at this . . . like right now, kids," Eddie said from the back. He passed us his old cell phone from the Midst. Of course, it didn't work as a phone and there was no Internet service. But the camera still functioned.

In fact, he had just taken a selfie with Bitty. "Look at the picture," he demanded.

Around both of their bodies, heads, and faces was a grayish-clear outline of their entire beings as if something had escaped from within, but it wasn't gone. It was shadowing them.

"Maybe we should pull over," Cass said. "Or never pull over. WTF."

He wasn't the only one with that bright idea. The DeSoto jerked to the right, too, as the left back tire sprung a leak and went pancake flat.

I knew it my soul not to believe anything at face value here. There were no coincidences here; no accidents.

3.

Daniel did the potentially tragic right thing, slowing our car and pulling over. "Everybody stay inside and lock the doors," he insisted. Three seconds later, we were all standing in gravel and staring hard at what the day put in our path.

The driver was an older teenage girl in a bright swing skirt and white blouse that appeared to be wet in front for some reason. She wore seamed nylon stockings that were not yanked up evenly, no makeup, and had shoulder-length hair dyed blonde and worn with a flip on the bottom. The front was smoothed to the sides in soft waves that didn't take away from the severely shaped brows that practically jumped off her creamy white face. Her perfectly innocent mouth was punctuated by a slash of the most perfect ruby lipstick. Firetruck red.

It only took a moment to see that the liquid on her shirt was tears, and it must have required a lot of waterworks to get it that damp. I didn't mean to pry, but as a concerned human type, I peered into her car to make sure there, um, wasn't a dead body back there. It was empty if you didn't count the newspaper in the empty passenger's seat.

We had—it couldn't be true—but the proof was right there.

One look. Two. Five.

We had driven north all right, but somehow, we had motored our way straight into December 8, 1941.

I wasn't exactly a history buff, but I was desperate to get a journalism scholarship to Northwestern University, which meant I paid attention. December 8, 1941, made it exactly one day after the attack on Pearl Harbor that jettisoned the United States into World War II.

I didn't want to be right. But there it was on the banner headline: President Roosevelt Declares War. US Enters World War II.

The girl looked vulnerable, hysterical, and totally freaked out when Cass approached her. The fact that he was wearing non-period clothing of black jeans, a white cable-knit sweater, and had a mass of blond hair tied back must have made him look like what her generation dubbed "a hipster" or someone quite fashion forward. The actual word "hippies" wouldn't be invented until the 1960s.

"Miss, we could fix your tire. You could wait in our car. It has air—" I knew he was about to say air-conditioning, but he had seen the newspaper, too. Cars didn't have air-conditioning in those days.

The girl looked at Cass like he was some West Coast freak, thus dangerous. Maybe this needed a female touch.

"Of course, cars have air," I covered, but she just shook her head. How could we explain our car anyway . . . the Cadillac Escalade looked like a futuristic army tank to those who dwelled in a time when gas cost twelve cents a gallon, a new house ran you about four thousand dollars, and presidents weren't on TV, which was why a man in a wheelchair, FDR, was our fearless leader.

"We're in the USO," I informed her, knowing that if she thought we were a group of performers it might make our differences a bit more palpable.

In fact, she didn't seem a bit perturbed by the vehicle. That was odd given that we were from some eighty years in the future.

"I would have driven a Hummer to get through these parts," she stated. "It uses less gas and the Governator, Arnold, drives them."

We had run into many things in past loops, but never another time traveler. No one knew what a Hummer was in 1941 and Arnold Schwarzenegger wasn't exactly on the public radar during WWII. He wasn't born until July 30, 1947.

I could see that Cass had his hand in his pocket, near his knife.

Loping a hand into my jacket pocket, I felt the piercing point of one of my throwing stars.

4.

There was another possibility.

There would be helpers, Dr. King always told us. Turns out, she was a Lurker, a soul that floats between different decades, never content to truly stop to smell the proverbial roses in one place. They were spirits with wanderlust. Lurkers loved to roam for the sake of seeing and re-experiencing something they hold dear. They want to visit people or events that ripped their hearts out while alive.

We had met them during out former mission into the past. After we saved children from the Our Lady of the Angels Roman Catholic grade school inferno in 1958, a Lurker on the streets of New York handed me a warm coat and pockets filled with antibiotic ointments to soothe my burn wounds.

Lurkers were road warriors of the afterlife and most had a soft spot for the young dead who lost their way. Dr. King promised that Lurkers would appear when needed or sent by higher powers. "Consider them friends. Accept their gifts," he said. "Above all, believe what they say."

I had a few questions.

"Are we in a past loop?"

"You're in Kansas City, Missouri, 1941. Given no choice, you drove into the past and into a time loop. They're everywhere in The Other."

"Is it a test?" I asked.

"Bingo on all fronts, sister," she said.

Dr. King schooled us in the fact that the past always and forever continues on and on. It kept spinning and existing. You could—if you knew how or made a mistake—jump into a fold in time and return to the past without even knowing at first that you did it. Many people who disappeared in current times, never to be seen again, fell into a past loop and just decided to stay. Some fought their way out; some settled down, which was tricky.

One had to be very careful in the past not to change even the smallest event or detail, which is almost impossible. A new soul arriving was change enough.

I knew this much: The past doesn't suffer fools. Change it and it changes you.

5.

"You're a Lurker," I said, and she smiled.

"I'm Alice."

But I didn't have the time to unwind her own personal history because a red flatbed Chevy had pulled up behind us. Lurkers rarely came in pairs, which meant that I was fingering the throwing stars in my pocket again.

What emerged from that truck seemed harmless enough, but you never knew in the past who was going to take you in . . . or take you out.

Out of the truck jumped the most handsome young man sporting a fresh buzz cut on his pale blond locks. He was broad shouldered with a wide smile and he swooped the Lurker girl up in a big hug. "Alice, I thought it was you . . . I was going the other way, but I saw my girl in distress. How am I going to leave if you keep getting in these pickles?"

I could see it on her face. *Don't leave. Don't leave me.*

Then, it dawned on me. She wasn't going to *tell* us about her past. She was going to *show* us.

"Johnny Amberson," he introduced himself to us like we were long lost friends who just couldn't remember each other's names. We returned the favor.

"Walker, odd name," he said, looking past the obvious differences in our clothing and vehicles. He wore a white tee covered by a collared navy-blue shirt, high-waisted blue jeans with turned-up cuffs, white socks, and brown penny loafers.

"My mother's maiden name," I said.

"What a gas," Johnny said.

By now his eyes were on Alice, who looked like a picture with her hair blowing in a cool breeze.

"Now, I'm going to fix that tire and you're going to follow me to the train station for a proper good-bye," he said.

"I'm shipping out today. Basic training in Texas and then gonna go kill Hitler," he told us. "It's going to be killer diller. And afterward, I'm coming home to marry this girl—unless anybody here knows otherwise," said Johnny with a twinkle in his eyes.

But I could tell from the tears on her shirt that there was no afterward. He never came home. Almost as if she could read my mind, she told him, "I will kiss you in a way to last forever at that train station." *Because there was no forever.*

My heart began to race; my stomach churned.

If there was ever a time to tell a young man to not get on that train . . . I could tell him not to go to war, but it would fall on deaf ears. Even worse were the repercussions of changing the past. Johnny Amberson's fate was to be killed in the war. It couldn't work any other way or I'd be paying the historical tab.

I looked down. And I remained silent for the next unbearable minutes when Daniel and Cass changed her tire.

"Very good restraint, which means we move onto the next step," Alice whispered to me. "In case you're wondering about the next part of your mission, here it is: You will travel through several historical periods of time before you get to where you need to go. You will be tested – morally and physically. You must rise to these challenges as a group. Just like today. Don't change history or it will change you," she warned.

It meant we couldn't tell Johnny to run, hide, and never leave this town. We couldn't warn anyone in any of the time periods of impending doom or historical events. We were observers in the past—and the past didn't take kindly to future visitors. It temped, teased, and threatened until it expelled you like a sliver of wood stuck in a throbbing finger.

"This next part will require your balls, your guts, and your expertise," Alice said.

"And Johnny?" I whispered because stories needed endings.

"They blew out the back of my skull after I crash-landed. The Germans didn't take many prisoners. I was only eighteen," Johnny said, holding his girl's hand now. Turns out, I didn't need to warn him. He was part of this test. "No one saw me again after that day, but it's all right. Them's the breaks when you dance with fate—and we all do."

"I come here again and again to see my girl," he said. "I come here almost every single day to feel the hope of a soldier shipping out and a girl who bets that love can bring him back."

He was a Lurker, too.

"I didn't check out until age eighty-two. Thunderclap heart attack," Alice said. "Married and had four kids. But my heart never left that train station down the road. My whole married life, I lived less than a mile from here. Snuck out every morning to walk to the train station in the name of exercise. But, it wasn't what it seemed.

"I never loved any boy like I loved my Johnny. I named my first son after my true love."

"You should be going," he said to us. "Just get back on the road and make a right at the stop sign. Follow it until you get to Joe's. Write that down. When you get there, get out of the car and go in. Follow the prompts—and resist the urge to satisfy your moral compass by changing things."

"I'm so sorry, Johnny," I said.

"Don't be," Alice said. "Some people have a lifetime; we have the rest. But you already knew that, dear."

Somewhere in the distance, I heard a train's whistle blow. Our car raced the train until it disappeared into the sky. It took only seconds, but once we were on Main Street again, I glanced at Daniel and then at Cass in the rearview mirror.

I wasn't sure if we were in 1941 anymore, but we certainly weren't in Kansas.

Welcome to California read the sign.

As for the year, it was anyone's guess.

6.

Joe's Hardware was a single store on Main Street, among many other little shops that reminded me of the quaint, central drag in the Midst.

We were nearing a two-story building, painted a mossy green color, and featuring a *very* old-fashioned Coke machine out front. "Pay dirt," said Cass, who in lieu of the actual nickel it cost, gave the machine a slight kick. The drink popped out in a thick glass bottle and Cass gave me the first swig despite Daniel's glare.

It wasn't like the thin, bubbly, sugary cola we were used to now, but deeper and richer, boarding on a delicious, cold milkshake. I licked my lips when reluctantly handing it back. Nothing tasted like this in current times, which made me wonder about progress.

Did we change things just for the sake of change?

Parked outside of Joe's was the coolest car I had ever in my entire existence. It was a white convertible, top down, with the number twenty-three painted on the driver's side door.

"Porsche," Daniel said. "A Super Speedster 23F. You don't see these anymore in our age of Hondas and Hyundais."

Something about the car looked familiar, but I couldn't exactly place it.

7.

Joe's wasn't the public library, but there were answers inside of that one-room store that smelled like buttery toast and fresh bacon. If there was a Joe, he was one of those guys who had a big chalkboard on the wall behind his large, gold-plated register. One glance and he was having a sale on nails and paint on this day . . . *September 30, 1955.*

We had driven into another time loop. Into the past.

A quick glance down at the local paper and we were in a town called Salinas, California, near a town called Monterey. The news of this day wasn't good: United States to Send Advisory Group to South Vietnam to Monitor Conflict. President Eisenhower Promises: No War.

Being from the future, I knew that the actual Vietnam War existed another twenty years until 1975. Almost 60,000 Americans died in the war along with 250,000 South Vietnamese.

I caught some familiar lyrics being played on a big jukebox covered in Christmas tinsel. Bill Haley & His Comets were crooning "Rock Around the Clock" followed by the Chordettes singing "Mr. Sandman."

Mr. Sandman, bring me a dream. Make him the cutest boy that I've ever seen . . ."

"Hey, Daddy-o," said the teenage worker behind the counter in back, but he wasn't talking to us. He was talking to *him.*

There was a young man in a starch-white V-neck T-shirt and mirrored sunglasses sitting there. His faded blue jeans were tight and a cigarette dangled from his mouth, small curls of smoke blurring ocean-blue eyes. He had tawny blond-brown hair slicked all the way off an extremely familiar sculpted face. Those intense eyes were framed by thick brows and lower were a killer pair of pillowy lips.

His facial expression was stuck at one setting: brooding.

"Burger, fries, and a vanilla shake and we'll be made in the shade," he said in a low voice.

I sat down next to him on one of those swivel, red vinyl stools. Bitty sat on his other side and the look on her mug could only be described as she was making love to him with her eyes.

When he turned a few degrees, I got a good look at his face and tried to contain every cell that was dying to do some kind of happy dance.

No, it couldn't be . . . but it was!

8.

"And you, missy? Yes, you, the one with the classy chassis," said the soda jerk, a pimple-faced kid with a nameplate that read Alvin. He was making it clear that if I was going to sit there, I was required to actual order something while he made comments about my booty.

"Do you want a milkshake? Word from the bird, I make the best strawberry shake you will find in *Cal-i-forn-ni-yay.*"

"Knock yourself out," I said. "Can you use fro-yo?"

"Fro-what?"

"Never mind."

I continued to stare at that angular face next to me. I wracked my brain for every word of '50s slang that might have embedded into my fan-frenzied brain.

"Sounds good, Daddy-o! And turn up the tunes," I said, sounding like a complete and utter moron. The fact that I was in black leggings and a long sweater just made me stand out even more.

"What did you say about the sound?" asked the soda jerk. "You want me to turn it up? Joe gets mad if I play the music too loud . . ."

"There is no such thing as too loud," said the man sitting next to me. *He spoke!* He was probably used to girls in A-line skirts and poodle sweaters. I caught him staring at my pants and felt my face flame bright red.

There was a scream stuck forever in my throat now.

It's not every day that you get to sit next to an actor who defined teenage angst. It was a good thing that my Aunt Ginny lived to watch the TCM cable channel where they frequently broadcasted the three movies he did in a short life —*East of Eden, Rebel Without a Cause,* and *Giant.*

He wouldn't live to see any of them on the big screen.

James Dean would die later today.

He was twenty-four.

9.

I couldn't resist making small talk with him, but he didn't mind since the soda jerk was slow with the food.

"Mr. Dean," I began.

"Jimmy," he said.

"Jimmy," I replied.

"Walker." I filled in the blank. He smiled. "A family name . . . my mom's side . . . never mind," I blurted again. *It was official. I sounded like a total idiot.*

"Jimmy," I began again. "Is that your car outside?" *I knew the answer.*

"Yes."

"Sweet wheels," I said.

"Thank you."

"Where you going in that super fine ride?" Bitty blurted.

"Darlin'," he said, swiveling to face her. "I'm driving down to the Salinas Road Races. Studio banned me from doing it. I'm filming this thing called *Giant,* but I don't care. My stunt guy Bill and I drove down from Los Angeles to break that car in. Racing is the only time I feel whole," he said.

"How fast does that car go?" I asked.

"Little Bastard—that's what I call it—goes about a hundred and fifty," he said with a laugh. "Already got me a speeding ticket, but I wasn't going over a hundred. Just eighty-five. Some say the car is cursed although I don't believe the nonsense."

He laughed as my eyes widened—and then he leaned closer.

"I like to say, 'Dream as if you'll live forever. Live as if you'll die today.'"

He would punch out of this thing called life in about two hours. One hundred and twenty minutes of life left . . . then fade to black.

That devastatingly handsome young movie star would be on US Route 466, near San Francisco, around six tonight when a big Ford car, a steel tank, turned left into his path. Dean was speeding, but couldn't stop in time. Maybe it was the twilight and the glare from the setting sun, but he slammed into the passenger's side of the Ford. The end result was Dean's car bouncing along the pavement until it rolled off the highway.

Jimmy didn't stand a chance. He would be trapped inside of the car with a broken neck and die on impact. Some would later say that his head was cut off his body, but that was too much. No one wanted to think it ended that way.

We prefer our icons whole.

The driver of the Ford would walk away with only minor injuries. Wasn't that always the bitch?

As for that cursed car . . . After the accident, Little Bastard's remains rolled off the back of a truck that would haul it. It crushed the legs of a mechanic standing nearby. Later, parts of the car, sold to buyers all over the country, would contribute to strange incidents. All of those cars taking in a piece of LB were involved in deadly crashes. The chassis was saved for a highway-safety exhibit, but the truck carrying it skidded off the road, killing the driver.

The chassis disappeared that day never to be seen again.

10.

"Well, I gotta go. The food is taking forever," Jimmy said. "Give it to one of your friends." He slapped a five dollar bill down on the shiny white counter.

This was the moment. All I had to do was tell him that he was going to die. That he should drive . . . the other way. Or just sit here. Eat a burger. Just take a few minutes. The timing would be off. Fate might get confused.

Maybe if I spoke to him for another ten minutes then the car that would hit him would hit someone else. Life was in the minutes.

But, damn it, I could not. This was a test. It wasn't real.

It. Was. A. Test.

"Jimmy," I said as he began to button his jacket, "what's the best part of being a movie star?"

I don't know why I asked it except for the fact that I really wanted to know.

"Work's good, darlin," he said. "But the best part is I bought my Uncle Marcus and my Aunt Ortense some new lawn furniture for their farm in Fairmont, Indiana. They took me in as a kid when my mom died. Never enough dough to buy lawn furniture. I got them the good stuff. All metal. Red. They really liked it."

"Godspeed, Jimmy," I said.

"Godspeed, Walker Callaghan," he replied.

He stopped. Turned. "One last thing, well . . . actually two. Start with this: if a man or woman can bridge the gap between life and death, if he or she can live on after death, then maybe that was a great man or woman. Think about it.

"Second thing: you'll want to take the gang out the back door, walk down the street, and go into the movie house for your next experience," Jimmy said.

"Jimmy, you're a Lurker?" I said in an astonished voice.

"Gotta win that race. I go there and try to win it almost every single day," he said, walking away with a hand held high and his head firmly on his shoulders.

TWENTY-SIX

1.

"We're going to the movies?" Eddie challenged me. "I mean, it's okay with me because of the popcorn, but don't we have more important things to do?"

"Eddie, please," I begged. "We're doing this together. When I know, you'll know."

"Maybe there will be nudity," Eddie mused. You had to hand it to the guy. He was tryng to tap into the positives.

There was no ticket-taker at the movie house door, which was open wide. No one was at the candy and popcorn counter either. "I hear music," Auggie said with glee. The former band geek didn't hear our warning before he burst through the double doors of the theater, where the screen was flickering with light although the rest of the place was dark.

You know what they say about walking toward the light.

We raced after him and a blink later and we weren't in that theater anymore. It was a cool evening wherever we were located now. The place was defined by an expanse of grass smack in what looked like a major city. Again, we were violating the dress code, which was mostly tie-dye with headbands. There was a definite aroma in the air and the people sitting on blankets were young and looked like they were living their bliss.

"If we're literally going to walk into the next time loop may I ask: What year is it?" Flick pondered aloud. His voice was somewhere between thrill and awe.

"I could spend the rest of my existence floating around the past," he said, doing a complete 360 to take it all in. "I'm high on history!"

"Hey man, that's boss," said a passerby who flashed Flick a quick peace sign.

A girl in long braids with beads at the bottom hugged our handsome Freak Island friend and then planted a hard kiss on his lip that became softer and deeper. He didn't seem to mind. When they came up for air, she said, "It's 1967, man. Are you on the make?"

"Excuse me?" Flick said.

"This never happens to me. Hot foreign girls never kiss me," Eddie griped from behind me.

"Eddie, I think we're in California," I said.

"USA, right?" he pondered.

"Excuse me, we've been trippin' a bit. Where are we again?" I asked the same girl who smiled and then kissed me hard on the lips. She didn't answer, but Auggie did. I don't know where he wandered, but he was now wearing a purple, yellow, and white dyed tee and a large sunflower in his hair.

"Walker, can you dig it?" he said in an excited voice. "We're in San Francisco. 1967. Do you know what that means?"

It was Cass who answered, smiling at me. "They called it the Summer of Love."

2.

We weren't just "there." We were standing at the epicenter of the "free love" mentality, the corner of Haight and Ashbury. Some called it "the

Height" or the "Upper Haight." No matter how you said it, this place was known as ground zero of the hippie counterculture.

Flower children or young dreamers with their enviable mile-long tresses danced in the streets, their tie-dyed T-shirts and peace signs waving in the air. They brought guitars, love beads, and a hope for a better future. As a rule, they didn't like the government, hated consumerism, and opposed racism, hatred, and killing. They rejected conformity and the materialism of a house in the suburbs, marriage, and two perfect kids. They certainly didn't want to get their head or legs blown off on foreign shores for a war they didn't understand—and someday nobody would.

"Let my freak flag fly!" cried Eddie, who was suddenly in full beatnik mode. He was suddenly wearing army boots, army surplus pants, and a field jacket. He had a thick strand of purple love beads around his neck. Bitty danced with him on the sidewalk in her long purple peasant dress and brown flat sandals. I had never seen either of them look so free.

"You don't have a miniskirt in your backpack, Callaghan? Some suede boots, baby? Any threads with fringe?" Daniel whispered into my ear. He kissed my neck while placing white flowing ribbons in my hair.

"Outta sight," I said.

3.

For the first time in my existence, I longed to burn my bra. So, I did. I took it off and threw it into a small fire in the park across the street. I don't know why, but just doing that made me feel like twirling madly in circles with my arms over my head. I wasn't high on anything beyond this feeling of pure joy.

"Free love! You bet your bippie!" yelled one of the girls in a crowd that I estimated to be in the several thousand tonight. They believed in communal living, political numbness, and dropping out of the so-called rat race. They sat on sidewalks, dangling their legs from the curbs, and filled any grassy parks.

They didn't just look happy, but serene and unburdened—and it wasn't just the drugs.

"It was a great summer for music," Auggie rambled. "Just listen." I couldn't be sure, but I swore I heard The Who in person, playing from some nearby bandstand. Keith Moon, Pete Townshend, and Roger Daltrey weren't the old men I knew, but were in their twenties, young and rocking on full blast. When I listened, I did hear lyrics insisting that I wouldn't be "fooled again."

"Last night, we jammed to The Mamas & the Papas and the Dead," said a young guy with long brown hair held back in parts with long, leather ties. He wore dirty jeans and a flannel shirt. There were about ten strands of beads around his neck, each with a deeper meaning.

"Don't forget. If you need anything, go to the Free Store. Everything's free, foxy lady," he said to me, swinging me around in a circle. "Can you dig it?"

"Yes," I said, "I think I can." For some reason, it didn't seem odd for people to touch you; we were one out here; brothers and sisters in a movement to change our consciousness.

"Do you think it will always be this way?" he asked in a dreamy voice.

I couldn't stand to tell him that all the way in the future, 2020 specifically, kids like him would still be marching and trying to find some justice in the living realm. A cop would kneel on a man's neck and kill him in the daylight on a public street. Kids from other places would be locked in cages and ripped from their parents' arms.

This was the test. Would I change history by telling him that all of this collectiveness provided no real solutions in the future? If I did, would it get around? Would they still gather? Would they still dream and call themselves free thinkers?

"Yeah, it will always be this way," I lied, because sometimes a lie is all you have in your pocket. "Power to the people."

Just not all the people. I saw the ghost of a boy named Eric in the distance. He was standing next to Breonna.

"Turn on, tune in, drop out," he said. "By the way, my name is Timothy. I'm a Lurker who needs to get back to the party. You need to split. Walk down Ashbury and when you get to the end of the road, go left. It's righteous where you're going, kids. All you need to do is hang out."

"Groovy," I replied.

4.

We walked that way Timothy suggested as day morphed into night. The familiar outdoors melted away. A breath later and we stood in a pitch-black room filled with loud screaming.

The music was thumping hard, the place was filled with people our age. And the floor, well, it was moving quickly underneath my feet. That was because during the past loop adjustment, we hadn't just been transported, but somewhere along the line we had changed our footwear. I was wearing roller skates and a band of serious musicians called Earth, Wind & Fire was shouting that I had entered what they called a place foreign to me: Boogie Wonderland."

I did not boogie.

"Roller disco!" Eddie yelled, wheeling away from me like he was an Olympian of the sport. I wasn't ever quite sure what his upbringing in Alabama was all about, but apparently Eddie had spent his fair share of time *rolling*.

"You gotta be shitting me," Cass said. And when he grabbed me by the waist from behind, I wasn't sure if it was on purpose. A half roll later and he was this-close to not only invading my personal space, but declaring victory.

"Sugar, if you move even an inch, I'm going to end up with a broken ass," said the man who had been to war on several fronts, personal and universal.

"I don't boogie!" he yelled. "And I do not skate."

As the bright disco strobe lights flashed red, green, and blue in our faces and the Bee Gees began to insist *"you should be dancing, yeah,"* I tried to do the math. My mother would never admit it, but she was in love with John Travolta. That song came out in . . . what?

Maybe the late 1970s.

Daniel was sitting on the wood bench, refusing to stand up. Turns out, he rarely rolled. "I've never skated in my life," he insisted. Auggie was another story. He took both Cass and I by the hand and before I could realize what was happening, he had me out on the main floor. Bitty, another rolling wonder, saddled right up to Cass who was hanging on for dear afterlife.

"Bitty, please, don't dump me," Cass begged.

"Has anyone *ever* dumped you, handsome?" she teased.

As I dug my nails into Auggie, he began to go faster.

"Let's see if the reset works!" he yelled over the "slow song," "Afternoon Delight."

As I sat on that highly shined wooden floor, humiliated after falling, I realized that my ass was in one piece.

Reset, on.

A glance up from my spot below revealed something else: the AXL Roller Rink had an advent calendar on the wall. It was four more days until Christmas Eve—*ho, ho, ho.* December 20, 1978. *What was the big freaking deal with that date? My brain spun. Nothing registered as historically significant.*

Confirmation of the time loop came in the form of a fellow skater whose words echoed, "Can you believe what I'm getting for Christmas? It's the latest in technology. A Walkman!"

5.

My toes were fine thanks to the reset, but there was only so much boogie in me. I found it even more interesting to just sit on the little wooden bench, slowly take off my skates, and listen to all the conversations around me. The reporter in me loved a crowd for this reason and tonight's didn't disappoint.

My ears tuned into the plight of two seventeenish guys sitting next to me in worn jeans and the kind of molting shirts that were worn a few days too long and needed a good washing. One was in a brown one covered in tiny flowers and the other wore blue silk. Scratch that. It was polyester and so were their pants.

They smelled like old cigarette smoke and bus stations. The taller one had a baby face with long, reddish-brown hair that feathered back off his face, warm brown eyes, and freckles, while the other one was a bit stout with shoulder-length brown hair, bangs, and lazy, halfway closed eyes. He had rock star lips and wore a big gold cross.

It was so '70s that I began to smile inside . . . until I didn't.

"Where we gonna stay tonight?" asked the one I would call Red. I watched as he nervously pulled a worn leather wallet from his pocket. He opened the flap to reveal five dollars, tops.

"Beats me," said the other who tapped his pockets in the universal signal of *brokedy- broke-broke*. "I'm out of green. We didn't meet any chicks here like you said. But we can always stay with that guy."

"What guy?"

"You know, the one from the Greyhound station. Remember, he offered us construction jobs that pay five dollars an hour. That's twice what I made at McDonald's at home," said Red. "And he promised to throw in lodging for a week until we got our first check."

"I dunno," said the stout one. "All that clown shit in the back seat of the car really creeped me out. I hate clowns."

I'm not sure why—but in that moment, I knew.

And it felt like I couldn't breathe anymore.

6.

"So, he does little kid's birthday parties for fun. Who gives a shit? He said he would come get us—anywhere, and give us a couch and three squares," said Red. "Anyway, he doesn't seem like a perv, I can sense a perv and he isn't. And there is two of us. We could beat the shit out of that old man . . . if we had to get out of there fast."

My mind was like a rocket. The words began to howl. He has guns and knives in that house. He will hold you at gunpoint. Force you. Maim you. Kill you.

You don't go to the devil. You run from him.

"Just one night . . . what could it hurt?" Red said.

As if it were decided.

Everyone who grew up in Illinois, like I did, knew. He was a shadow now that cast over the city, one that would never lift. I studied the horrific living days of the man-monster who liked to dress up like a clown. He also liked to chloroform young men unconscious, rape and kill them, and then stuff their remains into his trunk and dump them in the Des Plaines River.

Others were buried under the concrete floor of his garage and in the house's crawl space where later they would find the spare parts of upward of thirty bodies.

They were young men like these one . . . promised jobs, a bed, food . . . and then brutally killed.

I knew about John G because I met him at our prison school, ITT, in the afterlife. He was serving some kind of penance where he would be forced to control his killing impulses although control in his case had a way of slipping. No one could explain the ones at ITT who disappeared forever.

He didn't have a crawl space anymore to hide the bodies.

He simply had teeth.

7.

"We're gonna freeze our nuts off if we sleep outside," Red said. "I'm going to go call the guy. What was his name? It will sound bad if I don't remember his name. He was so nice to us."

"The guy in the black Olds? I guess he was friendly enough. He said to call him John. John Graves."

Pause.

"No, no, that's not it."

"Gacy. That's it!" said his soon-to-be dead friend who then did the impossible. Whipping around with the bravado of someone with a plan, he sweetly asked me, "Honey, do you have a dime, so I can use the phone? I'll be grateful for life."

He didn't realize his own was slipping away.

8.

I could deny them loose change, which I did. That wasn't changing history because I wasn't there the first time around.

"I'm sorry, I don't have any cash on me," I begged off. And then my bottom lip began to tremble hard. The words were stuck in my throat because I knew that if I changed history then I would fail this test—or worse—history would change me.

But, what if it wasn't a test?

My brain began to roar. I had to tell them. I had to shout it from the rafters or grab the mic the DJ was using to spin those tunes. I had to scream and shout that they were walking into a literal death trap. No one should ever go off with the devil willingly. No one should just sit there and watch as young men with their entire lives spread out in front of them make one wrong call. His last and his last.

The devil wins.

I had to tell them that the police wouldn't find all of them. Maybe an arm. Or a leg. The he had a trapdoor to a crawl space underneath his little suburban ranch house. It was a tomb for his prey.

I had to tell them that they would soon be a part of a club with the other young men who entered Pogo the clown's lair. Their naked bodies and carved limbs would be stuffed down there with rotting leaves and other dead things. Many had men's bikini underwear stuffed inside their mouths while others still had ropes around their necks.

And when he was done, John G would go back upstairs, stare at his clown portrait on the wall, and make himself dinner.

I remember what the Chicago Tribune *said when they caught him: "He always had a lot of kids working around his place, but they never stayed long."*

And they never left.

But that wasn't the worst quote that hit ink during those days before and after Christmas of 1978.

"If the devil's alive, he lives here," said a worker who helped pull the bodies.

What was left of them.

9.

It began with Eddie.

He "found" some money and had bought himself a Chicago dog with all the fixings. "Hey, Walker," he said, plopping down next to me. "Can you hold the change? You know how I lose things."

Temptation.

Fate was such a bitch.

Before I knew it, I had five shiny new dimes in the palm of my hand. This was still the days of pay phones where a local call would only cost twenty cents.

As Eddie wheeled himself away, dog in mouth, Red looked at me with fresh, hopeful eyes.

"Hey, sunshine," he said to me. "It's getting late. We're desperate to make a phone call. With circumstances now changing could you spare a few?"

His eyes focused on the glistening change in my hand and he flashed his I'm-good-with-girls smile.

Was there a girl who gave him the change in the past to make that fatal call? I would never be sure. I had to force them, one digit at a time to close. First, my index finger and then my middle one covered the change followed by the last stick and then my pinky.

"I don't think so," I said.

"Dang, help a dude out," said Red's friend under his breath. *As if that would change my mind.*

And then came the epiphany.

"We don't need her. Just go get change for one of your dollars," Red said.

My mouth opened because I *had* to say it. *It was now or never. For them. And for me.* And that is when I felt a hand on my arm. It was Cass who was standing over my shoulder the entire time, looking just as remorseful. Daniel sat down next to me and put his hand on my knee.

He knew that need in my eyes.

"They'll make change for you over at the shoe rental," Cass said while my head swiveled around to stare at him. Cass shook his head at me ever so slightly. There was nothing that we could do unless we wanted to face the consequences—and if we had any luck so far on this side, it was bad luck. Daniel laced his fingers in mine and remained wordlessly in the prison of our situation.

A beat passed. Then another.

I watched as the dollar bill floated to the floor.

It was Red who finally ducked low to say in my face, "Dy-no-mite, Miss Callaghan! I know your heart wanted to warn us, but you knew these weren't normal circumstances. And by the way, the authorities will arrest that son of a bitch . . . today . . . because it's after midnight. They took him in on December 21, 1978."

"So, you're not real," I gasped.

"*Psyche!* We're Lurkers," Red said. "Gacy killed my brother Frank. My mom dropped him off at a concert and we never saw him again. I was supposed to go with him, but it was my birthday and I blew the kid off. All they found was his blue nylon jacket and Boy Scouts wristwatch under the floorboards of Gacy's haunted laundry room.

"Frank was only fifteen," Red said. His voice choked.

"My cousin Tommy and I like to be here each and every time they take that bastard away—second only to the day they give him the juice," he said, reminding me that our favorite janitor in the Midst died by lethal injection.

"Faked you out," Tommy said with a big grin. "The truth is we'd like to linger and hang out with you kids, but we gotta go see a man about a new Walkman and some Van Halen tickets."

"You'll want to walk out the back exit and go east until you know . . . well, you will know when you get there," said Red as he waved a quick good-bye.

"Good night, John-Boy.

Catch you on the flipside," Tommy said before they walked across the rink in street shoes and disappeared into all things past tense.

10.

We walked out of that roller rink in Des Plaines, Illinois, and onto the streets of Manhattan, year unknown. I knew New York. It was my dream to live there someday, and now here I was standing on 72nd Street and Central Park West in the Upper West Side. Confirmation came in the form of high arched gables of the building's infamous main entrance. In fact, the doorway arch and vestibule would be seen on the front page of every single newspaper in the world because he died *right there. Famously.*

A stray *New York Times* poking out of a strolling businessman's grocery store bag confirmed it.

December 8, 1980.

There were many fabulous people who would call the Dakota, a famous Manhattan co-op apartment building, home over the years including singer Rosemary Clooney, actress Lauren Bacall, and football star Joe Namath. And then there was the icon.

His name was John Lennon.

A quick glance at my watch, which was working and on Manhattan time, showed me that it was 5:40 p.m.

In some kind of haze, we stood in the archway of the building, joined by six autograph seekers and history. The people of 1980 were simply waiting for them—John and his wife, Yoko—to appear outside of their New York home. Next to me was his shooter, Mark David Chapman, a partially bald middle-aged man who would soon fire five shots at Lennon with a Charter Arms .38 special revolver.

Right now, in this very moment when John Lennon was very much alive, his shooter/assassin stood with his hands in his pockets, obviously hiding the gun. The gunman wasn't much older than us. Was he twenty-four or twenty-five? A security guard from Honolulu, I knew he planned to murder John Lennon once before, but simply changed his mind—as if he got to choose if the legend lived or died.

Today, there would be no going back. He had been lurking since midmorning in this exact spot and even rushed Lennon's then five-year-old son Sean and the family nanny at one point during the day. Specifically, Chapman reached out to touch the boy's hand. It was out of line to touch someone else's child, a stranger, and the boy and nanny recoiled. It wouldn't be the only horrible moment of the day.

I felt a rush as their limo, which was late, finally swung around to take them to their recording studio. Chapman silently walked forward. The gun remained in his pocket. He reached out to hand Lennon a copy of his epic album, *Double Fantasy*.

It was just a prelude to what Chapman really wanted. A longtime fan of the Beatles and Lennon, he had turned against Lennon in particular. It would be revealed later that Chapman had experienced a religious conversion of sorts and was livid about Lennon's highly publicized 1966 comment that the Beatles were "more popular than Jesus."

"Is this all you want?" Lennon asked his future killer that morning, glancing up to smile at me.

Oh, John Lennon, no. Go. Run. Get out of here.

I am selfish. I needed so much more from you. I need your music in present tense, not past.

Most of all, I wanted to scream, "Do not be here later!"

It begged the questions: *If you do not show up at your own death then do you really die?*

11.

We left without speaking to Chapman. We could have easily taken him out in any number of ways. A concussion. A broken bone. Anything that would have put him in the hospital. We could have simply dragged him away and detained him, but that was against the rules.

We watched and then we wandered around New York City oblivious to the cold and the task at hand. At 10:30 p.m., we returned to the Dakota. I knew what would happen by heart and it would break me.

It broke the world.

On that night, Lennon decided to skip dinner so he could come home earlier than normal and tuck his son into bed. On 72nd Street at 10:50, John and Yoko got out of their black limo and didn't see that Chapman was standing in the shadows by the archway of the building. As Lennon passed, he glanced briefly at Chapman, maybe recognizing him from earlier. Maybe not.

It was my call.
All I had to do was say his name.
"Mr. Lennon," I could call out. I might wave my arms high in the air.
A glance. A step. A cough.
It could change a man's death into life.
Daniel would use the time to kick the gun out of Chapman's hand.
New York's finest would then cuff Chapman.
It would be good. John Lennon would live; the world would be a better place for it.

We could take out his killer.
As in out – all the way out.

My feet rocked in my boots. I was ready to launch, but I remained paralyzed as the small explosions lingered in my ears. Five shots rang out as Chapman pulled the trigger, jettisoning five hollow-point bullets from that .38 revolver. Four tore into Lennon's back, ripping flesh from bone, but the poet of his generation was still standing. Until he wasn't.

Lennon finally tumbled, bleeding profusely from his wounds, but he would use the little life in him to crawl the five steps to a security guard where he whispered the obvious, "I'm shot! I'm shot!" And then he would utter his last word: "Yeah."

Things that you will never forget: his breath lingering in the winter wind, his life force pouring onto cement, the cassettes he had been carrying that were now scattered everywhere.

Meanwhile, Chapman remained at the scene. He didn't run. I flinched as he pulled something else from his back pocket, but *all it was . . . was a book?* Dropping the gun on the ground, he began to *read* as he leaned against the building, furiously flipping the yellowed pages of an old copy of *The Catcher in the Rye*.

What else?

New York's finest roared onto the scene and paramedics swarmed the music legend, placing his now-still body on a stretcher. History told us that it would be a short trip before he was officially pronounced DOA at Roosevelt Hospital.

He never regained consciousness.

But, not tonight.

It didn't go down the same way because *this was a test. Just a test.* In the next moment, he sat straight up, swinging his perfectly functional legs off the stretcher while I stood there weeping.

"Walker," he said. "Everything will be okay in the end. If it's not okay, it's not the end."

"You're a—"

"I'm a Lurker now," he said proudly. "Maybe I was in life, too."

And then came the words I never expected to come out of John's mouth: "Would you like to come upstairs for some tea?"

12.

He lived the last seven years of his life in this building, but one apartment wasn't enough. John and Yoko purchased five additional apartments in this building using one for storage, one as a studio, and two as guest apartments.

Tonight, John Lennon not only invited us in, but brewed a pot of tea and motioned for us to follow. He sat on the couch next to Yoko, rocking his young son Sean who was now in his lap. I watched as he oh-so-tenderly gave him a goodnight kiss on the forehead. No one could see him – or us.

These were the priceless moments of his life that he relived again and again—even if those alive in his life were mere holograms from his memories.

I could see how you could get stuck in remembering.

He smiled.

"Sit a big longer," he said with a smile. There's nowhere you can be that isn't where you're meant to be.

"But, back to business," he continued, "Please know that you passed all tests and the X-catcher will contact you. Just follow along from this point on. To start, you will walk down the fire escape and back into your own time in The Other. Your car will be waiting. There will be a map of where you will slumber tonight, which will be outdoors. Your next escort will arrive by morning to place you on the right track as you journey north.

"As for tonight's escorts, please don't look them directly in the eye."

"Why?" I asked and stopped myself. *I was asking John Lennon questions! Pinching myself wouldn't be enough.*

"Just don't," he replied.

"Let it be," said Eddie who slapped his knee. Then he looked around the room. "Really, like, no one thought it was funny?"

TWENTY-SEVEN

1.

Time passes. You can't hold on to it. It's relentless. It grabbed at us on that New York fire escape like it had tiny tentacles and yanked us back to that lone Route 167 in our own present day and current time.

Daniel had wild brilliance and not only kept those car keys close, but he found where they hid the car in about five minutes because he left his watch inside and borrowed my watch, which also worked as a tracker. "Score one for Dr. King," I said as we found the car parked in a field behind a large sign promising that the rest stop exit ahead would "blow your mind." For once, after all that time tripping, I wanted my mind to simply coast.

But, we had come this far following the rules, so why not go a little further?

All of us tumbled into the car, grabbing seats that felt familiar, and drove for about five minutes until the highway abruptly ended. We found ourselves on a small country road with white arrows pointing north, but we remained in current time as John said. Our watches were clear indicators of time marching forward for once, which felt oddly normal.

Not sure where it was safe to stop for the night, we finally pulled the car over into just what we did not need. It was a cemetery, but at least there was no one there to bother us.

"*Carpe noctem*," Bitty said, adjusting her oversized sparkling sunglasses, which she wore in the dark.

It meant "to seize the night."

2.

Twilight and the purple-pink sky would not be shared by humans alone. My eyes focused on several flying black dots, maybe a hundred of them, swooping in to wait in the bare trees that surrounded The Other's version of a boneyard.

They were small vultures, predators, who were here because they hoped dinner was pending. What were they expecting tonight? Perhaps the birds were dreaming of what was buried. Or they were waiting for the newly arrived or what would soon be buried. That was an easy meal served nightly as most small towns only had one burial ground.

I watched as the birds called to each other, wondering if we were nothing more than a passing snack. I knew it wouldn't be long before the birds would begin fighting each other for limited resources. As with all beings, their greed would turn them into carcasses.

Daniel went with Eddie and Flick to look for firewood to keep us warm, which left Cass, Bitty, and I in charge of taking any snacks from the car and creating a small buffet. The birds cried overhead from the unfairness of it while Cass used the time to lure me into a short walk. We were still too blown away from our time travel journey to engage in much more than small talk.

Cass stopped at a limestone rock foundation amid the old-fashioned, intricately carved headstones. The rock sculpture was shaped like a witch with a crooked nose and protruding chin. "I read about this, sugar," he said, catching his second wind. "Lore has it that in the eighteenth century, there was an old woman who was misunderstood and labeled evil. A local monk sprinkled her with holy water turning her into stone."

"So, who was the true evil one?" I posed.

"I can't think straight because I just met John Lennon," he said with a wink.

It was true that my senses were turned up here. I could smell the fear. His and my own.

3.

We built a small fire and gathered around it to eat the chips and cookies we had left along with bottles of fresh water we borrowed from Griz and stored in the back.

Daniel spread his legs open and I fit perfectly in the safe space he created with his bones and flesh. My back relaxed on his chest; my fingers worried their way up and down his lower leg until he whispered in my air. "Baby, you keep doing that and we're going to go sneak off behind a gravestone."

I did it one more time.

"Callaghan," he warned, but it was more like a promise.

Our packs were either behind our heads or between our feet as we drifted off for a few hours not knowing exactly what the morning would bring. The iced breezes of late September provided enough heat although I felt that the reset was indeed doing a fine job.

There were parts of being here that were unnerving including a playground in the middle of the cemetery. More than once, my eyes lifted open because I heard those swings moving on their own. When I looked closely, I saw glowing circles of bright light behind the swings. Maybe it was my imagination, but they seemed to be filled with mysterious voices and laughter.

D woke me up in the middle of the night with a question. "Why are you breathing so hard, baby?" he asked.

"I'm not," I whispered.

In the next breath, I heard the *rat-a-tat-tat*.

Someone or something was drumming.

4.

It was so wildly quiet with the exception of a lone being who had found the beat. The constant rhythmic pounding in the distance played on every nerve—a constant pounding reminding me that what was far away was coming closer with each beat.

"Daniel," I whispered so harshly that the word made my throat hurt.

When I looked hard in the distance, it was the unimaginable: hundreds of lit torches in a row with their flames dancing high and caressing the night sky.

These torches crackled, swayed, and quivered in the light wind. My eyes felt heavy under their spell, my brain was muddled as my eyes focused almost hypnotically as they got closer and closer. In the far distance, I heard the steady and unrelenting clomping of what looked like a line of black horses. They took on an eerie silver glow under tonight's full moon.

I saw outlines of humans riding those wild beasts. A shaking hand naturally snacked into my backpack to feel for weapons.

"I might just be spitballin' here, but don't think the dead are going to rise up to protect us," grumbled Eddie who was now practically in my lap.

"Spread out," I whispered.

"I don't like to spread," said Eddie who just moved closer as the thunderous sound of horse hooves invaded the graveyard.

Hot air on the back of my neck made the hair rise until I realized that it was Bitty talking in my ear.

"Lower your eyes. Whatever you do . . . do not make eye contact as they come closer. They're called Night Marchers. Ancient belief has it that if anyone or anything looks directly at the Marchers then they will perish violently," she instructed. "Do it NOW!"

"I'm looking right at them," Eddie bragged, narrowing his eyes so they adjusted to the darkness and gazed straight up. But Bitty was faster and ripped his head to the ground. "Take off your clothes and lay facedown in the dirt. Do it now, Ed! NOW! You must get naked, lie facedown, and avoid any eye contact. Or you will perish forever!"

"What a bunch of horseshit," said Cass, staring right at them, too. "You have to look when the enemy seriously outnumbers your unit."

He didn't say anything else. I wasn't sure if it was because Bitty basically tackled him to the ground or that he actually took into account the hysteria in her voice. It wasn't long before she had ripped his shirt off and I saw her hands making fast moves on his pants.

"I like strong women, Bitty," Cass murmured, "but I don't think we know each other well enough."

In the frenzy of the moment, I looked down at more Cass than I had ever seen. His perfectly sculpted, exposed behind was pointing directly toward the moon while naked, massive shoulders and much thinner waist were also bathed in star glow. And that was when he turned his back to me, which he didn't do for long.

Full frontal Cass had no inhibitions although he was given a warning.

"Don't stand there, idiot," a frantic Bitty cried. "Facedown in the dirt!"

"I'm done with this nonsense," Cass hissed.

"You must show proper respect, fear, and deference if you want to be spared," she insisted.

I couldn't believe it when Cass actually complied.

"Now I've seen everything," Daniel grunted.

He was at the ready with long fingers curled around the small sword that he grabbed from his pack.

Cass's hand had also snaked over to grab a device from his pack, a clever little gizmo that spewed flames.

"Night Marchers are spirits or ghosts of long-gone warriors who rise up from their burial sites or from the ocean for night traveling. They're always dressed for battle and carry spears, clubs, and beat war drums," Bitty explained. "They appear in the dark and travel in a line on horseback.

"They hold their torches high to announce their arrival. Their job in death, as in life, is to protect sacred beings."

"Hell, Callaghan," Daniel whispered into my ear. "I was just going for special."

The piercing sound of their drums stirred my spirit. I noted that as they became closer the war drums became so loud that my ears began to ring. There was also a foul, musky "deathlike" odor that was strong and made my eyes water. But that wasn't the oddest thing. As they approached, the men and their horses illuminated from within.

Their only obstacle now was the haphazard rows of gravestone. I knew it wouldn't stop them.

"They do not recognize barriers," said Bitty, who stopped talking after those words although her eyes insisted that she was still in some sort of conversation. Was she communicating telepathically with them? Perhaps that was the case because it didn't take long before she informed the rest of us, "Grab your things. They want us to follow them. No car."

"Eddie, pants up," I said in a breathy voice.

5.

The drumbeat began again although it was much softer this time.

"We're lucky," Bitty whispered to me because we were the first ones ready although Daniel and Cass hurried to step in front of us.

"This cemetery has a back door lined up with the front entrance. That means that we had lost our path. They find the lost."

"And is this a good thing?" Cass said.

"Undetermined," she said, clearly mesmerized like she was looking up at her favorite rock stars. Only Springsteen wasn't up there planning to kill you.

I placed a throwing star in each hand.

6.

We kept our eyes on the ground and walked in front of them, which was not the best defense position because there was no defense. We were targets.

Cass and Daniel bitched about the stupidity of it, but Bitty was so sure and there was something about her. She had that voice of authority similar to Miss Maude Travis, our admission's counselor in the Midst and/or my second mother. I missed my own mother so much and Miss Travis filled in the nurturing blanks when she could and it didn't seem like she was overstepping. How I wished she was here now.

"We will survive," Bitty said with awe. "Which brings me to a slight confession, especially to Walker. I'm a Hybrid. And since you probably don't know what that means, it means I have more than one 'gift.'

"I don't just possess speed," she said. "I have a knowing. When it comes to history. Always had it. Inherited from my mother because she was jealous that my dad gave me the speed thing. They were both gifted, thus I'm a Hybrid."

"Can we get the condensed version before these things kill us?" I whispered.

"I have an amped-up version of the power of psychometry," she said. "In a nutshell, the user obtains historical memories or sensations concerning beings and objects they observe. And we can communicate via telepathy with people from ancient times. I got that last part from my grandmother Sadie who also made wicked-good chicken noodle soup."

"What's the amped-up part?" Cass asked.

"Some psychometry types need to actually touch the object, but I just have to be about fifty feet around it to know, for instance, that Walker was a lovely girl with a long history with her captor," Bitty said. "Honey, I actually saw your entire history with him before I decided to befriend you. Same thing with Griz. I knew he was harmless when I got within the desired range. Same thing with you, Cass. I know why you're really here."

Cass's gaze remained steady.

"We'd all like to know why," Daniel grunted.

"What's important is they expect us to walk in front of them," Bitty continued, getting back to the situation at hand. "It will be an insult if we don't."

"Bitty, I don't know you," Daniel whispered. "But you better be right."

"Does your gut say that I am?" she challenged him.

"My gut says this is bullshit," Cass said although he reluctantly listened to Bitty, too.

Daniel had already formed a plan to run toward the sides and regroup in the light. "Hide until dawn," Cass said. "And then walk north until we find each other again," Daniel said.

They were actually working together for the greater good although I wanted to scream a violent "no" at the idea of splitting up. That hadn't served us well here. And when would we reunite? In a day? A month? A century?

And so, I walked.

One foot moved in front of the other on a path where little dust clouds were created by my every step. There was no question who was behind me. The torches provided a heat that made my backside feel as if I was on fire.

"Are they marching us off the ends of this realm?' I whispered to Daniel.

"You're working overtime here, baby," he said. "For some reason, I choose to trust them. If they wanted to harm us, they would have done it already."

"Unless they want to take us to their camp and eat us," I joked, but not really.

"We know you taste good," he said under his breath.

When I was lagging, Daniel grabbed my hand and I had to double-time it to catch up to the point where I was practically jogging.

This reminded me . . .

On these long, dark nights, there was always the runner and the chaser. I wasn't sure which we were tonight, and I had a feeling that the roles could change on a dime.

7.

I'm not sure how it happened. Did they arrange it? Move it? Teleport it? We walked miles in a new direction . . . only to see our car in the distance.

There was our lovely SUV, stolen from Edward's house of pain.

There was no physical explanation in the mortal world of how the car, parked near the entrance of the cemetery, could move this far without any driver, plus Daniel had the only keys in the pocket of his blue jeans.

"Bitty?" I said.

"Obviously, they know how to control electrical currents," she whispered while I nodded. *Thank you, Bitty. Stupid me, electrical current conversion. So blindingly obvious.*

The temporary diversion of the car was enough to actually change the playing field. It only took a few more seconds for me to realize that the heat was gone. When I dared to turn a bit around, I didn't see torches anymore. It was as if they blew out in the night wind.

The horses had vanished. The Marchers had all but evaporated. A few more steps and we walked onto actual concrete and I noted that we were standing on the shoulder of an empty highway again.

The Marchers had obviously done their job, which was to march us from point A to point B. Now, all we had was the symphony of that night breeze that featured several solo performances. I wasn't exactly nature girl, but I swore I heard a wolf howl in the not-so-distant background. He was accompanied by friends who had glowing eyes that stared back, if you dared to turn around for a panoramic view.

Night time was feeding time.

One thing was clear: we were the runners.

8.

The only thing that made sense was to dive into the car and lock the doors. Daniel didn't wait long to put the key in place and rev the engine.

He drove out of this rural area onto a two-lane highway where the speed limit didn't seem to exist.

Civilization never felt this good, although I didn't see any buildings, signs, or even a lone middle-of-the-night exit stop. The good news was we weren't alone. At least not for long. There were several cars and a few long trucks, the kind that stock places up, going in both our direction and filling the oncoming traffic spots.

At one point, about twenty minutes later, we got stuck in a line of cars behind a slow driver. Finally, the traffic broke free and we entered another stretch where passing was allowed.

There was a woman—maybe forties, blonde bob, big eyes—driving one of those long Chevy SUVs, and we sped up to zip around her, which is when it happened. She sped up, too.

Daniel, who had been driving since age ten, slowed back down to go behind her, but she slowed down at exactly the same time. He tried it again. He sped up when there was a break in oncoming traffic; she sped up. He was forced to go behind her again. And then again, he revved it, jumped into the oncoming lane and she did the same. But this time, when he tried to fall behind again, she slowed.

It was a game they played at eighty-five miles an hour driving against traffic. My heart raced as I spotted the glare of high headlights coming at us.

At that point, I motioned to the woman, begging her to let us back in. I noticed she wasn't alone. A pale-faced young man sat in the back seat. He had albino-white skin and bleached white hair that stood straight up.

Tor. But I couldn't be sure.

He was staring right at me. Grinning.

The semitruck was barreling right at us.

"Daniel!" I cried.

9.

He swung the car violently onto the shoulder of the oncoming lane and the semi only missed us by several hairs. My entire body began to shake. *I died in a violent car crash and it began coming back to me . . . the shattering glass . . . my body a small missile . . . ejection from my seat and into the great yonder.*

It happened in a blink.

As she passed, the woman put up a hand and in it was something that glowed silver.

"Gun!" I screamed.

Her windows were down and the first shot took out our right tire, which exploded on impact. Was it Bitty screaming? Or was it Auggie?

I braced as the car skidded sideways toward a ditch.

I didn't hear a second shot. And despite Cass bellowing for us to brace and duck, I grabbed the roll bar and remained in place with my mouth wide open and eyes peeled at the show.

She crashed headfirst into a flatbed truck parked the long way across the highway lane. There was something in the back of that truck that made the explosion Hollywood pretty. It dawned on me. Someone had filled that back with fireworks—the big kind.

Her car? Gone.

The driver?

The passenger?

Undetermined, but probably gone.

What remained was a goliath red, white, and blue fireball that saturated the sky.

10.

I'd never remember who jumped out of our car first, but we did so on limbs made out of water. By now, there was only a little bit of traffic speeding by as we somehow made our way across the highway to examine the remains.

"I can't be sure," I rushed.

"I saw him, too, Callaghan," Daniel said.

Two figures cut through smoke that was heavy and hung low. I braced in case the driver and passenger had somehow jumped out before the *kaboom*.

I tried to remember our training. It calmed me although my hands were violently shaking.

Make a fist. Instead of striking with fingers in front, strike down with the underside of your hand at the five areas of the body that are the most vulnerable. The face, the throat, the knees, the feet, the groin. Where were my stars? Right. In my pack. In the car. Nice work, Walker, you freaking idiot.

I watched in shock as a human form broke through the smoke: black leather jacket, black T-shirt, black jeans, black shit-kicker boots. She was stunning.

She was singing.

"On a dark desert highway. Cool wind in my hair."

11.

Daniel's steel-gray eyes spotted her. He was in turbo mode, flying forward on feet that were made of jet propulsion.

He would use hands. He gripped her by the shoulders, violently pulling her in. She pushed back to survey the damages.

"They done get this black girl magic today whether they wants it or not," Bertha Jackson said.

12.

"The years dry up the tears," Bertha reminded me, smoothing down my hair with one hand and using the other to push me back and really look at me. Then I fell into her arms and she hugged me fiercely.

"I knew I'd see my sister again—shining and on your grind with your cute self," she said.

Bertha was one of my best friends at the Academy, but I hadn't seen her for months. Principal Dick "graduated" many students as a lesson to those who even dared think about defying him. He basically banished those students to parts unknown.

It was too much to ask, but I still wondered.

"Are you . . . ," I began.

"You think I was about to let her do this all by herself?" said Big Bad

Izayah who materialized as the puffs of mist and smoke cleared around him.

Daniel and Iz locked eyes; they crashed palms and arms.

"My man," said Daniel as I flew into Iz's arms.

Find your tribe. Love them hard.

13.

Bertha condensed her story in one big blurt. "When Principal Dick made me do all that grad-u-atin, Walk-*her*, I ran away before I could be sent anywheres," she said. "Hid out in the woods—and you know I'm good at the art of the vanish. Iz joined me and we weren't sure what to do. Then, one night the wall between the two sides opened. We crossed over."

"We ran. We swam. We walked. We snuck around until we found Dr. King and his house," Iz said. "You had been gone for about a week and we had to stay there to regroup. When we did, we came looking for you for many reasons. One is that we have some key information from home."

"Dr. King got some intelligence from Miss Travis at home," Bertha said. "They know the X-catcher is in the very most northern tip of The Other. In some kind of tower situation. They're not a hundred percent, but he lives in something that looks like a lighthouse."

"How have you survived this long on this side?" I asked her.

"'Cause I know one thing about life, Walk-*her*," she said. "Everything is temporary."

"And I know one thing," Cass added as he walked with us.

"What do you know, handsome?" Bertha teased.

But Cass was dead serious. "Pain shapes a woman into a warrior," he said. He wasn't looking at her but me.

"And what do you know, Iz?" I asked as a quick subject changer.

Our favorite hockey player friend loped a friendly arm over my shoulder and I melted into the familiar.

"I know that your faith has to be bigger than your fear," he said, adding, "This is fun. And you, Walker. Know anything?"

"I know absolutely nothing," I insisted.

I kept walking and blushed although no one could see it in the dark. They were obviously waiting.

"When I was four, a mean girl named Heather beat me up one day because she wanted my chips at lunch and I wouldn't give them to her," I blurted. "She punched me and pinched me, and I never wanted to go back to school.

"The next day, my dad scooped me up in his arms, carried me almost all the way to school, and then put me down on the sidewalk about a block away, so I could finish on my own two feet. When he put me down, he kissed me on the forehead and said something I would never forget."

I had to take a breath. My bottom lip trembled.

"He said, 'Sky above me. Earth below me. Fire within me,'" I recited.

"So, what's our battle cry for this mission?" Auggie asked.

Iz took his place next to me on the other side.

"Do no harm. Take no shit," he said. The hoots that followed were loud and proud and came with a heady round of high-fives.

I put my hand up. It was Cass who pressed his flesh to mine.

14.

It felt so good to walk, talk, and just be. Time didn't matter. Neither did distance from everything that was familiar. Under a lopsided moon, we hiked a good two miles before I saw what might have been a settlement beckoning in the distance. Or, it might have been a firefly convention.

On this side, nothing was marked, so you could never be too sure.

I linked my pinky finger to Daniel's. I felt a spark and gazed at one more visible off in the near distance. "There is something up ahead if you look hard enough," I said. "I see tiny specks of light."

"How do you witness everything, Callaghan?" Daniel asked.

"Reporters. We're trained observers," I said, but as we got closer there were no words to put with the picture. No caption. No cutline to explain a big, wide, unexplained world.

There was just a sight to behold.

"After you," I shouted, racing him for the future.

TWENTY-EIGHT

1.

We entered a serene valley that felt both familiar and wildly imaginative at the same time. It was so dreamy, so cozy. I could hardly contain my joy. It wasn't exactly Christmas morning, but as close as you could get on an early September day in a distant realm.

Golden light filtered out of windows and perfect smoke puffs rose from blackened chimneys. A massive evergreen tree was riding shotgun on the roof of a car. It was surrounded by sky morphed into a color undefined, but best described as purple pink.

Doors to the stores were open as in "come on in, stay awhile." Dogs stretched out sleepily on sidewalks and I bent down to pet a friendly golden retriever.

It actually looked a lot like the Main Street we enjoyed in the Midst, but this was more than a wonderful slice of small-town Americana life.

It was a painting come to life. Auggie knew it well. "*Home for Christmas*, created in 1967 by one of my favorite painters," he marveled. "Only, we're not just staring at it on some museum wall . . . we're living it."

The painter in question had moved to Stockbridge, Massachusetts, in 1953 at age fifty-nine and spent the last twenty-five years of his life in that small town.

My eyes feasted on the public library, the insurance office, the barbershop, the antiques and gift shop, the old town offices and down to the rambling Victorian hotel and a red-bricked town hall.

Each interior seemed to glow.

We were surrounded by snow-draped mountains and a little of the white fluff coated these streets although it wasn't particularly cold outside. A woman passed me in the same bright green Sears Roebuck catalogue coat that my own Aunt Ginny received as a Christmas present in the seventies and kept in pristine condition from decades of dry cleaning. It seemed like a current fashion here. Not vintage.

The rest of the town was like stepping back in time—a time none of us had experienced but knew existed.

"Look at the end of the street," Auggie said.

As we got closer, I saw it. On the far right of the painting was the artist's studio and home created on canvas by his own hands.

"See that . . . he lives there," I said to the others. "Cool factoid. He set up his office up there, but knocked out the main window on the first day. He replaced it with a five-thousand-dollar picture window that gave him a steady northern light. He wanted to make it dreamy and cozy."

"He who?" Auggie asked.

"Norman," I whispered as I ran up his front step. I could hear him way up top and took the next staircase in twos, which was highly illegal, I supposed. I did just walk into his home although the door was unlocked and the welcome on the front mat seemed authentic.

2.

It was a short race up the stairs to a small room painted white with warm wooden beams on the ceiling and slabs of oak on the floor. In the middle was a simple brown wood easel complete with speckles of old, dried paint on a ledge that held a single wooden brush.

In front of it was a basic wooden chair with side arms that wound around. It was a dining room table reject and didn't even feature a set cushion, but a wayward pillow. Next to the setup was a small wooden table in a lighter wood. It held a wood cup filled with about twenty-five brushes and a black pipe.

He was hunkered over a small architect's table that was void of the chair. It faced a cream-colored wall that was a gallery of his works of art and those of other artists he admired.

A big gold bell sat on a thin, tall table in the corner. Did he ring that bell when he finished each painting? Or was it just something pretty and shiny that gave him a little daily thrill?

Bright sunlight poured from a row of windows onto a thin man who was standing but hunched over a painting with a brush in his hand. He had on tan pants, a long-sleeved brown shirt, and even indoors wore a winter scarf around his neck.

He had sunken eyes and a swatch of light-colored hair that revealed a wide forehead. The pipe was in his mouth now when he looked at our motley group and asked, "Now, why do I have the pleasure? Did the high school let out early?"

"No, Mr. Rock—" I began.

"Norman," he corrected.

Norman. All right, if he insisted.

All I could do was stare at his fingers because they contained genius. When his index finger shot out to beckon me closer, I couldn't believe my luck. I counted the four nervous steps I took in his direction. When I was close enough, he gazed up and looked at me hard. He wasn't just looking. It was more like an examining.

"You have an interesting face," the artist said. "Midwesterner? Yes?"

"Yes."

"The character is strong," he continued to examine. "Unshakable."

"How do you know?" I asked.

"I'm a professional observer of people," he shot out. "You might know someone with the same disposition."

3.

"Do you want to see?" he offered and I glanced deeply at the canvas in front of him. It was mostly white spaces with a few deep green trees. "The secret to so many artists living so long is that every painting is a new adventure," he informed us. "So, you see, they're always looking ahead to something new and exciting.

"The secret," he said, "is not looking back."

I don't think we were talking about art anymore although it was all around us. His famous Thanksgiving work, *Freedom from Want*, with the family gathered around the table and Mom and Pop serving the turkey was propped against a wall. It was the *original*. It was destroyed in a fire when he lived in Arlington, Vermont, before moving here. But here it was.

"But why these places?" I asked him. "They're so common yet so inviting that you want to move into your paintings."

"You picked the right word: *common*," said Norman. "The truth is, commonplaces never become tiresome. It is we who become tired when we cease to be curious and appreciative.

"We find that it is not a new scene that is needed, but a new viewpoint," he said. "But that's why you're here.

"You've had a rough time in these parts," he said with a small chuckle. "The Other isn't an easy experience. You have been tested. But the good news is that you made it this far. Not many do, which is the idea. We cannot accommodate all young, wayward spirits. For starters, we don't have the dorm space."

I opened my mouth, but he interrupted.

"It's time for a blank canvas now," he said, pointing to any of the white new beginnings leaning against a wall. "You'll find that once you leave here. But, take your time. Have a look around. As in most things you will cherish forever, there is no rush."

Almost on cue, we heard a voice from downstairs.

"Lunch, Norman!" cried his wife.

"You kids better skedaddle and leave an old duffer like me with his imagination and his tuna fish sandwich," he said.

He winked at me as we walked out. "I always strive to capture everything I see as completely as possible, Walker," he said. "It's good advice for you, too."

"Sir, I didn't . . . ," I began.

"I was expecting you . . . eventually," he said. "It's all prewritten."

"And how did you know that we'd find our way here in the dark?"

"Because," he said, "you have a light within. We all do. We're all just stars wrapped in skin."

4.

We ended up on the street in front of Norman's lovely house, half in awe and mostly wondering what the heck we were doing here in the first place. Was this place called The Other finally softening?

"Would have been nice if she made us a tuna sandwich," Eddie complained.

"Wargo, does everything revolve around your stomach?" Cass asked.

On the way out of Norman's house, his lovely wife Mary handed me a typewritten piece of paper.

"Walker, dear, you had an email. I printed it out," she said. "Receiving that correspondence and my reporting back to Dr. King are two of the reasons why you're actually here."

We chose a mound of snowy grass in a charming wintry park for a pause.

I read aloud the email from the only one who had universal web service in life and death. It was from our computer teacher, Steve, who started that fruit company so long ago:

Today, Current Time, Hopefully . . .

Kids, if you've made it this far, and I pray that you survived,

I'm sure you're wondering what's next.

Damned if I know the complete answer, but I do know what's immediately next after you spend time in Norman's beautiful small American town. It's not really a town at all, but a gateway to an afterlife necessity. They just give you a little R&R in his utopia before moving on.

I won't ruin the surprise. But I will tell you this: Embrace what you're about to be embraced by. It will blow your freaking minds.

Please read that last sentence again. Blow. Your. Freaking. Minds.

It did mine.

—STEVE

P.S. Read the next page only if you want to know what has happened in the Midst.

I needed to know and flipped the paper.

Steve wrote:

"Sadly, things are dire here in the Midst. Principal Dick has declared martial law. Students are not allowed to leave their rooms, learn in classrooms, or gather in groups of more than two and then—if, and only if—that duo has been approved by the administration.

About three-quarters of the Academy's population has been sent to ITT to serve jail terms for offenses as heinous as sneaking out to see a friend, talking a walk in the woods, daring to look Principal Dick directly in the eyes, and stealing food or drink beyond the bare minimum now allowed each day.

Everyone is on sparse rations and not because there isn't abundance. It's about control. All war is about control.

But maybe I'm jumping too far ahead. Students are not allowed to have personal dalliances at the Academy. Falling in love is strictly forbidden.

Principal Dick has also taken away TV, movies, and phones. If he could deny breath, he would.

Faculty members who help students have been told that they will be sent into a past loop *indefinitely.* You might run into a few of them on your journey.

It will be your choice if you ever want to return. Many maverick types settle in The Other never to be seen again. They take their chances and visit the past loops for excitement. Your chances of living free might be better there—especially for Daniel and Walker who will be tortured by Dick in order for him to obtain the Omorrow papers. If you do wish to return, I will give you my secret email on my own web server. Only use it once. Under the most severe circumstances.

My advice is to stay there. Save yourselves.

Miss Travis, Harold, and I have started an underground group that we're calling the Revolt. Dr. King is a key member, but he probably wouldn't want you to know that. He wants you to stay on your mission and find the X-catcher, so you can open the wall. His plan is that you stay at the cabin in The Other while he uses the open door to return to the Midst to help save the Academy.

One thing about Dr. King. He's one brave, obstinate, never-say-die . . . well, you know him better than most.

The mission now is to open that wall and guard those Omorrow pages. There is no telling what Principal Dick and his minions will be able to do with the power of the Academy, plus Einstein coordinates.

When things are bleak please think of these words from Dr. King that help me face each and every day now:

If you can't fly, then run.

If you can't run, then walk.

If you can't run, then crawl.

But whatever you do, you have to keep moving forward.

—STEVE

P.S. Walk to the outskirts of town. Prepare to have an experience amongst friends.

P.P.S. I knew you'd read the second page, which is why I saved the instructions for now.

PART III

TWENTY-NINE

1.

We not only walked out of town, but *out* of the outdoors. A few steps past the city limits, all of the fresh air, trees, and birds singing disappeared. A blink later and we were inside of an actual building that had the faint musty odor of decaying books and burned coffee.

It was actually a beautiful turn-of-the-century structure with stunning pine wooden ceilings and creamy-white textured walls. Deeply sunken couches were made of busy floral fabrics and they were framed by thick maroon leather chairs and coffee tables that were artfully aged, scratched, and chipped thanks to years of service.

Auggie saddled up to me. "So, um, I chose the road less traveled and now I don't know where the hell I am," he tried to joke, but his nervousness betrayed him. And then came the confession. "My jokes get worse as my anxiety increases."

I had to admit that Augs had a point. There were goosebumps on my arm for no apparent reason and soon the small sign that said toilets might be visited.

But not yet. Because she had arrived.

"Sorry, sorry, sorry, I'm late. Sorry, sorry, sorry for your terrible time here," she said in a rapid-fire way that reminded me of both a machine gun and that guy selling strawberry pies at a state fair.

"Are you here for our freshman program or for a doctoral degree or just to brush up on some skills? Although, you do look like first timers? Does anyone need a current course catalog or do you have some kind of Internet access and read about us online after you were given access by Norman? He's quite a gatekeeper isn't he. He doesn't like you and he sends you back to the Night Marchers to be escorted away forever. And by forever, I mean *forever*. You gotta love those guys and gals as our security system. Who needs a pit bull? Marchers don't poop on the carpets."

"Some of our requirements have changed, but most of the classes come with a lab, which we all know is the good part," she said. "I promise that our school lives up to its name. It's the only school of its kind in any realm and we put you through hell to get here, so you might as well enjoy it."

"Enjoy what, ma'am?" Cass asked.

"Where are my manners? I'm sorry. My name is Zan," she babbled on. "Zan Mac. Welcome to the Astonishing School of Ghostly Needs."

She had me at *astonishing*.

She was a tall woman with short, pure-white hair and an upturned nose. Her mouth was large and covered in blinding pink lipstick. Her heels were sky high despite the fact that she was dressed in a long robe of black silk. She accented "the look" with a black silk scarf around her neck.

Her skin was almost translucent and she wore no makeup whatsoever except for the lipstick, which really didn't matter because her face—for lack of a more beauty specific word—shimmered.

Zan walked briskly up to me and snapped a silver pen in my face, but it probably wasn't really a pen. She waved it around wildly as it blinded me

"Interesting aura," she said. "But makes sense. Do you have any questions I can answer in under thirty seconds?"

"Where are we?" It was my best opening offer when it came to inquiries of a crucial kind.

"We call it the Astonishing School of Ghostly Needs," she said. "You are here to learn all the shadow arts such as—but not limited to—walking through walls, manipulating shadows, or visiting loved ones who still draw breath."

Now I was glowing.

"Older folk who die also must learn the ghostly arts. Thankfully, they go somewhere else because . . . don't get me started when it comes to a Boomer set in his or her ways. No thank you. Ick. You're young. Untrained. Unknowing. Which is why we have to teach you here at what I lovingly call Ghost U."

2.

"We will also dispel the ghostly myths here in Myths and Falsehoods Class," Zan rambled as I forced myself to take perfect mental notes.

Flick was also in his element. "Such as?" he posed.

"Such as many of the living believe that every time you get dressed you must remember if you died today that outfit could be your ghost outfit forever down to your underwear," she said. "All myths. Ghosts have a wide variety of fashion choices."

"Although I think some of you were born and died in those jeans," she said, sniffing the air. "But let's get back to your course schedule, shall we?"

"Has anyone done any orb travel? Haunted a house?" she posed. "Walked through a wall. Traveled through time."

Daniel and I held our hands up because we did walk through a wall once in the living realm at the Lake Forest Airport when we saved Bobby. The main terminal was locked and my temper had me kicking the wall. I was shocked when my leg easily went through the wall, but it was gooey and dense on the way through like walking through thick oatmeal mixed with watery concrete. I didn't stick the landing, but fell to my face on the other side. I got the job done by accident, and it wasn't pretty.

"Ever save a life with your guardian angel skills?" Zan posed.

This time most of the group held their hands up because we saved an entire elementary school from a burning building in the 1950s during our mission to New York.

"Interesting group, and I like it. I like it very, very, very much," said Zan who scolded as quickly as she praised. To Eddie, whose lips were at the water fountain stream of liquid, she cautioned, "Don't drink that. It will keep you drunk for an entire year."

"I like this school," Flick said.

Eddie took three more big sips.

"Wargos are born drunk," he said.

3.

"We don't just let anyone in," Zan explained. "Some spirits do online or learn it on their own. Those with promise are admitted here for formal training if they can figure out how to arrive in The Other. You have been chosen for actual on-campus courses."

"Will I learn to move objects with my mind?" Eddie asked.

Zan nodded, as in yes.

Eddie gave me the highest of fives while staring into my eyes.

"Ed, you don't know how to do it, yet," Auggie poked the bear.

"Telekinesis," Cass marveled. "I've always wanted to make objects move. I'd also like to take on pyrokinesis or the ability to manipulate fire."

"I'm a natural pyromaniac—living and dead," Eddie interrupted. "And I never went to any school!"

"Hydrokinesis," said Zan, filling empty water glasses with the stream of water that materialized from thin air.

Zan put her hands up high and the sun pouring through the large picture windows shined brighter.

"Photokinesis, or the ability to manipulate light. Don't get excited about it. It's only for seniors. You're here to learn the basics as freshmen."

"This is not the Academy," she warned. "Smart isn't good enough here. We have smart kids here. We also require a certain physical prowess along with a mind that fires in all directions. Do you understand?"

I did for some reason.

Almost on cue, the principal of the Astonishing School entered the room. "Harry," he said, introducing himself with a bowing motion. "And this is my wife, Bess."

They made a lovely couple. He was around five foot six with dark, tamed hair parted just a little off center. In life he was known for his intense gaze, and he didn't disappoint now.

There was an old-fashioned timepiece hanging from a gold chain resting at his waist. His wife had short, curly black hair, a literary nose, and a small smile. She wore an elaborate lace shirt that migrated up her neck and a long black skirt.

It was appropriate that he helmed this school. In life, one of his many nicknames was "the Man Who Walked through Walls."

"Harry was known in life to have an obsession with death," Zan explained. "He vowed once to be the only dead man who would ever return to living form. He promised to make contact once he had crossed over. He established this school to practice his art and plan his big comeback—the biggest the human race has ever seen."

"Here, you will learn the afterlife arts through what I like to call deliberate practice or various real-world exercises," he said.

"Can you explain, sir?" I asked and he nodded.

"When I first started practicing magic as a young man, I'd have my brother tie me up in ropes and then I would spend hours on the roof of my family's tenement building attempting to free myself. I worked until my toes could untie knots with the dexterity of the average man's fingers.

"Deliberate practice makes perfect," he said. "This is a safe place. Your Dr. King is thrilled that you are here. Safe. Enjoy your time . . . and, if you really learn the ghostly arts, it will serve you well for all eternity."

Cass's smile stretched wide. "So, we're in basic training as ghosts?"

"It will be anything but basic," Harry insisted.

4.

Our other worldly possessions were delivered to a series of dorm rooms in a high-rise built in 1802 called Vander Hall, which required a quick walk through a campus so green and lush I swore we were at the Harvard of the afterlife education.

Tall elm trees lined cobblestone walks and small black-and-white signs pointed out thrilling areas of studies from portals to psychometry, which was the art of touching an object or human and then an immediately knowing its entire history.

A teenage resident assistant with family ties named Beau Vander (tall, friendly, helpful) made sure to show us to our individual rooms, which were exactly similar to college dorms. They were small, overheated, and contained just a single, uncomfortable twin bed, a miniscule desk, a back-killing chair, and a tiny closet that smelled funky like old athletic shoes.

My room was in the middle of Daniel and Cass's with the rest around us. Bertha was already making plans for Iz to sneak into her dorm for some undercover studies while Daniel was giving me a look that had me blushing. Even worse was a few minutes later when I found Cass mistakenly in the ladies' room washing up.

"I wasn't thinking and just walked in," he said.

"Cass, since you're here . . . ," I began.

"You have some use for me, sugar?" he said with a wink as he leaned against a sink. "I'm easy. Use me."

"Seriously, I think we should ask around a bit about that place where MC could be living if she was in this realm. It's a longshot, but we have to take the shot," I said. "If there is any place dealing with matters of the very youngest spirits, it could be this one."

"Already on it," he said, putting out his fist. During the bump, he reached out and took my hand in his hand. "I can't wait until you meet my baby," he said in a soft voice.

5.

When I returned to my room a few minutes later, I found Daniel napping on my bed. We snuggled together for several minutes and the way he looked at me made me felt like I was being devoured.

There was no time for anything else because Beau was tapping on the door. "It might be nice to take a walk around campus," he advised, "before dinner. And then you should turn in early. Tomorrow will be a big deal."

It was late summer now and the larks sang above us as we took an early evening stroll. For the first time in a long time, I felt like I could take a deep breath.

We were all right here. Secure. How wonderful it felt to be able to close your eyes all the way shut.

Not that there weren't potential pitfalls. We passed building that looked so interesting Daniel almost had to pull me away because we didn't have access quite yet. One that really sparked my interest was one called the Ghost Containment Society. Another building proclaimed itself A Place Called Anguish.

In the main quad area, the grass was just mowed and the weeping willow trees danced in a light warm breeze. A few tables were set up on the sidewalk gauging your interest in various activities. It was up to you to explore the possibilities.

"What is the bane of your existence?" asked a fellow student who represented a club called Have an Experience.

At another table, a girl asked me, "Would you like to return to the sight of your death and explore those last fatal moments to have some closure? Join the Conclusion Society because we will be conducting "closure tours" for the next four weeks. First, you must sign a waiver in case of demon devouring." *In life, on a field trip, all they could do was lose you temporarily. This was a bit more extreme.*

I just smiled. I wasn't ready. Maybe I would never be.

"Daniel Reid—the one who can remove pain in others and replace it with healing energy?" announced a young man whose group dabbled in mind reading and future predictions.

"Yeah, okay," Daniel said. He never ever talked about his little "extra."

"Full disclosure is the only kind," said the mind-reading type A personality.

"You're a journalist. You . . . um . . . yes, come from a home missing a father, poor little broken bird," he said to me. "That makes for a lonely childhood with no real sense of security even if your poor mother busted her butt trying to make you feel safe. This lack of safety in your soul is why you relish taking wild chances."

"No, none of that is true," I lied.

"Liar," said the reader who added, "Appreciate your uncommon white aura."

"Thank you. I think."

"The healer has a red aura. Very impressive. Very hot when you put it all together."

"Jerry," moaned his partner at the table. "Stay out of their personal life."

"Well, sue me. It is hot between the two of them," he griped.

The tables went on and on. One promised that they would help you "unlock your Book of Life."

"Which means?" I asked, fascinated.

"You can go back and watch your life in movie scenes including tap into your Karmic Record to see exactly how you treated every single person you ever encountered." Pause. "Can you dig it?"

Are. You. Kidding. Me?

I could dig deep into it.

6.

We went to bed in separate rooms although there was no major checking system by anyone in power. Around midnight, my sweet dream picked the lock and then tried to fit his large body into my twin bed. It basically required Daniel lifting me and placing my body on top of him. This was possibly against the rules, but totally economical.

He put his lips in that sweet spot, the crease in my neck, in a way that made me feel like my bones were melting. I swear I floated.

"We could use a good night's sleep," Daniel said, lips on the sensitive skin between my breasts. "But first, a student body rebellion."

Strong arms bandied around my back before he kissed me with the kind of promise and reckless abandon that made me believe in the morning. I ached for him. And my soul split open as we tumbled, clothes raining off that raised bed and pooling on the floor underneath us.

He was the best thing that I never planned.

7.

Morning light and an alarm sounded inside the dorms.

It was our wake-up call.

My pulse bounced because maybe, just maybe, this was the highest education of all.

I could barely get through cold scrambled eggs in the cafeteria and a tasteless bagel.

"Little bird," Flick said under his breath. "I want to pinch myself. Not everyone gets to go here. It's like the Harvard of this kind of thing." Then he leaned in and said, "I feel like I'm five years old going off to first grade."

"Do you think the other kids will like me?" Auggie fretted.

"I don't care if anyone likes me," Eddie piped up. "I'm going to learn how to do some wicked hauntings." And then to me, he asked, "You gonna eat those eggs?"

"So much for Casper, the friendly Wargo," Cass teased him.

Turns out, we didn't have to sign up for classes because a full day of courses was presented to us under the door after midnight. A quick comparison and I sighed a deep breath of relief because *all of us* were together Period One for a self-explanatory course that required meeting in the field house in a black Astonishing School uniform. It was a loose-fitting black jumpsuit and athletic shoes (also provided in the correct sizes).

Zan herself knocked on each door to make sure everything fit, although she insisted her eyeball method of sizing rarely failed her.

This wasn't like any gymnasium or workout facility I had ever seen. Inside, there was a bit of space around the perimeter and then thousands of *walls* of all varieties—stone, concrete, plaster, bricked, retaining, masonry, you name it. If a wall could be made out of it . . . it was here.

It made sense. The course: Walking through Walls (for Beginners).

Our teacher was . . . no, it wasn't. But, it was. It was the Man in Black although he also wore a white shirt along with that black sports coat and jeans.

He said to call him JR and began our lesson telling us about his beloved brother Jack. True story: They grew up on a farm and one day were cutting wood. Jack got pushed into a table saw, which mangled his midsection. The boy lingered for a week and then died. He was twelve, which just made it extra sad and tragic.

"Day of the funereal I grabbed the shovel and buried my brother. I got my good funeral clothes dirty, but I didn't care. Didn't wear any shoes either since my foot was still swollen from walking on a nail," said the man who would later entertain at Folsom Prison among other career highlights.

No wonder he spent his post-time walking through walls. Walls of grief, of the prison variety, and self-imposed ones thanks to his substance abuse issues, trapped him for most of his life until they didn't anymore, which was a relief.

"All my life, I was always determined to connect with my brother," he told us. "He was a guiding force for my entire life. Some people would ask, 'What would Jesus do?' I'd always ask, 'What would Jack do?'"

"Now, he doesn't have to ask," said a voice that came from behind the tall wall.

A twelve-year-old boy in jeans, whole in limbs and spirit, now stood before us.

"Hi, I'm Jack," he said. *The weird part of it was that he never grew up. He was still in boy form, which was his choice. Maybe he just didn't know any other way.* "JR and I are here to show you how to walk through walls because we grew up with very few of them in our house. It was a small house. Everybody on top of everybody. You couldn't escape our dad when he was angry. Man, we would have loved to walk right out of there into the world, but it wasn't possible then the way it is now."

"Are we going to stand here telling old stories?" demanded his older brother.

"Yeah, yeah, yeah, we're getting to it, bossy," he said, pointing to Bertha.

She raced for her first wall, bashed into it and fell backward onto a mat. Our Bertha wasn't much one for public exhibitions and I could see her poor demoralized face.

"Shit!" Bertha yelled, followed by a quick apology. "Sorry, kid, but I was not raised to be subtle."

"You have to *believe* it can happen. *Will* it to be true. Kick the shit out of any doubts," JR said with a grin. "Once you get some kind of control of your feelings then anything can happen."

"Which means?" Bertha said.

JR and Jack told us exactly what it meant when they explained the process in detail. In a nutshell, we needed to meditate before walking through walls, but not sit in a corner and say "om." We had to find a quick way to simply shut out the rest of the noise of the world, travel inward, and say our own personal mantra to calm ourselves. Once we were in that third-eye state, well, they promised us that anything was not only possible. It was probable.

"After you get into the proper state, focus on the task at hand. Imagine your foot through that wall. Do a future projection of how proud you are of yourself that it happened. How does the pride of true accomplishment feel?"

"Will you give us the mantras?" I asked.

Jack shook his head. "Nah, that's between you and you, Walker. I'd advise you not to tell anyone your mantra. Think of it as your existential password."

I could have easily thought of a million of them, but one kept sticking in my head. Daniel said it a long time ago. It meant to take big chances in the hope of great rewards.

Embrace the vole.

Embrace the vole.

Embrace the vole.

"When you're in the living realm as ghosts, you must think of yourself as smoke," JR said. "Smoke can travel anywhere. Stop. Meditate by closing your eyes or staring into the distance. Say your mantra. Then try whatever you want to accomplish."

"Believe—and do," he said. "Believe—and be."

8.

I was taking mental notes as Bertha approached the brick wall again.

"Why not?" she said, staring off into the distance. "Had a lot of those brick walls in my life." She walked in tiny, tight circles as she meditated. *Hey, whatever worked.*

A professor wandering through these parts—one who made my jaw drop—stopped by the watch. He was a famous writer named Jack K who wrote a lot about being on the road.

"I saw that my life was a vast, glowing, empty page," he told Bertha. "And I could do anything I wanted."

That was when she finally closed her eyes hard and the next thing I knew her shoe, leg, and pelvis were moving through the bricks as if they were made out of Jell-O.

This was a nifty element to put into our bag of tricks. We no longer needed keys or front doors. It would prove especially useful if we ever visited the past.

"How does it feel, sister?" JR asked.

"Sticky, like I'm walking through a red velvet cake," Bertha said, adding, "I'm not kidding. I don't sugarcoat. I'm not Willy Wonka."

"Do it a hundred more times until it feels smooth as running through silk," Jack insisted and he led the way by racing around the room and exploding through the walls.

JR pointed at Cass who went next and ran through that wall like he had been doing it forever. Daniel blasted through it, first with his fists and then his body. Auggie was the best walking-through-walls student. Even though he was a big guy, he could still do crazy gymnastics moves. His backflip through a wooden door, all the way to the other side, was a sight to behold. Our music-loving friend decided to do a triple and landed on his ass, but through hard concrete.

"I think I lost a butt cheek in transit," he joked.

I was up. A steel retaining wall. Of course, I would never get the easy wall like Iz did when he simply had to walk through a thin piece of plywood from a shed. Hell, Iz could probably have done that prior to this training with sheer brute force.

Fears not. Focus on. Go inside.

Embrace the vole.

My big toe went first and I saw that hard steel as nothing more than silver water. One hard push and the rest of me plowed right through in record time. It did feel a bit gooey and cold, but parts of it were like walking around a swimming pool—soft, slippery, and oh-so sleek. *Hey Ma, look at me now!*

It was on. We raced around that room, exploding through those walls one after another and sometimes in twos and threes. Daniel lifted me in his arms and we went so hard that we blasted the concrete stone to pieces that fell at our feet.

"Sorry about your wall," Daniel said.

JR looked at Jack.

"It's not him," I heard him whisper. "It's her."

"You got mad skills," the kid said, shaking his head. "Just beyond. You needed this education because along with your throwing powers, it's—"

"Nothing," I interrupted.

"Okay, Miss No Nothing," he said. "The longer you're here, you'll find that it's all connected. *Nothing* we are given is random, you know."

"No, I don't know," I said.

"But you will," he said.

9.

Next period: Communication with the Living.

If I was a dog, my ears would have perked up because finding *any* kind of way to speak with my mother again was one of my major post-life goals.

Our teachers began with a disclaimer: "We've been called ghost hunters. Paranormal researchers. Wackos," said Ed.

"But we prefer to be known simply as Ed and Lorraine," said his wife, who promised, "This class will be easy for those loving souls. If you're a hateful spirit, there's the door. We'll give it a minute for everyone to figure out their intentions."

A few students stood up and walked out.

I knew from my love of movies that these teachers were the real deal who solved many infamous, terrorizing haunting cases. Now the rub: in the afterlife, they were dedicated to instructing young spirits on how to conduct themselves in kind, gentle, and appropriate ways. Annabelle, eat your heart out.

My hand shot up. I only had about *five billion questions*, give or take one or two.

"Can you communicate via Ouija boards?" I asked.

"We were always warning the living NOT to use Ouija boards, not to go into séances, and not practice the occult," Ed said.

"Seventy-five percent of our most heinous cases came about through the use of the Ouija boards," said Lorraine. "We beg all of you not to listen to any calls of the Ouija, even if it seems like you're being asked to make a friendly visit. It never ends well for the living or the spirit."

"Visiting the living realm is something we will take slowly. It was forbidden at the Academy to think about it or try to make that visit because of the demons," Lorraine said. "It is still forbidden unless we give you permission as it remains fatally dangerous for Younglings because of those devils left behind, which many of you call demons. I call them devils because if the shoe fits. Maybe I should say *horns*.

"One day when you're older and the demons can't haunt you anymore, you will be able to visit the living realm like Casper the friendly you-know-what," she added. "You will even be able to try one of our favorite jokes on them."

"I'm game," Iz said. "My dad always loved a good practical joke."

"For instance," said Ed. "When one of the living talks to you, just look at them sort of shocked and whisper quietly, 'You can see me?'"

A chorus of laughter followed and he wasn't really that surprised. "Gets the Younglings every single time," he said to his wife.

"We call those who passed before age twenty-four—when your brain is fully formed— Younglings on this side," Lorraine said, reading me. I had the distinct feeling that you could keep absolutely nothing from her. "Nothing wrong with being young, of course. But you're a unique group given your age, which is why you're here with us. You can be molded."

If I wanted to ever make real contact with my mother, I knew I'd have to study what they were about to teach us. The journalist in me began taking copious notes and I vowed to do further research in the school's expansive library.

Lorraine didn't mince words.

"Sadly, we long to regularly visit the living realm and have a real conversation over a cup of coffee. We pine to communicate with our loved ones who are still alive. That isn't how it works—at least not now, although we hear that Albert Einstein was working on something major before his death. Something that would provide this kind of scenario. A game changer for the living and dead."

"Not that anyone in here knows something about that situation, now do they?" Ed asked.

The room was suspiciously silent.

"I didn't think so," Lorraine said, looking hard at me and then at Daniel who stared right back at her. I preferred the view of my toes because I wasn't born with a poker face. I had the Irish, blushing, confessing mug and arm hair that stuck straight up at the worst possible times— and there were only so many times you could blame central air-conditioning.

"The good news is that spirits can communicate with the living right now in our own limited ways if you focus on the five senses," Lorraine picked it up from there.

"We'll start with smell," said Ed. He pointed at Auggie. "Do you have a loved one who adored a particular scent . . . someone who is still alive and perhaps is still mourning you?"

"My mom, Carol," Auggie said and I saw a little tear drop. "This might sound weird, but every Thursday night before the marching band played at a football or basketball game on Friday night, it was a big deal for her to make her mother's spaghetti sauce. She didn't miss a Thursday."

"Excellent," said Lorraine.

"It had a lot of garlic and basil in it," Auggie said. "I can still smell it. I'd come home from school and the whole house smelled like an Italian restaurant."

"Close your eyes, Auggie," Ed said. "What did it smell like?"

"You know how garlic smells when it's frying in a hot skillet full of oil? And then she grew fresh basil in the yard, so it was really fresh and fragrant when she put it in the sauce," he began.

In the next moment, the impossible happened. The entire room began to smell like an Italian dinner including just a whiff of parmesan cheese on the top of freshly made pencil-point noodles covered in tangy tomato sauce. Our friend was like the Olive Garden of the afterlife.

I couldn't see it, but I sure could smell it.

"Very good, Auggie," Lorraine said, putting her hand on his wide shoulder and handing him a tissue. "Very good, son."

10.

Over the next week, everyone got their chance—whether they wanted it or not.

I shot my hand up. "My mother is alive and I think one of her favorite scents in the world was this banana bread that she would make with really ripe bananas and cinnamon. I don't know why, but I always associate it with home on a cold winter's night."

"It's the same as walking through walls," Lorraine said. "Go into your safe place, meditate, think of your mantra, and then actually force yourself to smell that smell. It will come through your very pores."

It didn't work. One time. Ten times. *Nothing.*

Discouraged, I was about to give up when Cass grabbed my hand. "She made me the banana bread once," he said. "When I was working for your mom while she rehabbed. Let's go together."

A breeze went through that room of cinnamon, bananas, and even the chocolate chips she threw in for a special occasion.

Daniel wasn't in that class, which was why Cass was crouched down in front of me, holding me tightly when I began to bawl.

Oh, God! Anything but this . . .

"Class break," said Lorraine.

"Sugar, it's okay," Cass said as he held me hard. Then he told me, "She told me after that one time of making it for me that she would never make it again because it was too painful. Imagine how she will feel if you make it for her—even just the scent."

"Oh, Cass," I said, burying my face in his neck for just a second.

I'd never forget how he smelled.

Like sweet sea air mixed with that sunbaked salt that clings to your skin after a day playing in the tall waves. Cass contained the scent of the ocean carried on the wind and on the wings of seagulls.

"You don't have to pull away," he said into my ear. "You have a permanent spot."

11.

"Another way to communicate is to make computer lights blink or a phone act up. Lights can turn on and off. These are all signals that a spirit has come to visit," said Ed. "You can do this two ways . . . either use your hand and physically mess with these things or you can will it in your mind.

"My favorite, which takes real concentration, is to lower the temperature in a room," he said. "I take great pride in not touching a single thermostat. Added plus: always catches their attention.

"By the way," he added, "we don't recommend hiding in closets or under beds. You don't want to give them a heart attack. There are other schools in other realms for those who prefer to live on the darker side."

We broke into small groups to practice. Lorraine came to check up on mine, which included Iz, Cass, and me. "Just calm down . . . think hard . . . believe so deeply that it simply manifests . . . and practice," she said. "If you can smell it, hear it, or feel it then they can, too."

Ed said, "Quick tip: I like to turn on radios and TV without any human attention. This is easy because you can just walk up to them and literally turn them on. Always a game changer if you do it a few times."

He brought a small radio over for us to try. I guess Bitty thought about it so hard that all of a sudden Springsteen was singing "Badlands" at ear-splitting volumes without having to touch any dial. Ed took her aside and removed the radio from the room.

"Now, try it," he instructed.

Bitty reached Radio Moscow.

My notes from that day:

*Recreating smells is a way to reach them. Even foul smells, which Eddie enjoyed. (The living are "them" now. Weird.)

*Radios and TV can be turned on without any touch. (We are the ultimate remote controls now. Also, weird.)

*You can touch the living person, thus lowering their body temperature, which in turn will give them the chills or goosies. (Mom would love this. She wouldn't have to pay the electric company or, as she said, "We are not alive to support Commonwealth Edison.")

*Focus. There is no such thing as over-thinking,

over-trusting, over-loving when it comes to trying to reach those in the living realm. But DO NOT try this at all until told to do so b/c of the frickin' demons. (Demons, the gift that kept giving and we learned today that demons evolve until you're twenty-four and then they move on. More on that later.)

*Trust Your Gut Always. Lorraine said: "In religion, we call it spirits. In science, we call it energy. In the streets, we call it vibes. Trust them. Always." (She was so badass!)

12.

"Field trip," our teacher suddenly called.

A few days later and we found ourselves in the middle of nowhere that looked a lot like a suburban Chicago train station although we were the only people here. There were railroad tracks, a small red train station building, and a crossing equipped with bells and those long arms that warn drivers not to cross the tracks when a train is approaching.

"Is this real?" Bitty whispered.

"No clue," I said. "It's physically here, but it feels odd because it feels like there is nothing around here for miles. Rail stations take people to other places where people congregate."

"Riddle me that one," Auggie said, but he was interrupted by the arrival of a large yellow school bus that pulled up from far away. Two teachers walked down the three tiny steps, which meant it was time to gather around.

Daniel, in a black leather jacket and blue jeans, pulled down mirrored Ray-Bans to take a second look.

"Real courage is knowing what is right to do and doing it," said our teacher Sally who in life worked as a civilian teacher. She was joined by a US congressman named John who knew exactly what it was like to be self-sacrificing because he was a freedom rider in his lifetime.

"If guardian angels do exist, mine was off having a beer," Daniel said, looking back on his life.

"Might be the first time ever that I agreed with you," Cass, in a white cabled sweater and black jeans, muttered.

"Don't get in the habit," said Daniel.

Our first exercise involved a school bus that materialized in front of our faces and was headed toward the train tracks in front of us. Some of my friends gasped, but not me.

"I'm from Chicago," I said. "You see this kind of stuff all the time."

Chris Flicker was behind me and whispered, "Look closely. There's little kids on that bus." And it was true because on my second glance, I could see that the bus was filled with elementary school children no older than eight or nine. Some were as young as five or six, and there was about twenty of them. My heart began to race.

This course: The Guardian Angel Gig.

I heard the distinct sound of a train in the near distance followed by the bells at the crossing issuing a warning sound before the arm came down.

"This school bus is experiencing mechanical difficulty," Sally called out as the bus began to cross the tracks. Halfway across, it stalled to a stop as the train approached.

"The conductor slams on the brakes, but it's too late," John yelled. "The train cannot stop. But . . ."

Sally walked forward, pushing Eddie and Flick to go with her.

The train was getting closer.

"We go to the crossing," Sally instructed. "We step onto the tracks and push the bus the rest of the way."

Amid the brakes of the train screaming as they tried to stop, I watched as Sally, Eddie, and Flick gave one mega push, which finally sent the bus completely over the tracks." The train blasted through the intersection, a blur of forward motion as it disappeared into the night.

"Everyone," Sally called out. "I want you to look."

In the dust and dirt on the bumper of the bus, I saw three sets of fresh fingerprints.

"We leave the prints. It's our calling card," Sally said. "Plus, it's good to freak them out a little."

13.

We practiced for several days and I relished hearing Sally's stories between our life-saving simulations including burning buildings, plane crashes, and other train adventures.

"Spending a few years post-high school doing the guardian angel gig before moving on is a very worthwhile endeavor," said John, who even showed us how to save others in need during big crowd events like school shootings and protests.

As a bonus for doing a good job all week, Sally drew a portal with her hand and a large circle formed midair. We walked through it right into America—San Antonio, Texas, circa 1930.

"A bus driver is taking a load of ten children home. Unfortunately, on this day, his bus is having some difficulty. It stalls out . . . right on these railroad track crossings.

"Before the driver can get the bus to move, a train approaches. The conductor hit the brakes, but it's too late and all ten kids and the driver perish in the crash when the engine explodes into a fireball.

"Come with me," Sally said as the bus approached. About a block from the tracks, it stopped and I watched her go to the back of the bus and sprinkle something on the back bumper. Then, she asked us to get in *the damn bus.*

I hesitated as did Daniel. "If you die in the past, you're never born in the future," I said.

"You won't die. Get in," she said.

Reluctantly, we did and took our seats as did Sally. *She wouldn't put herself in this kind of danger because she'll perish, too.* The bus chugged up to the track and stalled out. I heard the whistle of the train announcing a momentary arrival with a bus stuck where it would soon be crushed into oblivion.

We stood to jump out the windows, but then a funny thing happened.

The bus driver turned the engine off. And something was *physically pushing us hard from behind.*

I closed my eyes, but Sally just laughed.

"You can still go to this crossing near the San Juan Mission in San Antonio. If, by chance, your car or bus stops on the tracks, a mysterious force will still push the car or whatever off the tracks before tragedy strikes. Every. Single. Time."

I braced. Eddie cried. Daniel threw his body over mine.

And then I felt the gargantuan shove followed by an announcement made without a hint of panic.

"Come with me, kids," Sally said as we walked off the bus. Unharmed.

What she sprinkled was baby powder. On it was ten sets of small prints and one set of large ones.

Those belonged to the original bus driver.

Our little tour de force wasn't over. Not by a long shot. Our teacher pointed to a nearby playground where we stood in front of a very normal-looking setup of four swings.

She pointed at Iz and whispered something into his ear.

"I can't do it. I mean, I can't imagine," he began.

"Yes, you can," she said encouraging him to focus and see it with his "third eye."

I almost stopped breathing when the four swings simultaneously started swaying in alternating directions while Iz stood in front of them. His mind made them move.

"You never know what you can do," Iz marveled, "until you do it."

14.

When we got back to the dorms, there was security everywhere. "We're on lockdown," I was told by a stout man named Hal or Security #46. "Disrupters." And then into a device on his wrist, he barked, "Notify all students to stay in their room until we ring the dinner bell. And tell the other officers to bring firearms and flame throwers."

"What's happening?" Daniel asked.

"Do you have a room?" Hal asked and he nodded. "Then, you should be in it with a locked door and the Sword of Mercy that's taped under your mattress in your hands."

"You see a seven-foot, half-alien, half-human-looking thing with entirely translucent skin and long black claws for nails coming into your room, and you stab it in the heart or go for the eyes to stun it and then you go for the heart."

"A heart shot makes them explode?" I asked.

"Now, we're cooking," he said.

"A quick follow-up," I said in a frantic voice. "Why is it called the Sword of Mercy?"

"It's just a name," he said. "There is no mercy involved."

15.

"I'm sorry," Cass interrupted. "What is a Disruptor?"

He was asking a more intellectual-looking guard named Gil (Security #12) who stopped for a moment to explain some of the particulars—as if a mental picture wasn't enough.

"An extremely violent spirit who never rests. They come forth in pale moonlight in late afternoon to feed on other spirits. The only way to kill them is with—"

"A heart shot. We know," Daniel said. It was a wild guess, but if it worked on demons, it was probably good enough for these things.

"We don't really excel at fighting here," Gil said.

"But we do," Daniel shot out.

"They come in twos," said Gil.

"So, do we," Cass said, tapping Daniel on the shoulder.

"No bullshit," Daniel said, staring at him hard.

"No bullshit," Cass agreed, returning the laser gaze.

And to me, they both turned rabid.

"I swear to God," Daniel hissed.

"You stay *in* your dorm room," Cass demanded. "The definition of 'in' is behind a locked door. Do you hear me?"

"Callaghan?"

No answer.

"You and your friend should start in the basement," Gil said.

"He's not my friend," Cass griped.

"Let's go dipshit," Daniel said.

Daniel briefly stopped by the room and in his presence, I pretended to sit on the edge of the bed and look uninterested.

"Callaghan." He pointed at the dead bolt lock.

Yeah, right. Because the supernatural always respected a purposely locked door.

The door closed and I counted to one hundred backward, which didn't really work because I skipped half of it. It was only natural to stand up and even downright normal to check that dead bolt. It slid open quite easily. A quick peek outside of the door revealed neither man nor monster, which meant it was a perfectly good time to grab a sword from Daniel's pack and then take a slow walk through the hallways.

I never really promised.

Hand on my throwing stars and senses given a boost, this was the closet I felt to normal since we arrived. I loved Daniel and thought fondly of Cass, yet there was something about being "all in" as a party of one that made this fight primal.

Now, where were these things? I overheard one of the guards say they were translucent in skin although their internal organs were visible, as if their hearts, spines, and innards were floating in the air. The odds were stacked: two of them, one of me. Yet, my brain screamed that this was the kind of challenge that set my blood on fire.

I asked myself the following: If you were a disgusting-looking see-through monster hell-bent on a human food frenzy where would you hang out? Forget classrooms because it was too late in the day for class. Never mind school's cafeteria, which harbored a scent that hovered between burned grease and charred starch. You could call it eau du tater tots.

The dorm made perfect sense because there were so many Younglings, as they called us. To "them" aka the intruders—the dorms were fancy and plentiful eating. Human sushi. So much uncooked red meat, seasoned with fear and presalted with the sweat of worry.

We were student stew.

16.

A lone stretch of hallway on the fifth floor of the dorm provided only the stench of too many living in such close quarters. Security had already cut off the elevators, so I was forced to take the stairs with my back on the cinderblock wall and my eyes peeled for anything supernatural or beefy including Cass and Daniel who were going to kill me if the monsters didn't do the job first.

On floor eight, which was under construction and had no students living there, I stopped to take a deep breath and get my bearings.

That's when I saw it. There were four, bloodred, long scratch marks on the white wall.

Next came the site I would remember for the rest of my afterlife.

A nose poked through those scratch marks followed by three perfectly white teeth, wide-palmed hands, albino in color, sporting three ten-inch digits each, and long claws grabbed at the split and began to pull hard, prying the barrier away. There was only one reason why. *They were inside the walls.*

Until . . . they weren't.

Out of the plaster stepped seven-feet-plus, mostly females including breasts and privates that weren't covered at all. Their pelts were almost completely translucent and I was transfixed on their pumping hearts and thick rib cages.

Faces were marked by black orb eyes, two tentacles poking out on top, plus large folds of skin on the top of their hairless heads. I had never seen deeply into brain matter until this day and it fascinated me to watch the sparks of ideas travel along thin highways of thought and intention.

They communicated in high-pitched wails and obviously hunted by scent. Sparkling bits of afternoon dust traveled from where I was standing at the ready, throwing stars in both hands. But I couldn't move. Fear rendered me paralyzed; the incessant high decibel cries made my head feel like it would explode.

One zoomed, hurtling herself behind me while the other remained stationary and tilted her head in awe. They were rating their conquest, maybe even divvying up the parts as they slowly began a circle dance, inching closer and closer. And in that moment, I found a roar buried so deep inside I never knew it was there. It was the pain of a thousand hurts coagulating together into a battle cry that not only cleared my ears, but created space in my head and heart.

Still, I didn't move.

There was purpose to my pause.

It was to remind myself . . .

I was a supernova in a human body.

Super jacked.

The one in back was the obvious first choice, but I missed her heart as the star embedded in the bottom of her lung. Yellow goo erupted as the she projectile vomited while white-colored blood poured from her nose. This was not a lay down. She almost stood again, lifting her claws close enough to my face for me to nail her a second time under her armpit. Her scream: thunderous. Her claw: villainous as she removed a chunk of flesh from my upper arm.

My blood pooling on the white tiled floor was a scent that invigorated them. Webbed feet flying across the slippery tile, claws were raised and perfectly white jagged teeth were unveiled. I needed to wait until she was closer. I needed to see molars—and then I did.

I sunk two stars into her aortic valve. She exploded on sight, which isn't what startled me to the point I actually jumped.

The ding of the elevator.

Oh crap.

"Mother f—" Daniel said, sidestepping some nasty stains as he approached. He put the finishing touches on the wounded monster by plunging his long butcher's knife into her left ventricle. Cass had his six and rammed aliens with fast fists and cutlery.

The cavalry. Yep, that was them.

"Are you okay, Walker? You're bleeding, damn it!" Cass yelled. Then he looked at the monster carnage down below. I saw his neck bulge and wondered if he would hurl. That was a negative, but close.

Stomachs settled, the boys both turned on me, physically by looming large and verbally by expressing their displeasure at the fact that I didn't go into lockdown mode.

"I had to pee," I said.

"Three floors above our dorm room," Daniel demanded.

"Didn't we tell you to—"

"No one tells me," I shouted, racing upstairs to tend to my wound, which Daniel would later fix. It was almost a shame.

A cool claw mark beats a hot tat.

THIRTY

1.

One free afternoon after an intense Examining Past Lives class, I wandered between the stacks of the Astonishing School's expansive library and spied a table way in the back where Daniel, Cass, Iz, Flick and Bertha sat amid a pile of thick books and towers of papers and notes. We didn't have any written homework, so this could be filed under: hell freezing over.

Studious wasn't exactly the word I'd use to describe *any* of them although I couldn't be too sure about Flick who was still a major mystery to me.

"What are we doing?" a voice from behind whispered in my ear. It caused me to jump almost to the moon.

My BFF who didn't like to be left alone, ever, just gave me one of his puppy dog stares.

I pointed straight ahead, shocked that they hadn't seen us by now.

"I didn't think any of them except maybe Flick read books," Auggie said under his breath.

I had been through this routine before in the Midst. If Daniel was in the library, he was most likely researching something entirely illegal. I'd give Cass a pass because he was likely to be looking into ways to find his daughter, MC. Flick? Jury was out.

"Augs," I said, rubbing his arm, which immediately made him suspicious.

"You want something," he retorted. He was sweet, but he wasn't a fool.

I whispered into his ear exactly what I wanted and then handed him a small notebook and pencil. "In return, I want you to help me find clothes for the big school dance on Friday," he said because this was obviously going to be a quid pro quo situation.

"I'm your new stylist," I said because they did spy us. "Just remember. Write every word down."

2.

It was déjà vu . . . all over again.

Daniel knew enough to scoop some of his papers up, but he simply wasn't fast enough and some fell onto the floor and under the big wooden table. Auggie "helped" while crouching down and taking photos of every page with the camera on his phone. He took forever to retrieve the documents and also took copious notes.

Meanwhile, I did a slow reporter's scan of the table's surface making mental notes.

"San Francisco. Interesting," I said, looking down at the table. *He was obviously on the hunt to find the realm that hid his sister Jenna. I told him everything I found in Edward's office about his sisters.*

"And Cass, you're investigating . . . realm orphanages," I stated.

"Sugar, the politically correct way of stating it is Habitations for Awaiting Foundlings."

"Callaghan," Daniel began.

"Callaghan, what?" I challenged. "Oh right, 'Callaghan, I couldn't imagine doing this without you because we already proved that during one of these little vacays to Illinois."

"It's not safe," he said.

"It never is," I reminded him.

Plopping down, I grabbed his pen and a piece of paper and wrote, "Once upon a time, in an infuriating misunderstanding stood two lovers . . ."

"I'm not going to win," he sighed.

"I'll need a soy latte to go along with the paperwork you're about to put into my hands," I said with a big smile. "Cass, if you want my help, avocado toast would be lovely."

Both grunted; they were becoming . . . something. Not friends. Not enemies.

But, something else.

3.

Daniel was looking for two needles in a historical haystack.

He was studying how to find his beloved sisters that Edward stashed in past time periods probably in America, but we couldn't be so sure although clues were pointing to the city of San Francisco for Jenna.

Most people didn't just pick a random day to jump into a past loop (which required complex portal training). Most chose major events to visit not knowing how dangerous it would be . . . and how one could possibly never return to their current time period. Just try finding a portal to your time when in the middle of the Civil War or even experiencing free love at Woodstock. All of it should have sounded scary, but nothing made my personal freak flag fly as high as the idea of entering history as a true participant.

Oh yeah, one more thing. Change the past and it changed you.

4.

Knowledge was power, but the sum total of what we knew already about the girls is what I learned at Edward's Reid's house of horrors.

I searched his computer and found a yellowed, vintage photo that had been scanned into a file. It was pretty Jenna with her glossy, dark hair in an old-fashioned bun and her gray eyes tomato red from crying. He labeled it: San Francisco, the past. Occupation: child bride.

There was a stamp over her face that read: Sold.

"Thirteen and sold into marriage to whom?" I said under my breath. "It must be an arranged marriage in San Francisco when this sort of thing was commonplace."

Cass looked up. Impressed.

"Aunt Ginny made me watch PBS every Sunday," I said.

Edward had scanned in a handwritten note from Jenna, but it wasn't to him. She wrote it to someone unknown to me who went by the name Wister Reid.

It read:

"I, Jenna Reid, do not accept that the die has been cast. I am of sound mind. Of sound body. Of sound will. I will not be led to marriage. Not to that man. Not in this time period. Not in any lifetime."

She signed it . . . in Latin.

Flectere si nequeo superos, Acheronta movebo.

Translated: If I cannot bend the will of Heaven, I shall move Hell.

5.

I had memorized Jenna's student file from Principal Dick's office during my clandestine missions there. Inside there was a file photo of a beautiful girl with stick-straight dark princess hair and eyes too wise, and certainly a shade too haunted, for someone who had only lived a decade and change before her father killed her in an airplane crash.

Her file, which I read about a hundred times, contained basic facts like her height, weight, and straight-A grade point average. On the bottom, in a man's chicken scratch handwriting, someone with ice in his veins had scribbled numbers and a few words: 19067.8. There was also an odd clue: the words *ham and eggs*.

"Who is Wister Reid?" I asked Daniel.

"I wasn't even that sure myself, which is why I came to the library to look it up in what they call *The Book of Life*. Every single person to ever draw breath is listed in that book, which has been in existence since the beginning of man and womankind," Daniel said. "It has just about every family tree in the universe—and this particularly came in handy because Edward never talked about his family of origin except to say that his father also beat the shit out of him on a regular basis . . . like his father did to him."

I rubbed his hand, knowing he had suffered terribly his entire childhood from his father's belt and fist. The Reid children lived in a mansion, but it was a haunted life filled with fear and dread.

"Wister Reid was my great-grandfather," Daniel revealed. "We could go back further, but Wister started the American line of the Reid family after relocating from England where he was dirt poor. A few years later in America, he not only struck oil, but also became a shipping magnate. A real rags to riches story. The American dream."

"When," I said, my blood pumping hard. I hardly even remembered sitting down.

"He was at the height of his power around the early 1900s," Daniel said.

"And he lived in?" I didn't need him to answer.

"San Francisco."

"And what happened in San Francisco at the turn of the century?" I asked.

Flick grabbed both ends of the table and began to violently shake it.

"Earthquake," I whispered. "At 5:12 a.m. on Wednesday, April 18, a 7.8 magnitude hit the San Francisco Bay Area. Some three thousand people died that day from the quake and the fires that followed when the gas mains ruptured."

"One of the largest fires," I continued, "was accidentally started in a house on Hayes Street by a woman making breakfast for her family. This was known as the Ham and Eggs fire."

"It makes sense now," I chimed in. "19067.8 stands for 19067.8 was the magnitude of the quake. Ham and Eggs."

Daniel grabbed my hand.

"Oh, there's more," he said, revealing a piece of paper copied from *The Book of Life*, which also featured historical tidbits. It was a yellowed wedding invitation with curled edges and swatches of expensive lace on top and bottom.

It read:

Mister Wister Reid cordially invites you to the wedding of his beloved granddaughter Jenna Elizabeth Reid to

Lord Horace Redvers Arnault of the British House of Arnault, London, who will also be celebrating his glorious 56th birthday.

Wednesday, April 18, 1906

The Palace Hotel, Market Street, San Francisco

6.

It didn't take long to look up Lord Horace Redvers Arnault.

He was fifty-six and she was thirteen. The horror factor was in the red.

Much older British men married young and rich American debutantes because it was how "winning" was described in those days.

In a nutshell, he had a young bride for those cold nights in London when hot tea just didn't do the trick and a young woman from a rich American family who infused a boatload of crispy colonial cash back into poverty stricken, formerly rich lords and counts in England. Many of these men had lived it up for years and, sadly, funds had run dry. Castles were about to go into foreclosure. Young, foreign, English-speaking booty fixed the problem.

The American family received a British title for their social-climbing needs, which meant the formerly poor oil barons and business magnets weren't just "trashy new money" but respectable members of society with deep European ties.

Poor little Jenna would be expected to perform all wifely duties including hosting dinner parties and hosting her husband in bed when not giving birth to his late-in-life children. Someone had to inherit the castle.

This bit of wedded bliss, I figured, had a unique twist.

Jenna's father Edward knew that there would never be a ceremony because the entire bridal party at 5:12 in the morning on earthquake day would be staying at the location of the wedding: the Palace Hotel. Most people inside the hotel died due to a massive fire inside caused by the quake.

"Bastard," I sputtered.

Daniel was keeping his rage inside. He proved me right when he passed over the next sheet he had copied from a vintage newspaper. It detailed how the historic hotel collapsed when the ground began to shake. The remains of the brick-and-stone structure was immediately gutted by several blazing fires that erupted inside the ruins due to gas leaks. It would be rebuilt several years later, which didn't help the 256 "visitors" buried under rock and incinerated. Most of the bodies would never be identified.

The wedding was on a Wednesday. Edward planned it that way with his grandfather Wister, whom I assumed was another prized member that someone should have dumped out of the Reid family tree. He used the excuse of the groom's birthday as why one would have a midweek morning wedding. Not that the groom cared. He wasn't paying for the nuptials, plus the minute he said, "I do," he would be bringing gold, jewels, and cash back to England along with his child bride.

"We have Portal Drawing class next week," Daniel told me late that night in bed. "I'm going to study hard, figure out how to dial in an exact date, and go back to San Francisco a few days before the quake and find my sister," he said. "It shouldn't be that hard. Find her, sneak her out, return here.

"No," he said before I could ask. "Not in a million years."

"Well, you better find a million and one years," I retorted.

"Stop."

"I will have a complete dossier on the earthquake to you in the next twenty-four and *our* packs at the ready."

"Yes," he vowed, rolling over me because there was nothing else to say.

7.

At 3:00 a.m. we were wide awake, so we confronted an even wobblier topic, which was the whereabouts of his eleven-year-old sister Andy.

Edward left few clues on his computer about his youngest daughter's whereabouts. Poor Andy, alone and stuck somewhere where she didn't know anybody, I assumed.

Her location was listed as Colorado: the past.

"It could be pioneer days in Colorado or two days ago," I said. "We'll have to figure it out as we go and hit the library again. I don't know much about that state. Did your dad have any friends there?"

"He has no friends anywhere," Daniel said. Then he read my mind.

"One thing, baby. We tell no one about this—not even Iz and Bertha," he said. "The more people involved, it derails. We do this together, alone."

I lifted my pinky finger.

8.

There were plenty of diversions at the Astonishing School including the social activity of the season.

Bertha and Bitty were right on it, hustling me out of the dorm room and to a row of quaint stores just off the quad.

"We're gonna deck this one out, baby," Bertha promised. "I'll do your hair and Bitty will do your makeup. But first, we're going to find a dress so beautiful that the beautiful man in your life will drop dead, which he can't because already is. Bad joke. Let's go."

That Friday, in my dorm room, there was a knock on the door.

"Girls," Bitty said. "I have makeup, skin care, hair stuff, and a bag of Oreos for motivation."

"You are my kind of people," Bertha said, embracing her warmly. How quickly we went from two friends to three and how easy it was to slide into our future as a trio. The girls insisted on finding my dress, which would remain a surprise until now.

"No, absolutely not . . . no," I said staring at the silk, floor-length, black halter dress with the open back down to *there*. It was fitted on top, but billowed out on the bottom for a romantic flourish. "She gonna really hate this part," said Bertha, who pulled out "big gal" black high heels out from under the bed.

"This sends a message," I fretted.

"Yeah, it says, 'I'm here. I'm sexy. I'm flaunting it,'" Bitty said. "If this thing fit me, I'd wear it every single moment of my life including when I was cleaning my room and baking pies."

"You do that?" Bertha chimed in. "You bake pies?"

They looked so hopeful that I agreed to try it on. That's when the train left the station. Before I knew it, my lower back was getting a draft and so was my right leg thanks to a slit in the dress that went from ground zero to where I put my hands on my hips. A blink later and my hair was long, curled, and flowing . . . except for the ruby-red crystal butterfly clips that held a small section on each side. This guaranteed that long loops fell naturally in my face like I just ran across a field of spring flowers in a deodorant ad.

"Just a bit of makeup . . . she's better natural," Bitty insisted. "A little powder and cheek tint and perfume. We need sexy perfume. No one wants to smell natural at these things."

"Almost-sheer lip gloss to catch what I assume will be candlelight," Bertha said. "I would do a petal-pink shadow. And tasteful lashes. Classy hot lass next door. Not step-into-my-dorm-room-to-study-my-naked-body, although that's guaranteed for later."

"Hello," I said from the desk chair where they were making me over. "I'm right here, you guys."

A few minutes later and Bitty looked like she just gave birth.

"Our work is done," she cooed.

9.

I told Daniel I'd meet him outside by the lily pond at twilight and found him under a midsummer sky blazing purple and pink.

One glance and it dawned on me. I fell in love with his soul before I could even touch his skin.

Words clogged in my chest as I got closer—ones that I might never tell him. Ones that were locked away in my own personal treasure chest. Ones that said, "I'm so glad you exist."

The love of my life stood tall in a forest-green tux, black shirt, and black silk tie. On his feet were spit-shined black wingtips.

"Walker," said the man who rarely used my first name. Tonight, he was using it as an entire sentence.

I closed my eyes and he slid both hands across the sides of my face. Then he kissed me and it felt like stars were dancing across my lips.

His lips moved effortlessly down to my top lip, which he captured between his lips and then he devoured my entire mouth.

"Is this heaven?" he lifted long enough to inquire. So what if he borrowed a line from one of our favorite movies. There was always a twist.

I gasped, moaned, and even managed to speak.

"No, it's just some ghost high sc-sc-hool."

"No, I think it's heaven." He pressed his lips to my neck while his hand settled at the top of the dress's slit. My breathing became summer soft and a smile melted away from my face. A soul connection this strong was made for serious pondering.

Maybe it was . . . just maybe.

What was the question?

"Look," I stammered

Daniel's intense eyes gazed so deeply into my own that it wasn't the dress that made me feel naked. It was his stare.

But there was no choice but to do a fast head jerk because when you're standing by a calm lake and suddenly a black-and-white horse, along with a gleaming black buggy, emerges from the middle of the water, well, that falls somewhere between *holy shit* and a second glance.

I peeked again and . . . yes, it was still absolutely right there down to the unmistakable happy bray of this majestic creature.

I blinked a few times when the ghost of an old man in a tux and top hat put up his "wait a sec" finger as the horse shook off the water and the drops rolled off his own frame.

It was touching how he focused on the details and gingerly dried off our seats. He patted the horse's rump with great affection.

"Milkshake knows the way to the party," said our driver, and I didn't doubt it.

I breathed in that jasmine-scented air and let . . . it . . . all . . . go. This wasn't my natural state of being as I was a worrier, but damn it felt good to just exist.

Daniel stepped in first and hoisted me in the rest of the way like proper gentlemen did in the olden days.

I heard the wind through the trees and it held an easy tempo. The clomping of horse hooves served as drums and the evening birds sang soprano as he gently placed me sideways on his lap. I couldn't help but put my head on his shoulder.

You lean into love. And if you're very lucky, it leans back.

10.

The "wow" factor swept over me as we got closer and found ourselves on a white stone path lined on both sides by hundreds of tall pillar candles whose tear-shaped flames danced in the night breeze.

Young butlers in white tails and supper club tuxes, model-like men who were maybe nineteen or twenty, bowed grandly, offering a hand to help me out of the carriage. They waited until Daniel descended to open heavy double wooden doors.

The big reveal of an indoor wonderland left me breathless.

Spanish moss and greenery dipped down from a wooden ceiling that was highly glossed and lit by rows of crystal chandeliers that sent prisms of rainbow colors onto the dance floor below. Strings of small twinkling lights decorated all of the walls making it appear as if a black sky of real stars were lassoed and relocated indoors.

Richly hued flowers had been placed on tables with pure-white linen coverings—peonies, orchids, and garden roses in deep pink and vivid burgundy tones. They provided the pop next to the snowy-white tablecloths, centuries-old ivory china plates, and black crystal goblets that would serve later for a midnight "snack" of wild turkey, stuffing, cranberries, and the rest of a lavish meal in preparation for days.

Bertha, stunning in a floor-length beaded lilac gown, tapped me on the shoulder and whispered, "Damn, girl. It's like somebody stole a royal wedding and brought it here. I'm the black Princess Diana."

A quick glance and I saw Bitty, wearing her own deep pink princess gown with miles and miles of tulle. She was on the dance floor, moving slowly with one of the assistant teachers named Maren.

Over a spirited discussion of lip gloss earlier that evening, Bitty told Bertha and I that she considered herself nonbinary and then talked about a tiny crush she had on an assistant professor who read auras. Bitty was, of course, unique in that she had a rainbow aura—found in healers— and documented as shards of colorful light resembling a sunburst. It marked a highly evolved individual.

Iz was crooking a finger to have Bertha join him out there. Eddie was already stuffing his face with bite-sized "ho derves" as he called them. I had to force myself not to laugh because it was just so Wargo. He wasn't used to formal events, but I learned that evening that no one could rock a 1970s powder blue tux like Eddie.

"You look very handsome," I said, adjusting his blue-and-white plaid bowtie.

"More hos?" asked the waiter.

"I don't mind if I do," said Eddie while getting lippy with a few shrimp puffs.

Daniel was always touching me subtly. His hand was on my leg under the table. His arm was around my back when we were just standing there. He kissed me in front of everyone to see.

One of the faculty monitors even told us to cool it on the PDAs.

"Outlaw love since day one," Daniel murmured.

We spent the next hour talking and mingling with other friends but keeping each other in clear sight.

I didn't know much about relationships, but I figured the good ones had some kind of natural pull, where you're drawn in.

We return to each other in waves.

11.

The guest list was strictly A-list.

I didn't want to interrupt, but stood silently as a new physical education teacher whose daughter was also a student here was talking about his life philosophy. "You are responsible for how people remember you," said K. "So, leave everything on the court. Leave the game better than you found it. And when it comes time for you to leave a place, I hope you left a legend."

In another corner, I near lost it when a famous writer held court while several of all ages took his words to heart. "You can cast all the protective spells you want at this school," said the man who now went by E. Waldo. "I've always said the best lightning rod for your protection is your own spine."

"And what if your spine isn't at max strength—at least not yet?" I blurted out.

He spied me and took a step closer, so we could lock eyes. "Then, young lady," he stated. "Adopt the pace of nature. Her secret is patience."

Over a Sprite in the heaviest crystal glass I had ever held in my hand, I met Sophie, who was executed in 1943 for leading a student resistance against Hitler. She was maybe twenty or twenty-one then and now and had a wide smile that occupied half her face, gleaming brown hair swept to one side, and extra-long bangs falling into her eyes.

Her words made my heart race: "At the time of my death, I said, 'Such a fine sunny day, and I have to go, but what does my death matter, if through us thousands of people are awakened and stirred to action?'"

It made me want to go. Do. Fight.

My spine was strengthening.

We boogied to the song stylings of a man named Richard, an American musician, singer, and songwriter who was on the top of the pop charts for, oh, seven decades and counting. Some called him the Innovator or the Originator or the Architect of Rock and Roll. He didn't deny us that pounding backbeat or raspy shouted vocals when he launched into vintage dance hits like "Tutti Frutti" or "Long Tall Sally."

He was beloved by audiences of every race as he broke color lines and brought people together. Now, he was the most popular music teacher at the Astonishing School although his friends Buddy and Jerry Lee would argue that title for hours over burgers, fries, and shakes.

During a band break tonight, he grabbed the mic and explained, "Kids, I decided to come here and teach goodness, not music, although music is goodness. The truth is I really came here to teach love. Music is the universal love language."

"Amen," fan-girled Bertha.

To which Richard called out, "Live full, my friends. Live full."

12.

Cass had a way of making an entrance.

He was wearing a midnight blue tuxedo with a darker blue collar, navy bow tie, and white shirt. His dirty blond hair was combed back off his face, but long and untamed on the sides and back.

Our eyes locked. Daniel was temporarily gone. HH needed him to help secure a French door that had fallen off – or some non-emergency sounding emergency.

Fingers were looped into my hair for the second time that evening. "Your butterfly is falling out, sugar," he said, placing his other arm lightly around my bare back. It was an overly air-conditioned room, I reminded myself, and not tingles that raced down my back.

"I got it," I insisted, but Cass was a bit of a perfectionist. It took far too long to hear the butterfly pin click back in. His fingers stayed in place until he used them to cup my face.

"Dance?"

No, absolutely not, cannot.

"Sure."

The music swelled and it was one of those drippy love songs that played along every heartstring.

"Great song," Cass said as someone insane on the AV crew dimmed the lights to almost darkness.

The Waterboys were playing on my heartstrings with a vintage song called "The Whole of the Moon." *"I pictured a rainbow You held it in your hands. I had flashes. But, you saw the plan. I wandered out in the world for years. While you just stayed in your room. I saw the crescent. You saw the whole of the moon."*

I was always hopeless at the art of eye contact. My eyes betrayed me and met his in the center.

"Nice music they're playing tonight," I hedged.

"There's music?" he replied.

"Cass," I began. "Why are you so late?"

"Story of my life," he bit out.

He twirled me around, once and then twice, until I was dizzy. And until I rested too closely in his arms.

"You know what, sugar?" he said, dipping me low. "I'm late because I didn't want to see you tonight. Not looking like . . . perfection. I'm late because I'm selfish. I'm an impatient bastard. I was going to stay away from the dance tonight to avoid you. I was going to spend my time in the library, but there I was all alone just thinking about the taste of your mouth and how you felt that one night naked in my arms. And I don't want to wait for it to happen again."

"Please," I begged. "Cass."

"And then I thought, 'What if we never get back to the Midst? What if we never see tomorrow? What if I never say the things I want to say to you? What if someday I'm just the sum of a few particles of brain matter that torture me for all eternity by running lists of words I wished I had said to you?"

"Friends," I began, setting the record straight. "Good friends. The best."

"Fuck friends," he said.

"That's what you can't do," I said.

13.

"We shouldn't talk about this anymore," I begged.

"We shouldn't talk," he demanded.

Swiftly he spun me around as the room, which blazed with real stars due to a retractable roof on their ballroom. The night sky was alive with lightening streaks searing through endless blackness.

"No, we shouldn't talk. Because the words you speak become the story of your life," I said.

"Chapter one," he said, pulling me so close I felt his heart pounding. "I'm Cass and I wish I could hold your hand. I wish I could run my hand through your hair for hours. I wish I could press my lips against your naked back as the sun rises. You have no idea how much I want to just kiss your lips because I remember last autumn in the woods when you melted into me. They call it fall for a reason. You didn't think about consequences or repercussions. You didn't think about him. You only thought about us."

Oh, Cass.

"It will end that way," he said. "You plus me and MC."

"Stop saying it," I begged. "Like you know."

"I do know. Your heart already knows it. And someday, when you can admit it, I will pick you up and carry you home," he finished.

Fiercely, I shook my head. It was a lovely dream—his own, but he had the wrong girl.

"Walker, your door might be closed, but it's not locked. I feel it. You feel it. Know one thing. I will keep knocking. And when you finally open that door I'll be standing on the other side of it."

Cass took a step back, which threw me off balance and I swayed forward.

He caught me by placing strong fingers around my waist.

And when he took my hand to his mouth to kiss it, a tear fell.

His.

He was swift with his reaction, which was to gingerly place my arm at my side, turn his back to me, and stride away. Cass's body slammed the double doors and disappeared into the obscurity of the dark.

14.

I tried to follow Cass, but it was too late. I saw Daniel walking back toward the ball at exactly the worst possible time. He was in a great mood and put up a hand to wave hello to me. It was why he didn't see Cass emerge from nowhere and shove him hard from behind.

"WTF, man," Daniel yelled, wobbling forward.

A second was frozen in time. The particulars were accessed.

My mind screamed for them to walk away before it started, but the words clogged in my throat. And it was beyond too late.

Cass launched again, coldcocking Daniel in the face with the perfect hammer fist that left an ugly gash on his bottom lip and rattled his teeth, if he had any of those left.

Daniel bent at the waist this time, put his hand to his mouth and spit a spray of blood and enamel into the dirt.

"Son of a bitch!"

"Poor little misunderstood rich boy," Cass taunted, circling him, but he wasn't fast enough. Without ceremony, Daniel stood up straight in Cass's face, smiled, and spit blood in his eyes. It was the last thing he expected, which gave Daniel the edge to drag Cass's right arm forward and then upward, jamming it hard into his armpit.

My stomach lurched as Cass's arm hung by what seemed like a string. The limb was still in play. Daniel grabbed that same arm again in both hands like he was lifting a log. The snap that followed was loud and garish, and I knew it was broken.

Undaunted, Daniel grabbed the jellylike flesh and cracked it again, satisfied only when the second blunt snap was louder and even more garish.

Cass should have howled in pain, but the reset took care of it, setting the bones and fixing the dislocation until it was like nothing had ever happened. He was fast and lethal. A lefty, Cass used his dominant fist to land body punches that sounded like a semitruck just bashed into Daniel's middle. I imagined blood vessels bursting.

Fearless, Daniel gagged as he reached for shallow breaths. He righted himself just in time to avoid the knee that almost hit his nose. The fire of his rage turned those gray eyes into glistening ash.

"Is that all you got?" Daniel growled.

They circled again and again. Legs breaking and fixing. Ribs cracking and repairing. Wild responses included skull cracking that should have knocked either out, but they only staggered back and waited until the reset made them whole again.

In a daze I tried to run to them, but it was futile. Chris Flicker, in a steel-gray tux, white shirt, and black tie was right behind me, reigning me in, stopping me.

"Let them," he said. "This was inevitable."

"Flick!" I yelled.

"I'm a pacifist," he offered, refusing to let me go.

"You're a lunatic," I offered, twisting hard to no avail.

"That, too," he said with a smile.

481

15.

It was primal.

They dropped to the ground, pummeling and punching. They were bloody and their fine clothes were covered in grass and mud. Mouths were twisted in hate. "Where were we? Oh yeah, the rich boy with the abusive father, the one who used to knock him around. Didn't see you save the kids from him. Don't see you saving her. People end up dead and gone around you, trust fund. You're a walking death wish," Cass taunted.

Daniel wasn't above taking his best shot.

"Not that anyone dares mention the Cass body count. We'll start with your dead girlfriend and your dead kid and your dead mother—shit, I just mentioned it—and we haven't even gotten to the part about your psycho bitch sisters, also dead," Daniel shouted back, sinking another fist into Cass's jugular.

The former marine returned the favor with a vicious knee to Daniel's chin. I winced as his head snapped back and felt queasy when Daniel planted the very tip of his elbow into Cass's now-bleeding-and-hanging-off-his-scalp right ear.

A blink. Reset. And they were ready to go again.

"Just a matter of time before you get Walker extinguished – an inevitable conclusion," Cass said in an even voice as he tossed his tattered and ripped suit jacket to the ground. "You've tried so many times already. The motorcycle rides. The jumps off cliffs. You got her a maximum-security prison stint at ITT and then probably a one-way ticket here, if we're not kidding ourselves."

"Better than boring her to death," Daniel taunted. "Isn't that what you did last fall when I was gone? You couldn't close. Must be cold at night in a land called Just Friends."

"I should have let you bleed out in the cabin. I will regret it until the end of my days. I could have cut you open and nicked just the right spot. You would have been history," Cass snarled.

"A few tears and a short mourning period—and then you would just be another memory like her life, like her mother and father, like everything she has ever known. She's good at putting those memories away in order to exist. As the years passed, she would forget you. She would barely remember what you looked like . . . what you sounded like . . . how you moved . . . what you said, which I'm sure is forgettable," Cass fumed. "You would just be a fading dot on the horizon. What's his name? Remember him? But we don't. And you want to know why?"

"Enlighten me," Daniel growled.

"Because you're not her story. You're just a footnote to remember on a hot summer night after I piss her off. She will storm out of our lovely, loving home because she needs space. And maybe she will remember you. But then I'll be there in the flesh. Between the I'm sorries, the flowers, and the lovemaking, she'll put you back in the photo album of time and slam the cover shut."

"We'll have to add novelist to your eclectic list of non-talents," Daniel bit out. "Marine. Psychic. General pain in the ass. Novelist. But you know what you really are, Cass?"

"This should be good," Cass snapped.

"You're a stalker. Someone stalking a girl through space and time—a girl who doesn't want you. She didn't want you alive. She certainly doesn't want you dead. That makes you one thing."

He waited a second.

"Pathetic," he said.

This time Daniel ducked when Cass came for his jugular.

"Poor Cass, the waiting prince. Always on the bench. Always coveting. You sure that was really your kid that your girlfriend had back in high school? Because I can't imagine you, King Virgin, seducing more than your right hand."

Cass let out a primal yell, put his head down, and advanced, but Daniel was a far dirtier fighter. He picked up a garden rake and jammed it in Cass's midsection. The favor was returned when Cass found large shears also left behind by a landscaper and stabbed Daniel in the leg.

The reset was strong and neither was worse for wear.

"You want to re-live the glory years? The worst mistake I ever made was not saving you from your lunatic sister on that rooftop in New York

City," Daniel said with a freezing calm. "I should have made sure you lived. I should have healed your sorry ass. And every single damn time you were about to die for the next eighty years, I should have shown up like your guardian freaking angel. Just to make sure you lived until a hundred—and you weren't on this side. Her side," Daniel bellowed.

By now, students began to pour out of the double doors and quickly took sides.

"Fight! Fight!" they screamed. Finally, I broke free from Flick and began screaming at both of them as they rolled on the lawn and eventually plunged into the lake. Cass pushed Daniel's head under, but not for long. Daniel twisted and had Cass in a headlock while he pushed his face into the thick mud.

"May hell rise up to meet you," Daniel taunted.

In the end, it was HH himself who was faster. He fetched them out, one at a time, and then shoved them both in again until both were covered in muck and seaweed.

"This is moon water, specifically under a waning moon. The water helps with releasing, letting go, and banishing," HH said.

He shook his head in disgust.

THIRTY-ONE

1.

I left them both in the water to cool off and attempted to walk back alone to the dorms. Geographically challenged, I took a major wrong turn because all the stone paths looked identically alike and a tree was a tree was a tree.

There was a light burning inside from what looked like a small barn. It was perfect. I would go inside, pet a horse, and figure out how to explain to Daniel that Cass was just a friend who wanted him gone. Or maybe I'd tell Cass later on how he was a very, very, very good friend with no benefits ever although he had a ripe fantasy life that this might change for some reason that made no sense to me.

He was psychic. Not a fortune-teller.

Horses made perfect sense, thank you, because they were knowing creatures. Only this barn was devoid of any animals. It looked like some kind of high-tech center with a slick, dark floor, long tables, and rows of computers. In the middle was a large silver stage.

Just as I was leaving, a man stepped out of a side room, glanced at

485

me, and said, "Are you my midnight ride? If so, I'm Luke."

Yes. He was.

Is.

"Go stand on the stage. All I need to confirm is where and when— and your name," he said. "You'll have ten minutes, Cara. Buckle in. Fly safe. Is that what you're wearing? It's sort of formal, but whatever floats your orb."

"Ye-yes," I said. "I have my own style. I'm not a Brenda or a Kelly." *Where was I going with this runaway mental train?* "I bet you get that a lot."

He just grinned.

"No, never," he joked. "I was on this show. We had a prom episode. I went with Brenda or was it Kelly? But, we digress. How much do you know about flying an orb?"

"Everything," I fibbed.

2.

"I was expecting you, Cora," he said, handing me something to sign. In life or death, there was always freaking paperwork.

"Cara," I corrected him, playing along. *Nice way to make sure.*

He was maybe nineteen in jeans, a white T-shirt, and a cool, black leather jacket. He looked like James Dean's younger brother with the slicked-back hair. Sounded like him, too. Luke had that way of making his voice and breath mix.

"Where do you want to orb to tonight? St. Louis to go visit your brother? Is this the right address? 1820 Appleton Court?"

"Yeah," I said, followed by, "No. There has actually been a change of plans."

"You are Cara Qualley, aren't you?"

"Of course," I lied. "Do you want to see some ID?"

Please don't ask for ID.

I patted the sides of my dress. "Sorry, hard to fit ID into a girlie dress," I said.

"Are you visiting an old boyfriend?" he asked.

Visiting. Who would I be visiting? Who would I want to pay a call on? And where? When? Why?

"My mother. And she has moved. To Illinois," I said.

"That's really sweet," he said. "I got a lump in my throat—for real, Cora."

"Cara."

"Could I also change the address because she has moved. I'd like go to Wheeling, Illinois—one of the Chicago suburbs," I lied.

"Whatever you want, Cara. That's what we tell all the quantum physics grad students."

"I've been looking forward to this for a long, long time, Luke."

"Yeah, that's what you all say," he said. "A quick warning: until you finish Advanced Orbing 501 and can control and create your own orbs, we'll be using the rudimentary orbs to get you used to the actual travel part."

I had absolutely no freaking idea what the hell he was talking about. But if I could go visit my mother, I'd ride a dragon out of hell.

He motioned for me to stand on a small stage in the middle of the room. On shaking legs, I climbed ten stairs and stood stone in the middle.

"Don't stand in the middle," he said. "It has to come down. You're blocking."

Story of my life. Always in the middle of something. Where I didn't belong.

Quickly, I moved to the edges, which is when Luke pulled a silver lever on one of his panels. What "came down" looked like a large, clear bubble—like the kind you would blow from plastic rings from soapy water.

When I looked closer, I saw there was a translucent bench inside and two seatbelt-like devices, which were nearly invisible.

"The Ford Intergalactic Orb," Luke said in a triumphant voice like he was introducing me to the first airplane.

"It will sense your aura when you approach it. In fact, it refuses to open for certain types with dark auras. No need to inflict that on the living. They have enough problems," Luke said.

I stood there paralyzed, hoping that a translucent egg would find my aura A-OK.

Suddenly I felt like that kid on the playground praying, "Pick me."

"You have a white aura, very nice. Rare," he said, looking down at his computer, which was triangular in shape. "Very pure. Open to heightened stages of consciousness, wisdom, and intuition. Ready to ascend.

"In fact, you've been preparing for it," he said. "You're also a new soul, unschooled when it comes to the cycles of life, typically on your first lifetime."

I was fascinated, especially when the bubble cracked wide open in the middle.

"Tell me," I stammered, shocked that I was a chosen one.

"Negative energy can easily be diminished by your presence alone. You love deeply and you want to bring positive change to the world that you're in—and the ones you have departed."

I had to stop him before anyone came looking for me.

"What do I do with this machine?" I blurted.

"An orb is a ticket to the living realm," he said. "Spirits use them all the time as ghost transportation between realms. Think of this orb as your wheels, but it doesn't roll. It flies through realms, pierces the line between life and death."

"A-and what happens when these orbs arrive in the living realm?"

"They're mostly invisible to the living eye although once in a while the living swear they are 'seeing' something supernatural—and they are one-hundred percent correct," Luke said. "If you look really hard at night only, and especially over a body of water like a lake or the ocean, you might see a sky full of them—these almost translucent bubbles or little white circles in the night sky—floating in the air. Or perhaps you'll capture some in a picture although people will tell you it's just a malfunction with your camera.

"We like to wait until you spirits are older to authorize this kind of travel," Luke said. "But we do teach it to select students at this school, so they can prepare for future visits."

I nodded, mind blown.

"Get in," Luke said, *like this was a done deal.* "Here's the rules, kid. You will be invisible. The living can't hear you or see you. Also, this visit isn't against the law in any of these realms because it is sanctioned by this school and you're under our rules now, which include exploration of anything we choose to explore."

I hadn't even thought of the ramifications. The first time we went back, Daniel and I landed at a prison school called ITT. Luke should have added "rushes blindly into situations" to my white aura traits.

"You have six to seven minutes at your destination. Don't mess with fate and take longer," he said. "The travel there will take a minute; the travel back here a minute. In total, you will be gone nine minutes. Not a minute longer."

"Got it," I said, looking at my blank wrist. A watch didn't exactly go with my formal wear. Luke shook his head, took off his watch, and strapped it on my wrist after setting nine minutes on the digital clock.

"Don't mess with me on time," he said.

I shook my head.

"Remember to use what you learned as an undergrad when it comes to reaching the living—manipulate temperature, play with lights, etc."

"Why only seven minutes with the living?"

"You know why, Cora, because it was covered in class," he scolded. "Anything more and the demons will sense that you are there and arrive to attack." Pause. "I assume you have a knife or two in your pockets? You are weaponless. Do I need to do the math for you?"

I had one throwing star in my purse. It wasn't enough to fight an army of winged devils, hell-bent on eradicating a young person's soul.

"Personally, I prefer motorcycle travel," Luke said, strapping me in. "But this will do."

Gingerly, I stepped in with one foot and then the other. The translucent seat was shockingly comfortable and rose to meet me. A see-through seatbelt wrapped around my middle.

"Hit this button when you want to release the belt. No bumper car crashing with other orbs, which means do not lean hard in any direction.

Just sit up straight. You don't drive. You just hit go and stop. I'll be sending you back and forth, plus I'll drive. I can see everything you see on, but on my computer screen.

"You're not allowed to operate the vehicle on your own until you take orb driver's ed here," he reminded me.

"Loved that class," I lied.

The rules were never ending.

"When you park the orb, try not to put it in a public place. Remember, the living can't see it. But they feel like something is off, so don't torture them. We like our living sane—or as sane as possible."

I nodded like a bobblehead toy.

"What will happen?" I asked him in a breathless rush.

"Well, Cora, it's a waning moon. Anything can happen. So, enjoy your ride."

I watched as he climbed off the stairs. The list of people who would be upset with me for doing this was miles long—and at the same time I couldn't wait until I jettisoned back to where I started.

3.

Luke counted it down. It was my last chance to step out of the bubble and return to my senses. In that moment, I heard my father's voice. "Babe," he would say, "never take a step backward. Not even to gain momentum. Fall forward. You get a little bit closer to your destination."

"Three, two . . ." I never heard the "one."

I was in full speed rush, carving through the heavens, sailing through the darkest black and severing time and space. My orb then began to float with the bright stars that had their own special choreography as they shot through the pea soup summer fog over Lake Michigan.

Welcome to Chicago, 2021, present time.

4.

I parked at the end of Dover Lane, a charming suburban street in a blue-collar town called Wheeling, Illinois. The perfect place for the orb was at the end of a circular cul-de-sac in the driveway of a dark house that was for sale and looked hauntingly uninhabited.

It was easy to pop the top of the orb, but awkward to climb out. A few uncomfortable seconds later, I practically fell out of the thing and was able to take those first few wobbly steps on living earth.

Ditching the high heels and barefoot now, I walked down the middle of a street, which was out of habit. My mother always told me to do that at night. "Walk down the middle of the road, Walker," she said. "That way, you can run in either direction."

I had a PhD in urban living while I was alive—I was poor, hungry, and extremely driven. My father died of cancer when I was a little girl and mom and I lived a life of evictions and moving from one low-income house to another. After my death that changed for her in a major way. She sued the trucking company involved in our crash and there was insurance money. Basically, they paid her off for killing me and for causing her spinal cord injuries that were long since healed.

It was more than enough to buy that charming dream house at 610 Dover Lane, a lovely white bungalow that made my eyes tear up. It was a "first," the only house owned only by my mother. The rub was that I would never live in it with her.

Because. Of course. Life indeed does go on.

5.

The dead daughter didn't have a key to the house. She didn't have time to fuss with locked doors either. I had exactly six minutes left.

Shutting out the noise of the world, I closed my eyes, calmed myself, and imagined my foot moving through the solid object, which was the cherry-red wood front door.

Embrace the vole! Embrace the vole!

I imagined my feet on the other side, manifesting it, which apparently worked because I was standing in my mother's hallway. A lone light burned in the kitchen.

Just when I thought a trip upstairs would be necessary, I saw the flicker of a candle on the back porch and as I moved closer, the outline of a figure sitting in one of those big white rockers became clearer. I touched a glass of wine on a small table and fingered the baby monitor, slowly turning the volume to zero.

She looked lovely in a summer skirt in light blue and a matching tank top with her white sweater draped over her shoulders to ward off a tiny night chill. Her hair was pinned back in a ponytail. Her sparkling hazel eyes were bare, except they were covered by new brown glasses. *My mother wore glasses now. Even minor changes were like stab wounds.*

I cupped her face in my hands. She felt so warm, and when I pulled my hands back, she put her own in the exact spot because she felt something unknown. In my desperation to be known, I waved my hands in her face. *Nothing.* When I did it again, an acorn fell right off a tree and landed by her feet.

"How odd," my mother said.

Five minutes.

There was another small chair not yet painted out there. It must have been a new treasure and the seat was missing a few long pieces of wicker, which made it look sparse and ready to be junked. I sat down in it and crossed my legs tastefully. It was what my mother would have wanted me to do in such a grown-up dress.

She couldn't see or hear me, which made me want to scream. But then the teachings in Communication with the Living began to flood my mind. It was my job and mine alone to make my presence known.

Four minutes.

I went deeply inside, focused, and then blinked hard through what many call the proverbial third eye.

And then I focused on a few "calling cards."

The flame from the candle went out at the same time the temperature in her screened-off garden room dropped twenty degrees. (Steven Spielberg time!) I blinked again and again until the overhead fan turned on by itself (nifty) and the tiny lamp in corner began to flicker (classic).

Okay, maybe I overdid it.

I didn't dare touch her face again: I did slip my hand into her soft, left palm.

"Walker," she whispered.

Three minutes.

6.

I brought my hand forward to touch the icy-cold glass of lemonade she had on the table. It felt frosty cool. I took my wet fingers, reached forward, and lightly ran them up her right arm. The fact that she now had the chills caught her attention again. There was one more thing on that table: a black mask.

"Oh my," Mom said to herself on her second shiver. "I hope it's not the chills."

I watched the tears run down my mother's sweet face and placed my hand over her hand.

"Walker, are you out there?" she said to the night sky. "Where are you, my girl?"

"Mom," I said to deaf ears. "I'm right here."

I gazed at her phone, which was dark. She had the song programmed in as her number one and sang it to me when I was sick or afraid. I clicked the "on" button without touching it.

"I've got sunshine on a cloudy day . . . ," it began. "What can make me feel that way? My girl . . ."

7.

Two minutes.

There was no time to see the rest of the house including the nursery where the Claires as babies dwelled. The she-devils were adopted from a local orphanage by my loving mother. These girls died at age seventeen, only to be reborn to a new family. They always killed their last mother before their demise.

Never again. Not on my watch.

I turned up the baby monitor although it would have been easier to let them rot up there. They sensed my presence. *Boy, did they know.*

"Get out of here, you bitch," whispered V in a little girl's voice.

"Or you can come up here," C taunted. "We've been waiting for you, sweet sister."

Before my mother could readjust the frequency or run away to check on them, I gave that monitor a hard kick off a wrought-iron table. So sad that it hit the ground hard and the batteries fell out. *Goodnight, girls! Go piss yourselves!*

I kissed my mother on the right cheek and pressed my face into her folded hands.

"Not good-bye, Mom," I said, lighting the candle again with my mind. "Just so long. I'll be just above you. Walking in the clouds."

8.

Furiously, I darted out through the house, past my favorite old plaid living room couch and plowed through the wall of the living room until I was splayed on the front lawn with my bare feet in wet grass.

Wiping out in my long dress wasn't the plan—and neither was finding a hand behind me that lifted me to my feet in the middle of my mother's front yard.

"You look good enough to kill tonight," said Tor, laughing as he grabbed my other shoulder so I couldn't move.

The only option was to tilt my head slightly upward to the upstairs bedroom window.

Four little girls, about four years old, had their hands raised in victory as they silently jumped up and down. One cracked the window open.

"Kill her," V cried.

"Kill her! Kill her! Kill her!" they began to chant.

One minute.

9.

Tor, in a white suit, black shirt, and dark dress shoes twisted his albino face sideways, so I was forced to look at the profile of his platinum blond hair and pointed chin. Slowly, he rotated forward, pointing his steel-blue eyes in my direction.

He specialized in probability manipulation. It was the power to alternate the perception of things. One look into his eyes and he had you on lock. And then the real fun began.

"Reality-warping piece of shit," I bit out, my eyes downcast on my feet.

One glance and he had you. It was no wonder that his real name was Distortion. He would distort current events just enough to force your hand, alter your reality, and make sure your decisions were the worst ones possible.

"I thought I'd shot you—and that you'd bleed out," Tor said.

"I hoped that I strangled you in New York," I replied.

"No such luck," he said.

"Disappointed," I countered. I kept my eyes low, which is when I heard it, a loud whoosh under my feet. It was as natural to these suburbs as breathing. First, the wheezing of air and then water rushing through underground pipes.

Turns out a girl's best friend is a solid underground sprinkler system. This one was powerful and the shock of freezing cold water threw Tor off his game. One hard push and Tor was on his ass. It was enough for me to twist away and soon I was running at Olympian speed down the street.

I heard his feet pounding behind me.

My orb gleamed in the distance and then I was upon it. The only thing: it was occupied.

And one more thing:

Time was up.

10.

Inside, they sat. Four little demon girls in footie pajamas who wanted to go for a ride.

Who the hell were they kidding? They weren't babies. C's face looked like she was six going on twenty-six. V looked about as innocent as a mountain lion with a sheep in her mouth. They were over a hundred years old—maybe a million—if you counted it in *bish* years.

Bish years were faster years. Why were they aging so rapidly here? To my mother, they were infants. I wondered how they learned to age themselves both physically and mentally.

They were too old for the little pigtails they wore; they were too evil to claim any shred of childhood innocence.

And they were too dangerous to claim my mother as their own.

11.

Tor didn't have to run any longer. He walked up to me. Towered over me.

He didn't have a gun tonight, but I watched as his gaze was directed upward, which was strange. This was the moment where he usually forced eye contact with his victim.

Instead, he reached long arms backward to the chain link fence separating properties and viciously poked a black crow relaxing on his evening resting spot. He did this with his bare hands. Startled, the animal took to flight, but was still low enough on takeoff for Tor to reach out and grab it from the sky. What happened next, I would never forget. He reeled the bird in and bit the head off, chewing vigorously, and then swallowed it. Casually, he chewed on the body and even ate several feathers.

Tor did this while backing up. One step, two steps, three . . .

A blink later and Tor was gone. All that was left by my feet were three black feathers.

The girls had enough of the show. They were standing on the lawn now in a line, forcing me to back up once and then twice. A few steps back and we were getting farther from the orb. I heard the roar of a car as I stepped back onto the asphalt and watched as a sleep, black vehicle, a Mustang Cobra, came barreling down the blacktop.

Hurling left, I had to jump out of the way. The Claires went left: I went right At least, I rolled in the most desirable direction.

Even the girls weren't fast enough to stop me as I pushed forward, raced to the orb and jumped inside.

The Mustang parked half an inch from the orb. I hit "GO," but Luke wasn't responding.

I hit GO ten more frantic times.

The door to the Mustang slowly opened.

It wasn't a guy in the driver's seat. It was me in a distorted demon form of myself, face hideously wide and bloodied accompanied by another deviation where my teeth took up half of my cheeks. They didn't put the car in park, but jumped out as it rolled, walking on spindly legs toward the orb.

I had overstayed my welcome.

"GO, damn it!" I screamed.

12.

Luke's voice filled the small bubble.

"Three, two . . ." He never said the "one."

Liftoff with the push of just one button. The return destination had already been programmed in.

I could breathe . . . until I saw it.

An onyx bird of black shadowed me almost the rest of the way along with two massive winged demons with crimson feathers who pecked at the orb's outer glass layer. *Tap-tap-tap.* Tiny shatter lines formed, but it was indestructible. *Tap-tap-tap.*

What a great trip "home."

Wheeling: the Village with Feeling.

Epicenter of the supernatural world.

13.

By the time I returned, Luke was beside himself.

"It was nine minutes, Cora. I said six or seven. You flunk, but you could have been extinguished!" he fumed. "That's worse than getting an F."

"Sorry, but I walked through a wall, lowered the temp, and extinguished a flame. I might have even seen a guy turn himself into a bird," I said. "All in all, I think I at least deserve a C."

"C minus," Luke said. "Tell me more while I walk you back to your dorm."

THIRTY-TWO

1.

Daniel didn't need to know about my quick "road" trip in an orb. He had enough on his mind with his missing sisters and his altercation with Cass. I didn't think he needed another reason to worry and it wasn't exactly lying. I'd tell him . . . eventually.

I did tell Bertha, who swore the oath of sisterhood silence. "Walk-*her*, you gonna get your ass in a sling one of these days," she said, rolling her eyes. "My only worry here is I'd need two orbs after all the eating we did tonight!"

Daniel didn't return to the room until three in the morning and quickly stripped down to nothing to spoon me in bed.

"I'm sorry," I whispered. "I only have friendly feelings toward him."

"Callaghan," he whispered back, "you are my favorite feeling."

He kissed me silent. He kissed me stupid. And then we drifted for a few hours.

2.

In the morning, we took a quick class in psychometry taught by Lorraine who quickly schooled us in the art of things and what it meant when human flesh/soul touched objects. It was alarming to say the least.

"I always told the living to never—and I repeat never—buy antiques of any kind," Lorraine said, shaking her head. "Spirits attach to things and they can live in them for centuries. Antique rings? No thank you unless you want to original owner hovering by your bed at night. Old wooden boxes? You don't know who or what lives in them. Ancient dolls?"

"I saw that movie," Eddie piped up.

"Others saw the actual doll—and they're dead now," Lorraine said.

"Damn," Eddie replied. "I thought that doll was kind of hot."

"He doesn't get out much," I warned the class.

Lorraine wasn't done with her warnings. "This brings me to the special gift of psychometry, which certain special individuals possess," she said. "This is the ability to read the history of an object by simply touching it."

She nodded to her husband who brought a big white bag to the center of the room.

"One by one, you will come up to me and I'll hand you an antique that has been specially curated from various settlements in The Other and the Midst. Feel the energy locked within the object. Each time we touch anything, it absorbs a portion of our own energy and sometimes those vibes are stored for decades or longer.

"Hold it within your hands," she told Daniel after handing him a small tin cup.

He shrugged after a few minutes. "I'm out," he told her.

Lorraine smiled and handed me a wooden box. "A letter box," she said. "Where someone keeps correspondences. Filched or taken from someone on this side. I thought it might interest you, dear.

"Hold it, Walker," she implored. "Impressions might appear or perceived imagines. Hear the sounds of the box, taste the smells, hold the emotions close to your heart." And then she whispered the last part in my ear. "Do this, if you have the magic to turn dreams into reality, dear," she said, adding in an even lower voice. "It *is* your dream to find the sisters, isn't it?"

I took the box to a quiet spot in the corner of the room, free of noises. As usual, I went into a light meditation to free my mind.

Back in the front of the room, Lorraine told the class, "For some, holding any object will tell you the history behind said object and the person who owned or owns it . . . and the experiences that person has had while the object was in their possession.

"You will be able to sense what that person is like . . . how they lived . . . what they did with their time . . . experiences the person had while the object was his or hers . . . how they passed if they did," Lorraine continued. "See or feel it in that psychic way of seeing something that is not visible to the ordinary eye.

"Remember energy is stored in everything . . . living or not," she repeated.

I closed my eyes and clutched the box. Nothing happened—so much for my so-called superpowers. I was still a news reporter, which meant I did the most unpsychic, nonmagical thing possible as my next move. I opened the freaking box.

My hand began to tremble because inside were the initials EXR. Inside was a yellowed picture of a large gray house on the top of what looked like a hill. It was dated 1904.

My arm began to shake, which was fortunate. The picture accidently slipped into my jacket pocket. Spur-of-the-moment thievery is your friend.

So is a dramatic exit. I dropped the box and ran out of the room.

3.

"Callaghan," Daniel yelled, running after me. I gave him good chase until we were out of the building and sitting on a small bench under an oak tree on the quad. I wasn't sure that Lorraine wouldn't follow, but the coast was clear.

"Baby, what is it? Jack the Ripper's box?" he asked. "And can you do that thingy Lorraine was talking about?"

"Let's jump to the chase," I said, shaking my head. "It's worse than Jack the Ripper. That thing belongs to your father."

Every molecule in his body seemed to tense.

"And no—I have no powers—except apparently I know how to open a box, recognize his initials, and steal something important he placed inside."

I opened my pocket a little bit and he stared in curiously.

"We have homework tonight," I said with a smile.

4.

Later in our dorm room we jumped on the small laptop we checked out from the library.

Daniel was fast on the keyboard and quickly matched the one-of-a-kind gray-and-white Victorian house on the yellowed picture with the real thing built in 1894 San Francisco. The sprawling mansion with downhill views of the rollercoaster ride of a city occupied the corner of a prestigious street on what was then known as "Billionaire's Row."

The house at 2500 Broadway was commissioned by a prominent San Francisco businessman and mayoral candidate.

His name: Wister Reid.

"My great-grandfather enjoyed seven thousand square feet in his four-story manse with six bedrooms, a ballroom and six indoor bathrooms," he read from the pages of a book on historic architecture from San Francisco's past.

There was a series of photos from some sort of grand ball in 1900. You couldn't miss Wister Reid, a handsome, tall, fifty-something man with a shock of black-gray hair and stunning blue-gray eyes—fitting with how the Reid children looked today.

He stood in a receiving line in a grand parlor handsomely constructed with expensive inlaid wood designs on the ceiling and creamy white marble on the floors. Next to Wister was a tall woman in a high-collared blue lace gown with dark hair and brilliant violet eyes. She was much younger than him, maybe twenty-five or twenty-six.

"Great-granny Marguerite, imported from France for a touch of class," Daniel said. Since that day in the library, he had studied his family tree. "She was the mother of his three sons including the eldest heir to the fortune named Leland Reid, who along with his wife Violet had seven kids—all girls to everyone's stunned disappointment."

"Can you name them?" I encouraged him as he leaned back from the computer.

"Wait," he said with a smile. "It was Daisy, Dora, Betty, Maggie, Ada, Rose, and Doris."Leland and the first four of the girls died in 1904 when the bubonic plague swept through the city. San Fran was the major port between China and the US. The ships contained rats that infected the cargo," he explained.

We moved to the bed because it was so late and snuggled under the covers, my leg loped over his leg, his hands low on my hips.

"Everyone got the plague," said the world's sexiest historian. "No one knew back then that rats carried the sickness and then fleas on those rats transmitted the disease to humans. Ships were declared clean after a lengthy inspection, but no one cared about the rats or fleas, which were everywhere. "People started dropping of fever and pneumonia. It was the first recorded plague in US history and lasted for four years. Governor Henry Gage denied it existed for the first two years. He wanted to protect the city's economy," Daniel said.

"Wister lost his beloved son and most of his granddaughters, plus his daughter-in-law, Violet. I guess the hardest for him was losing one granddaughter named Daisy who adored him. She was fourteen when she died. He had high hopes for little Daisy who was smart, sassy, and excelled in sports."

"What about the other brothers?" I asked.

"The second-oldest son was named Wenford," Daniel said, tickling me when I laughed at the name. "He was a Yankee Doodle Reid who had a lucrative shipping business in England. And then there was Roosevelt Reid, my grandfather. He was the youngest, born a year after the quake. I never met him, but he was Edward's father. An American legend."

"Legendary for what?" I hated to ask.

"Lethal hands. Barbaric ways of caging children including Edward and his sister Goldie, who died mysteriously when she was seventeen. Roosevelt was an oil man, also made a ton of dough working alongside the great American businessman John D. Rockefeller. He was his second in command at Standard Oil. Died rich and left my father exactly one dollar. He gave the rest away to universities who established libraries and buildings in his name."

"Why only a dollar?"

"Because he didn't enjoy children, especially his own," Daniel said.

"Nice," I said.

"And motivating to Edward, who made his representing the mob in Chicago," Daniel said. "He came up at a time when there were already oil companies and railroads, so this was the next best thing."

Daniel rarely talked specifics about his past, but tonight seemed different since the family tree already had been given a good shake.

"When I was little, Edward would take a spatula from the kitchen, pull our pants down, and beat us with it. He said, 'You're lucky. My father used to beat us with firewood,'" he recalled. "He would make us place our hands on his desk. We'd clench thinking he would break them, but then he would crack us across the face so hard that it left welts and we couldn't go to school for two days until the swelling went down.

"I guess Wister thought that one up, passed down to Grandpa Roosevelt," he said. "But the worst were the cages. We didn't have dogs, but Edward bought those large dog cages—one for each of us—and kept them in the basement. If he was 'not pleased' by whatever we were doing, we were caged for days . . . forced to sleep in our own piss, no food or water.

"You want to know how I survived the Hole at ITT?" he said. "I had already been schooled in Edward's idea of a kiddie penitentiary."

"Oh, baby," I whispered.

"It wasn't so bad if Pete was down there with me in his cage," Daniel said. "He would cry when Edward would padlock the front. Even worse were the girls. They would beg, 'Please don't lock us up . . . please, Daddy . . .'

"And now he has them locked away in past loops experiencing God only knows what," Daniel lamented.

"Until we save them," I said, slipping my hand into his fingers. He closed the deal tightly.

5.

"Walker?" Cass said at dawn as I was walking double time to class. "Care to slow down for just a second?"

He looked so sorrowful—and older—with his hair swept back in a mini man bun, new facial hair, and his jeans tight and black. He had on a Harley-Davidson T-shirt in black. I was wearing a black button-up sweater, a light blue skirt, and black Wayfarer sunglasses I bought at a store in the student union.

"Cass," I said with a warm smile and gave him a quick hug. "I've been meaning to find you."

"Yeah, right back at you," Cass said. "First, I need to apologize for the other night, Walker. I was absolutely out of line. You want to slug me?" He pointed his chin in my direction. "Go ahead," he insisted. "Take your best shot, darlin'. I'll even try not to cry."

I gave him a platonic kiss on that chin.

And just like that I forgave him. It couldn't be any other way with Cass. He almost dared you to unlove him.

"You look like you have news," I said.

He nodded while putting a hand up to where the kiss had landed. "Been researching my ass off since we got here. Library is better than what we have at the Academy for this kind of thing. They're called Youngling Schools. It's where the kids wait for parents if they pass as little ones."

"Oh, Cass," I said, my eyes filling. *This is exactly what he needed to focus on. His daughter would take him to places far and wide—as it should be.*

"I need a few more days to try to find the exact location with coordinates and then I'm going there," he said. "It won't be good-bye, but just so long for now. My plan is to grab MC and get her to safety. Maybe I'll bring her back here or I'll try to get word to Dr. King. I don't want any surprises. Just a safe place to nest."

I put my hand on his arm.

"Sugar, I don't know what I'll do when I first see her," Cass said. "I just want to hold my baby in my arms again."

I couldn't tell him that I would soon be doing a little time traveling. Our paths were obviously going in vastly different directions. What if I never saw him again?

Something inside began to hurt.

He grasped my hand and squeezed. Our eyes caught, locked.

And then, he cupped my face in his warm hands.

"Damn," he said.

He didn't need to say another word.

6.

Things separate into individual parts. People fall out of step with each other. Best friends move on—never to glance into those once familiar eyes again—or if they do, it's like looking into the soul of a stranger.

At our age, it was a given that we would divide.

In the haze of a cloudy summer morning, I heard the magic words that would set my travels in motion.

"Draw your own portal," said our teacher, HG. "Or as I like to call it: You get in the afterlife what you have the courage to ask for. If you ask to go traveling, bon voyage."

He was a theatrical man and with hands sweeping forward dramatically directed us to form a circle in the middle of the room. We were to leave plenty of room in the middle.

"We could pussyfoot around it, but this class really isn't just about how to draw yourself a portal," he said. "It's basically Time Travel 101."

"If you're a homebody, it might be a good time to drop this class and show yourself the door," he boomed.

No one moved. Class was in session.

"Think of the past like a foreign country," he began. "Sometimes, your soul needs to do a bit of traveling and the past is as fine a destination as anywhere else.

"The question for this class is twofold," H.G. posed. "How do you draw a portal and how do you program yourself to hit the exact right year, in the exact right country, in the exact perfect spot that you wish to visit?

"Think of it this way: You don't board an airplane thinking, 'I wonder where it will take me.' You need a time, a year, and a destination."

His next words were the typical warning that we were not allowed to change anything in the past *deliberately* or the past would change us.

HG tried to explain portals in as simple a way as possible. He leaned forward and told us that the afterlife and the human world was full of many energetic "hotspots" that were really hyperdimensional gateways or doors to the past. Since our senses were revved up in The Other, he insisted it should be quite easy for us to find these spots. Science fact #1: intense energy attracts other intense energy.

"Walker to the chalkboard," he instructed.

Why me?

"Walk along it. Tell me if you feel any energy or a buzzing in your actual blood—like you just swallowed about a hundred nonstinging bees and they're using your vascular system as a highway. Moving and buzzing. Buzzing and moving."

I felt like a dork, albeit an excited one, as everyone stared at me. So far, there was nothing out of the ordinary as I walked the line of that board. No bees. No road. It was discouraging to know that maybe I didn't have the stuff to recognize an energetic boost when I supposedly was jolted by it.

"Now, I'd like you to go get my sweater," he said, pointing to the several hooks on the cinderblock wall to the side. *Why would anyone want a sweater when it was overly hot in this room?* I walked past some old coats, a pair of jeans, and almost reached a black men's cardigan when the hair on my arms began to stand up. It was the oddest feeling ever because my blood seemed to be *humming.*

"Walker, listen to me closely. I want you to think hard. The year is 1986. The living realm. The place is Arizona State University in Tempe, Arizona. You sent for brochures of that school when you were alive. You know what it looks like. Just punch it up in your mind. You will go to the Student Activity Center. Say the words out loud. Someday you will just have to say them in your head, but this is not that day. Now go!"

"Living realm. 1986. Arizona State. Student Activity Center," I said loudly.

"You don't have to give me a migraine," HG said. "Just keep walking toward my sweater slowly. Very good . . . now move faster, but as you do, take your finger and scratch a small X onto the thin skin of your outer hand. Not your palm. Scratch the outside of the hand. Now, touch my sweater pocket on the bottom left with the X and keep walking and breathing.

"Go."

I wasn't sure why I was doing any of the above, but I scratched the X and I walked and then I looked down and found that left pocket on the sweater and touched it with the X I etched on my skin.

The buzzing in my blood became a deep drumming.

And so I walked, vibrating all the way, as that black sweater became a big black hole and then a big wide universe that swallowed me whole.

7.

This wasn't the afterlife anymore.

It was a packed amphitheater at a raucous college and a sold-out show with an estimated twenty thousand cheering fans in thrift shop club-kid clothing complete with multitudes of hair ribbon and an endless amount of rubber bracelets.

The girl on stage was someone I knew—and she was certainly striking a pose.

She sang about being a virgin, but probably wasn't—no judgment. No one gyrated like she did/does and certainly not in a corset white torn wedding dress with her signature strand of beads, crucifixes, and pearls. It was elegant. It was edgy. It was cut up to way past her cha-cha.

Dead or alive, past or present, it was MADONNA!

8.

A blink later.

Auggie was dancing his ass off next to me. "I've been sent to take you back, but maybe after 'Papa Don't Preach,'" Auggie said, grooving hard while singing about "keeping my baby." We looked at each other hard as the faint strains of "Holiday" picked up tempo in the background. I couldn't stop dancing, which wasn't ever my thing, and Auggie twirled hard.

Eventually, we would have to force ourselves, but it was time.

Sad when eventually becomes now, damn it.

He touched the X he drew on the back of his hand to the X still on mine and began to repeat, "The Other. Present time. Astonishing School."

We arrived by the coat rack.

"How very *Back to the Future* of you," said HG who added, "Welcome back, children."

9.

"Portals are created by the interaction between the earth and sun's magnetospheres," he explained. "We don't know everything about them except that they are usually volatile and unpredictable, opening and closing in an instant."

He explained that the X was necessary to absorb the energy and fired up nicely when touched to another X that was experiencing the same current.

"These markers are called x-points or electron diffusion regions," said HG. "Without getting too technical, it's a way for magnetic fields to connect and explosively transfer energy, therefore opening portals and jettisoning you to the past."

"The key is to find the energy fields, which will require dedicated searching until you feel what Walker just experienced," he said. "Living people are naturally able to find these fields or hotspots, too. Many times, in life, you might have experienced that surge or tingle of your blood at a specific spot—not knowing what was happening. Or you've heard a weird, unexplained buzzing.

"Now," HG said, "you know. It's a portal to another time."

10.

I saw Daniel taking copious notes, fingers flying across the page so we didn't forget a single thing. He wrote these tips from HG:

*If you want to time travel, temples and churches are a good place to find energetic hotspots. Gothic spots also work such as eerie and/or medieval cathedrals built on sacred ground.

*Large rock formations or walls that have spots that are dug in or look like tunnels are usually portals to another dimension. Example: there is a spot in Peru called Hayu Marca that features a twenty-three-foot-tall rock wall with a carved door in the middle. It's really a gateway to other time periods and how the Inca's hid their gold in other worlds. They just walked through the door carved by . . . no one knew. Note: most of those who walked through that door were never seen again.

*Rocks are filled with portals. Find the rock where you can feel energy pulsing from the object into your veins. Test it by placing your hand in the center of the rock, but quickly withdraw your body part so you don't slip through an unintended door otherwise known as an unscheduled time jump. Those who are inherently clumsy slip through time many times over a lifetime, but often catch themselves while falling and return to their original time period. If you don't catch yourself, you won't hit the floor. You might just float to a different decade. Permanently.

*If you are in a spot where you feel elevated like you've been lifted off the ground, it's a particularly strong portal. Certain rock statues in parks are also portals as is Mount Rushmore in the living realm and the Angel of the Waters Statue (also known as Bethesda Fountain) in Central

Park. Also check out the Red Rock area of Nevada and Sedona rocks in Arizona.

*Areas in a home can also serve as a portal. Perhaps you'll hear a vibrating in a kitchen closet, glasses knocking together for no reason, or there is a place where it sounds like something odd electrically speaking is happening. Portals all, perhaps.

*There are multiple dimensions beyond the Midst and The Other. They require additional observation, but there are quantum signs that point to them. We might experience life and death in a gravitationally heavy fifth-dimension known as "gravitybrane." In a nutshell, of all the fundamental forces, gravity does a piss-poor job and is pretty weak. We exist on one of the branes with the weak gravity. Therefore, we can't see what's going on in the other branes. Unless we find the right portal to go there—past, present, and future.

I put my fingers to both ears and pretended that my head was exploding.

For the next hour, the others tried different time periods—going up and back quickly. Daniel did a quick visit to 1962 in swinging Los Angeles while Bertha and Bitty relived the days of Scottish clansmen and women. How *Outlander* of them.

HG cautioned: "These trips are only for this class. There is no homework. You do not do this outside of this class -- ever -- until I okay you to travel. There will be consequences. Do not cross me on this matter."

Daniel and I looked hard at each other.

Our time was all about consequences and aftermaths.

11.

By the way . . .

You bet I had questions that next day.

"So, what did Chris Flicker do that night at the house in the Midst when he drew a portal and took me to see my mom?" I asked HG.

"Chris is an advanced student in your realm. You probably didn't even realize that he scratched an *X* into your hand and his," HG said. "I'm sure he put on a show by drawing a fiery circle, which is also a technique, but one we save for grad students. It's just more razzle-dazzle. The important part is Chris drew the *X*; set the time, date, and place in his mind; and then ran with you over a supercharged area."

"We ran over this big black rock in our front yard. It was always there. I thought it was decorative," I marveled.

Flick knew otherwise. All that searching and Daniel and I had a portal in our own front yard *and didn't even know it*. It didn't really matter. We didn't know how to use it in those days.

"The portal you used at ITT in John's closet is so supercharged that you could just walk through it without any hoopla. Your mind was so focused on one event—finding Daniel's little brother at a specific place and time—that your collective frontal lobe powers still set the time, date, and setting," HG said. "Those master portals are around, too. But rare. You used one at the Chicago amusement park to get back to the Midst."

"Interesting," I said.

"No practicing out of class," HG warned.

Again.

Daniel and I didn't exactly practice; we called it training.

One night, we snuck off into the woods and found a buzzing rock. It was easy to go back to the eighties again because the music was the best. We had decided to hit Randhurst Shopping Mall in Mount Prospect, Illinois, on April 14, 1982. Funny thing was that many decades later, both of us as teenagers had both shopped there.

In 1982, I was dying to buy a pair of fluorescent green eighties jelly shoes and couldn't believe all the big, feathered, Farrah hair.

"Don't even suggest it," Daniel said with a smile as we stood outside a small barber shop.

Every single guy in it had the same do: the mullet!

THIRTY-THREE

1.

Another afternoon, we fought about it all the way back to the dorm room.

"Okay, here's the deal," he said. "I go into the past for a few minutes. San Francisco. 1906. A few days before the big earthquake. I check it out. Come right back. Get you, if it's safe."

"If that's what you need to tell yourself," I offered. "We're going tomorrow night; we're staying; we're bringing Jenna Reid home with us. We need to break up a society wedding, avoid an earthquake, and not roast like marshmallows in a city that burned down after the quake.

"What could go wrong?" I demanded in a semihysterical voice.

"Callaghan," he warned.

"Don't Callaghan me," I said sweetly, planting a kiss on his tight jaw. "And if we have any spare time and they have them in 1906, I'd sure like some hot clam chowder in a big bread bowl."

"They didn't have bread bowls in 1906," he grumbled.

"They had bread. We can form it into a bowl," I insisted with the smile of an adventurous heart.

He spun me around hard before we got to the elevator door of our dorm. And he nodded, which meant that the time of discussion was over. I was *going*.

"Baby, you are my center when I spin away," he sang under his breath and then identified the band. "Radiohead."

"Get your pack ready," I said, leading the way. "And I really don't think we should tell anybody about this either. Too many cooks, you know. And I don't need Eddie there trying to see if he can swim to Alcatraz Island."

"Tell anybody what?" asked Auggie with a popsicle in his mouth, a towel around his waist, in the dorm hallway.

It took two hours to talk him off the ledge. He was absolute in wanting to go because he loved Jenna, too. We only told him so someone would know where we were in case we never came back.

"All right," Auggie grumbled. "But, if you're not back in two days, I'm calling in reinforcements."

"Three days," Daniel said.

It was decided.

2.

We skipped dinner that night to shop in the school's stores for anything resembling early 1900s period clothing. We couldn't wear our modern gear, and for a long time it seemed hopeless until we spotted a tiny vintage clothing shop.

Daniel found an appropriate dark-gray three-piece vintage suit made up of trousers, a tailcoat or jacket, and a waistcoat or vest. A white shirt and slim tie completed the look.

I found a frilly, puffed white blouse and a fluted, high-waist "hobble" skirt, which was cinched in at the hem. It came with a corset, which almost left me breathless, and a crinoline, hoops, and petticoats to wear under the skirt thus making it very wide. I even found a small top hat fashionable with the richer ladies of the time.

I would pin my hair up, powder my face and neck milky white, and wear just a bit of mascara and soft pink rouge on my cheeks and lips.

Of course, we would pack our ass-kicking clothes because you never knew when we'd have to bring today to 1906.

By midnight, our packs were ready, our vintage clothes were hiding in the closet, and we couldn't sleep a wink.

3.

I'm not sure whose idea it was to take a walk at midnight. In the dorm bed, he whispered, "It's a sacred place where fire mixes with water." It took about three seconds to control my goosebumps, untangle every limb, and put on my clothes.

Daniel had heard of this place on the school grounds, past the acres of sloping terrain and framed by the hardwood forest.

It was called the Eternal Flame Falls, and I smelled it—an earthy odor of natural, fresh water mixed with the smoked smell of fire. I heard it—the thunder of a massive waterfall pounding on the rocks below. And then I saw it—the entire fall was backlit by fire naturally blasting from the steep rock walls.

All I could do is stare at the sight and wonder as the bright flames jutted back and forth behind the cascades.

"It's so beautiful," I murmured as Daniel stood behind me. He wrapped strong arms around my waist.

"A phenomenon," he said, moving my hair and kissing the back of my neck.

We got naked and made love next to the falls in a dry riverbed as the water rushed above us, misty drops caressing slick bodies; hot ribbons of orange-red flames leaping across the glowing night sky.

I knew this place would forever remain with me just as I forever remain in all of the places I have roamed. It worked the same with people who wandered in and out of our lives, especially the one who loved us and the ones we loved back.

People were like quilts, made up of tiny pieces—bits of dialogue, faces that drifted by, snapshots of places we've roamed, slivers of midnight talks, kisses under the moon, wisdoms we've collected like words in a song. My quilt gained another patch tonight when fire met water met him met me.

Tonight would be stitched into a spot that would fade, but could never vanish.

I closed my eyes. Not to sleep. The reset was working fine.

I closed them to savor.

4.

We left the riverbed at dawn. It was the beginning of summer now, and I turned my face to the sun. Larks were singing. A mama bird was pushing a small baby out of the nest because it was different. It was lucky though—big enough to find its feet and then spread its wings, proving once again that different can be brave and smart.

Behind the tallest trees, we dressed in our period clothing, hiding small weapons in the ample pockets. I was the one who insisted we bring *everything* with us. A lot can happen in a day and hiding out in a wooded paradise was a solid move. The less we were seen, the chances were better for a clean break.

Little did we know that our "trip" would take places earlier than previously scheduled and have nothing to do with a classroom.

We stumbled upon the rock the night before while walking through the woods.

"Do you feel that?" Daniel said, looking at the perfectly regular gray bounder plopped in the mud.

When I got too close to it, my blood began to hum. As I stood next to the rock, I felt my bones shake, my muscles throb, and my skin seemed to be *quivering in tiny shock waves. It was the oddest feeling . . . similar to leaving my body when I died.*

It was a portal.

In the sunlight, we stood before the rock again.

"The year is 1906. The past. The place is Broadway Street in San

Francisco outside of Wister Reid's mansion," I said.

"The past. 1906. Broadway Street, San Francisco. Wister Reid's mansion," he repeated.

"Keep walking toward the rock slowly," I echoed HG's words. "Move faster, but as you do, take your finger and scratch a small X onto the dorsal side of your hand. Touch my hand as I've done the same thing. Keep walking and breathing . . . Wow."

For what it was worth . . .
They were going to kill us for doing this.
But, we were rebels on a mission to save Jenna.
And there is no point to being a rebel . . .
Unless you have something big to fight for.

"This is probably wrong," I said.

"Wrong is the fun one," Daniel said as the current world became colorless.

THIRTY-FOUR

SAN FRANCISCO, 1906

1.

I n life, my mother gave me this advice: Practice the pause. Pause before judging. Pause before assuming. Pause before accusing. Pause whenever you're about to react.

I had pause interruptus. The awe on my face covered the entire landscape.

On shaking legs, I found my footing. A deep breath and I could taste the salt water. I could feel the Pacific Ocean.

San Francisco, Cal-i-for-ni-yay, USA. The Queen of the West. The Golden Gate City. Sanny Franny. The City by the Bay. Oscar Wilde said it best: "It's an odd thing, but anyone who disappears is said to be seen in San Francisco."

And suddenly, we were there, our feet on terra firma.

In 1906.

Around the turn of the century, SF was a bustling metropolis of 400,000 people who migrated here to test their life luck. Some came to escape the overcrowded cities in the East where their economic futures were bleak. Others arrived due to old-fashioned wanderlust that came with the battle cry: Go West, Young Man.

The American West was the greatest adventure of all with its expansive land, space to dream, and possibilities that seemed as endless as those wide, orange-yellow Pacific sunsets.

If you were especially optimistic and this was your time of life, you might dig up your fortune out here, although the ones who arrived to mine gold were always disappointed. History would show that no single person obtained lasting wealth from the native element. Many of those who came seeking it pivoted and started businesses. Why not? Even our friend John Lennon would someday say: "Los Angeles? That's just a big parking lot where you buy a hamburger for the trip to San Francisco."

Famous writers always lived here including Mark Twain, Rudyard Kipling, Robert Louis Stevenson, and Oscar Wilde. But you didn't need a pen to make a name or a fortune here.

Some got rich creating a complex railroad system through the American West including four Sacramento businessmen: Amasa Leland Stanford, Collis B. Huntington, Charles Crocker, and Wister Reid—the man, the bastard, and unfortunately the great-grandfather of Daniel Reid.

The sound of horses' hooves clomping on the cobblestone streets snapped me out of my historical head trip.

Daniel slipped a hand into mine.

"Baby, what did we do?" he whispered, letting it sink in. "This is where it all began."

"Where you began," I said, feeling his pulse in my hand.

2.

We climbed the breath-stealing hills of Telegraph Hill, which wasn't even the highest point in 1906 San Francisco city proper. I took the heavily sloped land in large, fast steps because the incline was merciless.

Along the way, we passed men sporting handlebar mustaches

making their way up and down artful cobblestoned streets. They had smiles on their young faces, the afternoon newspaper—when there was such a thing—was tucked under their arms. Leather pouches were firmly gripped in hands.

Many of the locals nodded a quick greeting, but were too busy to stop for idle talk. Or perhaps they couldn't talk because some of the streets were built on 284-foot hills.

Our frequent pauses had nothing to do with the physicality of navigating this rollercoaster of a city. We were young, trained, and in top shape, plus the reset seemed to be working splendidly.

We stopped when the world in front of us began to match the black-and-white photos we had studied in history books. Right in front of us, right at this moment, was a red brick building called Engine No. 1. It wouldn't be long before the eight firemen inside would be on the front lines of chaos. Many of those brave souls would cross to our side before the earthquake was over.

We couldn't linger, but we could gawk at the opulent white-and-golden front of the Tivoli Opera House. I could imagine all of the fashionable society ladies in their diamond tiaras and intricately stitched gowns holding the arms of men in black tuxes and tails. It was all so civilized, until it wasn't. Mark Twain attended these performances, often in his heavy coats proclaiming, "The coldest winter I ever spent was a summer in San Francisco."

I shivered because the fog coming off the bay on this April day made the place feel like you were walking through chilled spray from the ocean blue.

We rounded the corner of Market and New Montgomery and lingered in front of the Palace Hotel on Market Street, which was *the* posh place to stay if you were living the American dream. It was a seven-story structure with massive white columns in front and private gold balconies hanging from the front façade.

There was an elegant carriage entrance and lounge inside called the Palm Court. This was the place that poor Jenna's wedding would occur on Wednesday, which was just three days away.

A doorman greeted us. "Good afternoon," he boomed. "Can I be of assistance with your bags?"

It must have looked odd to him that we both carried just one brown satchel, which was a way to hide a modern invention: our backpacks.

"Thank you, sir, but we're not staying," I said. It wasn't like I could pick up my cell and call a hotel that existed in 1906 and make a reservation.

"We have seven hundred and fifty-five guest rooms," he boasted. "We even have a rising room."

Daniel looked at me quizzically, but thankfully my love of vintage vampire books would finally come in handy.

Later, these *rising rooms* would be called elevators. In 1906, they were made of the finest redwood from nearby forests and a pulley system. "Each of the guest rooms feature a large bay window," the doorman boasted. "And a private bathroom, as well as an electric call button to summon hotel staff.

"It's a palace, truly," he said. "The castle of the West."

"Happy anniversary, baby," Daniel turned and said to me as the doorman looked at him oddly. *It dawned on me in that moment. We had to stay somewhere.*

"He means, 'The baby is with my mother.' Right, my *beloved*," I replied in 1906-speak.

"Yes, *dearest*," Daniel said.

"Check-in is through the double gold doors," the doorman said, sweeping his arm to the left to guide us up a tall, white stone staircase.

Act like you belong . . . and you do.

3.

Stunning in its design, the hotel's lobby featured sculptured columns and large arches lit by a skylight above. Thin glass above drew muted sunshine into what was called the Grand Court—and it was magnificent.

We were given prompt attention by a young male worker named Henry in a black suit, dotted with gold buttons and punctuated with a small beige top hat. "Women can sit in the parlor while men conduct the business of checking in," he advised, pointing toward the artfully decorated sitting spot filled with elaborately embroidered Louis Quinze-style couches and chairs.

I wasn't the kind of woman to leave Daniel alone at check-in—but there was no other option but to observe the protocol of the time period.

It turned out that trust was as good as cash in 1906.

Daniel signed us in as Mr. and Mrs. Reid from Chicago, Illinois, and muttered something about being here for the big Reid "family" wedding.

"I'm sorry that we don't have a credit card," Daniel blurted while the clerk filled out the paperwork by hand.

"What is a credit card, sir?"

Credit cards weren't invented in 1906, but came later in 1950.

"Home address?" the clerk inquired.

He gave him our old address in the Midst, but for the town added Chicago to the mix. No one questioned it.

He was handed a large golden door key.

That was it!

The clerk lowered his voice to say, "We will settle your account upon checkout. Enjoy your stay."

Little did he know that there would be no checkout. This entire lobby would be rubble in three days.

"We'll see you Wednesday when we leave," Daniel lied again.

"Do you need directions to tonight's engagement party?" the helpful young man asked. "At Reid manor?" He glanced at the grandfather clock behind the counter. "It begins at sunset and I can order you a carriage."

"Please do," Daniel said in his most formal voice.

While waiting for the "rising room," we had our first brush with greatness.

"I'm Mayor Schmitz. You can call me Mayor Schmitz," he joked with Daniel. He nodded his head to me and said, "Ma'am."

It was an encounter I would later regret.

4.

Our room was turn-of-the-century opulence at its best, which meant a busy mix of patterns and explosions of color that made your mind swim. The carpeting was ornate with red-and-beige swirls complimenting lime-green wallpaper and golden velvet couches. There were paintings of several pensive-looking women and men on the walls. "Bitchin' times," I mouthed at them.

A large fireplace had been lit and the crackling wood gave the room a homey type of feeling. I smiled when I peeked into the bedroom. Even though we were a "married couple," there were two child-sized double beds. The eureka moment was when I opened the drawer of the bedside table. Someone had left a wallet in there and quickly I removed the cash, pressing a single dollar into Daniel's hand.

The baggage boy smiled from ear-to-ear at his "tip."

"Nice find, *beloved*," Daniel teased me after closing the door.

"No problem, babycakes," I teased, looking through a small gold telescope at our window. Daniel loped his arms around me from behind and I gazed at the sunset over the Pacific where the future appeared to limitless—if you could survive the present.

There was no need to be afraid. Daniel smelled like hope and adventure, which was enough for now.

5.

Our carriage driver arrived promptly at 6:20 p.m., which allowed us time for bath-time fun in the claw foot tub followed by a frantic press of our "help" button resulting in two very expensive stores providing fashion assistance of the highest caliber.

Our plan was to meet the illustrious Wister Reid, grab Jenna, run, and then figure out the right vibrational spot to create a portal. Anywhere near a natural body of water was a good place to start as our teacher at the Astonishing School had told us.

The driver helped me out of the carriage, which was helpful since I was wearing a pale pink dress made of soft, flowing silk that pooled well beyond the pointed velvet violet shoes underneath that weren't visible. It came complete with a low-cut bodice, fitted sleeves, and embellishments of pale pink velvet ribbon and wispy white lace.

The train of the dress wasn't garishly large, but refined, cascading into a small circle of an absolutely to-die-for trumpet-shaped wonder.

My Victorian-babe look included putting my hair in a complicated top bun and powdering my face, neck, and chest classic pale white. A tight corset made my waist super-duper tiny although I couldn't wait to rip the thing off and breathe normally again.

Daniel wasn't in the same kind of pain. He looked dashing in a black formal tailcoat that flapped down to his calf, black pants, and crisp white evening shirt with a detached collar, plus a white bow tie that took us half an hour to actually tie. He was enjoying the patent leather dress boots, but hated the white silk hat that sat on the top of some seriously slicked-back hair.

Our horse click-clacked along the city as it morphed into night mode. All too soon, we reached what I would refer to as ground zero, better known as Reid Manor.

The house sat on the corner of Broadway Street; a massive, white Victorian palace located in a part of town that would come to be known as Nob Hill.

Railroad barons lived on this block as the homes weren't just dwellings, but specially erected testaments to one's wealth or lack of cash.

It was the perfect spot if one's last name was associated with millions of dollars.

We had little time to practice the art of mixing with other rich types that were now emerging from gilded carriages flanked by black gelding horses. I did have advanced training in the art of listening to other people's conversations, handpicking useful information—and some of the ones I heard as we made our way closer perked my interest.

"Wister truly is a live wire," said one man in a white tux. "An engagement party on a Monday and a wedding on a Wednesday are two *humdingers*."

"A real *lollapalooza*," a thirtyish man in black interjected.

His wife, in a stunning ivory frock, replied, "Come on, dear, time for us to *skidoo*."

In 1906, it meant that it was time to grab your crystal goblet, adjust your ball gown, and party.

I wondered if Wister Reid cared about the lasting horrors of marrying off his thirteen-year-old great-granddaughter to a man in his late fifties. All I wanted to do was wrap my hands around Jenna and steal her away. Daniel took the stone front steps in twos like if he got there faster, he could minimize the damage.

There was a doorman at the top in a black tux with tails (and tales, I was sure) and he bowed in front of us as if we were royalty.

With one long arm, he pushed open one of the two front doors.

It was easy to get in.

Staying would be another story.

6.

The interior of the Reid mansion was the very definition of extravagant excess. On steroids, which weren't even invented, if one was keeping score.

The floors were made of white marble shipped from a castle in Europe. Real fourteen- karat-gold trim trimmed the walls in an enormous entryway marked by a large, dark table made with wood and inlaid ivory.

A grand Venetian chandelier sent tiny rainbow-colored sparkles to the ground while priceless crystal vases were overflowing with the freshest spring tulips, all the tightly closed bulbs in pristine white, to underscore the virginity and purity of the bride for sale.

The rest of the home felt ancient and thick thanks to the heavy, dark furniture. In fact, every step was like walk through a museum filled with the finest European furniture, stone sculptures, priceless antiques, and rare expensive paintings created by the world's primo artists.

Wister believed in conspicuous consumption as did his friends, which certainly included the owners of the newspapers, banking royalty, and all of the major and minor politicos and their heavily decorated wives. I noticed that most of the women were merely ornamental and didn't speak unless directly addressed. They were property like the couch or the horse waiting patiently in silence outside.

Wandering past the great room—or living room to modern folk—I saw a portrait over a fireplace that was big enough to create a five-star blaze.

It was Wister as a younger man with the trademark Reid dark hair and light eyes.

"Are you a Reid?" a man in his thirties in a black tux asked.

"Yes," said Daniel.

"Master of the house?"

"No."

Daniel leaned in and cocked his head in my direction. "She runs this bitch," he said.

"Excuse me," I whispered.

"Good evening," the man said, backing away. One did not speak this way in polite company in 1906. That fact inspired my next words pertaining to his great-grandfather.

"Let's go get this son of a bitch," I whispered in Daniel's ear.

Just another Monday night back, circa yesterday.

7.

It wasn't long before several young businessmen had infuriatingly attached themselves to Daniel, quizzing him about his "affairs" and how he was related to Wister. It was a fact: money smelled money.

He was so absorbed in deflecting this interrogation that I easily slipped away, intent on finding a bathroom. One wrong turn and I was in a different section of the house, one that fascinated me. There were floor-to-ceiling bookcases on all of the walls and they were filled with first editions.

I knew it was wrong, but I allowed my fingers to do the walking over those covers, which were cool to the touch and filled with the words of the ages.

"Should we toast to the happy couple who will be arriving soon?" blurted a tall, elegant man who sat in the far corner in one of those deep leather chairs. He was a handsome one, well-built for his midfifties, and paused to consider me while lighting a cigar with something called a "striker," a device that resembled a blunt pair of scissors with a treated piece of flint at one end. When he pushed the two together, a spark lit some kind of flammable material and created a flame.

I watched the fire twinkle merrily through the prism of a red Tiffany lamp on a massive desk.

He was on his feet in one swift move and stood at attention because men did that in those days when a woman entered the room. I was beyond entering. My feet kept moving until I was standing a few feet in front of him. The stink from the cigar swirled in my hair.

He thought nothing of pouring me a glass of the same whisky he was drinking.

"To the girl who sees dragons in the clouds and who feels most alive in worlds that are hidden," he said as a toast. It wasn't just that his words were odd. His smile lit a face full of lines, highlighting an intensity that served as a warning sign.

Did he know me?

No, it was impossible.

As sweet, cold fluid raced down and burned my throat, he had one more thing to say to me: "I'm Wister Reid."

8.

"Walker Callaghan," I said because this was no time to skip a beat. This man was lethal smart, which helped build his fortune. He would not suffer fools. *Why not use my real name? He didn't know me. We were several generations removed.*

527

"Of the New York Callaghans in the steel business?" he demanded.

I nodded. *Whatever floated his boat.*

"You're new to America?" he asked. "Your family immigrated from Ireland."

Maybe I should break out my school ID.

"Not exactly," I replied. "Our family immigrated long ago."

"And you're educated—for a girl," he stated. "Modern, if not subversive."

"Yes, education makes us dangerous," I snapped. Then, I reigned myself in. No good could come out of my challenging the "great one" at this point.

"I'm actually a reporter for the *Los Angeles Times* covering the wedding for the society page."

It was a good one—as far as pulling one out of your newly minted 1906 ass went.

"A woman reporter . . . from *where* did you say? Oh yes, the *Los Angeles Daily Times*. I didn't realize that they hired women. Progressive."

What a douche. But, I was also guilty of a rookie mistake. Apparently, it was called the Daily Times *at the turn of the century.*

"Why, yes," I said. "Someday, maybe we'll even have the right to vote. Maybe run for president."

Take that, hater.

"Let's not be ridiculous," he said, puffing hard on his cigar while he rubbed his stomach. It was if I had just said something so hilarious that I caught him suddenly off guard.

I forced myself to laugh through gritted teeth.

"Where is the bride?" I asked him, hoping my voice didn't sound too demanding or shrill.

"Waiting upstairs to make her entrance, of course," he said. His smile faded. It seemed to say that thirteen-year-old girls had spirits to break, and this one was not exactly broken.

"You must be so happy," I said, leaving out this part: *you perv child seller.*

He stood and walked closer, narrowing his eyes.

"You're a reporter, yet you're not writing anything down," he said. "I find that odd. Are you going to memorize my responses?"

He was going to question me as a reporter? Not happening, human trafficker.

"Sir, I didn't ask you to be on the record, yet, so that would be impertinent of me," I replied with a sweet smile.

Casually, I strolled over to the desk and picked up a few sheets of loose paper and a quill pen. "I'm assuming that the bride spells her name J-e-n-n-a."

"I certainly hope you spell the bride's name correctly," he blustered. "My beloved granddaughter. "

"Yes, sir," I said, adding, "First question: Why would a girl who is thirteen want to marry a man in his fifties?"

A quick intake of air was followed by silence.

When he spoke, his words were laced with contempt.

"A man in my possession must judge motives, especially when a woman arrives out of thin air to ask impertinent personal questions during his beloved granddaughter's wedding week."

He wasn't finished.

"It doesn't make a lick of sense that I'd be ambushed in this manner. Believe me, I will be speaking to the editor of the paper about your manner. What is his name?"

He was one of the wealthiest men in the country. He probably shared brandy with the editor of one of the major papers in his state. This was the moment that would get me thrown out of 1906—or worse.

"Harrison Gray Otis, founder and editor of the *Los Angeles* Daily *Times*," I blurted, thanking my lucky stars for the extra research I did before we came here.

"Yes, Harry," Wister said. "He will be arriving tomorrow. I'm sorry about my rudeness, but I had to be sure that you were really associated with the paper. Now, that I am feeling confident, I would love to escort you to the party, Miss Callaghan."

9.

It was a long walk to the ballroom—especially when one is being escorted by a hard-to-read Wister Reid—who held out his arm, and me who put my hand on it, as we walked with his own personal security force on what felt like a mile-long journey padded by the ornamental carpeting under our dress shoes.

Luckily, the industrialist loved to hear himself talk and his favorite subject was his own brilliance when it came to settling his family in the Paris of the West, San Francisco. He was also a vicious gossip, smiling at some of his guests and then leaning in to tell me, "He doesn't have a lick of sense." A woman in a shade of pink that was too deep received a hand kiss from Wister. When she turned away, he said to me, "She's a nut."

"Sometimes you feel like a nut; sometimes you don't," I shot back.

"Walker, you are most entertaining. You must save a dance for me," Wister said with a twinkle in his eye. He wanted to make an entrance, so we stalled in some living room area until the band was ready to play him in.

In that time, I learned that Wister was fifty-five years old (born in 1851) and in this moment of history was the father of two grown sons – Leland and Roosevelt with his first wife who passed from consumption several years ago.

There were other medical issues for the family.

The plague had established itself in San Francisco the previous year, ravaging Chinatown where Asians lived closely together in dismal conditions. Only Chinatown was quarantined due to the prejudice of the day labeling its residents "dirty people." White doctors would not go in to treat the sick. Eventually, scientists confirmed that those sick—Asian and white—suffered from a deadly form of bubonic plague. Wister lost Leland and several grandchildren.

Grandfather Wister never bothered with the little children during healthy times. They were merely incidentals around his holiday tables. He barely knew their names.

Edward was crafty and sent Jenna as one of the youthful survivors of the plague.

"My favorite granddaughter came back to me," he said, zero emotions in his gray-blue eyes.

"She came back from . . . where?"

He would not question it. "My beloved Jenna simply returned one day. I found her wandering aimlessly in my gardens. It was a miracle. A true, wonderful, miracle.

"I knew exactly what to do," he boasted. "I would make her a bride."

10.

I tried not to choke on my own spit.

"It was her destiny to return and marry a British count," Wister said. "I personally arranged the union after Jenna returned to her proper senses. She was a bit confused when she first came back to me, but now she is in tip-top shape. For a woman."

"A girl," I corrected him.

The glint in his eyes indicated that he would not be corrected again.

Daniel's bastard father Edward planned this well. He knew that the first young lady had died and was gone. He sent our Jenna, a different girl, back to the past knowing from the sheer luck that Wister would believe this was fate smiling on him. He also knew that in 1906, Jenna Reid of present-day time would have few, if any, life choices. She was simply her father and then her husband's property like a cow or a mule. Dogs were treated better.

Wister was waiting for the big finale.

"I personally arranged the union," he said. "Yes, he's a bit older and not conventionally handsome or good-looking at all. It's as if his father mated with a toad. But, he enjoys the company of younger ladies. And our family will have a countess now. I will have a royal title in the Reid legacy."

"How much did that cost?" I inquired in a sweet voice. Wister, who towered over me, took a step into my personal space, but I held my ground.

Jenna was going to be what they called a "dollar princess." In the most sinfully wealthy houses of American society circa 1900, rich residents of the USA sold their daughters abroad to British aristocrats for a title. We were a country without aristocracy. Every rich American family yearned for a duchess in the family. The young American women had no choice. The families bought nobility. The girls, as young as ten and eleven, were given to older British men, often the family rejects who couldn't find a proper bride.

The English were happy with the arrangement for several reasons beyond the idea of a young and fertile bedmate. Rich American brides came with fortunes and dowries and those funds helped to infuse the European economy and saved castle-like mansions overseas from foreclosure.

"Congratulations to the happy couple."

Those were the last words Wister said before he bowed his head and walked swiftly in front of me. His large steps were to make sure I was in his wake.

Our conversation was over.

11.

Daniel only caught sight of the old man's long black suit jacket as he entered the ballroom. We reconvened in one of the side rooms where I told him that we were right about Jenna—and she was upstairs being prepped for her big entrance tonight.

I wasn't shocked when Daniel reacted by taking large steps in Wister's direction until I stopped him with a firm arm grip.

"You're going to have to control yourself—especially when we see her tonight," I hissed, frantically into his ear. "Patience. Deep breath. Play the game," I whispered.

Inside the grand ballroom, the flamboyant decoration took my breath away. Wister obviously subscribed to the "more is more" theory of life and had someone paint what looked like a family crest on the ceiling and surrounded it with important symbols of the day: art, astronomy, literature, music, religion, the ocean, theater, and the art of commerce and war.

The walls were painted lighter gold with pillars a darker version as a tribute to his own great wealth. I counted eight large crystal chandeliers looming overhead and sending down sparkling prims over the richest creatures of the day. Swirling dancers made me dizzy. It was all so grandiose, so opulent, and so unnecessary.

It couldn't be called old money: in 1906, the money was new.

"May I have this dance? I'm playing the game, Callaghan," Daniel said with a deep bow as the orchestra ramped up for a rousing number. He placed a warm hand on the small of my back and used a strong stride to place us in the middle of those who knew how to spin.

The music was deep and rich, swirling around us like a blanket. When the violins began to cry, my bottom lip trembled.

I had zero ballroom dancing creed, but somehow Daniel knew how to waltz like he was a modern-day Fred Astaire.

"Arthur Murray dance lessons. My mom made us boys take them. Ninety-nine dollars for an entire summer—and Ma got her money's worth," he said, soaring on his feet the same way he did when we played air hockey.

I was literally swept off my feet as we whirled at a dizzying speed with the other beautiful people of the era. My hair broke free of some of the pins and was airborne.

Gravity be damned, I was flying.

There was a moment when I closed my eyes to spin and dream, only to open them to find him, gray eyes soft and warm, full lips smiling down me.

The room was a blur of colors; the music filled every inside spot that needed to feel. And somehow when I was only half conscious, half intoxicated without even one drink, I noticed that my hand had slipped into a warm palm.

It rested on his heart.

12.

Clapping was the polite way to end the dance, and I did so with a disappointed heart. Why did it have to end? The answer came in a soft drum roll and gazes that drifted up to a small balcony.

The future bride and groom stood above us. He was about six feet tall, balding, and had a belly that hung over his expensive black woolen suit pants. His smile was a thin one that appeared annoyed at all the pageantry.

She wore a Paris-bought dress and a face filled with fear.

They began to descend a long staircase. He was in the lead with a firm grip on her small hand. I noticed that she wasn't walking; she was being dragged. When she missed an entire stair, he allowed her to stumble for just the slightest moment and then yanked her back into her wobbling shoes.

Jenna! She was flying down those stairs too quickly, perhaps hoping to tumble. Anything would have been better than to remain in this nightmare.

13.

She was wearing her wedding dress, which hung off her body as if her bones formed no more than a human hanger. The expensive frock, often worn more than once during the time period, was white and featured an S-shaped corset, which flattened her nonexistent prepubescent stomach and pushed out what was supposed to be bosom, but was really just the flesh of her chest trying to do double duty. The bodice was decorated with lacy frills as if it was celebrating cleavage.

Bird-thin arms stuck out of what was known as gigot sleeves: white puffy clouds that tapered to a narrow forearm. The gown was marked by a high waist and long train. Accessories included silk opera gloves that trailed from her elbow to her fingers and a veiled white hat.

The "happy" couple was required to pay homage to the great Wister and then greet a receiving line of friends and family who certainly attended this little engagement shindig in order to approve of this union while being jealous of Wister's new title.

Daniel and I flanked the back of the line unsure what kind of response Jenna would have, if any, when her PTSD brain laid eyes on us for the first time in months.

As we got closer to the top of the line, I could see that Wister was agitated.

Jenna wasn't smiling. She wouldn't even observe proper posture and stand up ramrod straight. Moments ago, she had defied him and refused to dance with her husband-to-be.

Wincing, I watched as the great man pinched Jenna hard on her upper arm.

I had to use both hands to hold Daniel back.

"You would do well to mind your orders, young lady," Wister sputtered. "And smile for your guests, like your pointless, female life depends on it, damn it! Because it does."

14.

I noticed how she never made eye contact with him. She looked here . . . there . . . and then directly *at me*, although I had maneuvered to the back of the line again.

She passed me once . . . twice . . . and then the slow glance back.

Our eyes locked, but it wasn't what I expected.

Her eyes were hollow. Vacant orbs. I assumed that she could remember us, but maybe our appearance seemed unbelievable or just too painful to comprehend, so she put us in a box, maybe as a delusion.

Did the spirit of her still exist? Where was her energy? Her vibe? There wasn't even an echo.

If she wasn't going to react dramatically . . . I would move up.

And I did.

Finally, I stood in front of her now, giving her a light hug and then I whispered into her ear, "We love you, Jenna. We came from the Midst to save you. But, we have to be smart about getting you the hell out of here.

Bobby needs you. We need you. Don't react. Do you hear me, honey?"

I pulled back and saw tears form in her eyes, cursing myself at the same time. I whispered to her again, "Please don't, baby. Don't do anything. We'll figure out a way."

And then Daniel bowed to kiss her hand. He leaned in to kiss her cheeks and said in a hush, "Jenny, we're gonna embrace the vole, honey. One more time. Count on it."

The way her tiny hand squeezed his big hand was enough. And then in 1906, when it wasn't at all fashionable or even invented, she let her hand rest at her side and gave Daniel a delicate, but deliberate thumbs-up.

15.

Every ounce of me wanted to grab her, hug her, steal her—but not now. He had too many police "friends" milling around—most of whom were on the permanent payroll to Wister.

What was conventional, however, was the idea that the bride needed powdering after just one dance.

I watched as Jenna was guided to a ladies' commode just outside of the ballroom, and casually followed by a haggard-looking older woman in black who was her keeper or maybe a governess. Her handler turned in the hallway for just a moment in order to retrieve the powder from another servant, which gave me just enough time to slip into the one-room bathroom with Jenna. I locked the door behind me.

A wide-eyed Jenna shook her head and unlocked it.

I watched as our smart girl cracked the door open again, just a bit, and put her hand out. "I'm thirteen. If I can get married, I can certainly powder my face and pee in private—and, of course, I do have to pee with all the tea you keep pouring down my throat," she said in her sassiest voice.

Obviously, the governess knew that her charge was a dour, moody teenager, as if there were any other kind. She would allow a few moments of privacy. "I hope your sour mood will improve," said the older woman.

"Whatever," Jenna retorted, making it official once again. She was my mini-me.

I put a finger up to my lips because the handler was certainly outside and listening. Jenna led me to the farthest corner in a sterile white room that contained a family tub (everyone used the same hot bath water hence the phrase "don't throw out the baby with the bathwater"), ivory bowl and pitcher for washing, and a chamber pot in the corner to do number one. Even the richest families with the tony homes still used an outhouse out back for number two.

Jenna purposely splashed around in the bowl to drown out our low voices.

"Baby, we missed you so much," I hugged her hard and then cupped her face in my hands. Jenna all but melted into my arms.

"Please Walker, don't make me marry him," she begged, a fresh round of tears rolling. "He's old and disgusting—and he even tried to kiss me with these dry, cracked lips, but I refused, which is proper here until the wedding night. Then, I will have no choice but to submit."

"Honey, listen to me carefully before they come in," I rushed. "We will try to sneak into the mansion and get you later tonight. If it doesn't work then we will try tomorrow, which is Tuesday. If that doesn't work, I hear you'll be moving to the wedding hotel, the Palace, on Tuesday afternoon.

"If all else fails, on Tuesday night, you will wait until three a.m. to sneak out as our last resort. Wear whatever you can run in," I instructed. "We have to leave this city by four in the morning at the latest before—"

"Before the wedding," she gasped. "It's at nine and then we sail for England."

"No," I said, gripping her face in my hand. "Not gonna happen. You meet us outside of the hotel, in the back, by the big statue of an angel. We'll time travel home—and Edward won't even know."

"He put me here," she whimpered. "My own father had me sold to the highest bidder."

"I know, baby. We'll deal with him another time. We just have to get you out before dawn on Wednesday because they're going to have a little old earthquake. Nothing to worry about now," I said, trying to keep it low-key.

"The great earthquake of 1906," Jenna said. "The entire city crumbled and then burned, which is fine. I'd rather die again in it and never be born than marry that smelly old asshat."

I had never heard Jenna swear before.

"Well, pissflaps, I see him as more of a shitbagaholic, honey," I said.

Finally, she smiled. And then she laughed.

The governess pounded on the door.

"Where did you get that from, Walker?" she whispered.

"I'm from Chicago," I explained. And then, I finished it.

"We'll draw a portal and leave this place. We'll go home," I promised. "Now, you get out of here. Act exactly how you've been acting. You don't want to draw any suspicion. Turn off the light behind you. I'll slip out later."

She hugged me hard.

"When I'm gone, they'll all shit bricks," she said with a tiny smile that she wiped off her own face.

I gave her the thumbs-up.

16.

I waited a few minutes before exiting the bathroom. It wasn't long before Wister was in my face flanked by a miserable-looking old man with matted gray hair pushed behind his ears, a witchy nose, and a short pepper-colored beard. His eyes were narrow and framed by black-and-white brows that looked like inchworms.

"Walker, look who is here," Wister boomed. "And we were just talking about you."

"That's too kind," I said. But the truth was I drew a blank. Did Wister just shake another relative off the Reid family tree?

"Your editor," Wister said, going in for the kill. "The publisher of the *Los Angeles Daily Times*: Harrison Gray Otis."

"Sir," I said, nodding like I held court with the man every single day in our ink-stained office. "It's a lovely engagement dinner, isn't it?"

Harrison Gray Otis looked confused.

"Do I know you?" he asked.

"Just as I thought. You don't work for the paper. You're some kind of intruder," Wister said under his breath.

He nodded and two officers in blue wool army uniforms, black clubs at their hips, held me back while Wister and Harrison Gray moved forward.

Next, I heard words that were hauntingly familiar.

"You're under arrest."

THIRTY-FIVE

B odily, I was dragged outside and lifted into a rickety wooden cage latched to the back of a wagon. Turns out, I wasn't alone in my box.

Daniel was in there because Wister "had a feeling" that he was up to devilish things. And when Wister had a vibe, the officers he paid under the table arrested first and asked questions later.

There was no way to escape, so we held hands in our party clothes until the same officers removed the restraints and yanked us into the street in front of a two-story brick building with a wooden staircase in front. It was a jail on the northeast corner of Broadway Street, dating back to 1851. Only we knew that it was scheduled to collapse and then burn to rubble in two days.

Male and female prisoners were kept on different floors. Before we were forced to part ways, some seriously jacked up news was delivered. "Judge can't see you until next Friday," said one of our jailers.

"But that's several days from now," I blurted.

We didn't have several days.

"What are the exact charges?" Daniel demanded.

"So, Romeo, over here, is now a lawyer," laughed the cop who pushed Daniel toward the staircase and used his club to prod him into walking upward.

"What about our rights?" I shouted.

"Your . . . what?" asked my copper who pointed up, annoyed at how I took my time climbing fifteen stairs in party shoes.

This was 1906. You had no right to be silent. You barely had a right to breathe.

The jail was almost empty on a Monday night and we were separated and thrown into dark cells with a pot in back for bathroom business, no running water, and a scratchy red wool blanket on the floor. We weren't given uniforms. We could rot in our original clothing.

It wasn't long before another man in blue wool with penetrating eyes, the six-foot-three Sheriff Jack Hayes, came by to tell me the rules. I had already been to jail in the afterlife, and frankly San Francisco lock-up of yore didn't seem to be half as horrifying as the maximum-security penitentiary ITT with the Godfather in charge.

Sheriff Hayes gave me a slow once-over and explained his personal quid pro quo system.

"No one cares about you here. No one knows you're alive. The fact that your blood is flowing is at my discretion. We execute the ones who don't behave, missy," he told me. "There's an enclosed jail yard behind this building with a nice, shady place to hang those who are just too much for their own good.

"Are you surly?" he demanded.

"Aren't all women pushed to their limit?"

"Are you crazy?" he asked.

"Well," I responded, "not usually."

I imagined slicing his throat with one of the throwing stars in my pocket. One odd thing about jail in 1906: frisking was considered lewd.

I could have carried a machine gun under my dress – and wished I had one.

"But, if you're nice to Sheriff Jack," he cooed, moving his hand up and down the bars, "well, your time here can be memorable, if you know what I mean."

"I have enough memories. I need to see the judge," I said in a sweet voice. "Please and thank you. Now, that's nice, isn't it?"

"We'll see by Friday what that smart mouth can do," he replied.

By Friday, this place will be melted bricks and ashes.

"Until then I'll have my deputy check on you in the middle of the night. We're both young and single. And we're also both the only two people one earth with the keys to these cells.

"I'd be mighty nice to him, too, missy," he said. "A girl could get lost in the legal system, if you know what I mean."

"Shucks," I said evenly. "I do."

2.

In the middle of the night, a dirty rag was stuffed into my mouth and a burlap sack was placed over my head as I was dragged outside to the prison yard.

"Yeah, boss," he yelled. "I'll just scare the shit out of both of them. I got him tied to a tree."

In a pool of darkness I could barely breathe. I couldn't scream. The old sheriff laughed from an upstairs window, which I heard him slam shut. There was still a sliver of light, which meant that he was watching.

Someone else had the same idea.

A calloused hand flew across my mouth as thick arms wrestled me to the dusty ground. I almost bit him, but he pushed my hair behind my ear and hissed into my ear, "Scream loudly now! Make a show of it, *sis!*"

And I listened. Because I would have gone along with him anytime, any place.

In return, Peter Reid, held me tightly in a fierce hug, laugh. He shouted a shit-kicking "yah-hoo" into the air, which was enough for the sheriff in the window above. He turned off the lights. Daniel's younger brother—the one we had left with Dr. King—looked wild and rugged with a beard and almost twenty pounds of muscle on him. We had a way of enjoying our collective silences together, but this was no time to keep quiet.

"Stop. Please!" I yelled loud enough for interested parties upstairs to believe I was being violated.

Pete pointed toward the hanging tree, which was surrounded by enough foliage that it would be impossible to watch from upstairs. Under it, Daniel stood with Tosh who was sporting a chic platinum edgy bob. "I'm single-handedly trying to usher the roaring twenties in," she whispered, hugging me hard.

She pulled away to jump into Pete's arms and kiss him with the kind of passion that made me do a double take. It was clear that their relationship had developed during their time in The Other. "We did it. Pete and me for the save!" Tosh spoke softly, jumping up and down, which was normal.

The girl was perpetual motion.

"Are we going to stand here talking?" Daniel said. "Sooner or later, the Avenger upstairs is going to realize that his partner is inside . . . in another room."

No one answered as we ran hard into the San Francisco fog.

3.

The next morning, Daniel and I stood under a scattering of clouds in an otherwise blue sky. A hint of thunder rumbled in the distance.

We made one pit stop at the Palace Hotel, and sent Pete inside to retrieve our backpacks from our room. Staying there seemed too risky, as those who knew Wister were everywhere, so under fake names of Miss Britney Spears and Mr. Post Malone, we slept at the less glamorous Hotel Majestic, built in 1902.

It wasn't so much the accommodations. The Majestic was considered "modern and new" with its twenty-five bathtubs, thirty water closets, and fifty-seven guest rooms. It was four stories with bowls, pitchers, and chamber pots in the room (oh joy). Pete and Tosh were staying here and immediately they jumped into the bed. Tosh put her head on Pete's chest. We were relegated to a few blankets and one pillow on the floor.

It took the better part of the night for Pete, over candlelight and whispers, to bring us up to speed.

"Dr. King said it was becoming too unsafe at the cabin house, so we left and drove to the Astonishing School," Pete said. "Once we got there we found out that you were gone. It didn't take long for Auggie to rat you out."

"Damn," Daniel bit out. "I knew we couldn't trust him."

"Dr. King sort of knew it already," Tosh said, playing with Pete's hands. "He knew that the minute you learned how to draw portals that you would go look for the girls. He knows you. We all do. He knew Walker would be by your side."

"How mad is he on a scale of one to ten?" I asked.

"Around seventy-five and accelerating," Pete said.

"He figured out where you went because there are ways to trace portals," Pete said. "When he said San Francisco, my mind went to: What's the worst thing that ever happened there?"

"Rice-a-Roni, the San Francisco treat?" Pete, the purveyor of pop culture, posed.

"Of course, it was the quake and the fires," he declared.

"What do you know that we don't know?" I asked Pete, one of the smartest humans I had ever met in my life.

"I know that we can't get Jenna tonight. Wister, our great-grandfather, will have the place on high alert," he said. "We have to grab her at the wedding hotel and then we have to run before the city falls down around us."

"Oh, easy," I blurted. "Maybe we stop along the way for some clam chowder out of those cute bread bowls."

"Baby," Daniel stopped me. "They don't have bread bowls. Yet."

I told the other three about how Jenna was going to meet us—if possible—in the middle of the night outside of the hotel. Daniel and Pete looked at each other as if they didn't trust that Jenna had enough real-world street smarts to go through with it.

"She'll get caught," Pete said.

"No," Daniel slowly argued. "She's fierce and motivated."

"The groom wanted to get married in England. Wister refused that request because he wanted the press coverage and insisted that the ceremony be held in San Francisco with a major send-off later at a ship that would sail first to New York and then to England."

"What ship . . . the *Titanic*?" I said.

"*Titanic* was six years later in 1912," Pete said.

"How lucky for us," I replied.

Around five in the morning, when the first light of dawn remained a dream, sleep robbing "travel" issues began to creep in.

"And then there is the matter of drawing a portal home. We need a place that has maximum energy. We need vibrational wattage," I said. "We need to go there in advance to make sure we feel some kind of pulsation, which is what we should do at sunrise."

"I got a place," Pete said with a mile-wide grin.

Before dawn, we stood in our bare feet in the Pacific at a golden spot called Baker Beach. Tranquil and untouched, it stretched a mile below the rugged cliffs of the city's western shoreline with stunning views of the golden hills. The Golden Gate Bridge would consume the skyline, but not until 1933. Who needed a suspension bridge when there were so few cars?

Glacially cold water felt invigorating as it sloshed over my ankles. Churning waves capped in white foam slapped at my knees and thighs.

"The epicenter of the earthquake, which will strike at 5:12 a.m. local time on April 18, 1906—tomorrow—is right here, about two miles, out in the ocean. It will create a vortex of majestic energy, as a 7.9 quake does, that could send us to any time or place," said our historian Pete.

"Or, quite simply, it will send us back to our friends," said the hopeful dreamer . . . me.

I knew we were in the right spot. I felt my feet and legs tingle so hard with vibration that they were quaking.

When we walked back, fresh green leaves were swaying. Spring was here.

So was the beginning of the end.

4.

The day went by in a blur.

We re-packed jeans, tees, sweaters, and our running boots. Daniel lifted an extraordinary buckskin jacket from the back of a chair in the lobby and put it on my shoulders. After dinner that night, we put on our traveling clothes and began to go stir-crazy counting down the minutes. We had to grab Jenna, but not get arrested in 1906 in the process.

Arrest would mean death in this time period. None of the jails survived the fires.

Die in this time period and you would *never* be born in the next.

We were careful to stay outside of the Palace Hotel, hiding our backpacks in the far bushes of the garden in back. A larger period dress we stole from the laundry of our hotel fit over the travel leggings and tees Tosh and I donned underneath. Daniel and Pete wore suit pants with leggings underneath; suit jackets with white shirts hiding. They would ditch the more formal clothing when it was time.

We had to melt into the swarms of fancy people checking into the hotel late that afternoon and early evening. They were here to celebrate a wedding tomorrow morning.

"Are you part of the wedding?" they asked us.

I nodded because in a weird way, we were a part of it.

I caught bits and pieces of gossip from the ladies who lose their lunch to stay that skinny.

"I heard," cooed one stick figure in mauve, "that it's a stunning white wedding dress made by the House of Worth, one of the first couture designers in America."

"Well I heard," chirped her sister in sky blue, "that the dress is woven with gold and embellished with white feathers on the bottom and has thousands of small but real pearls sewn into the bodice."

"Darling, I heard," carped a friend in lavender, "the bride is to wear a diamond tiara and an enormous emerald necklace."

They gossiped about the age of the groom (acceptable), the trip to London (exciting), and the oddness of a wedding on a Wednesday (shock and bad luck).

The nuptials were set for a 10:00 a.m. morning ceremony followed by an extravagant luncheon for San Francisco's bluest bloods and society mavens. Wister was serving duck although the groom was so poor in England that he would have enjoyed crow. It was strange to have a wedding on a Wednesday, but the groom insisted as it was also his birthday and their ship sailed for England the same day at sunset.

He had reserved a private suite for the honeymoon splendors.

It sickened me to see the long white dress carried from a carriage by three different teenage boy servants. I was close enough to hear them say that it was made of real lace and "not to forget the brand-new black leather shoes."

Around 8:00 p.m., a grand carriage arrived and I watched the governess step out followed by a numb, expressionless Jenna. Her face was blank, but her words had meaning.

"No one will disturb me tonight," she sassed the governess. "Not even you—or should I say, especially not you! I must get my beauty sleep."

"You will look beautiful tomorrow," said her keeper. It wasn't a statement, but more like an order.

5.
3:30 A.M.

It was cool outside and the air smelled of salt and dread. Knowing the future made my stomach churn and not knowing Jenna's fleeing prowess left me pacing in a small thicket of trees behind the hotel that served as a way for guests to commune with nature.

The entrance to this little passage of green was marked by an angel with wings wrapped around her being in protection. I wasn't sure if that was a good sign, or a mark that those who trespassed here were in actual danger.

A few "what if's" hit us in the desperation of an endless night and the wait for Jenna to materialize. *What if she never made it out of the hotel? What if they caught her? What if she didn't have the guts to leave?*

"Screw this," Daniel finally said. "We storm the place and go get her."

"And get arrested," I said. "And try to survive an earthquake in a jail cell that's buried in the earth now."

Tosh fretted by doing the yoga tree pose.

"Walker, Daniel, and Pete," she finally gasped as both feet hit the ground, "You're probably wanted for your jailbreak. I'm the only one whose face is unknown. I'll go in and get her."

"In your travel clothes?" Daniel fumed.

One thing about Tosh. She didn't really wait for the answer to her suggestion. Before we know it, she was blowing Pete kisses and traipsing across the big lawn. The last I saw of her in the dim light was her feet racing down a back cement staircase where the maids and butlers entered, which was pretty brilliant. There would likely be maid's uniform's down there, which would give her access to all the floors including the top one, naturally the best and the one Wister would rent out for members of the wedding party.

The only question was: What room was the bride in and how would Tosh find out?

"I'm going with her," Pete finally said after a frustrating ten minutes.

"I don't think we should separate," Daniel said.

"Would you leave Walker in there?" Pete challenged.

He didn't wait for an answer.

6.

3:45 A.M.

It *only* took fifteen minutes before the trees in front of us began to rustle like someone was using them as a doorway. "Daniel!" whispered a frantic voice. And just like that the bride herself, Jenna Reid, fell into his arms, crying tears of pure joy. "I'm free," she whispered as he spun and hugged her hard. "Thank God, I'm free."

But we were not free because Tosh and Pete were inside and now the three of us were outside. We would wait another fifteen minutes although I had a sick feeling deep inside that Pete wouldn't leave the building without his sister. Tosh was another story. I knew she had zero attention span and would get herself arrested.

"I'll go," Daniel said under his breath.

"No, I'll go in," I fumed.

"I was in Room 815," Jenna said. "The only solution is I'll go. No one will question it if it's me."

"No!" we cried, although damn it, her idea made perfect sense.

"Go," I told Jenna.

No time like 1906 to grow up.

4:00 A.M.

Middle of the night time is slow time whether you're having a nightmare or sleep is being refused to you by whatever sprinkles that fine, temporary coma dust into our brains. I spent that time taking large leaves and making tiny pieces of them. Daniel paced our small space until I thought he would wear a ten-foot hole into the earth.

Finally, two figures emerged walking hunched over toward the trees. "Is that them?" I asked, frantically.

"Sorry to freak you out," Tosh said, wheeling a silver room service cart. Pete was at her side in a butler's uniform and sleek black shoes.

"We climbed the servant's staircase, ending up in the kitchen, which was empty," Pete said.

549

My eyes filled. "We just sent Jenna back in," I began.

"And here I am," she said, jumping out of the bottom of the cart.

7.

"Give us the short version," I said.

"Tosh and I dressed up like a maid and butler," Pete said. "We made it to the eighth floor with food, which delighted the guards. Tosh left one table and I wheeled the other to Room 815 where Jenna was staying. The guard let us in after we told him some story about how the bride needed hot milk to sleep."

"We wheeled in there—she wasn't in the room," Pete said, "which had me pissing in my pants with fear because how else could we find her? Then, I heard a thump outside."

"I knocked out my own guard with a book," Jenna said, proudly. "The way Danny taught me how to do. He fell like a clump. The other guards were in the bathroom."

"We put dishwater soap in their food," Tosh said. "Old trick. Works every time."

"We took the maid's elevator back down to the basement," she said. "Everything seemed to be happening in slow motion."

"But now it has to go fast," Pete said. "They're going to know something is wrong when they see her guard missing. The shit is gonna hit the wall."

A bright light from a lantern infiltrated the trees.

"Meet at the water," Pete said, grabbing Jenna and Tosh's hands and bolting.

Daniel and I would stand and fight.

8.

4:17 A.M.

The highest-ranking law man in these parts used his Colt Paterson revolver, a revolving pistol, as his partner, eyes, and third arm. Long silver metal parted the tree branches in front of us followed by a flood of amber rays.

His finger on the trigger, the sheriff snorted and said in an overjoyed voice, "Girlie, I can smell you. Honey soap and nerves. I knew you would be coming back to me. Now, it's just up to you if you want to return in one piece or two or three or ten."

I raised both arms high in surrender.

"Do you plan on reading me my rights," I said, echoing our first encounter. "You better hurry because a major earthquake is about to hit the city in about an hour."

"You want the earth to move? That could be arranged," he said. "But if you want rights, you have the right to die by this pistol or by hanging— and it's up to me which one we'll be pursuing tonight."

"You're right, sir, to seek an ending," I said.

I threw the first star, which hit him exactly where his jugular vein was located. That interruption caused the blood to drain from his brain, face, and neck and land in the mulch down below

Daniel finished it by knocking the sheriff out.

"Checkout time," I said, looking back at the hotel as we ran west as fast as our traumatized feet would carry us.

THIRTY-SIX

1.

4:47 A.M. Twenty-five minutes before the quake.

By 5:00 a.m., we caught up with the rest and it was clear that the ocean was still too far in the distance. Our options were narrowing. "We can't just bang on some door and say, 'Excuse me, it's the middle of the night, but please let us in because there is going to be an earthquake in fifteen minutes,'" I said.

"We can't stand here on the streets either," Daniel replied. "Who knows what streets will still be here?"

Pete's sly grin told me that he had a plan.

"I took us this way because this little park, Lotta's Fountain, is right around the corner," he said as we raced down Market Street. "It's on hard land. Not sand. Sand won't hold up and there's a lot of this city built on it as you get closer to the water."

In the pitch black, we entered a small outdoor children's park with a cast iron fountain in the middle commissioned by actress Lotta Crabtree as a gift to her favorite city. The tall gold structure was dedicated in 1875.

"Later today, this is the spot that served as a meeting place for the people who would suddenly be declared homeless and would walk the streets aimlessly searching for relatives, shelter, and hope. They gathered here at the statue because it refused to topple," Pete said.

"This patch of land was completely undisturbed," Pete said, opening the unlocked iron gate.

5:05 A.M. Seven minutes before the quake.

There was no one in the park at this hour. Three heavy wooden tables were completely empty.

I prayed we found a vibration to travel back *right now*, but nothing. It was too late to run for the water. All we could do is shelter under one of those tables. Daniel took me into his lap along with Jenna while Pete draped himself over Tosh.

The world was about to crack open.

2.
5:10 A.M. Two minutes before the quake.

There were many things I counted down in life: New Year's Eve, the last seconds of a school year, the time between when you ordered your pizza and it arrived at the table, but this was something different. This was the devil knocking.

Two minutes. One hundred and twenty seconds remained. My mind was a riot. *Did this one chunk of land really hold? Was it revisionist history? What about the debris? Just because no one died, supposedly, in this spot didn't mean they weren't maimed or de-limbed. A 7.9 nine earthquake was a killing force. It was the real end.*

One minute left.

My heart was pounding; my brain locked in on full speed rush.

"I want two things in this world. I want you and I want us," Daniel whispered hard into my ear.

His heart.

Endless.

I die.

3.

5:12 A.M.

A distant rumbling from far away gave way to the thunderous sound of rolling annihilation.

Across the street, two wood frame houses began to crumble while bricks rained down from collapsing chimneys.

The earth began its dance, violent shocks moving the ground punctuated by strong shaking from side to side that would last a teeth-rattling sixty seconds.

I heard the sound of destruction.

I smelled death all around me.

And then, it stopped.

We were flattened on the ground like pieces of paper. Jenna below. Me in the middle. Daniel on top of us. He held me, tightly covering my face with his hands.

Everything below us moved in underground waves called aftershocks.

I watched as the dirt on the ground rose in two feet waves knowing that the quake hit eight miles into the sea and shook the world fifty miles east and two hundred miles north to south.

"Shitballs!" Pete cried.

As the seconds ticked, the quaking got stronger again. People were running into the streets in nothing more than white dressing gowns and bare feet. Most of the bodies that were found were clad in only sleeping clothes.

The great Pacific Ocean seemed to scream during two aftershocks as this beast devoured San Francisco proper. And then . . . a switch was flipped followed by an uneasy quiet.

The city was done trembling, but the aftermath was just beginning.

4.

In the smoke and dust, different living creatures begin to crawl out of their holes. Animals burst through barn doors and humans climbed out of windows and cracks.

A city hospital down the street looked more like an anthill with humans pouring out into the night.

Up the hill, the large brick buildings were gone. Swaying trees waved in a slight breeze as if they were saying good-bye silly humans. "What you built," they whispered, "was no stronger than a child's toy."

5.

All eyes were on Pete who took his right hand and made the motion that it was over. We stood on wobbling legs and left the safe haven of the little park knowing there was little time before the city burst into flames. On unsure legs, we walk-raced over rubble toward the ocean, which was only two blocks away. Amid the crumbling brick and ruins, we heard the scream of people who were still alive but trapped in collapsed brick houses.

At one point, we stopped to help the police pull a big chunk of concrete off the top of a building and then joined a chain of those reaching down to pull those "lucky" enough to the top. We couldn't save them all, but prayed for the city.

It was still pitch-black outside and the hard jolts of 6.0 aftershocks nearly took us off our feet. An explosion half a block up from us had me burying my face in Daniel's shoulder.

We had to move. It wouldn't be long before those in power would find a "solution" in demolishing the downed buildings with dynamite. No one had a second thought about the gas mains. The fires over the next three days from the explosions would destroy 25,000 buildings on 490 city blocks. Some of the property owners deliberately set their own fires in order to make sure they received as much insurance money as possible.

When a three-story house collapsed inches in front of our faces, I burst into sobbing tears. Daniel pushed the dust and mud away from my eyes, which registered shock.

"It feels like the end," I cried, clinging to him.

"It isn't," he said, holding my chin in his hand. "We go on."

He grabbed Jenna's hand and mine. With a primal yell, he pulled us forward.

Morning light seemed eons away.

As we raced for the safety of another world, fire trucks slammed up to hydrants. But when they tried to hook up their hoses, there was no water. "Water lines to the city are broken!" one yelled. It's why 25,000 buildings were destroyed and 300,000 would be left homeless. Some eighty percent of the city would be leveled by fire by the end of the day.

Thin columns of smoke were already rising into the sky as we found ourselves outside of a small breakfast place, and Pete grabbed us by the arms.

"Run!" he yelled, pulling us hard until we were racing up one of the hills. We knew why when we heard the explosion. "The chimney above the stove was damaged," Pete said, "When the cook just lit the stove, a fire burst out in the kitchen. It's the actual start of the entire city burning."

They would call it the Ham and Eggs Fire. A woman started to cook breakfast, but didn't realize that the chimney was damaged by the quake. Within minutes, the entire house was on fire and then the block went up in bright orange doom.

6.

There was a man who was thrown from a third-story window and landed on his front lawn. His jaw was broken and his nose was bleeding. One eyebrow was hanging from a thread. A nurse next door told him to stay still. "You have a broken arm and two broken legs," she said.

"The end of the world is here," said a woman in a long dressing gown. And it was.

A man stumbled forth holding a black leather bag in one hand and wearing a tuxedo. I knew he was not of this era because if you looked closely enough the suitcase wasn't really black, but medium brown and was imprinted with the uber-expensive Louis Vuitton logo.

"I came for the wedding. I wanted to know that it happened. That we had British royalty in our family. I know how to draw portals, too. But I expected to be at the hotel before this started—in a safety zone," said Edward Reid. "This is just . . . too much . . . much too much. I don't know what to do. I need . . ."

Edward was in shock.

"Kids, can you give an old man a hand?" he rambled.

Daniel's eyes flashed red from soot and the dust. With a primal yell, he charged forward, swinging at his father's face with his bare hands.

"No!" I screamed. "You can't kill him. You can't or you'll never be born. No Pete. No Bobby. No Jenna or Andy."

Daniel's hands were around his father's throat now and the refugees on the streets just stared at them as they walked past. No one stopped.

"This is for Callaghan," he said, squeezing hard as the old man choked.

"Where is Andy?" Daniel screamed, pushing hard on his father's jugular. *Only this was a father who didn't seem in his right mind. He didn't recognize any of us.*

"I have a daughter . . . yes," he rambled, eyes glazed. "I sent her . . . away . . . to the mountains . . . to the sky . . . my little Andrea . . . she is buried in Littleton, Colorado." Edward gasped as if these were his last words. "Date of death . . . Nineteen hundred and . . ."

I couldn't make out the rest.

One last squeeze and Daniel shoved the body off the curb and into the street. He stood, towering over his father who lay bleeding in the gutter.

Edward wasn't moving.

"We'll leave it to fate," Daniel said. "If he doesn't make it to a portal, he will die here. Just remember that rat bastards always survive.

"And once we're on our own time, I will finish it—kill him—once and for all."

7.

On Fillmore Street, the buildings didn't crumble, but sank into the ground as if it was made out of quicksand. Heads were sticking up from the rock and ruins. I saw a man standing in the middle of the street with a five-year-old girl.

"Agnes," he told her. "I hope you never see a thing like this again."

I did the same slow turn as he did to reveal the panorama of a city in flames. Engine Co. One was comprised of eight men, two horses, and a wooden buggy. They were no match for a city that was an inferno. Wooden houses fell like they were made of toothpicks and then their gas lines took care of the rest and burned the wood down to charred sticks.

The dead stayed where they perished. The living stood on rooftops stomping out the burning embers with their smoldering feet. Others carried pots and pans and put them in pillowcases for easier transport, but to where?

There were three dozen fires raging through the city. By the next morning, headlines in the *San Francisco Chronicle* would read: The City That Was. The Old San Francisco Is Dead.

8.

Baker Beach looked remarkably untouched by the quake.

As we ran through the sand to the water's edge, I began to feel a strong vibration. Daniel scratched a X onto Jenna's hand and we did the same as we set our intentions of where we wanted to travel.

The humming became louder and stronger. Holding hands, we didn't think or ask, but ran full blast into the water.

Waves were crashing as we waded out waist-deep, hands still linked. Daniel squeezed my fingers.

"You trust me?" he asked.

"Beyond," I yelled.

"Your heart and mine are very old friends," he shouted.

Tosh was crying.

As we stood in the middle of the ocean, the sun began to rise, but our world turned black.

I was dry.

I was laying on my back.

On hard ground.

Face up.

Hands free.

Daniel rolled, kissing me hard. It felt like stars tiptoeing across my skin.

This moment reminded me of one thing: be happy in every moment.

That moment is your life.

THIRTY-SEVEN

1.

From my vantage point in a muddy, grassy field, I saw majestic mountains above me, piercing the sky and surrounding us like a picture frame. I stood quickly just in case we were in danger, but the only obstacle was avoiding the mulchy earth below.

We were in a rutted field that opened to a large valley. Craning my neck, I saw that the mountains were a combination of seasons with snow-kissed tops and small pink and purple flowers blooming in untouched black dirt. fresh dirt.

It smelled like new beginnings.

I took a deep breath. It was crispy cool with a sweet hint of jasmine floating on the breeze.

Everyone was accounted for in a place where gloriously the ground was solid and not shaking. I spied another who wasn't with us on the San Francisco trip. Eddie Wargo was wiping grass stains off his finest Walmart shirt and rubbing his aching backside with both meaty hands.

"Kiss my ass-teroids. That landing was a bitch," he said.

Daniel was helping Jenna to her feet. Pete and Tosh celebrated this major time travel jump by falling into each other arms.

Daniel scooped me up for a long kiss.

I was startled by a jackalope or desert bunny who ran by my feet at a leisurely hop. Jenna celebrated her freedom by doing a quick cartwheel while Daniel grabbed my hand.

We should have been "home" in The Other, but we . . . definitely . . . were . . . not. I didn't know how I knew, but I felt as if something was wrong.

There was nothing else to do but walk a bit over the rugged terrain until we saw a little green marker that provided a quick clue. It read: Rampart Range Foothills.

Not that I was some geography expert, but I had never seen it before although it sounded hauntingly familiar. Pete looked at Daniel in a knowing way. "He took us to Colorado a lot as kids. His idea of a family vacation was trying to kill us on a trail ride," Pete said.

"We're in the suburbs of Denver," Daniel said in an astonished voice—and then it dawned on me.

None of us were thinking about The Other when we dialed in mentally to travel. There was only one town on our minds because Edward Reid told us that he sent his other daughter there: Littleton, Colorado.

A panoramic view revealed a great expanse of housing and a downtown center that were just a hop, skip, and a trek away. When we got closer, a bank sign revealed that it was 10:45 a.m. I waited for the sign to click. And it did, providing today's date.

April 20, 1999. Daniel shrugged; even Pete looked confused.

I kind of dug the town. It was mountain utopia, a great place to raise a family . . . or maybe not so great.

There was a school in the near distance. The sign. It couldn't be true.

Welcome to Columbine High School.

Home of the Rebels.

2.

No one said a word.

"What time did you set? This isn't The Other," Tosh gasped.

"Callaghan? Daniel asked.

"He said that thing," I replied. "About Andy. I couldn't stop thinking about it."

"About Colorado," Jenna said. "I can't think about anything else."

I looked at Tosh.

"What the hell do you expect? Colorado," she said. "I was thinking of Colorado. Sue me."

"April 20, 1999, of course," Pete said.

Daniel only said one word: "Edward wants her to die in the school."

Eddie capped it. "Dr. King figured it out, too. He sent me for muscle. And he sent toys," he said, dumping his backpack at our feet. Inside were enough weapons to arm a small country.

"We can't change history, Dr. King said," Eddie informed us. "Since Andy isn't really supposed to be here in the first place, we can 'legally' slip her out. As for Columbine and, you know, the shootings, we can't warn anyone. We can't save anyone. We can't take anyone out."

"It's a rescue mission," Daniel said. "We got it. Even if we don't like it."

3.

It was surreal in a way. You read so much about what happened here, but now we were walking around the outskirts of the hallowed grounds of Columbine High, eventually past the football field and then over the sidewalk where the twelve students would die in the first major school shooting to receive an elevated level of world-wide attention.

They were just like us. Students with plans. Students with big dreams.

That was shot to shit because, like us, they died young.

We moved in close enough to touch the sign that still boasted about spring break, which had been over for a whole month. I remembered for a moment that feeling of spring break ending and how it seemed at the time to be the most horrible thing that could ever happen.

It was a big world. And there were worse things.

In a few hours President Bill Clinton would announce, "We all know there has been a terrible shooting at a high school in Colorado. I hope the American people will be praying for the students, the parents, and the teachers."

Every noise I heard here seemed garishly loud. A Pontiac Grand Am drove with Ricky Martin's "Livin' La Vida Loca" blaring from speakers. There was so much bass that the car was practically throbbing. I put up a hand and the driver stopped.

"Do you know where the cafeteria is?" I asked.

"You're looking at it, *chica*," she said, pointing straight ahead.

They shot up the cafeteria, the library, and the choir room.

Engrossed in my thoughts and trying to remember, I walked right into a young freshman boy who was going the other way.

"Excuse me. What period is it?" I asked.

"No worries. Fifth," he said. "Mostly everyone is at lunch or in the library. Don't tell anyone you saw me sneak out."

"Do you know Andy Reid. Andrea Reid?" I managed to say.

"Yeah, I know her," the kid said. "Pretty girl with long black hair. She's in choir with me this period, but I'm ditching. Please," he begged. "You didn't see me."

"I won't say a thing," I said with dead eyes.

They shot up the entire choir room.

"He sent us here to watch her die in the past," Daniel said. "He wasn't in shock after the quake. It was just part of the game."

"He is . . . the devil," I said, repeating Daniel's words.

"Next time," I began.

"He's mine, Callaghan," Daniel promised.

4.

And then there was a moment of clarity like smoke parting.

"Are we doing this?" I asked.

Daniel gave me the look with the glow behind it. He would lay it on the line for his sister—as would I.

But, we wouldn't be alone.

Sometimes in the most unlikely places you meet the kind of people who just stick to you.

I looked across the parking lot and saw a welcome sight coming straight at us: Cass was at the ready.

"We have to get Andy out before—"

"We know, sugar," Cass said. "Others know, too. We were sent here . . . as reinforcements. As in let's get that girl, not change history, and get the hell out of here. This isn't our business. Andy doesn't belong here, so she is our business."

I couldn't help but give him the biggest bear hug.

"Sugar, you missed me," he said with a Cass grin.

"I would have brought you flowers, but . . . ," Cass said, squeezing me hard.

He filled my pocket with throwing stars.

"Pete," I said in an oddly shrill voice. Something deep inside told me this would not end well. "Timetable."

"They arrive at 11:10 a.m. in separate cars. If you look down the street to your right, you'll see them right now entering school grounds."

5.

They were, of course, seniors Dylan Klebold, seventeen, and Eric Harris, eighteen, former Boy Scouts and pizza parlor workers. They liked to dress in long black trench coats, which as fitting as they were members of a clandestine group in these parts called the Trenchcoat Mafia.

They were fascinated with Goth culture, bowling, TV cartoons, and Adolph Hitler. In fact, they chose April 20 to bring down this school because it was Hitler's birthday.

It was perfectly reasonable for all of us to stand shooting the shit in the high school parking lot. Millions of kids do that every single day. I watched as they pulled in and parked a few feet from us. Eric's window was down and I zeroes in on his sick smile as he threw the car into park.

He said three distinct words as his grin became wider.

"Rock and roll."

6.

11:10 a.m. As history would have it, there was an interrupter. A fellow senior named Brooks came walking by for his fifth period smoke. He sauntered up to Eric's car and began to bitch at him.

"You skipped your morning classes," he said.

"It doesn't matter anymore," said Eric.

There was a pause.

"Get out of here," Eric told his friend. "I like you. Get out of here. *Go home.*"

It didn't take much and Brooks was walking away. He wouldn't be one of the twelve dead today or the teacher who was slain or the more than twenty critically wounded.

He would live. And for the moment, so would the kids in the cafeteria eating lunch because the bombs Eric and Dylan planted all malfunctioned. The plan was to bomb the school then shoot people and then throw bombs at the remaining survivors.

Those damn devices failed to detonate, which meant that Eric and Dylan were now getting out of their cars. They went to their trunks, emerging with two big guns each: a semiautomatic rifle and a sawed-off shotgun.

Plan B.

7.

The parking lot was a spot for stray students who needed to get back to their cars for various educational and recreational reasons. Jocks. Queens. Studios. Outlaws. "You need to leave school—now!" Tosh began to whisper. "Something really bad is about to happen."

No, Tosh, no . . .

A Columbine student circa 1999 looked at her suspiciously in her dirty leggings and muddy sweater from the 1906 San Francisco earthquake.

"Bitch, take it down the road," she said. "I don't fall for senior pranks."

"It's not a prank," Tosh said, frantically. "There is going to be a school shooting."

"You don't even go to this school," said her friend. "Get the hell out of here. It's not funny."

"You have to tell everyone," Tosh insisted, despite the fact that I grabbed her hard by the arm. She couldn't sound an alarm. Changing history had severe repercussions.

At the same time, I wanted to find a megaphone and scream for the student body to go home.

"How 'bout I tell everyone that some crazy bitch tried to scare the shit out of me today, but I didn't fall for it," said the nameless student.

"They will fire one hundred and eighty-eight rounds," Tosh cried as I dragged her away. "I'm from the future."

"Tosh!" I hissed.

"Okay, and I saw an alien last night," said the girl's boyfriend.

8.

Inevitably, the past and the future would brush up against each other.

Daniel and Cass had raced far ahead, but in my paralyzing fear of what was about to happen, I found myself walking slower and making sure that Tosh didn't screw up. She was onto me and took off running.

I felt someone bump into me. He was a tall, skinny kid with a thin smile and dark hair pushed back off a long forehead. His eyes were blue or green. It was hard to decide because he narrowed them into thin slits. The rest was unremarkable: faded jeans, a blue-and-white checked flannel shirt.

"Do you believe in God?" he asked.

"Yes," I said, trembling. It was the truth.

Eric, the mastermind of today's event, recoiled back, staring at me the entire way. He looked at me. *Really looked*. I felt so uncomfortable that I looked down to the ground, which was when I saw the long gun he carried close to his right leg.

Eric raised the gun until it was all that was between us, pointing it at my forehead. There was no time to reach for a throwing star. One move and I was gone-gone.

He looked straight through me for a second and then walked away.

His back to me, he clearly said, "I'm doing this because people made fun of me last year."

"Eric," I called out in a wavering voice, but his mind was otherwise occupied. He never turned around.

9.

Daniel was almost inside the school with his sister Jenna under his arm. He told her to walk calmly with him and they would find Andy, but when he turned his back she disappeared.

Daniel knew where the morally pristine Jenna was heading: the principal's office. Jenna believed in Santa, good intentions, and that authority figures like the principal could fix everything.

"We have to find her. We can't change history," Daniel said to me when I caught up. "I'll get Jenna back and we'll meet by the school sign in exactly six minutes. They don't start shooting until 11:17 a.m."

It was a good plan, only an unworkable one. Time seemed to have moved faster than his watch could clock it. It was 11:16 when we all finally walked into the school, which was remarkably easy. No passes. No door guards. No one questioned the fact that we looked dirty and some of our clothes were torn.

I watched Daniel ask a pretty, young teacher in a stained smock for directions to the choir room. It turns out she was an art instructor named

Patricia who was double timing it to class with one of her students who looked young enough to be a freshman or sophomore.

I heard the two distinct pops.

Eric and Dylan were inside now. They smiled and pointed. Then they opened fire, grazing that young teacher in her back and the boy in the chest.

"Choir room!" I yelled, grabbing Eddie to go with me.

Daniel raced toward the front office to tell them and find Jenna.

Peter, Tosh, and Cass vaulted for the cafeteria to warn the student body.

Enough was enough . . . damn the consequences.

10.

The choir room was just off the main hallway if you took a sharp right.

I didn't remember that Eric and Dylan set small bombs off around the school, but watched in horror as a fireball exploded a few feet away, which had Eddie and I bracing against the metal lockers for cover.

I had my throwing stars in one shaking hand. Eddie had some kind of weapon close to his hip.

A slight glance left, and I saw Eric and Dylan making their way down this corridor. Grabbing Eddie by the shirt, I yanked him into the girl's bathroom. Four young girls were hunkered down in the stalls and they were crying.

"Not a sound, girls," I whispered. "Not one sound. Hide."

"Pray," Eddie said.

11.

We waited a minute, maybe two, before we gazed through the open slot to see Eric and Dylan waiting outside of the music room. Eric grabbed the doorknob, twisting it hard, which made the kids inside scream on the top of their lungs.

From where I was standing I could see her. Andy Reid, in faded jeans and a pale blue shirt, her dark hair in a ponytail, was crouched behind a desk. Her eleven tumultuous years had not prepared her for this. The fact that she was even in high school must have required Edward to lie about her age.

"Who's next? Who is ready to die?" Dylan yelled.

Eric saw little Andy, too.

"Peekaboo. We see you," he said, cocking the gun her way.

I would slash his throat with one of the stars. It was the only way. As I ran forward, blade to the sky, the gunmen turned around to face me. The shotgun made a garishly loud click as it was cocked.

What happened next would always feel like a blur.

Eddie reached out with one of his bearlike arms, almost dislocating my shoulder as he ripped me violently back.

I hit the lockers behind me and bounced to the ground.

Through my blurry vision, I watched helplessly as Eddie raised his other arm. He had a gun, "borrowed from Griz," stolen from Edward Reid. It was a Walther PPK, the weapon of choice for James Bond, and now Eddie Wargo.

Eric and Dylan stopped in their tracks.

Two head shots.

The Columbine shooters.

Our Eddie Wargo took them out.

"See you on D Block at ITT, assholes," he cried.

12.

My mind was screaming, but a breath later I forced myself to calm down. "Andy!" I began to scream. "Andy Reid." On quaking legs, the little girl slid out from under the desk.

"Walker?"

"Run to me, baby," I yelled.

She was shaking violently, but made it into the hallway where I cupped her sweet, terrorized face in my hands. Then I nodded at Eddie who carried her as we ran.

I found Daniel, Jenna, Cass, Pete, and Tosh in the cafeteria.

"We have to go. Now," I yelled. "The *only* danger is us getting caught."

"What happened?" Daniel and Cass yelled in unison.

"Now!" I screamed before my legs pumped hard towards the flashing red EXIT.

Eddie and I blasted out the back door into the field where we were sitting ducks for law enforcement types who were about to arrive. There seemed to be swarms of John Q. Laws in the distance along with SWAT teams, paramedics, and firefighters who were about to assemble with lights and sirens blazing.

Columbine students poured from doors, but they were all alive. The kids from choir were outside now, too, and they surrounded each other in a big circle. I felt the vibration of that much youth and hope combined with the pure joy of *living*.

Quickly, I drew *X*'s on Jenna and Andy's hands, which we held in vice grips. There was no time to ask, but I knew enough of us dialed it in perfectly.

My last vision of Columbine was a girl, maybe fourteen, with tears rolling.

"Make it count," I mouthed to her as we ascended.

THIRTY-EIGHT

1.

I landed flat on my back in the most vulnerable position. My legs were twisted under me like some backward yoga pose; my face was parts fear and wonder. My mind was racing as I was one-thousand percent past desperate to see if everyone was still with us.

Were they lost in the past? Or flat on their backs in the present?

A man hovered over me in the most menacing way. He was around twenty, black, and extremely agitated. Desperately, I tried to lighten things up. "Are you my guardian angel?" I asked.

"No, I'm your principal," he barked in a deep voice. "What the hell have you done now, Miss Callaghan?"

"Dr. King," I stammered, because what else was there really to say. Of course, I'd ignore his question. Anyone with the word "teen" after their age learned evasion at an early age. It was in our DNA. My pressing concern was to do an accurate head count.

Those numbers were all I wanted in this world and beyond.

I wasn't good at math, so I counted three times. Just in case of user error. There were seven of us on the ground, struggling to stand, also ignoring Dr. King and his baiting questions designated to change our afterlife trajectory.

Pete. Check.
Tosh. Check.
Jenna. Check.
Andy. Check.
Daniel. Pissed, but check.
Me. Check. Scared shitless.
Cass. Check.
Eddie was gone.

2.

Life happens when you're busy lamenting.

The girls—gone for almost a year—flung themselves into Daniel's arms. He stood, spun them around, and then began to squeeze each of them so hard I thought they would start gasping for air. Pete repeated all of the above with additional hugs and kisses. I was still wobbly on my feet when the girls charged in my direction. We melted in place.

Sisters.

The yearning to do just this had been imagined so many times. The reality was even better as flesh pressed and eyes flashed pure, forever love.

The cherry on the sundae was when a force of nature came charging out of the main gymnasium at the Astonishing School.

Bobby Reid, five, barreled into his big sisters like a little torpedo.

It dawned on me in the moment that this was the first time the entire Reid family had been together in a really long time.

The huddled it up, laughing, crying, and whooping. For some reason, I felt shy and stood on the sidelines until I saw Daniel's long arm stretched in my direction. I took two steps until I was yanked forward and enveloped.

Home.

It would have been so easy to stay in that moment, and I did for what felt like a long time until I pulled back. And then I faced Dr. King.

"Where is he?" It was maddening to come out of the chaos to find that we were one less. One of us was gone. Wandering.

"What did he do?" I demanded of Dr. King, who still looked like he was eighteen. "He defeated the darkness!" I said.

"He changed history," Dr. King calmly said. "And now he faces consequences. The Council of Curiosities on this side will determine his fate." And with those words lingering, Dr. King began wandering away.

"Don't you dare turn your back at me!" I demanded, which caused Dr. King to turn sharply on the heel of his boots.

"WHAT did you say to me?" he demanded.

"Sir," I began again. "Please."

"Please, nothing. Mr. Wargo made a choice, and I will check in later with the council. As for now, you have a phone call inside the office."

As he walked away, I heard Dr. King mutter under his breath, "You will be the death of me."

"You're already dead, sir," I said under my breath.

"Details," he fumed.

"I'll go get the girls settled in," Daniel said. "See you in a few."

I kissed him lightly on the lips.

"Yeah."

3.

The phone call was from an old friend. It was actually a FaceTime call, and quickly the screen inside the dean's office filled with the softly lined face of a lovely friend. Miss Maude Travis, admissions counselor at the Academy, was impatiently tapping a pencil on a file folder.

She was staring at Cass, who had also been invited to join the call.

Looking at him quizzically, I wondered how he knew Miss Travis beyond his dealings with her on the first day he arrived at the Academy. Apparently, they were very good friends.

Four words that would change everything.

"Cass," Miss Travis said, "I found her."

4.

Cass grabbed me and hugged me hard. "Come with me," he said, eyes full.

In that moment, staring into his ever-hopeful face, there was only one way to repay him for all of his help, kindness and loyalty. He was the man who breathed life back into me at Ellis Island . . . who stayed with me all of those long nights when Daniel didn't remember . . . who lost his own earthly life trying to warn me about his demonic sisters.

It was a life-changing decision wrapped in one simple word. I would go with him; his daughter was a car drive away.

In the end, we had decided that I was necessary for moral support, plus he needed someone to remind him not to drive like a maniac. Our favorite principal confirmed that we were safer as a pair, but warned us that the terrain was rugged because the Younglings School was tucked into a mountain range about forty minutes away.

"This isn't the Midst. There's no radio here. No TV. If you sense snow in the mountain passages wait until it passes," he warned.

Cass would have driven to hell itself to find MC. It helped that Dr. King had a serious, all-terrain SUV Jeep we could borrow although wild horses would have worked for the former marine.

"Are you prepared for what's next?" Dr. King asked me. He inquired in such a way that it made me do a double take.

Next, we would find some cute little kid and bring her back here. Cass would have another focus, which was perfect. A little girl would have her daddy back. I knew how it felt to long for the father who punched out early. All the tears in the world were not enough.

"I'm not even prepared for today," I said before racing back to the dorms to change into clean clothes and wash my face from 1906 and 1999.

What I found was a sight for my time-traveling eyes.

The entire family had reassembled. Everything we had just done was in order to have this kind of moment. My timing to leave again wasn't just off. It was off the charts.

The laughter was loud and uncontained. Bobby was hanging upside down from the top bunk. "Watch me, Walkie," he said, allowing himself to fly to the ground. "My reset always works!"

Daniel grabbed me in a big bear hug and planted hard kisses on my lips. When I leaned back, it was Auggie now who hugged me hard, profusely apologizing for ratting out our little "trip" to the past, but no one was angry at him.

In his typical Aug-a-licious way, he used one long run-on sentence to catch me up on current events, "Edward sent his goons to the glam cabin, so Dr. King, along with the rest of us, hightailed it here to Ghost U. It's safe here."

I was half listening. My heart was bursting because I didn't want to leave them—even for a minute.

I heard Cass beep from the street down below.

Daniel was not infuriatingly understanding—to a point. "You'll be back in a few hours?" he repeated. "Word is there is an all-Reids slumber party in here. No sleep. Lots of pizza and cookies."

It was everything.

"It's important," I said.

"Maybe I should go with you."

Dr. King was sending us. It had the promise of safety. In the end, I faked some bravado because I didn't want to worry him. Or stop his celebration.

"I'll be back before you know it, so don't eat my slices of pizza. You know, the ones with the black olives, etc."

"Extra cheese and mushrooms with black olives," he said, eyes worried.

"Is there anything better?" I replied.

Daniel slipped my fingers into his own and walked me outside to the Jeep. He glanced at the map and noted that the destination wasn't far, if you didn't count one rugged part where you literally drove up a mountain range and then straight back down.

Daniel and Cass locked eyes.

"I got this," Cass said.

"Better," Daniel said as the car jumped forward and my hand slipped away.

THIRTY-NINE

1.

The Other, in its most northwest part, was a dreamland of austere and remote beauty. A lingering sweep revealed the high ridges of tall mountain ranges with glittering, snow-covered peaks that reached 15,000 feet skyward.

The natural wonder and enchanting beauty had an almost hypotonic effect and I found myself hanging my head and shoulders out of the Jeep's wide window. When I looked down, I felt woozy and drunk. Above me, sky. Way below, a valley of jagged rock. Light snowflakes teased my tongue in this dreamy setting. *So calming. So soothing.* I felt as if I had entered a real-life fairy tale if you didn't count the heaves and lurches of Cass trying to maintain control of the Jeep.

It was glory. But this was not a sightseeing mission. The hard line of Cass's jaw and how he was wordless on this trip was a man I had seldom seen.

Dr. King was precise in his directions to the Younglings School because The Other was a place of few signs.

My ears popped as the car made a too-fast race down the mountain to land that was evenly laid out and even flat. "He said to turn right at the first road, which must be the one we're about to pass," I said, quickly.

Cass didn't hesitate, almost rolling the car when he cut a hard turn.

"Sorry, sugar," Cass said. "I'm not in my right mind."

"You want me to drive?"

"I'm coherent enough to say absolutely not. You don't drive and this terrain is wicked."

We passed a clear, turquoise lake as Dr. King insisted would happen and just like planned, the land leveled to what looked like a sea of deep green grass all around us. The air was fresh and crisp. For some reason, I felt light as a feather and practically giddy.

As we got closer, I spotted a small town in the distance, bathed in amber light. It was late afternoon and the sun set early here. A steeple pierced the sky and as we motored closer, I smiled at the small valley framed by large white oak trees contrasting sweet, red-bricked buildings.

"If I can't find her, I don't think I'll be able to survive it," Cass said. His voice was thick and I watched as his hands shook on the wheel. The hard line of his jaw was Cass trying not to crumble.

"You survived every hard day you've been given," I reminded him, adding, "If you rush it, you'll ruin it. Pause, be patient. Pray."

It was official. Unofficially, my mother Madeleine Walker was in the car with us, at least in spirit.

"Thanks, Mom," I mouthed into the fresh darkness.

2.

There was only one road in, one road out.

If you looked hard enough, there was a small white sign with no words. The symbol was unmistakable: a small child's hand in blue paint.

No gate guard was present; there wasn't even a gate.

Cass slowed down and finally opened his window. I couldn't help but touch his right hand. He linked his fingers around me. Thick tears trekked down his cheeks, and he didn't try to hide the emotions threating to drown him.

I expected to stay in the car.

"Walker," he could barely say. "Walk with me. "

Just past the sign was a sweet public park. There was a white gazebo in the middle, plus a playground full of swings, slides, and monkey bars. The odd thing here was there weren't just three swings, but maybe three hundred of them—as far as the eye could see.

These children were waiting for parents. The message was clear: they would not wait for anything else including a swing to free up.

Cass walked for a short period of time until his knees buckled. His head lowered. I heard gasping sobs from his chest. He placed a big hand over his face because he couldn't stop the inevitable tears. All he could do was point at a tiny water fountain in the middle of the park. It came up to my knees.

I could see that it was engraved on the bottom, the words etched into stone. "To MC," it read, "and for all those who aren't big enough to get a drink without their Mommy and Daddy."

I rubbed Cass's arm for a second. "How?" I asked in a whisper.

"When she was very sick . . . MC asked . . . um . . . shit, Walker." I rubbed his arm.

"So, she asked, 'How will I get a drink from the fountain when I'm gone without you lifting me, Daddy?'" He cleared his throat. "I would tell her, 'Papa will build you a special fountain. Your size.' I must have said it a million times. I put it out there into the universe."

I ran my hand over the smooth stone of the fountain.

"Oh, Cass," I whispered.

3.

Mine wasn't the only voice.

"Papa," she said. "Well look at you."

4.

The first great love of Cass Danko's life was about three-and-a-half feet tall with long reddish hair and big hazel eyes. She was a fast one and as Cass crouched down, she raced into his arms. He stood tall, hugging her tightly, and then spun her around and around. He was laughing like I had never heard Cass laugh.

"We'll look at you, sugar," he said in a thick voice. A river ran down his face.

Megan Caspian Danko, or MC, put her small hand on her papa's face and then lifted one in the air. It was their signal. "High five," he said and she obliged. "Down low?" he said and they did a low five. And then they did a double fist pump. She roped twig arms around his neck and hung on.

"Baby, I would have been here faster," he began. "It just wasn't my—"

"Papa, trust the wait," she said. "That's what teacher tells us."

Cass laughed in that full throttle way of his that made me grin.

"We learned to say here: If not today, it will be tomorrow. If not in this world, then I will wait till the next."

"You're pretty smart, sugar," Cass said.

"And strong and brave," said MC. "Like you."

"No, like you," Cass said, snuggling her.

"Papa, will you push me on the swings?"

In that minute, with a little girl flying in the air, the world was stunning.

5.

I stood on the sidelines, bawling like a fool, while her curious gaze focused on me from time to time. Each time the swing came level with my eye-line, she stared extra hard like she was gathering facts. All information seekers are gatherers, afterall. She must have been wondering: Is she here with my daddy? Is she a friend? Foe? Nice? Mean? A stranger? A friend?

One thing was certain: she looked enough like me to be my child.

Lost in my own thoughts, I jumped when I noticed that a woman in a white skirt and black shirt was standing next to me. I would learn that she was a Guardian, one whose eternal wish it was to look after Younglings until their families claimed them in the afterlife.

Her nametag read: BETTY.

"We tell them to trust the wait. Embrace the uncertainty. And to enjoy the beauty of becoming," she said. "We tell them that someday someone will come for them and we have never been wrong."

"That's part of the secret," Betty said.

"Papa, there's a girl," she whispered. "She's watching us. Is she a stranger? Is that my mama? Her hair looks like mine."

"No, she's not your mama. But she's not a stranger, little boss," Cass said, scooping her up off the swings. "She is actually someone I'd like you to meet."

6.

It was *on.*

My inquisitor was small, wiry, and full of opinions. "You look like me, grown up. But, you're not my mother. You can't make a peach out of a potato."

"MC," Cass said in an exasperated voice.

"It's not a bad thing," MC said. "I like potatoes as much as I like peaches."

A philosophizing four-year-old. This would prove to be interesting. Together with Bobby, they could possibly rule the world.

Kneeling seemed appropriate, so I hunkered down to little-kid level. "I'm not a potato although I love french fries as much as I love peach pie," I said. "And, no, I'm not your mom, but I am your friend although we haven't really been introduced. My name is Walker."

She looked up at her dad.

"Megan Caspian Danko, but you can call me MC," she said.

Gotta admit, the kid had some badass 'tude.

Then, she crooked a small finger and I got lower.

"Do you like boys?" she asked.

"Sometimes," I whispered.

"I think he likes you," she with a top spin on her words. She pointed to her pops. "I can tell."

I beamed down at her. "Your papa and I are friends. He's a great guy. Now, how are you today?"

"It's not today. It's tonight, silly," she said. "It's a beautiful night in my soul."

It made me laugh. "My soul is having a pretty good day, too," I said. "I mean, night." Pause. "I don't know what I mean!"

"My Spidey senses were tingling all day today. I knew it was going to be a big day," she said.

"Spidey senses?"

"*Spider-Man: Homecoming*," she said. "We have Netflix here."

She leaned in. "It's everywhere."

Betty handed Cass a small pink travel bag. "We like to transition outdoors, so it doesn't require any additional good-byes," she said. "You're welcome to take her now and go on your way as to not upset the other children who are still waiting."

"How many?" I asked.

By now the valley was all aglow in a blanket of warm light emanating out of small windows. "All the buildings are filled," she said. "Toddlers in some; children grouped by ages. All extremely well cared for and loved as their parents would naturally demand. We enter the mother and father's dreams. We adhere to their wishes. That's why the fountain was built. Mr. Danko had a dream. We made it happen."

Cass put his hand on mine.

"Kiss her, Daddy," she gushed.

Cass just laughed and kissed me on the cheek.

"No, KISS HER," MC shouted.

She clapped and then did a fast cartwheel when Cass quickly put his lips to mine.

MC burned off energy with one last run around the park followed by a sip of water from her fountain. She hugged Betty and then climbed into the back seat of the Jeep where Dr. King had installed a child safety seat.

Out of earshot, Cass asked the big question. "Her mother?" he wondered.

"No contact," Betty said. "I know she's on this side of life, but it's not meant to be right now. You are meant to be with her." I saw his eyes shade in a downward cast. It would have been perfect if he could have connected with his first love. Or perhaps not.

"Typical of Annie," he said. "Always running."

The night sky was clear under a big blue moon. There was no snow in our path. "We should get going," I said, knowing the sooner we made it back to the Astonishing School, the safer it would be for all of us.

Another voice seconded that opinion.

"Come on! Come on, you guys!" MC cried through an open window. "Everything is waiting for us now. Come on!"

8.

Cass's approach to fatherhood was taking his big heart out of his chest and wearing it proudly on the outside.

The little girl was so easy to love and I felt my own emotions traveling down that slippery slope. She looped her arms around her daddy and he spoke softly to her as he secured the car seat.

He kissed her crinkled nose and then placed a blanket over her lap so she wouldn't get cold. Not that it was possible. Betty had told me that children have the strongest resets.

I gazed at the lucky little girl in the rearview mirror.

"Daddy, what about her?" MC asked, pointing her little finger in my direction.

"Megan, would it be okay if I caught a ride with you?" I asked her. She was the type who considered things, and I could see the wheels turning.

"Can we stop at McDonald's?" *Ah, she would ask for quid pro quo.*

I looked around this winter wonderland. By now, a soft snow was falling on our windshield. "MC, they don't do McDonald's here," Cass said with a smile.

"Taco Bell?" she shot out. The kid was whip smart and I had to admire how she not only drove the conversation, but had a solid short list of all the fast-food favorites. Just when I thought we'd stick to our tour of grease and carbs, she surprised me.

"You look like my mommy," she blurted to me as Cass revved up the big engine.

I didn't have a lot of experience with impossibly short humans, so I wasn't sure how to answer her.

"But my mommy was prettier than you," she rambled. "But I didn't know her, but I've seen pictures. She died when I was a baby, you know. I died of cancer. How did you die?"

"Car crash," I said in a matter-of-fact voice.

"Did it hurt?"

"No."

"Are you my daddy's girlfriend?" She switched gears.

"No."

Cass burst into a loud crash of laughter. "Not yet, baby," he said to the girl in back.

"Cass," I began. The sounds he was making tickled my funny bone. I shocked myself when I giggled. He was the dictionary definition of *persistent*.

MC looked at his face and then mine. "I see how it is," she said, settling back.

Both Cass and I were so full of joy that happy tears were now rolling down our faces. We couldn't turn it off and didn't want to let this pass.

I felt peace. I witnessed love.

I was soul happy.

9.

Reluctantly, Cass swung back onto the highway where a light snow was now falling. A breath later, the mountain passage around us faded to black as we climbed. I tried not to think about the sheer 10,000 feet drop-offs or the sudden, slick conditions. I grabbed a map in the glove compartment while keeping sharp eyes on the road in front of us.

You can look hard enough that the world becomes a blur.

"Maybe we should go back to the Younglings town. Dr. King said the mountains wouldn't be safe in the snow," I reminded Cass.

"Bullshit," he said in a good-natured voice.

"Bullshit," said a young voice from the back seat.

"Whoops," Cass said.

I shook my head and smiled. "Cass," I said in a low voice, "she is spectacular."

His smile went full wattage.

At the same time Cass micromaneuvered the car down the mountain terrain. A steady snow came down in fat flakes here, but he was an expert driver, and closely hugged the mountain wall. The rock face was so close, I could have rolled down my window to touch it.

"Do not," Cass said, "look down." To make me feel better, he launched into a story. "I remember this time in Afghanistan," Cass began, but I tuned him out.

There were no guardrails on my side at this point. Drift too closely to the edge and all you had was gravel followed by air. It would be so easy to make one wrong move and drive off the world and into oblivion.

The highway marker indicated that we weren't just high in the air. We were twelve thousand feet above this world.

"Music?" Cass said, turning on the hits of the eighties. The vein in his forehead was pulsing, which told me that he was afraid. It was pitch black now and there were no overhead lights up here. He was doing a bit of granny gripping as we slowly descended down the mountain as the only car on the road.

At 7,500 feet skyward, I spotted one of those mini parking lot lookout spots where families stop to take a million pictures and junior takes a well-deserved pee.

"If you don't mind, sugar, I'm going to pull over for a second," Cass said. "Nature calls."

I didn't mind, but I was sure curious about the black SUV parked at the farthest side of the lot. It was embossed on the back with gold letters that were familiar: The Astonishing School of Ghostly Needs.

There was a small red flare on the ground, and the car was jacked up because of a flat front tire.

"Look," I pointed to Cass. "I wonder if they sent someone to find us."

He was such a Boy Scout that he pulled our SUV up next to the stranded motorist. If there was one person who would help in an emergency, it was Cass Danko.

"Lock the car," he said, looking and me and then back at MC.

Her head was tipped to one side as she softly slept.

"Hey, man," I heard Cass say before he closed the driver's side door. "What can I do to help?"

"Thank God you're here," said a muffled voice.

"I'm gonna go take a leak . . . then if you need anything . . . ," Cass said.

10.

It began as a feeling that swept over my system like a giant red flashing light. I couldn't see or hear it, but I felt a tingling, queasy type of sickness spread across the core of my being and settle in my throat.

"Don't make a novel out of everything, Walker," I scolded myself. "This is a rest stop on a public highway. People are supposed to break down here. It doesn't have to be anything sinister, you book loving geek."

My arm hair, standing at attention, thought otherwise. My right hand wiped the condensation off my side window. An unremarkable man in a standard black wool winter coat was crouched down and began humming to himself as he continued to jack up a nasty flat.

I'll never know why I opened the window wider. Or why I looked down.

What I saw next to the man's car, tossed carelessly in the dirt by the front end of the vehicle, sickened me. It was an animal carcass, something large, maybe a cat . . . either a jaguar or a better bet was a mountain lion. But it was no more because this man was a hunter. There was a large pool of fresh, red blood next to his latest kill and it looked garish staining the pristine white snow.

I recoiled at the deep, still-bleeding wound on its neck, obviously near a major artery. Whatever gun had killed this thing had taken away a chunk of flesh.

"Cass!" I whispered, willing him to hear me. I didn't want to wake the baby.

My friend was far across the parking lot taking care of business.

The man in the trench coat must have had excellent hearing. He stood, slowly turned around, and I saw the large oval swatch of red blood covering half of his face.

He took a step closer to our SUV, but then turned on his heels. He walked back to the curb where the carcass was waiting. Kneeling down, he pressed his red-stained face onto the glassy-eyed dead animal's midsection. And he began to feast.

Quickly, I rolled my window back up. But I could still hear him.

"I do marvel at the power of the mountain lion," the man said. "They're shy. Elusive. Solitary animals—much like myself."

He craned his neck higher and began to drink from the bloody, open gash.

"Just like the mountain lion, I like to stalk my prey at night and plan an attack. It's so satisfying to see your work come to fruition," he said. "The wait is almost sexual. It's like foreplay."

My lips began to tremble and my fingers shook in every which way.

"This is what I love about The Other and their vast animal kingdom," he continued to ramble on. "There are so many interesting ways I can co-opt the DNA strands of magnificent creatures and blend them with my own.

"If you weren't such a dumb bitch, Walker, you would have noticed," he said. "At first, at Dr. King's cabin, I left you my skin because I ate a black mamba snake wandering through the grass. And then I slithered away. I digested any number of birds in Illinois and flew with your orb for a time when you went back. And now, I have shown you a deeply personal factoid.

"I'm not a dog person. I'm a cat person," Tor said with laugh. "As a great '80s group once sang, 'You might as well jump.'"

11.

"I don't understand," I stammered. To myself.

He seemed to hear every word. From inside the car.

Then it dawned on me. Who knows what he ate in the name of super hearing?

Dogs came to mind again.

"These cats are extremely powerful. They can move at forty miles an hour," he said. "After I absorb them, I can enjoy excellent balance and leaping abilities. I can do running jumps exceeding forty feet and standing vertical leaps of up to forty-five feet. And my bite power? Out of this world."

He proved it by jumping in front of the car and violently ripping off his trench coat by tearing the material with his teeth. If I hadn't observed the rest of it with my own eyes, I would have thought he was full of shit. But I watched as hybrid Tor went from a standing position to jumping in one leap well over our SUV. On the way back, he landed hard onto the roof, which had the worst effect of all. I heard a small voice from the back seat say in a groggy voice, "Daddy? I think I heard a monster."

Tor pressed his albino face, covered in blood, to the driver's side window. I suppressed a full-throttle scream when he tried the locked door.

"I left you so many clues that introduced a new side of me," he murmured. "You went oblivious. Dearest, oblivious can get you killed."

I knew there were only two outcomes now: If I sat, he would come into the car and grab both of us. If I didn't then at least Cass could protect MC.

I had to take the game away. I wasn't the fastest, but I put my head down and kicked the car door open all the way. I couldn't be sure, but I swore I broke his nose. Tor fell backward, screaming and swearing.

Outside of the car, I lifted my right leg and roundhoused him in the face.

And then I ran.

12.

The snow was falling in blankets now making it hard to separate the lookout from the actual road. My path was predestined. Sprint as far away from the little girl as my feet would take me, so I could kill that bastard. Once and for all.

But, where was he?

Tor was stealthy silent, and when I stopped—sure I was standing in the middle of the highway—I was alone. A quick scan left, nothing. Right, nothing. An eerie silence swept the space that made my senses ache. A rock tumbled from above. I jumped. Flakes of snow gusted in my face. I almost came out of my skin.

And then silence again until I felt the sickening need to look straight up.

Tor landed a foot in front of me.

"I live for this," he said, his short, spiked hair white from the snow, highlighting eyes that were fire blue.

He practiced probability manipulation, meaning one look into those hard black eyes and he would alter your perception of current events. Up was down. Right was wrong. Friends were enemies. His full name: Distortion.

The DNA morphing with animals was something horrifically new— or maybe it was his ace.

It was almost as if he read my mind.

"I just need to eat a few bites of the other creature and drink a cup or so of their blood to absorb their DNA codes and then borrow their prominent skills. It's called genetic mimesis. I'll get you a book on it, dear. Or, I'll show you later . . . after I take a bite out of you."

"I'm not so tasty," I taunted him.

"That depends on where I bite you," Tor retorted.

Just like a cat, I watched him curve his back and stretch as if he was getting ready for something. He narrowed his eyes.

"You overanalyze everything. All your questions make you doubt your intuition and then poor little Walker feels anxious and blames herself for allowing the panic in," Tor surmised.

I tapped the throwing stars in my pants' pocket. I had loaded up before we left the dorm room at the Astonishing School.

"I can cancel that shrink appointment now," I baited him. *If he would only stand still long enough.* Slowly, I slipped a hand into my leggings.

"Wait, darling. Let me get out my weapons," he said. "I'm sure you want this to be a fair fight."

Tor grabbed two silver knives out of his trench coat pocket. He held a dagger tightly in his right hand while in the other he clutched a large machete. It was a victory when he dropped the dagger into the snow, the point piercing the asphalt and the handle standing straight up now.

"Oops," I said. And then I smiled at his mistake to taunt him.

"Did you know that the human smile is primordial?" he inquired, examining the machete. "It's really just a way to bare your teeth. It's a warning."

I gave him my full tilt grin.

13.

Tor's back was to a large yellow headlight that was barreling down the highway in our mutual direction. The driver was reckless, going about sixty miles an hour, a crazy speed given the ice and snow.

Strands of bright light betrayed me and Tor whipped around. Blinded, I knew enough to drop and roll to the side where the lookout was located. What slowed my roll was the body of Cass, very much alive, and about to race into the road to fight.

"No," I screamed. "Just let it . . ." The word *happen* was lost in the howl of the wind.

Tor stood his ground in the center of the road. It was the ultimate game of chicken.

Man versus machine. Tor versus the world.

The vehicle sped up.

"Faster," I prayed.

Almost as if the driver was listening to me, he accelerated, rolling over fresh snow like he was trying to melt it in order to eat the road.

Maybe he was just some speed freak who didn't see the man standing in the middle of the twisting mountain track.

I take it back. He saw him. How did I know?

The driver gunned it.

14.

At the last minute, Tor jumped high in the sky.

The driver skidded to a stop, the Harley Davidson badass mobile hydroplaning sideways under him and crashing into the side of the mountain. The bike burst into a tiny fireball, but in the light of the blaze, I saw him walk around the flames.

In a dark leather jacket and black jeans with a helmet on, the driver stood in the middle of the road. A lone stream of breath floated into the sky.

The hard look on his face made one thing clear: the time for gathering was over. He was a hunter.

"Tor!" he bellowed at the top of his lungs. It reverbed through the trees, and the word seemed to shake the ground.

And then he announced his intentions.

"You better send your soul to hell because your ass is mine."

I'm not sure where the man-cat landed, but I did hear his voice: "Don't tell me it's your pussy boyfriend," he said.

And then I heard Cass.

"We finally found a fun group activity," he bellowed to Daniel. "Let's kill this son of a bitch."

FORTY

1.

We stood as three.

Daniel carried what looked like a long sword that he had strapped, warrior style, on the back of the Harley he "borrowed" from one of the Ghost U professors.

Cass had retrieved his backpack from the back of the SUV. He had what looked like an ax in one hand and bow draped over his big shoulder.

Gun shots rang out in the near distance and after the first round, I spotted the gleam of a semiautomatic handgun in Tor's right hand.

"As much as I love a good demon hunt with primitive weapons," Tor said as he moved closer, "I feel far better with one of these in my hands, locked and loaded."

"Simba speaks," I yelled as a bullet whizzed by my head.

On second thought: maybe it was better to curtail the chitchat.

2.

He took three shots into the dark, but we were fast on the scramble. It was almost white out conditions now, making a blind man out of every man.

Cass slipped as he took a shot with an arrow and it sailed into oblivion. I had my throwing stars in my pocket, but it was hard to aim because Tor moved at such breakneck speeds and we were operating in a blizzard.

One minute, Tor was hovering far left; the next he was leaning precariously close to the edge. Daniel advanced, sword in hand, and just when I thought he had a clear path to victory, Tor was high up in a tree. I screamed when Daniel dropped the sword and began to climb, obviously planning to use his bare hands.

Tor shimmied down several branches, landing on top of Daniel's fingers that were in a death grip around a branch. It was a short fall to earth, and Daniel reached forward, grabbing Tor by his neck, viciously ripping him toward the ground. They landed in a bloody twist of shoulders, elbows, knees, and feet with Cass racing forward, ax in his right hand. Daniel was on top of Tor now and Cass skidded on his knees in the snow to bury the ax in what he thought was a leg.

It was Daniel's leg and Cass stopped. Just before contact.

3.

Daniel rolled away, close enough to place motivated hands around Tor's neck. He wrapped them around like vines while Cass was on his knees, landing hard punches to Tor's gut. I took out a star and slipped to the ground.

I found his wrist. One deep cut and he'd bleed out.

Over.

Drained.

4.

Cats might have nine lives, but Tor seemed to have twelve. No matter how hard Daniel pressed, he wouldn't go lax. Cass punched him again and again, cracking ribs now, but he continued to breath. Each small puff was his personal victory in the frosted air.

My hand was shaking as I reached for his wrist, mentally preparing myself to push hard into the skin, past the veins and across the tendons.

With a primal scream—the shrill of a trapped cat—Tor shoved me away with one arm. He used the other to grab Daniel's face and push it into the snow. I was contained, so he grabbed Cass by his long hair and drew him in physically.

An icy wind whipped hard as both recoiled, dislodging themselves from their prey.

Daniel and Cass stood, but Tor didn't move. We were close enough to the edge of the mountain now, some 7,500 feet up. All they had to do was kick and punch him toward the edge—and then one last push. One ram. Tor would topple off our world, plummeting to oblivion.

No one moved.

Cass and Daniel—glassy-eyed as if they were suddenly possessed—stared at me, but they didn't see me. In a trance, both began taking reckless steps backward toward the mountain's edge. One and then another.

"Daniel! Cass!" I screamed. "Stop walking! Stop! Not another step!"

Neither heard me.

Tor's eyes flashed victory. Their brains were muddled. His distortion turned real time, space and distance upside down. They were sure their path was leading to safety, when in reality, their feet hovered on the edge of a sheer mountain drop-off, an ultimate demise and a twisted two-for-the-price-of-one murders.

My scream echoed in the trees, but they couldn't hear me.

One more step.

They ran out of earth.

5.

Cass and Daniel descended, plunging off the ledge as if they were skydiving without chutes.

Both were strong enough to impede the crash as they reached out and white-knuckled whatever land they could and as quickly as possible. Daniel grasped jagged terrain, fingers embedding in dirt and rock, while Cass could barely dig his fingernails into the rocky snow-covered mountain wall.

Falling to my stomach, I anchored my boots into the deep snow and reached out, giving one hand to Daniel and the other to Cass.

His feet flailing, Daniel looked up into my face. He swung hard, once, twice, three times, as one hand remained embedded in this existence and his other hand linked with my shattering bones.

A glance left and Cass was struggling. "Cass, slowly, move forward," I said while holding Daniel in a death grip. "Grab my other hand." Our fingers linked although gravity and desperation made it seem as if my skin would soon rip off the bone.

"Just don't let go," I screamed. "Do not . . . let . . . go."

I had to ask them.

"Do you have the reset?"

Cass was bleeding and his leg looked like it was broken. "No, sugar, I do not."

"Baby," Daniel said. "Ditto."

"I do," I whispered, but it was a lie.

6.

It was soundless here in this winter wonderland. My stomach was frozen to the ground and my fingers were turning blue.

We stayed that way for what seemed like an eternity—one of my hands holding up Daniel and the other holding up Cass. These men. They were my life after life.

I could hear Tor walking around behind me, enjoying himself. At one point, I saw out of the corner of my eye exactly what he was doing. Like a prowling jungle cat, he was on all fours doing stretches and forward tumbles. Thank God he didn't realize that a baby was hiding in the car.

Frostbite was setting in. My hands were completely numb; my wrists were ready to break. I knew I had hairline fractures in several small bones because I felt them snap and although the pain was breathtaking, I would not allow either to know how I suffered.

I damned the reset, which was still gone. I banished agony to force a smile.

"Baby, you have to let one of us go—probably both," Daniel finally said. "You can barely lift one, but not both of us. The bones in your hand. Are they broken?" Pause. "I know you don't have the reset."

"No," I sobbed. "They're fine. I'm fine. Someone will come."

"I love you, Walker," he said. His face was soft in the moonlight; his eyes were at peace. "My love for you doesn't go away. It will transcend to another place, another time. We will find each other again. I will find you. Again and again. It's meant."

"No," I sobbed. "Don't you . . . just don't. . . you . . . dare."

"One day, somewhere else, we will never have to say good-bye. Only good night," Daniel said with a full blast grin that was for me. Only me

I put my head down on the ground and began to sob.

"Callaghan, you are so loved," Daniel said.

I felt my wrist go—breaking into tiny pieces.

"When my mom was alive," Daniel said in a clouded voice. "She used to say this thing to me before I went to bed. I want to say it to you."

I lifted my head and fell into those silver eyes.

"Day is over. Night has come. Today is gone. What's done is done," he said. "Embrace your dreams through the night. Tomorrow comes with a whole new light."

"Baby," he said.

Arms reached out for the last time.

And Daniel let go.

7.

I watched him tumble forever, barreling through cracking tree branches. I kept mouthing "I love you" until he disappeared into the darkness of an abyss that seemed so low and big that I wanted to toss myself into it.

But, there was Cass. He still had my left hand although I couldn't feel it.

It was my right shoulder now. I couldn't be sure, but I think it was dislocated.

"Move a little to the left Cass," Tor taunted. "Let go. Otherwise you're ruining a perfectly good moment for me."

Cass smiled up at me.

"Sugar," he said. "Your hands are broken. Your right wrist is broken. There is no way in the world you can pull me up. Even the toughest marine knows that sometimes you have to face the end. You lose the battle."

"No," I wept into the snow. "Someone . . . will . . . come."

"Look at me," he said, and I got lost in the beautiful smile of my best friend. He wasn't without scratches. But I always gravitated to the people who were damaged.

I loved people whose eyes told tales, and whose hearts were weary, from trying and trying and trying.

"Sugar," he gasped as the wind made his legs sway like a pendulum. "How lucky am I to have something that makes saying good-bye so hard?"

"Oh, Cass," I began to weep.

"Walker, be her mother," he said. "And tell MC one thing from her papa. Say, 'Sugar, be happy. Go to sleep with a smile. Papa is awake watching you.'"

It takes one second to break a heart and eternity to fix it.

As Cass fell, he yelled, "Just look up."

I saw only blackness.

When I gazed down again, the glow on his face made it clear. He saw something else under the same blank sky.

FORTY-ONE

1.

K arma has no deadline—and with broken hands, wrists, and a shoulder that was hanging by a thread—I was going to kill him.

I wouldn't be afraid of Tor with his supercharged DNA.

Same game; different levels.

Same hell; different devils.

The pain was excruciating when I reached into my pocket for a few stars. When I pulled out my hand again, it dangled at the wrist like a child's yo-yo attached by a flimsy string. The stars dropped to the ground, which caused wild laughter in the distance.

Tor would not count on my injuries. He would pad his win, which is why he returned with a hostage.

"Look at me, honey. I'll show you a magic trick," he told little MC, who stared into his eyes.

"No!" I screamed. "Look away. Look at me."

He put her down much too close to the edge of the mountain.

"Take one giant step back. There's a playground there and cookies.

And your daddy. He's waiting for you," Tor told her.

"Don't move, MC," I begged her. "Do . . . not . . . move."

"Bring her to the car and I'll go with you," I said. "Anywhere."

Tor considered it for a moment.

"I have no need for a brat," he reasoned.

"We can drop her off somewhere. If we don't, I'll jump with her."

"How do I know you're not a lying deplorable?"

"Because Tor, you've taken everything from me. And I have nothing else to do but save her existence or revoke my own," I said.

"Then look in my eyes," he insisted. "Surrender."

"After you take her to the car," I insisted.

"Now," he challenged.

The pain was stunning and my eyes filled with tears. I could still force a head tilt—and point in the direction of the devil who was holding little MC or defy him and risk her.

"No tricks, Walker," Tor said as he placed the girl on the ground. "A deal is a deal. Plus, it will be an interesting union. My odd genetics and your keen mind. We can have it all, dear. In every decade. In every century."

I glanced back over the cliff. And then I walked slowly toward him. Tor was pleased.

"We should seal it with a kiss," he said when I arrived close enough to enter his personal space.

My head lulled to the side. And when we were just a hair apart, my face fell and he kissed my forehead.

"Not that kind of kiss," Tor said. "Look at me."

I moved in closer; pressed my lips to his neck. And with the star I had between my teeth, I pushed in hard and sliced his damn throat.

2.

The rest remained a bit of a blur. Dr. King eventually arrived since we were gone so long as did Bertha and Iz. "Where's Daniel? Cass?" Iz demanded. With the ounce of energy left me in I shook my head and then barely whispered, "Tor sent them both over the edge."

Iz followed my eyes and ran to look below.

"Bullshit!" he screamed and it echoed. The second time his words were laced with tears.

Bertha put my head in her lap, carefully avoiding my shoulder as I remained on the ground in the parking lot. She held me hard while Dr. King covered me with his own coat and then accessed the damages.

"Dislocated shoulder, two broken wrists, several broken bones in your hands and frostbite on your right-hand fingers," he said, shaking his head. "If the reset remains gone tonight, we'll have to set those bones. You might even need surgery."

"Just leave me."

"I can't do that, Miss Callaghan," he said. "You're like a daughter to me. Plus, you have gumption."

"I thought it was grit."

"That, too," he said.

A small face was in mine. "Walkie, it's me, Bobby," he said. "I snucked into the back of the car to come find you guys. Where's Danny?"

I couldn't answer him. The last I remember of Bobby that night was him standing near the cars holding hands with MC.

It was Pete who carried me into a warm SUV where I sat in the driver's side back. "Lay down," Bertha said. "There's nuthin' to see, Walk-her. Dr. King will sort it all out. Never you mind. You rest now. You're done."

Dr. King made a few calls and soon there was repelling equipment there, along with four students from the Astonishing School who were on the mountain climbing team. I heard them through a crack in the car's window. "We just have to hope for the reset," Dr. King said, standing by my side while Bertha took MC and Bobby into the other SUV to read to them.

And then—the impossible.

"We found one of them—breathing," Dr. King yelled.

"On the way down, one of them snagged a stubborn, thick tree trunk and held on for as long as possible," reported Ladd from the repelling team. "When he felt the reset working and his pains were gone, he swan dived again, falling into a deep lake down below."

It wasn't an easy fall, but the cold saved him despite the bleeding and semiconsciousness that followed for the next week. The prognosis was truly a miracle—a nasty concussion, deep bruising around his ribs, various cuts and eternal gratitude.

It would heal.

He would heal.

Although nothing for me would ever be the same again.

3.

One last thing. Before I passed out.

"Tor's body," I said in a shallow voice.

"What body, angel?" Pete said, checking on me.

"I sliced his throat," I whispered.

"Sleep," Pete said. "Just close your eyes."

"We have to be sure," I said frantically. "Remember, the greatest evil lurks within—jealousy, rage, furor. Some never shed it. Even in death."

"Give her the shot," Dr. King said. "She's hallucinating."

4.

I woke up three days later in a hospital bed at the Astonishing School with casts on both wrists and hands and a long, nasty scar from shoulder surgery. The doctor said I was "lucky," whatever that meant.

Dr. King mandated that I stay in that bed for two impossibly long weeks where I did some mild rehab and tried to become whole again—at least physically. I refused to see the Ghost U shrink. I wanted the soft cheek of my mother, a fact I would never share. Bertha was close enough.

All of my friends enveloped me with warmth and understanding that didn't require words. Auggie gave me back rubs and Chris Flicker told me about his past antics. Pete and Tosh looked after me at night, often holding hands when they thought I wasn't looking. Bertha and Bitty hovered like Mother Figures One and Two. "One more eye roll, Walk-*her*, and you're gonna need glasses for the back of your head," said Bertha while Bitty braided my hair.

Dr. King was personally seeing to MC's care although Bobby refused to leave her side as she grieved the second loss of her beloved father.

He filled in the gaps.

I had a small window in the hospital and when he came to see me each day before dinner and the knockout drugs we swore were in our food kicked in. A fugitive from his room down the hall, we would spend this healing time looking out into nature for answers.

I thought about the one we lost. He thought about it, too.

"Sunsets are proof," he said one night, "that endings can be beautiful, too."

5.

About two weeks later, a curious thing happened. My body "clicked in" and repaired what still hurt. Everything healed in a nanosecond, which wasn't a medical miracle. The freakin' reset finally kicked back in.

We were deemed "travel ready," and Dr. King made all the arrangements to move us as a group to a place where we could "just be" for as long as necessary.

Being sounded divine.

The Other called this place the Commune and it was a five-hour drive straight north into the highest of mountain ranges. The place wasn't on most maps, which made it safe, plus few desperados in The Other wanted to sit around with a bunch of far-out, let-your-freak-flag-fly hippies. I couldn't wait to meet them.

The Commune was just that—freedom lovers in bell-bottom pants and tie-dye shirts just living off the land and loving each other. Barefoot girls danced in the dirt causing swirls of dust to rise up to their knees. These counterculture mavericks almost changed the world in the 1960s, and now their children's children had set up an afterlife paradise.

There were no phones. No Internet. No TV.

It was like summer camp amid endless days of seventy-degree temps for those who needed rest and refused to conform.

We lived in a treehouse of all things, but not your standard homemade, one-room, clubhouse for kids. All of us had our own three-story structures created around giant redwood trees that shot through the center of the homes. The rest of the home was made out of thick glass and rustic brown wood, so the structure just blended into the forest.

There were fifty-foot waterfalls nearby, one of the largest cascades I've ever seen surrounded by pines. My reset was still perfect, and I washed in the falls because it was impossible for me to get frostbite now. One touch of my cold hand to warm coffee, however, turned it into an iced drink.

We grew our own beans, peppers, corn, potatoes, apples, peaches, pears, and rice as the diet here was all vegan all the time.

The other hippies were lovely to us, helpful and welcoming. "Hey," said a new neighbor named Eddie V who played a mean electric guitar and used to have this namesake band, "I heard about you, Walker. You got that whole purpose-driven warrior-princess save-the-world vibe. I dig it."

"That was a long time ago in a lifetime far, far away," I told him as he strummed the opening licks of "Why Can't This Be Love?"

Love. It was all around me.

Loss. It was thick scar tissue in my heart waiting to calcify.

My damaged being, however, had found a place where every ongoing moment made me want the next.

That was something.

Maybe it was everything.

FORTY-TWO

1.

Three months later.

"Tell me a happy story in four words," I would ask him. *It was our new thing.*

"Sugar, I met you," he would say with a big grin. When I was depressed, he would leave me alone. When I was sad, he would remind me, "It's a beautiful world because we can stand under any sky and make it feel like home."

I watched Cass in the field twirling his little girl. This was life.

Some hope.

And love.

And dancing. Lots and lots of *rocking out.*

In a long gauzy skirt that took flight, I twirled with him. My heart wasn't always totally in it, but my legs needed to move. My mind needed to clear.

When I was dizzy, like right now, he would even quote poetry: "'Sad soul, take comfort, nor forget. That sunrise never failed us yet!'—Celia

Thaxter," Cass said.

As for Cass, he expected nothing, but wanted everything.

He was nothing if not a patient man who tried to speed things along.

But, he hoped.

Oh, how he hoped.

2.

One night, friendship became something beyond. Megan was safely tucked in and snoring and we sat at the kitchen table talking about the day. My hand slipped from my tea and touched his fingers. Gently, he stopped me from pulling away and then lingered, skipping across the sensitive skin of my inner arm with his index finger.

My pain was still so deep that I did something hysterical. I reached out and ran a finger down the side of his face. The outside of a calloused hand gingerly brushed the side of my neck. Cass looked at me. Really looked. He was full of hope—and curiosity.

Under the table, I put one hand on his knee, which was sturdy and solid. There was safety and love in a man this substantial.

Cass leaned forward, kissing my forehead and then my nose. It seemed so harmless, but it wasn't. I looked up at him with clear eyes and moved the inches required to make it better. I pressed my lips to his own. At first, Cass didn't move. He didn't kiss me back. He was Cass. He had his own damage.

"Sugar, is this just good night or is it an invitation?" he asked me. "Either way, nothing changes between us."

"Or everything," I said, "changes between us."

He gave me a beat. It was *still* my choice.

"You are cordially invited," I whispered as Cass scraped his chair back. He wouldn't need to be asked twice.

3.

It was one of those beautiful late spring nights of still air that was humid and thick and left very few options that didn't involve the shedding of clothing. Cass already had a roaring fire in his room because he wanted it hotter. Impossible. Inside his warm, strong arms, I melted and soon he was carrying me to his bed.

He was six-foot-two, broad shoulders, and had a space by his neck where I could bury my face and linger.

The room smelled like spiced cologne and the small lilacs I had left in every room of our house in the Commune. Hope filled the molecules of breathing space as he sat down on the side of his bed and cradled me gently in his lap. His breath was already ragged as he studied me with loving eyes. I felt his hands wander as his eyes wallowed.

My world was spinning fast. Tonight, I would not be going back to my room across the hallway.

And it was fine.

As long as I kept moving. . . . Speed was my drug of choice.

He was a person of particulars, details, and second thoughts—and he would consider this for a moment. My breasts lightly pressed against his chest and for a moment I thought he would do nothing. Reason slipped and he began the intimate act of discarding clothes—his and mine.

His arms were so strong; his jaw firm; blue eyes blazing. I wanted to touch him, and I moved trembling fingers across his face and into his long hair. His shirt came off and sailed off the bed into some imaginary breeze. My shirt and bra were tossed in a heap in the corner. We had to stand to peel off the rest. My green gauzy skirt pooled at my feet. His blue jeans disappeared.

I had never been naked in front of another man, but now I stood bare. And I didn't know what to do with this predicament.

"Sugar," he caught the one part of me that was always naked, my hand, and placed it on his heart. "There's only one thing I'm going to ask you. Close your eyes. Clear your heart. Let it go. Just be . . .

"With me," he said. His voice was part molasses, all need.

"Yes," I said in a breathless rush.

He kissed me, deepening his invitation, until something inside of Cass began to shatter. All those soft kisses transformed into moans and hard sighs. The teasing scraping of facial stubble worked on every nerve ending as his lips, teeth, and tongue made their way from the soft fold on my neck to the sweet spot between my breasts.

When he took a step back, I swayed forward until Cass caught my body weight as if it was nothing more than a feather. He buried his head in my shoulder, a trail of hands across my back and bottom, making me tingle until my heart began to roar.

"Beautiful Walker," he murmured, hands in my hair and his voice rugged from the wait. "No demons to slay tonight."

"Did you always know?" I asked.

"I wanted you. I cursed you. I dismissed you in the middle of the night when you haunted my dreams," he said. "But, you wouldn't go. Didn't much want you to either. What happened went something like . . . this."

Gently, Cass placed me in his bed, his body following me down until all that was left was pleas to continue and promises not to stop. The scraping of a working man's hands and those first-time touches filled me with shivers.

I moaned when his lips returned to mine.

"Sugar, you don't have to say it, but I love you. We love you," he said, catching my eyes. "Welcome home."

A woman's hand touched my arm. She was in the room with me now. "I need you to sip some water, Miss Walker," she said. "The ayahuasca is a very powerful tea that creates hallucinations—but you're still hallucinating. You're moaning. It's time to return to reality as I count it down. One . . . two . . .

"Wake," she said.

4.

"Wh-what?" I said, feeling the icy-cold cloth she had placed on my forehead.

I wasn't in Cass's bedroom anymore. There was no such place in the Commune. I was in a small tent on a cot covered in an intricately woven blanket. The freezing water she was forcing me to sip felt good on my parched throat. She sprayed a light minty mist in my face until I was fully awake.

"You drank the ayahuasca and it's a powerful tool that helps with grief therapy. You've been able to experience the life that you haven't lived . . . will never live. The drink creates fantasy scenarios—so real that you can touch and taste them. It's for a greater purpose. Perhaps it will give you some perspective and alleviate your grief over the loss of your friend. You will find the power to let him go."

She was a shaman—someone who induced a trancelike state—in the Commune, and a powerful one.

"For years, this tea has been used for healing ceremonies," she explained again. "The drink creates hallucinations and has therapeutic benefits. I told you that you would experience intense psychedelic insights."

She smiled as I tried to sit up. I felt woozy, but conscious and calmer than before.

There was something odd and satisfying about *feeling* the life not lived.

It answered questions; provided relief.

"The drink is illegal in some places because you *technically* get high—higher than a lot of other drugs. But it's natural and you do gain a better sense of self and are better equipped to work through mental trauma," she said. "It leads to a better head space."

My new head space had to accept the truth. Dr. King had sent out countless teams to try to find Cass at the bottom of the mountain range. There was nothing, except a few swatches of ripped clothing, a road map of sorts, but no body, no skin, no bones. Eventually, Dr. King had to call it, insisting that the animals up there . . . well, he didn't need to go on.

The search had concluded.

Cass was gone.

5.

After a brief rest period to come back down to earth, I was dismissed from the tent and found myself wandering the grounds of the Commune.

I still didn't know what heaven looked like, but this place had to be close.

There was a lake that looked as if it was made of pure glass, large wooden cabins, and the protection of large redwoods that stood like two-hundred-foot-tall guards. We were still in The Other, but so far enough away from other settlements at this due north post that no one cared.

The hippies who called this place home had settled wisely under big puffy clouds that looked like cotton balls. They dipped down onto the tall treetops with roofs of emerald green.

No one bothered anyone here. You could live. Love. Prosper.

Speaking of the love part . . .

I heard Daniel in the deep forest playing hide-and-seek with Bobby, Andy, and Jenna and one other pint-sized contestant. There were shrieks, screams, and counting that was loud and rushed. I spied a little girl draped over his wide shoulders, her little legs hanging down onto his chest.

"Callaghan," he said, opening his arms wide so I could walk into them.

This was home. The only one I wanted.

"Did you get what you needed?" he asked, craning his head toward the shaman's tent.

"I have what I need, gratefully so," I said, looping my fingers into his for a moment until he handled me the squirming little girl who treated my one-hour absence like an eternity. *Our girl now.*

There was no infuriating misunderstanding or uncomfortable talk. Cass's daughter was now our child. She would exist in our care with her new brothers, sisters, and close friends.

Daniel and I never talked about if we would adopt her. It was decided with a nod.

She called him Danny.

She asked to call me Mommy.

6.

I kissed his lips hard and memorized that he smelled of an earthly mix of sweat and fresh morning dew. I could feel his heart beating in rhythm as mine. We could take a moment to breathe here, which was the point. It had been a long time since we dwelled in such giddy normalcy.

Of course, Bobby embraced MC like a long-lost best friend and sister. MC missed her own daddy, and it was terribly hard at first, but the small one was the most optimistic of all. "He is just busy, silly," she told me over and over again. "Daddy will be back. You wait and see.

"Nothing is ever gone," she reminded me.

She told me that the two of them "talked" at night.

"Daddy told me, 'Only those who care about you can hear you when you're real quiet.'" She pointed to a tall redwood with a groove in the bottom bark. "That's where I sit and talk to Daddy," MC said.

Trees kept your secrets.

I prayed she wouldn't . . . but she did . . . pick up some interesting traits in these three months here. One was thanks to her new "uncle" Pete.

"Shitballs, this PBJ is good," MC said one day with the sweetest of smiles.

"You're damn right, toots!" Bobby said with glee while teaching her how to fly.

God help us.

She was the easiest little girl with red hair, pale freckled skin, and this will of steel. She had been alone in a strange place and refused to crumble. It reminded me of someone else who came to the Midst not so long ago.

"Mommy," she would call out to me at night or when we were

reading stories. I fell down that slippery slope of love fast with her. It's why I didn't correct her although her own mother remained a mystery.

Our senses were dialed up here including my own writing skills, which is why I started a small weekly newspaper, perhaps more of a newsletter called *The Commune Times*. Daniel was stronger, leaner, meaner, and more active. I could smell, see, hear and think more clearly if that made any sense. One day, I found Daniel teaching the kids how to sled down a snow-covered hill. I watched MC tumble off her sled and raced to save her.

MC, however, wasn't crying. She was laughing.

"Kid, you are stronger and braver than you ever imagined . . . like your daddy," he told the little girl who raced into his arms.

I would not cry.

I would not.

7.

The joy of it was simple.

All of us were here—the girls, Pete, Tosh, Chris Flicker, Bitty, Auggie, Iz, Bertha, and Dr. King. We lived in cool cabins next to each other with our new digs at the end. We dwelled in a deluxe residence, a large treehouse, which looked like a multistory townhouse made of wood and glass and implanted into a large, multibranched force of nature.

"Peanut butter and jealous!" Auggie said when I gave him the tour including the top floor perch, which was made of all glass and had a queen-sized bed for Daniel and me.

"A tree house for grown-ups," I would say and I tried my hardest to turn it into a cozy home by making candles and picking flowers for every room. At sunset, a gorgeous, golden-amber light filled the entire house like it was lit by liquid gold.

The girls shared a room; the kids shared a room; Pete and Tosh shared a room. No questions asked. We bunked and loved on the top floor. Iz and Bertha had their own cabin as did Dr. King and Chris Flicker. Auggie somehow started sleeping on our couch and I never did a thing about it.

Bitty camped out on a couch. Pancakes were flipped every morning.

Time passed, happy time.

When Christmas rolled around again, four plus months later, Daniel made sure to fill each room with a tall evergreen tree that we decorated with pinecones, painted popcorn, and other treasures we found in the forest. The kids painted rocks red and green and made a path. It was special.

It was also official on Christmas Eve. We had been here, in The Other, an entire year.

Dr. King left his cabin and arrived with food that we would spend all day preparing in the small kitchen. The smell of roasting turkey with apple and bacon stuffing was enough to make your mouth water. Bertha helped make the candied yams, green bean casserole, and cranberry sauce made from berries the girls picked. I was on mashed potato duty while Flick lined up the homemade pies in pumpkin, apple, and pecan. Dr. King made his bread pudding and savory was replaced by the sweet fragrance of sugar and cinnamon.

The guest list . . . loose in the Commune. My rule was: got a hungry belly, show up for dinner. We had a long table and I liked to see every seat filled.

I always put two extra chairs: for Cass and Eddie.

One night an old friend showed up and no one thought twice about it. My eyesight was sharper here and when I saw Griz rambling down a dirt trail, I began to run toward him. He lifted me high and held me hard.

"Wa, Wa, Wa!" he yelled, putting Deuce down. "Watchu doin' fren?"

"Hello fren!" I yelled. "I love you, Griz."

I didn't not say it these days.

"Lov you my Wa," he said, blushing.

MC and Bobby stared way, way up at Griz once he entered the house.

"Shit, he's a giant," said MC in that way she had of understating things.

"Bitchin,'" Bobby said. "He sleeps in our room."

FORTY-THREE

1.

I didn't take anything for granted anymore and celebrated it all from the softness of freshly baked bread to that perfect sunrise over the lake to the tart burst of fresh orange slices on my tongue. Miracles were there if you looked for them.

One day, Dr. King, a man who didn't judge, sat down to eat lunch with me at one of the picnic tables in the woods. As usual, he waxed philosophical. "The further on down the road you go, the miracles will get sweeter. That's called evolving," he said. "It's that way even after they put you in the box."

I would not wait for the next level of maturity. I would create a lovely life in the now filled with laughter and love.

When people left my presence, even for a short time, I would tell them, "Good luck out there."

Trust me, we all needed a little luck out there – and inward.

I had all the choices in the world when it came to my physical and emotional being. I could hurt a little or a lot, love a little or a lot, depending on where I allowed my mind to roam.

I chose gratitude on most days. I would think about all of the love I gave and the love I took, erring on the side of giving. You can choose. You can rewrite the story. That's really what an existence is all about—all of the stories and moments that lead to this moment.

We are nothing if not walking photo albums.

2.

I was an expert now at the art of the linger.

Yet, there were no waste moments. I would no longer talk about weather or dredge up that same story for the ninety-seventh time. I wanted to talk about something real like death or aliens or sex. I just couldn't do a mindless "Have a nice day" or "What's on streaming?" That's just not as good as, "Why are we here?" Or even better, "Why are you here with me?"

I didn't want it to just be good.

Every life is capable of greatness.

I ran into reggae Bob wandering around the woods in his typical white gauzy shirt, unbuttoned most of the way, covered with a worn brown leather vest and his legs bound by almost-disintegrated jeans. *Of course*, he dwelled here—and with his typical swagger mixed with natural shyness—we talked about how he brought ska to the cool kids in Kingston and then the world. We weren't even really talking about music, which was the coolest part of all.

"WC, some people feel the rain. Others just get wet," he told me. "Think about it."

3.

I saw Chadwick wandering one day, a major force, and we had a deep conversation about what it meant to be cool. "Never try to be cool," he said. "Never worry about what the cool people think. I head for the warm people. Existence is about being warm."

Daniel and I would stay up half the night mulling over what *really* mattered. After making mad, passionate love, we'd sneak out to our rooftop deck in the tree and dig deep into topics of universal, if not perplexing, interest. Many nights all we wore were our shoes (or my shit-kickin' boots) because it was slippery up there. Our bodies, warm to the touch, glowed in the moonlight.

He kissed me hard, lobbing the big questions, and kicking open doors when they needed kicking.

"Do you miss being alive?" he asked.

"Parts of it . . . other parts not so much," I said. "I don't miss being on my own while my mom worked long hours. I don't miss not eating for a day or two. When I was a kid and Mom didn't have money for lunch, I'd fish out an old brown paper bag from the trash and fill it with two socks. It looked like I had lunch. In high school, sometimes all that counted was the appearances."

"Never again," we vowed. "It's not how it looks; it's how it *is*."

Seasons changed as we mulled over these topics. And since they also moved backward in The Other, it was fall again.

"My God," Daniel whispered, playing with my hair, "How I love autumn. And big fires. And the naked girl in the black boots."

Another night, Daniel and I embraced something in science called serein, which was that fine, light rain that falls from a clear sky at sunset or in the early hours of night. We found some clothes and walked through tall trees, getting soaking wet and just enjoying the evening serenity.

The reset was back, and we spent the 2:00 a.m. hour on that slushy night swimming in a frosty lake. It felt good to be this cold and have it not matter a fig. When I splashed him hard and then tried to make it better by kissing the side of his face, he growled, "Don't go there unless you mean it."

"Who said I didn't mean it?" I said with a smile.

When he kissed me, he murmured, "I hate that I wasn't the first guy to really kiss you."

He was, but he didn't know it.

"All I want . . ."

His face looked interested.

"Is nothing," I said, pressing my lips to his lips, my being to his being.

He kissed me slowly and then traced his fingers along my lips, eventually nibbling the soft spot on my neck and the groove under my ear.

Even when we weren't together, I felt him, which proved an ancient theory of mine established when I lost my father.

The love you never see is still quietly guiding you.

4.

I watched the summer flowers burst into bright pinks and purples and then bid farewell to the blood orange autumn leaves as they flew away to places unknown. Another Christmas passed and we were energized and strengthened by icy winds as they danced across that wide-open sky.

Moist white snow swirled around my face until it was spring again and the butterflies danced and darted around my fingers, trusting me with their fragility.

There was purpose in the pause. We learned how to self-sustain and remain happy with what was given. We made friends and grew.

I spent time with all of my loves and friends. I knew everything about them and vice versa. No one was a footnote to someone else's story. It begged the question: What if everyone got a turn at being the main event?

Yes, there were some famous mugs here. There was that actor River who blazed across the big screen and then flamed out. And I loved watching vintage TV with John and Bob, former sitcom actors who could still tell a wicked joke. Kobe and his beautiful daughter came over often.

The daughter made Daniel and I hold our new little girl even closer.

One night, MC was on her knees saying prayers when she smiled up at both of us.

"And God bless my mommy and daddy of the sky and my new ones," she said, her eyes darting from face to face.

"Amen," we said.

Daniel carried her everywhere on his shoulders.

The Japanese called this *ukiyo*, which meant living in the moment, detached from bothers.

Ukiyo.

5.

On Friday nights, we'd go to an old-fashioned outdoor cinema with rows of weathered and worn theater seats. A guy from Chicago named Roger was the projectionist and, man, he loved movies. They dubbed it the End of the World Cinema. He played old movies like *The Last Picture Show*, *Bonnie and Clyde*, and *The Godfather*—three of his favorites—and it was wonderful to sit in the dark, hold hands with Daniel, and dive into buckets of popcorn. Here, every seat in the house was the best seat and you didn't watch too many coming attractions.

There were none because the message was to just be. Live in the now. Life is not a trailer.

"Of all the spots in the universe and you wandered into a place where we breathe the same air," I whispered to Bertha who was my best friend, eternally.

"Walk-*her*, my queen—now pass the popcorn," she said.

6.

One morning—I wasn't sure what month it was—I wandered into Dr. King's cabin with some brownies I baked for him. The day possessed that kind of wind chill that sneaks into your clothes and chills your bare skin.

Spring was almost here again, which filled me with lightness until

I heard Dr. King's rich baritone voice sound dark while speaking to someone over a secured chat line.

"You need to just hold on," he said. "Promise me! I will find the new X-catcher and open the wall. I'll come back and we'll fight."

My stomach sunk to the floor.

"Marvin," a woman's voice screamed into a snowy screen of his computer. "I don't know how much longer we can hold on. He's trying to extinguish us . . ." There was the distinct sound of gunshots in the distance.

And with those words, Miss Maude Travis, the Academy's admissions counselor, faded to black.

FORTY-FOUR

1.

Dr. King had obviously been monitoring what has been going on in the Midst, which he had kept pretty close to the vest. The time for secrets, however, was over.

"Go find everyone," he said. "Meet me back here in half an hour."

With the exception of the kids who were playing a rollicking game of dodge ball with the other children of the Commune, we assembled, gathering around Dr. King's large wooden table.

I was freaked out when he gave us the update. "The Academy is not much different than the prison school, ITT. All in-person classes have been cancelled. The few course offerings are mostly online as students are in lockdown in their dorm rooms. The houses off campus have been evacuated to house troops that Principal Dick and the Higher Authority have stationed there to police the situation. All students must live on campus, so Principal Dick can keep this strict control over their non-existent existences.

"There is no fraternizing with other students, the opposite sex, same sex. It doesn't matter. No coupling. No meeting in groups of more than two now. He considers any grouping of more than two bodies, a mob situation," Dr. King said. "I fear that Principal Dick is planning something quite heinous, which is why he needs to keep the student population under control while he does it."

"What is his endgame?" Daniel asked.

"He's trying to strip the Academy of all magical elements and repurpose them at another location for himself," Principal King said.

"He's nothing more than a common thief," Daniel interrupted.

"But a good one—a lethal one," said Dr. King. "Imagine what he could do with his own Hall of Yearning to name just one universal game changer."

"What about those who strenuously object?" Tosh asked.

"There have been a few—and they're sitting in glass cells at ITT under the thumb of the Godfather," said Dr. King. "Speaking of which, my intelligence informs me that the GF operates by his own rules. He's not a fan of Principal Dick and remains out for himself. At least that's something. Two crooks out for number one. Add Edward Reid, your father, as the third crook. I hear he's back in the Midst."

"The other objectors who have evaded a maximum-security eternal prison sentence aren't organized," Dr. King said. "That's why I plan to go back in a few days looking like this—a seventeen-year-old new student— and form an elite team of young people to fight Principal Dick."

"A gang," Iz interrupted.

"I don't care what you call it—a gang, a crew, a bunch, a pack, or a company."

"I like pack," I interjected, adding, "One thing to consider, sir. You look completely different because you de-aged. But if you're suggesting that any of us go with you . . . well, Principal Dick would arrest us the minute we returned."

"You're right, Miss Callaghan. I would welcome a few of you to join my pack. You're an accomplished fighter, and you have personal knowledge of the enemy, which isn't just Principal Dick. Our mission would be to remove—by any way possible including extinguishment—every member of the corrupt Higher Authority including Principal Dick."

This wasn't the response I expected. I assumed Dr. King would want Daniel and I to stay put, but that wasn't the case.

"Is that—" Pete began.

"Legal?" Dr. King retorted. "Given what they plan to do if they ever get their hands on the Omorrow Project, the mission is legal and sanctioned by the Council of Curiosity on this side."

I would never forget his next words.

"This is war," Dr. King said.

I had so many questions that I felt dizzy.

"If one was to go back," I began.

"Walker," Daniel interrupted. "Not happening."

"But if," I reapproached. "How would we do it?"

"You would be fugitives," Dr. King said. "We could live way up in the North Country in the Midst. No one goes up there. The terrain is rugged enough that if you kept moving, you could evade your captors. And you could sneak down to the Academy for short, clandestine missions and disruptive bursts including the removal of Principal Dick."

"What is the level of danger here, sir?" Pete asked.

"Off the charts, as you like to say," Dr. King said. "We can try to pretend, but the truth is we're about to have a war in the Midst. It will be the teenagers – rebels, outlaws, nerds, jocks, cheer queens, brains, emos, and more -- versus the corrupt administration that seems to hold all of the power."

"What are the Vegas odds?" Daniel asked.

"For shit," replied Dr. King.

The choices were obvious at this point. We could stay in the utopia of the Commune and spend our days walking in the woods and having wonderful family and friend time. There would be few challenges, but we could manage to fill the days.

Was that living?

"One more thing," said Dr. King. "The actual opening of the wall might make this entire plan moot. I do believe that our old friend AE was the X-catcher. He's at the Observatory, up north here. It's a school for kids who have committed suicide or tried. They're under constant watch or surveillance—a teenager's worst nightmare. But it's likely his time to hold those numbers that unlock the force field wall is over.

"He was a perfect X-catcher because he is stationary and cannot leave," Dr. King rambled. "But not anymore. We've been here over a year now. There is probably a new X-catcher and he or she could be anywhere in The Other.

"It's very likely we can't go back until we went on another exhaustive search," said Dr. King. "Thus, the decision would be made for us. We are forced to remain stationary for now."

For the first time ever, I saw a furious Dr. King make a fist and slam it against the table.

"What's happening at Freak U?" Flick managed to say as I got Dr. King some ice. He waved it off because his reset was strong.

"Son," Dr. King addressed Flick. "You don't want to know."

At that moment, the cabin door opened.

A young woman with big curious eyes and shining dark hair, black, and maybe eighteen, entered in a flowing purple and white gauze dress that touched the floor. The presence of a newcomer caused immediate silence, especially given the subject matter.

I had seen her walking around with Dr. King here and a few times I found her reading to Bobby and MC, but he never introduced her and she always skittered away before I could talk to her.

Was this just a friendly visit?

She certainly didn't feign ignorance when it came to the important topics at hand. "Don't fret. Struggle is a never-ending process, dear. Freedom is never really won, you earn it and win it in every generation."

She turned on a dime to introduce herself. "I'm . . . Scotty. Yes, it's a boy's name, but we have no time for family stories."

"Walker," I said, taking her hand.

She looked at each of us deeply, stopping to lock eyes with me for several beats and shook her head. "The failure to invest in youth reflects in lack of compassion and a colossal failure of common sense," Scotty said. Then, she touched Dr. King on his shoulder and laughed.

"M, you invested wisely," she said.

He looked at her in a very different way.

"Yes," he said. "I did."

2.

That night was honeyed from a wash of warm air with a threat of thunderstorms in the air. Summer lingered with shadowy mysteries lurking. I wondered if it was still that peaceful in the woods at the Academy.

The answer came from Pete who told us, "They have snipers out at night in case anyone tries to escape the school grounds. Dr. King told me that students who run are shot down and given to that janitor on D Block at ITT. The one they call John."

What about Harold? Miss Travis? Our teachers—Kurt, Steve, Miss Elizabeth, Heath, Jerry, Walter and Robin to name a few. The list went on and on. "Any teacher conspiring with students to defy Principal's Dick's martial law is in lock up at ITT."

"If we return will the world end for us?" Tosh posed after we put the kids to bed. All of us gathered in our living room.

"The world has ended for me so many times and then began again in the morning," said Flick.

Daniel had paced like a caged animal for most of the day. He finally had everything he wanted—his family back—but he couldn't find a peaceful moment.

"If you don't fight for what's right then don't cry for what you've lost," he said, raking his hand in his hair as he continued to burn up the floor.

"We could just stay here—safe and in love," Tosh begged.

Something inside of me began to hurt.

The door cracked open.

Could we fix it? Why was it our job? Why wasn't it our job?

"Imagine all those kids who died last night—arriving in hell now," Bertha said. She had done her time at ITT when she first arrived in the Midst. Under Dick's new plan, the Academy was nothing more than lockup, too.

"And Miss Travis," I worried. "She will not go quietly. Principal Dick will have to extinguish every ounce of her."

Bitty gave it a little bit of perspective. "My powers of zooming from one place to the next in sonic time have returned," she offered. "I could take Daniel and Walker to that suicide school. You could talk to this AE kid. It's not committing to do anything. It's just finding out if he has the numbers to open the wall. Maybe he knows who has been named the next X-catcher. Just in case you go back. Someday."

I nodded—and I don't know why.

As I did, I looked around the room. Pete and Tosh nodded. Flick did, too. Iz and Bertha did the north and south head tilt. Daniel was still.

These heartbeats were from my people and they didn't play small.

3.

Later that night, I looked out onto purple lilac covered fields with Daniel just as intoxicated by the sweet smell. He reached for my hand and twined our fingers. Daniel Reid. Transforming the enormous into the intimate.

"How hard do you have to fight?" I said. "When do you ever make your way through the bullshit?"

"Baby, you tell me after you figure it out," he said.

I wanted to wrap the moon around us for protection. I wanted to dance naked in the breeze, unburdened. I wanted to keep the party going here, but it felt different now. There was something else now. Some called that feeling spirits. Some called it energy. In the streets, they called it vibes. I called it wonderings.

I had too many wonderings now to remain still.

Life-changing questions were usually answered in the sunlight, which is why we made love that night under the moon in the woods.

"For all of time, I will search for these moments that are full of you, baby," a naked Daniel said at three in the morning as we curled up under a redwood tree.

I knew we were going. His kiss wasn't one of staying put.

And that's when I cried.

4.

I woke up covered artfully with my clothes. They were tastefully put on my bits by a third party who had obviously crashed our party while we were sleeping.

He was sitting under the next redwood tree, about a foot away, reading not just a book, but had his hands on *War and Peace*, a novel by Russian author Leo Tolstoy, published in 1869. The novel revolved around the French invasion of Russia and the impact of the Napoleonic era on Tsarist society through the tales of five Russian aristocratic families.

The young man was absorbed in his story. He looked up when we opened our eyes.

"Um, hi," he said, adjusting his black nerd glasses. "I saw you out here without clothing although I have a photo of you with clothing. The bottom line is they said to find you. I have some important information to share."

He was about six feet tall, slimmer, and the wild hair of the past was now artfully combed off his forehead. The glasses made him look like the kind of appealing geek I would want as a friend. Above all, *he could read*, which wasn't unusual for most seventeen- or eighteen-year-olds, but this one was different.

"Russian literature," I said slowly, making my way behind the tree to put my sundress back on. It took only a minute because I had so many questions for the young man who obviously didn't recognize or know us.

"Um, yes," he said, pulling a little notebook out of his pocket.

"And you write," I said, slowly.

"I like to write down my thoughts before I forget them," he said, standing up to shake my hand. His grip was firm and full of confidence.

"I'm Edward Wargo," he said. "These people who were helping me gave me a photo of the two of you and said I could find you at the Commune."

"You're Eddie Wargo?" Daniel said, slowly, shaking his hand like we didn't know him.

And maybe we didn't in this state.

"Edward," he corrected.

"Yes, yes, that's what they said was my last name, but I don't remember," he fretted. "I don't know. Maybe I had a concussion or spent some time in the hospital. My memory is a little bit foggy."

"I've been there," Daniel said to the new and improved *Edward* Wargo, who put down his book. We chatted about nothing for a minute while I tried to make some sense of it. *If you changed history then history changed you.* It followed: Eddie did something impossibly heroic at Columbine High School that day when he saved my life and took out the shooters.

History did change Eddie Wargo—for the better.

"Oh yeah, I'm supposed to give this to you," he said, ripping the last page out of his notebook. It was filled with numbers.

"It will open the force field wall . . . I mean, really? There is one?" he said in a low voice. "Oh, and I am the new X-catcher. Whatever the hell that means."

And then he said something so un-Eddie, so un-Wargo that it made my heart hurt.

"Courage will always find a way," he said, "in the quiet moments."

It made me want to go. Do. Fight.

5.

Sometimes the most important thing on earth is the decision we make between two breaths.

"I'm going," I said.

I didn't need to explain to him my inner sense of justice. I was that girl who fought against the bully. Certain traits were imprinted on your DNA.

"I know you're going—as am I," Daniel replied in our bed, in the dark. "But you already knew that I was going."

"But the kids? The girls?" I posed.

"Will stay here with Griz, Auggie, Bitty, Bertha, Deuce, and Tosh," Daniel said. "We will go—along with Dr. King, Iz, Flick, and Pete."

"And new and improved Eddie," I said.

When things got tight, I knew where my friends were at . . . close enough to touch them.

"Walker," said a voice from the floor, "you're my best friend. I will do anything you want me to do."

I looked down and saw Auggie next to our bed with a too-small blanket over most of him, but not his big feet, which were sticking out. It made me melt.

"Auggie, have you been here the entire time?" I whispered. "Boundaries."

"I sleep in here a lot," he said. "And I'll guard those kids—with everything I am. Do or die."

He didn't even want to pretend anymore, and slid in bed next to me. It wasn't a threesome for long because soon the girls and the kids were next to us in one giant pretzel of legs, arms and hearts.

I shared my covers. I gave my existence to a cause. I slept next to a man who would always stand with me.

I was going, but I wasn't going alone.

I had friends at my side and a purpose in my veins. Freedom trumps fear.

"Let's go get this son of a bitch," little Bobby shouted.

"Word," seconded MC.

6.

Saying good-bye to the girls was like taking a bullet. We did this two nights later, in the woods near a roaring fire. They weren't surprised at the news—not at all. Bobby was a natural spy as was Andy. They hid in corners, absorbed our words, knew our past deeds and future ones, and then provided a gossip column to the rest.

As a family, we were used to being pulled apart although we promised this was for the greater good.

Griz lifted me high into his arms and promised he would stick around as the head of security.

"Be saf, Wa," he said.

Bobby pretended to squirm out of my arms, but he didn't fight me when I drew him in for a tight hug. "You're a Reid," I told him. "It's your job to stay frosty and protect everyone."

He nodded and whispered into my ear, "I still like cuddles and I want a puppy. I'm the biggest and littlest boy at the same time."

"Me, too," I said, "except for the boy part."

MC was tough because she was newer to the bunch and had dealt with so much loss in her short life. Her spirit, however, was fierce and unbroken.

"Daddy will look over you," she told me. "He's here at night. I've seen him walking around, you know."

"In your dreams, baby."

"No, in my window, silly," she said.

I would let that ride for now.

Jenna and Andy motioned for me to join them apart from the others picnicking now near the river bend. "We want to go, Walker," Jenna said. "Just hear us out. We've been to the past. We've survived alone—bad, bad things. We've been training on our own and with others in the woods. Flick—who I want to marry someday, but don't tell him—taught me real good."

Jenna, my doppelganger or the young version of yours truly, held out her small hand. I slapped her a high five.

"You know that's not what I want," she stated in quite a grown-up voice.

Gingerly, Jenna reached into the pocket of my jeans and pulled out one of my throwing stars. Just as I was about to fret that she'd cut herself to smithereens, Jenna rolled the thing over three of her fingers like a true pro.

She grinned. "My personal training started with rocks as I worked my way up to little plastic carvings I made by myself. I cut them in the shape of stars."

"And then, she started stealing the real stars from your pants in the hamper," Andy filled in with glee. "She's a natural thief."

"We're not little girls anymore," Jenna huffed, pulling her hand back to throw hard, nailing a falling leaf into the bark of a tree.

"We're Ninjas," Jenna announced. "Hormonal teenage girls with payback on our minds."

I showed them the goosies that just crept up my arm.

"We have a little visit in mind for Principal Dick and our dear Daddy Edward," Andy said. "And no one will suspect girls who are eleven and thirteen. They'll either think we're too innocent or too dumb. And that's our winning hand."

"We're also flexible, cunning, and whip smart. Not my words," she continued, crooking her finger at Flick who gave me a blank look before uttering, "What? They need to know how to defend themselves."

Flick backed up far enough that when Andy sprung in the air and roundhouse kicked him in the jaw, he had room to fall on his ass in the mud.

"Cobra Kai'd you, Chris Flicker," Andy yelled.

"My reset better be working," Flick moaned.

"You're not going," Daniel told the girls.

I didn't like the lightning-quick look that traveled between them.

Not one bit.

"The minute it's safe, we will open the wall and come back for you," Daniel said. "Eddie's code is good for an entire year. We will." His voice began to crack.

Everything comes down to lasts.

One last sunrise.

One last day.

One last dinner.

One last embrace.

One last moment before you're gone.

7.

Violent rushes of water blasted at killer speeds near the ocean's edge. We stood on a low cliff, feet submerged in icy wash as the violent *whoosh* of the sea tried to tear our skin from the bone. Our wildly beating hearts sounded like a percussion session; our hard faces were as serious as death itself.

Griz was the one who helped us use the caves nearby to find the right watery passage where the code box was located and could be punched into the wall in a primitive way with sticks and a lever system.

Dr. King would do so, but only after he made sure that our little group would not be torn apart during reentry.

He used long, reinforced zip ties on our ankles to make sure we stayed together. "If you have to cut the ties, use the small knives in your pocket," he advised. "But do not cut the ties unless you're drowning. The reset, which we all have as of now, will provide you with hours of underwater clarity and breath."

Glancing at the lineup, I felt a surge in my chest as I stood with Daniel, Pete, Iz, Flick, Dr. King, and our new friend, Edward "Eddie" Wargo, who insisted on coming along for the ride.

These are my friends, I thought. These are my people.

And before I was ready, we walked closer to the place in the force field known as the Line. It was actually the border between the Midst and The Other—and as water lapped at my thighs, I felt the rock underneath me tremble.

I found myself at one of those crossroads. Who knew what was next?

The answer was somewhere between the shadow and the soul.

8.

Dr. King punched in the code as Daniel grabbed me hard. I held on with everything that was me as the blast of churning water in front of us became deafening.

"A long time ago, you told me to embrace the vole—risk it all for great rewards. Now what?" I had to yell.

"Here's what, baby," he said. "We'll cap the climax."

"Meaning?"

"To beat it all," he replied.

"One hundred percent."

With one hundred percent of his will and strength, he grabbed my face and kissed me as hard as possible. He gave me unconditional love and unwavering support. There were two things I could do about it.

Allow it.

And love it back.

9.

We stood on a tiny ledge of rock. It wouldn't be long now before the roaring waves licked higher and harder, swallowing us whole, while plundering our surrendered mortal bodies down into a liquid abyss.

We could stand here until we were washed away. The other choice was to jump feet and heart first into the drink.

"If it excites you and scares you at the same time, it probably means you should do it," he said, repeating his words of long ago.

"What do you want, Daniel Reid?" I asked him.

"I want to hold your hand and say we made it," he yelled as a stinging slap of liquid slicked back his jet-black hair.

We were here because the fire that burned inside of us was tougher and mightier than the fire around us.

In lieu of blood, I knew that formidable fuel ran through my veins. A force lived, yes *lived*, in the lining of my skin. I knew that everything I needed to do was on the other side of my wildest fears.

"Let's count it down. Five, four, three, two . . ." Daniel screamed. Those clear gray eyes were intense and had me on lock.

He didn't want to wait for the ocean. He was the ocean.

"Three . . . two . . . banana!" I shouted.

And we jumped.

10.

The churning water was arctic cold, but our resets were working fine as the entire group flipped up and down, sideways and back, over rock and sea creature and then past the Avenue of Ghost Statues. We fell through layers, body surfing black holes and hard, deep undertows, as dark became darker and we continued to tumble through the curtains of time and realms.

All I longed for was survival. It dawned on me that I had been chasing that ever since I died. *I did it by the seat of my pants, on a prayer, and with grit I didn't know was there.*

I knew I would never say sorry again for my inner wild. I owned my afterlife force. There was nothing left to save for *special occasions* either.

Existing was a special occasion.

I knew if I didn't make it then someone, someday, somewhere would say that I, Walker Callaghan, tried.

That's all you can do. After all, I was a Callaghan.

And my father told me once that you live for your name. And after . . . it lives for you.

11.

There was a door at the bottom of the ocean.

Daniel couldn't open it alone, so I wrapped my hands around his and Flick added another layer of skin. *We* twisted hard, fingers twining as my heart raced, which was the only setting that was appropriate.

You can't always achieve calm.

But, you can always generate brave.

12.

I could read Daniel Reid's mind by now. I knew he was thinking what lovers do at the possible end: I just want to look at you one more time in this light. I brushed my unencumbered, open hand against his familiar face. He put his lips on my hand. To imprint. One last time.

Then, we pulled hard until the door was ajar and we swam through and across realms.

Determined, possessive hands moved to my waist in case he had to physically pull me back.

The grip was strong.

Sometimes it doesn't matter what is in front of you. All that counts is who is behind you.

FORTY-FIVE

The night air was glacial, which should have sent wintry shivers, but the reset was working magnificently. I felt hard, hungry, and alive as the water spit me out.

Butt planted hard in the sand, I smiled. Behind me, the waves shimmered with an opalescent sheen as I stood on wobbling legs, and tremble-walked out of the wet sand, crouching behind a large, dry sand dune, big enough to hide all of us.

We were stealth silent for several long moments, damn lucky, and looking for our bearings. This could have been a Mars landing for all we knew although smart money was on the fact it was the Midst beach that took you to Freak Island—and several blinks later, I knew that it was terra familiar.

"Are you prepared for what's next?" a soaked Daniel finally whispered in my ear.

"I'm not prepared for right now," I said in a low voice.

The waves gently lapped at the shoreline creating a soft, dull sound designed to lull visitors into a mesmerizing, almost hypnotic state. Alas, that was just the preview and it was false advertising. That stillness and exquisite quiet was followed by hard thunder that boomed relentlessly in the near distance.

It was going to be one hell of a storm.

Turns out we weren't alone. ITT prison guard and infamous serial killer John G, in his full Pogo clown suit (red hair, white makeup, and flamed nose) stood in the middle of the sand with a shovel that seemed to glow in the moonlight. He looked like a man possessed, which is why he didn't see us. He didn't even smell us—yet.

We watched him dig for a long time until eventually he threw the shovel in the sand and removed the rest with his bare hands. I watched as he pulled hard on what looked like some kind of contraption below. When the clouds parted, I could see that the hole wasn't really that deep. And his prize was a door that was underneath all that grit.

Pete looked at me, puzzled.

"I don't know," I mouthed.

But, he knew. For how long, I couldn't be sure. Not that it mattered now.

As he flung open the warped wood, he looked at the sky and screamed four words I would never forget.

"We are all clown!"

Something was *coming through* that tiny door in the sand.

One feather. Two. Three. Enormous in size, they struggled, contorting to fit through such a small opening. By the tenth tuft, I realized that these were large wings specially designed for flight with a central shaft created with an interlocking microstructure.

This was an evolved biological structure. Black. Slick.

The most heinous of them were born for flight.

I heard the words of Dr. King in my head: *Portals exist all over the realm. They link us to the living and the dead. They keep in what's meant to be kept in. They keep out the devil.*

John G had opened a portal that provided passage *into* the Midst. And they heard it. They were waiting for it because monsters know when the universe has a crack in it.

The demons from the living realm were made out of what we – the teenagers who departed -- left behind. It was our rage, our jealousy, our evil—normal teenage emotions—that we shed when we died. They lingered behind, fueled with the frenzy of abandonment.

They transformed and grew into rubbery creatures with black wings. The more they waited, the more they stewed in their own lunacy. Their powers simply intensified.

Because no one likes being ditched.

They had been waiting for the ultimate reckoning. *If we wouldn't go back to them, they would come to us. If there was an opening.*

A heart shot from them to us or vice versa meant soul extinguishment. No existence. In any form.

Ashes to ashes.

Dust to dust.

Gone-gone.

3.

Heads up. Wings out. The rest of the demons ripped the door off, smashing the wood to pieces with long, rotted nails.

"What the fuck, Daniel?" Iz whispered.

"Do we have any weapons?" Dr. King asked, knowing the truth.

"Hands," Pete said. "We lost everything else in the water. We have our hands." Dr. King said. We left the bulk of the weapons with the kids for their protection. Plus, it would have been too cumbersome to try to carry the packs and weapons across the Line between realms.

Daniel formed fists as did Dr. King.

I could smell their noxious, putrid breath in the breeze as I watched the shadow of a tall, winged beast walk the shoreline. The demons were ferocious, ruthless, and merciless, monsters of such high order than only man could have created them from man.

Ear-piercing shrieks echoed as more zoomed across the sand on agile webbed feet. One of the larger beasts took to the air to fly lazy circles in rubbery skin amid furious wails. He scorched the night sky and then hovered over the shoreline. The razor-sharp beak was always pointed downward. Always hunting.

It was only a matter of time before our stink entered their whiff.

"Callaghan!" Daniel whispered harshly. "Level up!"

Someone's hands were shaking and I knew they were my own. Sweat drops fell from my forehead. In the near distance, I heard the distinct sound of marching.

4.

I held my only throwing star in my trembling hand. I packed one in my pocket. For good luck, but now that was shot to shit.

And then I waited.

On the beach, I could see dark green breath in the air rising along with talons, claws, and teeth that looked like silver swords in the moonlight.

I steeled myself to the inevitable remembering what I was once told: magic happens when you don't give up. The universe always falls in love with a stubborn heart.

5.

I have to sign off now as the edges close in. Let's end this on a positive, shall we? In case we never meet again.

I . . . I left a note on the treehouse door for the girls and Bobby. I knew if the worst happened, it would be part of my tale. Because, in the end, we're all just stories.

"Kids," I wrote, "wander often, wonder always. In other words, you don't need to solve it. Just ask the right questions. WC."

There is a reason they call them famous *last* words.

Silky and waxy, I felt a feather poke through the sand dune, grazing the velvet steel of my upper arm.

"Oh wow, oh wow, oh wow . . . *oh*," I gasped.

END

ASCENDERS I AND I (Book Six)
2022

ACKNOWLEDGEMENTS

My deepest gratitude to the people I'm blessed to have in my life including:

Fonda Synder, Fonda Snyder, Fonda Snyder. In the most inspiring way in the world, you are a writer's dream come true. Thank you for bringing your genius talent and keen sense of story to my life and my work. I don't know what I did to deserve both you and Rick Mischel in my life, but it must have been something good. Thank you both for your never-ending belief and for making bigger things come true when it comes to all things Ascenders.

Mary Altbaum, an amazing and extraordinary editor, friend and keeper of all things Ascenders. Thank you for all the years and your creativity in helping me tell this story. I'm such a lucky writer to have you in my life.

Shelley Chung, another phenomenal editor, and new to our team and most welcome. Thank you for jumping right in and being the brightest light. Stunning job. I can't wait to work with you again – and we are! Yay!

Adrijus Guscia from RockingBookCovers.com. There is a thrill that cannot be described in getting a new book cover from you. Thank you for always dazzling me and for thinking outside the box. Best cover artist ever. Thank you, my friend, from day one and into the future. I can't wait to show people the Book Six cover!

Emily Tippetts and her wonderful team, Tianne Samson and Stacey Tippetts. Your inside design is always so beautiful and creative, plus you have to deal with my pain in the ass-ness at the end with my last-minute changes. Thank you for putting up with me and for your artistry and patience. I promise I won't change one more thing . . . well, wait a second . . .

Nola Song. It took me a long time to find a fabulous map maker, and then I found you --- someone who exceeded any expectations. You hit it out of the park.

Thank you to Elena Stokes of Wunderkind PR for her insight and vision, plus her amazing team including Brianna Robinson. Thank you to Vickie Rose for the fan chats. Welcome Sara Cunningham to the team. You know how to hit the ground running. Hey Nat, your Mom is cool, but nothing cooler than having you do book reports on Ascenders. A plus, plus, plus for you!

The lovely folks at LA Comic Con and the Los Angeles Times Festival of Books. I always feel like I'm playing in the big leagues when we do your festivals.

Carol Watson at the Four Seasons Los Angeles. Thank you and the entire staff for your hospitality and for providing such a calming, gorgeous atmosphere for meetings, calm afternoons for editing and late night bursts of creativity.

To dear friends for always listening...Sally Kline, Joyce Persico, Vickie Chachere, Carrie Healy and Stephen Schaefer. Love to my family Gavin and Jill Pearlman, plus Reid, Cade and Wylie Pearlman.

To Jack "Buzzy" Gaber thank you, thank you, thank you, for manning the home front, for being such a wonderful brother-in-law and for taking care of the fur nieces and nephews when we're out of town. Appreciate it more than you know.

To Colt, our big boy who ascended during the writing of this book. We miss you. And to my two assistants on four legs --- Princess Georgia and our new guy Auggie Bee (yes, named after Auggie in Ascenders). Thanks for being here and for not deleting too much when you jump up.

To my parents, Paul and Renee, who have ascended, but I still feel you always.

To all the Ascenders fans and our fan group Ascenders Nations. We've laughed and cried together while sharing these books and our lives. I love you guys so much. Hearing how these books impacted you means everything and more to me.

Sabrina, my bonus daughter, who is killing it at college. I am so proud of you and your drive to make this world a better place. I'm so excited about your future. Love you always.

Ron, my love, my heart, my husband and my everything. He also sets up all the booths at events and tells me to just "be an author." This is usually after I've bumped into a pile of books and knocked things down. For the third time. Thank you for sharing your laughter, your life, your heart and our days and nights. Love you more.

Made in the USA
Las Vegas, NV
04 April 2022

46840934R00361